"Ask not what
your country can
do for you..."

BLACK PEOPLE:
53% OF THE DEAD,
2% OF THE
BREAD...WHY?

STOP THE WAR NOW

VETE
FO
PE

Vietna
wa
to end a
peace

"The answer is
blowin' in the wind."

I have a drea

PROMISES TO KEEP

George Bernau

Promises To Keep

WARNER BOOKS

A Warner Communications Company

Warner Books, Inc., 666 Fifth Avenue, New York, NY 10103

 A Warner Communications Company

Printed in the United States of America
First printing: October 1988
10 9 8 7 6 5 4 3 2 1

Library of Congress Cataloging-in-Publication Data

Bernau, George.
  Promises to keep.

  I. Title.
PS3552.E7277P76   1988   813'.54   88-5465
ISBN 0-446-51453-5

Designed by Giorgetta Bell McRee

For Laurie and Erin

AUTHOR'S NOTE

Promises to Keep is a work of fiction. Although it is set in what may seem to some readers as a recognizable historical context, its characters—their actions, dialogue, and motivations as portrayed by the novel—are entirely imaginary.

PROMISES TO KEEP

PART ONE

November 1963

CHAPTER
1

Dallas— November 22, 1963

The room was chaos.

At the center of it, a man lay on a gray metal emergency-room table. A starched white sheet had been thrown across his body and his eyes were closed. The man was John Trewlaney Cassidy, the thirty-fifth President of the United States.

White-clad emergency-room personnel moved around him in anxious but restrained activity, responding even now as they had been trained. And at the fringes of the crowded room near the doors stood the reporters and the other frightened onlookers, all pushing and shouting, pressing nervously forward, fighting for a glimpse of the man lying on the metal table at the center of the room.

Next to the President stood his wife, Suzanne. She was wearing a bright pink suit and fashionable matching hat, but there were fresh bloodstains exploded across the front of her jacket and trailing down dark crimson onto her skirt. She held the President's hand tightly in her own. Her eyes had the faraway look of shock in them.

The President was dressed in a dark gray, medium-weight wool suit, a white cotton dress shirt and dark blue tie, but the emergency-room personnel had cut away the top of the expensive suit coat and then torn away the shirt to expose his neck and shoulders and chest. There was a single, small, neat bullet hole in his throat, a smaller wound in his upper back, and the side of his head was blown open, leaving a mass of blood and damaged flesh and broken bare white skull.

The doctors took command of the room. They motioned for it to be cleared and a reluctant edging began toward the door.

"Mrs. Cassidy," the doctor standing closest to the President's wife said quietly, but she refused to acknowledge him. Instead, she continued to look down at where her hand joined her husband's hand.

"Please, Mrs. Cassidy," the doctor said. "We're going to operate on the President now."

Only then did she turn her gaze toward him. "Is there a chance?" she asked.

"Yes," he said, "there's a chance."

The horror of what had happened only a few minutes before still clung to Dealey Plaza. Police cars had sealed off the ends of the street and uniformed officers combed the tall buildings that surrounded the square below. Rumors spread like wildfire through the stunned crowd. The President was dead. He was alive. Mrs. Cassidy had been hit. The Governor was dead. Men and women knelt in the street praying silently to themselves or out loud for everyone to hear, while others walked around aimlessly in a stunned silence. A policeman slammed his fist in rage against the heavy trunk of a tree near the grassy hillside at the far side of the square, as the static-filled voice of a police dispatcher came over the air from the radio of his motorcycle that he had left abandoned by the side of the road nearby.

Special Agent James O. Sullivan stood on the steps of the old brick building where the search was beginning to focus now and looked out at the confusion of the people in the plaza before him.

Sullivan was FBI and he looked it. He was tall, with wide, powerful shoulders under a tightly fitting, dark gray suit coat. His blond crewcut stood up stiffly above a pair of bright blue eyes that looked out of a square-jawed young man's face.

Sullivan and a dozen other agents were on special assignment in Dallas during the President's visit. He had been riding in one of the trail cars behind the President's limousine only minutes before. Sullivan had been watching the big gray cement freeway overpass coming up in front of him and thinking that the danger of the small plaza was almost past, when he'd heard the uneasy stirring in the crowd by the roadside and then the little pops that he recognized immediately as gunfire—three, maybe four sudden explosions. And then he'd looked ahead and had seen the right side of the President's head explode in blood. He had drawn his own weapon then and turned toward the hillside in front of the President's car, where the young agent thought that the shots had come from.

As the President's limousine sped off, Special Agent Sullivan had jumped out of the trail car and had been among the first of the agents to reach the sloping hillside at the far side of the plaza. With his gun drawn, he had proceeded into the grassy area that bordered the road. In front of him, people moved at random—families, bystanders. It was impossible to make any sense out of it. There was a short stockade fence partially hidden behind some overhanging trees about halfway down the hillside. Sullivan had straddled the waist-high fence and then jogged down the hill behind it to the asphalt parking area beneath the overpass. A squat, dark-skinned man with grease-laden hair was leaning almost nonchalantly against a car a few feet away. The man was dressed in a blue plaid shirt and shapeless light blue trousers. Sullivan approached the man warily, and as he did the man reached into the breast pocket of his plaid shirt. Sullivan tensed, but the man removed only a thin leather wallet and flashed it open. Inside were Secret Service credentials—the stamp, the photo, the familiar seal. Sullivan glanced briefly at the man's face. It had surprisingly delicate, almost feminine features for such a thickly built man, with dark, heavily pockmarked skin and large dark brown eyes protected by long black lashes. The man's face matched the photograph precisely.

"There's nothing back here," the man said, and Sullivan turned from him and continued on under the cement overpass, but the man had been right. Sullivan found nothing.

Something still bothered Sullivan about the man in the plaid shirt. As Sullivan stood looking out at the plaza, he tried to remember what it had been about the man that disturbed him. Then he saw it again. The man's hands, holding the Secret Service credentials for Sullivan to examine, had been the hands of a mechanic or a workman, not of a government agent. The skin had been rough and damaged and the fingernails had been dirty and uncut. Sullivan made a mental note to check it out later. The Service would know which of their men could have been in that position at that moment —if any.

For now though, Sullivan forced himself to shake the memory out of his head. Then he turned away from the scene spread out in front of him in the plaza and started up the front steps of the building to join the search that was in progress on its upper floors. A few minutes later he watched as the police found a rifle and three spent cartridge cases near a window on the building's sixth floor.

Suzanne Cassidy knelt in the darkness of the small chapel on the top floor of the Dallas hospital. They were operating on the body of her husband only a few short yards away.

She was all alone, her hands clasped tightly in front of her, praying in the flickering light of the candles that burned on the simple altar at the front of the room.

She kept her eyes closed, ignoring as long as she could the noises at the closed chapel doors behind her. Finally she heard the doors open, and she turned to see the tall figure of the Vice President striding down the center aisle of the sanctuary toward her. The Vice President was a large man with a sad, deeply lined face. In dramatic contrast to his conservative, pin-striped business suit, he wore fancy leather cowboy boots and in his hands he held a ten-gallon hat. Behind him, Suzanne could see one of his aides closing the chapel door against the swarm of reporters, Secret Service agents, and hospital staff that filled the hallway.

"Mrs. Cassidy, I'm terribly sorry," Vice President Gardner said as he approached her.

"How is he? Do you know?" she said, standing and turning back to the Vice President. He could see now for the first time the blood on the front of her bright pink suit. He looked at it strangely and then up at her expectant eyes.

"Are you all right?" he said slowly in his deep Texas voice.

"I'm fine. Have you seen Jack?" she said.

"No," the Vice President answered, shaking his head. "They had me shut up in some damn . . ." The big man stopped talking for a moment as he looked at the woman's face. "I'm certain that he's goin' to be all right. The Governor's fine and Mrs. Clemmons. I saw them on the way up," he said, and then he let his voice trail off.

"They're operating on Jack," Suzanne said, and then she sat down on the narrow wooden pew that she had been kneeling in front of, leaving the Vice President standing awkwardly behind her in the middle of the short chapel aisle, his arms held stiffly down at his sides.

"You were with him?" he said.

"Yes."

The Vice President walked down the aisle then and sat on the row of wooden seats behind her. He hesitated only slightly before he asked his next question. "Was he conscious?"

He watched then while the bright pink fabric that covered her shoulders drew itself up and back in a deep shuddering movement before she answered. "No," she said finally. "No, he wasn't."

There was a commotion at the door to the chapel then.

"Bill!" the Vice President snapped at a young man in wire-rimmed glasses, who was standing at the back of the room. "Tell them to simmer down out there, would you?" But as his young aide started for the chapel door to do as he'd been told, the Vice President held up his finger, gesturing for him to stop. The young man froze in his tracks and watched as the Vice President bent down and lightly touched the shoulder of the woman sitting in the narrow chapel pew in front of him.

"Mrs. Cassidy," the Vice President drawled slowly. "I've got to ask you a favor, ma'am."

Suzanne listened, but her eyes stayed on the figure of Christ mounted on the altar above her at the front of the room.

"Would you mind if I had a phone or two brought in here? Maybe a television monitor, if we can scare one up? I'm afraid there's no other place to go. You see, it's a little wild out there right now." The Vice President gestured toward the chapel door and the hallway crammed with reporters and Secret Service men behind it. "I know your husband would want us to take care of business," the Vice President said quietly, but firmly.

"Yes, of course," Suzanne said, keeping her voice low and under control. "You do whatever you have to do," she said. "I should be with my husband." She stood then and started down the aisle of the chapel toward the door at the back of the room.

"No, Mrs. Cassidy, you can't go out there," the aide standing near the closed chapel door said gently. "The Secret Service is trying to seal off the hall. They won't let you."

The woman turned back to the Vice President. He nodded his confirmation of what his aide had told her.

Suzanne paused for a moment and then crossed to the very front row of the small chapel and walked down its aisle to the far distant corner of the room and knelt down, closing her eyes in silent prayer.

The Vice President watched her for a brief second and then stood quickly and started toward his aide, who was still standing by the door at the back of the room.

"Bill, do what you can," the Vice President said. "I need a phone or two brought in here. Have them hooked up back there," he said, pointing at a low table at the rear of the chapel that held a few worn prayerbooks and an empty brass collection plate. "Then get me Summers and Rozier, in that order. I'll want to talk to the Attorney General, too. But first Summers and then Rozier."

The aide nodded and started for the door.

"Is there some place to set up a television camera?" the Vice President called after him.

"I'll find out," his aide said.

"And get right back here. We've got work to do," Gardner said sharply.

Only a few minutes later, a command center filled with telephones and television sets had been set up in the small chapel on the top floor of the Dallas hospital, and the government of the United States began to be pulled together by the tall, sad-faced man who was its Vice President. Only a few yards away, the woman in the bloodstained pink suit stayed kneeling at the front of the darkened room, praying for the life of her husband.

Tim Cassidy had taken the morning off. The Attorney General had worked far into the night before and he'd let himself sleep late that morning. He was walking now, all alone, up a steep green hill at the far edge of the grounds of his home in the Virginia countryside, just outside the nation's capital. He was walking slowly, his head down, with his slim body bent slightly forward at the waist and one arm locked tightly behind his back, thinking about the afternoon's work ahead of him.

He turned toward the house as he heard his wife's voice calling out to him. But strangely, Kay was running now, down from the house across the long, sloping grass lawn toward him, her face uncharacteristically alarmed.

"Tim," she called out, and he ran the several steps to her, taking her hands in his own as they met each other at the base of the short green hillside that led back to their home.

"It's Summers on the phone!" she said.

"What is it?" he asked, but he brushed by her before she could answer and then he sprinted up the hill toward the main house.

The receiver of the extension was lying on the patio table near the uncleared coffee cups from lunch. He stopped and looked at the little plastic instrument lying at a crooked angle on the white-linen-draped table for a moment without picking it up. Somehow he knew with a certainty then, the way he had only a few other times before, that his entire life was about to change suddenly and dramatically. But he permitted himself only a short moment's hesitation before he reached down for the receiver and lifted it to his ear, his hand knocking silverware and used napkins off the table in front of him as he did.

"Mr. Attorney General." It was unmistakably the voice of the Director himself, on the other end of the line.

"The President has been shot," the voice said and then went on coldly, as if it were merely reciting the closing numbers on Wall Street. "It may be fatal. He's in Parkland Memorial Hospital in Dallas. The doctors are operating on him now." Then it paused dramatically before adding, "We have reason to believe that it may be part of a Communist attempt to overthrow the government of the United States. Operation Torn Sky has been placed into effect. I repeat, Operation Torn Sky is now in effect," the voice said again, terminating the call.

The Attorney General started to ask one question of the thousands that moved through his head at that moment, but he was holding a dead phone and there wasn't any use.

"The son of a bitch," the young man hissed, as he slammed the phone down into its cradle.

His wife was at his side now and he turned to her. "They've shot Jack," he said, making his own voice artificially calm.

His wife gasped involuntarily and her eyes widened in shock as she heard her husband's words.

"He's alive. He's at a hospital in Dallas. They're operating on him and . . ." The President's brother shook his head in disbelief before he went on. "And Summers is playing war games with us," the Attorney General said, gesturing with his thumb back toward the telephone. "The son of a bitch!" the young man said again at the phone sitting on his lunch table.

"Tim, I love you," his wife said and she stepped forward and they held each other close for a moment. Over his wife's shoulder the young man could see the dark outline of the first of the government's Secret Service cars already drawing up over the crest of a distant hill, and behind it several more government cars began coming into view, moving like giant, rolling, unstoppable, hump-backed insects toward them.

"We've got company," he said and broke the tight embrace. "Back there." He nodded past his wife toward the outline of the caravan of cars appearing over the green hills and speeding down the road toward the front gates of their home.

"I don't understand," his wife said.

"Summers," the young man said, gesturing again toward the telephone. "He has within his discretion the power to place the government on alert. If he believes there's a danger to the country's internal security, he can put a plan into effect. He calls it Torn Sky," the Attorney General added, smiling wryly for a moment at Summers's love for these kinds of "cloak and dagger" things.

"And?" his wife asked, just as the first of the government cars pulled to a stop in the driveway behind her.

"And, my love," the Attorney General said, "we—you and I—have just become the property of the government of the United States of America. The Secret Service is supposed to keep us here, or at Summers's discretion we could be moved to one of several secret hiding places." The Attorney General shook his head in anger. "Only the President, or in his absence . . ." he said the words painfully, "or in his absence, the Vice President can call off the plan."

"I'm going to try to get through to the hospital," he said and picked up the phone again, but before he dialed it, he looked across the patio at his wife. Behind her he could see the first of the somber dark-colored cars pulling to a stop in their home's long gravel driveway.

"The children," his wife whispered anxiously, as two Secret Service men jumped out of the first of the cars and began jogging across the driveway toward them.

"Mr. Attorney General," one of the men said, "Operation Torn Sky."

"Yes, I know," the Attorney General answered and then turned back to his wife. "The children will be brought here," he said and the Secret Service man overheard and nodded his own confirmation at her.

"We'll get them as soon as we know this area is secure," the agent explained.

"I'm going with you," Kay said.

The man hesitated. More agents were pouring out of a series of government cars that had pulled up into the driveway. The men were fanning out, some with their revolvers drawn, and moving across the long sloping lawn of the Cassidy home. Kay stared with disbelief at the spectacle being played out in front of her.

"We're fine here," she said to the agent. "I want to get my children," she said firmly and started toward the government car parked in the driveway behind him. The Secret Service agent hesitated for another moment, but then hurried after her.

"Be careful, Kay," her husband called out. "You know even Summers can be right sometimes."

"I will." His wife smiled back at him. "Tell Jack and Suzanne that I love them," she said and then she ducked into the waiting car and within seconds it was speeding down the Virginia back roads toward her children's school.

* * *

Somewhere over the Pacific a government VC-137 holding seven members of the Cabinet of the United States was drifting above the clouds. It was eleven o'clock Pacific standard time. For a moment the clouds broke and the plane found clear, sun-filled, blue skies.

Allen Rozier, the President's press secretary, glanced out the window at the November sky. Rozier was a big man with a round face, ringed at his jawline by a faint double chin. His dark hair was cut short and combed neatly to the side, letting his intelligent brown eyes dominate his face.

He had let himself forget for a few seconds the importance of the journey that he was on, and about the President's trip to Dallas that he had warned him against taking, and about all the petty concerns of the approaching election that normally occupied his thinking these days, and he had become for that moment just a man looking out an airplane window at a beautiful blue November sky. But as he sat enjoying the moment, the steward's voice interrupted him and returned his thoughts to the interior of the plane.

"Sir, you're wanted up front," the steward said and Rozier nodded and slid his bulky frame toward the aisle, not even glancing back at the skies outside the window again. There was his job to do now.

He moved toward the front of the plane, passing by the other powerful men, who sat quietly talking to each other or reviewing documents for the Japanese visit ahead of them or just dozing in their seats.

Rozier walked to the thin gray curtain that separated the cockpit of the big military aircraft from the passenger compartment. Then he moved the curtain aside and ducked down into the small instrument-laden area at the front of the plane.

As he entered the cockpit, the copilot stood and held the radio's microphone toward him. The two men brushed awkwardly by each other in the small space and Rozier settled down into the seat at the front of the aircraft that the copilot had vacated.

Rozier sat leaning forward, his head down, looking at the instruments on the panel below him rather than up at the bright cloudless sky outside the big curved cockpit window while he caught his breath. He clicked the microphone on then and spoke into it. "This is Rozier."

"Carpet, this is Liberty," the voice answered, and, hearing the official voice of ground control, Rozier snapped to attention. Sitting bolt upright in his seat, he looked across at the pilot's face set in grim profile only a few inches away from him.

"Yes, Liberty," Rozier said into the open microphone. "This is Carpet."

"Carpet, please stand by," the voice responded over the crackling speaker.

Rozier sat frozen in the copilot's seat for what seemed to him a very long time, the steady low drone of the aircraft's powerful engines the only sound. "Liberty" was the code name for the Signal Corps' Midwestern Center. They were apparently hooking the call through to the President, but it was taking one hell of a long time, longer than it needed to. Something had happened.

"Are you on there?" It was Gardner's voice. Rozier felt a sudden, warm rush of blood surge through him, settling in his head, filling it and then beginning to press in a loud pounding rhythm against the inside of his skull. What the hell was it? Why Gardner?

"Sir," he said slowly, drawing the sounds out, and then immediately wondered why he'd chosen that word. He wasn't in the habit of calling Gardner "sir," or thinking of him that way either. That was a term he reserved for the President. "Sir, this is Carpet," he said, finally completing the identifying code.

"Who else have we got on here?" the Vice President's voice asked confidentially.

"This is Pyramid," came back the reply, the voice under control. The sound of the words angered Rozier. A trained soldier, he thought. "Pyramid" was the designation for the Joint Chiefs' Communication Center near the Capitol, locked at the base of an inverted concrete skyscraper, a dozen isolated stories beneath the earth, the information pumped to it as rare and sanitized as the air that filtered down to it through the miles of twisting metal ducts that led back to the Maryland sunlight.

"Good, you go ahead, Pyramid," came back Gardner's slow, deep-throated reply. Rozier shook his head and smiled grudgingly at the Vice President's obvious shared discomfort with the official communications techniques, but Pyramid's next words removed the brief smile from Rozier's face.

"Carpet, this call is to inform you that Operation Torn Sky is now in effect," Pyramid said simply and, as it did, Rozier clutched tightly at the microphone in his hand and closed his eyes with the pain. When he opened them again, he could see the face of the pilot moving forward, his eyes focused on the instrument panel in front of him, already beginning to activate the maneuvers that were his initial portions of Torn Sky.

"Carpet." It was Gardner's exaggerated, honey-modulated Texas voice again. "You let everybody know, now, that everythin's under control."

Rozier nodded at the microphone in his hand that he would. Then he slowly clicked the button on to open the channel. "What is the condition of Front Office at this time?" he asked with apparent calm.

"He's been shot, son," came back Gardner's reply.

Rozier nodded again. Of course there would be very few other reasons to put Torn Sky into effect, but as much as he wanted to, he didn't ask the other question now—the obvious one. This was not the proper channel for that. It could be monitored too easily to use it for anything other than what it was designed for, to tell them only those facts that they had to have now in order to proceed with the plan.

"We'll be back to you, but let them know that everythin's under control," Gardner said again, meaning that Rozier should inform the members of the Cabinet in the rear of the plane of what had happened.

"Yes, sir," Rozier said automatically, and then he handed the microphone up to the copilot, who was still standing above him. There would be other communications from Pyramid, but they didn't need him for that. His job was to walk back now into the main cabin and tell the others.

Rozier sat for a moment steadying himself and looking ahead at the stern profile of the pilot, who was correcting the plane's course, sweeping it up and out in a great banking turn and beginning to return it to the east, back toward the capital. Soon the escort jets from Honolulu or Guam or wherever they would be dispatched from would be visible around them in the once-clear November sky.

The breakers rolled up on an Atlantic beach. They rolled up long and slow and white. The early afternoon light sparkled off the water and on the shore behind a low wooden fence and then across a long sweep of green lawn to where an old man lay on the porch of a big two-story Cape Cod home. The man lay across a couch with a blanket wrapped tightly around him and looked out to sea through a pair of round horn-rimmed glasses that had been his trademark when he'd been younger. The man was Ben Cassidy, the President's father.

Inside the house, a few yards from where he lay, his wife set the phone down into its cradle, and then she stared across the room at the dull gray-green surface of the unlit television screen that could tell her the remainder of the terrible news. But she was afraid for now to turn on the set and learn the truth, and she could only stare at its blank surface. After a few seconds, she looked outside at the man lying across the couch on the front porch of their home, the man she had lived with and loved for over fifty years—all of her adult life. How could she tell him? His own body had been irreparably weakened by a massive stroke only a few months before, and now the once dashing, energetic man could no longer speak or even move short distances unaided. He could only sleep fitfully through the nights and during the days lie wrapped in a blanket and look out to sea and know that he would never again be the man that he once had been. His children were his legs now, his eyes in the world, his voice. How could she tell him that one of them had been stilled? The other time it had been different. There was a war then and part of you walked around half-expecting . . . The woman couldn't finish her thought without remembering a second flood of pain. She needed to be with her husband. They should be together now. She would find a way to tell him when she saw his face. And so she stood and went to the double glass doors that led to the porch of their home and walked outside.

It was a surprisingly warm afternoon in Hyannis, but there was a cooling breeze coming up from the ocean—the kind of a day that her husband and their children had always loved—and when she smelled the cool sea air, the memories began to flood over her, pictures of her children and her husband in a series of family portraits, their children growing bigger year by year, stronger, more confident, more beautiful, and then she had to close her eyes against the flashing series of images, because it hurt too much to remember them now. She was happy that she had them, though. She would take them out and look at them again, when she could.

She crossed the long porch and knelt down next to the thin, damaged, old man who was lying beneath the heavy wool blanket.

There was a spot where the blanket rose up and exposed a patch of pale white skin to the afternoon breeze. Instinctively, she reached out and began arranging the cover, tucking it in below her husband's frail body, so that cool air would not disturb him. Then her fingers touched his narrow, weakened shoulder and she left her hand with the wedding ring on it resting against him as she tried to find the words.

He moved his head slightly then to look into her face, and their eyes met. She could see in them that somehow he already knew. Of course, she thought, remembering now that other time. He'd known then too, even before he'd been told. They both had.

She said the words anyway, more for herself than for him now.

"Jack's been shot," she whispered hoarsely, surprised and frightened by the terrible thickness in her throat and then she sobbed, just once but uncontrollably. The old man reached up with his long, bony, age-spotted fingers and touched the side of her face and brought her close to him, until her cheek was buried against the side of his chest and his own head was resting on top of hers, trying to comfort her as best he could without words that he was unable to speak. She began weeping then, spilling tears onto her husband's chest, as those images of her children returned before her, jumping out unasked for from deep inside her head, where she had tried to store them until she was ready to see them again.

A blue-and-white taxi pulled up in front of a boardinghouse on a tree-lined Dallas residential street and a young man got out and clumsily paid the driver. He did not seem like a man accustomed to taking taxis. He was dressed cheaply in a dark blue windbreaker and khaki slacks and he moved anxiously, barely under control, as he closed the taxi door and walked up the boardinghouse's front path and went inside.

In the entry he was greeted by the hushed tones of a television reporter on vigil on the front steps of the Parkland Memorial Hospital at the outskirts of downtown Dallas, only a few miles away.

The young man paused uncertainly in the entry hall at the base of the short staircase that led to the boardinghouse's second floor. As he stood awkwardly between the front door and the staircase, his landlady's excited voice called out to him.

"Mr. Strode," she said, "they've shot the President."

Arthur Strode stood and nervously unzipped and then rezipped the front of his dark blue windbreaker. "Yes, I know," he said and then fled up the front staircase to his room.

The key to his door didn't seem to fit and he fumbled with it for several seconds before he was able to force it deep into the lock and feel the metal tumblers move against his wrist and fingers. He leaned on the door with all of his weight and fell forward into the room.

The shade was up in the small furnished room, but the window was closed and locked and his bed still unmade. The room smelled faintly foul, and strangely he closed his eyes against the smell. Then he turned back to the thin wooden door and closed it, locking it from the inside only as an after-thought.

He stumbled quickly across the room to the small window and undid the metal catch that had kept it locked and opened the window wide to let in some fresh air. He knelt down by the windowsill then and took several hurried breaths of hot, dry Dallas air. Only after feeling the slight breeze in his face for several seconds did he lean forward and look through the trees that grew up close to the window, staring intently, his face pushed forward toward their leafless November branches, at the street in front of his boardinghouse, but it was empty. And so he stood and went to his dresser, unzipping again the front of his dark blue windbreaker as he walked hurriedly across the room. He paused at the mirror above the dresser and looked back at his reflection in it. His skin was pale white against the dark black stubble of his beard and his eyes were filled with fear. He ran a hand uncertainly through his ill-cut light brown hair and then reached into the top drawer of his dresser and removed a black forty-five caliber pistol from it. He opened the pistol clumsily and saw the chamber clearly for a fraction of a second. It was jammed full of shiny brass-seated cartridges.

He reached into the drawer and quickly emptied a cardboard box of extra shells, spilling them out in a crazy-quilt pattern onto the top of a stack of neatly folded underwear that was lying at the bottom of the drawer.

A horn tapped twice, lightly but unmistakably, outside his window on the tree-lined street below.

The young man crammed handfuls of cartridges into the pockets of his wrinkled khaki pants and leaned forward and waved his hand at the dark car parked beneath the big trees on the other side of the street. When he did, the car moved on slowly.

The man turned from the window and pulled off his jacket. He removed the long tail of his shirt from his pants then and let it drop down and cover the .45 pistol that he now wore tucked deep into the waistband of his khaki slacks.

He raced around the room for a few minutes, throwing some things into a cheap plastic flight bag—a shirt, socks, and fresh underwear, some papers, a photograph, and finally a small diary bound in imitation red leather. Then he started for the door, but he stopped before he left the room and looked back at it again. The drawers to his dresser were out, the closet door thrown half open at a wild angle to the room, the window up, the bed unmade, some of his things left scattered on the floor—an unholy mess his mother would have called it—just as he'd made of his life, he added for her. But she was wrong, he thought. He had everything that he had ever really wanted in life now. And he closed the door angrily, not stopping to lock it, and then he ran down the front stairs.

The television was still playing loudly in the sitting room and he glanced in at it as he passed. His landlady was bent over, watching it intently, and she didn't seem to notice him as he moved by her open door.

He walked outside. Down the block a car engine started and the dark sedan slid out from the side of the curb where it had been waiting and disappeared silently around the corner of Beckworth and Tenth. The dark sedan was the same City of Dallas police car that had been parked in front of his boarding-house only a few moments earlier.

"Mr. Vice President, the Attorney General is holding for you on the hospital's line," Bill Mallory, the Vice President's aide, said.

Gardner looked up from the command center that he had established at the back of the small, dark hospital chapel. After a few seconds of thought, he nodded at his assistant to put the call through.

Gardner stood then and walked down the chapel's narrow aisle to the kneeling figure of Suzanne Cassidy.

"Mrs. Cassidy," the Vice President said softly and then continued without waiting for a reply, "I'm going to be talkin' to the Attorney General now. Would you like to speak with him when I'm done?"

Suzanne turned slowly back to him. "Yes, thank you," she said.

Gardner nodded gently and then returned to the rear of the chapel. As he approached the growing row of phones on the low table at the back of the room, he pointed briskly at his aide to punch in the call. Mallory held the phone out to the Vice President then and Gardner took the instrument firmly in his hand and immediately spoke into it. "Mr. Attorney General," he said solemnly.

"How is he?" the President's brother snapped at him, without any preliminaries.

"He's been shot, at least twice, maybe more. I'm not sure. He's unconscious, has been since it happened. I don't think it's good. They're operatin' on him now about three doors away."

"What are the doctors doing?" Cassidy asked impatiently. The Vice President wasn't telling him anything more than was the television set that he'd been kept waiting in front of for the last twenty minutes.

"Everythin' possible's being done," Gardner said reassuringly.

"And Suzanne?"

"She's fine. I'm with her now," the Vice President said and then, with the spotlight of history pointed straight at them, the two men fell silent. The noises from the people in the hall could be heard through the chapel's double doors, the frenzied, anxious, clamoring sounds of a country waiting to know its direction, but the two men on the phone, who held a big part of that future, had nothing to say to each other—and the silence continued between them for a long time, surprising them both.

"I'm coming there," the Attorney General said finally, but even as he did he looked around at the figures of the FBI men that surrounded him, monitoring his every move, and then he looked out his window at their parked cars that blocked his driveway and at the dozens of agents with their drawn weapons scattered around the perimeter of his home. He was a prisoner in his own house. "I'm coming there and I'm taking Jack out of Dallas," he added defiantly then.

"No, son, I don't think that's right," Gardner drawled, but there was Texas steel at the base of his message. "We don't really know the extent of this thin' yet. Until we do, I think it's best we all keep to the plan, jus' the way it's been mapped out for us. Don't you?"

"No, I don't," the Attorney General's tense New England voice came back slow and firm. "The hell with Summers's plan," he added then in the same cold, deliberate tone.

Gardner was quiet for a moment, looking across at the figure of the dark-haired woman kneeling at the front of the chapel a few feet away. When he began again the Vice President's voice was confident. "It's a governmental order, son," he said. The chill in the silence that followed between the two men was almost palpable, but Gardner was the first to try to warm it with a little Texas syrup.

"I'm goin' to need your help, son. The whole damn country's goin' to need it. So, let's start out right for everybody's sake," he drawled and then waited to let the words and the reality of the new power that they stood for sink in on the President's brother. "Now I need to talk a little business with the Attorney General of the United States. That's who I'm talkin' to, isn't it?"

There was quiet. Then came the stern, disciplined answer in the tense New England voice again: "Yes, Mr. Vice President, it is."

Gardner reached into his inside coat pocket and removed his glasses case. He kept the man on the other end of the phone waiting then while he set the case down in front of him and deliberately removed the small half glasses that he used for reading, flicked them open, and placed them low on the bridge of his nose. On the table in front of him was a letter. At the top of the page the letter bore the official seal of the office of the President of the United States and at the top right-hand corner it was marked PERSONAL AND CONFIDENTIAL.

"I want to read you somethin', Mr. Attorney General," Gardner drawled. "I'm goin' to read to you from a letter I've got here in front of me. When I'm done, I want to ask you a couple of questions." Gardner cleared his throat again as he found his place on the sheet of paper in his hand and then he began to read in a solemn, gravelly voice. "The President and the Vice President have agreed that the following procedures are in accord with the purposes and provisions of Article Two, Section One, of the Constitution, dealing with presidential inability." Suddenly he stopped reading. His aide was quickly approaching him down the chapel aisle.

"It's the doctor, sir. He wants to talk to you and Mrs. Cassidy, right away," Mallory said. The Vice President nodded and reached up and removed his reading glasses and spoke the rest of the short letter by memory into the phone.

"Paragraph one—In the event of inability the President would, if possible," Gardner underlined the phrase "if possible" with his voice for the Attorney General and then went on, "so inform the Vice President, and the Vice President would serve as Acting President, exercising the powers and duties of the office until the inability had ended."

Gardner paused then and watched as Mallory walked to the front of the chapel and knelt by the figure of the President's wife. Then the Vice President continued on in a dry, calm voice. "Paragraph two—In the event of an inability which would prevent the President from so communicating with the Vice President, the Vice President, after such consultation as seems to him appropriate under the circumstances, would decide upon the devolution of the powers and duties of the office."

Suzanne was standing now, her back to the Vice President, as she stopped before the crucifix at the center of the chapel and acknowledged it by making the sign of the cross with a lightly cupped hand across her forehead and chest. Gardner continued talking as he watched her turn and start back down the darkened chapel aisle toward him. "And the Vice President would then serve as President until the inability had ended. That's signed John Trewlaney Cassidy, President of the United States," Gardner said into the phone, looking at the President's wife who was standing only a few feet from him now.

Gardner stood then, holding the phone steady in his hand. "Are you familiar with that letter, Mr. Attorney General?" the Vice President drawled into the telephone.

"Yes, I am," the Attorney General said quietly.

"The doctor wants to speak with us now," Gardner said. "But we'll keep this line open and I'll get back to you as soon as I can."

The Vice President handed the phone to his aide then. "After I speak to the doctor, I'll want to talk to the Attorney General again," he said. Then he turned to Suzanne. "Are you ready?" he asked.

She nodded and reached up and touched the front of her suit to smooth it and, as she did, her fingers came across the edge of the sticky, drying splash of crimson that had seeped now deep into the garment.

"Are you all right?" Gardner said as he watched her drop her hand from the stained cloth.

Without thinking, and reacting gallantly as he had been taught many years before, the Vice President whisked off his suit coat and reached forward to place it across her shoulders and hide the dark red stains on her jacket and skirt.

"No, I don't think that will be necessary," she said with great composure, as she raised her head to look directly into his face.

The tall Texan standing above her looked back deep into her dark brown eyes before he spoke. "There'll be photographers in the hall," he said.

"It's my husband's blood," Suzanne said and lightly touched her stained jacket. "I'm not ashamed of it."

"I'm not either," the Vice President said quickly and then replaced his coat onto his own shoulders. "Well, les' see if we can find a way to talk to that doctor without half the reporters in the State of Texas jumpin' all over us," he continued, and then the two figures, the tall, sad-faced Texan and the slim, elegant, dark-haired woman in the bright pink suit with the almost dried bloodstains splashed across the front of it, started out the chapel doors into the crowded hospital hallway.

In the hall, Secret Service men swept the two figures through the noisy central corridor to a dimly lit back staircase and then down the stairs and into a small room in a secluded corner of the floor below.

The doctor was already inside, standing at the window, looking out at the hospital grounds, where a large crowd was gathering with a police line forming and strengthening in front of it.

Through the curtainless window behind the doctor Suzanne could see the flagpole at the front of the hospital. The American flag was still flying at full staff, rippling open in the light Texas breeze at the very top of the metal pole.

The doctor turned from the window as he heard the door open behind him. His once starched, snow-white surgical gown was unbuttoned at the neck and the front of the cloth was awash in a sea of red. "He's alive," the doctor said simply.

CHAPTER
2

"I don't want to mislead you, Mrs. Cassidy. The wounds that your husband has sustained are very severe, particularly the head wound. There's been a great deal of damage." The doctor leaned forward and looked only at Suzanne as he spoke.

"Is he conscious?" she asked softly.

The doctor shook his head no, and out of the corner of his eye he could see the tall figure of the Vice President stiffen and then begin to move anxiously toward him, but the doctor continued talking only to the President's wife. "So far, all we've been able to accomplish are some very preliminary emergency measures. But we have specialists coming in from all over the country. We're going to need to operate again very soon though, probably within a few hours. I can assure you, Mrs. Cassidy, that everything that can be done is and will continue to be done, but, of course, you may want to bring in your own people to work with us or to take over completely, if you prefer. That's entirely your decision."

Suzanne nodded her head that she would consider it. "Thank you, doctor," she said, "but that won't be necessary for now."

"Mrs. Cassidy, I want you to understand, your husband's condition is a moment-by-moment proposition. He's been very badly injured. The most serious damage is from the bullet wound to his head," the doctor said, touching the place on the side of his own head where the bullet had struck the President. "It did not enter the brain itself," the doctor said emphatically. "But it does appear that it shattered a small portion of the skull, and when it did it sent several small fragments of bone into the outer layers of the brain. Had the

19

bullet been a fraction of an inch . . ." The doctor didn't finish his sentence. "Even as it is," he continued instead, "your husband may never regain consciousness again. Head injuries, particularly something like this, are extraordinarily unpredictable. In your husband's case, it's made even more difficult by the complicating factor that he has sustained two other wounds, one to his chest and one to an area between his neck and shoulder. Neither of these wounds alone would normally be life threatening, but the three together," the doctor paused again, before adding, "well, there's just no way to know exactly what's going to happen yet. All we can say with any certainty is that for the moment, he's alive." The doctor's face, as he finished, showed how difficult it had been for him to say what he had.

"I understand," Suzanne said evenly. "I'd like an opportunity to thank everyone involved. I thought they were magnificent. Can that be arranged?"

"Yes, of course," the doctor said.

"Doctor, I need to speak with you," the Vice President said, stepping forward again, until his presence could no longer be ignored.

Suzanne turned back to the Vice President then. "Rance, everything that needs to be said can be said in front of me."

The Vice President nodded and then looked up at the doctor, who had sunk down in weariness now and was half seated on the edge of a small metal desk by the window at the far side of the room.

"In your judgment, doctor, is Mr. Cassidy presently capable of performing his duties as President of the United States?" Gardner asked, in a cold, calm voice.

The doctor looked up slowly from where he was seated at the other end of the room. His face looked puzzled, but the question continued to hang unanswered in the room, floating anxiously in the air between the two men. "No, of course not," he said finally.

The Vice President nodded and then followed up like a good prosecuting attorney making his case. "Doctor, in your medical opinion, is he likely to be capable of performing those duties again in the near future?" he asked.

Before he answered, the doctor looked again only at Suzanne, and she returned his look steadily and with deep composure.

"No," he said, looking into her dark brown eyes. "No, it's not likely," he added. "Even if he survives the next few hours, there will be damage. Speech problems perhaps, probably some serious memory loss, at least temporarily. These things can take years. Even with a vigorous man like your husband," he said, still speaking only to Suzanne. "The best we can hope for is a long recuperation period."

"I want you to prepare a written statement to that effect, signed by you and by every doctor who was in that room. I want that statement typed and signed in the next ten minutes. My staff can help you with it," Gardner said sharply, the honey and cottonwoods almost totally gone from his speech.

The doctor shook his head in confusion. It was all happening too fast for him. "You have to understand, we're still in a highly speculative area here," he said. "It's extremely difficult to estimate what the President's condition is going to be twenty minutes from now much less in a week or a few months," he said and turned toward the President's wife again. All three people were silent for several long seconds then.

"Please do your best," Suzanne said finally, breaking the awkward silence.

"Yes, of course. I will," the doctor said. "You'll have it in a few minutes," he added and then stood wearily and started for the door.

"Doctor," Suzanne said.

"Yes," he answered, turning back to her.

"As soon as you've done what the Vice President has requested, I would like to see my husband."

"Mrs. Cassidy," the doctor began uncertainly, but then, seeing her steady gaze, he let his voice break off and only nodded his head. "Yes, of course," he said.

There was a report out now for a young man in a dark windbreaker and light-colored slacks. He worked at the School Book Depository building in Dealey Plaza where the police had found the rifle. The man even had a name—Arthur Allen Strode—and an address.

Special Agent Sullivan knew that the proper procedure was for him to call in and be told by someone at headquarters what to do next, but headquarters here in Dallas would be a shambles and it would probably just be a waste of time. He could call Washington, he thought, but he didn't want to. Technically he was under the jurisdiction of the Dallas office until Monday morning, when he was scheduled to return to the capital. Under the circumstances, he could probably get away with a minor breach of procedure and just go ahead and follow this thing out and see where it led. It was worth the risk, he decided after he'd thought it through; the Bureau should be in on this.

So he followed the two Dallas police officers who had gotten the call down the steps of the Book Depository and returned with them into the confusion of Dealey Plaza. He caught the second of the two uniformed officers just before they reached the patrol car that was parked in front of the building.

Sullivan flashed his identification materials and without asking jumped into the back seat of the squad car. The young officer looked at Sullivan closely for a moment, but he left him alone. There was obviously nothing in the police rule book either that covered a situation like this one, Sullivan thought, as he watched the young officer's puzzled face.

As soon as the patrol car managed to thread its way through the stunned remnants of the crowd that remained in the plaza, the Dallas streets were clear and Sullivan leaned forward and listened intently to the squad car radio, while the car flew down Commerce and across the Floodway toward Beckworth and then turned south down the tree-lined, residential block that led to their destination.

The static-filled radio repeated the description several times of this man, Strode, whose boardinghouse they were headed for now, but then for no apparent reason the dispatcher called out for the officers to also be on the lookout for a second individual: male, mid-twenties, dark hair, maybe a Latin, short, five-six or -seven, but heavily built, and wearing a blue plaid shirt. Jesus, Sullivan thought, that's a description of the man he'd seen in the parking lot at the back of the hillside right after the shooting.

"What was that?" Sullivan asked and leaned even farther forward toward the front seat, hoping that he could hear it again, but the police radio didn't repeat the description a second time.

The cop in the passenger seat turned back to him then and shrugged his shoulders.

"I saw that guy," Sullivan started, but there wasn't time to talk now. The squad car was stopping in front of a two-story rooming house in the middle of a quiet residential street on the outskirts of downtown Dallas.

The three men jumped out of the patrol car and the young officer who had been sitting on the shotgun side raced up the driveway and disappeared around the corner of the house. The driver waited for his partner to get into position and then went quickly up the boardinghouse's front steps with Sullivan following only a few short steps behind him.

The officer knocked on the door and then waited. Inside the house, a television set was playing out the news of the drama at the Dallas hospital. Reluctantly, a heavyset, white-haired woman wearing a once brightly flowered housedress and a shapeless, light blue sweater came to the door. When she saw the uniformed officer and the tall, neatly dressed young man with the short-cropped blond hair standing on her front porch, she quickened her pace and opened the screen door wide to let the two imposing-looking figures come inside.

"Yes, is something wrong?" the woman asked, puffing with the effort it had taken to get from her television set to the front door.

"Does Arthur Strode live here?" the policeman asked.

The woman nodded, but her big round face looked bewildered above the faded flowers of her housedress. "First door on the left, up the stairs," she said, motioning toward the staircase behind her.

"Is he in?" the policeman asked.

"Yes, I think so. He came in about twenty minutes ago. We talked about the President," the woman said, backing away toward the safety of her television set again, as the two men moved past her toward the front stairs.

She watched from the doorway as the uniformed officer started up the staircase and then, drawing his gun and holding it at the ready, he double-timed up the last few steps to the landing at the top. He was followed a half second later by the tall young man with the short-cut blond hair. As they approached Strode's door, the young man drew his gun as well, removing it carefully from a neat little black holster that was strapped at an angle to his waist and hidden, until that moment, under his suit coat.

The two men positioned themselves at either side of the upstairs doorway.

"Arthur Strode!" the police officer called out. "Arthur Allen Strode! Police!"

he repeated, even louder, and when there was no response, he reached forward and tried the metal doorknob. It turned easily and the two men whirled from their positions at the sides of the door and rushed inside the small upstairs bedroom.

The room was empty and quiet. A gentle breeze blew in, disturbing the sheer light curtains at the window. The closet door was open and the police officer flew to it and braced himself against the wall at the side of the opening before spinning his body into it, crouching low, his service revolver in two clenched hands out in front of him, but the closet, too, was empty. The officer turned back into the room. The drawers to the bureau were open, clothes and papers scattered on the floor.

Special Agent Sullivan went to the open drawers and looked inside. Brass cartridges from an overturned cardboard box glinted up at him through piles of gray-white underwear. He gestured for the police officer to look inside.

The officer crossed the room and without touching anything scanned the contents of the open top drawer.

"Our boy packed in a hurry," Sullivan said.

The officer nodded his agreement. "We better call in and let people know he packed something that holds forty-five-caliber cartridges," the officer answered, and the two men backed carefully out of the room and closed the door and then returned down the staircase to the first floor.

When he reached the front hall, Sullivan stepped inside the parlor where the television was announcing another twist in the already tangled Dallas afternoon. The woman stood spellbound, looking down at her television set, her back to Sullivan.

"What is it?" the FBI agent asked.

"A police officer's been shot," she said, without taking her eyes off her television set even for a moment. "Right close to here."

"What?" Sullivan turned to see the startled face of the uniformed officer standing behind him.

The woman shook her head in bewilderment, her eyes still not leaving the television screen. "I don't . . ."

"Ma'am!" The police officer's sharply official voice finally brought the woman back around to face the room. "We're going to leave an officer here with you. If Mr. Strode returns . . ."

The woman's eyes blinked several times, not understanding. "He's not there," she stammered.

"No, ma'am. He's not."

"You should have come in right away," she said.

It was the police officer's turn to look confused. "What do you mean?"

"I mean, the first time you pulled up," the heavyset woman said again even more insistently, and then she walked across the room to a window at the rear of the television that was still spilling out a series of pictures of the police-officer shooting only a few blocks from her home. "Right after Arthur came in. I saw your car over there," she said and pointed out across the street at where the long branches of the sycamore trees growing near the curb dropped down and shaded the far side of Beckworth Avenue.

"A police car?" the officer said, trying to understand.

"Yes," the woman said firmly, as she turned back into the room. "It honked twice, kind of like a signal. So I went over and looked. When I did, it pulled away."

"It wasn't us," the officer said.

"Well, it was somebody. A black-and-white patrol car, just like yours."

"And Strode was here then?" Sullivan asked. "Are you sure?"

"Oh, yes. It was right after we talked and he went upstairs. Less than a half hour after the President was shot. I'm sure of it," the woman said.

Vice President of the United States Ransom W. Gardner had returned to the temporary command center that he'd established in the hospital chapel. He held one of the series of phones that had been set up along the back wall of the darkened room.

On the other end of the telephone line was General Greer, the Chairman of the Joint Chiefs of Staff, in Washington. He was giving Gardner a complete report on status—worldwide. And his message was clear. In the one hour and . . . As he listened, Gardner glanced down briefly at his wristwatch now for the first time since it had happened. In the one hour and sixteen minutes since the shots had been fired in Dealey Plaza the Joint Chiefs had been in almost constant communication with each of the nine combat commands of the United States that surrounded the globe. Each of these commands had been placed at their highest state of readiness—Defense Condition One—as had dozens of other elements of the nation's defense systems throughout the world. Command planes and bombers had circled constantly in the skies over Europe and at certain strategic locations above the Pacific and Persian oceans as well, but immediately after it had happened and consistently thereafter messages of reassurance had come in from Moscow. There was no attempt at a coup, no attack, the Kremlin had communicated over and over again, the Chairman of the Joint Chiefs explained to the Vice President now.

And across the world, the Chairman continued, every American patrol had reported back a message of status quo, and no failure of official communication of any kind had been reported anywhere. "The nation is at peace," the Chairman of the Joint Chiefs reported in summary. Operation Torn Sky could go back to where it had come from, back into locked black ring binders in secret vaults in the big cement blockhouse buildings deep in the defense maze of the complicated nation that had created it.

"Sir, we believe it's appropriate at this time to withdraw from Defense Condition One," the Chairman of the Joint Chiefs said as he completed his report.

Gardner held the command phone steady in his hand and looked across the room to where the President's wife was speaking into one of the hospital's extensions with her brother-in-law, the Attorney General. The Chairman of the Joint Chiefs was awaiting his instructions. The world was waiting at alert.

"Thank you, General. Your people have done an excellent job," the Vice President said, and then he looked up at his aide, standing above him, and spoke to both him and to the Chairman of the Joint Chiefs at the same time. "I want this line held open. The general and I will need to speak again in a few minutes. Thank you, General," Gardner said and then stood, handing the phone to Mallory, who took it and immediately began issuing instructions to the hospital operator.

Gardner crossed the room toward the weary figure of Suzanne Cassidy and, as he did, she glanced up at him and said a hurried good-bye into the receiver and then held the instrument out to the Vice President.

"Tim," the Vice President drawled gently into the phone. "Your brother's unconscious and he's liable to be that way for a while."

"Yes, I know," came back the tense reply.

"Have you been thinking about that matter we discussed earlier?" Gardner said.

"Yes, of course," the Attorney General answered.

"I'm going to need your support and the support of Mrs. Cassidy as well," the Vice President said, looking straight ahead at Suzanne, who was standing only a few yards from him at the side of the chapel and looking up at its single, small stained-glass window.

"I want to come there," Cassidy said, his voice showing the strain he felt from being kept practically a prisoner in his own home, surrounded by Secret Service men while events in Dallas moved forward without him.

"We have to do what's best for the country," Gardner said, and as he did he could hear a sharp intake of breath on the other end of the line. It didn't sound like the Attorney General was in any mood to listen to lectures on patriotism at the moment, Gardner thought as he heard the angry sound.

"You and I both know there's no Communist conspiracy, except maybe inside Summers's head," Cassidy answered tensely.

"I'm goin' on television in a few minutes," the Vice President said, ignoring the Attorney General's comment. "The country needs to know that it has a leader. It needs to know there's no danger and that everythin's all right," Gardner added. "I'm goin' to tell them that I've spoken to Summers, to the Joint Chiefs, to members of the Cabinet, and to all appropriate command centers, and that I've spoken to you, Mr. Attorney General, and that we've determined," Gardner paused then and repeated it, so there could be no doubt what he was asking for now, "and that we've determined, in accordance with President Cassidy's own desires, that I should immediately become the Acting President of the United States and assume all of the powers of that office. I want Mrs. Cassidy to stand with me and Mrs. Gardner when I deliver that message to the American people."

"I see," the Attorney General answered.

"Yes, but do you concur?" the Vice President snapped back at him.

There was a long pause—then Cassidy's clipped New England voice again. "And I come to Dallas," the Attorney General said. "You put the pieces back together again, right now. Operation Torn Sky is called off as of this moment, and the world goes back the way it was," Cassidy lashed the words angrily into the phone.

"Only the President or in his absence the Acting President can do that," Gardner said pointedly.

"I understand that," Cassidy said and then paused.

Gardner was silent for a moment now too, looking again only at Suzanne's straight, tense figure standing in front of him.

"I have the Joint Chiefs on the other line," he said finally. "If they're in agreement, Operation Torn Sky will be terminated effective as of this moment. I'm going to ask each of the other members of the Cabinet to return to Washington then, but you do whatever you believe that you should do."

"I'm coming there," the Attorney General said without any hesitation.

"I'm going to put Mrs. Cassidy on the phone now. I want you to explain to her what we've decided," Gardner said and then set the receiver down on the table.

"Mrs. Cassidy," the Vice President said, and, when she didn't move, he turned away and walked to the far side of the room.

Only then did Suzanne walk back the few short steps and lift the receiver slowly to her ear. "Yes, Tim," she said, without needing to be told anything further. "I understand."

The police car at the intersection of Tenth and Patton was parked at a hasty angle to the curb. Its driver-side door was open and the fallen figure of its driver lay on the street nearby.

The sound of gunfire had brought a store owner and his wife out onto the sidewalk across the street. Behind them a woman carrying a sack of groceries in her arms stood frozen in the store's doorway and an old man peered out in fear at the scene spread out in front of him from the porch of his home next door. Blood was flowing freely now from the head of the fallen officer toward the rain gutter at the side of the road.

Down the block a man wearing khaki slacks and a long white shirt that hid a forty-five caliber pistol beneath it walked hurriedly toward the intersection of Tenth and Denver and then disappeared quickly around the corner. The man was Arthur Strode.

A second man walked calmly past the abandoned police car then and stepped into a waiting gray sedan. He started the car's engine without looking either to his right or left, but only straight ahead through the car's dusty windshield. He swung the sedan out into the street, taking a wide berth around the spot in the road that held the fallen officer.

The gray sedan continued on down Tenth and then out of sight. Its driver had been short, but compactly built, with dark black hair, and he had been dressed in a blue plaid shirt and faded light blue pants.

By now other people were beginning to slowly appear from out of nearby shops and from the row of small wood-framed homes that faced Tenth Street on the north. A motorist passed and slowed but didn't stop, continuing on at a faster pace toward downtown Dallas. Finally a young man appeared from one of the shops across the street and, seeing the fallen officer, he ran over and knelt down near the body, but he was careful not to touch his own clothes to the trail of blood by the officer's head. The young man looked down, puzzled by the thing that lay in front of him. He reached out tentatively to touch it and then quickly withdrew his hand. The young man had never seen the body of a dead person before, but he knew somehow with complete certainty that this fallen man in front of him was dead.

Soon the others began edging closer to the body in the middle of the circle they were forming, while motorists began to stop and block the road on both sides of the small, hushed crowd around the policeman's body. In the distance they could hear the sound of sirens now, only faintly at first, but then growing closer and louder.

A few hundred yards away, around a corner and down Denver Avenue, Arthur Strode half walked, half jogged along the narrow, nearly empty sidewalk. He looked anxiously back and forth several times, glancing across the street, and then he turned his head to look behind him. He stopped for a moment by the glass front of an appliance store that featured that day a tired array of washers, dryers, and TV sets. He pressed his face nervously up against the glass and looked inside. A television set showed him the latest pictures from Parkland Memorial Hospital.

He hurried erratically on, passing a dress shop, a magazine stand, a drug store, and finally spotting the sanctuary of a movie theater.

The theater doors were open, but the ticket booth was empty. There was no ticket taker at the front door or behind the refreshment counter and so he went unseen into the darkened lower mezzanine. The long neat rows of seats were almost empty, but he sat near the back, staring blankly up at the screen, where enormous Technicolor images moved in some strange parody of life in front of him, but their movements and their words were meaningless to him.

He scanned the small audience and examined with care the twin exits at the base of the brightly lit movie screen. He looked away from the screen then. Below it and to one side, an exit door was opening and the shadowy figure of a man appeared. He was carrying something in one hand, held high. It was a compact metal object that glinted brightly in the light.

Someone in a front row screamed when he saw the object up close and then the other exit door opened and another shadow figure appeared. It was a policeman. A real-life drama was beginning to be played out beneath the fantasy story on the giant movie screen.

More uniformed officers began pouring in through both exit doors and they spread out and slowly began moving up the aisles, examining closely the few frightened faces that they passed.

Strode stood and started down the aisle closest to him toward the rear of the theater. As he did, he reached under his shirt and removed the forty-five caliber pistol from the waistband of his pants. He carried the pistol low, letting it drop down hidden behind the side of his leg, like it was his own little secret.

One of the officers saw him and yelled "Stop!" Strode did and then he turned back very slowly to face the sound. As he pivoted on the worn surface of the theater carpet, he began to raise his weapon into the air, but he heard the sounds of other officers behind him now, running down the narrow aisle, and in front of him there were suddenly other uniformed figures. He was surrounded.

His body was turned back toward the enormous silver movie screen. Strode's pistol was up, pointed at nothing in particular, and then, seeing the drawn weapons in the hands of the uniformed figures that surrounded him, tense and steady, pointed straight at him, he dropped the heavy pistol that he'd held in his own hand down onto the theater aisle.

"It's all over!" he shouted wildly, as he watched the uniformed figures, their guns still drawn, closing in around him.

The gray Chevy sedan sped down Tenth Street away from downtown Dallas and then turned up onto the expressway. Its driver kept the vehicle moving efficiently through the light afternoon traffic, approaching but being very careful to never exceed the speed limit.

He played the radio low, so that at all times he could hear the sounds of approaching vehicles or the whine of a closing siren behind him. He kept his angry dark black eyes straight ahead, only occasionally glancing up at the rearview mirror to assure himself that there was nothing out of the ordinary following him.

His lane of traffic slowed behind a painfully immobile truck, but he didn't speed out around it dangerously or attract attention to himself by sounding his horn. Instead he stayed disciplined, as he knew that he must, and used the time to search the radio dial for the news that he hungrily sought, but the stations refused to tell him what he wanted to hear—only more waiting, more uncertainty. Was it possible that they could have failed? He slammed the radio dial in anger with the heel of his hand and the dial jumped to static. He settled back in the driver's seat then and fought to bring his emotions back under control. After a few seconds he reached up and adjusted the radio back to a local station that was reporting the news directly from the hospital.

The truck pulled off at the next exit and the traffic began to clear away and the man breathed out deeply, exhaling a big load of tension, trying to relax, and then he edged the gray car up close to the speed limit again.

Soon he was at the far outskirts of Dallas. He pulled the car off the expressway and began working his way from the main streets and onto the narrower back country roads.

A small airport emerged out of the miles of flat Texas countryside and the man turned the gray car into its empty parking lot.

He parked the car and turned the engine off, but left the single ignition key in place. Then he reached over and opened the glove compartment. Inside was a long-barreled thirty-eight caliber Smith & Wesson revolver. He wrapped the revolver carefully in a black windbreaker that lay on the passenger seat next to him.

Then he carried the neatly folded package to the trunk of his car. The trunk opened without a key. It contained a small brown paper sack and a cheap blue vinyl flight bag. The disconnected metal rods of a marksman's rifle protruded from the sack and dark oily spots appeared on its brown paper surface. The man refolded the top of the sack, so that the metal gun parts were no longer visible. Then he glanced down at the vinyl bag. Impulsively he opened it. A tangle of underwear, papers, and a sprinkling of brass-seated cartridges stared back at him. He swirled his hand quickly through the hastily packed contents and uncovered a small red imitation-leather-bound book— a diary. He checked its contents briefly. There was excited scrawled hand-writing on several of its pages. Jesus, the man thought and lifted the diary up and stuffed it into the breast pocket of his own blue plaid shirt. Then he carefully rezipped the flight bag and closed the lid of the trunk down over it.

A few moments later, holding his windbreaker-wrapped parcel in one hand, he crossed the parking lot to the break in the aluminum cyclone fence that surrounded the almost deserted airfield.

A single-prop aircraft waited for him a few yards away at the edge of the runway. Its engines were turned on, whipping its twin propellers in noisy circles, and a pilot waved to him from its cockpit as he crossed toward the small plane. The man waved back and then quickly climbed on board the aircraft.

Immediately the light plane taxied into position and within seconds began its burst of speed down the narrow desolate runway. Then it exploded into the air and glided up toward the bright blue Texas sky.

Only after it was far out of sight did another man emerge from the shadows of the airport's abandoned hangars and cross the parking lot to the gray car. The man went to the trunk first, opened it and checked its contents. Satisfied, he closed the trunk again and then walked around and opened the driver's side door and started the car's engine.

A few seconds later, the man pulled the car onto the Texas side road and drove it east into the dusty back country away from the deserted airfield.

The downstairs cafeteria of Parkland Memorial Hospital had been converted into a makeshift newsroom.

Reporters milled around talking to each other, or stood watching the screens of the television sets that had been brought in and placed around the perimeter of the room, while a few waited for their chance to use one of the small bank of telephones that had been set up on a row of tables near the cafeteria's back door.

A member of the hospital staff would occasionally appear on the stage at the front of the crowded room to make a short announcement concerning the President's condition or to give the press the name of some new medical specialist who was being brought in to examine him, but something else was stirring now and the buzz of noise in the small room was growing louder.

Frank O'Connor, one of the President's assistants, a tough Irish pol from South Boston, appeared at the room's back door and started for the temporary podium. He was followed closely by Bill Mallory, one of Gardner's people. Something was happening, and the television lights flashed on and the cameras moved into position as the men and women of the press shuffled forward toward the stage.

Behind Mallory and O'Connor came two lower White House assistants. The assistants were carrying stacks of photocopied handouts and the reporters began scrambling for them. They were copies of a letter signed by Cassidy with the big presidential seal at the top and marked PRIVATE AND CONFI-DENTIAL, but O'Connor's scratchy, Boston-accented voice sounding through the hastily set up P.A. system brought the reporters quickly away from the handouts and back to the small stage at the front of the room.

"Ladies and gentlemen," O'Connor said over the loudly reverberating sound system. And then the reporters saw the first hint of what was to happen as a small cadre of Secret Service men pushed through the back door behind O'Connor, and the Vice President and Mrs. Gardner emerged from out of the pack of Secret Service agents, and then the crowd gasped as the President's wife came into view, still in her bright pink suit, the bloodstains on it shockingly apparent.

The reporters' questions shouted out O'Connor's introductory words and, in the bedlam, Gardner stepped to the microphone while Mrs. Cassidy and the Vice President's own wife took their places quietly on either side of him.

Gardner waited for the crowd to quiet before he began talking in his slow, solemn, but soothingly reassuring Texas voice. "My fellow Americans," he drawled slowly and then stopped and looked down with mournful eyes at the trio of television cameras that were aimed at him from the top of the ingenious arrangement of stacked cafeteria benches set up at the front of the room. "It is with deep regret and great sadness that I come before you today. As you know, President Cassidy has been gravely wounded," he said, and the crowd gasped again, as if the event that they had known about for well over an hour now had just been announced for the first time. "The President's condition remains critical at this time. But we are all confident that in due course and with the help of Almighty God, he will survive this crisis and soon be strong enough to resume his duties as the leader of our great nation." Gardner paused again and looked directly out at his audience. "However, even as we confidently await that moment, the business of our government must continue, and in accordance with President Cassidy's own wishes, as the Vice President, the powers and responsibilities of his office have temporarily passed into my hands." Gardner held up his hands for the television cameras then, to show their size and strength. "And let me assure you that at no time has our nation been without executive leadership. Since my arrival here at Parkland Hospital, I have been in constant and direct communication with the Joint Chiefs of Staff that represent each of our great military branches, and with the directors of both the Federal Bureau of Investigation and the Central Intelligence Agency. They have reported to me that our nation has been and is at this moment totally free from any danger whatsoever. Further, I have just spoken with the chief of police here in Dallas, and I can announce to you now that the tragic event that has happened here today appears almost certainly to be an isolated act perpetrated by a sole individual, and that individual has been apprehended and is at this very moment in the custody of the Dallas Police Department. Let me repeat, we are certain that at no time was our national security in any danger whatsoever from the actions of this single, tragically misguided individual." The Vice President paused for a moment then and looked out at the reporters that surrounded him in the small room and out at the greater audience that he knew was watching and listening anxiously to his every word around the country and throughout the world. "I have discussed these matters with members of the Cabinet including the Attorney General, who I've asked to join us here, and they have each pledged to me their complete support in the hours and days ahead. And now I invite you to join Mrs. Cassidy and Mrs. Gardner and myself in our prayers that the President will soon be restored to his full health and once again resume his position as the leader of our great country."

And as he finished, the Vice President bowed his head in a moment of silent prayer and without a vote being cast the leadership of the most powerful nation on earth quietly passed from one man to another.

They led the President's wife down long, narrow back corridors, up a freight elevator, past checkpoints manned by grim-faced, dark-suited men, and finally into a small, cheerless room.

The President lay on a hospital bed, surrounded by doctors and medical technicians. The metal blinds were drawn across the windows of his room and outside Secret Service men crouched with rifles resting across their laps on the slanting roof of the hospital's top floor.

Suzanne looked through the tangle of white-clad bodies that surrounded the bed to where she could see her husband's face just barely visible above the starched white sheets. His eyes were closed, his features calm and peaceful. The top of his head was wrapped in thick bandages and a clear plastic breathing apparatus labored in his nostrils. She looked at the face of her fallen husband for several seconds as she waited for the white-clad men and women to slowly file past her into the hallway. A tall, gray-haired man in a white surgical gown was the last. He stopped in front of her. "Mrs. Cassidy, I'm Doctor Abramson," he said quietly, and she extended her hand and shook his long precise fingers. Her gaze was steady and intense, but her dark brown eyes refused to disclose even a hint of what she felt now.

"Please just take a moment," he said.

She crossed the room and knelt down by the side of his bed and buried her face in his arm and shoulder, being very careful not to disturb his handsome damaged head wreathed in the thick cushioning of sterile bandages.

"Oh, Jack," she whispered through her tears. "Oh, dear Jack, what have they done to you?"

CHAPTER

3

Tim could see it from the air through the lightly misting rain. Parkland Hospital was close to Love Field and the pilot had brought the Attorney General down low and circled the field once, so that he could see a picture of it from above. And there it was spread out below him for miles, stretching out in every direction below the plane— thousands of twinkling lights glowing in the dark night, lighting his way into Dallas.

The hospital had released an announcement in the late afternoon that the operation on the President had been successful, but that he was still unconscious and that the night ahead remained critical for him. And then thousands of sparks of hope had flamed up in the vast crowd that had been standing vigil around the hospital grounds. Soon, all over America, the people were out on the streets holding single candles, or small glowing flashlights, or briefly flaming matches, anything that would burn brightly against the darkness of the night.

Tim looked down at the sight below him, the cabin lights in his plane turned out, the seemingly endless sea of lights a warm golden yellow color under the slanting line of rain, and he closed his eyes for a moment and let his own prayers join those of the people on the ground.

After a few seconds, he opened his eyes again and looked across at his wife, who was sitting next to him. She was crying softly, making no noise, only letting a few tears drop down over her cheeks, but as Tim turned toward her, she looked up at him and smiled. He smiled back and then he glanced across the aisle to where Jack's two children were sitting, both looking down with

33

wonder and awe at the beautiful sight spread out below them in tribute to their father. And then, finally, Tim turned to look behind his brother's children to where the rest of his own family sat, all of them making a quiet pilgrimage to Dallas together.

The military jet circled once and then followed the flickering lines of light gently down onto the wet tarmac of Love Field.

The Attorney General and his wife were the first of the passengers out the door of the aircraft, and they stood for a moment then, lit up in the bright television lights that surrounded the plane, and looked across the cement airstrip to where thousands of people were pressing up quietly against the aluminum fence that separated them from the airfield. The people were silent, most of them holding single brightly burning candles in their hands.

Tim didn't wave at the crowd, but he stood respectfully, solemnly looking at it, exchanging the love and affection that he felt directly with the people in it, and then he held out his hand for his wife and they walked together down the ramp to the waiting limousine.

The children followed, one by one—the boys of the Cassidy family dressed that night in neat dark suits and the girls in dresses of whites and grays. None of them wore raincoats or any concession to the blowing rain. The President's son and daughter came last, holding each other's hands tightly, their nurse following closely behind them.

Soon a short procession of limousines led by a squad of slowly moving police motorcycles began to move along the airfield's wire fence. The people in the crowd pressed up close to the barrier as the limousines passed, and Tim drew down the bulletproof window next to him and sat forward, so that he could see clearly the faces of the people standing at the roadside. A Secret Service man seated across from him reached out to stop him, but the President's younger brother ignored him and continued to look directly out at the faces of the people in the crowd, as the limousine traveled along the long wire fence. After a few seconds, Kay, too, sat forward and rolled her own bulletproof window down and silently acknowledged the people standing on the sides of the road as the limousine continued slowly down the wet Dallas streets.

At the hospital, the short motorcade stopped and the family members spilled out of the limousines and started up the front steps of the modern glass-front building.

The Attorney General's younger brother, Brian, was already there ahead of him, waiting in the mild rain at the top of the hospital steps that were lit up by more television lights and by the glowing ring of candles held by the people pressing up against the police line that surrounded the front of the building. When he saw Tim, Brian came quickly down the steps to his brother and the two men embraced in front of the crowd and in the full glare of the television cameras, holding each other the way they would have within the privacy of their own family.

"I'm glad you're here," Brian whispered hoarsely into Tim's ear. Then the

"What kind of time do I have in New Hampshire, Tom?" Granderman said, even though he knew the answer perfectly well himself even before he asked it, right down to the hours and minutes, but he wanted everyone else seated at the dinner table that night to know just how serious he was now.

"You have a little over two weeks to file," Bargley said, picking up on the cue. "But Longwood's been in and out of the state for the last six months," he added, looking around at the rest of the dinner table. He knew that none of this was really news to any of these men, but it seemed to him a good way to remind them all of the size of the job ahead. "We can't afford to be so careful that you lose it to him. Senator Longwood's own peculiar brand of Republicanism sells pretty well in some parts of our neighbor state," he added, looking back at Granderman himself, as he finished.

"That kind of Republicanism died with Taft," Granderman said.

"Robert or William Howard?" someone down the table quipped. They'd all heard the small joke before, but the table full of elegantly dressed men laughed now with appreciation at its timing and with a general sense of their own new well-being. When they stopped, Granderman lifted his glass of wine toward the candlelight and peered through its crystal surface at the brightly dancing flame. "Here's to a whole new ball game," he said and lifted his glass even higher in a salute to his dinner guests, and then he took the sparkling crystal glass to his lips and drank thirstily from it.

It was late evening in the bayous of Louisiana too, and a light plane soared over the dense swampy ground below.

The man in the blue plaid shirt, who was sitting in the plane's passenger seat, looked over at his pilot.

The pilot's hands were steady on the wheel as the plane skimmed low, just a few hundred yards above the treetops of the Louisiana swampland. He was dressed in an olive-drab military shirt that had too many oversize button-flap pockets sewed on to the front of it to belong to any real army, and his aging freckled face was tense and determined, showing just how deeply involved with his role he was, but the cheap, ill-fitting red toupee that he wore at a slight angle down over his forehead and the thick continuous line of bright red eyebrow that flowed out above his eyes made him hard to take too seriously.

"What do they call you?" the red-haired pilot asked.

"It doesn't matter," the man in the plaid shirt said. But then a few moments later he added casually, "Lopez sometimes."

"I'm Regan."

"This is the longest goddamned flight in history," Lopez snapped suddenly.

"I'm supposed to keep you on schedule," Regan answered him.

"Right," Lopez said without much conviction. "How far out are we now?"

Regan glanced down at the huge, round, luminescent dial of his military watch. "Twenty-two minutes," he said without even looking over at his passenger. The less he knew about this guy the better, he thought as he kept his gaze fixed straight ahead.

The guy's a fucking walking army supply store, Lopez said to himself, as the pilot studied the face of his complicated compass-watch. Then Lopez reached down and picked up the bundle of his windbreaker that had been lying on the floor of the plane by his feet. It was time now.

"New Orleans is out of the question," he said, as he withdrew the long-barreled Smith & Wesson revolver from inside the folds of his jacket.

Regan stared over at the gun in confusion. It was pointed straight at his stomach.

"Jesus, put that thing away," he breathed out in fear, but Lopez kept the barrel of the gun pointed at its target.

"It's all been arranged," Regan said.

Typical supply-store hero, Lopez thought as he watched his pilot's lip begin to tremble.

"You stupid fucking bastard." Lopez spit the words angrily out at his pilot now. "What do you think? They're going to let us live happily ever after?" he said and then paused. "We're not goin' to New Orleans," he added after a few seconds, looking away from the bizarre frightened profile of his pilot and down at the marshy land below the plane.

Regan didn't answer him. He'd been afraid of the same thing, although he'd refused to admit it even to himself until now, but shit, he was scared too. The men waiting on the ground for them in New Orleans were capable of anything.

"We're less than ten minutes from the Gulf," his passenger said, interrupting his thoughts. "We could be in Mexico in a few hours."

Regan shook his head no. "They'll pick us up on their radar," he said.

"Not if we stay low enough," Lopez said.

"The Gulf is full of ships, Coast Guard, Navy . . ."

Lopez raised the long barrel of his revolver and aimed it at his pilot's head. "New Orleans is out of the question," he said again.

Regan looked at the open round mouth of the lead-colored metal pistol for a moment and then turned back to his instruments and began making the adjustments necessary to swing the small light aircraft to the south and start it out over the Gulf toward Mexico. "You're going to make some people very unhappy," he said.

Lopez shrugged his shoulders and then he laughed. "I don't give a damn who I make unhappy," he said, smiling, and then he let the barrel of his pistol drop away, back down toward the floor of the aircraft.

"Unhappy and angry," Regan said, keeping his eyes straight ahead, still not wanting to look at his passenger too closely.

"Fuck them. Fuck all of them," Lopez hissed softly, directing the words out over the swampy bayou country that led to New Orleans.

The television people were doing some of Sullivan's legwork for him. He watched as they interviewed an elderly couple who had seen Strode walk away from the shooting of the police officer in South Dallas. Sullivan jotted down the couple's name at the bottom of another sheet of notes and waited to see if the couple would mention the rest of it, but they didn't.

Sullivan was back at the FBI's Dallas office now, and he had to sort through the growing pile of notes and papers on his desk to find the report he was looking for. He finally found it in a manila file that he had marked temporarily in pencil "Second Gunman." He reread the police reports that contained the interviews of the other witnesses to the shooting. Two of the eyewitnesses had mentioned a second man who had been on the sidewalk near Strode and had driven off immediately after the shots had been fired—driven off in a light gray car. Sullivan thought again of the Secret Service man in the blue plaid shirt that he had come across in the parking lot behind the grassy hillside right after the President had been shot. He'd been leaning against a light-colored car of some kind. Could he have been the same man? God, Sullivan wished that he'd taken his time with him, but it had all been happening too fast. It was either something very big that he was on to now, or more likely it was nothing, Sullivan decided as he set the reports back down into the tangle of papers in front of him. Still he wanted to check it out with the Service as soon as he could.

He sat back then at his borrowed desk and closed his eyes. He ran his fingers through his hair and breathed out deeply several times.

The crowded office around him was full of heavy, fatigued activity. It had been a long day, growing longer.

"Sullivan! It's Washington," came the voice from the next desk, and the big blond agent wearily leaned forward and punched in on the call. It was Hollis, his supervisor back in the capital. Sullivan could imagine his impassive stone face talking into the phone in his office two doors down from Summers himself.

"How are things down there?" His boss's voice came through as cold, and efficient, and precise as Sullivan remembered it.

"Quieting down," Sullivan said. "But it's not as neat as they say on TV," he added after a few seconds, and then he looked at his own crowded desk. "This Strode character himself isn't much, though. Just some psycho who probably could have used a little more target practice."

"He may have gotten the job done anyway," Sullivan's boss said.

"Yeah, I guess so." Sullivan exhaled tensely.

"Have you seen Strode up close yet?"

"I was going to go over there now," Sullivan said, sitting up in his chair and trying to rub his eyes awake with his free hand.

"Good, you can tell your kids you saw him."

"Yeah," Sullivan said, but he knew how unlikely the possibility of his ever having kids was at the moment, and growing even more unlikely every day he decided, as he thought about it some more. "By the time I have kids, I can tell them I made the arrest," he said into the phone.

"Yeah, mine think I got Dillinger," Hollis said, and Sullivan had to smile.

"The Dallas police on top of it?"

"Seem to be. They picked up Strode quick enough. Maybe too quick," Sullivan said.

"What do you mean by that?" his supervisor asked coldly.

"Oh, probably nothing. There're just a couple of angles I'm working on, that's all. Strode may have had a little help. I'd like to stay down here for a few days. It's getting pretty interesting. I'm looking at the police reports now. Some of the eyewitnesses seem to think they saw a second . . ."

"Write it up," Hollis said, cutting him off.

Write it up, the Bureau's answer to everything, Sullivan thought. "I have," he said, but then, looking down at his pile of scattered handwritten notes, he corrected himself. "I will," he said instead. "I'll get you something by tomorrow. I could use a peek at the Strode file here, though."

"What file?" Hollis said.

"The file on Strode that we had to be keeping down here. He was a defector, a known Russian sympathizer. We must have something on him. Could you clear that for me?"

"Jim," his boss said coldly, "get one thing straight, okay? There's no Strode file. Never was. Do you understand? The Bureau has no connection, no awareness of any kind about this guy prior to about eight hours ago."

Sullivan paused for a moment, disappointed that they were going to play it that way, but he wasn't really surprised. He'd been half expecting it. The Bureau had to come out as clean as it could on something as big as this. "Sure," he said wearily, and then, remembering: "Yes, sir."

It was time for a new subject. "Write up what you got and let me see it. And try to clean up the loose ends as quickly as you can. I want you back in Washington," the voice on the phone said sharply and then continued on in a more conciliatory tone. "Jim, look, Summers is happy. I know that's hard to believe, but he is. He's got a living, breathing, proven Communist to hang this on. By the look of it, the evidence is piling up on this guy Strode faster than the police can pick it up and count it. They've got a gun, matching cartridge cases. The guy works right there where it happened, a political nut, pro-Castro, pro-Russia. What else can we ask for?" But Sullivan's boss didn't pause for an answer. "Gardner's happy too. The press is happy. They're all happy. Bring it on in and we can go on with the battle, right?"

"Right," Sullivan said. "I'll write it up and bring it on in."

"Good. Get me that report by tomorrow," Hollis said, ending the call.

Sullivan sat at his desk with the phone at his ear for another moment and looked around at the weary room, its occupants working in slow motion around him.

"Okay, coach," Sullivan said to no one in particular. Then he flipped the phone onto its hook and stood up, reaching back to lift his suit coat off the back of the chair where he'd thrown it several hours before. He stopped only long enough to fit the tightly cut Ivy League jacket over his broad shoulders. He started for the door, but just before he got there, he turned and headed back, ducking into the file room at the rear of the big floor of offices. He smiled at the primly dressed young woman who sat at a desk that barred his way into the long, narrow room packed with files. The woman was working furiously at her typewriter, but when she looked up and saw Sullivan's handsome blond head she stopped and sat back in her chair and caught her breath.

"Where's the Strode file?" he asked casually and smiled at her.

The woman breathed out a great sigh and glanced over her shoulder at the rows and rows of tightly packed file cabinets, making it clear that she didn't want to go through the motions of looking for anything more that night, not even for someone with as nice a smile as Sullivan's. She turned back to him after she was done with her act. "You can look if you want, but just between you and me, I don't think you'll find anything."

Sullivan nodded. He knew damn well that the office had a file on Strode and he could guess where it was now. Yancey would have pulled it and hidden it in his own desk. Sullivan had seen him do it before. Then the Bureau could deny ever having a record of Strode and the press couldn't make them look like complete fools for letting someone that they supposedly were keeping an eye on come within a few inches of murdering the President. No, there was a file, Sullivan thought, returning his gaze to the file clerk. "What if I looked on Yancey's desk," he said, turning to the Dallas Section Chief's private office at the far end of the floor.

"I wouldn't do that," the woman said and returned to her typewriter.

"I wouldn't either," Sullivan said and started toward the door. "I'm too much of a team player," he said. And then he opened the office door and walked out into the hall and pressed the elevator button. "I guess," he added, as the elevator doors opened in front of him, but his voice, as he said it, sounded surprisingly unconvincing, even to him.

Lopez kept staring over at his pilot. The long-barreled Smith & Wesson lay haphazardly across his lap and he was trying to make up his mind whether he should kill the red-haired man.

The lights of Monterey were visible now in the distance across the last few miles of dark Gulf waters. Regan had done his job and gotten him to Mexico. Now what?

"How're we going to work this?" Lopez asked the pilot casually.

"What do you mean?" Regan said, looking nervously out of the corner of his eye at the dangerous little dark-skinned man sitting next to him. "I can land us in Monterey with no trouble. For a couple of bucks they won't even log us in. Refuel, get some food, and I can fly myself out at dawn," the red-haired pilot added uncertainly.

His passenger was quiet, for a few seconds weighing the options. "You'd be on the phone to New Orleans as soon as I left you alone, and I don't think I want our friends knowing where I am just yet," he said finally.

Regan stayed quiet. He didn't have any answers for this lunatic who was sitting next to him.

They were both silent for a long time. Finally, Regan burst out: "What are you going to do, kill me?"

Lopez shrugged his shoulders. "You'd be dead already if I'd let you land us in New Orleans," he said matter-of-factly.

"You don't know that." Regan's face was flushed almost as red now as his phony hairpiece.

Lopez just laughed and then went back to figuring the angles as the scattered lights of Monterey began coming up below the plane. He reached his left hand up and fingered the small red imitation-leather diary in his shirt pocket. Then he removed it slowly from his shirt and let it drop into his lap.

"What's that?" Regan said.

"This?" Lopez said nonchalantly and then looked down blankly at the diary on his lap as if he hadn't even noticed it before. "This could be your ticket back to the States, I guess. I haven't decided yet."

The two men flew on in silence for several more minutes, the aircraft's droning engines the only noise in the small cabin.

"You got an answer for me yet?" Lopez asked finally.

Regan shook his head nervously. "No, not really. I can promise you that . . ." He stared, but Lopez cut him off with another burst of hard, cold laughter.

"You can have the plane. You could get yourself another pilot in Monterey. Have him fly you out, wherever you want to go. I have money." Regan reached up for one of the oversize, button-flapped chest pockets on his paramilitary shirt then, and as he did, Lopez sat bolt upright in the passenger seat next to him and pressed his long-barreled gun tight against the pilot's neck. Regan's hand froze and he stared straight ahead at the lights of Monterey, wondering if they would be the last things that he would ever see.

Lopez reached forward then and unbuttoned the pilot's pocket for him and removed a thick sheaf of American cash. He laughed again when he saw it and withdrew the long barrel of his pistol from Regan's neck.

"I'll think about it," Lopez said, as the light plane began its descent into Monterey.

CHAPTER
4

"Do you really have this thing under control?" Sullivan said, and Deputy Chief of Police Jacob Boyer leaned back in his chair and smiled. They were in his private office on the second floor of the Dallas Police Department building on Main Street.

"It got a little hairy there for a while, but it's comin' together now," Boyer said with more than a touch of pride.

"Can I see him?" Sullivan said. "I've got a few things that I'd like to ask him."

"You and everybody else."

"Well?"

"I don't know," the deputy police chief said slowly, thinking about it.

"Where is he now?"

"We're interrogating him."

"Still?"

The deputy police chief smiled again. "There's some things he ain't told us yet."

Sullivan looked across the small windowless room at Boyer's big, beefy face, not quite understanding what the deputy police chief was telling him now.

"Like what?"

"Well, like he's the one that done it," Boyer said and then smiled broadly. "Things like that."

Sullivan smiled back at the big, heavyset man, who was sitting contentedly behind the desk across from him.

"There's a federal man in there now, anyway," the deputy police chief said casually.

"No, I don't think so," Sullivan said. "Nobody from the Bureau anyway."

Boyer shrugged his shoulders, as if one federal man was like another to him. "Whatever. I'll tell you what, though," he said. "Why don't you write your questions down and I'll see if I can't get them answered for you. It's about the best I can do right now," Boyer added, smiling.

"Why are you playing this one so tight?" Sullivan asked. "I just need a couple of minutes."

"Well, like I say, we almost got ourselves embarrassed pretty bad back there this afternoon. The President almost got himself killed right here in Dallas. We don't want to take any more chances right now, none that we don't have to, anyway. Maybe in a day or so."

"Okay," Sullivan said, remembering his own boss's warnings not to push too hard. "I'll write down what I've got. I'd appreciate it if you'd see what he has to say about it, though. I'm working on some angles you may not have yet."

"You know what else I can do," the deputy police chief said, standing up then and trying to match Sullivan's six-foot-plus frame, but not quite making it. "We're goin' to let the press take their pictures and look this boy in the eye for a few minutes. I can probably squeeze you in when we do it."

"Thank you. I'd appreciate that," Sullivan said, reaching out to shake the police officer's hand and end the meeting. "Congratulations again—your people did a real good job."

"Thanks." Boyer smiled.

"How did you do it, anyway? You had a patrol car at Strode's rooming house practically before Strode got there himself," Sullivan said.

Boyer's face hardened and the smile faded out of his eyes. He placed his hands on his wide hips and stared across the desk at Sullivan. "What the hell are you talkin' about?" he said.

"I talked to his landlady. She saw one of your people outside her place less than twenty minutes after Cassidy was shot. I just don't understand how you put it together that fast."

"She's wrong," Boyer said abruptly.

Sullivan shrugged his shoulders to show that he wasn't sure of it, but he returned Boyer's angry stare with a puzzled look. "Maybe so," Sullivan said. "I'll check with her again, but she seemed pretty clear on it. She said your officer honked his horn twice. What was that all about?"

"You want to see Strode or not?" Boyer said, angrily cutting Sullivan off. Then he moved around his desk and started the young FBI agent for the door.

"Yeah, I do," Sullivan said and followed the big man out into the hallway, leaving the office of the City of Dallas's deputy police chief with even more questions than he'd had when he'd walked into it.

* * *

The Vice President of the United States was in his pajamas, his size-eleven feet bare and propped up on the edge of his hotel-room bed, his long bulky body leaning back deep into the biggest, softest chair in the room. He was talking on the phone when the Attorney General was led into his presence.

Gardner pretended not to notice Tim at first, and then, slowly and without missing a beat in his phone conversation, the Vice President looked up at the younger man and nodded.

Cassidy stayed standing awkwardly at the far side of the hotel bedroom waiting for Gardner to finish his call. When he was finally done, the Vice President hung up the phone and then punched a signal into it to the outer rooms of his suite that he didn't want to be disturbed for now. Then he looked up at Cassidy again and motioned for him to sit down.

"How is he?" Gardner asked, as the President's brother took a chair at the center of the room, a long way from Gardner's turned-down bed.

Cassidy nodded his head affirmatively several times before he answered Gardner's question. "He'll come through it," Tim said simply then.

Gardner waited to hear more, but the Attorney General stayed silent, reluctant to talk about it with the older man. And the two men were quiet with each other for several long seconds, Gardner inspecting the younger man carefully in the silence. Finally Cassidy stood and went to the window of the hotel bedroom. Below on the street surrounding the entrance to the hotel stood a small crowd of curiosity seekers. "The doctors seem to think that the next few hours are going to be very important," Tim said thoughtfully, as much to himself as to the pajama-clad figure sitting behind him.

"What do we know about this man Strode?" Cassidy added, in a sharper voice, and then he turned from the window to face the Vice President directly again.

"A nut, a commie, defected to Russia a few years ago. The Dallas police are on top of it. So is Summers. You don't have to worry about any of it."

Cassidy couldn't help laughing, a little bitterly. "Sounds like it's right up Summers's alley."

"I reckon it is," Gardner said.

"Rance," Cassidy said and then stopped. "I don't want to get cut out on this. The man shot my brother," he said after a few seconds.

"You're the Attorney General," Gardner said.

"Yes, well be sure and tell Summers that, would you?" Cassidy said, and then he walked back toward the chair in the center of the room and sat down in it again.

"If you think that's necessary," Gardner said finally, after watching Cassidy's sudden energetic movement across the room.

"I do," Cassidy said, his steel-blue eyes looking straight ahead at the big man sitting behind the unmade hotel-room bed. Both men were quiet then for several more seconds just staring hard at each other.

Finally, Gardner put a good-sized Texas smile on his face. "It got a little rough back there this afternoon, didn't it, son?"

"Yes, it did," Cassidy said calmly.

Gardner suddenly looked away from him and picked up the telephone. "Has the Secretary of State called yet?" he said into the phone and then paused. "All right, when he does, put him right through, will you?" He hung up the extension and turned back to Cassidy.

"I'm checkin' with every member of the Cabinet, askin' them to stay in Washington and not come here. Makin' certain they all know just how much the country needs them, how much I need them, too," Gardner said. Then he added pointedly, looking straight at the Attorney General, "I need the undivided loyalty of every member of the Cabinet right now, with no exception."

"Where's Mrs. Gardner?" Cassidy said, ignoring Gardner's words.

"She's out at the ranch. We thought that was best. I've got a lot of work to do tonight," Gardner said. He paused. "Like to have you and your family out there after this all simmers down—meanin' to do that for a long time now."

Cassidy nodded and then Gardner went on. "We're plannin' on flyin' back to Washington tomorrow. It's my judgment that the country'll feel better to see us gettin' on with the business of government as best we can. 'Course we'll stay, if there's reason to."

"You're moving pretty fast, aren't you?" Cassidy snapped.

"Fast?" Gardner stood up then. "Fast? Maybe you've forgotten, but there's a country that still has to be run here. We can't let our personal feeling get in the way of that. Now, that's somethin' your brother has always understood." Gardner crossed the room to the long formal bar built into the wall behind the Attorney General.

"Rance, for God's sake, let's not fight," Cassidy said to the older man's broad back.

"I think you and me were made for fightin'," Gardner said, smiling slightly and pouring himself a tall bourbon. He turned to Cassidy and pointed at the bottle and an empty glass, but the President's brother shook his head that he wasn't interested.

"I was hopin' that maybe you and I could say a few words to the TV people tonight," Gardner said. "Mebbe have one or two of them up here for a short little talk."

Cassidy shook his head. "I've got to get back to the hospital," he said. "The night's going to be difficult for everybody. I want to be there."

"Of course," Gardner said, covering his disappointment.

"As soon as he can travel, I want to take Jack back to Boston," Cassidy said suddenly.

"Good God, son, it's a little early to be thinkin' about that, isn't it?" Gardner said.

"No, Jack will want it that way," Cassidy said decisively.

Gardner crossed the room slowly, holding his tall glass of sour mash bourbon up high near his chest. "Texas ain't the villain, son," he said, and then he sat back down in the big soft chair by the side of his bed.

"I know that."

"No. I don't think you do. This state didn't shoot your brother, some lunatic did," Gardner said evenly and then paused to take a long drink. "You remember why your brother came down here in the first place?" he said when he finished his bourbon.

Cassidy nodded, but Gardner went right ahead and reminded him anyway. "Pol-o-tics," the Vice President said, drawing the word out as far as it would go. "Pol-o-tics with a capital P. And we've got about two chances now of winnin' that election that's comin' up eleven mighty short months from now, and one of those chances is spelled T-E-X-A-S and the other is sitting right here in this room. You and me are goin' have to start workin' together to hold this party and this country together, until whatever is goin' to happen, happens. You think I'm movin' fast, but what the hell do you think your friend the senator from Arizona is doin' tonight? Or Mr. Marshall T. Granderman, the very rich, very handsome Governor of New York State, for that matter? I'll tell you what they're doin', whether you want to hear it or not," Gardner said, pointing his drink at Cassidy. "They're lickin' their chops, that's what. And don't you think they're not. They're sayin' whatever happens now, they got themselves one hell of a fightin' chance all of a sudden. Now you go and pull your brother out of here and start runnin' away to Boston, Massachusetts, and makin' us all look like a lot of damn fools down here, and you're on the way to givin' the Republicans even more of a shot at winnin' that election than they've got already."

Cassidy didn't even try to answer him. He just stared across the room with his hard blue eyes at the Vice President's face.

"You know, this afternoon, you read me your letter," Cassidy said finally. Gardner nodded. "Yes, I did," he said.

"Well, you forgot to read me all of it," Cassidy went on. "There's a third paragraph we didn't talk about then, but I want to talk about it now," Cassidy said, and then he paused before reciting from memory: " 'The President, in his sole discretion, would then determine when the inability had ended and at that time would resume the full exercise of the powers and duties of the office of President.' " He paused again before repeating the phrase: " 'The President in his sole discretion,' Rance."

The two men looked at each other for a long time then. Gardner finally broke the silence between them. "Let's be honest though, son, we're a long way from that, aren't we? One hell of a long way! You, me, Longwood, Granderman, nobody knows what's goin' to happen now," Gardner said.

"My brother's a strong man," Cassidy said.

Gardner only snorted a short, cold laugh then. "Hell, son, that don't matter. We're all strong men."

* * *

Sullivan showed his I.D. at the door and shoved his way into the crowded press room in the basement of the Dallas Police Department. He elbowed his way through the noisy crowd to a place by the side of the raised platform at the front of the room where a single microphone had been set up.

A few minutes later, the door opposite Sullivan opened and two uniformed police officers came into the room, followed closely by Strode and more uniformed Dallas cops behind him. Strode looked bad. He was handcuffed and he moved slowly and stiffly, pushed along by the crowd of blue-uniformed officers that surrounded him. He was unshaven and his heavy dark beard stood out in striking contrast to his puffy, pale-white face. His left eye was bruised an ugly blue-black color and swollen closed. There were more cuts and bruises on the side of his face and he wore a rumpled gray sweater with one shoulder faintly spattered with blood.

He was led to the podium while flashbulbs popped around him and news cameras whirred. He stood for a moment in front of the noisy crowd and squinted out at the people in the room through his damaged eye. After a few seconds, he cocked his head slightly toward his good side to see the people standing around him a little more clearly. In some strange way, Sullivan thought, as he watched him, Strode seemed to be enjoying the attention of the moment.

The questions began, the reporters all yelling at once, but one came through louder and more insistent than the rest. "Did you shoot the President?" came the single urgently repeated question.

"I haven't been charged with that," Strode said, cocking his head even more dramatically to one side, searching out the questioner with his good eye. "No one has said that I've done that," he added in the same strangely formal, but seemingly half-pleased way.

"We said no questions!" Deputy Chief of Police Boyer shouted, moving his heavy body in front of Strode and trying to cut off the flow of noise that was pouring up from the crowd onto the small stage. "Just the pictures for now, boys!" the deputy police chief bellowed into the microphone, but he could barely be heard above all the noise and confusion in the small chaotic room.

"Do you have a lawyer?" someone shouted from the crowd of reporters.

Strode turned his head to let the news cameras see the full extent of the damage to his eye and the severity of the bruises and cuts on the side of his face. "As you can see, I'm not even being allowed to . . ." Boyer cut him off then, reaching out in front of him for the microphone, and the assistant police chief motioned for the uniformed officers to lead Strode off.

"The suspect is being given every opportunity to exercise his constitutional rights," Boyer said, leaning into the microphone, but no one was listening. The crowd followed Strode to the door, pressing in on the circle of police officers that surrounded him, yelling more questions, almost in a frenzy now.

Strode turned just before he reached the door and shouted his last words back at the room. "I'm a patsy!" he yelled, and then the ring of police officers pushed him through the door and out into the hall.

Sullivan stood for a moment looking at the confusion in the small room. It was getting out of control, Sullivan thought, just as the bullet exploded in the hallway outside the door—the door through which Strode had just disappeared.

Sullivan leaped across the low stage and past the startled figure of the deputy police chief. The big blond FBI agent was one of the first through the side door and out into the underground hall. When he got there, he saw a circle of police officers kneeling around something. It was Strode. There was a bullet wound in his crumpled and now deeply bloodstained sweater, and his eyes were closed. From where he stood at the far end of the underground hallway, Sullivan couldn't see whether he was still breathing.

Two dazed Dallas police officers were holding a heavyset man in a shiny, dark black suit. The man was only a few steps from Strode's fallen body. There was a small handgun at the man's feet.

It was the dead middle of the night when Sullivan left the Dallas Police Department—3 A.M. Sullivan drove the dark, empty streets watching the lightly misting rain fall in neat thin lines under the yellow streetlights. As he drove, his thoughts kept returning to that file on Strode that officially didn't exist, but that he was pretty sure he'd find in Yancey's desk, if he went looking for it. Sullivan drove first to the theater on Denver Avenue where the police had picked up Strode earlier that afternoon. The neon lights on the marquee were dimmed, but Sullivan could still read its announcement of Doris Day and James Garner appearing in *The Thrill of It All*. Sullivan cruised on past and took the turn onto Tenth Street to the spot where the police officer had been killed. He slowed his car and looked across the street to where the police reports had said that witnesses had seen the gray car and the second man. Sullivan could see nothing there now.

He retraced the route back to Strode's rooming house, taking the streets Strode himself had probably taken. When he got to it, Sullivan parked in front and looked up at the second-floor window and the room that had been Strode's. The agent imagined a Dallas black-and-white parked under the trees across the street. He listened, trying to hear its horn tap twice, but the neighborhood was at quiet peace, sleeping through the troubled night.

He drove around aimlessly for a while then. The radio reported in a low Texas voice that the announcements from the hospital were still the same and that the President remained in critical condition.

Sullivan finally stopped at an all-night doughnut shop and ate his dinner and his breakfast—two stale buttermilk doughnuts—and then he carried an enormous paper cup full of black coffee back with him to his car. The hot liquid burned his hands through the thin white container and he set it down on the floorboard of his government car to cool while he drove.

There was a police line at Dealey Plaza, but he flashed his I.D. and they let him through. He parked his car and walked into the square holding his container of coffee and looking up at the light mist falling against the ring of tall buildings above him. He stood for a moment on the empty sidewalk and sipped tentatively at his coffee. It was drinkable now. He strolled on after a few seconds and watched the brick front of the School Book Depository building coming up in front of him.

There were two officers sitting on the front steps of the high building. Sullivan held his I.D. out to them as he approached. He offered the big container of coffee to one of the uniformed men as the other checked his credentials.

"No thanks," the officer said, waving the coffee off.

"You want to go up?" the other said, after he satisfied himself with Sullivan's FBI card.

"What would I see?" Sullivan said, smiling.

"Boxes full of books," the other officer said.

"It was a pretty good shot," Sullivan said casually, glancing up at the sixth-floor window where they'd found the rifle, and then back down at the street to where the President's limo had been.

"Maybe not good enough," the other cop said, motioning down at the portable radio by his feet, and then he laughed. Sullivan looked over at him, wondering what he'd meant by that, but the officer's face didn't give him any more clues and Sullivan let it go.

"Some day, this'll all be history," Sullivan said and drank from his coffee, trying to relax, but he couldn't. The cop's comment had made him almost angry enough to make the decision about Strode's file for him and Sullivan wasn't so sure that he liked the way that his choice was starting to come out now.

"Yeah, someday we can tell our kids," the other cop said.

Sullivan laughed then, remembering his own words to his boss. "Tell 'em what?" the agent asked.

"That we were here, that we saw it happen," the cop said. "You saw it, didn't you?" he asked Sullivan.

"Oh, yeah," Sullivan said and looked back out onto the square at where his trail limo had been when he'd heard the shots.

"I thought it came from in there," Sullivan said, pointing out at the short grassy hillside at the far edge of the plaza.

"A lot of people did," the cop said.

Sullivan turned to leave, but first he stopped for a moment and looked down at the grassy hillside again.

"Anybody down there now?" Sullivan asked the two men who were guarding the Book Depository building that night.

"No, no reason," the other cop said.

"Mind if I . . . ?" Sullivan asked, gesturing toward the hillside with his half-full container of coffee.

"You know what you'll find?" the first guard said.

"Unh-unh," Sullivan answered, as he turned toward the square.

"Grass, trees, and dog shit," the cop said and laughed.

Then both officers started laughing loudly. Sullivan looked at them, puzzled. It must just be a slow night, Sullivan decided finally, and he forced his own expression into a smile that he didn't really feel. Then he walked down the sealed-off street, past the place in the road where his own limousine had been, and to the spot where the President's limo had taken the fire.

Sullivan turned after a few seconds and looked back up at the high floor of the Book Depository building. It was a long way off. The two officers were lounging on the building's front steps again, listening to the radio and paying no attention to him. So Sullivan set his coffee container down and pretended to sight with an imaginary rifle back up at Strode's window. He closed one eye and sighted along his extended fingers until he had a steady picture of the dark window just above his own outstretched thumb and forefinger. He pretended to squeeze off a few rounds back at the window then.

"A hell of a shot," Sullivan said after he finished firing off his phantom rounds, and then he bent down and picked up his coffee and walked with it into the sloping tree-shrouded hillside a few yards away at the edge of the road.

Sullivan walked around under the protection of the overhanging trees for a while, drinking his coffee and looking back occasionally into the dark, empty plaza. There was a low stockade fence near the spot where he had seen the man who didn't seem like a government man. Sullivan stopped when he got to it and squatted down behind the fence, looking at the square again through the overhanging tree branches at where the President's limousine would have been. This was the spot he would have picked, he thought, as he sat on his haunches. Right here, he told himself.

He looked up at the sky. The first faint rays of light were just beginning to appear. Soon it would be dawn. If he was going to do it, he had to do it now, before the night was over, he decided.

He stood and with certainty started back across the square. He passed the police line without saying anything and got into his car.

It was a short drive back to the FBI's Dallas office. When Sullivan got there, he went upstairs and used his key to go inside. The main room was empty. He could hear a typist down the hall banging out an endless report, but Sullivan didn't hesitate. He walked straight to Yancey's office. Without turning on the light, Sullivan shuffled through the papers and files on the section chief's desk. What he was looking for wasn't there, but he kept trying drawers until he found what he wanted. He opened the file and glanced at its contents briefly before he carried it out to the open bay near his own borrowed desk and began to use the Xerox machine at the center of the room to copy its contents.

The noise and light of the machine brought a tired-looking agent down the hall to take a look.

"Sullivan, that you?" the agent called out.

"We're earning our pay tonight," Sullivan answered calmly and continued his copying at a rate only as fast as the deliberate machine would permit.

The other agent began to approach him, weaving his way slowly through the maze of desks in the big open room. "And I thought Dallas was going to be slow." The agent laughed wearily. He was only a few steps behind Sullivan now.

Sullivan looked down at his work. There were only three more sheets to copy, but the Xerox machine was still grinding through its mechanically controlled manipulations in its own painfully slow way and Sullivan kept his back to the other agent, blocking his view of the machine.

The agent stopped and sat on a desktop a few feet behind Sullivan. "What have you got?" he asked, seemingly only half caring.

"A headache and about twelve pages of notes that I told Washington I'd already had written up and was on its way," Sullivan said calmly.

"The check's in the mail," the other agent said and laughed.

"And I'll respect you in the morning," Sullivan said, mostly to himself and looking down at the last of the sheets marked: STRODE, ARTHUR ALLEN at the top that he was running through the laborious Xerox machine.

"What?" the other agent said, but Sullivan didn't repeat it for him. He was too busy, removing the last sheet and replacing it in the official file and then stacking his own copies and inserting them into a clean manila folder from the stack on the table next to him. Then he placed the second folder on top of the official file, before he turned back to the other agent.

"You want to get some breakfast or something?" Sullivan asked.

"Yeah, why not," the agent said. "Maybe some real coffee. Let me get my coat," he added, and then he stood and began threading his way back through the long rows of empty desks.

After the other agent disappeared down the hall Sullivan replaced Strode's file in the bottom drawer of Yancey's desk. Then he walked back out to his own desk and inserted the fresh manila folder filled with photocopied pages into an FBI lock bag that agents normally used to transport sensitive material from one Bureau office to another. He locked the bag and put the key into his pocket and then, carrying the bag with him, he hurried out to meet the other agent at the bank of elevators at the end of the hall.

"Yancey asked me to take some things back to Washington for him," Sullivan lied, as he saw the other agent look questioningly at the bag.

The other agent turned away and nodded in understanding, but Sullivan couldn't be sure whether he had believed him or not.

The President's eyes were closed, but when he concentrated he could occasionally hear the whisper of concerned voices near him.

The pain that he felt had become strangely secondary to the fear now. It seemed bigger, more powerful somehow. Sometimes though, he could put the fear aside and try to focus on the heavy insistent pain inside of himself, checking it, measuring it against other moments of physical pain that he had known, trying to decide if this pain was different, bigger, grander, more horrible—maybe even capable of killing him. Each time he let himself do it, though, he decided that it wasn't, but there was no way to be certain and soon the fear would sweep over him again and he would have to reach in and check the pain once more, measure it, feel its power. He would grow angry then and very brave, determined to fight it through, but soon the anger would exhaust him, and he would grow calm, becoming thoughtfully philosophic for a while, almost ethereal in his understanding. Sometimes in that peace he would pray for grace and feel it come, starting in his heart, and then spreading slowly through the rest of his body, but then, suddenly struggling against a new surge of pain and darkness, he would find himself confused again, asking for mercy, begging for his life, forgiving everyone, needing forgiveness himself, full of love, full of a desire to live and see his children again, as the horrible searing pain would begin burning through him and set the chain of feelings off once more, of fear and anger, bravery and hope and then the brief temporary peace, all kaleidoscoping through him in turns and then all at once. And as it was happening, he was barely aware of who he was, or why he was there. He had become, even to himself for that time, only a man, a man without any real identity, just a man who wanted to go on being alive.

Finally though, he remembered faintly from somewhere deep inside himself that he still had promises that he couldn't leave unfulfilled, and the thought seemed to help him stay alive and fight against the darkness. As hard as he tried though, he couldn't yet remember what those promises were, or who he owed them to, or why. He could remember clearly only the blinding moment of impact, the inside of his head suddenly lit up in a bright explosion of light, and then as if through a thick veil, all the faraway motion and movement and people and bright lights shining right down on him.

And now he was all alone in the darkness again, a woman who he knew was his wife, near him somewhere. And it was night, deep, dark, powerful night. He remembered now that he'd heard a voice tell the woman who was his wife, "We'll know more in the morning." The morning, thank God, he thought there was a goal, a goal that he could understand, something to fight for in all this swirling confusion of feelings. He would fight the pain and darkness until it was morning, he decided, and then in the light of day it would be easier, but it was so dark now—the deepest, darkest night he'd ever known. Could anyone ever stay alive through such a darkness?

He slept then, fitfully, but with more peace than he'd known in hours. He slept fighting the darkness, mistaking it for something else, afraid of falling into it forever, and then coming out of it briefly, but still not opening his eyes, wondering if he'd slept, praying that if he had, that he wouldn't again, because of what it could mean, and then trying with all of his courage and imagination and strength to remember somehow what a dawn looked like. How it felt. Its sounds and smells. And then he sensed that his wife was sleeping herself, below him at the foot of his bed, and something made him open his eyes, slightly at first, just flickering his eyelids so slightly that the nurse sitting in the chair in the far corner of the room watching him couldn't see it at first, but then a little more pronounced and the nurse began to waken herself and lean forward, focusing on what she wasn't sure that she really saw.

"Mrs. Cassidy," the nurse whispered, finally waking the dark-haired woman lying awkwardly across the foot of her husband's hospital bed.

"Yes," Suzanne said sleepily, not yet remembering where she was and then suddenly all of the horror of the day before rushing back to her in a fearful blur of remembering.

"Mrs. Cassidy, your husband," the nurse said and Suzanne slid off the foot of the bed and leaned forward over her husband's face. His eyes were open slightly, looking up at her.

"It's morning," his wife said quietly and behind her he could see below the window's metal blinds, dawn's first soft shafts of sunlight filtering into the room.

CHAPTER
5

Tim Cassidy's slim figure was bent slightly at the waist, his back to the unlit room. He had removed his suit coat and his shirtsleeves were rolled up, his hands thrust deep into his pants pockets. The hospital bed next to him was untouched—still all crisp, clean, white linen. He was standing at the far side of the small hospital room looking down at the crowd of people below the window. It was dawn, but the flames from the sea of brightly burning candles still glowed in the fading darkness.

Suzanne appeared at the door behind him and stood watching him for a moment. Finally she spoke, saying the words that he most wanted to hear at that moment. "Jack's awake," she said, and Tim turned back into the room, removing his hands from his pockets as he started toward her, his face full of excitement.

"The doctors are in there now, but we can see him in a few . . ." Suzanne stopped off in midsentence, her voice finally breaking. "He's better, Tim. He opened his eyes and looked at me," she said and smiled at her own words. "I wasn't sure I'd ever see him do that again," she added and then she began to cry, sobbing only a little at first, low in her throat, but then freely and openly.

Tim walked to the window and stood with her, looking down at the crowd again and, as they stood silently together, a doctor appeared at the door behind them. "You can go in now," he said. "He's much better. Your husband's a very strong man, Mrs. Cassidy," the doctor added, the admiration showing in his voice.

"And he has a lot of friends," Tim said, smiling and gesturing back over his shoulder, down at the vast crowd that surrounded the hospital grounds.

The doctor nodded and then stepped aside to let the President's wife and brother enter the corridor and walk the few short steps to the small hospital room next door.

Jack was there, lying in bed, fresh bandages running back over the right side of his light brown hair. The morning sunlight was pouring in through the window behind him and Tim watched as the sun's rays shone across the room in a thick beam, illuminating a bright tumbling dance of tiny dust particles in the air.

The two visitors moved to the side of the bed. The President's eyes were open, and he looked first at his wife and then up into his brother's eyes.

"How are the children?" the President said slowly and haltingly, barely getting the words out, and then he smiled at the startled but pleased look on his visitors' faces. These had been the first words that he had spoken since the day before.

"They're fine. The doctor thinks it would be all right if they came in to see you in a few minutes," Suzanne answered. "But you're not supposed to talk."

"He's a Cassidy," his brother said, his voice suggesting the impossibility of the doctor's instruction. "You're telling an Irish-Boston politician named Cassidy not to talk. That's against nature." Tim smiled across the sunlit room at his brother.

The man in the bed smiled back. He didn't say anything though. The effort of his earlier words had already made him feel surprisingly drained of energy, but he looked at his wife for a long moment, remembering how she'd slept at the foot of his bed the night before, telling her now with his eyes what he wanted her to know.

"I love you too, Jack," she said back to him, the words passing only between the two of them.

They were all three quiet for a few moments then. In the silence, Tim walked to the window and stood looking down at the crowd standing around the hospital grounds. It was growing even larger now in the strengthening sunlight.

"I wish you could see this, Jack," he said. "There are people out there everywhere, as far as you can see in every direction. They were there yesterday and last night, praying for you, and when we brought the children in from the airport the people lined the roads. They were spread out around us in every direction and it seemed like they each lit a candle as we passed."

Tim turned back to his brother. The President's wife was holding his arm very tightly and there were tears in both their eyes.

"I thought the son of a bitch was going to kill me!" Regan blurted into the phone. "He's crazier than a goddamned . . . I don't know what. Where the hell did they find a guy like that, anyway?" Regan rambled on. He was closed into a phone booth in the lobby of the American hotel in Monterey. He'd had two quick drinks at the bar before placing the call, but his hands were still shaking uncontrollably.

Outside the booth a mariachi band in full costume was already playing an early morning rendition of "La Cucaracha" for the tourists, and the exotic rhythm was making the man's stomach roll over with each throbbing beat.

"Where is he now?" came back the tight, disciplined voice on the other end of the line.

"Jesus, Case, who knows? I left him at the airport. I thought he was going to kill me," Regan said again, wishing that he hadn't stopped at just two drinks. "He had a gun the size of a howitzer. The only reason he didn't use it is . . ." Regan stopped then and felt in his pocket for the torn piece of paper that the man had thrust into his hand right after they'd landed in Monterey. "He gave me something that I'm supposed to deliver, personally," Regan said. Then he added nervously, "He was convinced that if we flew into New Orleans last night they would have killed us both."

"He may have been right," the steady, flat voice on the other end of the long-distance call said.

"What, what do you mean, he might have been right?" Regan stammered.

"I mean, they killed Strode, that's what I mean," the voice said back to him.

"Strode?"

"Strode. In Dallas. They got to him."

"How could they? The Dallas police had him. I heard it on the radio just before we flew out of there. The cops arrested him," Regan said, still not understanding what he was being told. "What are you saying to me? Cassidy's alive and Strode's dead?" He laughed at the absurdity of that. Was this Case's idea of some kind of a grisly joke?

There was a long silence on the other end of the line then. And in the silence Regan began to realize that it was no joke and the final outcome of the operation of the day before finally began to sink in on him. "It's big, isn't it?" Regan said in awe, after he'd thought about it for a few seconds.

"You're goddamned right it's big," the other man answered. "One hell of a lot bigger than either of us thought."

"So, what do I do?" Regan asked.

"Shit, I don't know. The whole thing's so fucked up now," the voice on the other end of the line said, sounding a lot less composed than it had before. "I'll see what I can find out," the voice added after a few more seconds. "I'll wire you some dough and you sit tight until you hear from me, okay?"

"Okay," Regan said and started to hang up, but before he did he mumbled hastily into the phone. "Case, you be careful."

"We all better be careful now," the voice said, closing the call.

"Oh, God! He's really going to do it," the senior Secret Service man said to his partner as he saw the Attorney General slip his wiry body down off the hospital steps and start back into the crowd that was pressing up against the front of the building.

The people near the President's brother were in a jubilant mood now, the agent thought, as he watched them begin moving forward to surround Cassidy. The tension of the long candlelit night had been touched off into celebration in the early morning by the public announcement that the President's condition had improved dramatically. And then a sound system had been set up on the front steps of the hospital and Suzanne Cassidy had appeared and said thank you to the crowd, thanking them personally for their prayers. Her short simple speech had been followed by a few words from the President's brother, but then, feeling that words weren't adequate, he had suddenly walked to the edge of the steps and jumped right down into the tumultuous crowd.

"Goddamn politicians," the senior agent mumbled under his breath to his partner, and then the two men sprinted down the steps toward the figure of the Attorney General. He was reasonably safe for the moment, the agent thought, as he sized up the scene in front of him. So far, Cassidy had only managed to work his way into the fringe of the vast sea of people that was surging up around the hospital grounds, but this was the moment that the agent had feared all morning. He'd been advised by Cassidy staff people that the President's brother might want to thank the people of Dallas directly, but the agent had hoped right up to the last second that he wouldn't actually do it, and now that it was really happening he was caught unprepared.

"Get some backups! There's thousands of people out there," the agent yelled at his partner. "Get the goddamned National Guard, if you can!" he added to himself as his partner turned and ran back inside the hospital's front doors toward where the Service's command post was set up on its first floor. Then the senior man took a deep breath and jumped down off the steps to follow Cassidy.

As he fought to stay close to the President's brother by twisting and turning through the crowd in an imitation of Cassidy's own fluid, unabandoned style, the agent tried to search each approaching face for any of the telltale clues that he'd been trained to detect, trying to watch the people from every angle, looking for any sudden movements, unusual packages, known faces, anything out of the ordinary, but it was impossible. The entire event was out of the ordinary, he thought finally with a strange mixture of anger and exhilaration. A wild burst of applause sprang up all around the Attorney General's moving figure everywhere he went and Cassidy was soon surrounded on every side by eager, pressing hands and faces.

Finally security backups came and formed a double ring of protection as best they could around the Attorney General, one ring of moving bodies a few feet from Cassidy, clearing his way immediately in front of him by pushing forward themselves into the swarming crowd and a second ring of trained agents doing their best to filter and restrain the crowd in a wider circle, ten to twenty yards out in front of him. It was all standard procedure, but it barely seemed to work as the people continued to thrust themselves forward, pushing and tugging at Cassidy, ripping at his clothes.

It was a hot, sunny morning and it was hard work. The agent began to sweat heavily and so did Cassidy, and soon the Attorney General loosened his tie and then removed his coat and handed it to a Secret Service man, who had stationed himself directly behind him. And then Cassidy rolled up his shirtsleeves, but he didn't take his eyes from the people near him as he tried to smile at every face, touch every hand that was thrust out toward him, say thank you to each person that he passed.

And for almost the next hour, Cassidy continued moving through the happy crowd, as people pounded him on the back and shoulders until he was bruised and cut, called out to him, as if he were an old close friend, shook his hand over and over until it was swollen and bloody. His body was weary and near exhaustion, sweating freely, and his eyes were red and raw, their surface bright with a thick blur of unreleased tears. Then, like an athlete passing the finish line of a long, grueling race, his knees began to buckle and his legs gave out and the Secret Service man following behind him had to race to him and take him in his arms before he fell and hold him until other nearby agents could help move him forward through the last of the crowd to a waiting limousine. After they helped him into the limousine's back seat, the driver started the vehicle through the crowd that pressed around the edges of the slowly moving car, but even as he drove away, Cassidy leaned forward, reaching his own hand out of the open window of the limousine's back seat to touch the hands extended toward him, until the driver found a sealed-off exit and accelerated past the last of the crowd and returned the exhausted man up the Dallas side streets to the back doors of his hotel.

Gardner watched it all on television. He watched the early morning bulletins on the sudden, dramatic improvement in the President's condition. He watched Suzanne Cassidy's short speech from the steps of the hospital building and then the phenomenon of the crowd and Tim Cassidy. All three networks had stayed with it. "It was an event like nothing ever before experienced in American politics," one commentator had said. "A totally spontaneous, mutual outpouring of love and joy and celebration between the people and the President's family." And it was happening right there in Gardner's own state of Texas. The Vice President watched the television screen with a sense of puzzlement at first and then with a growing feeling of frustration and helplessness.

"Jesus, he's a fast learner," Gardner breathed out finally. The living room of the Vice President's hotel suite was full of aides and assistants that Saturday morning, but no one seemed to know what the Vice President was trying to say. So Gardner continued. "Last night, he was ready to tell Texas to go screw itself. This morning he looks like he's runnin' for Governor," Gardner explained angrily.

"They're saying it's the single most-watched event in the history of television," said Ted Mazeloff, Gardner's press secretary, as he finally hung up the phone he had been on most of the morning to the network people in New York. "The early reports are that over ninety percent of the television sets in the country are tuned in to it," the little gray-haired man added.

Gardner shook his head in disbelief and started to answer him, but then the Vice President only sighed deeply and looked back at the television screen. He stared at it in silence for a long moment. It showed Cassidy's limousine disappearing down an empty, blocked-off side street toward downtown Dallas.

Gardner finally turned to Mallory, who was seated directly across from him. "Call the hospital. I want to talk to that doctor. What's his name?"

"Abramson," Mallory said.

"The man in charge," Gardner said crisply. "Tell him I want to see the President this morning, right now."

Gardner's head pivoted around the hotel suite then. It stopped only when it reached the face of his press secretary. "Call the networks, Ted. Tell them I'm on my way to the hospital. Tell 'em that the President and I will be holdin' a short meetin' before I return to Washington. And from the hospital, I'm goin' straight on to the airport. I want full coverage of my leavin' on *Air Force One* around two o'clock Dallas time."

"Sir!" Mallory interrupted him. "I've got the doctor on the phone," his aide said, holding the telephone out toward him.

Gardner nodded and stood up and crossed the room toward the phone in Mallory's hand. As he did, Mazeloff tried to brush by him, but Gardner reached out one of his big hands and caught his press secretary by the shoulder of his shiny silk suit.

"Ted, I'm goin' into that hospital, up the front steps, an' I'm doin' it in the next thirty minutes. And when I do, I want that Texas crowd to know I'm comin'," Gardner said, and then he released Mazeloff and dropped down onto the bed and punched into the doctor's call.

Sullivan ate breakfast seated across from the other agent, with the FBI lock bag containing a copy of Strode's file lying on the restaurant's curved red vinyl booth between them, and then Sullivan returned to his motel room. He was tired, but he tried to take a quick look through the copied file before he let himself fall asleep, and, to help himself stay awake, he kept the motel room's television set on and let it show him the dramatic scenes of the Cassidy family at the hospital that morning.

He managed to read Strode's file through twice, but he was too tired for it to make much sense to him, and he slumped down onto his bed, the contents of the file scattered on the bedspread around him, and he slept for several hours with the television set still on.

When he awoke he was still dressed in his suit pants and short-sleeved white shirt and tie. Only his shoes and his dark gray suit coat had been removed and lay in a pile on the floor beneath his bed.

He rearranged the contents of the file and placed it carefully in the top drawer of his nightstand before he went into the small sanitized motel bathroom to shower and shave.

He was going to have to find a safe place for that damn file, he thought as he showered, either that or get rid of it. He sure as hell couldn't keep lugging it around Dallas with him. And the more he thought about it the more he wished that he hadn't taken it at all. Making copies of unauthorized files was no way to get to be a thirty-year man in the Bureau. He decided he should walk out there right now and burn the goddamned thing. But instead he turned off the shower and dried his six-foot-plus frame, using all three of the thin white motel-room towels to get the job done, and then he went out and turned up the volume on the television set so that he could listen to the news as he shaved.

Vice President Gardner's limousine was just pulling up into camera range on the street leading to Parkland Memorial Hospital in the heart of downtown Dallas. Sullivan stood for a moment and watched as the limo moved slowly down the same route that the President's ambulance had taken the day before, but instead of the rear emergency-room entrance, the Vice President's car slid to a stop at the big main front steps of the hospital building where the television cameras were positioned. The Vice President stepped out onto the sidewalk in front of the hospital and went directly up the front steps, pausing at the top and smiling back at the cameras. A reporter asked a question and Gardner turned to him. "This is a joyous morning for all of us," the Vice President said, and then he walked quickly through the hospital's double doors, where the television cameras were forbidden to travel.

Sullivan shaved in his bathroom, returning just in time to see *Air Force One* taxiing into position on the tarmac at Love Field. It was scheduled to leave within the hour and return the Vice President to the capital. End of story, Sullivan thought to himself as he watched the pictures of the big government plane preparing to take off. And the young FBI agent reached down and removed the Strode file from his nightstand.

A metal wastebasket stood in the corner of the room, and without hesitating Sullivan walked over and tossed the stolen file into it. Then he began looking around the room for a pack of matches. He was tempted to start burning the file right there in the room and then carry the remains out to the empty lot behind the motel and finish the job.

As he looked, the scene on the television screen behind him switched to the Dallas jail. Deputy Police Chief Boyer was making a short statement to the press in the same basement room that his department had used to show off Strode the night before.

Sullivan found a little cardboard box of matches in a motel ashtray. He carried the matches and the metal wastebasket with the file in it over to the edge of the bed and sat down. He was about to light one of the matches and drop it on top of the file when he heard Boyer beginning to explain the events of the night before to the American people. "The man who shot Strode was a local nightclub owner named Green," the deputy chief began. "And from what we can tell so far, it appears that Mr. Green was extremely upset by the assassination attempt on the President and he wanted to spare the Cassidy family the pain of a long court trial." I guess that's possible, Sullivan thought as he listened, but for some reason it didn't make one hell of a lot of sense. "Whatever his motive, though," Boyer continued, "we're confident that Mr. Green acted entirely alone, just as Strode did himself. Of course, our department is working very closely with federal authorities, particularly with the Federal Bureau of Investigation, to ensure that every possibility is completely explored." Sullivan laughed at the television set.

He dropped the cold match on top of the file in the little metal trash can beneath him without striking it. Then he reached up and switched off the television set. He looked at the file for a moment and sighed deeply before bending down and lifting it out of the trash can and setting it back on the bed next to him.

He dressed in khaki slacks and a red Banlon shirt that had a white penguin stitched on it. Wearing loafers without any socks, he walked down the hall and used the hotel vending machine to get two small plastic containers of coffee. He carried the thin manila file with him as he went for the coffee and he kept telling himself that he was still making up his mind what he was going to do about it, but he knew that he was only kidding himself. He already had. The Dallas deputy police chief had made his decision for him. He was going to keep the file, keep it and study it, and follow out any leads that it might give him.

When the elevator doors opened onto the hospital's top floor, the Vice President stepped out and looked around. The halls were quiet and empty, except for the dozens of Secret Service men hiding in their shadows.

"The family's left to attend a special church service," one of the doctors that had escorted Gardner up from the hospital lobby said, and the Vice President nodded as if he'd known. God damn it, why wasn't I told? he thought. He wondered what the networks were carrying. His visit to the hospital? Or the whole Cassidy brood tromping up the steps of some Catholic church somewhere? But his face didn't betray even a trace of his feelings. Gardner walked down the hall toward Cassidy's room, and a moment later he was ushered inside by the duty nurse.

Cassidy smiled weakly across the room at his Vice President when the tall Texan appeared at the door.

"You're lookin' good, Mr. President," Gardner said as he approached the bed and sat down on the chair next to it.

"The doctors told me to do all the talkin' and that's somethin' I kin probably manage," Gardner said and smiled broadly, his big crinkly face breaking into a series of relaxed folds and deeply etched wrinkles. Cassidy returned the older man's smile.

"I want you to know how I feel. I want you to know that me an' my family are prayin' for you an' I . . ." Gardner stopped then and reached into his inside coat pocket and removed the letter with the big seal of the United States and Cassidy's own signature on it. "I don't know how much your brother has told you, but yesterday I released this to the press," Gardner said. He held the letter out toward the President so that he could see it, but Cassidy's eyes didn't leave Gardner's face.

"It did its job, Mr. President," Gardner said then. "The country's concerned about you, deeply concerned, sir, but it feels safe. It feels secure as hell, I think. Everythin's changed, but nothin's changed, if you know what I mean."

Cassidy nodded his head that he did.

"Well, I . . ." Gardner was having difficulty with his words now. "I thought that I should check with you. As I'm sure you're aware, sir, it's entirely your decision when to resume your duties. I thought it was important for you to know that I haven't forgotten that."

The two men were quiet then, and the leadership of their country hung in the air between them.

The young man lying on the hospital bed shook his head from side to side to indicate his decision that things should remain as they were for now, the power, the country, the presidency in the other man's hands.

"Well, I . . ." Getting ready to leave, Gardner looked at the door. "I promised them that I'd only be in here for a few minutes. I've said all that I wanted to say. I'm leavin' for Washington in about an hour. I think it's best if I'm there right now, don't you?"

Cassidy nodded his agreement again.

"I talked to every member of the Cabinet last night. They're all good men. Every last one of them wanted to come here and be with you, but I asked them to stay at the capital for now. We'll take care of things jus' the way you'd do it, till you get back," Gardner said, burying the emotion that he was beginning to feel by standing up quickly by the side of the bed as he finished talking. "You've got to hurry though," he added, smiling down at the young President. "Longwood and Granderman are both startin' to circle. The State of New Hampshire's goin' probably get pretty busy, real damn soon." Gardner smiled.

He walked to the door and reached out for the metal handle, but he stopped in midstride when he heard the faint but unmistakable New England voice coming from behind him.

"Mr. Vice President," the voice said, and Gardner turned back to face the weakened young man lying in the hospital bed. "You made the right decision," Cassidy said.

Gardner nodded his head, deeply touched. "Thank you, Mr. President," he said, and then he turned and left the room.

When he returned to his motel room, Sullivan double-locked the door behind him, first with the deadbolt and again by latching the chain at the top of the door to the wall.

Then he sat down and started to pore through the Strode file, drinking both cups of coffee and managing to read it all thoroughly this time. As he did, nothing jumped out of the facts and figures of Strode's past and connected up to anything else that Sullivan had learned about the case so far, but he knew that was the way it usually was this early in an investigation. For now, all he wanted to do was to study the background of Strode's life, and Sullivan carefully memorized each of the dates, places, and names in the file.

All that really emerged from Strode's file for the moment was a pathetic picture of a rather sad, ineffectual man probably mentally ill, who could have been desperate enough to do almost anything, and when Sullivan was finished reading about him, he felt vaguely upset and lonely himself. There was something important in the file that didn't add up, too. Sullivan couldn't quite put his finger on it yet, just something, and it was starting to bother him. Sullivan was hungry though, and he was tired of thinking about it. He looked at the clock by his bed. It was a little after three.

There was a girl in Dallas. A lot of cities had a girl for Sullivan. The one in Dallas wasn't as pretty as some, but she was good company and, more important, Sullivan smiled to himself as he remembered her now, she had a great quality. She could always be ready on short notice.

Sullivan set the file down and made the call. The girl's roommate answered the phone. There was a baby crying in the background. The girl had been married, or something. She was always a little vague on that part. Anyway, she had two kids and one or the other of them always cried whenever Sullivan called or came by, but what the hell, he needed the company, he thought as he listened to the kid cry and waited for her to come on the line.

The girl finally made it to the phone and she agreed to be ready in a half hour. Sullivan smiled as he set the phone down. She hadn't changed, he thought. It would be good to have a girl like that in every city where the Bureau had an office. That would be a good goal for a thirty-year man to have, he decided.

Then he set the phone down to clear the line. He had one more call to make before he drove over to her apartment and picked the girl up. He dialed the number and Strode's landlady answered the phone.

"Hello," she said, tentatively.

"Mrs. Riordan, my name is Jim Sullivan. I'm the FBI agent that spoke to you yesterday afternoon."

"Oh, yes, I thought for a moment that you might be a reporter. I'm sorry," the woman's voice said with a little more confidence, and then there was a click and another voice—this one a man's, heavy and deep-throated. "Everything all right?" the man's voice asked.

"It's okay," the woman said, and after a few seconds the phone clicked down again. "They have a policeman staying with me," the woman said proudly.

"Tell me again what you saw yesterday," Sullivan said, reaching for a pen and a fresh pad of paper.

"I told you already," the woman said.

"Tell me again, please," Sullivan coaxed.

"I saw a police . . ." The woman stopped and then continued in a lower voice, "I saw a Dallas police car parked out in front of my house."

"What did the police say when you told them?" Sullivan asked.

The woman didn't answer for a minute. "You were here," she said finally.

"You mean, nobody's followed up on it since then?" Sullivan said, slightly incredulous.

"Not about that," the woman said.

"And it—the police car—" Sullivan said, "it did what again?"

"It honked twice, kind of soft, like a signal," the woman said.

"A signal?"

"Yes, like it wanted someone to know it was there."

"Like Strode?"

"Maybe, I don't know," the woman said.

"And then it pulled away?"

"Yes."

"Just the driver, nobody in the passenger seat?"

"That's right."

"Was the driver in uniform?"

"I couldn't see."

"What time was that?"

"Twelve thirty or so," the woman said with certainty.

"And Strode was upstairs then?" Sullivan asked.

"Yes, I think so."

"Are you sure?"

"Well," the woman hedged, "I never did see him go out. We talked briefly about the President and all and then he went upstairs."

"And then you saw the car," Sullivan said.

"A minute or two after that," the woman said.

Sullivan waited for more, but the woman was quiet.

"That's all?" Sullivan said.

"Yes."

"Would you be willing to sign a statement under oath to that effect, if I were to bring one by later on tonight?"

"Sure, why not?" the woman said.

"I'll have one prepared and bring it by then."

"Okay," the woman agreed easily, as if she didn't care what Sullivan did, and he started to hang up, but the woman's slightly troubled voice stopped him before he could close the call. "Is it important?" she asked.

"Maybe," Sullivan said, trying to sound casual.

"You know, ah . . ." the woman started, but then she didn't seem to know how to go on.

"Yes," Sullivan said and waited.

"There was something about what happened last night that I didn't like," she said.

"You mean when Strode got shot?"

"Right there in police headquarters. I didn't like that," the woman said, her carefully lowered voice sounding its first signs of real alarm.

"Look . . ." Sullivan began, "let me give you a couple of phone numbers." He repeated the Bureau's numbers in Dallas and in D.C. "You can always call me if you want to talk," he said.

The woman was quiet for a few seconds as she wrote the numbers down.

"It'll be okay," Sullivan said reassuringly then. "Just bad luck having Strode for a boarder," he said.

"You can say that again," the woman said wearily and sighed once very deeply before hanging up her phone.

Sullivan found a sport coat then and started for the door, but before he could leave he remembered the file. He sure as hell couldn't leave it there. He turned back and grabbed it off the bed and replaced it in the FBI lock bag. He walked outside with the heavy fabric bag under his arm and then threw it onto the passenger seat of his car.

As Sullivan pulled away from his parking place, a cream-colored car that had been waiting in the shadows across the street slipped into traffic behind him and began following him through the Dallas streets toward the girl's apartment.

CHAPTER
6

The girl's place was a cheap garden apartment in the Kenwood section of Dallas. Her roommate answered the door. The roommate was taller, slimmer, and more attractive than the girl, but she seemed like the type that would never be ready on a half hour's notice, even if she had nothing better to do, and the hell with her, Sullivan decided, but he couldn't help noticing how her long brown hair fell down loosely over a skin-tight, black nylon top.

"Hi, I'm Katie. My friends call me Kit. Denise'll be right out," the girl's roommate said and smiled at Sullivan, but when he smiled back at her he could see her eyes roaming over his shoulder at the parking space in front of the apartment where Sullivan's government-issue, beige-colored, no-frills Chevrolet was parked. Screw her, Sullivan thought, but he watched closely as she turned and walked slowly in her black stretch pants back into the apartment.

Sullivan stepped into the living room just in time for the girl's six-year-old son to buzz him with his tricycle. But Sullivan still had a few old football moves left and the kid's rear tires only nipped his ankles and Sullivan didn't back off. He waded ahead into the array of scattered newspapers and toys that littered the floor of the little apartment, while in a far corner of the room a toddler gripped firmly at the low wooden bars of its playpen and wailed loudly at Sullivan's advancing figure.

The girl's roommate turned quickly and caught Sullivan staring at her stretch pants. "You a cop?" she said and pretended to smile at him through very thick, very red lipstick.

"No, Katie, I'm not," Sullivan said and smiled back halfheartedly at her.

"But you work for the government, huh?" she said and sat down in front of the television set that dominated the small living room. On the screen, *Air Force One* was just landing in Washington and the members of the President's Cabinet were waiting on the runway in a faintly falling rain to greet Vice President Gardner as he arrived at the capital. The announcer was busy listing the agenda of issues that awaited the Vice President: "Cuba, civil rights, Vietnam, Berlin, inflation," the announcer droned on.

"What makes you think I work for the government?" Sullivan said, trying to be heard over the blaring TV.

"'Cause in Texas only fools or government people drive around with blackwalls on a light-colored car," Kit said, dangling her long legs over the side of the TV lounge chair that she was slumped into.

"That's something to be proud of, anyway," Sullivan mumbled.

"What?" the girl said.

"It's the same in Pennsylvania. We're crazy about whitewalls in the East too," Sullivan said quickly.

"That where you're from?" Kit said, but Sullivan didn't have a chance to answer, because Denise appeared out of the bedroom then. She'd probably learned from past experience to never leave her roommate alone with her dates for very long, Sullivan thought, as he watched her quickly cross the living room toward him. Denise had red-blond hair cut to mid-length and loosely curled. Her skin was very pale and there was a light scattering of freckles across the bridge of her nose and her eyes were a special light blue color that Sullivan had never seen on any other woman. Her cheeks were a little full, but her mouth and nose were small and pixielike and there was something about her that made him want to smile whenever he saw her again.

"Jim, have you been mixed up with any of this?" she said, motioning at the television set.

Gardner was coming slowly down the steps of *Air Force One* now and stepping firmly onto the capital's soil. His wife and daughter were behind him. Sullivan looked briefly at his new boss before he turned from the television set and nodded his head at the girl.

"I knew you were a cop," Kit said, and she untangled herself from her armchair and turned the TV lower, hoping to hear a little of what was really going on with the investigation from Sullivan, but he didn't give her a chance. After the girl's kid took one more quick run at his legs with his trike, Sullivan began backing toward the door. Denise knelt down, pecked a kiss good-bye at her son and then at the tiny howling prisoner in the playpen, and then started for the door after Sullivan.

"How late you going to be?" her roommate yelled after her, but Denise only turned and shrugged her shoulders, made a comic face at her friend, and then trailed after her date.

She caught up with him outside on the short sidewalk that led to Sullivan's government car. He glanced over at her as she took the last half-running step to come alongside.

"Kit's pretty, don't you think?" she said and then watched Sullivan's face closely while he answered.

Sullivan pretended to think about it for a long beat. "A knockout!" he said finally, emphasizing the words, and then, looking down at her, he smiled broadly until she returned the smile. "But you have your own good qualities," he said, looping a long arm around her soft waist and gliding her toward the car.

"What did you think of Danny?" she said, letting herself fall softly against Sullivan's heavily muscled side and chest.

"A young George Washington," Sullivan said as he opened the car door for her. The lock bag containing the Strode file was on his passenger seat and he picked it up and held it in his hand, looking at his date and thinking for a moment. There was something else about this girl he had always liked, too. What was it? He tried hard to remember as he tossed the bag into the back seat and helped her carefully inside, being extra nice.

"What is it, Jim?" she said. She wasn't used to this kind of treatment from him, or from any of her other dates for that matter, she thought, looking up at him with a slightly puzzled expression.

"Oh, nothing," Sullivan said, but he was still thinking hard, trying to remember what else it was about her that he liked so much. He walked thoughtfully around to the car's driver's side and got in and then started the car back toward downtown Dallas.

"Where are we going?" Denise said.

Sullivan glanced over at her. She was wearing a dress made out of a soft, loose-fitting, synthetic fabric and it was cut very low and her body showed at the top of it, looking very comfortable and inviting for a Saturday afternoon.

That was part of the reason he liked her, Sullivan remembered now, as he looked at the low-cut front of her dress, but what the hell was the rest of it? He knew there was something more. Sullivan glanced at his watch, thinking about the Bureau's office downtown and the unprepared affidavit that he needed to have Strode's landlady sign as soon as possible. There probably wouldn't be any secretaries at the office this late on a Saturday afternoon, even today, he thought, and if there were, they'd be busy as hell. He looked over at the girl then and smiled broadly. He remembered the rest of it now. She could type.

"Denise." It was the first time he'd used her name. "I need a favor," he said.

She sighed deeply in her soft, low-cut dress and shook her head in disappointment. God, it was the story of her life.

"Sure," she said without even asking what it was. She knew there wasn't any use. She'd probably wind up doing whatever he asked anyway.

"Would you mind typing up one short little affidavit? I need to nail something down before it disappears on me. I've got a typewriter in my room, but I can only do about six words a minute on it myself. You don't mind, do you?" Sullivan said in the extra-sweet voice that he saved for moments like this.

"Unh-unh. I don't mind, but you did ask me to lunch," she said a little sadly.

"We'll make it dinner," Sullivan said, still smiling over at her and trying very hard to look as boyishly appealing as he could.

"I'm hungry," she said.

"An early dinner," Sullivan said.

Denise sighed again. "And then what?" she asked, sounding hopeful.

"Oh, just a little light filing," Sullivan said and smiled again.

The girl hit him playfully with her open hand against his leg, but she left her hand on his thigh then and looked over at him, the playfulness leaving her eyes. "Okay, whatever you say," she said.

Sullivan glanced down at the low-cut front of her dress and at the lightly freckled skin appearing above it. Maybe her roommate was a little prettier, but there was a lot to like about this girl, he decided. And he accelerated the government car down the expressway back toward his motel room where he'd left his portable Royal, and a half-full box of typing paper, and his unmade bed.

Allen Rozier, the President's press secretary, met the Vice President near the steps to *Air Force One*. A light November rain swirled around the nation's capital that late Saturday afternoon, and Rozier carried a big black government umbrella that he held up over Gardner's wife and daughter as they followed the Vice President down the long reviewing line of other Cabinet officials that had assembled on the runway to welcome Gardner back to Washington.

Before he got into a waiting limousine, the Vice President turned to Rozier and signaled for the press secretary to join him. Gardner's own family dutifully shuffled to a trail limo then, as Rozier carefully moved his own bulky frame past them and into the limousine's roomy back seat next to the Vice President.

Then Gardner leaned out his window again and motioned for Secretary of State Holland and Secretary of Defense Forbes to join him as well, and the two men climbed inside and sat facing Gardner on the limousine's double rear seat.

A small bar was built into the rear compartment of the vehicle and as soon as the limousine was safely out of television camera range the Vice President poured four large bourbons into heavy cut-crystal glasses and handed them around without asking.

Rozier held the heavy glass in his hand while he watched Gardner drink a big slug of bourbon from his own. When the Vice President was finished, he made a loud, satisfied noise and then turned toward Rozier.

"I hope you didn't mind me asking you to stay in Washington," Gardner said, looking directly at Cassidy's press secretary for an answer.

"I understood," Rozier said, not quite responding to Gardner's question.

"I need your help," the Vice President said then, reaching out with one of his big hands to tug at the well-tailored sleeve of Rozier's topcoat.

Rozier nodded, but Gardner ignored him, turning instead to the other two men sitting across from him in the back seat of the limousine, trying to balance cut-crystal glasses full of bourbon on their laps. "I know how you must feel," Gardner said to them. "I know how you all must feel," he added, pointing out the back window at the other Cabinet limousines in the long, solemn procession that was following him back to the White House. Gardner paused then for effect before adding dramatically. "But, I want absolute continuity," he said forcefully. "Absolute!" he said again. "We can't afford to lose anybody right now. I don't want a third-level clerk at the OMB stirrin'. Do you understand that?"

"Yes, sir," Secretary of State Holland said in his slow, thoughtful, Virginia voice, and the Secretary of Defense nodded crisply, but instead of answering right away Rozier used the break to drink from his glass of bourbon. What the hell was he doing here? he thought. He worked for Jack Cassidy, and what he did for him was hardly vital to the national interests of the United States. He'd never fooled himself about that, unless you just happened to believe that keeping Jack Cassidy looking good for the voters was as vital to the interests of the country as just about anything else was right now. Rozier did, but he knew that didn't explain being asked to sit in the back seat of Gardner's limousine with the secretaries of State and Defense at a time like this.

"Isn't my function a little different, sir?" Rozier said finally, and then he paused, trying to find the right words. "I mean, at some point soon I think that the President is going to need me," he said.

Gardner didn't answer at first. Instead, he just stared across the back of the limousine at Rozier's face and eyes for a long moment. "Don't be too sure about what the President is going to need. You haven't seen him," the Vice President said finally.

"What do you mean?" Rozier asked.

"Just this," Gardner went on. "This morning, before I left the hospital, I talked to the President's doctors for a good long time. And I'm personally convinced now that Jack Cassidy is never goin' to be able to complete the last year of his term or be in any condition to run for reelection either. Now, that's somethin' that the public should only very slowly become aware of . . ." Gardner said. "Very slowly. It's absolutely imperative that we give this country a feelin' of continuity, but the truth of the matter is that Jack Cassidy will probably never be healthy enough to really be President again, not for a long while, anyway," Gardner said flatly.

All three men traveling with him down the wet capital streets remained very quiet after the Vice President had finished. Outside, the limousine was just passing the Lincoln Memorial. Rozier kept his eyes tightly focused on its outline, slightly blurred by the misting rain that fell around it, as he responded to Gardner. "Have you spoken to the President about this?" Rozier asked finally.

"No, not yet, not entirely," Gardner hedged. "He's not in any shape to discuss it right now, but I do think he's goin' have to face it very soon." And then Gardner paused and looked directly at Rozier again. "And I haven't spoken to his brother about it yet, either," the Vice President said, and Rozier finally understood why Gardner had asked him to join this little loyalty meeting in the back seat of the vice-presidential limousine. Gardner knew that he'd report back to Tim everything that was said and that was just what the Vice President wanted. Well, he'd sure as hell get it that way, Rozier decided, and then he drank again from his heavy crystal glass full of bourbon.

"I'll be meetin' with every member of the Cabinet, and I'm goin' to tell them jus' what I'm tellin' you. It's up to us to run this country now, day by day, minute by minute, and forget about Jack Cassidy—and if we don't, we're jus' not doin' our duty," Gardner said. "Do you understand that?"

Rozier nodded, but he still couldn't bring himself to look back across the interior of the limousine at Gardner's long, deeply lined face. Instead, the President's press secretary kept his eyes on the statue of Lincoln fading behind him in the November rain.

Special Agent James O. Sullivan rolled over and stretched. Then he looked at the plump, freckle-faced girl sleeping sweetly in the motel bed next to him, her eyes closed, a curl of reddish-blond hair down over one eye, the motel sheet up, only partly covering the nipples of her very full and beautifully shaped breasts. She was smiling happily in her dreams.

Some women look better with their clothes off than they do with them on; with some it was the other way around. He'd always preferred the first kind, Sullivan philosophized, as he watched her sleep.

Denise sighed deeply and then curled her body higher in the bed, uncovering a few more inches of herself above the sheet.

Sullivan looked first at the girl's body and then across at the remnants of the early dinner that he had promised her lying on the nightstand behind her, wax sandwich wrappers and a nearly empty cardboard pint container of milk with a plastic straw in it and some uneaten wedges of dill pickle. Then Sullivan looked across at his old battered Royal portable.

Mrs. Riordan's affidavit was still rolled around the typewriter's carriage, neatly and professionally done. Sullivan glanced at his watch. He should get the damned thing signed, he thought. If there was one thing he'd learned about witnesses, it was to get them tied down fast, because they all had a way of fading on you—both their memories and their nerve. Just then the girl stirred and rolled her body slightly so that both her breasts were pointed straight up at him, their nipples a bright, fresh rose color. Sullivan looked down at her for a moment and then moved closer, pressing the front of her body almost flat against his own naked chest. He bent down then and kissed each of her breasts tenderly, running his lips and tongue across their creamy surface for a long, slow time. As he did, his hand searched between her legs. Her underwear was a forgotten memory, disposed of somewhere after she'd finished the typing, but before the first bite of roast-beef sandwich, and Sullivan's big hand grasped her tightly and began a firm, steady, rubbing motion.

She moved even closer to him, not quite opening her eyes, and they held each other in a lush, clinging embrace for several long seconds, and, somewhere in the middle of it, Special Agent Sullivan entered deep inside her.

The girl sighed and laid back against the hard, flat, motel-room pillow beneath her head and Sullivan moved up hungrily after her, pushing himself even deeper into her still sleepy, but wonderfully warm and accepting woman's body.

"Jesus," Sullivan breathed huskily at her face, as he closed in next to her. "You sure can type," he said and then licked at her full upper lip as it began to curve in a playful smile back at him.

It wasn't until almost midnight that Sullivan managed to lead the girl to his car and start her back for West Dallas.

She had moved over completely onto his half of the front seat now, her body pushed up against him and her head with its reddish-blond curls in complete disarray dropped down onto his shoulder. She was breathing rhythmically and smelled faintly of onions and dill pickles.

"Denise, would you mind if I just made one quick little stop before I take you home," he said a little uncertainly, but she only smiled absently at him and nodded.

"I don't mind anything right now," she said contentedly.

Sullivan patted her head softly. Or any other time either, he thought to himself.

"I just want to swing by and see if I can get this affidavit signed. Mrs. Riordan's probably asleep, anyway," he said out loud, moving his government car into the far right-hand lane and signaling for a turn.

"We can be together longer then," Denise said, snuggling her head more comfortably into Sullivan's shoulder—and she kept it that way the entire time it took to drive across town to Strode's boardinghouse.

The lights were out in the old two-story wood-frame house when Sullivan finally pulled his car across the street under the branches of a big overhanging sycamore tree, right where the landlady had said that she'd seen the police black-and-white the afternoon before. As late as it was, there were still a few sightseers out on the street in front of the rooming house. Sullivan carefully removed the girl's head from his shoulder before he got out and crossed the street. An amateur photographer was kneeling on the front sidewalk, pointing his camera up at the now infamous wood-frame building, and a few other passers-by were stopped on the sidewalk nearby looking up at the house and talking quietly. This town was getting to be like a damn circus, Sullivan thought as he stepped by the cameraman and started toward the rooming-house entrance.

"Hold it," a voice said from the shadows of the front door, and Sullivan froze in his tracks, as a uniformed Dallas cop emerged from the darkened porch and started down the front steps toward him.

"I'm FBI," Sullivan said quickly, trying to make it sound like what a Dallas cop would probably expect it to sound like, and then he reached very slowly for his I.D. card and flashed it at the figure that was moving out of the shadows toward him. The cop inspected the card for a moment and then nodded.

"I just wanted to see Mrs. Riordan for a minute. I called earlier," Sullivan said. "But I guess she's sleeping, huh?" he added, gesturing up at the house's darkened second story.

The cop turned away from Sullivan and started back for the shadows that surrounded the front door.

"She ain't here," the cop said, with his back still toward Sullivan.

"I just spoke to her a few hours ago," Sullivan said.

The cop shrugged his shoulders to show that he couldn't help that and then he sat down heavily in a sagging porch chair right next to the front door. The thick wooden door behind the outside screen was closed and no light shone through the door's double glass inserts.

"She's at her sister's," the cop said from the dark place where he rested. "Too much hassle here, reporters, gawkers, assorted riffraff, and now G-men." He pointed at Sullivan.

"Where's that?" Sullivan said.

"What?"

"Her sister's."

"Fuck if I know," he said.

Sullivan took a deep breath and then started again.

"I talked to Deputy Chief Boyer last night . . ." Sullivan said, but the cop didn't let him finish.

"So talk to him now," the cop said and stared through the darkness at Sullivan.

"Okay," Sullivan said and turned back for his car.

"Hey, you got any magazines in there, anything to read?" the cop said, pointing at Sullivan's car.

Sullivan remembered the Strode file sitting in his back seat then and he laughed at the thought of giving it to the cop.

"Fuck if I know," Sullivan said and walked away.

Back on the sidewalk in front of the house, the man with the camera was at a new angle and when Sullivan appeared out of the shadows of the front lawn, the photographer knelt and snapped a couple of views of the house that included Sullivan.

The camera's flashbulbs exploded almost in Sullivan's face and he looked over at him angrily, but the kneeling man quickly pointed the camera away from him and Sullivan let it go and returned across the street to his car.

The girl was waiting sleepily in the front seat. "No luck, huh?" she said wearily and leaned forward, but as soon as Sullivan got in next to her she just collapsed back onto his shoulder and closed her eyes.

"No problem," Sullivan said, glancing quickly at the lock bag lying across the back seat. He was beginning to feel very uneasy about a lot of things and he wasn't sure that he wanted to keep lugging Strode's file all around Texas with him while he shadow-boxed with the local police, but keeping it in his motel room was even worse—and there was nowhere else in town that he could leave it. He checked the rearview mirror. There was a car with someone sitting in it parked about a half a block behind him. Was someone watching him? It was probably nothing, he told himself, but he could feel his heart beginning to pump hard and fast.

Sullivan started his car's engine and began driving slowly down the darkened Dallas streets toward the girl's apartment as he tried to think it all through. As he drove, he kept glancing in his rearview mirror. He couldn't be sure, but it looked like the car that had been parked behind him was following him now. He needed to make some decisions fast.

"Denise," he said, and the girl stirred with Sullivan's unexpected use of her given name for only the third time the entire night.

"Sure, whatever it is, sure," she said without a struggle. She was too tired to even try to pretend that she wasn't going to give in to him, in the end, anyway.

"Do you have someplace to keep valuables? You know, a safe-deposit box or something?"

"No," she said flatly. But then after she thought about it for a few seconds she added, "I've got a jewelry box in my bedroom."

"How big?"

She showed him with her hands.

Sullivan nodded. "In the back seat there's a locked FBI bag. Do you see it?"

Denise slowly disentangled herself from Sullivan's shoulder and turned to the back seat.

"Uh-uh."

"Could you keep that for me, just for a little while?"

"Okay," she said and lazily sank back down onto Sullivan's shoulder. "Don't you have places for that kind of thing?" she mumbled sleepily.

"You have to promise me that you won't look at it, that no one will, and you'll give it up only to me," Sullivan said emphatically. He hated getting the girl involved, but she was the only thing he had right now. If there really was someone following him, like maybe the local poiice, they could easily decide to pull him over on the long lonely drive back to his motel, and if they did he didn't want the file with him. And it should be safe enough, he decided. There was probably no way that anyone could know about the file, but just to be certain, he added, "And if anything happens to me, just burn it. Do you understand? You don't tell anybody about it and you burn it," Sullivan said, and when he didn't get an answer right away he almost shouted at her. "I said, do you understand?"

"Okay, sure," she said, finally straightening up a little to get a better look at Sullivan's face. She could sense the urgency in him now.

"But, I mean, don't you have official places and things?" she said.

Sullivan was quiet for a second, his face growing tense, as he thought about what he'd done. "This is unofficial," he said finally.

He looked back up at his rearview mirror, but now all he could see was a long, dark street empty of even a trace of anyone trying to follow him.

"You know, I wasn't going to say anything," Denise said, as they made the final turn toward the low row of apartment buildings that she lived in. Her voice had lost all its sleepiness now.

Sullivan turned to her in the half light from the darkened city streets. "What?" he said.

"Well, a few minutes ago, when we stopped at that rooming house, I thought it was strange." She paused for a moment then, not knowing how to say it. "Do you remember that man taking pictures of the house?" she asked.

Sullivan nodded, listening hard now.

"Well, after you went inside, he turned around and took a picture of your car."

Sullivan stayed quiet, but he could feel his stomach begin to churn.

"Isn't that strange?" Denise said after awhile.

"No, it's nothing, just some nosy jerk. Dallas is full of them right now," Sullivan lied.

He pulled up in front of her apartment and walked with her to the door. She held the FBI bag under her arm proudly. Sullivan looked at her and then at the fabric bag, wondering if he was doing the right thing.

After they stepped carefully around the toys on the sidewalk in front of her unit, Sullivan had second thoughts, and he reached out and grabbed the bag. As he tugged at it, Denise only tightened her grip and then turned to look at him. "No," she said, shaking her head. "It's okay."

Sullivan took his hand off the bag and looked back at her. Her curling reddish-blond hair was dropping down loosely over her forehead, some of it almost reaching to her pale blue eyes. "Remember what I said then," Sullivan told her again. "Only me."

Denise nodded. "I'd like to invite you in," she said and smiled shyly. "But I got a roommate and . . . ." Her voice trailed off.

"And two kids, I know," Sullivan said, moving up close to her and holding her around the shoulders and softly kissing the top of her messy reddish-blond hair. "And I'm sure they're both terrific kids—they probably just want to keep you all for themselves," Sullivan said. He paused before adding, "I don't blame them either."

"I had a nice time," Denise said and turned back for the door.

"I'll call," Sullivan said.

"I know," she said, lifting the FBI bag and showing it to Sullivan under the porch light. "I've really got you this time. I've got your secret whatever-it-is." She smiled.

"Take good care of it," Sullivan said as Denise unlocked the door and went inside. "And take care of yourself too," he breathed to himself, as he walked back down the narrow path.

He got into his car and started for the motel. Even though as he drove he checked in his rearview mirror several times, he never got another glimpse of the car following about a block and a half behind him. It was a cream-colored, no-frills American car, maybe a Ford or a Chevy, with four cheap, blackwall tires. Just like Sullivan's.

CHAPTER

7

"Jack, I think there are some things that we should talk about." Tim said the words carefully, watching his brother for any sign of strain. He was sitting by Jack's hospital bed, leaning forward, talking quietly to him. They were alone, early on the Sunday morning two days after the attempt on the President's life.

"I spoke with Dad. He's fine." Tim paused then and laughed. "Mom's convinced that he knew somehow even before he was told that you were hurt." The two men smiled at each other, remembering fondly other similar times with their mother, but the President knew that this wasn't what his brother really wanted to talk to him about now.

"Dad's raising hell with his doctors, but they won't let him leave home." The President nodded his head slightly to let his brother know that he understood.

"He's in Hyannis," Tim said slowly, watching his brother's eyes, seeing how much of it he remembered. The doctors had said there would be memory lapses for a while, but that they would probably disappear with a few months' rest. Tim had kept that fact out of the statement that the hospital had just released to the press, but he knew that it would be only a matter of time before the public found out.

Jack nodded slightly in response. The pain and the thick wrapping of bandages made it impossible for him to do anything more.

"They're thinking of going to Palm Beach after the holidays," his brother said, and the President nodded again and smiled. He knew that Tim was testing him. The doctors had already played some of the same games with him.

"Well, Suzanne and I thought that you . . ." Tim stopped and then tried it another way. "Most of the doctors seem to think that you shouldn't leave here, but hell, Jack, I talked to Dr. O'Neil and he thinks that as long as we're careful . . . There are hospitals in Boston, too. Some of the best in the world. He thinks that maybe in a week or so . . ."

At the word *Boston* Jack's eyes lit up and he tried to nod again, but the pain that he felt kept him from making the movement too emphatic.

"Dr. O'Neil thought . . ." Tim started again, but then stopped when he saw the small smile beginning to light up his brother's face. Tim caught on to the joke. "You're right, Jack. I got to the one Irishman in the crowd. Hell, he'd probably send you to Dublin, if I asked him to," Tim said, laughing at himself. "But I can't help thinking that being near home might be the best thing for you right now. I know how much you hate hospitals, and maybe we could sneak you into Hyannis for a day or two around the holidays. You'd have Suzanne and the children close by, and Kay and I thought . . ."

The President shook his head, interrupting his brother in midsentence. "No, Tim," the President managed painfully. Both men were quiet then, but they understood each other completely without the words.

"You want me in Washington, don't you? You want me to watch Rance for you?" Tim said finally and his brother smiled weakly at him that he had guessed right.

"Well, maybe I can come up to Boston on the weekends then and we can talk about a few things, like what's going on at the White House in your absence, for example," Tim said, smiling back at his older brother. "I wonder if being President will be as easy as Rance always seemed to think that it would," he added then.

The two men smiled at each other for a moment, guessing the probable answer to Tim's question, but then Tim looked away from Jack, avoiding his eyes, and the President's face tightened in concern. Something about Tim's manner had bothered him all morning. The President's requests for a television, or a radio, or even a newspaper had repeatedly been denied as well, and he was certain now that he wasn't being told something. "What is it, Tim?" he asked and his brother continued looking away from him for a moment, but then he finally began to explain in his tight, clipped Boston voice.

"Jack, the man the Dallas police arrested yesterday . . ." Tim paused again then, barely believing what he had to say next. "He was murdered," he said finally.

The President's expression turned to puzzlement.

"He was in custody and he was shot down, right in police headquarters," his brother said. "I know it's unbelievable, but it happened. I'd feel one hell of a lot better with you in Boston right now, Jack."

Tim looked at his brother for a long moment before he said the rest of it. Tim hadn't told anybody what he had really been feeling since he'd arrived in Texas, and he had to weigh whether he wanted to tell Jack now, but he finally decided that he had to say it. He didn't care how it sounded. He had to get his brother out of Dallas and safely back to Boston whatever the cost. "I don't like any of this down here," he said finally. "I don't like what's going on with the local police. I don't like Summers being in charge of the investigation. I don't like you still being in this city," the Attorney General said. "To tell you the truth, Jack, I'm not sure we can keep you safe down here."

Regan flew his light plane out of Monterey early Sunday morning. He didn't take it into New Orleans, though. Instead, he brought it into Baton Rouge and a balding, solidly built, middle-aged man in a khaki suit met him in the airport's passenger lounge. The two men shook hands briefly.

"Case, Jesus, are you sure this is okay?" Regan asked, nervously looking around at the crowded terminal lobby. The man in the khaki suit nodded and the airport lights reflected off the top of his balding head as he did. "I got it all cleared. They just want you out of New Orleans for a while," the man said. Glancing over his shoulder, he added, "Come on, let's get out of here. I've got a car."

The two men walked together to the airport parking lot and got into a dusty, light green Plymouth sedan with Texas plates.

"You been readin' the papers?" the balding man asked as he started the car's engine, and the red-haired man next to him nodded his head.

"The TV up here has been full of it, too. It's all they've got on. Jesus, what a fuckup!" Case said.

"Are they angry?" the red-haired man blurted out and Case looked over at his companion's worried face and shrugged his shoulders. "Yeah, they're pissed off, but not at you. I told them it wasn't your fault with this guy, that he pulled a gun on you. That's right, isn't it?"

"Yes, of course," Regan answered impatiently. "Did you tell them I couldn't I.D. him, even now? I mean, if I ever saw him again I wouldn't even recognize him. Greasy black hair, that's all I saw, probably a spic, but I didn't even look at his face. Almost twelve hours in the air with the bastard and I just kept looking straight ahead. Gave me a goddamned headache staring straight ahead like that." The red-haired man laughed disgustedly at the memory. "But I never even looked at his face. Did you tell them that?" Regan asked again.

Case didn't answer for a few seconds. "You can tell them yourself," he said finally.

"What do you mean?" Regan stammered.

"Shit, they've got to talk to you. What do you think? They're not going to talk to you?"

The green Plymouth was speeding down a narrow two-lane highway toward the outskirts of Baton Rouge now. The hot, humid Louisiana air was blowing in through the open windows and both men stayed quiet for a while and just let the moist bayou air blow over them.

"Case," the red-haired man said softly after a few minutes.

"Uh-uh?"

"I've got something I'm supposed to show them," Regan said. "He gave it to me."

"Who?"

"The spic I flew to Mexico! Who the hell do you think?" Regan exploded, and then he reached into the front pocket of his shirt and unbuttoned it, removing a single piece of paper. One edge of the paper was ragged, as if it had been torn out of a binder or a book of some kind, and it blew erratically in the air of the open car.

"What the hell is that?" Case said, nodding at the flapping piece of paper.

"I think it's a sheet out of Strode's diary," Regan said.

The balding man at the wheel turned to him in a flash. "What do you mean?" he said.

"The spic had a little book. He said it was Strode's diary. He told me that Strode wrote it all down, the whole goddamned thing. It's all in there, everything." Regan paused, and then he added pointedly, "And everybody."

Case kept looking at him for a few seconds and then he reached up and tore the little sheet of paper out of the red-haired man's hands and stared down at it. "Jesus. They're not going to like that," he said finally. Looking back up at the road, he added, "What does he want for it?"

"He wants back in," Regan said.

The balding man in the rumpled suit was afraid to look at him. Instead he kept his eyes straight ahead on the narrow Louisiana road that led to the hotel.

"He wants a new contract. Half the money now, half when he finishes the job," Regan said and then went on. "When he gets the first installment, they get the rest of the diary. He gave me instructions on how the money is to be delivered."

"And you're supposed to tell them that?" Case said, almost laughing at how the people that they had both been working for during the last several months were going to take the news, but he was too frightened to do any more than barely manage to twist his face into a grimace. Big bright spots of moisture began to show on the fleshy parts of his bald head.

"That's the only reason he let me live," Regan said. "What the hell should I do?"

"Tell them. What else can you do?" Case said. Then he fell silent for a long time before he added, "They're at the hotel."

"Oh, sweet Jesus." Regan clutched at the door handle next to him in fear as if he meant to leap out into the sugar-cane fields at the side of the narrow road. "I didn't even look at his face, I swear to God."

"It'll be okay," Case said. "They just want to hear it from you, that's all."

Regan slowly loosened his hold on the door handle and let his hands rest limply in his lap. "You know what else?" he said then.

Case looked over at him.

"I think that spic wants to finish it, no matter what," the red-haired man said. "Money or no money, diary or no diary. I think it's personal with him now."

The Attorney General sat on the edge of a metal desk at the front of the room. His coat was off, his shirtsleeves rolled up, and his tie undone. The men sitting in front of Cassidy on the rows of folding metal chairs all had their coats on and buttoned, their dark ties pulled up tight, clutching their throats, their chins freshly and closely shaved, their eyes respectfully fixed on the front of the room. They were all waiting for the section chief of the FBI's Dallas office to finish speaking.

The meeting was being held in the big main bay of the FBI's offices in downtown Dallas. It was Monday morning.

Sitting in two tight clusters near the back of the room and looking a little out of place were the Secret Service and FBI agents from Washington who were on special assignment in the city for the President's trip, and sitting even farther back, in the last row on the aisle all by himself, was Special Agent Sullivan. Sullivan's eyes were red, his shave not as close as the others', and his body slumped a notch lower in his chair than anybody else's in the room. He was tired and angry and he looked it. He'd been up all night chasing leads, but his investigation wasn't going anywhere. He was.

Yancey had called him earlier that morning and told him that he was being pulled out of Dallas. Sullivan didn't know where it was that he was being sent yet, but he knew that he'd find out soon enough. And as he sat in the back of the room and listened to Yancey drone on about what a thorough job was being done on the investigation and some other bullshit, Sullivan kept trying to tell himself that he didn't really care about getting pulled out of Dallas now, but the lie was only making him angrier and the anger was starting to show very clearly on his reddening face. Finally, Yancey introduced the Attorney General and let him talk. And Sullivan forced himself to sit up a little in his hard metal chair and listen to what Cassidy had to say.

The Attorney General stood and looked quickly around the room for a moment, smiling at the Secret Service agents that he recognized.

"The President asked me to speak with you this morning," the Attorney General began. "He wants you each to understand just how much he appreciates what you've done. He knows that he wouldn't be alive this morning if it weren't for the coordinated efforts of the people in this room, and he asked me to thank you on his behalf." Cassidy wasn't certain just how to go on with what he wanted to say next, and so he looked away from his audience for a moment trying to collect his thoughts.

"Now, I know that we've got a delicate situation down here," he said and then paused again. "With the investigation, I mean. Mr. Yancey and I have talked this morning and he's told me that you're beginning to run into some jurisdictional problems. Now, the Dallas police . . ." At the mention of the police, the normally polite men sitting on the rows of folding metal chairs in front of him began a low collective groan. Cassidy laughed then and held up his hand to quiet them. "The Dallas police," he said again, still smiling.

"—have not exactly done a hell of a job," an agent at the back of the room said, finishing Cassidy's sentence for him, and everyone laughed.

"A little Texas justice," another agent said, and the laughter started again.

"Well, you're right, we've got a little work to do with them," Cassidy said. "And personally I'm convinced that the best way to deal with the problem is to do what some of the press have been suggesting." Cassidy paused again for a few seconds before he went on. He knew what he was going to say next was not what the people seated in front of him that morning wanted to hear, but he said it anyway. "I'm going to ask the President to establish an independent committee with its own staff and with full authority to investigate everything that's happened down here during the last few days."

There was no more laughter in the room now. The men's faces were grim and serious—some even openly hostile.

"I'm sure that many of you have your own feelings about a commission of that kind, but I want to assure you that my position on this is not intended to reflect in any way on the ability of the people in this room to do the job." Cassidy looked out at the silent, openly unhappy roomful of men. Only the smattering of Secret Service agents at the very back returned his gaze, as the other faces grew busy looking down at the floor or at the tops of their own highly polished shoes. Special Agent Sullivan just looked vaguely up at Cassidy, waiting to hear the rest of it, and as he did the young agent could feel his own role in the investigation disappearing deep into this political tangle.

"I believe that an independent commission is the most efficient way to overcome the jurisdictional problems between the state and federal authorities on this case and to quickly get at the truth," Cassidy said sharply, trying to bring the faces in front of him back to attention. A few heads snapped up at his words. "But at this time, Director Summers is in complete charge of the investigation and I can assure you that no commission of any kind will be established without his full cooperation, and then only after taking into account all of the Director's thoughts on the matter. Please be confident of that," Cassidy said. He turned back to the long wooden table behind him and reached for the suit coat he'd left lying across it.

"As you probably know," the Attorney General said, turning toward the room again. "There's a very good chance that the President will be leaving Dallas in a few days." At the words "leaving Dallas," the Secret Service men at the back of the room began to applaud and Cassidy grinned at them before he went on. "As soon as his condition permits, he will be taken to a hospital in Boston to continue his recuperation there. I'm sure that you'll all be pleased to know that he's getting stronger every day, and we're confident that with sufficient rest he will recover fully." Cassidy paused. "One last thing," he said, holding up his hand to the room again. "I want you to know, too, how grateful I am personally to each of you for what you've done for my brother and for our family, in the last few days," he added emotionally. "And if I can be of any help to any of you in the investigation, or if my office can be, please feel free to contact me directly. Thank you again." Cassidy turned back to the Dallas section chief standing next to him. "Mr. Yancey and I will be in constant communication, I'm sure," he said and then he folded his coat over his arm and began threading his way through the rows of folding chairs toward the door.

As Cassidy approached him, Sullivan straightened up in his hard metal chair and leaned forward toward the Attorney General. The two men caught each other's eye for a moment and Cassidy paused in his stride, as if he expected Sullivan to say something to him, and Sullivan half wanted to himself, but he just nodded politely at the Attorney General and Cassidy nodded back. The cluster of Secret Service men folded quickly around the Attorney General then and the small entourage exited by the room's rear door. Hell, what was there to say, Sullivan thought to himself as he watched Cassidy's lean, white-shirted back disappear into the hall. What else could he have done, anyway? Blurted out his suspicions right there in front of everybody? He would have looked like a goddamned fool, with only the sketchy half facts he had so far. What he needed was another couple of weeks in Dallas running out leads before he was ready to say anything to anybody, much less to the Attorney General of the United States.

"Sullivan!" It was Yancey's voice snapping him out of his thoughts, reminding him that he didn't have a week. He probably didn't even have the rest of the day.

"Sullivan, I want to see you in my office!" Yancey snapped again, and Sullivan stood up then, and, as always, he hurried across the room to do as he'd been told.

Cigarette smoke curled up over the fuzzy black-and-white pictures flickering on the little pull-down movie screen at the front of the room.

Special Agent Sullivan was sitting in the dark, drinking hot coffee from a paper cup, his feet propped up on the back of the chair in front of him. He was looking across the room at the little screen, where an unshaven, wild-eyed young man with dark brown hair, wearing a crumpled, short-sleeved white shirt, moved erratically back and forth on a street corner handing out pamphlets to passers-by. Then the film ended abruptly and the screen went blank.

"Let's see it again," a voice called out in the darkness, and the projector at the back of the room began to whir, rewinding the film for another showing.

They were in Yancey's office—Sullivan, Yancey, and two other agents temporarily on special assignment in Dallas from the Washington office.

"We got a blowup of those pamphlets?" a voice asked in the dark room.

"Better, we think we got one of them," came back the answer. It was the section chief's voice this time.

"Pro-Cuba?"

"Pro-fucking-Cuba, pro-Castro, Moscow, you name it, Strode was for it, as long as it wasn't American," another voice answered.

"Son of a bitch should have stayed in Russia," a third voice said, as the film started again.

"Where is this?" Sullivan asked into the smoky room and pointed at the screen as it lit up again with the white-shirted young man holding a big stack of pamphlets in his hands and walking slowly toward a crowded street corner.

"New Orleans," someone said.

"I know that, but where?" Sullivan asked.

"Somewhere in the French Quarter. The TV station that took the film has the scoop on it."

The film ran through again and then stopped.

"What else we got?" someone asked.

"There's a clip of him on a local call-in show."

"Let's see it."

A few seconds later Strode's face filled the screen at the front of the room. He was talking fast, excited, his dark eyes darting wildly, as he explained in overly complicated terms the differences, as he saw them, between the beliefs of those currently in power in Moscow and his own brand of what he called "radical dialectic Marxism."

"Quite a scholar," a voice said.

"Fuck him," another answered.

"This New Orleans too?" Sullivan called out.

"WTRQ—Channel Ten—New Orleans, Louisiana," came back the answer in the darkness. "Interesting aside." It was Yancey's voice again, as the film stopped and Sullivan could hear another reel being placed on the machine. "But they sent this along too," Yancey said and flicked on a new strip of film.

"State troopers found this deep in the bayous outside Baton Rouge late last night," Yancey said. On the screen a short piece of news film showed a once-green Plymouth sedan being towed slowly out of a bayou swamp. Thick brown mud clung to the outside of the car, half-covering a set of Texas plates.

"They found two men inside it," Yancey went on. "They each had a bullet hole in the back of their heads, big, ragged bullet holes, at close range."

"Mafia?" a voice asked.

"Maybe," Yancey said. "It's got that kind of a look, doesn't it? Anyway, both bodies were identified. One was a private detective of sorts, named Case.

The other worked for him sometimes, an ex-pilot named Regan. James Regan. Earlier in the day, Regan had logged in a flight to Baton Rouge. He'd come in from Mexico—Monterey, Mexico. Could be something."

Sullivan took another drink of his hot coffee and watched the screen at the front of the dark room as the green Plymouth sedan finally came unstuck from the oozing, brown bayou mud that had surrounded it and the outline of the two men inside became partially visible. The man closest to the camera was bald and his mouth was open wide in obvious terror. The other man's head had slumped forward onto his companion's shoulder and the cheap red wig that he'd worn had flapped forward and fallen comically down over his eyes. It almost made Sullivan want to laugh. What a silly-looking bastard, he thought and took another sip of his hot coffee, but as he did his eyes never left the flickering images on the little movie screen.

"Anyway, here's the good part," Yancey said. "Both men were from New Orleans. And not only that, but on the morning of November twenty-second, the Baton Rouge flight logs show that Mr. Regan left there with a planned destination of Dallas. Now, there's no record of him arriving at any local airport. I checked it out myself, but we all know that doesn't mean he wasn't here. He could have set down at a thousand places within a half hour of the city, and he could have been standing by to fly Strode out of town or to help him in some way. Personally, I don't think any of it means a damn thing. New Orleans is a big town and there's no way to assume any connection between Strode and Regan just because they both happened to live there. And God knows people get killed and their bodies dumped in the bayou all the time and for a hell of a lot of reasons, even pilots, who maybe did or maybe didn't fly into Dallas last Friday, but if there is anything that ties Regan to Strode or to any other part of this thing, I want to know it before the press does. If they get the story first, they could wind up making us look pretty goddamn bad if they want to, and usually they do. So I want us to get it first, understood? The other thing I want to know is what Strode's contacts were with the Communists down there and anything else we can learn about what he was up to in New Orleans over the last few years."

"Pack your bags, Sullivan," someone called out to him in the darkness.

"Not just Sullivan," Yancey said then. "All three of you are booked on a five o'clock flight to New Orleans."

The President looked out the window of *Air Force One*. The big aircraft was doing double duty now. The Air Force had shuttled it back to Dallas and it stood on the runway at Love Field ready to take President Cassidy and his family to Boston.

The President could see Tim, standing alone at the side of the runway and looking up at the plane. Several Secret Service men stood nearby. It was dawn in Dallas, a few minutes before six in the morning, and the move was a surprise to everyone, including the press. The President's doctors had finally given in to the pressure being applied by the Cassidy family and had agreed to let the President continue his recuperation at a hospital closer to his home. There had been no announcement of the flight, for security reasons, it would be explained later. But it was also a concession to the Vice President. Gardner hadn't wanted any fanfare when the President left Texas, and the Vice President's political instincts were right, Jack thought now. The state didn't need a reminder of just how eager he and his family were to get out of it and go home. Texas would be crucial in the next election. Gardner was right about that, too. But crucial for whom?

The President raised his hand and waved to his brother. Tim waved back and *Air Force One* began to pull away from the gate, leaving Tim alone in Dallas. The President smiled. He knew that was a condition that his brother would remedy soon enough. There was probably a plane close by even now, ready to take the Attorney General and his family back to Washington, as soon as the President's own aircraft was safely off the ground.

Air Force One taxied to the head of the runway and waited for clearance. The President looked out the window at the trees by the edge of the runway and, as he did, he enjoyed being by himself for a few minutes. He was strapped tightly into a soft, reclining airline chair that had been adapted into what had become almost a full-length hospital bed for the flight. His head was heavily cushioned by an arrangement of foam-rubber supports that the doctors had designed specifically for the trip, and two nurses sat attentively nearby. Up front, three of the best doctors in the country, each a noted specialist in his field, sat belted in for takeoff. Suzanne and the children were the plane's only other passengers.

The President looked across the interior of the aircraft to where his wife was sitting with their children, one on either side of her. She was watching his every move. The aircraft began to accelerate down the runway then. This was the moment that the doctors had warned him against, the time of maximum stress on his wounded body, as the plane reached its top ground speed and then thrust itself up, into the air. He could see the tension in his wife's face as she looked over at him while the plane gathered its full speed and began rushing forward down the runway.

"Say good-bye to Dallas," he mouthed to her over the sound of the plane's engine, and then he could see her smile as she relaxed slightly while the shapes outside the window behind her began to blur.

"Good-bye, Dallas," Suzanne mouthed back to him and they both smiled as the powerful jet plane exploded up into the air, jolting them against their seats.

Jack kept his wife's eye as the aircraft continued climbing at a hard angle into the Texas sky, letting her know with his look that he was fine. Then he dropped his glance to his six-year-old daughter, Erin, who sat staring over at him and clutching her mother's hand at the same time; then Jack looked at his son, John Jr., half Erin's age, sitting on Suzanne's other side, the little boy's head resting comfortably against his mother's arm.

"Hello, Boston!" Suzanne said, loudly enough for Jack to hear as the plane began to level off above the early morning clouds.

A nurse seated behind him unbuckled her seat belt and started down the aisle toward the President, but he waved her off.

A few seconds later though, two of the doctors approached him. He nodded at them, and as he did one of them knelt down and looked deep into his face. "I'm fine," he said, and the doctor's eyes watched him carefully as he spoke.

"Really," Jack said. Satisfied only for the moment, the two men returned grudgingly to their seats.

Cassidy looked over at his wife. She pretended to look stern and he reached his hand out across the aisle and touched her arm. He left his hand there for a moment and then turned and looked out the window to where the clouds were breaking and he could see the city of Dallas beneath him. The pain in his head was much stronger than he wanted anyone to know, but he was grateful in some strange way that he could feel it at all.

He watched the city sail by beneath the plane for a few moments and then he saw it. It was unmistakable, the interconnection of expressways, the cluster of tall buildings with the green square in the middle of it. Dealey Plaza was spread out below him. Suddenly, it all flashed back to him, the hot, windless morning, the motorcade, the friendly crowd. It had been very warm in the back seat of the open car, the black leather seats swelteringly hot in the sunlight, and he remembered now, looking ahead at the shade of the cement overpass coming up in front of him, how he was looking forward to the coolness of passing through the short tunnel before the motorcade emerged on the other side of the expressway. He'd wanted to say something to Suzanne and he remembered turning to her and seeing her beautiful alive face above the bright pink color of her suit, but he'd forgotten now what he had wanted to say to her and then the loud whirring sound coming at him so fast that he couldn't focus on what it was, followed by the sharp tearing pain in his back and chest, and then the heavy slam of the big explosion against the side of his head. And finally all that darkness, great, black darkness. How had he ever made it through all that darkness? Why had God let him come through it?

"Jack?" he heard his wife's voice, snapping him back to the present, back to the big plane flying him away from Dallas and away from Washington too, the plane taking him back to Boston, where he'd begun his journey. He focused his eyes again, looking out the window past the wing of the aircraft. They were on the outskirts of Dallas now, Dealey Plaza somewhere behind them in the clouds.

"Jack, are you all right?" his wife asked.

He turned toward her faintly alarmed face. His daughter's blue eyes were looking at him now too.

"Yes," he said. "I was just . . ." he began, but then turned to his daughter instead. "Are you happy about going back to Boston?" he asked her, knowing the answer before he heard it.

"Uh-uh," Erin said. "It's sort of like our home." He could see the agreement in his wife's eyes, and he smiled at them both.

Air Force One continued on, heading north and east now, flanked by twin fighter escorts, flying from Dallas toward Boston, carrying a tired and wounded but living President of the United States, flying him and his family toward their new destiny. The date was Thursday, November 28, 1963. It was Thanksgiving Day in America.

PART TWO

December 1963—August 1964

CHAPTER
8

The rioting broke out all over South Vietnam right after the American day of Thanksgiving. Ambassador Luce could see some of it from the big round reception room on the second floor of the American embassy. When he stepped right up against the glass of the terrace doors he could see the bright orange flames leaping into the air above the city streets, and even with the doors closed he could smell the harsh wood smoke seeping into the room. Saigon was in flames.

"And the reports are that it's worse in Hue," General Harwood said from behind him. "And in the provinces," Harwood added glumly, a moment later.

Luce turned from the window to face the general. Above an elegantly tailored, double-breasted, dove-white suit, the ambassador's face was beginning to show the strains of too many months at this post.

"Cities in flames," Luce said, shaking his head in disbelief and trying to refuse the reality of the very thing he could see if he would turn back to the window behind him and look, but he forced himself not to do that. Instead, he moved to a richly brocaded gold-colored chair that stood near the center of the room and sat down, crossing his leg gracefully over one knee.

"I had lunch today with General Trang," Luce said, using his voice to draw General Harwood's imposing uniformed figure away from the window and back toward the middle of the large reception room.

"I still find him to be a very impressive man," Luce said.

"Yes, so do I," General Harwood said, crossing the room now and sitting down next to the ambassador.

A white-jacketed servant came into the room and paused by the door, waiting for instructions.

"Do you want something?" Luce said. The general hesitated for a moment, not knowing if he should. Luce could see the hesitation in his face.

"I'll have a scotch, tall," Luce said, showing the servant with his hands what he meant. "And ice," Luce added.

"Yes," the general said gratefully. "I'll have the same."

"General Trang believes that his government can control all this," Luce said disdainfully, his hand fluttering back to the windows at the far side of the room and the chaotic Saigon streets beyond. "He says that all he needs is a little more time, but I'm finding it more and more difficult to believe him." Luce paused to hear what his ranking general had to say.

"Well, God knows, it hasn't been that long," Harwood said.

"No, it certainly hasn't," Luce half laughed at how preposterous it was for them to even consider the possibility of another change so soon. It was less than a month since General Trang himself had come to power in Saigon. Trang had been backed by American support for precisely the same reasons that Trang's own presidency was now being threatened. His predecessors hadn't been able to control the country and their fall was inevitable. Luce was wondering if history were repeating itself now, less than a month later, and if it were, what he should advise Washington to do about it.

"Good God!" Luce said angrily as he thought about it. "The students and the Buddhists riot because they think every government that comes to power here is too corrupt. And at the same time, the Army is opposed to the same damn government, probably because it's not corrupt enough. And all of them hate the Communists and the Communists hate them.

"It's worse than Boston politics," Luce said wryly. "Maybe I should put that in my dispatch. Tell the President that it's just like Boston politics over here, and maybe he and I should change places. I can go back home and take his job, and Cassidy can come out here and tell me what to do about all this. He always was better at getting the vote out of Boston than I was." Luce laughed coldly, thinking about that now, fifteen years and half a world away. Then he turned back to the general. "The trouble, of course, is that this is Southeast Asia, not South Boston, and not even a couple of old New England boys, like Cassidy and I put together, can seem to figure where the votes are out here."

General Harwood nodded his head, but the general's eyes were blank. He knew that there was a great deal of talk back in the States about Luce going home and taking a run for the Republican presidential nomination, but Harwood didn't really understand what the ambassador was getting at now. Was this his way of telling him that he was actually going to do it?

Luce could see the blank look in the general's eyes. "Don't worry, General," Luce said, reading his mind. "I haven't made any decisions yet. We've got some problems to solve here, before I can even think about going home."

The general looked relieved. "There's something else I think we should consider," Harwood said then. "We've lost over a hundred American boys out here ourselves. One hundred and three to be exact. We've got our own stake in this thing now," the general said grimly. Then he repeated the number of American deaths for the ambassador's benefit, so there could be no mistake. "Over one hundred American lives."

"Yes," Luce said. It was an argument he'd advanced himself with Washington, but it was beginning to grow thin, with governments toppling in Saigon like bowling pins.

"I think that's what bothers me the most," Luce said. "If General Trang falls so soon after taking office, there are plenty of people back in Washington who'll want to use that failure as an excuse to desert our commitment here. And I just don't think we can let that occur."

Harwood nodded in agreement.

"What happens after Trang? Who comes out on top?" Luce asked the general then.

"Jesus, who knows," Harwood breathed out. "It's anybody's guess right now. There are at least a half a dozen possibilities in the Army alone."

"Well that's something that we have to know," Luce said.

The servant reentered the room holding a silver tray with two tall frosted drinks on it. He bowed first before General Harwood, offering him one of the glasses. The general took it without looking at him, and then Luce did the same. The small brown-skinned servant left the room silently, unnoticed.

Luce could smell the smoke from the street now, and he could taste its harsh wood flavor in his mouth. "Sometimes I think that the country doesn't even know that we're out here. I'd almost like to bottle up that smoke," he said, gesturing back toward where it was leaking in below the terrace door. "Bottle it up and send it home, let them smell it in New York and Chicago and Los Angeles. Let them know that it's real," Luce said, but then he stopped and laughed coldly at himself again and at the absurdity of flames and smoke from a street in a place called Saigon in Southeast Asia, a half a world away, ever really reaching his own country.

"I see no other choice but to continue to back General Trang for now, but we've got to prepare Washington for another change out here. We've got to find someone who can pull it all together for us. And when we find him, we're going to have to convince Washington that he can do the job," Luce said, coughing slightly at the traces of ashes and wood smoke in his throat and lungs.

"And then we've got to make very certain that he does it," the general added, and Luce nodded his agreement.

"Then we can all go home," the ambassador said.

The general lifted his glass to Luce and the ambassador returned the salute and both men drank deeply from their iced glasses, but when he was finished drinking, Luce found that even the cool whiskey didn't wash away the faint taste of smoke and ashes that lingered in his mouth.

* * *

The President's health continued to improve through the early weeks of December, and a few days before Christmas he was transported from Boston to Hyannis by ambulance—an unmarked vehicle, almost pitch black in the rear compartment, with its windows taped shut. The visit home was only to be for a few days, but he'd been looking forward to it with as much anticipation as almost anything that he'd experienced since he was a child. Accompanied by a half dozen unmarked Secret Service cars, the ambulance moved quietly down Boston side streets, avoiding the press by using an unannounced secondary route. There was nothing for Jack to see in the ambulance's sealed-off rear compartment. After a while he tried to sleep, but the stops and starts and jostling bounces of the road against his injured body kept him painfully wide awake throughout most of the journey, while two doctors hovered nearby, watching his every movement. There had been three doctors on the plane that had flown him in from Dallas less than a month before; now there were only two. That was some kind of progress, he thought, but as the two men continued watching him, Jack made sure not to let the pain that he felt so intensely show too deeply on his face.

The preliminary operations had only cleared away the surface debris from the wounded area on the side of his head. There were still shattered fragments of bone and bullet left embedded beneath the damaged area that the doctors were not yet ready to remove. The procedures to accomplish a final closing of the wound would be long and debilitating, and the doctors had reached a decision that Jack should rest and regain some of his strength before they continued with them. The other wounds in his neck and shoulder were clean and healing quickly, but the head wound left him in almost constant pain; typically a dull throbbing coming only from the damaged area, but occasionally a sharp slicing wave that would cut through his entire head and then move down the length of his back and spine. But even at the worst of these moments, Jack kept the knowledge and the intensity of the pain to himself, not sharing the truth with his doctors or Suzanne, or with anyone else.

He knew by instinct when the ambulance had turned off the main highway and had begun winding its way back down the smaller, less traveled roads toward the Cape, and it made him feel better just to know that he was approaching his home.

Soon the President felt the ambulance begin the descent through the final set of sloping hillside roads that led to his family's compound on the eastern shore of Cape Cod. He hadn't realized before that his body had memorized the way back to his home with such precision. Looking only at the dark metal roof of the moving ambulance, he could feel the Atlantic Ocean off to his left below the road, with the gray December tides rolling up onto the brown sand beach, and the tall shore grass blowing back in the wind. He closed his eyes and first imagined the tide to be high, licking up and rolling over the tall dark green shafts of grass and matting them down heavily against the wet sand. Then he imagined it to be low, and he could see the wet muddy scoop of land that had been the sea's shore at the edge of the waterline now and in his mind's eye he could see the gulls and the other smaller shorebirds swooping and exploring the newly exposed land at the point of the low tide.

The weight of the ambulance shifted and he knew they had turned through the gates and that his father's rambling, two-story, Cape Cod–style home with the long wooden porch in the front was appearing before the ambulance, and below the porch the sweeping front lawn where Jack had played as a child.

"Is it snowing?" Jack asked the doctor closest to him.

"No, I don't think so. It looks to be a beautiful, clear, New England day," the doctor said, as he tried to peer out of a small crack in the black tape that sealed the ambulance's rear windows.

"How do you feel?" the other doctor asked the injured man lying in front of him, but the doctor didn't get an answer to his question.

"It's saving up to snow on Christmas day," Jack said instead, as the ambulance came to a quick stop. He felt again now like the little boy who had played on the big lawn in front of this house years before, and in his excitement he raised himself painfully and awkwardly onto his elbows.

"Easy," the doctor warned. "You've been through a lot today."

"But I'm home now," Jack said and, as he did, the rear doors of the ambulance swung open and displayed it all just as he remembered it, the white frame house, the rolling green lawn, and the long wooden porch with his mother standing on it. His mother was wearing a bright red wool dress with a string of pearls at her throat, just the way he often pictured her. She stood looking intently at the back of the ambulance where he lay, and as the doors to the vehicle opened, she reached down and grasped the hand of her husband, who was sitting below her on the porch of the home he'd built overlooking the Atlantic, the house that he'd built for his family, his children, his daughters and sons, one of whom was coming back to him now, injured and damaged, his body full of pain, but through the grace of God still very much alive. The old man stood on weakened legs and leaned close to his wife, his arm draped around her waist, as the attendants lifted their son out of the rear of the ambulance.

Suzanne and the children stood at the side of the path that led up to the front of the Cassidy home, watching as the attendants carried Jack up the front steps and onto the porch.

"Jack," his mother said simply, her eyes misted over but smiling as she bent down to kiss him, careful of his bandaged head. As she drew away Jack could clearly see his father, standing above him. The older man was holding himself with great difficulty, valiantly fighting the pain that he felt from his own damaged body. He looked down at his son, and their eyes met for a moment in a private partnership of pride and strength. As much as he wanted to, his father couldn't speak now; the stroke that had paralyzed the side of his old man's body had deprived him of that pleasure, but his eyes and the portions of his face that he could still move in response to his thoughts and feelings told his son what he wanted more than anything else in the world to hear at that moment. Welcome home, his father's face said with perfect eloquence.

Sullivan sketched in first the rough shape of the man's head. Then, as he waited for the answers to his question, Sullivan filled in the hairline from memory as best he could—low over the forehead and shiny dark black. Then the broad flat nose and high, delicate cheekbones. Pretty good, Sullivan thought as he stopped to admire his work, but he hadn't gotten the jawline right and he was erasing it when Tolliver came back on the phone.

"No, definitely not," Tolliver said simply.

"Let me get it straight," Sullivan said, flipping the crowded notebook in front of him to a fresh page and beginning to jot down some notes. "The Service had no one stationed in front of the President's motorcade. No one on the hillside west of the Plaza or in the railway overpass area directly behind it." Sullivan wrote the time, date, and source of this new information down on his memo pad.

"I'm looking at the reports now," Tolliver said. "Every man we had in Dallas that day is accounted for. None of them was in that position, or anywhere even close to it."

"How many did you have?" Sullivan interrupted.

The other agent went on in a low, determined voice. "The only thing I'm going to say is that our people are all accounted for. We had a dozen men in the limousines, the rest in a couple of places I'm not even going to tell you about," the Secret Service man said.

"But I saw a man and his credentials," Sullivan said.

"You gotta look close at those identification cards . . ."

"I know Service credentials," Sullivan interrupted him again.

"Well, not this time," Tolliver said. "I'll tell you something else too. The description you gave me. We don't have any five-foot-eight, dark-skinned agents with greasy black hair and dirty fingernails. Period!" Tolliver laughed. "I think you had yourself a gate crasher," he added after a few seconds.

"Yeah, I do, too," Sullivan said, flipping his notebook back to the sketch of the man's face that he'd begun on its top page.

"You should have grabbed him while you had him," Tolliver said.

"Yeah, thanks," Sullivan said sarcastically.

"I'll need this in writing, you know. Whatever you saw, we should look into it. Faked credentials or whatever they were, you're telling me that they were supposed to be ours. That makes it our jurisdiction," Tolliver said.

"Yeah, sure," Sullivan answered, only half hearing. All of his attention now was on the rough black-and-white pencil sketch in front of him. "Thank you. I'll write it up and you'll get it through channels," Sullivan said. "Unless you want it direct."

"No, I don't want it direct. I don't want it at all. We've got enough to do here without looking for phantom agents, but since I know about it now, I gotta ask," Tolliver said.

"I'm sorry," Sullivan said, although he wasn't sure what for, and then he hung up the phone.

He looked down for a few long seconds at the half-finished face that he'd sketched on the paper below him, and then he reached down and drew in the broad flat chin and jawline as best he could, completing the portrait. He ripped the finished sketch out of the notebook and tacked it angrily onto the white-painted wall behind him. Tolliver's attitude had pissed him off, but Sullivan knew that the Secret Service man had been right about at least one thing, anyway. He'd had him, whoever the hell he was, and he'd let him go. And Sullivan knew, too, that in his business, when you screwed up once, you usually didn't get a second chance.

"I feel like a double agent," Rozier said.

"I do too." Tim laughed across the small dinner table that had been set up in the den of his Virginia home. A fire was blazing in the Colonial-style fireplace next to the impromptu dinner table. Outside it was a blustery, cold Virginia night in mid-December, and as the two men spoke big flakes of snow occasionally blew past the window behind Rozier and settled on the Cassidy backyard.

"But I think it's pretty safe to assume that Rance doesn't tell you anything that he doesn't want Jack and me to know about," Tim said.

Ignoring the grocery-store wine at the center of the table, Rozier nodded and reached for the bottle of French Bordeaux that he'd brought with him. He poured several inches of the good wine into his own glass and then set the bottle back down on the table next to him without offering any to Tim. Rozier had long since given up on trying to educate the Attorney General on some of the finer things of life.

"Rance has one speed and it's just full speed ahead," Rozier said, before he took the first sip of the dark red wine. "There's no such thing as Acting President to him. As far as he's concerned he is the President now, and he intends to keep it that way for just as long as he can."

Tim moved nervously in his chair, turning his body toward the fire in the copper-framed fireplace.

"He's convinced that Jack won't be able to run for reelection next year and he wants him to make that clear to the Party and to the country as soon as possible. Then Rance will be free to start his own campaign," Rozier said.

Tim nodded and leaned closer to the fireplace.

"He's not even being subtle anymore," Rozier said. "He's talked to every member of the Cabinet about it, and he's beginning now to even let some of the press know his feelings."

"He's not a subtle man," Tim said into the crackling flames.

"The one thing that he needs as soon as possible is for Jack to take his name off the ballot in New Hampshire. Then the way will be cleared for Rance to announce his own candidacy," Rozier continued. "He says that he won't make a move until Jack does, but he wants it pretty badly, Tim. I think that's what I'm supposed to let you know, and then I think you're supposed to convince Jack that he should do it, for the good of the Party," Rozier added, smiling at the awkward role he was being forced to play among the three powerful men.

Tim sat silently for several long seconds, saying nothing, just watching the orange flames leaping in front of him. "Maybe it would be for the best," he said, but he said it very softly, as if he might be embarrassed by the words.

Rozier set his wineglass down on the small antique wooden table. "Are you serious?"

"Yes, I am," Tim said, turning his hard blue eyes back toward Rozier. "There's something I think we're all forgetting about here," he added angrily, but then stopped himself and finished in a quieter tone. "I almost lost a brother four weeks ago," he said.

"I haven't forgotten that," Rozier answered.

"Well, a lot of people have. He's a man, not just a politician," Tim added. "He's a man and we almost lost him. I lost a brother once. I don't want it to ever happen again."

"I don't want to lose Jack, either," Rozier said. "But it's early, Tim. I know it looks doubtful now, but it's months before the first primary. A lot of things can happen between now and then."

"I'm not just talking about how quickly Jack can regain his strength and be healthy enough to begin a presidential campaign," Tim said, and then he couldn't go on.

"I'm supposed to be the Attorney General of the United States," he continued a few seconds later. "The chief law-enforcement officer of the country—and I can't even keep my own family safe. I can't even protect my own brother."

"Good God, Tim, you can't blame yourself for what happened down there," Rozier said.

"Maybe not, but what about now?" the Attorney General asked sharply and then paused, trying to find the right words to express the frightening new visions that had begun to haunt him since he'd returned from Texas. "Promise me that you'll never tell Jack or Suzanne this, but what really scares me isn't Dallas. It's now. It's my job to make certain that nothing like that ever happens again, and I'm not certain that I can." He stopped again, fighting against the jumbled flood of feelings inside him. "I'm not sure half the time of what's happening with the FBI investigation. Summers is telling me that everything continues to point away from a conspiracy of any kind and that all the evidence confirms that Strode was some kind of Communist radical who acted entirely alone that day—but I don't know if Summers is giving me all the facts, or if he and Rance are more concerned about how it looks to the country than they are at getting at the truth. I'm afraid that if it's left up to the Bureau we'll never know what really happened down there. I asked Jack to do something about it, but you know him, he refuses to dwell on the past. He doesn't want Dallas to change the work that he sees left to be done by the administration. And he doesn't want . . ." Tim laughed, remembering his brother's exact words now. "He doesn't want any 'unnecessary dissension' with Rance. If Jack's going to break with him, he's decided it will be over issues that he considers to be more important to the country. And that's the end of it, as far as he's concerned. I don't think there ever will be a real investigation of what happened in Dallas. So maybe it would be best if Jack does withdraw. At least, that way, I could be sure that nothing more was going to happen to him."

Tim walked to the window and stood with his back to the room, looking out at the snow that was falling lightly. "What worries me the most, Allen, is that maybe there was a conspiracy, or just something more that we don't know about—and what if we never find out?" Tim said, looking out at the dark winter night just a few feet away from the warm glow of his firelit den. "My own brother, and I don't even know if I can keep him from being murdered," he said, shaking his head angrily as he thought about it again, as he had little else since he'd returned from Dallas.

It was very dark in the last few moments before dawn in Hyannis Port, but the President could sense that there was somebody or something in his bedroom.

The President's eyes were closed, but he could feel a faint stirring at the foot of his bed, as if someone was actually pulling himself up on to it, and then suddenly there was a second, even more powerful tugging near the President's feet. He opened his eyes, but it was pitch black in the closed-up bedroom and he could see nothing but darkness. Outside the windows, Secret Service men moved on the white frosted December lawn, and in the hall outside his bedroom door a nurse had stayed in attendance throughout the night. What could have slipped past them?

The President reached out tentatively and felt first the soft warm shoulder of his small son, who was pulling at the blankets near his chest, and then he felt his daughter coming up over the side of the bed and landing on top of his legs. She began giggling then and bouncing up and down on the metal-frame hospital bed that he slept in now. Suzanne woke slowly, lying almost next to him, but all alone in the big double bed that she and Jack had once shared. She turned on the light near the bed stand and in the soft glow saw her daughter about to jump on the President's unprotected stomach. Erin was giggling wildly and John Jr. had a hold on his father's hand and was trying to use his own three-year-old strength to drag him out of bed.

"Be careful of your father," Suzanne said firmly, reaching out to restrain Erin. But she couldn't keep from smiling down at her daughter's beautiful little six-year-old face.

"You said it was okay today," the little blond girl said in her excitement.

"It's Christmas," her brother added happily.

Jack smiled and slid his body up in bed to get a better look at his attackers. He wasn't sure what was going to happen next. He hadn't left the big upstairs bedroom since he'd arrived home, but the doctors had said that he could go downstairs and be with his family on Christmas morning. But how? He looked down at his children's faces and he knew that he couldn't disappoint them, but it wasn't going to be easy.

"I think it's time to give your father his Christmas present," Suzanne said, slipping into her long silk bathrobe.

Erin sprang into action then, followed by the shorter, hurried, determined strides of her younger brother. Together they flew to the door. Jack could hear furtive movements in the hallway outside the room and then the door came open again and into the bedroom came a high-backed, rolling wooden chair. The chair was magnificently carved out of soft, blond, polished wood, with the deep sweeping outlines of flying fish, and beautiful four-masted schooners, and mysteriously voluptuous mermaids emerging out of the outline of a series of high-crested ocean waves—an antique wooden wheelchair beautifully restored, polished and gleaming as if it were new. It had a big red bow tied around it and hidden somewhere behind its high wooden back were his children, but then only a few feet into the room his son stopped and ran around in front of the rolling chair and jumped up into the seat, getting a free ride to his father's bedside at the expense of his laboring sister, who noisily pretended to grunt and groan and strain her way across the room.

"Merry Christmas," Suzanne said. "Do you like it?"

"It's magnificent," her husband said, smiling at his son, who was sitting now deep in the old chair like a young prince being brought before his father, the king.

"Who's it for?" Jack said, smiling at his children.

"You, silly." His daughter laughed, jumping out from behind the big chair.

"Oh, I thought it was for his majesty," Jack said, pointing at his son, who was crossing his arms in front of his chest now in great royal comfort.

"My brother's crazy," Erin said, and she moved forward to sit on the edge of her father's bed.

"Do you really like it?" Suzanne said, coming in on her husband's other side and kneeling to kiss his cheek.

"Yes, I do," Jack said, turning to her.

"It was made for an old whaling captain in Nantucket who lost his legs on a voyage off the Cape," Suzanne explained. Then she turned to her son, who was sitting deep in the old chair, listening closely to his mother's every word. "And they say, after that, he just sat in it, on a hillside overlooking the ocean, and stared out to sea. They say it's haunted even now, by the old sea captain's ghost," she said in a spooky voice, and she lunged forward and tickled her son in the stomach. Her son dived from the chair to the bed to bury himself safely between his parents and his sister. The four of them stayed there together then, laughing and admiring the antique chair.

"Merry Christmas," Jack said to his family, as he saw the first light of the morning beginning to appear just outside the window. "Is it snowing?" he asked.

"I hope so," Erin said happily.

Suzanne crossed to the window and opened the drapes. Down below on the lawn a Secret Service man stood, looking up at the window, while big lazy flakes of snow dropped around him.

"Merry Christmas," Suzanne said, and she waved down at the man who had spent his Christmas Eve on the cold front lawn of her home, keeping her family safe through the night.

"Merry Christmas," he called up to her and smiled. Suzanne turned back into the room to tell her family what a beautiful morning it was, but as she turned she could see the three of them close together, their arms around each other, looking across the bedroom at her, and in the steadily increasing light from outside, she could see from their smiling faces that she didn't have to say a word.

CHAPTER

9

It was snowing in Hyannis on New Year's Day—good, solid, New England snow. Jack looked out the window as it fell on the sloping front lawn of his family's home and on the grassy Atlantic beach across the road, and out over the ocean itself, the flakes melting as they touched the great, high-crashing gray-green waves of the Atlantic. There was a wind, too, rough and strong, like the wind across the shore rocks of the Irish Sea, Jack thought. It made him feel stronger and more powerful just to sit by the window and look out at the way the land and sea and the great swirling forces of air came together on a day like this, on the eve of a new year—an election year in America.

There was a knock on his bedroom door and he turned to it.

"Yes," he called out.

"Telegram!" came back the cheery bantering reply. It was Allen Rozier's hearty voice.

"Just slip it under the door," the President called out, smiling.

"I can't. I think it's from a woman," Rozier said, and he came into the room smiling himself. "And I think she may still be in it," he added, and he winked across the room at his friend, then closed the door behind him. Rozier was in a dinner jacket and formal black bow tie, wearing the formal clothes as naturally as other men might wear a sweater and slacks.

"I'm not disturbing you, am I?" Rozier said, pausing at the door.

"Not at all. How's Washington?" Jack said hungrily.

"What, don't you believe everything you hear on television?" Rozier said, pointing at the big set in the corner of Cassidy's bedroom.

"Not everything," Cassidy said and grinned at his friend, as Rozier moved his elegantly dressed body across the room toward Jack, who was wearing a pair of dark blue silk pajamas, half covered by a heavy, Irish-green, woolen blanket.

Rozier sat down in the wooden rocking chair that stood empty next to the President. The press secretary fell into it with a sudden heavy dropping move, pinning the rocker immobile to the floor. He grinned over at Jack.

"I've always wanted to sit in this damn thing," Rozier said, "but you were always hogging it."

Cassidy looked at Rozier's bulky frame filling the rocking chair and laughed. "It seems as if everyone wants to sit in my chair these days," he said to his friend.

"Not me. I just want to test this rocker for a few minutes," Rozier said. He looked out the window at the snow falling on the grassy lawn of the Cassidys' Hyannis estate. "But just think, even tonight, as we sit comfortably in this room, there are men, not many miles from here, rich, grown men, one of them perhaps even richer than you, if that's possible," Rozier said, smiling at his friend.

"It is," Cassidy said firmly.

"Grown men," Rozier continued, "marching through that snow, shaking hands, making speeches, looking at other men and women, and in some cases even little children, square in the eye and asking for their support for a job that has two other grown men already doing it."

"Kissing babies, wearing funny hats," Jack said and laughed and then both men fell thoughtfully silent for a few seconds.

"You miss it, don't you?" Rozier said as he watched the expression slowly change on the President's face.

Cassidy only shrugged his shoulders and looked away, but his eyes had betrayed the truth. "Tell me what's really going on in New Hampshire," he said then.

Rozier paused for a moment to assemble his thoughts. "The Republicans may be coming down with a very strange and for them what might even be considered an almost unprecedented disease," he began after a few seconds. "It's what we Democrats have always called 'pragmatism.' "

"The Republicans think they can beat Rance," Cassidy said, finishing his press secretary's thought.

"Well, at the moment, they seem certain they can beat Mr. Gardner, if it comes to that," Rozier said. "Now, you and I both know that they may never get the chance, but . . ." Cassidy held up his hand to cut Rozier off, and the big man stopped and changed the subject quickly.

"Oh, Jesus! Can you believe it?" Rozier said, looking out the window, where, charging across the snow came a heavily bundled Brian Cassidy and, following not far behind him, his brother Tim and a high-spiraling brown leather football. Brian leaped into the air, making a tumbling circus catch of the ball, and rolled over and came up grinning in the window at Rozier.

Brian held the ball triumphantly up in one hand toward Jack's window, but in the middle of his triumph, Tim suddenly flew through the air and slammed into him, blind-siding his younger brother and knocking him down onto the icy ground. The football bounced off crazily across the lawn toward more heavily bundled Cassidy family members, who were spilling out of the house and filling the grounds below Jack's window with shifting, bright winter colors.

Tim jumped quickly to his feet and pointed up at Jack, gesturing with his arms for him to join them. Jack smiled and pointed at the bandage wrapped around his head.

"Oh, that's right, you're the one who got himself shot, aren't you?" Tim called up, smiling at his older brother.

"This is a hard place to get any sympathy," Jack said turning to Rozier. Seeing the elegantly dressed man sitting comfortably in the rocking chair next to him, Jack then raised his hand and pointed at him. Tim smiled and reached down and tapped his younger brother on the shoulder, gesturing in toward Rozier. Brian nodded back and the two of them began running for the house.

Rozier stood up awkwardly and turned to the door barely in time to see the two men entering the room behind him. Tim was holding a football in one hand and he looped it underhand across the room at Rozier. The big man caught it in his stomach against his neatly pressed dinner jacket.

"We need one more," Brian called out.

"We're talking politics," Rozier said.

"It's football season," Tim said, brushing snow off his bright yellow ski sweater and smiling. Then he crossed the room and took Rozier by the arm, just as Brian closed on the press secretary from the other side and began pushing him toward the door.

"I'll referee," Rozier said as the three men moved into the hall in front of Jack's second-story bedroom.

Tim stuck his head back into the room just before he closed the door. "You've got a great seat there," he said to his brother and pointed at the window.

Jack laughed as the door closed behind his younger brother. The President turned to the window where he could see the group forming into two teams on the lawn directly below him. Tim, Brian, and Rozier came down the front steps and joined the others. Rozier had the football and he walked with great dignity to the center of the two teams, taking charge and solemnly removing a coin from a pocket of his dinner jacket. Then, brushing a little touch of snow off the shoulders of his tuxedo, he turned to Tim.

Jack leaned forward and opened his window, and a blast of cold air greeted him.

"Captain Cassidy," Rozier called out loudly enough for Jack to hear through the open window. Then Rozier turned to Brian and repeated the introduction, using his best referee's voice, and the two brothers shook hands.

"They've already met. Let's get going, I'm freezing," Kay Cassidy called out, blowing out a big puff of frosty air and clapping her hands vigorously, and other voices joined in, yelling insults at the ponderous ceremony.

But Rozier continued undeterred. "Please call it in the air, heads or tails," he said to Brian, and then the press secretary flipped the coin up into the snowy New England air.

"Heads!" Brian called.

Rozier let it fall to the ground and then with great dignity he stooped down to read its shiny metal surface. "Heads it is."

"Let's play," Kay called out again and other voices joined in.

"We'll receive," Brian bellowed and Tim pointed down the long snow-swept lawn at the imaginary goal that held the wind coming in off the Atlantic at its back, and then he led his team in a spirited run toward it across the front of the Cassidy estate.

Suzanne stayed with Brian's team, nearer her husband's open window. As the other players hurtled toward each other at the kickoff, she turned toward her husband. She wore a small red knit hat perched on the top of her dark brown hair, and little drifts of snow settled down on its bright red surface as she smiled up at him. As he looked at her, Jack thought that she had never been more beautiful.

"Close the window," Suzanne said, and he leaned over dutifully and did as he was told. A nurse entered the room behind him then and glanced out the window at the action on the front lawn.

Jack turned to her and smiled. "We've got great seats," he said, gesturing to the unused rocking chair next to him. The woman hesitated for a moment, looking at the President's famous chair, but Jack only smiled at her and motioned again for her to sit in it. Finally she did and the two of them sat together and watched the snow lightly falling on the brightly colored Cassidy family below the window through the remainder of the late winter afternoon.

There was snow and a cold wind and a setting orange-colored winter sun in New Hampshire. And a man stood in it, feeling the cold wind through his topcoat, standing at a factory gate at quitting time. The man was a long way from his home. He was tall and lean, with a strong, determined, resolute western face, set with heavy, dark-brown, horn-rimmed glasses that he peered out of at each man who approached him to shake his hand at the end of the long, harsh, New England day.

"My name is Longwood. I'm running for President and I'd appreciate your support," he said, or some variation of it, over and over as the men passed by him. He stood firmly, his legs spread solidly apart, and looked any man who would raise his face to him in the eye and returned their strong workman's handshake with his own firm grip, until his hand ached, and blistered, and finally split open, and the New Hampshire wind whipped into the open wound and blew it raw.

A small scattering of reporters and campaign aides stood off to one side, watching the man go through the ancient political ritual, adding his own uniquely independent western brand and style to it as he played out his role in the old American theater of democratic politics. When he was done and the last blue-collared, tough-eyed, lunchbox-carrying worker and potential voter had walked past him and sized him up, he turned to the reporters and smiled.

"Happy New Year," he said, and a television cameraman who hadn't bothered with the ritual at the factory gate raised his camera and turned it on the Senator, its bright light illuminating the outline of Longwood's dark-suited figure against the now phosphorescent-white snowbanks behind him. But Longwood only raised his hand and waved the camera off. "Not tonight," he said. "It's New Year's Eve. I'll buy you a drink," he said to the cameraman and then, turning to the other reporters, he said, "I'll buy all of you a drink." And the small group of tired men, all of whom were a long way from home, trudged across a dirty, snowy street to where a tavern sign burned in red neon against the darkening New England sky.

Inside, the crowded room smelled like generations of stale beer and the hearty sweat of workingmen, and when Longwood walked through the door, there was only a mild fluttering of recognition and acknowledgment. The Senator walked to the bar undisturbed and ordered two pitchers of beer. A few minutes later he carried them with him, one heavy foaming pitcher in each hand, across the center of the room to a vacant corner booth. His small party followed behind him, an aide carrying a tray of assorted glasses and beer mugs.

"Hey, Longwood! Welcome to New Hampshire," a workman called out to him, and the men at the nearby tables laughed. The Senator raised one of his pitchers of beer at him in a salute. As he did, golden foamy liquid spilled down the outside of the glass pitcher and Longwood laughed, too. He set the pitchers down on the table and then, as the others in the party took their places around the booth, he took off his coat and hung it on a peg on the wall nearby. He rolled up his sleeves then and accepted a big foaming mug of beer from his aide. Longwood waited for everyone at his table to be served and then, still standing, in his shirtsleeves now, he lifted his brimming stein of beer into the air. "To New Hampshire!" he said and then drank for a long time from the big mug of beer in his hands. When he was done, one of his aides added, "And to victory in 'sixty-four!" And Longwood drank happily to that, too.

There are streets in most large Mexican towns that no one walks with comfort, and the city of Tampico near Mexico's eastern coast is no exception. And on a New Year's Eve just before dark the discomfort can quickly spread to cold fear.

But the squat, dark-haired man with the heavily pockmarked face who walked those streets now looked strangely comfortable as he moved along, smelling the harsh mixed smell of gasoline fumes, spicy Mexican cooking, and overflowing garbage cans. A pack of dirty barefoot boys eyed him from an alley as he passed, and Lopez turned to them and bared his teeth like one of the wary smiling jackals in the hills above the town. When he saw the boys, he moved forward onto the balls of his feet, leaning toward them, as if he were eager for their attack, and as he did he had to restrain himself from throwing himself into them and tearing at them, and his legs began to shake as he barely held himself in check. The boys let him pass. There would be better game soon, easy drunken New Year's Eve game. They could afford to let him go and he moved by them grinning fiercely, disappointed at the quiet passing.

A little farther on, Lopez stopped at a seemingly abandoned storefront marked with the number nineteen. When he knocked on its front door, a man appeared. The man's name was Ortiz. He was a supplier of things— drugs, information, new identities, whatever was needed, even the woman, who waited for Lopez at his hotel now, had been supplied by Ortiz.

Hidden in the shadows of the doorway, the two men quickly exchanged envelopes, each carefully checking the contents of the packet he received to be certain he hadn't been cheated. Their business over, Lopez returned to the street.

In the next block, he stopped at a sidewalk café and ordered tequila. When the girl brought it to him the first fireworks went off in the narrow dirty street in front of him, signaling the start of New Year's Eve in Tampico.

Lopez sat sullenly at his table while all the noise and activity of the street burst around him. He stared at the small crowd celebrating the start of another squalid year in this squalid town and then he reached into his pocket and removed the pack of new identity papers. He didn't open it though, not here on the street for everyone to see. Instead he left it on the tabletop in front of him, letting his hand rest securely against it. Another year, another name, another identity, another man perhaps, Lopez smiled to himself for a moment at the thought, but then suddenly he grew angry and landed his fist hard on the greasy wooden tabletop next to the small neat packet of papers. A new man maybe, he said to himself, but with very old business to settle. He stood up then and walked inside the cantina and bought more tequila, this time two large quart bottles. He carried them clinking together in a net bag, letting them dangle low at his side, as he walked along the street toward his hotel. He stopped for a moment at a corner and drank from one of the bottles, letting some of the fire-hot liquid drip out of the corner of his mouth and spill over the front of his open shirt.

He didn't drink from the bottle again until he had crossed the small squalid lobby of the place he lived in now and rose in the creaking metal-cage elevator to his floor and found his room, but before he could walk inside, he stopped outside the door and took several long swallows of the white-hot tequila. Then he opened the door and stood in the hall, looking in at the woman lying on the dirty, unmade bed in the middle of the small hotel room. The woman got up from the bed wearily and crossed the room to him. She clung to him briefly, neither of them saying anything as he took another drink from his bottle. And then he let the woman rub him between his legs with the palm of her flat open hand, while he looked down blankly at her face. He felt himself becoming aroused, but the woman turned away from him before he gave in to it, and she returned to the bed in a slow, languid walk. He watched her walk away, her too-big ass moving deliberately under a graying synthetic slip, her long black hair tumbling down loosely over her bare shoulders as she moved confidently across the room. He walked to the table and set both bottles of tequila down on top of it. As he did, he could hear the woman settling into the messy unmade bed behind him, its rusted springs squeaking and groaning with her weight. The woman lives in that bed, he thought, and she has two positions on it—her legs closed and her legs open—but either way, who gives a damn.

Outside the open window next to her, a string of firecrackers went off and some people began shouting at each other, then another loud explosion—a cherry bomb, or someone killing someone else, in this town you could never know which. He removed his long-barreled pistol from underneath his jacket and set it down on the table where the woman would see it. She looked over at it lazily, unimpressed.

He reached back into his open shirt front and withdrew the small neat packet of papers again. He emptied the packet's contents onto the table and sorted through them. The man that he'd gotten them from did good work. There was a passport, credit cards, a Florida driver's license, a Social Security card, some with his own picture on them and all with his new name—Antonio Lopata. It felt good to have a new name again.

"Wha' do you have?" The woman asked from her place on the bed, interrupting his thoughts.

"A half a hard-on," the man called back angrily, and then he shuffled through the forged cards and papers proudly one last time before returning them to their envelope.

"This is my business. You understand?" he said, tapping the envelope and turning back to the woman on the bed.

"Sure," the woman said vaguely, and a pinwheeling red-and-silver skyrocket whined by the open window and then crackled into a circling series of sparking explosions only a few feet from where she lay.

The man picked up the long-barreled gun off the table and pointed it out the window at the firework display. He pretended to squeeze off a few rounds at the last of the smoke curling up near the window.

"Hey, are you goin' fenish wha' we start'd, or not?" the woman asked. The man turned slowly toward her, still holding the gun in his hand, and smiled. Then, smiling even more broadly, he swung the long barrel of the revolver around and pointed it at her.

The woman looked at the gun's open round gray-metal mouth, uncaring, only lifting her dirty slip up in the air, opening her legs widely apart toward the man and his pointed long-barreled gun. "Fuck you," she said casually as she pointed herself at him. "Either fenish wha' you start'd, or sen' someone over here who can," she said with cool, practiced savagery.

The man stood up then and let the gun drop to his side. He carried it across the room, dangling heavily toward the floor, and sat on the edge of the bed next to the woman. Then, suddenly, he raised the long-barreled pistol and jammed it angrily into the opening made by the woman's widely spread legs, thrusting it up hard inside of her, but the woman didn't protest. She continued looking coldly bored, as if she'd seen it all many times before.

The man lifted her graying slip then, exposing her heavy thighs and buttocks. He looked down to where the long, black, metal barrel of the gun was buried deep in the dark lush tangle of hair between the woman's legs. He cocked the long-barreled pistol and smiled at the woman. She looked calmly back at him through dull black eyes.

"I always finish what I start," the man said, raising the hard metal mouth of the cocked gun up and rubbing it roughly against the soft raised ridge near the top of the opening between the woman's legs. "Always!" he said defiantly.

He removed the long-barreled pistol from between her legs then and let the heavy metal revolver drop to the floor, and as he did the woman reached over with both of her hands and grabbed two big fistfuls of the man's greasy black hair near the back of his head and rammed his face down, burying it deeply into the place where the pistol barrel had been.

Behind her the brightly colored fireworks continued to whistle and explode on the narrow, dirty Mexican street outside the window.

At a few minutes before seven on New Year's Eve, three well-dressed men appeared at Jack's bedroom door. They were followed by Allen Rozier, whose dinner jacket now looked as if he'd refereed a touch football game in the snow while wearing it and then had tried to brush it back into shape. The other three men were the President's brothers, Tim and Brian, and the President's friend and assistant, Frank O'Connor. Brian carried a long garment bag in one hand and a small brown paper parcel under his other arm.

Suzanne was dressed and downstairs, but Jack was still sitting by the window in his blue silk pajamas, the thick blanket spread across his legs.

The four men were all grinning broadly at the President as they entered the room. Brian lifted the packages into the air in direct sight of his older brother.

"Okay, what do you have in the bag?" Jack laughed warily.

Tim reached over and unzipped the garment bag, displaying a black dinner jacket.

The President smiled. "I like the pajamas," he said, gracefully moving his hand down over the blue silk that covered the tops of his legs.

"Not on New Year's Eve," Rozier said, and the four men started toward him with determination written on each of their faces.

Brian quickly removed the blanket from the President's legs and Tim began unbuttoning his brother's pajama top.

"Wait a minute, have you asked the doctors about this?" Jack said.

"There'll be two at dinner," Tim said. "You can ask them yourself."

"Okay, okay," Jack said, and he reached up to finish unbuttoning his pajama top himself. And from out of nowhere then Rozier held up a magnum bottle of Dom Perignon and three fluted champagne glasses, their stems neatly nestled between the fingers of his big hand. O'Connor brought two other glasses out from behind his back, showing them to the President.

"I feel like I'm getting married," the President said, trying to force a smile as he fumbled weakly with the last button on his pajama top, but as his hand got more tangled up with the stubborn button, a deeply frustrated look appeared on his face. Seeing the problem, Tim swooped in and finished undoing the button without a word. Jack pulled off the pajama top, leaving his chest bare. A thick bandage was wrapped around the side of his chest, covering the bullet wound that had passed through his chest and back, and his upper shoulders were softer, whiter, and far less powerful than his brothers had ever seen them, shockingly weaker than they had been only six short weeks before. There was a smaller, neater bandage on the side of his neck too, covering the almost healed second bullet wound, and of course, the heavy bandage pressed tightly against the side of his head. Jack saw the others looking at his weakened, bandaged body and he turned away, embarrassed, but a champagne cork popped then, and Rozier poured frothy golden champagne lavishly into the five crystal glasses.

"Mr. President," Tim said, holding a glass of champagne toward his brother, and Jack turned back toward the group and reached out for it, a smile returning to his face. He took the glass in hand and held it out in the air in front of him to join the other toasting glasses.

"To better days!" Rozier said, lifting his glass above the others.

"There's no such thing," Jack said, looking at each man in turn before lifting his glass and drinking deeply from it. Fresh pain throbbed in his head and down his spine from all the movement and excitement, but he was grateful to be with his friends and he had meant his words.

The room was quiet for a moment, but then slowly, thoughtfully, the others followed his lead and a few seconds later Rozier poured more champagne and Brian undid the second brown paper package that he had been holding, revealing a dress shirt and stud buttons and a shiny black cummerbund.

"You were telling me about New Hampshire," Jack said to Rozier, as the other men began to busy themselves with the task of dressing the President in the formal dinner clothes. Only Rozier sat back down on the rocking chair across from Jack and idly drank his champagne.

"New Hampshire, ah, yes," Rozier said, comfortable again, in a warm room, looking out at the snow falling on the darkened lawn, talking politics with his friends, and sipping expensive French champagne.

"The Vice President has the results of a poll that he had commissioned and

I think that I'm supposed to tell you what it says. Even if I'm not, I'm going to," he added. "It shows Granderman coming on fast and strong against the rest of the Republican field in New Hampshire. It's scaring the hell out of Rance, too. He doesn't want any part of a race against Mr. Granderman. He wants to run against our old friend from Arizona, Senator Longwood, and nobody else. I can hardly blame him, either. If Rance can beat anybody in November, it's probably Bill Longwood," Rozier added with a chuckle, and he sipped at his champagne again.

"But Granderman's spending a goddamned fortune," Frank O'Connor said then. O'Connor was an organization man raised in the politics of the wards of South Boston, and the enormous sums spent in modern national politics always bothered him. His tough Irish face showed that distaste now.

"I think it's wrong to outspend your opponent in an election, don't you?" Jack laughed as he reached for his own champagne glass.

"Not me," Tim answered.

"Yeah, but you're a ruthless bastard," Rozier said, smiling at his friend.

Tim had finally completed the process of getting the dress shirt on over Jack's bandaged shoulder and it hung loosely, unbuttoned and only partially covering his brother's weakened chest, but Jack was breathing hard, deeply fatigued by the effort he'd already expended, and not yet ready to complete the difficult job of getting dressed in the formal clothes.

"More champagne," Rozier said, taking the attention away from the President's labored breathing, and then the press secretary took his time refilling everyone's glass.

"But here's the part I really like about the Vice President's poll," Rozier said as he poured the champagne. "It's this. What do you think the number-one reason is that the New Hampshire Republicans are swinging away from Longwood and over to our friend, the Governor of New York?" Rozier asked, and then he paused dramatically.

But before he could go on the President stole Rozier's punchline. "Because they think against a divided and confused Democratic Party, like the one that Rance and I might just hand them in the fall, Granderman can win and Longwood probably can't," Jack said.

"Right," Rozier said, nodding at Jack. "They think Granderman might just be that rare political phenomenon, an actual 'Republican Winner,' but that Senator Longwood shoots from that famous right hip of his a little too fast sometimes and that even Rance might be able to take advantage of that. So it might not be the time for conscience after all, but maybe for a little pragmatism in the Republican Party in 1964."

"You mean, if they were going to lose anyway, they didn't mind letting Longwood do it for them, but if there's a chance they can actually win it, they might just risk going with Granderman," O'Connor said.

"That's right," Rozier agreed. "And it's all making Rance nervous as hell and he really wants to get started badly, Jack," Rozier said, his voice a little more serious now. "He wants to get his own campaign out in the open, as soon as possible. All he's waiting for is for you to officially withdraw from New Hampshire. Then he'll be off and running himself. He's not going to do anything until you do. Privately though, he's telling anyone who will listen that when he talks to you about policy matters that you can't remember details of conversations from one day to the next." Rozier's voice and face were plainly angry now.

"I know, you've told me that before," the President said. "But I keep forgetting," he added and then smiled.

"I don't think we should do anything yet," O'Connor said. "As long as Jack's in the race, Granderman has a much better chance of getting the nomination, and it seems to me that's exactly what we want. A Granderman nomination really keeps the pressure on Rance. Jack can beat him and maybe Rance can't. The Party knows that and it also knows that Rance certainly can't win without Jack playing a major role in the campaign."

"There's only one problem with that strategy," Tim said, and the attention in the room shifted to him. "There's someone else who might just get into it and change everything. It's just possible that our old friend Ambassador Edward Todd Luce is going to come home and announce his own candidacy. And if he does, it would really shake the Republicans up. Luce, Longwood, and Granderman. God knows who'd come out on top of a fight like that."

"One thing is certain though, it would give Rance what he'd dearly love to see," Rozier said as Tim finished. "A divided Republican Party, slugging it out over a long hard primary season between three or four solid contenders and maybe even Longwood coming out on top in the end." Rozier paused then, fingering his long-stemmed wineglass and smiling, clearly enjoying trying to work out the five-sided presidential puzzle of Cassidy, Gardner, Longwood, Luce, and Granderman.

"But Luce knows damn well that there's no sense for him to make a run at the nomination as long as Jack's in the picture," O'Connor said confidently. "I'm sure he and his people understand they won't be able to convince the Republican Party that he can beat Jack Cassidy in November, when he's already proven that he can't even carry his own state against him."

"All the logic says that you should stay in the race for now then, doesn't it?" Rozier said, turning his gaze back toward the President. "It keeps Luce in Saigon and probably gives the Republican nomination to Granderman, and that should strengthen your hand within the Party and in dealing with Rance, whatever you decide to do in the long run about your own candidacy."

The President nodded his head at Rozier then, to indicate that he had put the pieces of the political puzzle together in exactly the same way.

"You're way ahead of me, aren't you?" Rozier said, looking with great respect at the handsome man in the dress shirt and blue silk pajama pants seated across from him. "You've already decided what to do. You're going to keep your name on the ballot in New Hampshire, aren't you? That way, even if in the end you do have to withdraw, you'll be in a better position to get what you want from Rance," Rozier said, glancing briefly at Tim.

"Like helping him pick a Vice President," Brian said.

"Don't look at me," Tim said, but everyone in the room was.

"I don't think there's any doubt about it. Staying on the ballot keeps all of Jack's options open for later," O'Connor said.

"Timmy, what's bothering you?" the President said, turning to his brother, who was standing away from the rest of the group, saying nothing, his champagne glass resting on a table next to him.

"Jack, you know what the problem is as well as I do," Tim began. "If you stay in it now even for a little while, you could split the Party in half. Then if you do decide to withdraw later and the Party winds up losing in November, you'll be blamed for it just as much as Rance will be, maybe even more. And then, there's always the chance, if you don't get out, that Gardner might call your bluff and take you on in the early primaries. He knows that you can't really mount much of a campaign yet. He could let his people go forward with some kind of a write-in effort on his behalf in New Hampshire or even file himself and let his name go on the ballot directly against you. Then what?"

"He won't," O'Connor said. "He hasn't got that kind of guts."

"Yes, but what if he does? What if we're not as smart as we think we are and we can't keep it all under control, just the way we've planned," Tim said, angrily turning to O'Connor, but the President answered, guessing what was really on his brother's mind.

"Tim, I promise whatever happens, I won't campaign in New Hampshire. I won't leave Boston. I won't kiss a single baby," he said, smiling at his brother.

"No funny hats?" Rozier said.

"Well, maybe just one or two," the President said, touching the bandage near the top of his head.

"You're going to do it. You're going to stay in the race, aren't you?" Tim said.

His brother nodded. "I'll need your help though, Tim," the President said, looking directly into his brother's eyes.

Tim paused only for a moment. "Of course," he answered. "It's your decision, Jack. I'll do whatever you think is best."

Sullivan was in New Orleans, spending New Year's Eve at a different motel, by a different airport, but it looked pretty much like all the others to him, except for the pictures that were beginning to cover the wall behind his bed.

The room was one that you could rent cheap by the week and it didn't have maid service and it was definitely beginning to show the lack of care, but that was the way Sullivan liked it. He didn't want anyone poking into his business, particularly not now. The wall around his bed was plastered with a wild collection of photographs, notes, and sketches. The bizarre design was dominated by a big full-color artist's rendering that Sullivan had asked a Bureau artist to do from Sullivan's own quick sketch of the man he'd seen in the parking lot below Dealey Plaza, the man Sullivan now called the "second gunman."

Sullivan looked up at his second-gunman collage and tried to make up his mind if he should leave it now and go out somewhere and get New Year's Eve—drunk like he was supposed to do. So far, all he'd been able to manage was to drink a half a bottle of beer while he'd reread the report that he'd received from the Dallas Bureau earlier in the day. And as he thought about the report's conclusions again, Sullivan glanced over at the now-famous newspaper photograph of Strode clutching his stomach as he was gunned down in the basement corridor of the Dallas police station. Strode's face was contorted in pain, his arms folded in front of him as the bullets from Green's gun tore into his stomach and chest. Sullivan slowly moved his gaze to a series of photographs of the President. The pictures showed Cassidy's head being jolted backward and then forward in the back seat of his limousine in Dealey Plaza. Even to an untrained eye, the photographs suggested that the first impact had been from the front, not the rear. Sullivan looked ahead of the motorcade. There was that grassy hillside again, the area that the press was calling the "grassy knoll." Sullivan's glance drifted to the photo above it, to the picture of the police officer lying on his back near the gutter of a South Dallas street corner, and finally he looked over to the blowup from the TV news film of the two men being pulled out of the Louisiana swamp. Strode, Green, Cassidy, Officer Towne, Justin Case, and James Regan—Sullivan's own private New Year's Eve party, with its mysterious guest of honor—the dark-haired second gunman.

Sullivan turned away from the macabre design plastered on the wall of his motel room and picked up the report from the Dallas Bureau again and began reading it. The goddamned thing was useless. He'd hoped that somehow he'd misread it the first two times, but after only a few minutes of flipping through its safe, unquestioning pages, he knew that he hadn't. He slammed it down on the floor next to him and went back to just staring at the violent disjointed images taped on his wall.

Hell, he'd written it all up for them before he'd left Dallas, he thought then. He'd even given them the leads to follow, the questions to ask, but no one was doing very much about checking any of it out. The official Dallas report was a bunch of crap as far as he could tell, agents just going through the motions. They already had their case and they were just building facts to fit what they thought they already knew—that a lone gunman, acting with very little advance planning, had come within a fraction of an inch of changing the course of history, and then a second half-crazed man had appeared out of nowhere and, in full view of a dozen armed officers, had been able to murder the only suspect right in the middle of police headquarters. Sullivan shrugged his shoulders. Well, maybe. Maybe that's the way it was. Maybe the Bureau knew some things that he didn't, Sullivan thought. Or, maybe, they just didn't want to rock the goddamned boat enough to find out what had really happened.

But that's not why I signed up for the job, Sullivan told himself. It seemed to get harder all the time though to remember why he had signed up, but who gives a damn. It was New Year's Eve and he was in New Orleans, the party capital of the world. It was his patriotic duty to go out and get drunk like everybody else and leave the thinking to the people in charge.

Without stopping for anything except his coat, he started for the door, but before he left the room he walked back and retrieved the fallen report and then he locked it in his briefcase and slid the briefcase into a far dark corner of his closet. But then, still not satisfied, he bent down for the case and put it under his arm. He'd lock it away in the Bureau's safe downtown, just like he was supposed to do, before he went out and got drunk. Summers would have been proud of him, he thought angrily as he walked out of the room, slamming the door behind him.

The Cassidy family was gathered downstairs near a long buffet table spread with dishes brimming with holiday foods. A servant made last-minute arrangements at the festive table while the family and their guests stood around the room talking quietly among themselves.

Jack sat near the Christmas tree at the corner of the big living room where he could see all the activity. He was in the antique wooden wheelchair that had been his wife's Christmas gift to him. He said that whenever he sat in it he could feel the presence of the sea captain who had owned it, and Jack had told the press that he planned to send the chair to Castro when he was done with it. Everyone knew that it would probably really wind up in the Smithsonian or at a Cassidy presidential library somewhere as a piece of American history, but Jack was just sitting in it for now, manipulating it skillfully to face the people around him, while he talked to them and balanced a small plate of food on his lap at the same time. He was dressed in his dinner jacket, with only a small white bandage decorating his carefully cut light brown hair. From a distance, he looked good, relaxed, talking freely and slowly drinking from his second glass of champagne, which was one more than the doctors had permitted him for the evening.

Across the room Suzanne was standing and talking intently with Allen Rozier; she had positioned herself so that she could keep an eye on Jack without appearing to do so. Only Rozier could tell that he didn't have Suzanne's complete attention.

"Maybe this was a bad idea," Rozier said.

"No. It was a lovely idea. I just want to be certain that he doesn't overdo, that's all," Suzanne said. She was dressed in a long ice-blue satin gown and the front of the dress was laced with tiny shimmering blue and white rhinestones that reflected the light from the candles on the long buffet table next to her.

"He looks fine," Rozier said.

"Yes, he does," Suzanne agreed. "Coming home has been good for him."

"When's he going back into the hospital?" Rozier asked.

"In a day or so. They want to watch him for a while, make certain that everything's going as well as it appears to be," she said, smiling faintly. "Konstantine's invited us to go to Greece in February. I've talked to the doctors about it and they think that it might be a good idea. I hate to think of staying here much longer," she added, glancing out the window at the snow falling in the New England night. "After everyone leaves, it will be a little dreary."

"Konstantine presents some political problems for Jack," Rozier said cautiously. He knew that the wealthy Greek businessman had impressed Suzanne with his considerable charm on his brief visit to the White House earlier that year.

"I don't believe what people say about him," Suzanne said defensively.

Rozier shrugged his shoulders, not wanting to be judge and jury to one of Suzanne's friends, but in the end the press secretary's loyalty to the President outweighed any other concerns, and he began making the case against Konstantine as gently as he could, reminding Suzanne why Jack chose to keep the Greek shipping magnate at a distance. "Suzanne," Rozier said, "Konstantine Mykanios isn't just another multimillionaire—he is one of the richest men in the world, and some of the methods that he used to accumulate that enormous wealth are suspect, to say the least, perhaps not illegal, but . . ."

"And it's not good American politics to be seen as too close to people like that," Suzanne said, cutting Rozier off. "Particularly Democratic politicians who depend on the support of labor unions and working people. I understand, Allen. Jack's been over the same ground with me, but we don't have to worry about politics right now. What we have to worry about is getting Jack well."

"What about going to Palm Beach instead?" Rozier asked. "Greece is a long way off."

Suzanne turned to him and looked directly into his eyes. "I know that," she said firmly. "I also know the date of the New Hampshire primary. And the Oregon and California primaries as well," she added after a moment. "But what you may not know and what he seems to be trying to conveniently forget," she said, gesturing at her husband, "is that sometime in the very near future, he's going to require at least one operation and probably more, in order to rebuild the area underneath that very dashing bandage that he's wearing."

"Plastic surgery?"

"No, it's more serious than that. I don't think you or anyone else realizes just how much pain he's really in. I know that he hides it from his doctors and he tries to keep it from me, too, but I can tell. I know him and I know it's still very hard on him. There are some fragments of bone that the doctors need to remove from the head wound, but they don't even want to begin until they're confident that he has his strength back. Until that's done, he's still at risk. The danger is that the shattered fragments of bone could work their way into . . ." Suzanne stopped then, reluctant to say anything further about it even to Rozier. "Allen," she said, holding out her hand to him, "I don't care what the official reports are saying—I'm still very worried about him. A month or two in Europe with some rest and some sun before the doctors begin on him is precisely what he needs now. And then after the procedures are completed, he's probably going to need an even longer rest. If we're lucky, the best we can realistically hope for is at least a year before he's completely recovered. I don't know what the five of you were plotting up there before dinner, but . . ." She stopped then and looked away from Rozier, back toward the corner of the room where her husband was sitting quietly talking now to a small group of friends and relatives who had gathered around him. Rozier reached out and touched Suzanne's hand, trying to let her know that he understood.

"Allen," she said turning her body away from the rest of the room for a moment and directing her words in confidence only to her friend. "It's deceptive. You don't see him every day the way I do. I know he jokes about it, but he does have memory problems. They're only slight," she added, quickly holding up her hand to the press secretary, afraid for a moment that she'd given away a family secret. "The doctors say that it's natural and he'll get over it in time, but it scares me sometimes. I know they gave him some tests, perception, reflex, I'm not certain what they all were, but I do know they weren't entirely happy with the results. As hard as the doctors try to reassure me, I know that they're really every bit as worried as I am. And all the pressure he's under. It can't be helping him, and, if we care about him, we've got to be certain that he doesn't let it get any worse."

"The Vice President calls him every day?" Rozier said, half question, half fact.

"Yes, they talk in the mornings, sometimes again in the evenings."

Rozier nodded his head, and then he and Suzanne were both quiet for a moment. "All he needs is rest and time," Suzanne said finally. "And I'm going to make certain that he gets them both. Politics or no politics. And if he isn't able to understand that, this will be one campaign that you'll have to run without Suzanne Cassidy to kick around," she said, smiling, but her eyes remained hard and determined.

"Have you told him that?" Rozier said, and Suzanne's smile widened at the question. "I will," she said. "Unless you'd like to do it for me," she said, pointing her champagne glass toward Rozier's broad chest.

"Who, me?" Rozier said, pointing at himself with his own wineglass. "No, thank you, my life already has enough intrigue in it. You can tell Jack that you won't let him be President yourself," he said, but as he did Suzanne took a step back from him and turned instinctively toward her husband. She could tell from the sudden quiet in the room that something wasn't right, and across the festive living room she could see her husband's body tensing, fighting the pain and exhaustion of the long day. He was trying valiantly not to show how he felt, but his discomfort was clear to his wife, and she moved away from Rozier and wove her way through the party to her husband's side. She knelt down by him then and quietly removed the small uneaten plate of food from his lap.

"Just a little tired," he said, looking over at her, trying to disguise the pain and fatigue, but up close it showed clearly in his eyes.

"I don't want to ruin the night for everyone," Jack whispered to his wife, and he gestured out weakly at his family and friends, who, by continuing to go about the business of the party and pretending not to notice his sudden dramatic loss of strength, were trying hard not to embarrass him.

"Two minutes to midnight!" Tim suddenly boomed out through the awkward silence that had begun to grow up in the room.

"Quick, champagne everybody," Kay added, and then there was a general rush to fill the glasses.

Jack laughed despite the pain as he looked up at the big grandfather clock at the far side of the room.

Tim moved to his brother's side then and filled his glass with champagne. Jack smiled up at him gratefully. As he did, the lights in the room went out, leaving the big living room full of Cassidy family and friends all in darkness. Only the candles from the long holiday buffet table and the Christmas tree lights glowing out red and white and a warm soft green illuminated the smiling faces of the people in the room.

"Ten, nine, eight," began the count, and the President laughed out loud now, but more voices joined in drowning out his laughter. "Seven, six, five." And the man in the wheelchair turned to his wife and smiled as she loudly counted "Four!" And, giving in now, he counted with them. "Three, two, one." And then the voices exploded in a room-shaking "Happy New Year!"—and then laughter and toasting, drinking and more warm laughter.

"Should auld acquaintance," began Frank O'Connor in his mellow Irish tenor voice, and the room quieted and listened in the candlelight to the beautiful old lyric. "Be forgot? And never brought to mind?" O'Connor sang, and then, slowly and very softly at first, but growing to a rich shared melody that filled the room with feelings of love and faith and hope and commitment to both the past and to the future, the other voices joined in and sang the words together: "Should auld acquaintance be forgot / And days of auld lang syne?"

And when the song was over, the oldest brother lifted his glass to them. "Happy New Year!" he said to his family, and the hands of the big grandfather clock at the far side of the room clicked another notch. It was four minutes after ten, eastern standard time, but in the glow of the candles in the darkened room you couldn't see the clock's painted face clearly and through the laughter and shouted toasts of "Happy New Year!" in the room, you couldn't hear it ticking.

A few minutes later, Jack waved good-night to his family and Suzanne helped him up to his room.

Less than two hours later, when the big grandfather clock finally clicked its way to midnight, Jack was sleeping peacefully upstairs, regaining his strength for the year ahead.

CHAPTER
10

Tim agreed to meet with Summers in the Director's office. Summers was easier to talk to in his own office, and Cassidy had decided that what he had to say to him might sound less threatening that way, maybe keep Summers a little less defensive. But Summers had never enjoyed serving under a man more than thirty years younger than he was, and he'd never made a secret of it.

Cassidy wanted to take a short walk before going in to see the Director. And so he waved off the long black limousine that had been brought around for him and started down Pennsylvania Avenue at a good clip. Walking gave him a chance to think and exercise at the same time, and after a few minutes he started to enjoy the feel of the blood moving inside his body and he began picking up his pace even more, moving forward with his head pushed into the brisk wind that was coming in off the river. It was still winter in Washington, a particularly cold and snow-filled January, and Cassidy had to thrust his gloveless hands down deep into the pockets of his suit coat to keep them warm. It was a day made for topcoats, but he hadn't worn one, and as he turned off Pennsylvania and started up Fourteenth toward the Washington Monument into the full blast of the wind, he began to wonder if he'd done the right thing and at the corner he caught just a quick peek at the monument in the distance before he turned back and half ran, half walked the rest of the way back to the Justice Department.

He took the elevators up to Summers's office and was escorted immediately inside. Summers didn't stand when Cassidy came into the room. He simply motioned instead with a carefully manicured hand for Tim to sit down in one of the small hard chairs that were lined up in front of his desk. A photograph of Cassidy's own brother smiled down at the Attorney General from the wall above the Director's head, and the long, narrow, windowless office was filled with numerous other reminders of the long string of Presidents that Summers had managed to both serve under and survive.

"You're here to be brought up to date on the investigation, I presume," the Director said.

"That would be a good way to begin," Cassidy said, trying to match Summers's formal, almost somber way of doing business. Tim knew that he had to be careful. This couldn't be made to look like what he had to say was merely a personal conflict between the two of them. It was too important for that.

"There really is nothing new. We're following out some threads down in New Orleans and a few places, alleged Cuban connections and things." Summers spread his soft, well-cared-for hands out in front of him to help demonstrate to the younger man that everything was under control.

"I've seen the reports," the Attorney General said. "Thank you for keeping me up to date. Your office has done a good job with that," Cassidy added, and Summers nodded back, accepting the compliment.

"So, why have you come?" Summers said patiently.

"Two reasons," Cassidy said and then paused. "I want to talk to you about establishing a commission to investigate Dallas," he said and stood up anxiously, but then, seeing that there was no place to go in the narrow room, he moved to the back of his chair and leaned forward, the palms of his hands pressed against the chair's high leather back.

Summers winced slightly at the undecorous way that the younger man suddenly got up and moved energetically around the room, right in the middle of their conference. To Summers, it felt unseemly and he held his own body even more rigid as he looked back across the desk at him.

"We've decided that it won't be necessary," Summers said.

"Who has?" Cassidy said carefully, still not wanting to let his true feelings show.

"I've spoken to the Vice President about it," Summers said, folding his hands together on his desktop. "The Bureau will report its findings fully to the American people very shortly. There'll be no surprises in it. I can assure you that there is nothing to be concerned about."

"Shortly?"

"A few months at the most."

"Before the convention?"

"The convention?"

Cassidy smiled at Summers's pretense of ignorance. "The Democratic convention in Atlantic City in August." Cassidy went along with the game.

"Perhaps. That hasn't been decided yet. We have to be certain that we've fully investigated all possibilities before the report is released," Summers said, spreading his hands out across his desk again in a display of his total reasonableness about these things. "We will, of course, supply your office with a copy of our report before it goes into final form," he added, as if to close the discussion once and for all.

"I believe that a totally independent commission of some kind is appropriate under the circumstances," Cassidy said, ignoring the finality in the Director's voice and returning to the front of his visitor's chair and sitting down on the very edge of it this time.

"Yes, I know you do. You've expressed yourself in the newspapers quite thoroughly on that subject," Summers said.

"I think it would clear the air," Cassidy said, leaning forward over the edge of Summers's long desk.

"The air isn't dirty, Mr. Attorney General," Summers said, moving back in his own chair to maintain the distance between them across the long desktop. "Have you spoken to your brother about this?" Summers asked, although he could guess the answer.

"Yes, briefly," Cassidy said.

"So has the Vice President," Summers said, and then he paused to watch the younger man's reaction. "The President seems satisfied with our handling of the investigation. He sees no reason for an independent commission. All it could accomplish right now is to stir the American people up unnecessarily."

"Well, I disagree," Tim snapped.

Both men were quiet then.

"Perhaps you should be having this conversation with the President then."

"Perhaps I should," Tim said, and then he fell quiet again and let Summers continue.

"The President sees the same reports you do, as does the Vice President. It's a very simple case really. Of course I can understand your emotional involvement. After all, it was your own brother that this man Strode tried to kill. I appreciate your feelings, but that's why we have the law, isn't it, Mr. Attorney General—to ensure that our emotions don't rule us at times like these."

"There are newspaper reports every day," Cassidy said, interrupting the Director before he could go on.

"They're all being checked out," Summers said calmly, and then he sat looking across his desk at the Attorney General, saying nothing.

In the silence, Cassidy weighed his next step. "I received a telephone call last night," he began, and Summers's big, round, Buddha-like face remained impassive.

"*The New York Times* is bringing out a story tomorrow morning charging that the Bureau had a file on Strode long before the shooting, and that he was known to the agency to be dangerously violent and possibly a threat to the President. But when my brother visited Dallas that information was not given to the Secret Service or to anyone else, and no precautions of any kind were taken to protect the President from him. Is any of that true?" Cassidy was showing a hint of anger now, but he fought to control himself. "And if it is," he said, "I want to know what else you're keeping from the President and from me concerning the investigation."

Summers carefully placed the tips of his fingers together in an orderly pyramid in front of his face. "Mr. Attorney General," he said, "I'm not in the habit of responding to every whispered rumor, every half truth, and every distortion that the press can manufacture. I can only tell you that a very thorough, competent, and professional investigation is being conducted into all aspects of the case and that the Bureau has absolutely nothing to apologize for or to hide."

Cassidy angrily pointed his finger across the desk at the older man. "I asked you if there was any truth to those reports. Because you and I both know that if there is such a file, it has not been made known to my office, and I don't appreciate . . ."

"And I don't appreciate being given a lecture," Summers cut him off. "And I'll tell you something else I don't appreciate, I don't appreciate it when I hear reports that you've personally spoken to some of my agents and instructed them that they can forget about the chain of command and just deal directly with you on this matter," Summers said.

"In Dallas, right after the shooting, you mean?" Tim said, uncertainly. He knew he had been wrong about that, but he couldn't bring himself to apologize for it now. "I simply—" Cassidy paused for a second to catch his breath in the middle of the heated exchange and then continued, "I simply told those agents, who were assigned to the case, that if there was anything I could do to expedite their investigation that they could contact me or my office."

"Yes," Summers said. "And I'd like to remind you that there are rules and regulations and procedures that have been established through the years in the Bureau's dealings with the Office of the Attorney General and those procedures have served this country well in the past, and, as long as I'm the Director, I will do everything in my power to ensure that we continue to conduct our business in that manner."

When the Director had finished, Cassidy looked at him for a moment and then took a deep breath collecting himself. It was obvious that this meeting was going nowhere. "Yes, of course," Cassidy said. "It won't happen again." He stood up and started for the door.

"Just out of curiosity, Mr. Attorney General," Summers's voice stopped Cassidy before he could leave the room, "who would you have proposed to head up this commission, if it had been approved?"

Tim thought about the question for a minute, weighing whether or not to tell Summers the truth. He'd come this far, though, and he decided that he might just as well go all the way. "If an independent commission of inquiry is authorized, I'll ask the President to put me in charge of it. At least then I could be confident that the job was getting done," Cassidy said, letting his full anger and disrespect for the older man finally show.

"Yes, I thought so. Good day, Mr. Attorney General." The Director turned his attention back to the files on his neatly organized desk, leaving the Attorney General with nothing to do but to awkwardly close the door and return to the cold, windswept capital streets.

Tim wanted some time to think and, as he walked along, his head bowed into the wind, he was more certain than ever that Summers was hiding something important about Dallas from him, something more important than the Bureau having not disclosed their file on Strode to avoid some embarrassment with the press. No, it was something far more important than that, but what the hell was it? And how was he going to find out about it?

It was at least thirty degrees warmer in New Orleans than it was in Washington and there was something about the city that always suggested a slower, more relaxed pace to Sullivan, and he could feel himself beginning to adjust to it now, maybe too well.

He'd been to New Orleans once before, with his college friends for Mardi Gras, not that many years ago. He'd come then to get drunk and, if humanly possible, to get laid as well, and he had accomplished one of his two objectives six times in five days and returned to University Park with a very bad hangover.

This trip to New Orleans wasn't turning out much different so far: no women and a big headache, he thought, as he parked his car on the edge of the French Quarter and began to walk. He moved along the tourist streets then, using both Bourbon and Royal, trying hard to fit in with the rest of the morning traffic and not look too much like what he was—a junior FBI agent on a case that was several sizes too big for him and that had led him to a city that was probably far too old and far too clever for him to even begin to understand how to penetrate its mysteries.

He took his time, moving along the quaint narrow streets, watching the way they fit together, trying to memorize the faces of those who lived and worked on them, noticing exactly what the people did, how they acted and talked, even what the moist air smelled like. This was the way the city was teaching him to work now, slowly, from the outside in. His first few weeks in New Orleans, he'd tried it the old way, the way the Bureau had taught him, efficient and precise, like a scientist collecting facts and testing hypotheses. But this city didn't reveal itself to scientists, poets maybe, but it was more than just a collection of its facts and figures, dates and places. It was proud to be a slow-moving creative mystery, and it had refused to yield to standard Bureau methods. Sullivan had decided that if this city held the secret locked inside of it of what had really happened in Dallas on November 22, the only way to find out was the way the city demanded, and he was forcing himself now to move at the city's own pace—a slow, intimate mating dance.

He turned off the main tourist streets of the Quarter, moving away from the freshly painted black-and-white wrought-iron balconies and neat storefronted sidewalks, back into the dirtier, rundown side streets where the people of the Quarter really lived. The tall, conservatively dressed agent knew that he stood out even more dramatically now than he had on the wealthier tourist streets. He still wore the standard Bureau uniform: dark gray Ivy League suit, crisply laundered white shirt, and narrow black tie, and his blond crewcut was still tightly trimmed, its hard, flat edges matching the neat square lines of his jaw and chin. On the outside he was still standard-issue Bureau stuff, but on the inside he knew it was getting to be a different story. Something about this city or this case was changing him, and he wasn't so sure that he liked it.

He forced himself to amble slowly by the address that he had for Strode's childhood home. Strode's mother and stepfather still lived there. Sullivan didn't go inside. He'd been in once a few days before, but the answers he'd been given had added up to nothing and there was no reason to go in again, better to just walk by slow this time, feel it, sense the . . . Shit, he cut himself off. He decided he was getting weird, and he picked up his pace. He had a destination, time to get to it, and he began striding now with long determined steps toward 311 Claire Street, making the disciplined, controlled movement of his body match his neat, precise outward appearance.

Sullivan moved quietly up a wrought-iron-framed exterior staircase to a circle of offices constructed on two levels around a small brick courtyard that was overhung with the drooping branches of several old willow trees, their fallen leaves building up in a dry stone fountain at the center of the courtyard. He went to 311 and peered in the curtainless window. It was empty, as Sullivan knew it would be. The Bureau had searched it and then put the office under surveillance as soon as they'd learned about it, but they'd found nothing, and so far no one had appeared to claim its contents.

The lights were off inside, but Sullivan could see the outline of a desk, a few chairs, and an old metal file cabinet pushed up against the back wall. There was no reason to go in. It was some of the other occupants of this old French Quarter building that Sullivan wanted to talk to now, some of Strode's neighbors. During the last few weeks Sullivan had been researching them, and they were quite a group. If New Orleans was harboring some deep secret about the mystery of Dallas, this building was as good a place to start looking for it as any.

Sullivan began with 313, directly next door to Strode's vacant office. Sullivan knocked on the door and read the small brass plate below the address: HIRAM R. GARRETT, ATTORNEY AT LAW.

A slow New Orleans woman's voice with the slightest touch of a lisp invited him to come in, and Sullivan turned the big brass knob in front of him and walked inside.

A man and a woman sat in quiet intimacy behind their desks in a small, leafy, plant-drenched room. It was brilliantly cool inside and the blowing manufactured air smelled heavily of the woman's floral perfume.

The desks were arranged one behind the other, almost entirely filling the small office space inside. The woman sat behind the desk closest to the door. She was in her mid-forties, with long brown hair falling over bare shoulders that held the thin straps of a lightweight, low-cut summer dress. As Sullivan looked at the summer dress he had to keep reminding himself that it was January now and that he was there on business.

Behind the woman a man in a rumpled white suit, wearing dark-rimmed half-glasses slid down very low on the bridge of his nose, pretended not to notice Sullivan as the woman greeted him.

"Yes," the woman said slowly, making the single word into a softly played Cajun melody.

"Good morning," Sullivan said to the two people in the small room, but the man continued working, reading the papers on his desk through his half-glasses as if he were far away, separated from the intruder at the door by several thick walls and a couple of glass panels and maybe a big conference room or two. Sullivan admired his style, but he knew how to break through it with one quick phrase.

"I'm with the FBI," Sullivan said abruptly, and he enjoyed watching the man's head pop up and his hand go to his glasses, removing them quickly so that he could inspect Sullivan adequately across the few feet of office space that separated them.

Sullivan showed his credentials to the woman, who bent exquisitely forward, showing her full front to Sullivan in return. Sullivan took it all in gratefully. He was a long way from home.

"Yes, I'll see," the woman said, and then she turned around as if to check on the man only a few feet behind her, pretending to find out if he was in or not, but he was already standing, showing the full length of his wrinkled white linen suit to Sullivan.

"Hiram Garrett," the man said, extending his hand. "How can I help you?"

Sullivan removed a photograph from his inside coat pocket. It showed the front page of one of the pro-Castro pamphlets that Strode had been passing out on New Orleans street corners only a few short months before.

"Have you ever seen one of these?" Sullivan said, showing the photograph to both of them.

"No," Garrett said, glancing down at the photograph and shaking his head. When Sullivan turned to look at the woman, she shook her head no as well, but she refused to meet his eyes. Sullivan felt a click inside his head. That was the kind of thing that he was trying to learn to trust in himself now. Instead of just jotting the answers down on the notepad along with the date, place, and time, as he'd been trained to do, he asked her the question again and watched her carefully as she answered. She did better the second time, glancing up at Sullivan's eyes and batting her long, dark eyelashes at him several times as she told him that she'd never seen the pamphlet before. Sullivan only nodded, saying nothing at first. "This pamphlet was published by something called the Castro for Cuba Committee. Ever heard of it?" Sullivan asked finally.

The man said no again, but Sullivan guessed that he might just be a better liar than the woman was. Lawyers had even more practice at it than secretaries did, the agent thought. Sullivan liked looking at the woman more anyway, so he turned back to her and showed her the other photograph that he had kept hidden until that moment in his inside jacket pocket. It was of Strode, taken in New Orleans, a month before the events in Dallas. "Know this man?" Sullivan said, shoving the picture suddenly in front of the woman's face. Her long eyelashes fluttered involuntarily at the photo several times, before she got the nerve to look up at Sullivan's eyes.

"Sure," she said, the faint lisp returning to her voice in her excitement. "Everybody does—that's the man who shot the President . . ." But before she could finish, Garrett cut her off by reaching for the photo in her hands and snatching it away.

"What's this all about?" Garrett said, looking up angrily at the FBI agent.

"You know him?" Sullivan said, tapping the photograph.

Garrett said nothing, only glaring back at Sullivan angrily.

"Do you?" Sullivan said, turning back to the woman.

"No, of course not," she said and then stood. She was at least a head taller than the lawyer, but still several inches shorter than Sullivan. "Why don't I leave you two gentlemen to your business," she said, some of the French Quarter languidness returning to her voice again as she started for the safety of the small office's front door.

"No," Sullivan said. "I'm done." And the big FBI agent brushed by her in the small space and started for the door himself.

"Oh, one other thing," Sullivan said, turning back into the room as if he'd forgotten. He removed another photograph from his inside jacket pocket and handed it to the woman, who took it uncertainly. It was a blowup of the back page of the pro-Castro pamphlet Sullivan had shown her earlier. The address: "311 Claire Street, New Orleans, Louisiana" was clearly visible at the bottom of the page.

"Next door," Sullivan said, motioning with his thumb toward the thick, white-painted stone wall that separated the lawyer's office from the room that Strode had rented during the fall of 1963. "It's the same address in the Parish business license records and in a couple of other places that I've checked up on, for the Castro for Cuba Committee. Arthur Allen Strode was its only member," Sullivan said. "That address is next door, right?" he added, looking directly at the short man in the white suit.

The lawyer bent forward and looked at the photograph in Sullivan's hands. "People come and go in this building," he said smoothly. "I couldn't even tell you who my neighbors are at this very moment."

"Some of them are your clients, and most of them are very active in Cuban political affairs," Sullivan said, letting the lawyer know for the first time that he'd already done some checking on him.

"They're not Communists," Garrett said angrily and pointed his finger at the FBI agent. "You check me out," he said. "You'll find I have never represented anyone with associations like this," the lawyer added, slapping his hand out at the photographs of the pro-Castro pamphlet in Sullivan's hands. "You check me out on that," Garrett said defiantly.

Sullivan looked down at him for a moment. "I have," he said, and then he slipped the photograph back into his inside coat pocket. There were two other photographs still in there that he hadn't taken out and shown to anyone yet, but this wasn't the time or the place, he decided. "Well, thank you both," Sullivan said and then had to fight with himself not to get caught glancing down the woman's dress, as she moved her head and the top of her body up and down at him acknowledging his thank you. "I'll just ask around," Sullivan said, pointing out at the other offices that surrounded the overgrown brick courtyard. "Maybe somebody else." Sullivan shrugged his own shoulders then and walked outside.

Alone on the balcony, he stood for a second in the humid New Orleans air and looked around at the dozens of office doors that surrounded the courtyard, but he decided against trying any of them for now. He was going to play his hunch instead.

He returned to the street and walked back through the French Quarter's residential streets to his parked car and drove to the New Orleans Bureau office. He wanted to find out what they had on Garrett's secretary, and how he could reach her again. He still had that final pair of photographs that he wanted to show her, preferably when the two of them were alone.

"Jack, I'm sorry I had to disturb you this time of the night," the Vice President said. "You feelin' all right?"

The truth was that the headaches that raged from the damaged area on the upper left side of his head were still far more numerous and severe than he was letting on to anyone, and Jack had made a decision to hide the truth even from his own Vice President. He hated making Rance's job any harder than it already was, but he just couldn't bring himself to tell him. He just couldn't show his weakness in front of his old political rival and strengthen Rance's hand in the delicate balance of power that had been established between them.

"I feel fine," Cassidy said quickly. He wanted to get on with business—whatever it was. The President was home from the hospital for a few days, and for the moment he was alone in the small study off the master bedroom of his home in Hyannis. As far as he could tell, Suzanne was still sleeping peacefully in the next room. The duty nurse had wakened him with the call. She had helped him into his wheelchair and accompanied him into the study. It was a few minutes after three o'clock in the morning, February 4, 1964.

"Just a minute, Rance," Cassidy said, and he covered the receiver with his hand. He looked up at the nurse, who was hovering with a worried, disapproving face above him.

"Ten minutes," Cassidy said. "I promise."

"Ten minutes or I'll awaken Dr. Grayson," the nurse said, and, still not satisfied, but knowing there was nothing more she could do about it, she walked out of the room.

"Yes," Cassidy said into the phone.

"Well, we've got one hoppin' right out of the fryin' pan tonight," the Vice President said.

"Saigon," Cassidy whispered back, tensely.

"Saigon," Gardner repeated. The two men had talked on and off during the last few weeks about the increasingly obvious inability of General Trang to take firm control of the South Vietnamese government and what, if anything, they should do about it, but they had always reserved a final decision for the last moment, hoping against hope that conditions might change, but apparently they hadn't, and it looked like that last moment was upon them now.

"Trang's finished," Gardner said flatly. "Our people are certain of it."

Cassidy nodded at the phone in his darkened room and reached for the sheaf of papers on his desk, but then he let them drop back down to the crowded wooden surface. They were just words, and old words at that, mostly copies of out-of-date cables from Saigon. They wouldn't do him any good now. He glanced at the date and time on the top sheet of paper.

"The last thing that I've got here is dated yesterday, noon, their time," he said.

"One hell of a lot's been goin' on since then," the Vice President said. Only stony silence came back to him over the line from Hyannis. "We didn't want to disturb you until we had a recommendation," Gardner explained, feeling the President's displeasure.

"And now it's out of control," Cassidy said icily.

"No, sir," Gardner said. "Not out of control. Trang's done, that much is certain. The Army started moving against him several hours ago, but so far there's been very little bloodshed, which is a small miracle considering the fact that, from what we can tell, every damn general in the South Vietnamese Army has turned on him. We're pretty sure now that General Giai is going to come out of it in better shape than anyone else. He's . . ."

Cassidy's fist smashed down on the desk top in front of him, rattling the phone, and Gardner could hear the explosion all the way to the capital. "God damn it, Rance! Why wasn't I told?" But then, not waiting for an answer, Cassidy moved on. "Is Trang safe?"

"Yes, sir. He accepted Ambassador Luce's offer to fly him and his family into Bangkok. That's being done now, sir."

"Thank God," Cassidy breathed. "We can't have a repeat of what happened three months ago. That has to be our number-one priority."

"Yes, sir. It is," Gardner said. "But it still leaves us with a problem in Saigon."

Cassidy laughed sharply and without humor at the understatement.

"We don't really know all that much about General Giai, yet," Gardner went on. "Except that he seems to be all we've got, but if we don't step in right away, it could all go to hell for him in one big hurry and maybe for us, too. By morning, there could be dozens of factions warring among themselves for control of the government and, God knows, within the week some of those factions will probably begin doing business with the Communists. The best we could hope for then would be some kind of a coalition government with the Communists playing a major role in it. Giai is probably the only way left for us now to keep that from happening. All our military people are waiting for is a word from us. They think that it can be done with a minimum of casualties, but frankly, Mr. President, my own gut feeling on this is that if we don't move soon, there could be one hell of a lot of trouble out there. If someone doesn't come out of it in clear control in the next few hours, it could turn into a bloodbath."

"I see," Cassidy said, taking it all in as calmly as he could. "What does Ambassador Luce say?"

"In so many words?" Gardner asked and Cassidy stayed silent, meaning that he wanted the Vice President to continue.

"Pretty much what he and General Harwood have been sayin' for the last couple of months. That General Giai can do the job."

"That's what he said about General Trang," Cassidy said coolly.

"I know that, sir," the Vice President said. "But what I think Luce is really sayin' this time is that if we don't back Giai now, and do it with plenty of new muscle, including a substantial increase in our military presence in the South, that Luce will feel compelled to resign as ambassador and come back to the States and make a real run at the presidency himself," Gardner said.

"What did he say, exactly?" Cassidy asked nervously, fingering the copies of the dispatches on his desk.

"That he couldn't stand by quietly while we lost Southeast Asia," the Vice President said.

Cassidy smiled wryly at Luce's old-fashioned phrase. It was vintage Edward Todd Luce.

"And do you agree with him, Rance? What you seem to be telling me is that the American government should back a military coup sponsored by a man we know practically nothing about against the very government that just a few months ago we helped put into power ourselves," the President said.

"We have information on Giai," Gardner said, his own voice flat and cold now, almost all of the Texas squeezed out of it. "For one thing, we're certain that he's strongly anti-Communist," the Vice President added.

All alone in the quiet darkness of his New England home, Cassidy nodded his head and thought of how often he'd heard that same hollow argument, but he said nothing.

"I've got the Cabinet in session," Gardner added. "They're in the next room. I just stepped out when we got through to you," he said, pushing Cassidy for a final answer.

"Is my brother there?" Cassidy asked, but Gardner didn't answer right away. "Yes, sir, he is," he said after a few seconds.

"I want to talk to him," Cassidy said.

"Mr. President, Giai is all there is. We've got to go on this one way or the other right now, or it's going to be too late," Gardner said.

"If Tim's there, I want to talk to him," the President repeated evenly, still in control.

"Of course," the Vice President whispered back, his voice growing even more tense.

Cassidy waited in his darkened room in Hyannis. Through the window he could hear the night sounds of the Atlantic. The inside of his own head pounded almost as violently as the ocean surf, and he was operating on thin reservoirs of strength now, but he was angry and the adrenaline surged through him and countered the pain as he tried to decide what he should do next.

The nurse reappeared and tapped her watch, signaling that the allotted ten minutes was up. Cassidy shook his head no, and then his brother's voice suddenly came through on the other end of the line.

"Mr. President," Tim said.

"Tim, what the hell is going on there?" the President thundered into the phone.

The Attorney General quickly summarized the situation for his brother. "It's getting bad fast. It may already be too late. The South Vietnamese Army is convinced that Trang was about to put some kind of a deal together with the Communists so that he could stay in power. The generals think he was ready to put a coalition government of some kind in place. Our own people aren't too sure about that, but it probably doesn't matter very much anymore, because Trang's gone, and the Army is looking for a signal from us. If we back General Giai, it will probably do the same, and it looks like we could spare a lot of lives that way. If we don't back him, there's no way to say now just how it would all come out, except that a lot of people will be killed. We can be certain of that much."

"Why the hell didn't someone call me?" the President asked tensely, but then the pain in his head forced him to close his eyes for a moment, his body exhausted, and he had to rest one elbow against the table next to him to keep himself from faltering.

"It wasn't my decision to make," Tim said, looking across the room at the Vice President, who was sitting several feet away, angrily waiting to pick up a second receiver and finish his call with the President.

"So, what you're saying is that we don't really have any choice, that it's already too late, and our only way to go now is with General Giai?" Jack said, still quietly struggling against the pain and fatigue surging through him.

"The consensus here is yes. Yes, it is," the Attorney General said.

"But what about you, Tim? What do you think?" his brother demanded then.

"Maybe it gives us a chance," Tim began. "This will be the third government in Saigon in less than three months. Maybe that gives us some kind of an opportunity to let everyone, the South Vietnamese, our allies, our own people, everyone, know that this is a South Vietnamese war, not ours." Tim stopped then and chose the rest of his words with even greater care. "But I guess what bothers me the most right now is that every step forward that we take, even for the best of reasons, only gets us more deeply involved and limits our options later. That's the other side of it. I think we can control events tonight, but maybe we shouldn't. Maybe this is our last chance to get out and let them settle it themselves. As bad as it might be for us to step away now, it might be even worse later on."

"Yes, I know, but how do we do it? How the hell can we afford to just pull out on them? Break our commitment? Our allies are watching every move we make on this, and so are the Russians," the President said, cutting his brother off. "And how can we afford to do it now?" he added, going over the old ground for what seemed to him like the hundredth time that week.

Both men were quiet then. Neither one wanted to raise the issue of American politics directly, but it hung heavily in the air between them. They both knew that if they moved away from Vietnam now and let it fall to the Communists that they were handing the Republicans the one issue that could win the election for them.

"Under the circumstances, I believe that we must back General Giai," Tim said finally.

"All right, put the Vice President on," Jack said, and then, in a softer voice, he added, "Thank you, Tim."

Gardner clicked immediately back on to the phone. "Yes, sir," he said.

"I want one thing very certain," the President said through tightly clenched teeth. "Nothing gets this far without informing me, ever again."

"Yes, sir," the Vice President said, squinting across the room at the President's brother as he received his reprimand.

Tim stood then, embarrassed, and walked back into the smoke-filled White House conference room next door.

"Rance, you know my feelings," the President went on. "The Vietnamese need every possible signal from us, that it is in the last analysis their responsibility what happens to their country, not ours. Every possible signal!" The President repeated the words with emphasis and then paused. When he resumed his voice was weaker, resigned to what he felt that he had to say. "But, from what I'm hearing, I see no choice tonight. We have to move and I believe on balance we have to support General Giai now. You're all there on the scene with up-to-date information, and if that's your judgment . . ."

"It is," Gardner said, interrupting him.

"Yes, and as I say, if that's your judgment I concur, but I want it understood that these matters are not to be handled in this manner, ever again," the President said, but his voice had lost most of its sting.

"But it has to be made clear to General Giai and to his people," Cassidy continued, "that the United States is not about to make any pledges of additional military aid at this time. And that will continue to be our position, until we are convinced that he has the political support of his own country, and in our judgment that will involve some very significant reforms on his part."

"Sir, in all likelihood the Communists are going to use this crisis to launch a new campaign of their own," Gardner said then. "We've got to find a way to put some kind of real military pressure on North Vietnam to combat their plans. Until we do, the situation in the South will only continue to get worse. The Joint Chiefs are recommending that, at the very least, we should begin bringing in American planes and pilots now, so that later we would be in a position to begin air strikes in direct retaliation for . . ."

"Rance," the President cut him off again, and, using the last of his strength, Cassidy issued his final decision on the matter. "I understand the position of the Joint Chiefs, but there will be no new pledges of American air power at this time or any increase in our military presence in South Vietnam of any kind. And if that . . ." Cassidy reached down and fingered the stack of old dispatches in front of him again. "And if that brings Edward Todd Luce home to run for the presidency, so be it," he said.

"Yes, sir," the Vice President said.

"Is that all?"

"It is," the Vice President answered curtly.

"I want you to call me first thing in the morning or sooner if necessary. I want this matter brought under our control. Good-night," the President said.

"Good-night, sir," Gardner echoed and then, after he had hung up the phone, he sat by himself for a moment in the small office just off the East Wing conference room at the White House. The Vice President breathed in and out deeply several times, regaining his composure. He was determined not to show even a trace of the anger that he felt when he returned to the big White House conference room next door and rejoined the Cabinet meeting that was in progress there. "Signals!" Gardner snorted out loud finally, but only to himself. "They need one hell of a lot more from us than signals," he said into the empty room. Then he stood to rejoin the others and issue the orders that the President had given him. General Giai would have his coup, the American Army and the CIA would see to that, and if they were lucky, no one else would die that night, but what about tomorrow night? And the night after that? the Vice President wondered. Only a strong American presence could ensure the stability of the area, but Cassidy still refused to bend on that, only advisers, a few thousand advisers. Signals and advisers, something had to change, or the next thing either he or Cassidy knew, Ho Chi Minh would be sitting in Saigon and some goddamned Republican like Bill Longwood would be sitting in the White House.

Five hundred miles away in Hyannis, President Cassidy placed the phone down into its receiver. He sat alone then, looking into the darkness. It wasn't Gardner's fault, it was his, he thought. He shouldn't have let the decision slide this long. He was either the President or he wasn't. There couldn't be any middle ground on it. This uneasy partnership that he'd formed with the Vice President had to end. Only one man could be the Chief Executive, or the whole system started to go to hell. Maybe it was time to end Gardner's term as Acting President, but he had to be realistic, too. He was in no position to resume his duties yet and the country had to have a healthy full-time leader, not a crippled part-time President. Maybe he should resign after all, he thought then. Cassidy looked down at the carved wooden wheelchair that he was a prisoner in, suddenly hating it. He slammed his hand down on its arm. The decision on Giai should have been made weeks ago, he repeated to himself, while there was still time to keep it under control. If only our own elections were over, he thought, and our hands were untied on this thing. Then we could begin to move on it, make it absolutely clear to everyone that we weren't about to commit ground troops or tangle ourselves up in a major military commitment way the hell out there on Red China's own border, but he couldn't saddle his party with that kind of an issue and expect to continue the progress they were beginning to make now in so many other vital areas. All he'd succeed in doing was electing Luce, or Granderman, or maybe even Longwood President. No, he'd done the right thing, but he had to be very careful now. It had to be kept under control. He was going to have to be certain that their commitment in Vietnam was in a position that there was still room to maneuver with it after the elections. He wanted to think about it some more but the pain in his head had become intolerable and he was very tired, and when the nurse came back into the room he nodded up at her that he was ready.

He reached down and tried to move the old wooden wheelchair back into the dark bedroom, but he couldn't do it. His hands slid off the runner onto his lap. The nurse pushed the chair back into his bedroom and helped him slide down into his hospital bed. He thanked her in a low whisper so that he wouldn't awaken his wife, and then he closed his eyes. Control Southeast Asia, hell, he couldn't even control his own body, he thought to himself angrily, but then sleep quickly reached up and took his weary mind down into it.

Next to him, Suzanne kept her eyes closed in the darkness, her breathing deep and even, pretending for her husband that she was asleep and at peace.

Sullivan waited on the outdoor patio of a small café in the French Quarter. The table he had picked was in a far corner under the long arching branches of a very tall, very old magnolia tree. He drank a short beer and then a second one. Finally the woman came. Her name was Leigh Hodges. The Bureau didn't keep a file on her, but she'd been easy enough to check out. She had been Garrett's secretary for the last two years and the word was that she was probably sleeping with him, or had been, or certainly would be soon, but that wasn't the part Sullivan cared about now. He was going to keep this strictly business. Sullivan wanted to check out those suspicions that he'd filed away for future reference when he questioned her at Garrett's office.

Sullivan sized her up as she approached the table. She was a big woman and the high heels that she wore made her appear even taller, but her body was round and lush and she moved it with a slow assurance that told Sullivan that she was well aware of her impact. That afternoon she wore a tight, red, zippered jumpsuit, with a red-and-gold paisley scarf at her throat. The zipper of the suit was drawn down very low, revealing the tops of her large white breasts, and her long dark brown hair fell softly over the suit's shoulders. She wore expensive square-cut dark glasses and as she sat down in the chair next to him at the little café table, a gold hoop dangled from the zipper of her jumpsuit for a moment just in front of Sullivan's face, swinging alluringly near the rounded tops of her breasts. Once she had settled into her chair, her knees almost touched his, almost but not quite.

She shook her long brown hair back from her face and ordered a double scotch from the waiter. When the drink arrived, she grasped the glass firmly in front of her as if it were an old friend. Before she drank, she used her other hand to remove her dark glasses, revealing dark puffy circles of sagging flesh around her eyes. With her glasses off she glanced furtively around the café, making certain that no one nearby recognized her.

"Thank you for coming," Sullivan said.

The woman laughed at that. Sullivan had put the fear of God into her over the phone.

"You said 'one drink,' " she said and took a big swallow of the scotch. "I drink fast."

Sullivan smiled at her and sipped at his own beer.

The woman's face grew even more anxious. "So, what do you want?" she asked, her faint lisp apparent again in her nervousness.

"The rest of it," Sullivan said.

"The rest of what?" she said.

"Whatever there is."

"The Quarter is very small. Anyone could tell you about Mr. Garrett."

"They already have," Sullivan said coldly, not giving an inch. "I just thought you'd like your chance."

"Why don't you tell me what you think you already know, and maybe I can . . ." She drank from the scotch again, rather than finishing her sentence.

"Sure, if it's easier for you that way," Sullivan said. He looked at the big gold hoop swinging tantalizingly at the top of the bright red jumpsuit with each movement of her body, and then he began wishing that they were having this drink under other circumstances. But he reached into his inside coat pocket and spread a half dozen photos out on the café table in front of her, dealing them out one at a time like a pack of cards.

"You tell me when to stop, that's all," Sullivan said, putting the first photo on the table face up in front of her. The woman looked over at Sullivan, puzzled.

"I'm looking for confirmation," Sullivan explained. "Anybody who knew Strode and may have known Garrett too. All you have to do is stop me, if you see a familiar face." He plunked down another photo. He had a dozen of them, collected from weeks of checking and rechecking, of running the local files and talking to people in the Quarter, but there were still those two photographs that he really wanted to know about. He was coming to one of those pictures now. He threw the photo face up in front of the woman. She lifted her scotch, drinking from it and nodding her head nervously at the same time.

"What's his name?" Sullivan said.

The woman shrugged her shoulders. "I've seen him around the Quarter."

"Lately?"

The woman shook her head no. "Can I have another?" she said, pointing at her glass with the long red tip of her fingernail. She was crunching ice now with her back teeth.

"Sure," Sullivan said, and brought the waiter back over. He picked the photos up off the table before the waiter arrived. Sullivan ordered two double scotches this time and then kept the pictures coming. The woman tapped down on two more of them with her long curving fingernail and then disappeared back into the scotch when it came.

Sullivan left his own drink untouched and shuffled through the photos, returning finally to the first picture that she'd identified, and he placed it back on the table in front of her. She looked down at it nervously. The scotch was beginning to take its toll on her eyes now, glazing them over and helping them to lose their focus.

"Let me get it straight," Sullivan said, knowing that he was probably pushing her further than she would be willing to go, but risking it anyway, because he already had three I.D.'s more than he'd really hoped to get from her that afternoon.

"These three men, you've seen each of them around Garrett's office at one time or another."

The woman nodded and set her drink down in front of her. She was very near her edge now and Sullivan knew it, but he kept pushing anyway, still figuring that he didn't have much to lose.

"You see any of them with Strode?" Sullivan asked.

The woman took it like a punch in the gut, letting out a sudden sharp burst of air. "No," she managed. "I told you, I never knew him."

"He rented the place next door for six months," Sullivan said.

"I can't help that," the woman said and began to push her way back from the table.

"Your boss," Sullivan said, "he's got some bad friends."

She was quiet for a moment. "Don't I know it," she said finally and then managed a half smile.

"Do you want to know how bad?" Sullivan said.

"No," the woman said quickly.

"How about these men you identified?" Sullivan said, tapping the photographs again. "Haven't you heard that two of them are dead, buried in a bayou swamp with bullet holes the size of grapefruits in the backs of their heads?" Sullivan said.

The woman was quiet then, just looking at Sullivan in fear. "Can I go now?" she said finally.

"You can do anything you want to do as far as I'm concerned," Sullivan said and smiled confidently at her.

"I want to go," she said and stood up.

Sullivan watched her walk away in her tight red jumpsuit and high heels, and he wished again that the circumstances had been a little different between them.

"Phone if you need anything," Sullivan called out to her as she moved away from the table, but she didn't turn around. He watched her body move all the way to the sidewalk and then cross the narrow French Quarter street and walk quickly on her high heels down the block.

Then Sullivan flipped through the three photos she'd recognized, leaving the one that intrigued him the most on top—Regan, James R., born New Orleans, Louisiana, June 5, 1918, working at the time of his death for a private investigator named Justin Case, a man with anti-Castro connections just like Garrett's and with an address half a block away from Garrett's law offices. Sullivan looked down at the picture of Regan's freckled face, wearing the obvious bright red wig at a low angle on the top of his head.

Jesus, he thought, was it possible? Could this man actually have been part of a conspiracy to kill the President of the United States?

CHAPTER

11

"Sometimes I'm afraid it's going to kill him," Suzanne said and then checked herself as she realized how un-Cassidy-like what she'd just said had sounded. She could read the displeasure all too easily on her brother-in-law's face.

They were in the living room of Ben Cassidy's winter home in Palm Beach. It was the first Tuesday in March—the day of the New Hampshire primary, and Tim had flown down from Washington to watch the returns on television with his brother.

"I'm sorry," Suzanne said quickly. "I know I'm being melodramatic, but I just don't have anyone to talk to about it," she said.

"You want to know a secret?" Tim said. "I get a little scared too, sometimes," he said and then smiled.

"You?" She smiled back in mock amazement.

Outside the living room's big picture windows a light breeze was blowing through the line of Florida palm trees that separated the Cassidys' winter home from the broad, flat sand beach in front of it, and directly below the window was a long swimming pool filled with blue-green water. Suzanne turned to the picture window and looked out at the swimming pool where Jack was standing at its shallow end, talking to their daughter. At that moment, Erin was poised at the edge of the pool leaning forward, her little legs tensing for a dive. Her father was half turned to her with a few-feet head start. It was that head start that the two Cassidys, father and daughter, were discussing now, Suzanne guessed, folding her arms in front of her chest in disapproval as she continued watching them, but then she smiled despite herself, as Jack shouted: "Go!" and Erin exploded in a determined dive from the edge of the swimming pool and began churning in great, exuberant, splashing strokes toward the other side of the long pool.

Jack looked up at Suzanne and winked. Then he dove after his daughter, swimming slowly and awkwardly as he tried to catch her and avoid soaking the bandage on the side of his head at the same time. He managed to close most of the distance between them though, and in a hurried finish he came even with her and they both seemed to touch the far side of the pool at the same time.

"I won!" Erin yelled, pool water running down her face.

"I won," the President shouted back, but he was breathing deep and hard after the short swim, one hand grasping the side of the pool for support.

"Erin won," Tim said, throwing the sliding glass door aside and calling out toward them.

"You're early," Jack said, looking up at his brother. "And I won, by the way," he added, forcing a smile as he continued to hang from the side of the pool still breathing deeply.

"I'm the chief law-enforcement officer of the United States and I believe that I'm in a position to say who won here, and I declare Erin Cassidy to be the winner," Tim said.

Erin yelled and clapped her hands and swam away accepting victory. Jack smiled at her and then looked back up at his brother.

"You want to talk?" Jack said, sensing Tim's seriousness.

"No. I want to make some telephone calls. Can I use your office?" Tim said.

"To New Hampshire?" the President asked, lifting himself slowly out of the pool and then reaching for a towel that he had left lying draped over a nearby patio chair.

"Yes. They should be able to tell us something by now," Tim said, looking at his watch and away from his brother's pale and still weakened body.

"I'll join you," Jack said.

"Are you getting out?" his daughter called to him, disappointed, and Jack turned back to her.

"I'll go ahead," Tim said, seeing his brother's dilemma. "Politics can wait," he said, and he stepped back inside the sliding glass door and into the house.

Suzanne was still standing near the window watching her husband as Jack walked back down to the shallow end of the pool and rejoined his daughter and the two began negotiating terms for their rematch.

"He's not supposed to get that bandage wet," Suzanne said, half to herself, half to Tim, and then she looked up directly into her brother-in-law's eyes. "I'm turning into quite a . . ." she began.

But Tim wouldn't let her finish. "You love him, that's all. How is he anyway?" he said.

Suzanne walked back into the living room and sat down. "Not as good as he pretends, but probably not as bad as I'm afraid he is, either," she admitted.

"But he's certainly not strong enough to start running a presidential campaign, if that's what you're really asking," she added, concern returning to her face.

Tim crossed the room to sit with her, saying nothing.

"Tim, it doesn't take a genius to know what he's thinking," she said, smiling faintly.

"No, I suppose it doesn't," he said.

"He puts up a brave front," Suzanne said, gesturing out the window at her husband. "But he's not really good enough right now to take the kind of stress he's putting himself through as it is. He's still trying to run the country over a telephone, talking with Rance at least two or three times a day, and it's taking all of his strength to do it." She paused then for a few seconds before she went on. "The doctors want to start the surgery as soon as possible, but he's been stalling them. He has to give them at least two uninterrupted months to do the work properly and he'll need to take a good long rest after it's finished. And you know what that means to Jack. He'd be forced to give up whatever plans he still has for November. But he has to do it, Tim. He doesn't really have a choice. Please help me make him see that," she said, looking up at her brother-in-law's face. "I know I was being overly dramatic before, but I really am worried. He just refuses to slow down. I don't know what's going to happen to him if he doesn't start taking better care of himself."

"Suzanne, I'll try," Tim said. "But you have to know, too, that in the end I'll support whatever decision Jack makes."

"I'm sure you will," Suzanne said, suddenly angry and letting some of the tension that had built up inside her over the last several months spill out at her brother-in-law. "It's all just a game to you both, isn't it? I mean, can either of you truly believe that it really matters that much, whether Rance Gardner or Jack Cassidy is President for the next four years? Their policies are the same, the same people in the administration, the same goals, the same programs. Sometimes I think it's all just your damn Cassidy ego. The great political adventure—you just have to be part of it, don't you? Whatever it costs the people close to you." She stopped then, too angry to find the words to go on, and tried to collect herself again. "I'm sorry, Tim."

She stood and went to the window and looked past the swimming pool, down the beach to where the big orange sun was just beginning to duck under the fringed outline of the palm trees in the distance. "Maybe it's just me," she said, turning back to Tim, her anger gone now and a kind of quiet despair taking its place.

"Maybe I'm the one who can't run again. Not now, not this soon," she said, touching the place on the front of her clean, white cotton dress where only a few short months before the scarlet stain of her husband's blood had seeped deep into the fabric of her bright pink suit.

"You haven't got enough for a tap here!" The head of the Bureau's New Orleans office threw the papers containing the request that Sullivan had been working on for the last three weeks back across the desk at him. "You haven't got enough here to listen in on Garrett if he was giving a public speech in Jackson Square on the Fourth of July!"

"The man lied to me," Sullivan began.

"You don't know that," his section chief shot back.

"He sure as hell did," Sullivan said. "He told me he'd never seen Strode, never heard of Cuba for Castro—that's bullshit. He had to. Its headquarters were right next door to him, and from what I hear Garrett's client list is almost exclusively people caught up in Cuban politics."

"Anti-Castro, not pro-Castro!" the section chief thundered. "That's a hell of a difference down here."

"Okay, anti-Castro, but Garrett also represents organized-crime people, politicians elected on Cuban money . . ." Sullivan tried to go on, but his boss wouldn't let him.

"So what?" the section chief said flatly.

"So what? So, he's swimming in it. That's so what. Your own people down here think the guy's running over the edge."

"Over the edge?" the New Orleans section chief said with a disgusted half laugh. "Over the edge of what? Where's your probable cause for a tap on Garrett's phone?" he said, pointing at Sullivan's thick file of carefully prepared papers again. "For that matter, where's your goddamned crime? There's no real evidence of a conspiracy to kill Cassidy, and you know it. What are you doing, Sullivan, trying to be a hero? Cassidy tried to be a hero, too. Look what happened to him," he added, and then he looked away.

"What is that supposed to mean?" Sullivan said.

The head of the New Orleans office was quiet for a few seconds then. "Nothing," he said finally. "I just don't get it, that's all. What the hell are you trying to do with all this?"

"I'm trying to find out what happened in Dallas, three months and . . ." Sullivan paused, adding up the days in his head. "And sixteen days ago. I thought that was our job."

"Me, I'm not in the hero business," Sullivan's boss said then. "We have to remember what's important here. Our job is to keep the lid on, nothing more, nothing less. Now you, you keep taking the lid off. You got it all mixed up," he added, but the young agent seated across from him just stayed quiet then and listened.

"Jim," his section chief went on, his voice quieter, more reasonable, "you got the word spread to every possible source, reliable and unreliable, from here to Mexico City, on this guy that you think you saw in Dallas right after the shooting—and it's turned up nothing. I mean, we haven't even had somebody come in and try to shake a few bucks out of us with a good hustle. That should tell you something."

"It tells me that the Louisiana State Troopers pulled two bodies with bullet holes in the back of their heads out of the swamp seventy-two hours after it happened and nobody else wants to wind up like them. That's all it tells me," Sullivan said.

"And there's another thing," he continued. "Strode's landlady saw a Dallas police car stop at Strode's rooming house within minutes after the shooting. No one in Dallas is following up on that. I've been reading the reports."

"Jim, look, New Orleans is New Orleans and Dallas is Dallas. We leave them alone, they leave us alone. That's how it works. Whatever they're doing over there, I'm sure they've got their reasons, and even if they don't, neither you or me can do a damn thing about it." His boss sighed deeply then before adding. "You got what, eight vacation days coming?"

"Twelve."

"Twelve. Good. You take them now, or you're going to lose them," he snapped, and then he closed the file on his desk and slid it back across to the young agent. "Okay?" he added.

"No tap?" Sullivan said.

"No tap."

Sullivan stood up and began picking up his papers from the section chief's desk. "Okay," he said.

"And, Sullivan."

"Yeah."

"Don't try going over my head on this," Sullivan's boss said. "I've already talked to Washington. This is policy I'm giving you. Do you understand?"

Sullivan nodded his head to show that he did.

"Now, just shut the fuck up and listen." The dark-skinned man, who called himself Antonio Lopata now, spat the words into the phone.

"I'm trying to tell you that the FBI has been in to see me," Garrett said, interrupting his unexpected caller again. It was late and Garrett was all alone in his small plant-filled law office at the edge of the French Quarter. The office lights were out, but the room was lit by the faint yellow luminescence from the Quarter's imitation gaslights.

"If you'll shut up, I'll be off the phone in ten seconds," Lopata said, and the lawyer stayed quiet and listened.

"I've got unfinished business with one of your clients. You know which one and what the business is. I want to finish the job that I started for him last November, and I want to be paid for it. One hundred thousand dollars. I'll let you know when and where," Lopata said.

"Wait a . . ." Garrett started.

"Shut the fuck up, I said." Lopata silenced him. "I pick when, and I pick where, and I finish the business my way this time. No more fuckups like last time," he said. "One other thing. I've got something your client wants, something that will blow the lid off this fucking country and its government," the dark-skinned man said, fingering Strode's red leather diary. "They know what it is. I'll throw that in for an extra hundred thousand and everybody will be happy. I'll give you a few days to reach your client before I call you back," he said, and then he hung up.

Garrett sat staring at his phone for several minutes in the cool dark office. He decided that he didn't dare use it, not with the FBI poking around everywhere. Jesus, he thought, this guy had to be crazy. He'd told the son of a bitch that the goddamned Federal Bureau of Investigation could be listening in on the call and the bastard had just gone right ahead and rattled out his demands. What the hell did they have on the loose out there, anyway? And what could he be talking about that was so goddamned valuable it gave him that kind of confidence?

He reached into his top desk drawer and took out a glass and a pint bottle of Bacardi. He poured the thick dark rum into the glass and drank it down in one quick swallow. He could feel himself sweating even more heavily into his rumpled white suit now. Shit, he should have never gotten into this in the first place. It was way out of his league, but he was in it now though, and he was going to have to see it through. He looked out the window of his office at the little bar across the street, remembering that there was a pay phone in its men's room.

Garrett put the pint bottle back in his desk. He left his office and crossed the little French Quarter street to the bar and walked through its darkened front lounge area to one of the twin doors at the back of the building.

The men's room was empty and Garrett went to the pay phone on its side wall and dialed the number by heart and then waited for the familiar voice to answer. When it did, Garrett blurted out his story, barely stopping to take a breath. Sweat was dripping through his shirt and beginning to stain the armpits of his white suit coat.

"Jesus, he's out of control," the voice on the other end of the phone breathed out when Garrett finished telling his story.

"What do I do?" the lawyer asked frantically as the voice on the other end of the line grew silent for a moment.

"You do what you've always done," the voice said finally. "You sit tight and take orders. We'll do the rest."

"What do I say when he calls back?"

"You tell him we can probably do some business, but look, Garrett, your number-one priority is to find out where he is. Do you understand? Find out where the hell he is right now," the voice ordered.

"To send him the money?" Garrett asked with disbelief.

"Just find out where he is and where he wants the money delivered—that's all you have to do," the voice said. "Then let us know and we'll take care of the rest."

The election returns were starting to come in and the Cassidy family and friends were gathered around the television set in their Palm Beach home, huddled forward, drinking beers or mixed drinks and talking loudly, as if they were watching a boxing match or a closely played football game.

Suzanne stood at the edge of the crowd with a drink in her hand watching her husband's animated movements at the center of the group. Frank O'Connor was on one side of him, Jack's brother Brian on the other.

"So, Frank," Jack said. "You're the politician. What's going to happen up there tonight?"

"I think it's really up for grabs, Jack," his friend said. The Republican's heart says Longwood, but . . ." O'Connor hesitated for a moment.

So the President completed his thought: "But with the mess I've put the Democratic Party in, the Republican's head tells him to go with a winner, and he thinks that Granderman might just be a winner," Jack said.

"Yes, something like that," O'Connor said. "But we Democrats like a good mess to clean up," he added proudly.

"What kind of impact do you think our ex-ambassador to Saigon was able to make with less than a month of campaigning?" Cassidy said, looking around at the group, inviting anyone to answer.

"Very little," Tim said with authority. He was just walking into the living room from the den, where he'd been making the last of his calls to the Cassidy contacts in New Hampshire. He had up-to-date reports now, as good as any television network's. "It looks like the write-in effort for Luce never really got off the ground," he added.

"Then it's Granderman," Jack said flatly and stood up. He walked to the back of the room then and stood next to his wife.

"You're that sure?" Brian said then.

"It looks that way," Tim answered for Jack. "It seems to be working out pretty much the way we guessed it might. Longwood's been scaring the hell out of the Republicans up there with some of the right-wing things that he's been saying and they don't seem all that happy with Granderman either. He's probably too damn liberal for them. But with Jack still in the race, they're afraid to switch to Luce, because they know that Jack has beaten the hell out of him before, and probably would again. So that leaves them nowhere else to go, only Granderman."

"Well, we'll know officially soon enough," Brian said, looking at his watch. "The polls closed five minutes ago."

"Any write-in for Gardner?" Jack said quietly to his brother, who was standing a few feet away. Tim shook his head. "No," he said. "It won't be five percent."

"Good," Jack said.

"Quiet!" Kay called out to the group. "Granderman's going to talk now."

Jack turned back to the television set. Marshall and Shelley Granderman were standing at the podium in a ballroom in Manchester, New Hampshire. Jack smiled at the familiar setting. He knew the hotel, the room, the podium, the way the microphone worked, the lighting, the names of more than a few of the people in the room, and, most important, he remembered from four years earlier the quickest way out the back through the kitchen after the difficult but necessary ritual of thanking the troops was over.

"It's still too early to . . ." Granderman was saying.

"God, look at his wife. She looks like someone's got a gun to her head," Brian said, laughing at the television image of Shelley Granderman.

"What a phony smile," someone else called out.

"How would you like to be six months pregnant, with everyone in the country analyzing everything you do?" Suzanne said sharply.

"Me?" O'Connor asked. "I wouldn't," he said.

After he said it, Suzanne set her drink down and started toward the sliding glass door that led outside to the pool area. Jack took a step toward her and she turned back to him.

"I just need to take a walk," she said, pointing out past the Cassidy patio toward the beach.

Jack nodded, understanding. "I'll be down in a minute," he said. "I just want to . . ."

"Shh," Brian said, "they've got some returns."

Jack looked back at the television screen again. It showed Chet Huntley's face in close-up. "Well, David, we do have one winner to announce. The NBC Decision Desk has determined that John Trewlaney Cassidy, the thirty-fifth President of the United States, is the winner of the Democratic primary in New Hampshire. Our projections show that he's captured over ninety percent of the votes in that state, which he . . ." The cheering in the room drowned out the rest of the reporter's words.

"Congratulations," Tim said, smiling across the room at his brother.

"Yes, congratulations," Suzanne said. Jack walked over to his wife and took her hands in his own and bent forward to kiss her cheek.

As their eyes met, Suzanne expected to see that look in her husband's eyes that she had seen many times before: hungry, driving, ambitious, ready to do battle, whatever the odds, but as she looked closely, she saw something else entirely. Perhaps something that only she knew Jack well enough to see. She saw only the fatigue and the extended pain and the uncertainty beneath the determination on the surface. "What are you going to do?" she whispered to him.

"How the hell can I stay out of it?" he said. Suzanne pulled away from him angrily and turned back toward the sliding glass door. She crossed to it quickly then and stepped out onto the patio.

Jack followed after her. "Suzanne," he called out, but she didn't turn around. Instead, she walked past the pool and out onto the darkened Florida beach.

"Running unopposed, except for some minor write-in efforts on behalf of Vice President Rance Gardner, and without making even a single appearance in the state or any public appearances of any kind since the tragic events in Dallas last November, President Cassidy has once again proven his tremendous popularity with . . ." Jack stopped and listened to the television commentator's voice behind him as he tried to decide if he should catch up with Suzanne or stay and hear the rest of the election returns.

As Jack stood by the picture window watching his wife's retreating figure, O'Connor called out to him. "Jack!" he shouted, "they've got it already."

"God, that didn't take long," Brian said, and Jack turned back into the living room and rejoined the others, who were still huddled around the brightly glowing television set. "In the Republican primary . . ." "Shh, shh," someone in the middle of the boisterous crowd admonished, and the general noise and hubbub began to subside to hear the words. ". . . has determined that Governor Marshall T. Granderman of New York is the winner in New Hampshire!"

"You were right!" Brian called out, and the noise started again for a moment and then suddenly quieted so the group could hear the rest.

"In what, we have to think, is at least a bit of a surprise," the reporter continued, "Governor Granderman has swept in here over the last three months with his organization—and let's not forget with his money as well—and won what appears to be a stunning victory. He was what, David? Ten? Twelve points down to Senator Longwood in the polls when he started?"

"Something like that," his co-anchor said dryly.

"And he's managed to hold off what some experts thought might be serious write-in challenges from two of President Cassidy's oldest political rivals, Ambassador Edward Todd Luce of Massachusetts, and former Vice President Simmons of California," Huntley added.

"Thank God for that!" someone yelled, at the mere mention of the former Vice President's name.

"I didn't think they'd do it!" someone else shouted.

"This could give the Republican Party a very strong candidate in November, David. If Governor Granderman can repeat his performance tonight in the Oregon primary next month, he could be very difficult to beat, whoever the Democrats nominate in Atlantic City five months from now."

Jack stood at the edge of the group near the open door to the patio. In the distance he could see his wife walking down the beach by herself, her solitary figure framed by a bright Florida moon that hung in the sky above the long row of palms near the water's edge.

"Quiet," Kay said. "Granderman's going to talk." And the room behind Jack began to settle in to hear the Governor's acceptance speech. The President took another half step toward the patio door, but then the sound of Granderman's challenging voice tugged him back to the television screen again and he stood at the back of the room watching as Granderman accepted victory. And then the President stayed as Longwood came on from another hotel ballroom across town, his honest blunt face openly acknowledging defeat, but when he spoke Longwood vowed to fight on in the western primaries, because "my conscience dictates that I must," he said.

Jack listened to it all before he finally stepped out onto the patio and walked down to the water's edge. The night breakers were rolling up and splashing on the wet sand near his feet as he looked down the coast toward where he'd last seen his wife's retreating figure, but the beach was very dark now and even the light from the big white Florida moon wasn't shining brightly enough for him to see where she had gone.

Sullivan drove his government-issue Ford over the Huey P. Long Bridge and then out toward Baton Rouge. He was in his shirtsleeves, his tie undone, and all four windows of his government car were rolled down. The radio was playing "I Want to Hold Your Hand," and Sullivan sang the lyrics along with it, loud and off-key. His only other company were the big bugs that kept spattering against his window in an endless series of kamikaze dives.

He was on his way to the airport in Baton Rouge to learn whatever he could about the flight from Mexico that Regan had logged in on November 24, two short days after the assassination attempt on the President in Dallas.

After the bridge, the highway was bordered by Louisiana back country, high, dense, deep-green vegetation that grew up by the side of the road, blocking any hint of a breeze. There were a few simple stores at the crossroads, but the only other buildings were the dirty one-room houses scattered in between the roads and fields. Shit, he was sick of Louisiana, Sullivan decided, looking out at the countryside as he drove, and he thought then about what his section chief had said to him about his vacation time. The radio was playing "Love Me Do" now, but Sullivan didn't know the words to it and he didn't try to sing along anymore. Thinking about his boss had made him angry anyway, and he no longer felt like singing.

When Sullivan stopped at the next light, he reached over and pulled a map from the glove compartment. He'd taken the map out of his "Second Gunman" file and for some reason had carried it with him that morning. He knew now why he'd brought it. Sullivan spread the map out over the empty passenger seat next to him. It was a map of Mexico, and Sullivan's fingers reached down and traced the outline of the country's gulf coast. The stoplight changed then and Sullivan glanced back up at the traffic as he pulled away from the intersection, but a few seconds later he looked down at the map again. There it was—about ten miles inland off the coast—Monterey, Mexico. What the hell had Regan been doing there the morning after Cassidy had been shot and less than a day before his own dead body was found in a bayou swamp? Monterey sounded like a pretty good spot for a little vacation, Sullivan decided impulsively.

Through the bug-spattered front windshield of his car the agent could see a Shell station. He slowed the car and pulled up into the station's service area next to a pay phone.

He rang the girl in Dallas. If he was going to take a vacation, he could use a little company, he thought. She might turn out to be useful cover too, if he decided that he wanted to look like a tourist in Monterey and not like an FBI man on an investigation.

"Hello, this is Kit," the girls' roommate said, answering the phone.

"Jim Sullivan," the FBI agent said into the service-station pay phone, pushing dimes and quarters into its metal slots as he did, but there was only silence on the other end of the line. "I'm a friend of Denise's," Sullivan explained into the silence. "You and I met the day after the President was shot."

"Denise isn't here," her roommate said coolly.

Suddenly, Sullivan thought of the stolen file that he'd left with the girl. "Is something wrong?" he said, anxiously.

"No, everything's terrific. I'm sure Denise loves hearing from you every couple of months," her roommate said.

"Kit, is there something you're not telling me?" Sullivan said as he caught the hard edge of the girl's voice.

"Denise is out on a date," Kit said.

"Something serious?" Sullivan asked. He tried to sound like he cared, but inside he only felt relieved. He had been afraid for a moment that something might have really happened, but now he knew it was okay. He'd been worried about leaving the stolen file with the girl ever since the stories speculating about its existence began to appear in the newspapers, but he hadn't done anything about it yet. He promised himself now that he'd get it back from her as soon as he could.

"Serious?" her roommate said. "Maybe," she added mysteriously. "I think you better talk to her about it yourself though, don't you?"

"Yeah, okay. Do me a favor would you? Tell her I'm taking a little vacation down to Mexico and I thought that she might want to come along," Sullivan said.

"I'll tell her," Kit said. "When are you leaving?"

Sullivan could hear one of Denise's kids screaming in the background. He waited for the noise to subside before trying to answer. As he waited, he thought about the question. Let's see, if she could be ready for a date on a half hour's notice, how long would it take her for a week in Mexico? he wondered.

"Oh, I don't know," Sullivan said finally. "I won't leave tonight, probably not until tomorrow or the next day," he added, casually.

"That's terrific," Kit said sarcastically. She could hear a car pulling up in front of her apartment and she knew that it was probably Denise and her date, but she didn't bother to say anything more. Not that it was any of her business, but this guy Sullivan was a loser, with his government car and his one call every three months.

"Tell her I called and I'll phone her back in a few hours," Sullivan said confidently. He set the receiver back into its holder without saying good-bye.

In West Dallas, Kit moved to the window and looked outside. Denise was coming up the front walk followed by a man wearing a dark gray Ivy League suit over a plain white shirt and narrow black tie, but Kit barely looked at him, glancing over his shoulder at his car instead. Shit, she thought, and she shook her head in disapproval. Another one. Probably another cop or government man, Kit thought with disgust. Poor Denise, she always gets the losers. This guy was driving another light-colored American product with four cheap black-wall tires. Just like Sullivan's.

Jack couldn't sleep. The pain that usually confined itself to the side and the top of his head had spread and had worked its way down his spine to his lower back. He looked at the pain medication in the plastic container on his end table. He hated taking any more of it, but he really had no choice, he decided, as he felt his head begin to throb even more intensely than it had a moment before.

Being careful not to awaken his wife, he carried the container of pills with him to the bathroom and closed the door, locking it from the inside.

Without turning on the bathroom light, he swung open the mirror mounted on the door of the medicine cabinet, so that he could see his reflection directly in front of him. He placed the container of pills on the counter and used both his hands to remove the tape and bandages from the side of his head. Alone in the half light of the bathroom, coming in through its single window, he looked at his wound. A series of scarred lines ran in an irregular webbing of cuts and ridges, holding the twisted, reddened flesh together. What if the voters of New Hampshire could see this? And what if they could see, too, the internal damage that lay beneath it, the remaining fragments of smashed lead from the assassin's bullet and the shattered pieces of bone embedded deep under the scarred tissue on the surface? What if they could feel the pain even for a moment? Who would they vote for then? Would they vote for the man who just smiled and pretended to his family, to his Vice President, to his country, that things were far different from the way he really knew them to be?

In pain and anger, Jack closed the mirrored door to the medicine cabinet, refusing to look at himself any longer. He knew the answer to his own question only too well. If the voters could see the image in the mirror that he had just seen, and if they knew the truth of the pain that he felt, they would move on and choose someone else to lead them, someone who could run the country with full health and energy, not half a man, not someone who deceived them, as he was doing. And history would pass Jack Cassidy by. Forty-six years old and history would pass him by, probably forever. But, damn it, he thought then, as he replaced the bandage and pressed the tape back into place, he had been taught that winning was important, that success defined a person's character, measured his contribution to the world. And he'd won the presidency, the biggest prize of all, and he couldn't be expected to just give it away without a fight. So many times before in his life, he remembered then, something had come along and changed everything for him—the famous "Cassidy luck"—and it might just happen again. Tomorrow or the next day or the next, he would wake up and the pain would be gone and then he would be spared having to endure the ordeal of months of operations that the doctors kept insisting were necessary. Those months that the doctors seemed determined to take from him were precisely the time that he had to have to save his presidency and perhaps mount a drive for a second term. They couldn't be wasted in a hospital. But even as he thought about it, a new wave of pain flooded through him, starting in the wounded area of his head and quickly sweeping through his neck and back, making him feel weak and vaguely nauseated. Quickly he filled a glass of water from the tap and used it to swallow two of the pain capsules. But if something was going to happen he thought then, as he stood for a moment by the sink waiting for the medicine to begin to work, it better happen pretty damn fast.

Finally the pain pills began to deaden the feeling in his head a little and he walked back out to the living room of the Palm Beach house. Through the window he could see the reflections of the silver-white moon on the surface of the ocean. Everyone else in the house was in bed. Suzanne had been the last, coming home from her walk very late and slipping into the bed next to her husband without saying anything.

Jack walked over to the television set and tried the channels, but he found only static and one loudly humming test pattern. He turned the set off. It didn't matter anyway. Granderman had won. In the end it had been close, less than four percentage points over Longwood, but Jack knew that by the Republican convention in July that four percent win would look like a landslide. So he probably had what he'd wanted now—a Granderman victory. But Jack couldn't help wondering if maybe he hadn't outsmarted himself on this one, or worse, that maybe none of it really mattered at all. Granderman would be a formidable opponent—the kind of an opponent that Gardner and the Democratic Party would certainly need his help in beating. But so what? Jack thought. Was that what was really important to him now?

He wandered out to the kitchen and looked into the refrigerator for something that might help settle his stomach. It was crammed full with plates and dishes left over from the party. He reached in and removed some cheese and some small round crackers from one of the plates and then closed the refrigerator door.

He needed to talk to someone. He walked slowly back toward the room where his father slept. He paused then, at his father's door, taking a few small bites of the food as he stood in the hallway. There was a light on inside his father's bedroom. Jack tapped lightly on the door and then peeked inside. His father was awake, lying in bed all alone, his head propped up on a high mound of pillows.

"Dad, I uh . . ." Jack said tentatively, but his father turned his head to the door and his eyes invited Jack to come inside. Jack crossed the room and sat on the chair by his father's bed. A small phonograph was playing classical music from a nightstand a few feet away—something from Mendelssohn, turned very low.

"How are you feeling?" Jack asked and his father let him know with his eyes and a slight movement of the right side of his body that he was all right.

"Can I get you anything?"

His father shook his head no.

"It was good seeing everybody, wasn't it?" Jack said. "It's going to be hard just going back to being a convalescent home in the morning," he added and smiled at his father.

Jack fell quiet then. Finally he whispered: "Dad, I don't know what to do."

Both men were silent for a few seconds then, the music of the Mendelssohn symphony the only sound in the darkened room.

On the nightstand next to Ben Cassidy was a tablet of paper and a pen, and he motioned for his son to hand it to him.

The older man scratched something on the little pad of paper, and when he was done, Jack looked down at it and read his father's words. In small, shaky letters his father had written simply: "Don't quit, Jack."

CHAPTER

12

Jack chuckled softly. He and Suzanne were having a poolside breakfast. The glass-topped table was laid with silver and china and clean white linen. They were in Palm Beach and the weather was good, but a big yellow-and-white striped beach umbrella protected them from the direct rays of the morning sun.

Jack had *The New York Times* in one hand, folded to a story about his brother's visit to Gardner's Texas ranch. His other hand was lifting a coffee cup to his lips, but the coffee in it was splashing violently as the President's hand shook with laughter at what he was reading. Finally he had to set both the newspaper and the coffee cup down and breathe deeply several times to regain his composure. As he did, Suzanne smiled across the table at him.

"I would give anything to see Timmy down there at the ranch," the President said and then pointed down at the *Times* article. "They're having a barbecue and square dancing tonight," he said and then began laughing again at the thought of his born-and-bred New England brother deep in the heart of Gardner's Texas, where Tim had gone at Jack's request to find out what Gardner and the politicians that the Vice President was in constant contact with were thinking now. "Jack, you're terrible," Suzanne said, but she was smiling too. "Poor Kay," she said, shaking her head as she thought about her sister-in-law.

Jack picked up the newspaper again and finished reading the story, shaking his head and laughing softly at it as he did, but he was in enough control now to safely lift the coffee cup to his lips without an accident.

"I'm going to have to ask Tim for his chili recipe when he gets back," the President said, looking up at his wife and smiling, but he could see that her face was serious now.

"We've had another invitation from Konstantine," she said.

Jack nodded, saying nothing.

"He says that his yacht is just anchored unused in Athens. We can have it for as long as we'd like. He could meet us on his island late in August or early September, if we prefer," she said.

"His own island," Jack said, shaking his head. "Maybe he should run against Granderman—at least it would be a fair fight." He looked off at the shoreline. A few early beachcombers were already out, strolling along the sand.

"Jack, I want to go," Suzanne said.

"Yes, I know you do," the President said. "The convention's in August though," he added, but he understood, even as he did, that he wasn't saying anything new to her.

"Konstantine's an opportunist, Suzanne. If he wants us to visit him, it's because he wants something from us, from me," Jack said.

"He's not that kind of man," Suzanne said in return.

"He is precisely that kind of man," her husband answered sharply.

"Jack, I talked to Dr. Abramson again," Suzanne said, looking down at her own coffee cup rather than at her husband as she said the awkward words. "You and I both know that you can't . . ." She stopped then to correct herself before she continued. "That you shouldn't try to push yourself through a long campaign right now. He thinks that it's time for you to go into the hospital and begin the surgery. In fact, he thinks it's a little past time," she said and then stopped again. "I know he's talked to you about it, too, but he wanted me to . . ."

"Convince me," Jack finished his wife's sentence for her.

She nodded. "He thinks you're strong enough now, Jack, and if you begin right away you could be out of the hospital before the convention. And I thought we might be able to go to Europe after that. I think we'll both need some real rest by then."

Jack continued looking out toward the sea. His wife could tell from his face that he was very far away.

Nothing had come along to save him, he thought. The headaches were just as frequent and just as severe as they had been, draining him of strength, but there was still hope. Not even the pain could take that from him. The only difference now was he was out of time. Jack could guess the answer that Tim would return with from Texas. Gardner and the rest of the Party had to have a decision from him as soon as possible. They needed to know if they had a healthy incumbent to lead the ticket in 1964, and, if they didn't, they needed him to publicly step aside and let the party get on with the job of selecting his replacement. Jack was still damned if he knew what his decision was going to be. He only knew that it had to be made now. Well, plenty of people had called him just an actor before, he thought. It was apparently time for another one of his great performances.

"Suzanne," he said finally, coming back to her, "I'm going to ask a few people from the press to come in. I think it's time that I made some kind of public appearance," he said.

"When?" she asked, her voice full of uncertainty.

"In a day or two, I think."

His wife nodded.

"Suzanne, I ah . . ." Jack started, and then he reached out for her hand and took it in his own across the plates and coffee cups on the white linen tabletop.

"Jack, I can't," she said and shook her head. "It's too soon. It's just too soon. It's not fair to any of us."

"Suzanne, I don't know what I'm going to say yet."

"Yes, you do," she said, looking back at him angrily. Then she took a deep breath and summoned all of her courage, finally telling her husband what she'd been wanting to say to him for months. "Jack, whatever you decide, the children and I are going to accept Konstantine's offer. We're going to go to Athens. I've already written and told him."

"But what about the convention?" Jack asked anxiously.

"We'll be here for that, if you want us to be, but then we're going to go on to Greece," she said. "And, Jack, come with us, please."

"Mr. Lopata." He liked that. He liked having a name again, a new name and a new identity—Antonio Lopata.

Maybe it wasn't that smart to use it until after he was finished with his business down here, but he had decided to risk it anyway. He would take care of any problems that came up later. For now he was just going to enjoy his new name.

"We have that package you've been expecting, sir," the postal clerk said, and the dark-skinned man smiled at him. In addition to his new name, he had let a small black mustache grow in a thin straight line above his upper lip and his sideburns now came down far below his ears, curving sharply inward just below his cheekbones until they almost touched the corners of his mouth. He wore the hair on top of his head greased back in a high full pompadour now, too, and the total effect with a pair of metal-framed, dark glasses covering his eyes was striking. Lopez had become a new man—Antonio Lopata of Miami, Florida. And he was thoroughly enjoying his new identity, even if it was only in this dirt-shit Mexican town, but this package should be able to change that part of it now, too, he thought.

The clerk handed him the simple brown paper parcel and Lopata took it, smiling, and walked back into the town square.

He sat at a café table in the uneven cobblestone courtyard, near the sidewalk, under the shade of the overhanging shop roofs, and ordered a beer.

As he waited, his eyes scanned the crowd in the market square warily. It was midmorning and the crowd was sparse and he was able to inspect every one of them carefully as he sat and waited for his drink to arrive.

He knew that this was the time of maximum danger. The package surely wouldn't have been sent from the States without someone being dispatched along with it—someone whose job it would be to see who would come for it. Lopata knew that at least one of the faces that he saw around him now worked for them and would in all probability try to follow him, or perhaps even try to kill him in the next few minutes.

Maybe the prosperous-looking Mexican businessman in the white suit? Or the American tourist with the camera? Or one of the members of the Mexican family eating in the café across the square? But surely someone. He was going to have to be very careful for the next few minutes, but the risk was nothing he couldn't handle, and he felt proud of himself and how well he'd manipulated events so far, and confident that he would be the one to continue setting the rules for the game ahead.

He had considered sending someone else for the package, but there was no one that he could trust, not even the girl he lived with, particularly not the girl. She had been acting strangely lately, he decided, as he thought about the day before when he had returned to his hotel room to find the girl alone with the man Ortiz, who was the only other person that he knew in Tampico. But he didn't trust him either, or anyone else for that matter. Lopata continued looking around suspiciously at the faces near him in the town's central courtyard.

When the beer came he drank it down thirstily before turning his attention to the small brown paper parcel. Finally he opened the package slowly with his thick dark fingers. Inside, under a heavy roll of tissue paper, was a single key. Lopata looked at the key and nodded, still smiling. They were careful men, too. He liked doing business with careful men, even if the cat-and-mouse game that they played might be designed to kill him. At least with careful men, if you played well, you had a chance to win in the end. With sloppy men, too often everyone would lose.

Lopata turned the key over in his hand. It had a number on it—a number Lopata guessed would correspond to a box at the post office that he'd just left.

So he returned across the cobblestone square and reentered the big, old, high-ceilinged government building at the heart of the Mexican city that he lived in now. This time, though, rather than approaching the row of postal clerks behind the small barred windows in the open, high-domed area at the center of the building, he turned down a narrow hall of locked boxes that were mounted on the walls on either side of a long side corridor. Each box had a number painted on it, and he walked along until the number of the key that he held in his hand matched the number stenciled onto the front of one of the boxes. He knew that in all probability he was being watched by someone now but he unlocked the box anyway. Inside was another brown paper parcel. Lopata bent forward slowly and removed the parcel from the box.

As soon as he did, he turned and fled into a door at the end of the hall marked EMPLOYEES ONLY, and within seconds he was in the alley behind the post office building.

Alone in the alley, he could wait no longer. He tore into the small brown paper package, and when the first of the freshly printed green-and-white American bills spilled out of it, his heart leaped for joy. He was back in business! But as he began to finger the crisp new bills, the truth became rapidly apparent to him—paper-only stacks of cut paper with a few sheets of American currency on top. It was a trap! The bait—a brown paper parcel containing only a few hundred dollars of American money. Lopata was enraged by the trick, and he jerked his head up quickly from the worthless bundle of paper in his hands. His eyes scanned the narrow back alley that he stood in.

It was empty except for a single man lying against the wall of one of the shops that backed up against the narrow alley lined with garbage cans. The man's eyes were closed, his arm resting on an overturned trash can, an empty bottle of wine lying next to him. Lopata pretended not to notice him, but as he approached the spot in the alley where the man lay, Lopata quickly removed his long-barreled Smith & Wesson revolver from under his coat and pressed it up against the side of the man's head. He was right, the man was one of them, and in the same instant that he saw the man reach for his own weapon, Lopata squeezed the trigger of his .38, and the man slumped back down into the pile of garbage from the overturned trash can that he had been lying on.

Then Lopata looked up to the mouth of the alley that led back to the square. He knew that any instant now there would be others. He ducked into the back door of one of the shops that opened onto the alley and rammed his body through racks of used dresses that clogged the interior of the store. Then he jumped out of the little shop's front door onto the busy Mexican commercial street in front of it. The street was crowded with people, but down the block he could see a taxi driver lounging across the hood of his cab talking lazily to a thick-waisted Mexican girl.

Lopata's pistol was back inside his coat and he carried the brown paper package cradled under his left arm like a football as he jogged down the street toward the taxi. He withdrew a hundred-peso note from his pocket as he ran and waved it in the air, using it to attract the driver's attention. When he reached the cab, Lopata threw open its back door and jumped inside. Once he was in the taxi's back seat, he looked behind him down the crowded shopping street. The prosperous-looking Mexican businessman in the white suit from the café was just appearing at the far end of the road. He had been running, and he was breathing hard, but he stopped now and his eyes began sweeping up and down the crowded row of shops, searching for Lopata's moving figure.

When he saw the man in the white suit, Lopata laughed to himself. He'd been right about that, too. He turned back to the driver. Lopata knew that he had to risk returning to the hotel, and he gave the driver the address and then glanced behind him just as the cab pulled away from the curb. The man in the white suit was only a few yards away from the taxi now and Lopata looked directly into his face, memorizing it. Lopata smiled at him through the cab's departing rear window as the cab accelerated down the street, and the man's expression revealed clearly that he knew he had been beaten.

The taxi returned Lopata the few short blocks to his hotel. When the cab arrived at the destination, he paid the driver and stepped carefully into the street, his hand reaching again beneath his coat to finger the handle of his revolver.

The hotel lobby was vacant, and he crossed it quickly and chose the elevator instead of the dark staircase to make the ascent to his room. Alone on the rickety metal elevator he thought about the dead man that he'd left behind in the alley and the final look of defeat on the face of the man in the white suit. There was nothing he couldn't handle, he thought then—nothing! They were careful men back in New Orleans, but they'd underestimated him and they had tried to end the business between them too cheaply. They would know now the kind of man he was—a dangerous man and a man who always finished what he started. There would probably be more cat and mouse ahead with them, but he would win in the end. He would finish his job and he would be well paid for doing it, he thought. And he left the elevator smiling, but he still remembered to be careful as he walked slowly down the narrow unlit hall and entered his hotel room.

The woman was there, just as he'd left her, still in her dingy gray nylon slip. She was lying across the bed, her legs spread apart and breathing deeply, her eyes closed, sleeping or faking sleep, he couldn't be sure which.

Lopata crossed the room to the single dresser and opened the top drawer. Inside was the reason that he'd had to risk returning to the hotel, but the small red leather diary that he'd taped to the upper shelf of the dresser was at the wrong angle and his new identity papers were not in the order that he'd left them in their envelope. Someone had disturbed his things during the night.

He looked again at the woman lying on the unmade bad. He remembered now how strangely she and the man Ortiz that she worked for had been acting lately. Slowly he reached under his coat and removed the long-barreled Smith & Wesson from its shiny black leather holster and undid its safety catch. He'd clean up all his unfinished business in this dirty little town now and tomorrow he would be a totally new man. Then he would be free to complete the job that he'd begun, he told himself, as he advanced toward the woman lying in the unmade bed, his cocked gun dangling down at his side, hidden for the moment behind the curve of his leg.

Less than twenty miles away in the Mexican city of Monterey, Sullivan pulled his rented car up in front of the Church of the Guadalupe, near the

Shrine of Miracles and right next to the statue of the Virgin Mary itself. He leaned over and kissed Denise lightly on the cheek and then moved away, waiting for her to get out of the parked car.

Denise smiled forlornly over at him. "You promised, two o'clock," she said, pointing across the small, hot, dusty, Mexican square to the restaurant where they'd agreed to meet for lunch for the second day in a row. Sullivan had broken their first date and after waiting for most of the afternoon Denise had taken a taxi back to the hotel alone. Sullivan had explained to her later that he had gotten caught up running a lead to a little farmhouse outside the city, but like all the others, it, too, had turned to nothing.

Sullivan had been painfully working his way through the long list of airport people he'd been given by the Monterey police. He was looking for any kind of a clue as to what might have happened on the weekend of November 22–24, 1963, the weekend right after the shots had been fired in Dealey Plaza and right before the flight log at the Baton Rouge airport indicated that this man, Regan, had flown his plane into the States from Monterey. In his spare time, Sullivan was busy getting the word out around town that he was interested in talking to anyone who might have some information about what Regan had been doing in Mexico and that he was willing to pay for that information, but so far nothing worth a damn had come out of that either.

They'd been in Monterey for over a week now and most of the time Denise stayed at the hotel by the pool getting her lightly freckled skin brutally sunburned. At night, she and Sullivan usually had dinner together and then made love, with Sullivan having to be very careful of her tender, lobster-red skin. Sometimes Denise would break the routine by going into the city in the afternoon to shop or to see the sights, but always alone.

"I promise, two o'clock," Sullivan said and then reached for Denise's hand. "Look, I know I've been a jerk," he said, looking into her light blue eyes. "But I've got just one last thing I want to check out and then I'll let it alone."

"We've only got another two days," Denise said, shyly looking away from him, down to where the long straight fingers of Sullivan's hand rested on top of hers.

"I promise, starting with lunch, we'll be on a real vacation," he said.

She looked up at him and smiled. "Okay," she said, and she slid out of the rented car.

Sullivan waved at her and then headed east toward the airport. There was a free-lance pilot coming in that morning who might know something. Sullivan had been waiting for days to talk to him, but the man had taken some tourists to the coast for some fishing. Fishing, shit, that's all he was doing, too. He was on a fishing trip to Mexico himself, he thought as he swung the rented car out of the dusty Mexican square and headed it west toward the airport at the outskirts of town.

There were a few tourists on a guided tour already congregated at the base of the shrine in the center of the square, and, as Sullivan drove away, Denise approached them and stood at the back of the crowd and listened to the guide explain the miracles that had occurred on this very spot throughout the centuries of Mexican history. The guide was a young Mexican man and he spoke first in Spanish and then repeated the miracle stories a second time in English for the benefit of the few Americans in the group.

When she was finished listening, Denise walked over to the edge of the shrine and said a short prayer and then waited for a miracle of her own, but nothing happened. So she just sighed deeply and crossed the barren square, already bake-oven hot at midmorning, and walked up the steps and inside the Church of Miracles itself.

She sat in the back looking around at the high arched ceilings and the brightly colored stained-glass windows and enjoying the cool, dark, faintly musty air, when a voice behind her whispered hoarsely in English, "Do not turn around!"

Denise froze, staring straight ahead at the crucifix with the dying Christ figure draped across it at the far end of the church's long center aisle.

"The man you are with wants some information," the voice behind her began again. Whoever was kneeling behind her was close enough that she could feel his hot breath against her sunburned neck and shoulders. "I am in the business of providing such information. He is looking for a man. I know of a woman, a friend of mine shall we say, who is living with such a man not very far from here. I was with them both only yesterday." The voice went on. "At sunset tonight, you come alone with an envelope. In the envelope you are to have one thousand American dollars. That envelope is to be placed on the church pew upon which you are sitting. When I see that this is done and I am certain that you are alone, you will have your information," the voice said and then paused to gather its breath.

Denise stayed frozen, staring ahead through the candlelit interior of the church.

"You are to tell all of this to the man. If he doubts, you give him this." She heard a small envelope drop on the wooden pew next to her.

"Until sunset," the voice said in parting, and then there was silence.

Only after several long seconds did Denise dare twist around to look at the pew behind her, but there was nothing, only the small band of tourists being led down the aisle next to it by the guide and a few veiled praying figures scattered around the darkened pews of the big church.

Denise picked the small envelope up off the pew next to her and held it in her hand. She stood then and forced herself by the pack of slowly moving tourists that filled the aisle. Finally she was able to reach the high double doors at the rear of the church and walk outside, but the big stone steps of the Church of Miracles were empty and the small Mexican square below looked like any other in the hot, dusty, Mexican morning in Monterey.

It was a cool, gentle spring morning in Palm Beach. The breeze from the ocean blew in lightly laced with salt spray and touched the cheeks of the reporters sitting on the rows of folding metal chairs set out under the gracefully swaying branches of the palms and cypress beside the Cassidy home.

The reporters were talking to each other, joking, a flow of bantering questions and predictions floating back and forth among them. Most of them were dressed in brightly colored vacation clothes, but, for all of their casualness, each of them was secretly proud to have been chosen to be present at this historic moment—President Cassidy's first public appearance since Dallas—and the tough, seasoned reporters surprised even themselves when they saw him. They jumped to their feet and began to applaud politely but with great intensity as he emerged from the main house through a rounded wooden arbor that was wrapped that morning in green vines and dotted with fresh yellow and white spring flowers. And they continued applauding as he slowly walked out onto the side lawn where the reporters waited. He smiled at them and raised a hand to wave and then kept it in the air to sweep his hair back from his face and even the reporters' tough, cold, cynical hearts leaped at seeing the familiar boyish gesture again. Most of them told themselves that it was just because he was such "damn good copy," but a few knew that it was more than that. He was tanned and looking healthy. The big bandage they had seen in the photographs was no longer apparent, but the sandy brown hair on the right side of his head was cut much shorter than the rest, and it grew down close to the scalp, and at the front of the close-cut patch of brown hair the reporters could still see a significant wrapping of white gauze.

Jack walked gracefully to the simple little podium with the microphone on it that had been set up beneath the trees in front of the rows of folding metal chairs, and the television camera lights flashed on.

He was followed by his wife, the epitome of springtime in a long, softly flowing pink-and-white flowered dress. She held each of her children's hands in her own, and as they came into view they looked up shyly but with great interest and excitement at the crowd, their little faces openly curious about what all those people and cameras were doing on the side lawn of their home.

Their father stepped to the microphone and grinned out at the small crowd that was still applauding respectfully. He waved again with his free hand, while his other hand stayed buried deep in his coat pocket. He was wearing a soft, light brown cashmere sport coat, a white knit tennis shirt open at the throat, cream-colored slacks, and dark brown deck shoes. All gloomy thoughts about his country or its future melted away as he stood there in front of them. But then, almost as if they suddenly remembered who they were and how tough they were supposed to be, the reporters stopped applauding almost in unison, and all but one of them sat down. Only Dan McGuire of the *Boston Globe*, the senior reporter present, remained on his feet.

"Mr. President," he began, and Cassidy smiled at him from the podium. "I've been asked by all those present this morning," McGuire continued, gesturing at the other reporters, "to welcome you back and . . ." McGuire paused and smiled wryly up at the President. "And to ask you if there's any meaning, sir, in the fact that you've chosen to make your first public appearance in almost five months less than a week after Governor Granderman has won the New Hampshire primary?" It was quickly back to business as usual and the reporters laughed as the President smiled down at them, and then he laughed briefly himself.

"Thank you, Dan," the President began as the laughter gentled and then he timed his answer, releasing the words at the perfect moment just as his audience had grown almost still again. "And the answer to your question is no. There's no meaning whatsoever," he said, and then he laughed at his own answer and the reporters immediately broke back into laughter with him again, this time even more loudly.

"Mr. President!" Nan Fairchild of the *San Francisco Chronicle*, one of the few female reporters present that morning, used the moment to stand and get the President's attention.

"Yes, Nan," the President said, recognizing her.

"Your brother recently returned from a visit to Vice President Gardner's ranch. Was he carrying any messages from you when he met with the Vice President?"

Jack chuckled again before he answered. "No, the Attorney General doesn't need to carry any messages from me. He has plenty to say on his own," he said, and the crowd chuckled softly too, relaxing even more deeply under his spell. It was a pleasant spring morning in Palm Beach.

"Mr. President," another reporter said, and Jack pointed directly down at him with his extended arm and hand.

"Sir, are you in agreement with Vice President Gardner's handling of the administration's policies over the last several months? I'm referring specifically now, sir, to his handling of such sensitive foreign-policy matters as Cuba and Vietnam?" the reporter asked.

The President took a moment before answering this time, his face growing serious and more thoughtful. "Jerry, as you know, the Vice President and I are in daily communication on all matters of vital national interest and he and I are in complete agreement on all areas of current administration policy, and this includes Cuba and Vietnam," he said. The President continued in his clipped New England voice, "I would also like to say at this time, that I, personally, and my family, and I believe the nation and the entire free world as well, owe a tremendous debt of gratitude to the Vice President for the outstanding manner in which he has conducted himself and the affairs of our government over the last several months."

"Does that mean you're endorsing him for the Democratic nomination for President?" someone called out from the crowd, but no one stood to take credit for the question. Cassidy looked around, pretending to try to spot the anonymous questioner, and the reporters laughed again. Smiling, the President responded to the question. "What it means is that I believe, as I have for the last three years, that Mr. Gardner is fully and admirably qualified to serve as President of the United States in my absence, and in my judgment he's proven that beyond any doubt by his conduct over the last several months." Cassidy grinned at the elusiveness of his own answer.

Another reporter stood up then. "Sir, will you seek your party's nomination for reelection?" he said, and the crowd stirred with the directness of the inevitable question, but few if any of the reporters expected the equally direct answer that Cassidy gave them now.

The President paused and looked almost imperceptibly at his wife and children before he began his response.

"No," he said firmly, and the answer seemed to surprise even him. Out of the corner of his eye he could see Suzanne's hand tightening its grip in excitement on their son's hand. "No, I won't," the President said again with even more certainty.

The reporters stirred. They hadn't expected anything like this. The reporter popped back to his feet, ready with his follow-up question.

"Mr. President, are you saying that you are not going to run for reelection this year?" he asked, his voice a little out of breath and his face looking slightly incredulous at the unexpected scoop.

"That's right," the President said flatly. "I've discussed the matter with my family and with my personal physicians and I've arrived at the decision that I will not run for reelection in 1964," he said, still smiling calmly down at the excited buzzing crowd.

"Over the next few months," the President continued, "I will be undergoing a series of rather extensive surgical procedures, and during most of that time I will be confined to the hospital. Further, I have been advised by my doctors that after the completion of these procedures there should be a period of recuperation." He turned to his wife. "My wife and I are considering a trip to Europe at that time." He paused before completing what he had to say. "In my judgment, these considerations preclude my ability to run for reelection to the presidency at this time."

"Is there any danger connected with . . ." a reporter began.

"No, there is not," the President answered crisply before the reporter could finish his question.

"Sir, does that mean you will resign?" a voice called out, followed by a barrage of other questions loudly springing from the crowd of reporters, but the man at the podium only smiled and lifted his hand to the noisy crowd, managing to almost totally silence it with the simple gesture.

"I have absolutely no intention of resigning my office," he said flatly. "Three years ago I took an oath to conduct the affairs of the nation to the best of my ability. I intend to continue to uphold that oath until January of next year. And I believe that the decision I have announced to you this morning, to withdraw my name for consideration as my party's nominee for President in 1964, is entirely consistent with that oath."

"Will Vice President Gardner remain the Acting President during this period?" another reporter called out.

"Yes, of course. The Vice President and I will continue to consult together on all major matters whenever possible, but the Vice President will continue to exercise all the powers and duties of Acting President throughout the period of my hospitalization, and he will continue to do so until such time as my health permits me to fully resume my duties. And he will, of course, continue to have my full and complete trust and support throughout that period," the President said. "That's all for now," he added crisply, and then with his wife and children following closely behind him, he returned down the side lawn and through the freshly painted white wooden arbor, bright with springtime flowers, that led back to the interior of his Palm Beach house. Disappearing from sight he left the small group of reporters and television cameras with the biggest news of that already crowded and exciting political year.

As soon as they had ducked through the privacy of the little wooden archway, Jack exhaled deeply, releasing an enormous load of tension. He could feel the familiar throbbing pain already beginning in his head and he knew that soon it would probably spread down his spine to his back and legs, but he'd done it, he told himself, remembering the reporters' approving faces. He'd given them one hell of a performance, not the role that he would have preferred to play, but one that reality had forced upon him. The President turned to his wife then. "That's the easy part." He smiled. "Now someone's got to tell Dad."

CHAPTER
13

Denise could see Sullivan's tall, broad-shouldered figure coming toward her from a long way off. His big blond head towered over the smaller dark-haired men and women on the busy Mexican street and when she saw him she almost cried out.

She had waited through the morning for him, all alone at a café table across the street from the Church of Miracles, and she had grown more and more frightened with every passing moment that he was going to stand her up again, but there he was smiling and relaxed, ambling slowly along, looking in shop windows, his suit coat off and thrown over his shoulder, his tie loosened. He looked ready for what remained of his vacation.

Denise stood when she saw him and left the restaurant table. She ran out the door and down the street, threading her way through the crowd on the narrow sidewalk, and when she finally reached him she threw her arms around his shoulders and held herself close to him. Sullivan held her back tightly, laughing down at her and touching the dropping curls of her reddish-blond hair gently, as he felt her warm soft body pressing up against his.

"What is it?" he asked as she clung to him.

Finally feeling a little more composed, Denise backed off and looked up at his face, but she still couldn't bring herself to say anything.

"I promise, we'll have a vacation, starting now," he said, not understanding.

She looked up then and shook her head back and forth at him to let him know that wasn't it, but she was still too out of breath to say anything. She reached into her purse instead and handed him the small brown envelope that she had been carrying. Sullivan took it, puzzled, and without opening it he led Denise back toward the restaurant. They walked inside with their arms around each other and then Sullivan helped her into the little hard-backed wooden chair that she had waited in for most of the morning.

"Open it," Denise said finally, pointing at the envelope, and Sullivan tore into it with his big hands.

"What is it? A present?" Sullivan began as he pulled the envelope apart.

"A man . . ." Denise began and then stopped and thought about the voice she'd heard for a moment before she started again. "I guess a man, anyway, somebody gave it to me this morning. They said if you wanted the information that you'd come here for, you were . . . I mean I'm supposed to bring a thousand dollars to the church tonight," she explained in a series of quick breaths and then gestured out the restaurant window at the Church of Miracles across the street. "Jim?" she said then. "I don't know if I . . . I mean, does this sort of thing happen a lot?"

But Sullivan was too busy staring down at the contents of the envelope to answer her. In his hands were several low-quality, hastily executed photocopies of some handwritten material. Sullivan shuffled through the pages quickly the first time and then went back through them again and slowly examined each page. He read and then reread several lines on each sheet before he finally looked back up at Denise's frightened face.

"I don't understand," he said.

"He, or it, or whatever it was, said that this would convince you that you would be getting your money's worth," she said and then she looked up suddenly, startled by the dark-skinned man standing above their table.

It was their waiter. Sullivan reached out and touched her hand, settling her down. They ordered quickly and then Sullivan made her go over her story again.

"What are they?" Denise asked when she was finished and pointed at the sheets of paper that were still tightly clutched in Sullivan's hand. But Sullivan only shook his head several times. "No, I've put you too deep into this already," he said.

Soon the waiter set down two big platefuls of Mexican food and a pair of fresh cold beers. Sullivan looked at the food for a second and then reached for the beer instead. He took a long, slow, thoughtful drink from the ice-cold bottle before picking up the sheaf of photocopied papers again and examining them even more closely for several minutes. Jesus, they really looked like they could be authentic. Maybe it was even worth a grand to find out. If he had a grand, he thought, and he reached into his back pocket and removed his wallet. He counted out its contents. It wasn't half of what he needed.

"Doesn't the Bureau?" Denise said, pointing at the money.

"There isn't time to get it authorized," Sullivan said, glancing at his watch. And then, thinking of some of the things his section chief had said to him lately, he added, "Besides, I'm not so sure they'd go for it right now. But if it does turn into something, I probably could get it back from them later on. I think it might be worth the risk," he said, looking down at the photocopies again.

"It's got something to do with the man who shot Cassidy, doesn't it?" Denise said, her light blue eyes a little calmer now.

Sullivan nodded.

Without hesitating, Denise bent down for her purse and placed it on the table in front of her and removed three tightly folded one-hundred-dollar bills from a small, secret side compartment and held them across the table toward Sullivan. Sullivan looked at the money for a moment and then without saying anything reached out his hand and took it.

"I'll pay you back," he said finally, feeling embarrassed, but looking directly into Denise's eyes to let her know that he was serious.

"You're damn right you will," Denise said and smiled back at him.

"It's still not enough, but maybe he'll go for it," Sullivan said, looking down at the money again.

"One condition," Denise said.

Sullivan looked back up at her sunburned face.

"I've got to know what was in the envelope," she said.

Sullivan hesitated for a moment, getting ready to tell her that it was against Bureau policy, which was the truth, but then he decided, screw Bureau policy, she was entitled.

"I'm not sure," he said. "But I think they're copies of pages out of Arthur Strode's diary, written in Dallas, maybe two or three days before he shot Cassidy."

"Oh, shit!" Denise said, the words just slipping out of her mouth. "I don't think I really wanted to know that."

Sullivan just shrugged his shoulders then and smiled at her. "It's too late now," he said.

The lights of the Capitol were coming on and Gardner could see them clearly from where he sat in his office at the White House. The Vice President had his feet up on his desk, the heels of his cowboy boots resting on the edge of a long manila file that was stamped TOP SECRET and CONFIDENTIAL in so many places that its once cream-colored surface had been turned into an almost solid, black-and-red plaid design. Gardner was drinking sour-mash bourbon out of a tall glass and looking out the window at the lights of Washington. With him were both Mallory and Ted Mazeloff.

"I surely do love it here," Gardner said, his eyes still directed out the window. "Yes, sir, I surely do," he said and then finally swung his head around to look directly at his two assistants.

"So, do you believe him?" Mallory said. This was the first time that the two men had been given a chance to discuss the announcement that Cassidy had made earlier in the day.

"I called him and set up a meeting. I don't think I'll believe it until I hear it from his own lips." The Vice President paused, thinking carefully about what he'd just said. "I probably won't believe him even then," he added a moment later. "Cassidys are born wanting to run for office, the way beavers are born wanting to build dams. So I guess I'm not really goin' believe it until I'm sittin' in Atlantic City and I see that gavel come down on a final roll-call vote without the name Cassidy on it. But I'll tell you this—I'm not so sure if it really matters all that much what I believe right now. He's given us an opening and we've jus' got to get to work now puttin' that convention together. We got to pack it so goddamned tight with our friends that Cassidy won't be able to get within twenty miles of it, without it squeezin' him."

"It might already be too late to do that," Mazeloff said. "Almost half the delegates have already been selected."

Gardner nodded. "We've got a little time though. We'll get it done, good enough," he said and then turned back to the window, letting his thoughts float out over the few short months that separated him now from the nomination that he had worked for all his life. "Cassidy's going to be in and out of the hospital between now and the convention. They've got to rebuild that entire area," Gardner said, touching the spot at the side of his own head where the bullet had shattered Cassidy's skull. "He tells me that he's not in any danger and I believe that, but he sure as hell's not goin' be in any position to be out hustlin' up delegates either," Gardner said. "And then, when that's done, he's supposed to rest for a good long time. So, the way he's talkin' now, it looks like we won't be able to count on him during the campaign either."

"That may be just as well," Mallory said.

Gardner nodded as he listened respectfully to the younger man.

"It seems to me that you're going to have to be very careful how you handle Cassidy now though," Mallory said.

"I know. He's put me in one hell of a tough spot, hasn't he?" Gardner said.

"Yes, in some ways, he has," Mallory went on thoughtfully. "By withdrawing from the race, but not resigning his office, he's left you in a very difficult position. You're going to have to mount a national campaign over the next few months and it's important that you look like your own man while you're doing it, but at the same time you're obligated to continue to follow and execute Cassidy's policies, some of which are going nowhere. That's going to be a very difficult line to walk."

"Well that's one of the things he and I have to talk about," Gardner said. "I need his support, but mebbe it would be best if I got it from a distance. I'm thinkin' now that it might be a good idea if he and Mrs. Cassidy did go along to Europe or somewhere, like they're plannin' right after the convention."

"You can't forget about him altogether. He's too popular a man," Mallory said, even though he knew that it wasn't exactly what his boss wanted to hear at that moment.

"I know," Gardner said then. "What I really need is some kind of public gesture from him first. He's gotta' let everyone know that the Party's truly united."

"Well, it seems to me that the best thing for us would be for him to make your nominating speech at the convention," Mazeloff said.

"Mebbe so," Gardner said slowly, thinking about it. "Trouble is, he's goin' have somethin' to say about that. Right now he won't even commit himself to attending the convention at all, much less makin' any speeches for anyone. He says there's no guarantee his doctors will let him." Gardner chuckled then. "'Course he's got a way of doin' what he wants to do, when he wants to do it."

"The trick is, then, to give him something that he wants enough that he's certain to be there and on our side," Mazeloff said.

Gardner smiled again. "I expect you're right, but if he wants what I think he does, I'm not so sure that I want to give it to him."

"His brother on the ticket with you, you mean?" Mallory said then and Gardner nodded at him.

"That's a damn high price," Gardner said. "Could do me more harm than good."

"There are advantages as well," Mallory said. "But one thing's certain, what you need as much as anything else right now is some room on policy. You've got to begin building your own record."

"You're right, but that's goin' to be tricky, too," Gardner said. "After all, he's still the President. He's made that very clear."

"I know, sir," Mallory said. "But Cassidy can't expect to be able to put the entire world on hold, just because at the moment he's not in a position to run things himself."

Gardner smiled then, slow and southern. "Don't ever underestimate what Cassidy expects," he drawled. "His daddy taught him to expect one hell of a lot." Gardner paused before adding in a slow and strangely sad voice. "'Course, he gets it most of the time, too."

The three men were quiet then, thinking of the enormity of the job ahead of them.

"Damn, he should resign," Mazeloff said finally.

"Well, he's not about to do that," Gardner said. "We've jus' got to work with what we've got." Suddenly the Vice President jumped to his feet, smiling broadly. "And that's plenty!" he said. And then, picking up the bourbon bottle from his desk, he started for the door. Startled and more than a little puzzled, his aides trailed hurriedly after him.

The three men walked silently in their shirtsleeves down the White House halls toward the Oval Office. They carried their glasses of bourbon with them and the Vice President let the big quart bottle of sour mash dangle down by his leg as he walked along the formal flag-draped passageway. They passed unchallenged by the Marine guards and Secret Service men into the President's unlit executive office.

Gardner crossed to the desk that stood empty near the center of the darkened room. He set the bottle down on the desktop and motioned with his half-empty glass for his aides to sit in the chairs that were arranged in front of the President's desk. Then he walked over and sat down in the President's chair. Behind him Mallory could see only a thin wedge of the twinkling lights from the capital's night skyline.

"You know, I'm not so sure that the view isn't a little better from your own office," Mallory said, smiling.

Gardner sat in the President's chair facing out into the room, looking at the two shirtsleeved men seated in front of him. "I don't know what it looks like from over there," he said. "But the view sure is one hell of a lot better from where I'm sittin'."

Sullivan and Denise sat at the café across the street from the Church of Miracles and watched the members of the late afternoon tour take pictures of each other standing in front of the shrine in the middle of the square, and then take pictures of each other in front of the church, and after awhile begin to filter back and take a last few shots of each other standing in front of their big green-and-white tour bus. It was almost sunset.

Sullivan went over his instructions with Denise one last time then. She was scared, but she was determined to go through with it anyway.

Sullivan hated not using the police, particularly with the girl involved, but he just didn't know who to trust in a town like Monterey and he didn't want to take the chance of one of the local cops making a clumsy move and spooking the contact.

At sunset, as the last stragglers were loading on to the bus, Denise crossed the square and returned to the darkened interior of the church. It was empty except for a small funeral in progress near the altar.

She walked to the same pew that she'd been in that morning and dropped the envelope onto its wooden surface just as she had been told. Then she knelt down and began to pray. Denise prayed for a long time and her prayers were very real. Suddenly, she heard the hoarse voice behind her again.

"There's only seven hundred dollars in here," the voice hissed angrily at the back of Denise's neck.

"That's all we had."

"Shit," the strange breathy voice hissed again and then paused. Denise knelt frozen in fear, waiting anxiously to find out what would happen next.

At the front of the church the funeral was ending and the small wooden casket at its center was starting up the aisle, followed by a short procession of weeping mourners, the men sad and uncomfortable in ill-fitting dark suits, the women hidden in somber black dresses and shadowy veils.

Denise could feel the presence behind her still trying to make up its mind what to do, but as soon as she heard something drop on the surface of the wooden pew next to her, she turned toward it in a flash. Behind her in the darkened church knelt a large figure dressed all in black. Its big body was covered by a dark, shapeless dress of mourning and over its face was a black lace veil, but behind the veil Denise could make out the rough heavy features of a man, and she gasped in horror.

The kneeling figure stood up fast then and moved to the center aisle, but its way was blocked by the passing coffin. Denise screamed just as Sullivan appeared out of the shadows at the far side of the church. The fleeing black-draped figure saw him in that same instant and it rammed its bulky frame out into the aisle, knocking into the procession of passing mourners who were bearing the funeral casket down the center aisle, and with the impact the casket slipped from their grasp and fell to the floor. The body of a young Mexican girl dressed all in virginal white spilled out of the overturned casket and on to the cold gray stone floor of the church. Some of the mourners trailing behind the casket screamed as the fleeing black-shrouded figure leaped over the fallen body of the young girl and started up the center aisle toward the high metal doors at the very back of the church.

Sullivan moved down a long row of pews and then started up the aisle after the running figure, but halfway up the crowded middle aisle his way became blocked by the chaos of mourners and the overturned casket and the fallen body it had once contained. So Sullivan ducked down a side row and then jumped on top of the high wooden back of the pew behind it.

He leaped from the top of one pew to the next until he landed at the rear of the church, but by then the strange figure of the man in the black veil and long black dress had disappeared.

Sullivan ran down the church's front steps and into the square below just in time to catch the exhaust of the tourist bus that was pulling away from the front of the church. He stood for a moment by the Shrine of Our Lady of Guadalupe and looked around at the network of twisting Mexican streets that fanned out away from the square. The neon lights of the local bars and nightclubs had just flashed on and the downtown streets were only beginning to fill with their nighttime traffic, but there was no hint of the dark figure anywhere.

Sullivan turned back to the church. Denise was coming down the steps toward him. Behind her, Sullivan could hear the sad confused wailing of the funeral party coming from the depths of the big stone church. Denise had an envelope in her hand, and she held it out toward Sullivan as she approached him.

"He dropped this before he ran away," she said.

Sullivan tore the envelope open. Inside was a handwritten note. On it was written only: "Room 409, Mirador Hotel, Tampico, Mexico."

The *Trewlaney Rose* pulled neatly away from the harbor and out into the Atlantic waters. The cameramen left on the dock caught their last flashes of white-water wake and receding polished oak bow. There were no reporters permitted on board, only the President and the Vice President and a small staff.

It was a clear, cool Florida morning and the skipper took the big yacht far out to sea to a place where the two men seated in the big swivel chairs in the stern could no longer see the Florida shore and their view became miles and miles of blue-gray sea water.

Lunch was served early, at a small table on deck, and after they'd eaten, the President lit a long, thick, black cigar, smoking it casually and letting the smoke curl up near his face and then blow out to sea.

"When do you go into the hospital?" the Vice President asked.

"Next week," the President said and drew in deeply on the expensive cigar, as if Gardner's words had been a reminder of the pleasures that he would soon have to forego.

"Well, I want you healthy for the convention," Gardner said.

Cassidy nodded a thank you and went back to puffing on his cigar, revealing nothing of his plans.

A steward appeared at the doors that led below deck. He had a big silver coffee pot in his hands. Cassidy nodded for him to refill both his and Gardner's nearly empty cups. The steward poured each cup less than half full in respect for the movement of the sea, and then he returned to the galley below deck, leaving the President and Vice President alone again.

"I envy you," Gardner said, looking out at the ocean. "A few months of rest," he said, glancing at Cassidy out of the corner of his eye to see if he was getting away with it.

He wasn't. Cassidy was looking at him and smiling, his handsome Irish patrician face lit up with a big broad grin. "Rance, I have a feeling that at this moment you don't envy anyone else in the entire world," he said.

"No, I expect you're right," Gardner said. "I wasn't made for this," he said, his big gnarled hand sweeping around at the expensive yacht and at the sunny Florida morning that was sparkling a few feet away. "I was made for smoke-filled conferences and dark Senate cloak rooms," Gardner said, smiling broadly himself now.

"And the White House," Cassidy said.

Gardner grew very serious then, and he turned his gaze slowly to meet Cassidy's. "Looks that way, don't it," he said.

Cassidy nodded at him and then the President took another long, slow drag on his thin black cigar. "Yes, it does."

"I'm assumin' that I kin count on your help," Gardner said, watching Cassidy's face and trying to gauge how far he could push him. Judging that it might not be very far, Gardner quickly added, "Funny how things work out sometimes, isn't it?"

Cassidy didn't respond for a moment. The ship pitched slightly to starboard in the silence and both men reached out to steady their coffee cups.

"I mean between you and me," Gardner said, after the sea's slight interruption. "We've done our share of fightin'. I'm not always sure just what about, but when push has come right down to shove, we've seemed to always realize that deep down we've got more in common than we really got against each other," Gardner said, and Cassidy nodded in agreement but said nothing for a moment. Finally, Cassidy decided it would be better not to make the older man ask the question that had been on both of their minds all morning, and so he told Gardner his decision without being asked. "Rance, I'm not going to make a public endorsement right now," Cassidy said, puffing on his cigar again.

It was Gardner's turn to nod his head and stay quiet. A few seabirds flapped by as the two men sat silently and watched. Finally Gardner was unable to contain himself any longer. "That could look damn bad," he said, barely disguising his anger.

"I'll make certain that it doesn't," Cassidy said. "I'm not going to be holding any press conferences where I'm going, anyway. So, it won't be awkward, but I just think it's too early. My judgment is that it's important that you have some time on your own first, that's all. There will probably be a better time for both of us down the road."

Gardner looked at him and waited for the rest of it. He knew there had to be more.

"During the next couple of months, my life is going to be pretty much just hospital beds, and doctors, and quiet naps," the President said, trying to make light of what he knew was going to be a painful and debilitating process. "For all practical purposes you'll be running the country, Rance, and during that time I believe you should be able to pull the Party and the country together under your own leadership. I'm confident that you can do it, and once you do, an endorsement from me will have a lot more impact. But until then," Cassidy went on, "well, I know how you must feel about me. And I know it'll be one hell of a lot easier for you if you're out from under my shadow for a while. And I think a political endorsement from me right now might just hurt you more than it would help."

"Sort of like a testing period," the Vice President said, not altogether pleased and letting some of his displeasure show as he spoke.

Cassidy remained silent. He knew that Gardner wasn't going to like his decision, but that wasn't going to change it. He wanted to keep as many of his options open as he could for now, and giving a public endorsement to Gardner without receiving something significant in return was against all of his political instincts.

"Well, if it is, it's a test I intend to pass," Gardner said.

"I'm sure you will, and we'll talk again soon," Cassidy said. "In the meantime there's one thing I'd like you to consider as well," Cassidy added slowly and turned back toward the older man. "I'd like you to consider the Attorney General as your running mate."

Gardner sat back deep in his deck chair then and thought about his answer carefully before he responded. The request was hardly a surprise, but thinking about it in advance hadn't lessened any of his own feeling about the inappropriateness of selecting the President's brother as his running mate. "He's a very young man," Gardner said, not letting his true feelings show entirely.

"He'll help you beat Granderman," Cassidy said.

"Mebbe," Gardner said. "Mebbe he will or mebbe it'll jus' be sayin' to folks that you were jus' tellin' me that I had to be careful of—that mebbe I can't run this country by myself without a Cassidy around to tell me how to do it."

"He won't be telling you what to do, Rance. You'll be the President," Cassidy said, leveling his steady gaze directly on Gardner's face as he answered him.

"Mebbe he's not the Cassidy people'll be talkin' about," Gardner drawled the words out slowly, Texas-style, giving himself more time to think.

"He'll help you, where you're going to need help. In a race against Granderman you're going to have some trouble in the East and in New England. I'm sure your polls must be showing you that. Tim would give your ticket the kind of geographic balance that you're going to need to win," Cassidy said.

"And the Attorney General's a Catholic," Gardner said, smiling and letting Cassidy know that he'd thought about it, too.

"And Tim's a good Catholic," the President agreed, smiling back.

"There are differences between us," Gardner said.

"Personal or policy?" Cassidy said.

"Policy," Gardner said, waving his hand to show his disregard of personal differences when he was talking about this kind of politics and power.

"Tell me what's bothering you. I'll speak to him," the President said.

"Well, mostly, it's this commission to second guess the FBI report on Dallas that he keeps stirrin' the press up about. Makes people think that mebbe things are out of control. It could make some real trouble if he keeps talkin' about it," Gardner said.

Cassidy nodded, letting the Vice President know that as far as he was concerned that part would be easy.

Gardner nodded back. "Good," he said and then paused. "Well, a Gardner-Cassidy ticket. It's certainly somethin' I'll have to think about. Let me talk to a few people and we'll see. I don't think I'll be makin' any final decisions, though, until convention time. Wouldn't be smart," Gardner added, underlining the word "convention" for the President's benefit and leaving little doubt between them what he wanted in exchange from Cassidy.

"And I'll talk to Tim," Jack said and then smiled, letting Gardner know that neither man was fooling the other about what he wanted now and what the price would be.

"We'll just see where it goes," Gardner said.

"Anything else?"

"Yes," Gardner answered, and Cassidy took a long slow sip of his coffee and listened.

"I need some room," the Vice President said, shifting his large body uneasily in his chair to demonstrate what he meant. "Between now and the election I can't have my hands tied on every last policy matter. I've got to be able to run on my own record, not yours."

Cassidy still said nothing, choosing first to hear all of what the Vice President had to say.

"Now, the way I see it, the only issue the Republicans have right now that could do us any real harm is located about five thousand miles away in Southeast Asia," the Vice President went on. "I need some room on that. I need some room in settlin' that down in my own way. I'm the one who's goin' to be takin' the heat on what happens out there now, and it seems to me that gives me the right to start callin' some of the shots," he said and then paused for Cassidy's reaction.

"No," Jack said sharply. "If you mean the Joint Chiefs' plan. The answer is no."

Gardner's face remained stoic, but inside he was beginning to seethe. "You've read the proposal?" he asked finally.

"Yes, I have," Cassidy said. "And the answer is not at this time," he said evenly.

"Sir, we've got to back President Giai or it's all goin' to go to hell out there. We've got to give him all the support he needs," Gardner said.

"I understand that, and we will," Cassidy said. "Financial aid, logistical support, but not an increased military presence."

"The Joint Chiefs' plan would put some real military pressure on North Vietnam for the very first time," Gardner said. "I thought that was somethin' that we both agreed had to get done."

"Not this way."

"The personnel the plan calls for is strictly South Vietnamese," Gardner said.

"Rance, it calls for our planes to fly reconnaissance missions in the north, our ships to sail within what could be construed and probably legally should be construed as North Vietnamese territorial waters. That is simply not acceptable."

"We do that now."

"Yes, I know, but not in direct support of South Vietnamese commando raids. All it would take is for one American plane to be shot down over North Vietnamese territory or one naval patrol boat to be lost as part of a joint South Vietnamese and American offensive into the north and we could be drawn into a full-scale war, a war that we're not really prepared to fight, and . . ."

"We've considered that possibility," the Vice President said, not letting Cassidy finish. "The Joint Chiefs assure me that, if the plan were fully implemented, we would then have sufficient American air power available to us in the area that we could immediately begin conducting a series of surgical retaliatory air strikes against whatever targets were responsible for . . ."

"And what if they're wrong?" Cassidy asked. Then he repeated in a softer voice, "What if they're wrong, Rance? God knows they've been wrong about this kind of thing before. We can't be drawn into this war any deeper than we already have been through a miscalculation."

"Unless we intend to win it," Gardner said flatly.

Cassidy's face showed clearly the anger he felt now, but the Vice President continued anyway. It was too important an issue to let it be lost without a fight. His own election could hinge directly on the decision, and he wasn't going to back down now.

"And there's the other part of it," Gardner said then. "If there were an incident of some kind, it would give us what we really need. We could go to Congress and finally get a War Powers resolution. You and I both know that a bipartisan congressional resolution supporting our actions in the area would remove the issue from the fall campaign entirely."

Both men knew that they were at the previously unspoken heart of the problem now—the need for Congress to authorize the administration's actions in Vietnam, actions that were beginning to look more and more every day like an undeclared and illegal war.

"If that's the only way we can get Congress's support," the President said, "then maybe we shouldn't have it. Rance, look, on purely political grounds I don't think you're going to want your hands tied on this going into November, anyway. In all likelihood the Republicans are going to attack you by taking the position that our policies are leading the country into an unwinnable war in Southeast Asia. I don't see how you can afford a miscalculation and a widening American involvement in the area against a campaign like that, and the Joint Chiefs' plan has just too much potential for a miscalculation."

"Sir, I'm willin' to take that risk. I know you haven't had much time, but I've studied the plan thoroughly and I believe it's sound," Gardner said.

Cassidy let his anger loose then. "It's not your risk to take," he reminded Gardner sharply. "I've studied it as well, and my judgment is no," he said.

The Vice President nodded to show that he understood.

"Good," Cassidy said to Gardner's acquiescence. "I'm glad we understand each other." The President stood up then and walked to the rail of the ship.

"Rance, I know how difficult it must be for you," he said as he walked away from the Vice President. "I know that you're in a position where you're being forced to carry out policies that you may not be in total agreement with. You must feel sometimes that you're having to take the rap for my mistakes, but the way it looks now, you'll have your chance," he said, and then the President turned out toward the sea and flipped what was left of his cigar overboard and watched it flow away from the side of the boat, swallowed up in its wake. "You'll have your chance," he said again as he watched the cigar butt float away in the tide.

"It's not fair," Denise said, but her heart wasn't in it. Sullivan could tell how she really felt by the way she'd said it and by the way that she clutched her flight bag tightly to her chest with both arms. Whatever it was that was waiting inside Room 409 at the Mirador Hotel in Tampico, she didn't need to know about it firsthand.

Sullivan had booked her on a flight back to Dallas, and they were waiting for it at the Monterey airport. They could feel the time between them running down quickly and Sullivan suddenly realized just how much he'd left unsaid over the last several days.

"If this lead doesn't work out, I'm going to ask for a transfer back to Dallas," Sullivan blurted out quickly. "God knows if I'll get it, but at least I'm going to try. There are one hell of a lot of questions that still need to be answered back there," he added.

"You're really committed to this thing with Cassidy, aren't you?" Denise said.

"It's not Cassidy. It's just . . ." Sullivan started, but then he couldn't find the words. "You know," he began again after a few seconds, "I didn't even vote for the guy." Sullivan paused then. "I didn't even vote." He smiled after he thought about it some more. "And if I had, I probably would have voted for Simmons, anyway. It's just that . . ." And then he couldn't find the words again, so he just shrugged his shoulders and gave up, his face showing all too clearly the confusion that he felt.

"Whatever happens, I want to see you again," Denise said and then jerked her head up quickly as she heard her flight being called.

Sullivan finally asked the question that he'd been wanting to ask her for the last ten days. "Kit said you're seeing somebody. Is it serious?"

"Serious? Nothing about my life is too serious," Denise said, laughing softly at herself.

Sullivan walked her to the gate. Outside the plate-glass window behind them a big, gray-bodied DC-6 was warming up, spinning its long powerful propellers, ready to fly Denise out of Mexico and back to Dallas.

"My lock bag okay?" Sullivan said, trying to sound casual, but it didn't fool either of them.

"I haven't opened it," she said, "if that's what you're asking, but I think I can guess now what's in it. I read the newspapers, too, sometimes, you know."

"Even if the Bureau doesn't give me the transfer, or whatever happens, I'm going to come visit you," Sullivan said. "I want to get my bag back," he added, before she could think that he meant anything more.

"Well, I'll see you then?" she said, shyly.

"Uh-uh," was all Sullivan could manage, but as Denise started away from him he ran after her and caught her. He held her tight then and kissed her with a power that surprised them both. Sullivan thought about that kiss on his short flight across the mountains to Tampico almost as much as he thought about what he was going to find in Room 409 of the Mirador Hotel.

Sailing together reminded them both of when they had been boys together, happy, alone, out past the breakers, running their skills against the wind and the sea. And as they let the small craft skim silently over the surface of the water, there seemed to be only water and sky and air and it made their bodies feel fresh and alive, flowing with life.

Jack had meant to bring up his conversation with Gardner as soon as they were under way, but it didn't seem right somehow. It was better to watch Tim's tense, lined face begin to smooth out and his narrow, overburdened shoulders begin to relax.

It wasn't until they were within sight of the coast again and they both could see the familiar outline of the Cassidy estate on the rising piece of land on the Hyannis shore that either of them mentioned anything even remotely connected to government or politics. It was Tim who broke the silence. "Jack, I'd like to talk to you about something before we go back in," the younger brother said, and Jack nodded.

Tim brought the small sailboat about and began sailing it down the coast away from the big wooden dock built on the Atlantic shore just below their home. It was almost sunset and the wind was beginning to pick up and it was becoming difficult to maneuver the small craft, but with Jack's help Tim managed to swing the sailboat to the north up the coast, running against the wind.

"You know that I'm worried about the investigation," Tim began, after he settled back into his position forward of Jack.

Jack waved his hand at his younger brother. This wasn't the way he wanted to deal with this subject right now, not after what he and Gardner had discussed.

"No, Jack," Tim said stubbornly. "I want to talk about it."

Tim paused for a moment, collecting his thoughts. The air was growing rapidly cooler and Jack reached up and turned the collar of his dark blue nylon windbreaker up to block the wind as he waited for his brother to continue.

"Rance is dragging his feet on appointing any kind of commission at all, and the few names that he has floated for it, they're . . ." Tim couldn't find the right words. "They're not investigators. They're politicians," he said. "I think it's pretty obvious that he's not interested in finding out the truth. He's just interested in it not becoming a political issue for him in November, but the press isn't going to let it go that easily, Jack. Strode is just too damn hard to buy as a lone assassin. There's too much that just doesn't add up, too many loose ends that point to some kind of conspiracy."

"Is it the press you're really worried about, Tim?" the President asked after his brother had finished.

Tim shook his head no and then reached up to unsnag a line that had begun to loop up in the growing wind and tangle with a piece of the mainsail.

"We should head in," Jack said, looking out at the whitecaps beginning to bounce higher around the sides of their small boat.

"In a minute," Tim said, but he kept the tiller steady, driving the little craft even farther down the coast away from Hyannis, right into the teeth of the wind.

"Jack, I'd like your help on this. You have the power to simply cut through all of Rance's stalling and just appoint the commission yourself, and I think that's exactly what you should do," Tim said.

"You didn't tell me what it is you're worried about," Jack said.

Tim didn't say anything for several seconds, but it was apparent that his brother wasn't going to let him off the hook that easily.

"Jack, I'm concerned about your safety," he said, turning his head back and looking directly into his older brother's eyes.

The wind was in full force now, catching the President's long brown hair and throwing it straight back, exposing the bandage that decorated the side of his head just past the hairline.

"Tim, there's a great deal going on right now," the President began, trying to find the right words himself, and as he did the wind began whipping even more furiously against the sides of the small boat.

"Turn this damn thing around," Jack said, suddenly, laughing at the fierceness of the wind. "We'll get blown up to Maine. Then where would we be? Neither of us could get elected County Clerk up there," he said, and Tim began working at making the boat come about, and then Jack joined in, the two men using the skills that they had practiced together since they were children to head the craft back toward the Hyannis shore.

Breathing heavily, Jack smiled at his brother when they had finished. "How do you feel?" Tim said, returning Jack's smile, his eyes though, showing more than a touch of concern for his brother's health.

Jack nodded that he was fine, but he settled back into his place in the bow of the boat, his breathing still deeply labored, while Tim stayed at the tiller and began working the craft against the swelling sea, back toward the Cassidy estate that they could both see again clearly now in the distance.

"Tim, we just can't afford to have any kind of major split in policy between Rance and ourselves right now, particularly on an issue as emotional as Dallas," Jack said a few moments later.

Tim's dark blue eyes flashed as he looked across the deck of the small boat at his brother. "Jack, for God's sake, I'm talking about your safety. I don't give a damn about the politics of it."

"Well, I do," Jack said weakly. "I've asked Rance to consider you as his Vice President," he said abruptly then, with a lot less skill and tact than he had planned to use.

"No," Tim answered flatly.

"Tim, this is something that we can accomplish right now. Rance needs us. And, in my judgment, it's something that we have to do," Jack said. "The chance may not come again."

Tim was quiet for a second. Then he began shaking his head in the wind-filled air. "Jack, if you're saying that I have to keep quiet about something that I feel this strongly about in order to become Vice President, something that risks your safety, then the price is just too high."

"Timmy, there's always a price," Jack said. "We both should know that by now. It's something that the world seems to demand for the things that are really worth having. And Tim, if you're truly worried that something might happen to me, it just makes that nomination even more important to both of us, doesn't it?" Jack said. He looked directly into his brother's eyes for a moment to let him know that he understood his fears.

"You've thought about it then, too?" Tim said. "The possibility that there still might be someone out there, I mean?"

"Sure," Jack said. "And no matter what happens, I want to be certain that the work we've set for ourselves to serve our country can continue. That's why it's important to me that you do it, Tim. Do you understand what I'm saying?"

Tim paused before answering. "Yes, I do."

"I'm betting that if there is somebody out there, he can't get us both," Jack said calmly, and then he smiled at his brother.

"There's more of us than there is of trouble, right?" Tim answered, smiling back and using an old family saying to let Jack know that he understood.

The two men were quiet then. They sailed the small boat toward the land, the sea beginning to rise dangerously high around them as they returned to the dock built at the water's edge below the big house on the hill overlooking the wind-swept Atlantic.

Sullivan decided to use the local police in Tampico. They sure as hell couldn't do much worse than he'd done by himself in Monterey, he thought.

After he landed he went straight to the central police station and when he told the local commandant that he was an American FBI agent, the commandant became more than cooperative. In fact, the police chief came perilously close to declaring it a local holiday. Sullivan had to tell him three times that the National Guard wouldn't be necessary. But the commandant insisted on accompanying Sullivan to the hotel. The chief even dressed in full gear for the occasion, with high polished black boots and a triple row of brightly colored medals displayed across the chest of his uniform.

As soon as they arrived at the Mirador, the commandant used his troops to surround the perimeter of the old hotel, three or four men at every door and a uniformed man at each first-floor window. Sullivan began regretting his decision to not go in alone as he watched the officers move into place, double-timing out of their police jeeps along the quiet Mexican street, their automatic weapons held at the ready across their chests and in full view of the building's upper windows. But then a loud, curious crowd began to gather on the street in front of the hotel and Sullivan knew it was too late to do anything about it.

"Okay," Sullivan said reluctantly over the noise of the crowd, and the commandant followed him in the front door of the hotel. They didn't stop at the front desk but promptly crossed to the elevator. The commandant stepped right to the elevator controls and then he began to maneuver the old rickety elevator up to the hotel's fourth floor.

The two men crept down the darkened hall with their revolvers drawn, and, without warning, Sullivan kicked in the thin wooden door to 409 and jumped inside, crouching low, his gun barrel searching the interior of the room as he had been trained.

It was dark, quiet, and motionless inside the small hotel room, and at first Sullivan's adrenaline was pumping too fast to let him smell the gagging odor that filled the airless room. The only movement was from a brightly lit-up sign across the street of a dancer kicking a bare leg outlined in red neon, but the room itself was not empty.

Sullivan crossed slowly to the bed that stood against the far wall of the dirty little Mexican hotel room. The bed's top sheet was pulled up, covering something, and the wrinkled linen was stiff and soaked through with a large dark stain. Sullivan pulled the sheet back.

Below it were the remains of a young Mexican woman dressed in only a soiled, gray slip. Her long black hair tumbled down over her face, her legs and arms spread out at disjointed angles, like an awkward dancing marionette on a broken string, and the woman's abdomen and stomach were torn open, exploded outward in a great torrent of drying, dark red blood.

The regularly scheduled flight from Tampico to Miami landed at Miami International at 10:30 P.M. The passengers disembarked and crossed under the bright lights of the runway and passed quietly through United States Customs and Immigration.

To the officials who searched luggage, looked at faces, and stamped documents on behalf of the American government that night, it was just another routine flight full of American citizens and a few Mexican nationals entering the country temporarily on properly issued visas. And the passports were all stamped and the visas all checked and verified as they always were and the passengers moved on to claim their luggage, and meet their friends, or to mount buses, or rent cars, or to slip quietly into a waiting Miami taxi as one passenger did.

The man who stepped into the taxi was a short, solidly built, dark-skinned man with long sideburns and a full high pompadour of shiny black hair above a broad, pockmarked face. He wore a neat, newly grown, pencil-thin mustache, and even as he sat in the back of the cab that sped him down the dark Miami streets, he wore metal-framed aviator sunglasses over his eyes.

The papers that he'd shown at Immigration said that his name was Antonio Eduardo Lopata, a naturalized American citizen, but in Miami that night no one had noticed and no permanent record of his entrance was kept, and like his fellow passengers from Flight 612 from Tampico, he would soon melt into the free flow of people coming and going, unnoticed and unaccounted for, within the borders of the great vast country of the United States of America.

CHAPTER

14

It was midsummer in Cape Cod and Jack stood at the seashore looking out at the blue of the ocean. It had been almost four months since he'd made his decision to not seek his Party's nomination for the presidency. Four months of hospitals, and operations, of long walks and doctors' offices, of reading and contemplation. Four long months of being the President of the United States, but of watching other men rise in the public eye around him, until now it seemed to him that he was almost forgotten.

First the doctors had cut back into the wounded area on the side of his head and removed bit by bit the last tiny stray fragments of the bullet that had struck him several months before. In the same series of delicate operations, they had also removed numerous pieces of shattered skull bone from the outer layers of brain tissue. Then the wound had been closed and resewn this time along one clean incision line and allowed to heal, while the President rested and regained his strength for the final series of primarily cosmetic surgeries where skin from the back of his head was to be grafted on to the damaged area.

He stood and looked longingly at the sea and wondered what he had become during those months of inactivity and what the future held for him now. The doctors had told him that the operations that he had submitted to over the last four months had been successful, but he knew that his body had been left weakened by them as well and that he needed more rest now, and the prospect of even more inactivity left him with very little joy.

He heard Suzanne approaching behind him, but he didn't turn to face her. He just stood for another few moments gazing at the far-off horizon.

"Jack," Suzanne said softly. He turned to her then very slowly and smiled. After a few seconds, though, his attention drifted back toward the ocean again and they both stood quietly watching the sea.

"I know what a difficult time this must be for you," Suzanne said, her voice showing traces of how awkward she had begun to feel with her own husband over the last few months.

Jack nodded his head at her and as he did the sea breeze blew his hair straight back from his face, revealing the series of healing scars on the side of his head.

"I feel sometimes like that Nantucket sea captain who owned the wheelchair that you gave me last Christmas," he said. "Just looking endlessly out to sea for the sight, for even the outline of a four-rigger, but knowing inside myself that I'll never sail on one again."

"You'll captain one," she said proudly.

He turned and held his arms out to her. She came to him then and put her head on his chest and he wrapped his arms tightly around her. It was near sunset and the air was growing cool and he was wearing a fisherman's cable knit sweater, and she could feel its heavy wool weave against her own skin. Nestling against it she could smell its good wool smell mixing with the familiar smell of her husband's body.

"Forgive me, Jack?" she asked, feeling for that brief moment like a very little girl again.

He nodded his head over and over, signaling that there was nothing to forgive, and then he left the side of his face resting against the soft, dark matting of her hair. "It was my decision," he said, and the words seemed to cut into him as he said them. He let go of her. "It was the right thing to do at the time. The only thing really," he said, stepping back from her.

"And now?" she said, and her hair, no longer protected by her husband's body, lifted up behind her in a long dark wave as it caught the full force of the ocean wind.

"I took an oath," Jack said. "To the best of my abilities. I promised," he said, his voice thick with uncertainty.

"Oh, Jack, you've never broken that promise. Don't you know that?" she said. But he moved even farther away from her then, turning his head toward the sea, and he didn't answer her question. He seemed to have drifted again into some other world of his own making.

"I wanted you back, and I feel now," Suzanne said, "in wanting it so badly that somehow I've lost you."

Jack came toward her and reached to touch her shoulders. "You haven't lost me," he said, and he took her face delicately between his fingers and kissed her gently on the lips. But then neither of them had anything more to say to each other and a few long painful seconds later Suzanne returned alone down the beach toward their home, leaving Jack standing on the rocks by the edge of the sea.

He watched her walk for a while, watching the wind swing her long dark hair back toward the land in a series of graceful swaying moves. Then he turned and looked out at the ocean again, and as he looked at the rising blue-green waves, he fought hard against the words that kept rising up inside his head, but they kept forcing themselves on him anyway, ruthlessly seeking their own expression, until finally he gave in to them. "But I may have lost myself," he whispered, so softly that even the shorebirds gliding and swooping in the wind above him couldn't quite hear the words.

"Ah, a touch of the old sod is all that you be needin'." Frank O'Connor broke into a little of his grandfather's brogue for the President's benefit, and it got the big smile back from his friend that it always did. "And Connemara, my boy. That's the true old sod. It's at the real magical heart of the country itself," O'Connor added. "How's a mere politician like yourself be knowin' a man like that, anyway?" O'Connor said, pointing at the letter of invitation that Jack was holding. "A man with the good sense to pack up and live in a grand place like Connemara again just as his ancestors did."

"He was a friend of my father's, in his bad old Hollywood days," Jack said.

"Jeffries's bad old days or your father's?" O'Connor asked, smiling.

Jack smiled, too. "Both, I guess. If I can believe the things I've heard about Dad."

"John Jeffries," O'Connor said respectfully. "He's a far cry from the rabble us poor Boston politicians are usually mixin' with. He's made some truly glorious movies in his day."

"He may still have one or two left in him," Jack said.

"I spoke to Bill Mallory about it," O'Connor said. "I told him that you were still thinking about going to Europe for a little while, maybe right after the convention." Jack's expression remained unchanged, giving no clue as to what he was going to do about it or the decisions that were going to be made by his Party in Atlantic City in just a few short weeks.

"And he about came through the telephone after me, at first," O'Connor went on. "All he could see was you and Suzanne stealin' the six o'clock news from his darlin' boy. While Gardner's givin' out Eagle Scout badges in the Rose Garden, or whatever the hell his idea of high theater is these days, you and Suzanne would be leisurely chatting with de Gaulle at a state reception in Paris or passin' the time with the Queen at Buckingham Palace and then maybe poppin' over to Berlin to address another cheerin' throng or two," O'Connor stopped then and chuckled at Mallory's discomfort. "But when I told him it was only Ireland, he thought that would be swell. 'Perhaps Ireland would be all right,' he said. The Tory bastard! They're still scared of you, Jack. They've been hustlin' delegates for over four months all by their lonesome and they're still scared of you," O'Connor said and smiled. "Pretty damned good for a man who's only made one public appearance—and only a press conference at that—in the last eight months," he added. They were sitting in the big living room of the Hyannis Port house, drinking pint glasses of Guinness. The television was on to the national news, but Huntley and Brinkley were being ignored for the moment.

"Suzanne's still talking about Greece," Jack said.

"That'd be okay with 'em too. As long as you're out of sight after the convention. Somewhere in Greece where there's no phone and absolutely no television cameras and they'll be happy."

"Konstantine has his own island," Jack said and shook his head in amused disbelief. He took a long drink of the Guinness then and let it wash away the need to make any decisions for the moment.

"Gardner's instincts are right, though," Jack added a moment later. "We've talked about it and I've agreed to keep a low profile during the campaign. It has to look like his show. With me around, it would only confuse everyone and probably wind up hurting him in the end."

"They'll be needin' you before it's all over," O'Connor said. "You can count on that."

Jack only smiled. "Perhaps, but maybe it's best if they learn that for themselves," he added.

"Ireland then," O'Connor said. "And if you'll be needin' any assistance over there, well," he lifted his pint toward Jack, "at your service." He took a long slow pull on the murky brown liquid.

"But you know what I'd rather be assistin' you with," O'Connor said with a twinkle in his eye, after he finished drinking from his pint glass.

Cassidy laughed out loud. "You and Brian, a couple of revolutionaries," he said.

"Well, it'd serve 'em right," O'Connor said defiantly. "They're so god-damned sure that you're goin' steal the nomination out from under them at the last minute somehow that they can't sleep nights."

"They should worry about Granderman, not me. He's going to give them a run for their money," Cassidy said.

"Oh, they're plenty worried about him, too, but it's you that's really got their goat. You and Tim," O'Connor said, the light twinkling even more brightly in his eyes as he thought about Gardner's discomfort.

Erin came into the room then and climbed up into her father's lap, and he reached out and held her in his arms.

"Well, if you can talk Tim into it, I'll vote for him. You can tell him that," Jack said.

"You're the real revolutionary, Jack," O'Connor said.

"Talk him into what?" Erin asked her father.

"Talk him into running for President," Jack said, smiling.

"You're the President," Erin said simply.

"You're right," Jack said. "I'd almost forgotten." He was quiet for several seconds, but even from across the room, O'Connor could see the pain in his friend's eyes.

"Mallory wants to talk to you, Jack. I think he wants to ask you again to make the nominating speech for Gardner at the convention," O'Connor said, breaking the tense silence and interrupting Brinkley's clipped television delivery that had been the only sound in the big living room.

"Yes, I'm sure they'll keep hammering on me for that right up until the last moment," Jack said slowly. "One good speech of unremitting praise, then lift Gardner's arm in the air a couple of times and smile for the cameras, kiss him on both cheeks, and then disappear until after the election," Jack said. "And then what? I can be ambassador to the country of my own choice, I guess, or maybe Secretary of the Navy?" His voice contained more than a touch of bitterness.

Erin was bored and she jumped off her father's lap and started out toward the kitchen.

"Jack, you've done," O'Connor stopped and then corrected himself. "You're doing all that anyone can reasonably expect of you," he said, looking at Jack carefully and trying to make the pain in his friend's eyes go away.

"Have I, Frank?" the President said. "I was elected to do a job and I'm not doing it worth a damn anymore. That's all I can see."

"Maybe in the end it'll work out for the best, somehow," O'Connor said.

"Maybe it will," Cassidy said. "I know if it was the other way around, I'd be doing, and saying, and probably asking for pretty much the same things that Rance is," Cassidy added, the reasonableness beginning to return to his voice again. "It's just not the way I want it, that's all."

"What do you want, Jack?" O'Connor asked then and Cassidy stopped and thought about it for a few seconds. "What I've always wanted, I guess," he said finally. "Everything. I want to be President and I want to be loved," he waved his hand off gracefully toward the other room where his wife and children were now. "And I want my friends," he said, looking directly at O'Connor. "And to drink Guinness," he said, lifting his glass again. "And to write poetry and make history and maybe to save the world too, in my spare time. Everything," he added, smiling, and when he said it, it sounded for a brief moment as if it were almost possible. "But for now, I guess I'll settle for what there is," he said, laughing softly at himself and snapping himself back into action.

"What should I tell Mallory?" O'Connor said.

"You tell him to find someone else to nominate Rance. You tell him just what we've been telling everybody else for the last two months, that for now it looks like my health is going to prevent me from even being able to attend the convention, as much as I'd like to, but . . ." Jack spread his hands out in front of him then. "You tell him, too, though, that I am getting better every day now and that, who knows? Maybe by late August, I might be in shape to drop in to Atlantic City for a few minutes, maybe even say a few words. We'll just have to see."

"Should I tell him that it might make it a whole lot easier for you to come by and say a few words, if there was a Cassidy on the ticket somewhere?" O'Connor asked, but Jack only stayed quiet, just smiling mysteriously across the room at his friend.

"You crafty Irish devil, you're after something, aren't you?" O'Connor said. "Are you going to tell me what it is?"

"I told you, Frank," Jack said. "Everything."

The Vice President handed the single piece of paper across the desk to the Attorney General. The date typed neatly at the top of it was Wednesday, July 30, 1964.

Tim took the paper and read it. Then he looked back at Gardner's face and saw the pleasure etched into the deep folds and lines of the older man's expression.

"I'm about to release that to the press," Gardner said, motioning from behind his long vice-presidential desk at the sheet of paper in the Attorney General's hand.

Cassidy knew that Gardner wanted him to react. Anger, acceptance, sadness, almost anything would do, that's why he'd been called here, so that the Vice President could read his feelings firsthand, but he'd be damned if he'd give him the satisfaction.

"Well, what do you think?" the big man behind the desk prodded him.

Humor was one thing that Gardner probably wasn't expecting, the Attorney General thought. "I'm just sorry I took so many good men over the side with me," Tim said, and then he smiled.

He was right. Gardner didn't like that. The Vice President reached out with both of his big hands at once and forcefully pulled the press release back across the desk and held it up close to his own chest.

"I've given it a great deal of consideration," Gardner said. "And I believe that I should select someone other than a member of the Cabinet to be my running mate," he said solemnly, as if the decision had some kind of internal logic to it that escaped Tim, some kind of logic other than the fact that it conveniently eliminated Tim Cassidy from consideration as a potential vice-presidential candidate, without saying it directly.

"I assume that means you've decided on Senator Putnam," the Attorney General said.

"Mebbe," Gardner answered, warming to the interest Cassidy was finally starting to show in the subject. "Mebbe, but I haven't decided that yet," he said, smiling.

"Senator Putnam's a fine man," Cassidy said and then began looking around Gardner's office, reminding himself where the exits were. Tim was ready to go now, but it was obvious that the Vice President wasn't done with him yet.

"How do you think your brother's goin' to feel about this?" Gardner said, waving the press release in the air.

"Why don't you call him and ask?" Cassidy said, pointing at Gardner's big, bright-red, vice-presidential phone and starting to betray some of the anger that he truly felt.

"The President's health seems to be a lot better," Gardner said.

"Yes, I think it is," Cassidy answered.

"I'd hoped that he would be able to attend the convention. He could give the Party a big boost, but he's still sayin' that it's not possible." Gardner watched the Attorney General closely for his reaction, but the younger man said nothing.

"Do you think he'd be able to come by and say a few words, if it were you and me running . . ." Gardner began.

Cassidy cut him off angrily before he could finish the question. "Whatever you do about selecting a running mate, I intend to support your candidacy and I'm certain that the President will do the same," the younger man said, his dark blue eyes flashing.

"Yes, I'm sure he will," Gardner drawled. "But then there's support and there's support, isn't there?"

Gardner picked the press release back up off his desk. "I spoke to your brother for a good long time a few months ago, jus' before he went into the hospital," the Vice President began again, his voice more conciliatory now. "And he said that he'd talk to you about a few things that were botherin' me."

"I know," Tim said. "He did and I've been quiet about some issues that I've felt very strongly about since then."

"Not enough!" Gardner thundered suddenly, slamming his fist against the desktop for emphasis. "That's what I mean about support," he said. "I have to choose somebody to be my Vice President who I can work with. Somebody who does what I expect him to do," he said, pointing his finger at Cassidy. "And after I talked to your brother, I expected you to let the country know that you'd changed your mind about the FBI investigation of Dallas, and I waited to hear it from you, and I'm still waitin'."

"I'll talk to some people, let them know," Cassidy said, but without much conviction.

"Not just some leaked story to a few of your special friends in the press. I want a public announcement. I want people to finally understand that all this conspiracy nonsense is all over, behind us once and for all. How the hell can your brother expect us to run together on the same ticket with something like that standin' between us?"

Tim steeled himself. "If you think that's best," he said finally, in a low tense voice.

"I do," Gardner followed up quickly. "And I want it done right away, before the convention. And then we can start talkin' about who's supportin' who for what," Gardner said and set the press release down on the desktop squarely between them again. "Do you know how many times Senator Putnam has come to me personally and asked for that job?" he said, tapping the press release loudly with his pointed finger.

"No," Cassidy said.

"Four times," Gardner said. "He sat there, jus' where you're sitting now, and told me how much he wants to do the job, four times."

"I want it, too," Tim said. "I want the vice presidency as much as Senator Putnam or anyone else does," he said.

Gardner's big body began to relax then, but he didn't smile. "I don't want you and your brother thinkin' you got me over the barrel on this Vice President thing," he drawled. "I don't believe in the long run it's goin' matter one good goddamn, who I'm runnin' with, or who says what about who at that convention. The voters are goin' get down in the long run to just measurin' me and my record, plain and simple."

Cassidy stayed silent after the Vice President's short outburst.

"But . . ." Gardner said, as he picked up the press release and tore it lengthwise in half in his big hands, "we still got a little time left before I have to say, for sure, who it is that I think is the best man for the job. Why don't we all just use that time wisely?" He dropped the torn sheets of paper into the vice-presidential wastebasket on the floor next to him. "I'm sure you'll do your part," Gardner said.

"I will," Cassidy said, fixing the Vice President with his hard blue eyes across the desktop.

"Good. We'll all just wait a little while then and see what happens," Gardner said.

Sullivan knew a dead end when he saw one, and the Mexican police photograph that he slapped up on his wall now to join the rest of his collection had all the markings to him of a very final dead end.

The picture showed the blood-soaked remains of the Mexican woman he had found in the Tampico hotel room, and Sullivan taped her picture to his motel-room wall now, right between the newspaper photograph of the murdered police officer in South Dallas and right above the autopsy pictures of the two men that the Louisiana State troopers had pulled out of the Louisiana swamp, but when he was finished the entire bizarre collection that Sullivan had built up of odd pieces and parts of the case just looked even more like one big dead end.

It had ended in that Mexican hotel room with a final mutilated and silent corpse, he decided. The dead woman had turned out to be just some local whore, who had no connection to anything or anybody that Sullivan could connect to the case. And no one in Tampico would identify the man that she had been staying with in Room 409. He was "just a man," the desk clerk had said over and over, either too scared or too well paid off to say anything more. And when Sullivan had shown him a copy of the sketch of his dark-haired second gunman the desk clerk had only shrugged his shoulders and said, "No, I don't think so."

The Bureau's final report on the Dallas assassination attempt had been completed and was scheduled to be released to the public in a few weeks.

Sullivan hadn't seen it, but he could guess what it said. Even the President's brother had held a press conference and announced his satisfaction with the FBI's handling of the case. That meant there was nobody left to turn to for help even if he found a good lead, which he hadn't—dead end, he thought again. He had prepared a letter and submitted it to Washington though, outlining the problems that he saw in the Bureau's case. As Sullivan saw it, the primary issue was that the Bureau's formal public conclusion—that Strode had acted entirely alone—ignored some pretty good leads, like the fact that Strode's landlady thought she had seen a Dallas police car outside her rooming house at least twenty minutes before it should have been there. Leads like that either had to be explained away by a far more thorough investigation than the one that had been undertaken so far, Sullivan thought, or an entirely new theory of the case had to be developed, a new theory that pointed to the possibility of some kind of a conspiracy behind the events of November 22. He could guess what Washington would do with his letter, though—another dead end. Well, he could live with that. He'd done his job, worked at it as hard as he could, and he'd just been overridden by his bosses—that's all. And this part of his life was ended now, he thought, looking up again at the grisly collage of photographs that he'd papered over the surface of his wall during the last few months in New Orleans—dead ends all of them he decided again. He might just as well forget about his leads and his theories and about his fantasy second gunman, because the sketch of him on his wall was as close as he was ever going to get to him now.

The Republicans held their convention in late July, three weeks before the Democrats.

They had chosen San Francisco as the site and Marshall Granderman sat in his shirtsleeves on the couch at the center of his living room, looking out the window of the big home he'd rented at the top of Nob Hill at the skyline of the "City by the Bay" spread out below him. He looked first at the sharp cluster of high-rises near the water's edge and then out at the long graceful expanse of the Golden Gate in the distance.

He stood up when he heard the knock on the door and took his suit coat off the back of the chair where he'd thrown it earlier that morning, and placed it carefully on over his wide shoulders. He took his time buttoning the coat carefully at his waist before he stepped to the door and opened it. Outside in the entry hall, all alone, was Senator Longwood, just as it had been arranged.

Granderman reached out and shook Longwood's hand. As he did, he couldn't help thinking how strange the Senator from Arizona looked to him now, standing there at the door all by himself, without his aides, without a microphone, and without a cheering crowd of supporters. They hadn't met with each other face to face since the Oregon primary almost three months earlier, and in that time Granderman had almost forgotten what the real man looked like. Since Oregon, Granderman had begun to confuse Longwood the man with the image that the television and the newspapers showed to the country, and Granderman wondered if that was what Longwood was thinking now, too, as the Senator stood in the doorway and looked back across at him through his heavy dark-framed glasses.

"Bill, come in," Granderman said, smiling at him, and the two men stepped back inside the rented home's big living room. "It's good to see you again," Granderman said.

"It's good to see you, too. I guess we've both been a little busy lately," Longwood said, smiling slightly at the understatement. He crossed the room to the big picture window and stood looking out at the same skyline that Granderman had been looking out at only a few moments earlier.

"It really is a beautiful city, isn't it?" Longwood said.

"Yes," Granderman answered, and he remained standing behind him. The Senator from Arizona finally turned from the window and sat down, not on the soft plush velvet couch at the center of the room, but on a hard wooden chair near the window.

"It was a hell of a fight," Granderman said.

"Yes, it was," Longwood agreed.

"I hope there are no bad feelings. No, ah . . ." Granderman spread his hands out in front of him then, as he had trouble finding the words.

Longwood interrupted his moment of awkwardness. "None," Longwood said simply. "It was all politics. I said some things, too. I just happened to lose, that's all."

"Bill, I've been asking people who they think my Vice President should be," Granderman said, but Longwood didn't answer right away.

"What do you think?" Granderman asked.

Longwood stayed quiet for a long moment, thinking. He'd known why he'd been asked to come, but he still wasn't sure what he'd say when and if the moment arrived.

"I think that you should choose the man whom you believe has political views that are the same as your own and whom you believe would make the best President in the event that something unexpected happened to you," Longwood said honestly, although he knew that the answer didn't help his own chances very much.

"Bill, let me be frank," Granderman said, his big handsome face growing very serious. "You and your people have put together a tremendous organization, particularly at the grass-roots level, and I don't want to see that organization lost. I also believe that the people of the Republican Party have a deep and sincere respect for you," Granderman continued, but it was obvious that he was still having difficulty finding the right words to express what he really wanted to say.

"Governor, let me make it easy for both of us," Longwood said, standing up and looking Granderman square in the eyes. "I believe that it's vital for the country that Rance Gardner not become the President of the United States, and if you think I can help stop that from happening by running with you as your Vice President, I'll do it," Longwood said.

"I think it would be the best thing for the Party," Granderman said, looking directly back at Longwood's sternly serious face.

"Then it's a deal," Longwood said, extending his hand, and the two men stood in the big rented house on Nob Hill overlooking the skyline of San Francisco and sealed their agreement with a firm Republican handshake.

"Granderman and Longwood, that's the strongest ticket they could have put together. I have to give the Republicans credit," the President said. He and his wife were in their bedroom at Hyannis with Suzanne's clothes and luggage spread out over the bed and chairs.

"What are you thinking about?" she said, eying her husband suspiciously.

"It doesn't matter what I'm thinking. What matters right now is what the voters are thinking, and from what I hear, they're starting to call me the Forgotten Man," Jack said, trying to smile bravely, but his wife could easily see through it.

"Jack, they haven't forgotten about you. And, anyway, even if they have, I haven't," she said, putting down the long dress that she had been folding and walking over to where her husband was sitting to kiss him lightly on the cheek.

"Speaking of not forgetting," Jack said as his wife turned and walked back toward the clothes-littered bed to finish her packing. "It looks like you're not forgetting very much of your wardrobe either," he said, looking up from the bed and out at the army of fashionable clothes displayed almost everywhere around the large bedroom. "You're only going to be there for five days," he said.

"Well, I've got to fill up all those closets at the Carleton. Frank booked us the top two floors, you know," Suzanne said and turned toward her husband. "That's an awful lot of closets for one poor woman traveling alone with just her children for company," she said.

"Well, just make sure you keep it that way," Jack said. "I don't want you slipping one of those delegates up to your room."

"I won't have time," Suzanne said, returning to her packing. "The Vice President has me scheduled right down to the second. He even has it written down when I'm supposed to smile and wave," she said.

"You haven't forgotten how, have you?" Jack said.

Suzanne turned to him, and she smiled and waved to prove that she hadn't. Then she stopped and stared down at her husband, who was sitting in his rocking chair by the window with his chin resting on his cupped hand, watching her.

"Damn it all, Jack," she said, "I don't want you to think for a minute that I don't know that you're planning something. I know you and I know you're not going to be able to just sit here and watch it all go by on television and do nothing." She couldn't look at him after that, and finally she just turned back to her packing. "I know that you're just waiting until the very last possible moment. So that you can squeeze whatever it is you want out of Rance," Suzanne said, looking angrily down at her suitcases.

"What is it you think I want?" Jack said calmly.

Suzanne was quiet for awhile then. "I think you still want to be President," she said, still afraid to turn around and face her husband and to see in his eyes that she might be right.

CHAPTER

15

"Well, I know Rance wants a peaceful convention, but this is ridiculous," O'Connor said and then flipped an old worn leather football across the lawn toward the President. Jack caught the ball gracefully with two hands out in front of him and then tossed it back across the front lawn of his Hyannis Port home to his friend.

As the two men talked, the platform and credential business of the Democrats' national convention droned on and on from the portable radio standing on the porch rail of the Cassidy home, only a few yards from where the President and his political assistant were playing a lazy game of catch while the television in the living room of the big house remained dark. Jack, like most of the rest of the country, had tuned the Democrats' uninspired convention performance off and gone on with other things. He had instructed the secretaries taking his calls in the telephones set up in his downstairs den to interrupt him only if the Vice President or one of his aides called, and then he and O'Connor had gone outside.

"I wonder if this is what the press would call 'hardball'?" Jack said, smiling and letting the football slap firmly into his hands. He hadn't spoken to Gardner in almost three days, neither of them wanting to show any weakness in his position, but the silence between them was growing tense and strained now as the time to reach an agreement was running out.

"I'll bet that Gardner can't believe it," O'Connor said then. "He'd never be able to understand how a politician could really choose to miss a national nominating convention. I'm sure he thinks that you're only bluffing."

"Well, if he does, he's doing a hell of a good job of calling me on it,"

Jack said, the smile fading from his face as he thought about the high stakes that he and the Vice President were playing for now.

"He's had everyone else in the Party try to reach you," O'Connor said, gesturing with the football in his hands toward the bank of phones set up in the Cassidy den less than a hundred yards away. "Every state chairman, every Governor. Rance has probably arranged to have almost every damn Democratic politician in the entire country call by now and ask you to make an appearance."

"Yes, everyone's called, except for the man himself."

"And he's the only one who really counts," O'Connor said. Then he paused to look at his friend's face and try to judge how Jack was taking the pressure. He looked calm enough, considering the circumstances, O'Connor thought, so the little political assistant decided to continue. "But, I've thought about it a thousand times, Jack," he said. "And I'm still convinced that you're right. The only way to really get anything meaningful out of him is to wait. He has to be the one to call and ask you personally."

Jack nodded and flipped the football back across the lawn toward his friend. He knew that he was doing the right thing too, but it was taking all of his discipline to stay in Hyannis in an empty house while the precious few hours slipped by from a distance.

"Tonight's the night though, that they've got to have you at the convention," O'Connor reminded the President. "They've committed to the networks to show the film that they had made about your life."

A film about his life—it was like he was dead, Jack thought as he listened to O'Connor's confident words.

"I hope you're right, Frank," Jack said, his face still outwardly calm, and then he looked briefly at his watch. "But if he's going to do it, he'd better hurry, or I could wind up looking"—Jack stopped as he saw out of the corner of his eye one of his secretaries standing at the front door of his home. "It's Bill Mallory," she called out to him. The President's face lit up as he turned and looked back across the lawn at O'Connor.

His aide took off running toward the house, bouncing up the front steps almost like a school kid, with Jack only a few steps behind him.

Jack watched anxiously from across the room then as O'Connor handled the call, the old politician listening mostly, responding occasionally in a solemn respectful Boston voice. But after only a few minutes of the nervous listening, Jack had to turn away and walk back out on to the front porch of his home to be by himself. Finally, O'Connor set the phone down and walked outside to join him.

"Right on schedule," O'Connor said happily. "Mallory says that the Vice President wants to see you."

Jack stood for a second looking out over the long rolling green lawn of his family's home toward the Atlantic in the distance. Then he turned to O'Connor, and the President's eyes had a look in them that his friend thought that he remembered from the old days.

"I think it's time, don't you?" Jack said intently.

"Yes," O'Connor said, almost laughing now. "It's either time, or it's way past time, one or the other. The only thing I know for sure is that it's not too early," he said.

"Well maybe we can liven up that convention a little then. Tell him I'll come there," Cassidy said.

"Tonight?" O'Connor said, making sure that he had it right.

Jack nodded.

"Sweet Jesus," O'Connor said. "That could be more than Gardner's bargaining for."

Jack shrugged his shoulders and smiled.

"Should I tell him you're feeling better?" O'Connor asked.

"I feel pretty good," Jack said, still smiling. He had fewer headaches and the hair had grown long enough in and near the healing area to be combed over and cover the scars that lay beneath it. Of course his strength hadn't been challenged yet. His body hadn't been placed under any real stress at all since he'd left the hospital. So it was impossible to know how he'd react to some real pressure, like the kind Gardner and a national nominating convention could apply, but it was time to find out. In fact, as O'Connor had said, it was probably way past time.

"And if he asks if you feel good enough to make an appearance or maybe even a speech?" O'Connor asked.

"Tell him that's something the Vice President and I should discuss."

O'Connor started back for the house then.

"Frank!" The President's voice stopped O'Connor before he could walk back inside. "No one is to know. Whatever you set up, it's just to be Gardner and me, no one else, not even Mallory. And whatever you do, the press can't know anything about it," Jack said.

O'Connor nodded that he understood.

"What about Tim?" O'Connor asked.

"No, Tim's fine just where he is. I want him on the floor of the convention the entire time," Cassidy said and then added, "Frank, be sure, now. Whatever you set up, let Gardner know that it's just to be him and me, nobody else," the President said again, and O'Connor nodded and then disappeared quickly into the house to make the arrangements.

The helicopter churned noisily above the New Jersey coast. In the distance the skyline of Atlantic City was visible, and at the water's edge, the long straight ribbon of the Boardwalk.

The President sat all alone in the back looking out over the water passing beneath him. O'Connor sat up front with the pilot. The aircraft was an unmarked presidential chopper with a military pilot dressed in civilian clothes. From the ground it looked like any other private helicopter, maybe rented for the afternoon by a wealthy convention delegate to escape the tedious politics going on a few thousand feet below under the round gray cement roof of the sprawling convention hall.

The craft swung by the low outskirts of the city and then nestled down onto a pad built on the top of the city's tallest hotel building. It was sunset and the last of the sun's rays reflected off the polished metal surfaces of the skyscrapers that surrounded the descending aircraft. The President waited until the chopper was firmly settled into place before he leaned forward and thanked the pilot; then he opened the aircraft's door himself and stepped down onto the hotel roof. The swirling air from the chopper's blades blew his hair as he passed beneath them and he reached up to pat it down and then lightly touched his tie to his shirt in a characteristic gesture, just before he moved forward to greet Mallory, who was waiting for him a few steps away. Behind Mallory was a small knot of Secret Service men, but there was no press anywhere in sight.

"Bill, it's good to see you again," the President said, extending his hand.

"It's good to see you, too, Mr. President," Mallory said.

"Have you got the Vice President stashed away around here somewhere?" Cassidy said, smiling and looking around the roof of the hotel, obviously enjoying the intrigue of the moment.

"Yes, sir," Mallory said, returning the President's smile. Then he extended his arm to show Cassidy a set of steps that led off the roof and down into the hotel building below.

Cassidy followed Gardner's aide down the steps to a long dark hallway where more Secret Service men waited outside a door marked PENTHOUSE at the end of a short side corridor.

The Vice President stood just inside the open door of the penthouse, his large frame blocking the view of the city and the setting sun over the Atlantic that would otherwise have been visible from the high glass windows at the far side of the big hotel suite.

Gardner didn't speak until he was certain that the door was securely closed behind the President. Then he stepped forward and extended his hand for Cassidy to shake.

"Mr. President," Gardner said as the two men shook hands.

Both men were quiet then for a few seconds, neither wanting to be the one to play the initial card in the high-stakes game that had developed between them.

"I didn't think you could stay away," the big Texan said and then walked over and sat in an armchair that stood on a raised carpeted area next to the suite's picture window. From there he could keep an eye on the convention hall—about a block away beneath the window—the television set in the far corner of the room, and Cassidy himself.

"Want somethin'?" Gardner asked, waving a long arm out at an array of bottles standing on the fancy mirror bar on Cassidy's side of the room.

"No," Jack said, as he crossed to the picture window and stood looking at the sunset over the Atlantic.

"Hotel did a pretty good job of stockin' the bar on pretty short notice, don't you think?" Gardner said, still hoping that Cassidy would be the first one to get down to business.

Cassidy continued silently looking out at the view. "It's a nice suite," he said.

"Good enough for horse tradin'," Gardner said.

Jack turned and nodded at the Vice President and then moved the few steps to the chair opposite Gardner and sat down in it. "Yes, it is," Cassidy said.

"I've been talkin' to those people that I told you I would," Gardner said, finally breaking the tension that had built up between the two men.

Cassidy only nodded.

"They don't like what we talked about any better than I thought they would, though," the Vice President said flatly. He looked across the room at Cassidy.

"Yes, I know the feeling," Jack said.

"Meanin' your friends didn't like me any better four years ago than my friends like your brother right now."

Jack nodded his head that Gardner had guessed right. "Tim's done everything you asked him to do," Cassidy said.

"Yes, I know, and I appreciate that," Gardner said. He glanced down at his watch then. "Tomorrow evening, seven thirty eastern time, ten thirty western, somebody's goin' nominate me for President of the United States," he said. "I was hopin' right up until a couple of days ago that somebody was goin' be you," he added and then slowly lifted his gaze to meet Cassidy's eyes. "You're lookin' pretty good, Mr. President. How are you feelin' these days?"

"I feel fine," Jack said coolly, and then the two men grew quiet again.

"If I were to ignore what my friends had to say and went on ahead and selected your brother as my Vice President, the press'll probably say that I caved in to you," Gardner said thoughtfully and then waited to measure Cassidy's reply.

"Whatever you do, the press will say something," Jack said.

Gardner nodded his agreement at that. "But if I did decide to choose your brother as my running mate, I would expect to have your pledge then," Gardner said, looking Cassidy directly in the eye. "And your brother's pledge as well that neither of you would publicly challenge any of my administration's policies now or after the election," he said.

"No," Cassidy said, shaking his head. "Until January, I'm the President."

"But I can't have a shadow government sittin' on my shoulder and expect to run this country," Gardner said sharply.

"I understand that, and after January it will be different, but not until then," the President said.

"And your brother?"

"He understands that it comes with the job," Cassidy said.

"It does," Gardner said, and then both men smiled at each other.

"But whatever happens, I am going to need some room to run this campaign in my own way. You understand that, don't you?" Gardner continued.

Cassidy shrugged his shoulders. "I'm willing to do whatever you think best about that. My family wants me to go to Europe with them for a little while," he said. "My doctors, too. We could continue to communicate by phone while I'm away, just as we have been."

Gardner nodded that he liked that. "And you'll make my nominating speech tomorrow night."

"No," Cassidy said. "But I'll make an appearance tonight," he said, pointing down at the gray-roofed convention hall. "Let Senator Putnam make your nominating speech. He deserves it."

"He deserves more than that," Gardner said, his eyes narrowing and his meaning unmistakable.

Gardner stood up then and walked to the window and clasped his big hands behind his back as he stood in front of it, looking down at the convention hall.

"Rance, it would be your campaign, your administration, you could run it your way," Cassidy said. "But you know what it is I want now. I want Tim to run with you, and I'm confident the two of you together can beat Granderman."

Gardner continued looking out the window, weighing his options. Just how much did Cassidy want his brother on the ticket? How much of a price would he really be willing to pay? the Vice President asked himself as he stood silently at the window and thought about his next move. He had to find out just how far Cassidy would go before he committed himself to anything, he decided finally, and so he turned back into the room to face the President again. "There is only one way," Gardner said, and Jack waited silently to hear his terms. "One way that I'd take your brother on the ticket with me, but only one," Gardner continued. "And that is if, effective immediately after the convention, you were to resign the presidency."

Gardner watched from the penthouse suite above as Cassidy ducked into a limousine that had pulled up to the side entrance of the hotel. It had less than a block to travel to the convention hall, but Gardner checked his watch for the third time in the last five minutes to see how they were doing on time. They were still okay.

Mallory was in the suite with the Vice President now and the aide was kneeling in front of the television set switching the channel selector back and forth with one hand and holding the phone with the other. The last five minutes had been filled with hectic activity as Mallory relayed Gardner's new instructions to the floor of the convention.

"Do they know he's in town?" the Vice President asked as he turned and gestured down at the image of a reporter on the television screen.

"They know something's going on," Mallory said, looking up from his call, but still turning the television dials back and forth, finally settling on Cronkite and CBS.

The convention had just heard a series of tributes to John Cassidy and then seen a short film about his life and before the lights had gone back on in the darkened hall, Suzanne and her two children had been escorted under a single moving spotlight to a private box located right below the podium.

Tim and Brian and their families were already seated in the box that was draped in cascading folds of red, white, and blue bunting, and the two brothers stood up and greeted Suzanne as she came down the aisle of the darkened convention hall with the single moving spotlight still focused on her. The band was playing the theme from *Camelot*.

> *Once there was a spot . . .*
> *for one brief shining hour*
> *known as Camelot . . .*

The convention applause for the Cassidy family was deafening, the delegates all on their feet applauding as loudly as they could and then, softly at first, but then growing louder, a steady chanting could be heard over the sound of the music. "Cassadee! Cassadee! Cassadee!"

Gardner sat down in front of his television set and watched. After a few seconds he leaned forward, obviously growing more and more nervous by the moment at what he was seeing beginning to happen on the television screen in front of him. When he had consented a few minutes earlier to Cassidy's appearance before the convention delegates, he hadn't counted on anything like this, and he looked over at Mallory in alarm, but it was too late to do anything about it now. His aide had hung up the phone and there was no time left to change the arrangements anyway. It was out of their hands. The moment belonged to the people on the floor of the convention, the people who had suffered through the boredom and discomfort of the last few days in the hot, overcrowded, overmanaged hall, but who were beginning to come spontaneously alive right before the Vice President's eyes.

"Cassadee! Cassadee!" The chant was growing louder and more insistent. It seemed as if it was coming now not just from the delegates in the hall, but from everywhere, from all over the city, all over the country maybe. "Cassadee! Cassadee!"

Suzanne helped her children into their seats and then in the full glare of the single bright spotlight she embraced first Brian and then Tim and the crowd roared even louder.

"Jesus, do you think we're being set up?" Mallory said and then walked to the window of the penthouse suite.

"I don't know, Bill. I think mebbe we've got a chance at a deal, but I'll tell you this, with him you can never really know for sure. In the end, I couldn't pin him right down on anything. He said he'd think about it, that's the way he works, he always leaves himself plenty of room to wiggle out later if he wants to. Anyway, there was no way that I could stop him from talkin' to the convention tonight. He knew that." Gardner's voice was full of concern, but it also betrayed a touch of his admiration for Cassidy's political skill.

Through the penthouse picture windows, Mallory could see the President's limousine pulled up to the back of the convention hall where a line of police and Secret Service men led one after another forming a human corridor from the sidewalk all the way inside the hall to the back of the podium.

"Are you sure of what he's going to do when he steps out and sees it all again, sees all the people and the lights and the excitement? Jesus!" Mallory said, nervously.

"Sure of him?" Gardner laughed. "Let me tell you a story, Bill," the Vice President said, trying to sound folksy and relaxed, but inside his stomach was twisting violently.

"Once there was a young Senator from the East Coast," Gardner began, slow and easy, hoping that the sound of his voice would help quiet his aide's obvious discomfort and maybe his own stomach at the same time. "Well, this young Senator was rich, good lookin', and as smooth as all get out. He'd been in the Senate about a year and a very important vote was comin' up and nobody, I mean nobody, knew what this particular Senator was goin' do. Well, old Sam Tyler, he was runnin' things then," Gardner kept drawling his story out in a slow easy Texas voice, but his eyes didn't leave the television set for even an instant as he spoke. Mallory had turned attentively toward him now and he was standing with his back to the window listening carefully.

"Old Sam says to me, 'Rance, why don't you go find out what this here, young, good-lookin' Senator's goin' do on this very important vote.' And of course, I went and did what I was told. Old Sam gave me a few things to horse trade and I did my horse tradin' and then this Senator looked me straight in the eye and shook my hand and said 'You got yourself a deal,' and I shuffled on back to Old Sam and I told him that he didn't have to worry anymore, because we had ourselves a deal. But Old Sam, he was a smart man. He'd been around young, good-lookin' Senators a lot longer than I had then, and he asked me the same thing you jus' did. He said, 'Rance, are you sure we can count on him?' And I said, 'He gave me his word, Sam, that's good enough for me.' " Gardner stopped then and smiled at Mallory. "Now, I don't have to tell you how that story turned out, do I?" Gardner asked, and the smile faded off his face.

"Cassidy broke his promise," Mallory said flatly.

Gardner nodded his head that he had guessed correctly. "And right now I don't know what we've got, but it sure as hell isn't any damn promise. So, you tell me," Gardner said, pointing at the television screen, "you tell me what he's goin' to do now."

The lights were on in the convention hall, the chanting subsided, and right on cue the head of the Alabama delegation yielded the floor to Senator Putnam of Minnesota and Putnam appeared at the podium. Then, just as ordered by Gardner a few minutes earlier, the head of the Massachusetts delegation stood and walked to his microphone and called out from his place on the crowded noisy floor of the convention. "Mr. Chairman!" he bellowed into his microphone, and his words reverberated throughout the hall.

"Yes," the chairman of the convention said into his own microphone mounted on the podium.

"Will the Senator from Minnesota yield?" the head of the Massachusetts delegation asked in the hastily prearranged way, and the chairman glanced over at Senator Putnam, who was standing next to him on the dais. The Senator leaned into the microphone that he shared with the chairman and looked out at where the leader of the Massachusetts delegation was standing on the aisle, about halfway back in the crowded hall.

"Yield for what purpose, sir?" Putnam asked, his big, happy, midwestern face breaking into its famous smile, and suddenly the crowd began to catch on to what was happening and started to buzz with excitement.

"Yield for the President of the United States? John Trewlaney Cassidy!" the head of the Massachusetts delegation shouted, and Putnam's reply of "Gladly, Mr. Chairman!" was lost in the bedlam of cheering voices, as the President himself stepped out onto the side of the stage and the delegates broke into a wild roar of approval, standing at once, cheering and applauding, the noise sudden and tumultuous in its spontaneous joy. It filled the convention hall and seemed to cascade off its roof, echoing across the country itself. Young housewives and their husbands sitting in front of their television sets in safe suburban houses turned to each other with unexpected exhilaration as they watched the graceful figure cross the stage and lift a regal hand to wave at the crowd. And in the same moment, in union halls across the country, millions of blue-collar workers, tired after their long hard day in plants and factories and on loading docks and assembly lines, looked up from their dinners or set down their drinks for a few seconds to catch the sight of this man that they'd voted for four short years before. And children watched their parents' faces, seeing something new in them, something unexpected, as the man on the television screen shook hands with the other men standing with him at the podium. And still the cheering didn't stop, still the people in the hall stood and applauded and shouted and waved their signs in the air in front of the television cameras. Signs saying GARDNER, signs saying TIM CASSIDY, signs saying anything jumped and waved spontaneously in the air, and then, as if by themselves, two nights early—balloons, red and white and blue balloons, began tumbling slowly down from a huge net suspended near the ceiling of the hall, brightly colored balloons spilling down through the air, beginning to fill the hall above the heads of the jubilant crowd, and you could hear the music now. They were playing from *Camelot* again but not the main theme. They were playing the love song. The orchestra was playing the notes that symbolized the show's deep true love story, and in their hearts and some of them out loud, as well, the people in the happy crowd began to sing the familiar words, as they watched the man on the podium in front of them.

If ever I would leave you.
It wouldn't be in summer.
Seeing you in summer I never would go . . .
No never would I leave you at all!

They sang joyously and the music poured out over the great hall on the Boardwalk in Atlantic City, and then the President smiled and raised his hand in a simple gesture and the crowd roared and he dropped it and the noise subsided, and then he raised it a second time, slightly lower this time, and he grinned broadly at them when they roared just as loudly. The chanting began again then as the red, white, and blue balloons descended, floating in slow motion into the roaring crowd. "Cassadee! Cassadee! Cassadee!" Over and over again and then again shouting out their hero's name, as if they would never stop: "Cassadee! Cassadee! Cassadee!"

And in an expensive townhouse in New York City, high above Central Park, another man watched the phenomenal events on his television screen and shook his head several times, barely believing them, as he began to wonder how what he was seeing in front of him now was going to affect his own future.

And in a bar at the outskirts of the French Quarter in New Orleans, a young man with clear blue eyes and short-cut blond hair sat on a bar stool and looked up at the television set mounted on the wall above him. He thought not about the images on its screen, but about the pictures plastered on the wall of his own motel room. And as he did, he began to ask himself again if those pictures meant anything at all, or if they were just his own private, ugly little obsession.

And from a box suspended over the podium in the convention hall itself, almost close enough to reach out and touch the man on the stage, a rugged old Irish pol wept and let the tears roll unashamedly down his reddening cheeks, as he yelled to anyone who could hear him. "Go, Jack! Go!" And he shook the arm of the man's brother, who was sitting next to him. "He's gotta' go, Timmy! He's gotta' go!" He shouted and Tim nodded back his own approval, as he stood and cheered and applauded for his brother, just like all the rest.

And the slender, dark-haired woman standing next to him applauded too, but in her eyes you could see the fear and uncertainty, as she looked back and forth between her husband standing before her in the full light of the convention hall, and the crowd, and then over at the two men standing in the private box next to her, one of them shouting at the top of his lungs now. "Go, Jack, go!" But as she heard the man's words, inside her own head she could only think: No! Jack! Please! No! And through the bedlam her husband turned and looked only at her for a moment. It was as if he could hear somehow her unspoken plea to him. And through the few yards of smoky air that separated them, he could see clearly the fear and desperation written deeply into her beautiful dark brown eyes.

And in a penthouse suite just a block away, a tall, sad-faced man who was the Vice President of the United States leaned forward and watched with growing fear the seemingly endless shower of love and joy that this other man had unleashed in the convention hall that until only a few moments before he had been able to control with his own iron hand.

And in a cheap hotel room on Cape Cod, only a few minutes from the Cassidy's estate in Hyannis, another man sat in front of a television set. This man was all alone and he was naked, except for a pair of tight dark-colored undershorts, and in his hand the man held a long-barreled Smith & Wesson thirty-eight caliber revolver.

As he watched his television set the man reached over and carefully selected a single, long-pointed Mexican bullet from a cardboard pack that sat on the end table next to him and jammed the single bullet down savagely into the chamber of his long-barreled revolver. He spun the chamber with the fingers of his small hand, letting the single cartridge fall randomly into place. He slowly lifted the pistol's long barrel then and pointed it at the television set in front of him, lining the pistol's high sculptured metal sights up with the image of the head of the handsome man on the television screen.

The man on the screen in front of him was smiling broadly now and raising his hand in another futile attempt to silence the crowd in the convention hall, but in response the voices just came back even louder, merging now into a single deafening chorus. "Cassadee! Cassadee! Cassadee!"

And the man in the motel room squeezed the trigger of the pistol then, holding the picture of the man on the podium tightly within the hammer sight of the long-barreled revolver. He tensed his body as the trigger mechanism collapsed against the squeezing flesh of his finger, but then there was only a dull metallic click of metal on an empty chamber and the man relaxed his naked shoulders and, softly and slowly at first, but then faster and louder, he began to laugh, and soon wildly out of control the picture on the television screen in front of him dissolved from his view, lost in wild cascades of uncontrolled laughter.

PART THREE

August 1964—November 1964

CHAPTER
16

"**W**hat the hell did he say?" Gardner was nearly shouting at the television set in front of him. Cassidy's speech to the National Democratic Nominating Convention had just ended and the thousands of delegates that had crowded into the steamy Atlantic City convention hall that night had reignited into a fresh bedlam of approval.

"Well, there were a few things that he definitely didn't say," Mallory reminded the Vice President, but it was hardly necessary. Gardner was already on his feet and halfway across the floor of the long penthouse suite. He began then to pace back and forth, his hands locked tightly behind his back and his reddening face showing all too clearly that he was very conscious of just what Cassidy had said and also what he had failed to say in his short but powerful address to the convention delegates.

"He didn't mention my name once!" Gardner roared. "Not one goddamned time in all that . . ." Gardner stopped his pacing then and looked again at the television screen as Cassidy began to weave his way gracefully through the crowd of politicians at the rear of the platform, shaking hands and nodding his acknowledgment at the familiar faces that surrounded him. Occasionally, Cassidy would turn back toward the crowd and wave a regal hand triumphantly in the air and each time that he did the audience in the hall would cheer even louder than it had the time before. Gardner watched it all with his practiced political eye. Cassidy looked happy to be back in action—too happy, the Vice President decided finally.

"What the hell are they carryin' on about?" Gardner said angrily. "Don't they know what they just saw could destroy the Democratic Party for a generation?"

The Vice President stopped talking only when Walter Cronkite's face finally appeared in close-up on the television screen. "This crowd," Cronkite began, his rich, melodic voice rising majestically above the noise in the packed convention hall, "has just been energized by what may well go down as one of the great dramatic moments in the history of American politics," Cronkite reported. Then he glanced up at the clock mounted on the wall of his broadcast booth. "Only eighteen short minutes ago," he continued, "this convention was rocked by the sudden and unexpected appearance of President John Trewlaney Cassidy . . ."

The telephone rang in Gardner's hotel suite, swinging Mallory back into action, and the young aide quickly turned away from the television screen and reached for the phone.

"Yes," Mallory said into the receiver.

"Although it is too early to say precisely just what political impact President Cassidy's words here tonight may ultimately have on the outcome of this convention, it would appear certain that he has left the delegates with some doubt about his own plans concerning the presidential nomination," Cronkite went on, and as he did Gardner leaned forward, listening intently to every word that the newscaster spoke.

"It's Mazeloff," Mallory said from across the room. "He's being swamped by calls. He needs to know how you want this handled."

Gardner turned his head slowly away from the television set, but he kept his ears trained on Cronkite's analysis of Cassidy's speech. "How do I want it handled?" Gardner said. "The man stabs me in the back and my own press secretary wants to know how I want it handled?"

"Yes, sir," Mallory said, straining to keep his own voice as coolly efficient as possible.

Gardner took a deep breath, shaking loose his anger and returning himself to the job ahead. "Like an endorsement," the Vice President said finally, drawing on his instincts developed over four crowded and action-filled decades of American politics. "Like a goddamned twenty-one-gun salute right out of that son of a bitch Cassidy's own mouth, that's how I want it handled. Here, give it to me!" Gardner said, and then he crossed the room in two quick strides and ripped the telephone out of Mallory's hand.

"Ted!" the Vice President shouted into the receiver. "You tell the press that you talked to me and that I'm happy as hell. You tell them that I think Cassidy made one damn fine speech tonight. It reaffirmed all of the great themes of the Democratic Party that he and I both deeply believe in, and then tell them that as far as we're concerned Cassidy has just unequivocally endorsed my candidacy for the presidency of the United States. And we're all mighty damn grateful to him for it," Gardner thundered into the phone. But even as he did, he could hear other voices coming from the television set behind him joining Cronkite's now, and beginning to raise the possibility of a very different interpretation of the speech Cassidy had just made. "And, Ted, the thing we can't do—" Gardner said, "we can't make it easy for Cassidy to break with us. If there's goin' to be a split, it's gotta look like he's the one who did it. Do you understand?" But Gardner continued on then without waiting for an answer from his press secretary. "Just make it clear to everybody how mighty damn grateful we are to Cassidy for his continued support. And just how much we're looking forward to working with the conniving son of a bitch in the fall campaign!" Gardner slammed the phone down then.

On the television screen, the picture now showed Cassidy standing talking to reporters backstage at the convention hall.

"Look at him," Gardner said. "He just can't stop, can he? He just can't let go of it," Gardner's voice, as he watched the handsome, energetic man pictured on the television set in front of him, was full of disgust.

"Get me Senator Putnam on the phone," Gardner said then, suddenly turning back to Mallory. "Tell him I want to see him. I think the Senator from Minnesota and I have some very important matters to discuss, like just who the hell is goin' be running this country for the next four years. If the Cassidys don't know when to let go, we're just going to have to teach them."

O'Connor was waiting for Jack by the back door to the convention hall. Reporters and well-wishers were still pushing in at the President from every side as his little political assistant held the door open for him and then followed the President out into the warm summer air of the New Jersey night. Cassidy's limousine was parked only a few steps away, but the President's shield of police and Secret Service agents was beginning to grow thin against the onslaught of the crowd that had formed in the normally quiet alley at the rear of the auditorium. "Can you get Tim for me?" Cassidy said and then he stopped to smile at O'Connor in the middle of all the noise and excitement that swirled around them.

"He's in the car," O'Connor said, motioning to the curb where Cassidy's limousine stood waiting. Jack nodded a thank you and then turned smiling at the crowd and walked the half dozen short steps to the waiting limousine. As he did, Tim opened its rear door from the inside and Jack ducked down, disappearing into the big car's rear seat.

"That was quite a speech," Tim said as the limousine started away from the curb, working its way behind a slowly moving police escort through the thick crowd. Jack could tell from his face that his brother was not entirely happy.

"Tim, I'm sorry that we didn't have a chance to talk earlier. There wasn't time," Jack said, trying to explain. "I wasn't really certain of what I was going to say until almost the last moment."

"I understand," Tim said, but his expression was still set hard and the muscles of his lean face tightly clenched. "Gardner's calling it an endorsement," he added then. There was a small radio receiver mounted on the door panel next to him, and Tim tapped on it now, indicating where he'd learned the news.

Jack nodded his head in understanding. "He's going to force us to make the next move. That's smart," Jack said.

"Well, everyone's wondering what it's going to be," Tim said, "including me."

"Including me," Cassidy said, echoing his younger brother's words.

Tim managed a small smile then. He knew Jack far too well to believe that his brother hadn't thought through a plan of action. The limousine had disentangled itself from the worst of the traffic now and was headed the few blocks to Cassidy's hotel. Jack's head was turned, watching the streets of Atlantic City pass by outside the car window. "I told Rance that if he agreed to put you on the ticket with him, I would endorse his candidacy and do everything in my power to see to it that you were both elected."

Tim nodded his head, the smile disappearing now. "And what did he say?"

"He told me that he'd do it on one condition," Jack said.

"That you resign," Tim said before his brother could continue.

Jack nodded his head that Tim had guessed correctly.

"Good God, Jack, you didn't agree to it, did you?"

"No," the President said flatly and then repeated himself. "No, I didn't."

"But you're considering it?" Tim said anxiously.

Jack refused to answer his brother's question directly. "What are my choices?" he said, instead.

"You mean, can you take the nomination away from him?"

"Yes," Jack said. "Or, at least prove to him with enough pure political muscle right here, right now, at his own damn convention, that it's us and not him that will set the terms for what happens next."

Both men were quiet then.

"I honestly don't know," Tim said finally, his voice betraying his feeling that, by not knowing, he was somehow letting his brother down. "We're not organized at all," he added a moment later in the same uncertain voice.

"Tim, I know that and I'm sorry that it couldn't be different, but . . ." Jack stopped then and looked out the window again at the streets of Atlantic City slipping by outside the slowly moving limousine. For that moment, the New Jersey streets reminded him of another set of streets and of another ride in the back seat of another slowly moving limousine. The ability to fully control events, or even to believe that he could, had ended for him on that day in Dallas, Jack thought, but he didn't share any of that with his brother now. "I just want to know what my options are, or if I even have any," he said instead.

Sensing his mood, Tim reached out and lightly touched the sleeve of his brother's suit coat. "I'll see what I can do, Jack," he said quietly. Then, shifting his tone, he added playfully, "I'll need to know what's in it for me, though. If I can convince you to resign, I could probably become Gardner's Vice President."

"Well," Jack said, turning back to his younger brother and smiling, "look at it this way. If I win, I can only serve one more term, but if Gardner's elected, you'd have to wait another eight years to become President yourself. You'll be an old man by then."

"Yes, that's a good point," Tim mumbled, barely hearing. His attention had been drawn to a yellow legal-size notebook that he'd removed from his briefcase, and he was already beginning to make notes for himself on the job ahead.

"Remember," Jack said, his voice serious again, "we can't do anything over the next few hours that will irretrievably divide the Party or seriously damage your chances to become Gardner's running mate, if later that becomes our best course of action. We have to keep all of our options open now."

"You don't make it easy, do you?" Tim said.

"I never have," Jack agreed.

Tim looked up from his legal pad long enough to nod, signaling that, as difficult as it was, he would still do it the way his brother wanted it to be done. "And just how long do I have to put this political miracle together?" he asked then.

"I have to have your best answer by midnight, tonight," the President said crisply, and then he looked at his watch. "Mayor Conlin has asked us to a reception tonight. Rance will be there as well, and I'm going to ask the Mayor to arrange a meeting."

"In other words, you're giving me a little over three hours to do a job that it's taken Gardner's people nine months to do," Tim said, looking back down at the pad of paper on his lap and beginning to scratch hurried notes on it again.

Jack smiled at his younger brother. "Yes. That's exactly what I'm asking you to do," he said simply. "A three-hour miracle—and, knowing you, I don't have any doubt whatsoever that it will get done."

The only face Jack could see when he stepped off the elevator was Suzanne's. She was standing at the far side of the crowded floor of connecting hotel rooms that was serving as the Cassidy convention headquarters. "Oh, Jack," she sighed as he approached her and then she tried to smile, but its energy failed to move from the mere upward curve of her lips to the tensely held muscles of the rest of her face.

"Where are the children?" Jack asked as he reached her.

"Safely asleep, thank God," Suzanne said, and she pointed through the dozens of Cassidy staff people who swirled around them in the halls and offices of the campaign headquarters, toward the comparative peace and quiet of the final door at the end of the long hotel hallway.

"Let's ah . . ." Jack began, but his voice faltered then and he couldn't find the words. So instead he grasped Suzanne's hand and led her toward an open doorway. Inside what had once been a hotel bedroom and was now a converted campaign office, a presidential aide was talking urgently into one of the several telephones that lined the room. As soon as he saw the President, the young man immediately stood and quickly finished his call.

"Thank you," Cassidy said as the staff worker hurried out the door, leaving Jack and Suzanne alone in the ugly, smoke-filled room. The hotel carpet beneath them was stacked with piles of papers and cardboard boxes jammed with files, and the single desk pushed into a far corner of the room was littered with coffee cups, ashtrays brimming with cigarette butts, and several constantly ringing telephones.

"Welcome home," Suzanne said sarcastically, looking around at the cluttered, disorganized room, reeking of politics.

Jack stood in the middle of all the ugliness of the staff room and looked down at the striking dark beauty of his wife's face for a brief moment before he answered her. He seemed to be trying to judge the depth of her unhappiness and perhaps find some kind of answer for it, but instead what he saw frightened him. Suzanne seemed unhappier than he had ever seen her before. "What did you think of the speech?" he asked tentatively.

"All it needed was one more sentence," she said, "and it would have been the best speech that I've ever heard you make."

"The line about: I will not seek and, if nominated, I will not accept . . ."

"That's the one," Suzanne said, cutting her husband off in midsentence. "You're not fooling me. I know how much this is taking out of you, even if no one else can. You're not ready for all of this yet."

They were both silent then, just standing near each other, but not touching in the middle of the ugly, brightly lit hotel room. They stood for several long seconds, listening to the noise of the ringing phones around them and through the thin hotel walls the clatter of typewriters and teletype machines coming from the other offices nearby.

"Jack, I'm sorry," Suzanne said, dropping her head away from Jack's face, so that she could speak honestly now, and search inside of herself for her own feelings without seeing her husband's strong brown eyes watching her every move.

"Sorry for what?" Jack said.

"Sorry that I'm not different, sorry that I'm not a better Cassidy for you," she said, forcing a small smile and lifting her eyes back toward his face.

"Suzanne, I love you," he said simply and began to move forward to take his wife in his arms, but he could see from the way that she held herself, her body stiff and tense under her brightly colored dress, that she didn't want to be held. She didn't want to be talked to and soothed down. She wanted, Jack guessed, only to let her feelings out, and to have him understand what it was that was frightening her now, and so he held his ground and remained standing across the room from her.

"It's different than it was," she said softly, her mind flooding back to the sight of the roaring delegates in the convention hall that they'd just left. "It's like they want a part of you, Jack, like they want a part of us both," she added. "Something's changed. There's a feeling that wasn't there before. It frightens me," she admitted finally and then looked away again, knowing that her words had still been inadequate.

"It's just politics," Jack said, smiling slightly, but in the back of his own head there was a stirring now, too, a stirring of something that he'd felt in the country since Dallas, but he didn't want to see it clearly and so he fought against it, denying it with the cool, confident smile that he formed for his wife, as he took the last few short steps across the room to her and held her close to him. Her body felt as cold and unyielding as it had looked from across the room, but then with his touch he could feel her begin to give in slightly, and then he could feel her body faintly trembling against him. In her hair, Jack could smell the strange mixture of perfume and stale cigarette smoke. He closed his eyes, hating himself for a brief moment for forcing her to this point, where she stood trembling in his embrace. "Maybe it's the war, maybe it's what happened in Dallas, maybe it's something else. I don't know, but something's changing the country, changing us," she said and then paused, groping for the words. "The truth is I'm afraid. I just don't want to lose you. I don't . . ." But she couldn't finish.

"Rance asked me to resign tonight," Jack said then. "Is that what you want?"

Suzanne hesitated for a moment before answering, and it was the hesitation more than her words that communicated her true feelings, Jack thought as he watched her. "No," she said finally. "No, I don't want that." Then she turned and walked slowly to the window that overlooked the Atlantic City street.

"I have to consider the possibility of challenging Rance for the nomination," he said. "But first, I have to know that, whatever I decide, you'll support my decision," he said.

Suzanne paused for an uncomfortably long time before answering. "Of course," she said finally, but when she spoke, her back was turned toward her husband and he couldn't see her face. "I'm your wife," she added, and as hard as she tried to disguise it in her voice, Jack could sense her true feelings of sadness and helplessness. "I'll do the right thing," she added softly. "I always do."

"Well, you've got half the country wondering what you're going to do next," Rozier said as he took his place in the living room of Jack's private suite on the top floor of the Atlantic City hotel.

For the moment, Jack appeared content to simply reach over and lift a half of a chicken sandwich off a room-service tray that had been set up on the coffee table in front of him. He took a small bite and paused for a moment before taking a glass of milk from the tray and sipping at it thoughtfully. It was the first food that he'd eaten in almost twelve hours, but he barely seemed interested in it.

It was even worse than Suzanne suspected, Jack thought as he set the glass of milk back down. His head was pounding again now with almost as much power as it had before the operations, and he was drained of energy. One speech, he thought angrily, one damn speech and I feel like this, how can I possibly consider running a campaign and an administration? He could see that Rozier was watching him carefully from across the room, and he forced himself to stop thinking about the pain then. He just couldn't afford to let anyone else know how he felt.

"Do you want something?" Jack asked his press secretary, gesturing at the room-service tray.

Rozier looked at the other half of the thin chicken sandwich briefly, not trying to disguise his own less than enthusiastic appraisal of Jack's late-night dinner. "No, Suzanne and I had dinner before we went to the hall," he said.

"That's what I like about the French," Jack said. "No matter what the circumstances, they find time to eat well."

"And the Irish always find the time to make a speech," Rozier said. "By the way, that was a damn fine one you made tonight."

"Thank you," Jack said. "God knows I had enough time to work on it."

There was a brief knock on the door and then Tim Cassidy's slim figure entered the room. He was carrying only the same long yellow note pad that he had begun working with earlier in the evening, but he was in his shirtsleeves now, his tie half undone and hanging loosely down and flapping against his shirt front. Jack tried to look across the room and read the notations on the legal pad that his brother carried. He knew that buried within the numbers scratched on those few sheets of paper lay his future and to some extent the future of his country.

Behind Tim came Brian, followed by O'Connor. They each found seats at various places around Jack in the comfortably furnished room and, when they had settled into position, Cassidy nodded and pushed the room-service tray out of the way, clearing the space on the coffee table in front of him. "Well, tell me, how does it look?" he said, gesturing eagerly at the legal pad in his brother's hands. Jack was dressed for the Mayor's reception in a black dinner jacket and white tie, with a small, neat, red carnation decorating his buttonhole. He grinned easily out at the roomful of shirtsleeved men who had gathered in a small semicircle around him, seeming to enjoy the contrast in their dress to his own, as he waited for his brother to respond.

Tim stayed crouched over his legal pad, jotting a last few numbers, and then he rechecked his notes one final time, being very certain of his calculations before he spoke. Down the left-hand margin of the top sheet of his yellow pad were listed the names of each of the fifty states. Earlier in the evening, Tim had written from memory next to each state the number of voting delegates that each had at the convention and then, with the help of his recent phone calls, he had begun inserting a breakdown of the probable first-ballot votes for Cassidy, Gardner, Putnam and "Others" in the four columns against the right-hand margin. Beneath the vote totals for each state was a section for comments and notes. Almost all the spaces on the yellow legal pad were black with numbers and notes now, all of them created by Tim over the last few short hours of intense work.

"Well, we're not as well organized as we were four years ago," Tim said smiling, and the men seated around him chuckled softly at his obvious understatement.

"We're not as well organized as we were eight years ago," the President said, joining in the soft laughter and reminding his brother of the hasty, ill-conceived bid for his Party's vice-presidential nomination that they had tried to mount at the last moment at the 1956 Democratic convention.

"Yes, well, that didn't work out so well," Tim said, and then he paused before giving his assessment of the votes at the current nominating convention. "Jack, I think we can stop Rance from being nominated on the first ballot," he said dramatically. "It will be a fight, but I believe that it can be done," Tim added, and then he looked up from his work sheets and focused on his brother's face. As he did, Tim could see a brief faint look of disappointment pass across his older brother's eyes, but, if it had really been there, Tim thought, it was gone in an instant.

"Are there enough votes to nominate me?" Jack asked calmly.

Tim shook his head. "Not on the first ballot, Jack. The best we could hope for is to stop Rance. We've got three states here," Tim said, tapping his yellow legal pad with a pencil point. "Three states with almost two hundred votes that I think we could convince to stay with 'favorite sons' on the first ballot, but they won't commit to you—not the way things stand now, anyway. They don't want to see a Gardner nomination, but they're not willing to take the risk of angering him either, not unless they're certain that you're really in this fight to stay and that you're committed to winning it."

Jack nodded his head, knowing without needing to be told which states Tim was talking about now.

"And Senator Putnam still controls Minnesota and maybe a hundred or so other votes," O'Connor said then.

"Yes, maybe as many as a hundred and fifty or a hundred and seventy-five in total," Tim added. "But I think we know where those votes will be before the night is over."

"Putnam has been meeting with Gardner for the last hour or so," O'Connor explained to the others then.

"Yes," Jack said coolly. He hadn't heard the news until that moment, but he knew that a Gardner-Putnam meeting under the circumstances was inevitable. "But what you're telling me," Jack went on. "Is that, even with the votes that Senator Putnam controls, we could deny Rance's nomination on the first ballot?"

"If you let us take the gloves off," Tim said urgently. "If, first thing tomorrow morning, you made an announcement of your candidacy, and then pulled out all the stops and let us make a real fight out of it. Yes. Without that . . ." Tim shrugged his shoulders. "I can't be certain."

"Jack, that's the most we can reasonably expect under the circumstances," O'Connor said then. "I mean, for God's sake, it is Gardner's convention. The mere fact that you stopped him on the first ballot would finish him. We could win it then on the second or third ballot without you having to promise Putnam or anybody else a damn thing."

Brian nodded his head sharply in agreement. Jack smiled at his youngest brother's enthusiasm, and then he shifted his gaze to Rozier. "What do you think, Allen? You've been pretty quiet," Jack said.

Rozier sat silently for a long moment, thinking it all through before he spoke. "I think that you could win the battle and lose the war, Jack," he said finally. "There's no point in having the nomination, if all it means is that we've put ourselves into a position to lose in November. If we take the nomination away from Rance now at this late stage of the game, what do we really have? We could just be handing Granderman the election on a silver platter."

"We've got three months to the general election—that's more than enough time to put the Party back together again," O'Connor said.

"Four years ago," Rozier went on making his case, after O'Connor's brief interruption, "Simmons came within a percentage point of beating us, and, in my opinion, Granderman will be a far stronger opponent than Simmons ever was. That means to win in November we're going to have to hang on to almost every state that we won four years ago. If we challenge Rance now and take the nomination away from him, what happens to our chances of winning Texas and the other southern and border states that we won in 1960?" Rozier paused then and looked carefully across the room at the President before he summarized his thoughts. "In my opinion, it's too risky. We're trying to move too quickly. Four years from now, everything could be very different. I say wait."

As Rozier finished, the door to the hotel suite opened. It was the small, neatly dressed figure of Ned Townsend, the President's brother-in-law. He had been making calls from a little room down the hall and he carried with him his own legal-size pad of notepaper, but his list wasn't of delegates and votes. It was a different kind of listing entirely, but one equally important, and Jack was eager to hear what was written on it as well.

"The money's there," Townsend said, as soon as he noticed Jack looking expectantly across the room at him. He crossed to the President then and set his notepad down in front of him. The President's brother-in-law was in charge of finances, and he'd spent the last three hours talking to contributors from the 1960 campaign and his list was full of names, and phone numbers, and dollar signs. Cassidy looked briefly at the list and, satisfied, he looked back up at the roomful of men gathered around him. "Anything more?"

The room was quiet for a few seconds and in the silence Tim decided to say a last few words in summary of their findings. "I think you can have the nomination if you want it, Jack," he said simply. "I agree with Allen that it will make some people very angry, but in my judgment, if you announce now, it's available to you on the second ballot or the third at the very latest."

"And in the fall?" the President asked.

Tim only laughed at the question at first. "Granderman's got too much money. The country will never elect him," he said.

Jack smiled and looked around the room one last time, his face asking for further comments. There weren't any. "Thank you, all of you," he said then.

As the men stood, Jack looked over at Tim, who was gathering his notebook and scraps of paper off the top of the coffee table. "Do you have a dinner jacket somewhere?" the President asked.

"A dinner jacket?" Tim said, not returning the President's smile, but just keeping his head down, looking only at the numbers he'd created on the long yellow sheets of paper that lay in front of him.

"You're going to need one at the Mayor's reception," Jack said.

Tim glanced down at his loosened tie and rumpled white shirt with the sleeves rolled up past his elbows. Then he nodded his head sadly that he understood. "Yes, Mr. President, I do have a dinner jacket," he said as he got to his feet.

"Good," Jack said and then stood himself, showing the full length of his own elegantly tailored formal wear to the roomful of weary, shirtsleeved men. "Thank you all again," he said, not giving a hint of what decisions he might have reached as a result of the meeting. "I appreciate what you've each done tonight and I've listened to your thoughts carefully. Now, I think you all better get some rest. I'd like to see everyone here again at five thirty tomorrow morning."

The groan that escaped Rozier's throat then was loud enough for the President to hear from across the room. "For Allen's benefit, we'll make it five thirty-five," Jack said, smiling.

"Thank you, Mr. President," Rozier said and returned the smile.

"Now," Jack said, turning to his brother, "the Attorney General and I have a party to attend."

There were fireworks in progress at the Governor's mansion when the presidential limousine pulled to a stop in the center of its big circular front drive.

Jack paused for a moment before stepping out onto the walkway that led to the old two-story Colonial-style mansion. He felt weak; the pain that he had fought against for the last several hours had drained him of energy, he realized suddenly. How the hell was he going to pull this off? He sat for a moment to collect his strength. A bright red burst of light exploded in the sky above the mansion's grounds then and illuminated the President's face for a brief moment as he looked out from behind the dark protective glass of the limousine's back seat. Tim was seated next to him, and as the burst of fireworks faded away the President smiled weakly over at his younger brother. "Are you okay?" Tim asked, seeing the signs of fatigue in his brother's face.

"Sure, it's just like going into combat," Jack said. "All you have to do is make sure you show up and then let your adrenaline do the rest."

Tim glanced up at the study on the mansion's second floor where both men knew that Gardner was waiting for them. "Yes, and the enemy knows our position," Tim said as he noticed the Vice President's big shadow briefly pass by the upstairs window.

At the front steps to the mansion, Jack could see the Mayor of Atlantic City waiting for them as well. So, without delaying any longer, the President stepped out of the limousine's back seat and crossed the driveway to shake hands with the older man.

"You asked for a diversion," the Mayor said as he stepped forward to greet the President, and Jack glanced from the Mayor's face toward the exuberant fireworks display exploding in the night air above them. "Yes, thank you," he said, and then he started up the steps into the mansion's front entrance. Most of the reception guests were in the courtyard at the rear of the mansion watching the fireworks display, and the main downstairs ballroom was almost empty, but the Mayor motioned Jack toward a back staircase that couldn't be seen from the floor of the main ballroom.

"How has it been?" Jack asked the Mayor as the two men paused for a moment and let Tim brush by them and start up the stairs toward the second floor.

"A little dull until now," the Mayor said, smiling and motioning out toward the fireworks display.

"Yes, well, that's nothing compared to what we have to face upstairs," Jack said, turning back to the private staircase that led to the second story. His brother was at the very top of the staircase now, just disappearing down the dimly lit second-story hallway. "Tim's going up to see him first," Jack explained. "We drew straws coming over and he lost. So, he has to go in on the first wave and try to establish a beachhead for me," Jack added, and as he did a loud whistling sound could be heard in the air above the mansion's grounds and then a rapid series of crackling explosions. "That's the Vice President now," Jack said. "I better get up there and give Tim a hand. I don't want any casualties." But before starting up the stairs, he paused and nodded his appreciation at the older man.

Jack turned then and started up the dimly lit staircase. Once he reached the top of the stairs, he turned and looked back down at the nearly empty ballroom. The Mayor was already crossing toward the garden at the rear of the mansion to rejoin his guests.

Jack continued down the long upstairs hallway toward the Mayor's second-floor office. He paused for a brief second outside the door, breathing in deeply and calling on his final reserves of energy to some-how get him through the next few minutes. Then he swung the door open and he could see Gardner standing at the far side of the room next to the Mayor's executive desk. A display of brightly colored fireworks was exploding outside the window directly behind the Vice President's tall figure, but he had his back to them, his attention fixed on the door to the office.

As Jack entered the room, Gardner's body stiffened noticeably under the dark formal clothes and neither man made any effort to shake the other's hand. They just stood looking at each other, saying nothing for several long seconds, until the door closed behind the President. Rance always looks slightly wrong even in the most expensive tuxedo, Jack thought, as he looked across the upstairs office at the older man.

"Your brother and I have been waiting for you," the Vice President said impatiently.

Jack only nodded coolly, and then he crossed the office to sit in one of the several formal antique chairs that decorated the room.

"The last two hours may have cost us the election," Gardner said without any further preliminaries. He moved around the Governor's desk then, not waiting for Cassidy to reply, and bent down by the first of three television sets that had been brought in at the Vice President's request and placed along the far wall of the office. The three modern machines looked strikingly out of place in the old-fashioned room that had otherwise been decorated exclusively with antiques out of New Jersey's Colonial past.

"You can't turn one of these damn things on without . . ." But then rather than finishing his explanation Gardner angrily bent down and by way of demonstration flicked on the first of the television sets. Immediately, its screen lit up showing a news commentator in tight close-up with a handheld microphone pressed to his lips. The reporter was standing in the darkened and now empty Atlantic City convention hall. "The speculation here tonight is that President Cassidy may be considering . . ."

" 'Speculation'!" Gardner shouted the word at the television set, but its meaning was clearly intended for the President. A great silver-and-blue explosion of fireworks flashed outside the second-story window then and the explosion seemed to energize Gardner even more dramatically. He suddenly reached forward, blocking the President's view of the first television screen, and switched on the second of the three sets. As soon as he did, another telecaster appeared and began mixing his opinions with those of the commentator on the first television screen. "Will Cassidy . . ." the second commentator began, but Gardner wouldn't let him finish either. Instead, the Vice President reached past the second commentator's image to the third and final television and snapped it on as well. Soon the room was filled with a cacophony of competing voices, each questioning, pondering, speculating, musing, and theorizing about the President's plans. It was ugly, discordant music to Gardner's ears and the distaste could be seen very clearly in the deepening lines in his long expressive face, but as he listened he held his body very stiff and straight, with his hands clasped tightly behind his back, and he let the sets blare away at the room, while multicolored fireworks exploded exuberantly at the window behind him. It was good theater, Cassidy thought, as he waited quietly and watched the other man perform.

After a few seconds, a Secret Service man opened the door and looked in to see what all the noise was about, but Gardner just waved him off and the agent hurriedly closed the door again, apologizing as he left, but his intrusion had broken the noisy spell and Gardner began reaching down then and silencing each stream of words in turn, until the room was thankfully quiet again, even the fireworks display outside the window momentarily spent.

"Speculation," Gardner said as he crossed the room to stand over the chair that Jack had chosen earlier. "Speculation, rumor, innuendo, and prognostication!" He spat the words out like an East Texas preacher from his home county revealing the four deadly sins of the modern world to his congregation. "Speculation is what kills candidates, and campaigns, and sometimes entire political parties," he said, and then he paused and looked back and forth between the President and his brother. The President could tell that he was getting ready to deliver his punchline now. "I didn't want to do this, but you forced me into it." Gardner's eyes finally rested on the President's face as he spoke. "I had to take control of this situation myself, before it became a disaster for all of us. So I've scheduled a press conference for first thing tomorrow morning and I'm goin' announce then that I've selected Senator Putnam to be my running mate." Gardner remained standing after he'd finished talking, trying to keep the physical high ground for himself. He looked down first at the President and then across at his brother. Both men's faces were coolly impassive, waiting to see if he had said all that he wanted to for now. He had, but still he stood over them, hoping to intimidate them, as he had so many other men by his very size and energy and physical strength. The fireworks remained silent in the courtyard below, as the crew assembled their ammunition for the grand finale, and the only sound for the moment in the upstairs study was the ticking of the tall grandfather clock that stood by the door. Gardner studied the President in the silence. He looked prepared to wait for hell itself to freeze over before he would give in and speak with Gardner standing threateningly above him. Finally, reluctantly on stiff, tense legs, the Vice President moved back toward the room's massive walnut desk and sat down behind it. As he stared across the desk's shiny wooden surface, he made no effort to disguise his anger and his belief that the two men were now playing by a quite different set of rules than they had been at their meeting only a few hours earlier. But still Cassidy said nothing, just returning Gardner's angry stare with his own unemotional, businesslike look. The Vice President finally grew uncomfortable in the lengthening silence. "I'm not saying that you and I agreed to anything this afternoon," Gardner said, interrupting the silence and pointing out the window behind him toward the modern skyscrapers of downtown Atlantic City where he and the President had met earlier that day. "I'm not questionin' anybody's honesty here, maybe jus' their wisdom," Gardner said. "I know you've had your people on the phone for the last three hours, testin' the waters for you."

"Rance," Tim said. "We owed it to ourselves and maybe to the Party as well, to explore our alternatives."

Gardner snorted a short laugh. "Well, I guess I just had to do the same thing then, didn't I? I had to explore my alternatives, and, when I did, I decided that I had to do somethin' to end all this speculation once and for all," the Vice President said, pointing back out at the now silenced television sets lined up in front of him. "I kin' count votes, too, and there's no way that anyone can do anything about my nomination now. It will be a Gardner-Putnam ticket, and that's the end of it," Gardner added, moving his eyes from Tim toward the older brother and glaring angrily across the desktop at the President's still coolly composed face.

"No," Jack said quietly, his voice very low, but self-assured. The word stung Gardner. Recoiling with its impact, he moved back in his chair away from the younger man.

Jack reached up then into the inside pocket of his dinner jacket exposing its elegant white satin lining to the Vice President for a moment before withdrawing several sheets of yellow legal-size paper. Without taking his eyes from Gardner's face, Jack unfolded the sheets of paper slowly and then leaned forward to spread them face up on the desktop that separated him from the Vice President. As he did, Gardner reached into his breast pocket for his half-rim reading glasses and hurriedly placed them on the tip of his nose. He stared down then at the sheets of paper, trying to catch even a glimpse of the numbers written on them.

"I'll tell you what they say," the President said calmly. "They say that I can deny you the nomination on the first ballot and they say that I can win it on the second."

"We don't see it that way," Gardner said, his face not betraying his true feelings. "I have the votes to control this convention. You must know that," he added quickly.

Instead of answering him with words, Jack boldly pushed the legal-size sheets of paper filled with Tim's confidential and highly valuable calculations across the table toward Gardner like a poker player so confident of victory he would offer to show his opponent his cards before the final bets were made. Gardner had played political poker long enough to feel the drama and the power of Cassidy's confident and unexpected move. "You don't have the votes, Rance," the President said evenly, and Gardner refused to look down either at Cassidy's eyes or at the long yellow sheets of paper on the desktop in front of him, choosing instead to wrap the long fingers of his hands together in a bridge near the front of his face, pretending to study them carefully instead. He knew now, without reading the numbers, that Cassidy wasn't bluffing.

"If you do it, you'll split the Party for a generation and you'll end up destroying your own career in the bargain," Gardner said finally, his eyes still studying his own hands.

"Rance," Cassidy said, ignoring the Vice President's predictions, "we discussed some things this afternoon." The President reminded Gardner of their meeting earlier in the day. "We couldn't reach a final understanding then, but I think we were close, and I'd like to reach that agreement now," he said coolly. Gardner began to relax the tangled web of his fingers that blocked the view of the President's face and slowly he lifted his eyes above them to meet the younger man's gaze again.

"The Attorney General is the best possible choice to be your running mate," Cassidy said calmly.

"I can't do that, Jack. I've already agreed to put Senator Putnam on the ticket," Gardner said.

"Rance, you need us more than you need Senator Putnam," Jack said. "The truth is, Rance, we need each other," he added confidentially.

Gardner continued to return his look. This was not the way he had wanted it, not the way that he had dreamed of becoming his Party's candidate for the presidency. The goal that he'd worked for all his life was within reach now, but it wouldn't be truly his. If he gave in now, it would be forever shared by the two men sitting with him that night, but he didn't dare to say no, either. The numbers on the long sheets of yellow paper stared up at him, mocking him. "And you'll resign?" Gardner said, but his heart wasn't in it any longer. The words lacked the power that he'd said them with at his meeting with Cassidy only a few hours earlier.

Cassidy shook his head no, refusing to even say the word out loud to the other man.

"Jack, don't you see the position this puts me in?"

"Yes, I do," Cassidy said. "But those are my terms. It's a Gardner-Cassidy ticket, and I will serve out my term in its entirety. That's my only offer."

There was total silence in the room then.

"And you'll support the ticket right down the line," Gardner said finally.

"I'll play whatever role you ask me to play in the campaign," Cassidy said.

Gardner nodded his head and then lowered his eyes to the tangled web of his fingers again. "All right," he said slowly. "But I can't afford to have you running off somewhere after the convention now. I'm goin' to need you right here for the next few weeks. We're both going to have to work hard to undo the damage that's been done tonight."

Jack thought first of Suzanne before he answered, but he knew what Gardner was asking for now was fair and it was a necessary part of the agreement that he was seeking with him. He had done damage to the ticket and it was only reasonable to expect that he be the one to correct it. "I'll stay as long as you want me to," he said.

Gardner's head and eyes rose again then and he looked directly into Cassidy's face. As the two men's eyes locked, the agreement was finalized without any further words passing between them. As if on cue then, the technicians chose that moment to fire off the grand finale, and multicolored fireworks of red and white and blue all exploded at once, lighting up the Atlantic City skyline beyond the window of the second-floor office. And in the middle of the bright flashing display of whirling colors, the two men stood and faced each other, shaking hands against a backdrop of red, white, and blue fireworks, and the Gardner-Cassidy ticket was complete.

CHAPTER
17

"The campaign may be beginning, but it's beginning without me," Suzanne said, tossing a copy of *Newsweek* on the coffee table. The cover picture, taken on the convention's final night, showed her husband holding Gardner's hand high in the air. She and Jack were alone in their suite at the Waldorf, high above the streets of New York City.

On the low table in front of them was an assortment of newspapers and news magazines, all proclaiming the start of the 1964 presidential campaign: Granderman-Longwood versus Gardner-Cassidy, and after the Democrats' emotional and chaotic nominating convention in Atlantic City the experts now were calling an election that had once tilted decidedly toward the Democrats a toss-up.

"We've got a hell of a lot of work to do," Jack said absently. He had a magazine and a copy of *The New York Times* both open on his lap. "No one's being very kind about last week," he said, finishing one editorial and beginning another.

"They rarely are," his wife said, but Jack only continued reading. Suzanne stood and walked to the window of the suite and stood looking down at the lights of the city beginning to shine against the late summer night sky. She suddenly became very aware of the silence in the room. For the moment, she could hear only the steady hum of the air conditioning pumping out regulated oversanitized air for her to breathe, and in the distance she could hear very clearly the faraway street sounds from below. Suzanne reached up and placed the palm of her hand on the thick pane of glass that separated her from the freshness of the real night air outside the window. She wanted to go for a walk outside, maybe along the river where the hot day's air was gentling and cooling. But the Secret Service men would have to accompany her and she wouldn't make it through the lobby without the reporters and photographers blocking her way, shouting questions at her, firing bright lights in her eyes. She let her hand slide slowly off the window and the heat from her skin left a tracing of smudge marks on the otherwise clean surface of the glass.

"The *Times* thinks New York is the key," she could hear her husband saying, but his voice sounded a million miles away. "Of course the *Times* always thinks that New York's the key," Jack continued. "But this time they might be right."

Suzanne didn't answer. She wasn't even certain of what he'd said. Her thoughts were somewhere else, outside on the street, at the beach in Hyannis or at Palm Beach, but not in that cooped-up, air-conditioned, oversanitized hotel room perched high above New York City.

"What I think is important is to fight him for it. Go right after it. We can't let Granderman take New York or any other state without a fight. If we can make him spend his time and his money in his home state . . ." Suzanne could hear her husband's voice making sounds somewhere out there past that vast gulf that had grown up to separate them, but they were just words to her without much meaning, just politician's words, and she'd heard too many of them over the last few years. She kept her body turned toward the window and the New York skyline and her thoughts seemed to drift by themselves again to the streets, to the river, to the cool green areas to walk along in the city on summer nights, and she was surprised when suddenly she sensed her husband standing behind her.

"Jack," she said, startled, as she turned back to him and then, without guarding against it, she blurted out the truth of what she had been thinking. "Would you think I was terrible if I took the children and . . ." But she couldn't finish, and then she could feel Jack's hands touching her shoulders.

"Can't you wait, just a few weeks?" he said, but his voice showed that he already knew the answer.

"No," she said, so softly that she could barely hear the word herself as she spoke it.

"Suzanne, everything's changed," Jack said. "I promised Rance that I'd help get the campaign back on the right track. After what I did to him at the convention, I owe him that much." Jack paused then, hoping that he'd said enough, but he knew from the expression on his wife's face that he hadn't, and he tried to explain. "If I leave now, it will look as if I don't really support him, and that could be very damaging. You can see that, can't you?"

Suzanne shrugged her shoulders. It wasn't important what she saw, she thought. She stayed silent, lacking even the strength to reply, and the silence quickly became more eloquent than words. "Maybe you should go," Jack said then.

"And you could join us in a week or two?" she said hopefully.

"Perhaps," he said, but with no real conviction.

"All those people," she said, looking down at the busy, crowded Manhattan streets below her.

"I'm just going to make a few speeches," Jack said quickly.

"Jack, don't lie to me. You've promised to appear in the Labor Day parade," Suzanne said sharply, catching him at his deception.

Jack only smiled then. "You have a better intelligence network than the CIA. Who told you that, Allen?"

"It doesn't matter. Jack, please don't do it . . ."

"The parade route will be fully protected," Jack said, cutting her off. "Besides, I only intend to walk a few blocks at the most . . ."

Suzanne sighed deeply, disbelief showing in her face. "Jack, you've said that kind of thing before. But then you hear the band and you see all those people cheering and . . ." She didn't finish her sentence. When she looked back up at her husband's face, he was smiling slightly, although his face was struggling not to show his amusement. "You think that you know me pretty well, don't you?" he said, finally letting the smile that he had been fighting come through and light his face.

"Jack, I think that the only way that you're ever going to listen to me about any of this is for me to show you just how serious I am," she said.

Jack shook his head. "Suzanne, I listen to you. I just can't do anything about it right now, that's all. I have to stay here. There's just too much at stake."

"It doesn't ever stop, does it? I mean, there's always something, isn't there? Some state that needs your special touch, some congressman who needs to see only you and no one else, some big contributor who can only talk with you. Jack, I'm exhausted," she said, letting her arms drop flat to her sides and her shoulders slump down in a way that Jack had never seen before. "We, you and I, our family, have just survived the most . . ." She ran out of words then and crossed past her husband, not letting him touch her as she sank back onto the big hotel couch at the center of the room. "I'm not like you," she said then. "I don't get an unlimited supply of energy from the air of a political gathering, any political gathering. I'm just a person, or I used to be," she said sadly. She began shaking her head over and over, back and forth wearily, as if the movement might be able to erase all the things that she didn't want to deal with in her life now, and, as she did, she could feel the fatigue and trauma of the last year and the anxiety that she felt about the future, all the things that she had fought so hard to hide from the press and from her friends and her own family, and maybe even in some way from herself, finally begin to rise to the surface. "But you know the worst of it, Jack," she said. "The worst of it is that I'm not me anymore," she said. "I've been strong, strong for you, strong for the children, for the country. I've acted at being brave for so many months now, that I've forgotten who I am when I'm not acting." She was silent once more, and in the silence her husband moved toward her and sat down next to her, putting his arm around her shoulders.

"Jack, I want to go to Greece. I can take the children and visit Konstantine and . . ." She stopped in midsentence and looked directly up into her husband's eyes, hoping that he understood that she had finally reached her limit. She didn't try to explain any more of it though; she just waited for his answer, hoping that no more words would be necessary.

"If you think that's best," her husband said, but his face betrayed his disappointment.

Suzanne sighed. "I do. I have to," she said. "We're very different, aren't we, you and I?" she added after a few seconds, her voice full of a very real sadness.

"In some ways," her husband said.

"Jack, please come with me."

"I can't, but I think it would be good for you. I'll be all right," he said, putting a smile that he didn't truly feel back on his face for his wife's benefit.

"Will you?" Suzanne said. "I hope so. I hope we both will be."

"Jesus, the guy's got balls, doesn't he? No one can say that he doesn't have balls," Costello said, and then he looked again with disbelief at the photograph that Garrett had insisted on bringing across town and giving to him personally. It was hard to decide which one was stupider, the bastard in the photograph or Garrett himself, Costello thought as he looked down at the picture of the short, dark-haired man that lay on his desk.

"Look at that fucker," Costello commanded, swiping at the photograph angrily with the back of his hand. "What did he do? Stop some fucking tourist and say, 'Hey, would you mind? I'm going to waste the President of the United States and I'd like to have a picture for my friends of me standin' outside his house? Just push this little button right here.' The guy must be nuts!" Costello tried to laugh then, but the laughter seemed to become trapped somewhere in the heavy rolls of flesh that rippled down from chin and throat and it was lost in a thick choking sound long before it escaped from his lips.

"That's Hyannis, ain't it?" Costello said finally, shoving the picture back at the lawyer. Garrett nodded without looking at the photograph again. He didn't have to. He'd memorized every angle and shadow on it when it had arrived in the mail that morning, memorized it while he'd worked up the courage to call Costello and tell him.

"And that's our boy," Costello said, tapping the image of the short man standing in front of the Cassidy estate in Cape Cod.

As Costello looked down at the photograph, he remembered briefly the first time that he had met the dark-haired man, who had called himself Lopez then. They had met in a bar in the French Quarter. The meeting had been at Costello's request and had been arranged by a mutual acquaintance. Costello was always on the lookout for people like Lopez, and from the first moment that he'd looked into the man's dark, remorseless eyes he knew that he had found someone who would be useful to him.

Garrett turned the photograph over, showing Costello the other side. On the back "$250,000" was scratched in dark black ballpoint pen, and beneath it the name of a Costa Rican bank that they had used to do business with the man once before, paying him for the service that he had never accomplished, but that he was obviously preparing to finish now. Costello nodded to Garrett that he saw the sum printed in bold black numerals on the back of the photo. Then Costello reached forward and grasped the photograph with his short thick fingers and tossed it back across the desk to the lawyer.

"Burn the fucking thing!" Costello said angrily.

Garrett scooped the photograph up off the desktop and began to stuff it into his inside coat pocket.

"Now!" Costello said and Garrett pulled his hand out from under his white suit coat and reached for the big silver-plated lighter that decorated the front of Costello's desk.

The silver lighter worked easily and Garrett moved the edge of the photograph into the long golden plume of flame that escaped into the air, and only when the photograph was burning dangerously close to his own fingers did he drop the flaming paper into a big glass ashtray. Garrett stood then and watched the fire eat away the last of the image of the man who called himself Lopata now, standing proudly in front of the camera, the outline of the famous Cape Cod home clearly visible over his left shoulder.

"Flush them down the fucking toilet," Costello demanded, pointing at the bathroom a few yards away across the carpetless cement floor of the converted warehouse space overlooking the New Orleans harbor that served as his office. And Garrett carried the heavy, bluntly cut glass ashtray into the bathroom and flushed the pile of ashes down into the New Orleans sewer system, and then he returned to the big warehouse room and set the ashtray back down on Costello's desk.

"Look, I'd like to get out from between . . ." the nervous little lawyer began, but Costello cut him off before he could finish.

"There's nothin' to be afraid of," the big man said angrily. "Anything else?" Costello said and wiped a finger full of sweat from his upper lip, flicking it onto the cement floor as he waited for the lawyer to answer his question.

"No, that was it," Garrett said.

"How about the envelope?"

"What?" Garrett was confused.

"The fucking envelope that the picture came in," Costello said. In the silence that followed, a ship's horn wailed low and mournfully in the New Orleans harbor behind him.

"Oh, yeah," Garrett said. He reached back into his briefcase that he'd left lying by his feet. His fingers fumbled for the envelope that had arrived in his morning mail, and when he found it he handed it to Costello.

"Anyone else see the envelope?" Costello said.

"No, no one," Garrett said. "Except for my secretary, I guess," he added after a few seconds.

"You guess?" Costello said.

"I don't know. It was on my desk," Garrett answered, but from the look on Costello's face he could tell that his answer wasn't satisfactory. "I'll find out," Garrett said quickly.

"You do that," Costello said, not changing his expression. Costello looked down at the envelope that the photograph had arrived in, turning it over in his thick hands. It was a standard white business envelope. The postmark on it was "Hyannis Port, Massachusetts." The only other thing on its clean white surface was Garrett's address in New Orleans. Costello inspected it closely. The handwriting on the envelope seemed to match the hastily scrawled $250,000 on the back of the photograph.

"Burn it!" Costello said, and Garrett hastily repeated the movements that he had just completed a few moments earlier of burning, and then flushing the envelope's ashes down Costello's private toilet, while the big man stayed wedged behind his desk, watching his every move. "Your secretary see the picture?" Costello said as Garrett walked back out of the little bathroom at the rear of the office.

"No, of course not," Garrett said, and as he did Costello looked carefully at him to see if he was lying, but with Garrett it was impossible to tell, he decided finally. The lawyer's nervous, sweaty face was always moving and twitching, his eyes darting around like those of a man who had lied so much, over so many years, that his face and eyes and body no longer knew the difference between lies and the truth.

"What's in there?" Costello said, giving up on trying to read Garrett and pointing instead at the lawyer's bulging leather briefcase.

"Oh, yeah," Garrett said and began to unload several inches of legal-size documents onto the desk in front of Costello. Typed at the top of the first of the long sheets of paper was the heading: *"United States of America vs. The Allied Dock and Warehouse Workers of The Southeast, Joseph A. DeSavio, Thomas R. Costello, et al."*

"The fuckers don't quit, do they? What is all this shit?" Costello said, pulling the big pile of papers toward him and beginning to flip through them.

"Interrogatories, admissions of fact . . ." Garrett said.

"We don't admit nothin'!" Costello cut the lawyer off in midsentence. "The fucking Justice Department," Costello said, letting his squat, fleshy hand drop away from the government's latest batch of legal papers.

"Maybe it will be different after the election," Garrett said, pointing to a newspaper that lay on Costello's desk. The paper's front page showed Rance Gardner, the Democratic Party's presidential nominee, holding aloft the hand of his running mate, Tim Cassidy, who stood on one side of him, and the hand of Jack Cassidy, who stood on the other. The caption below the photograph read: "The Campaign Begins."

Costello looked from the newspaper to the pile of government papers standing on the desktop next to him and then back up at Garrett's face. "Nothing's changed," Costello said. "Not a fuckin' thing. Cassidy's still runnin' things, don't kid yourself about that. He's the one calling the shots."

"So what do I do about . . ." Garrett stopped and pointed back to the spot on Costello's desk where the photograph had been a few minutes earlier.

"Find out who else saw it," Costello said. "I'll let you know what happens next."

The lawyer nodded his head nervously several times. He wanted to say something more, but he knew that it would be useless. He was in this thing so deep now there was no getting out.

Well, here he was back in Dallas. The Bureau, in its infinite wisdom, had returned Sullivan to Texas, not Washington, and he could guess why. It wasn't just because they wanted him out of the capital and far away from the Washington press corps when they released the final report on the Cassidy assassination attempt. And it wasn't just to show him who the boss was and teach him a lesson for sending the letter that he'd sent to headquarters questioning the Bureau's findings in the case. Both of these things were part of it, but if they had been the only reasons, they could have sent him to L.A. or Denver or some other place a million miles away from the action. No, the real reason was because in Dallas they could keep a nice tight eye on him. Sullivan glanced behind him to the glass-enclosed front of Yancey's office. The man with the lean, hawklike face was busy talking on the telephone while his eyes roamed the roomful of agents at his command. The Bureau trusted Yancey to keep him under control, because Yancey's own career was on the line, Sullivan thought, and that's why they'd sent him back to Dallas—back under Yancey's watchful eye.

He'd had almost a week between assignments to visit his family in Philadelphia and get himself straightened back out. It was amazing just how much this Cassidy thing had affected him, but he was feeling better now, ready to go on with his career. His father was retired and they'd had plenty of time together to talk. Sullivan found that he couldn't quite bring himself to tell his dad everything that had been bothering him, particularly how badly his confidence in the Bureau had been shaken by its actions in the Cassidy case. His dad wouldn't have understood. He was the son of an Irish immigrant and his faith in a country that had given him a job and a home and a college education for his son was almost unquestioning. But still, just being with his dad and listening to him talk about how proud he was to tell his friends that his only son was a member of the Federal Bureau of Investigation had reminded Sullivan of why he'd joined the Bureau in the first place and eased the doubts about his own future in government service that had begun creeping into his mind over the last few months. And before Sullivan left Philadelphia, he'd promised both himself and his father that he would give his career a fresh start. After all, he owed his dad at least that much, he'd told himself. If it hadn't been for his father putting him through college, he wouldn't even have a job with something like the Bureau in the first place. He'd be in the factories back in Philadelphia, like most of the people that he had grown up knowing. So, the important thing now, he'd decided, was to go on with his life and try to get things back to the predictable safe way they'd been before that day in November of 1963, when everything had started to go a little haywire.

The Bureau had chosen the week of his return to the Dallas office to release its report on the Cassidy shooting, and releasing the final report to the public meant that the case was permanently closed. You could even buy copies of the damned thing in bookstores. They had it stacked up right next to the diet books and all the other crap that they sold these days, Sullivan thought as he reached out and touched a copy of the slickly bound report that lay on his desk. He hadn't bothered to read it, but its conclusions had been in all the papers. According to its summary pages, Strode was nuts, a Communist sympathizer, and he'd acted alone—end of story. Sullivan picked up the heavy, impressively bound book and dropped it into his desk drawer. Well, if that was the way the Bureau wanted it, he didn't like it, but he wasn't going to kill off his own career by chasing endlessly after some hopeless cause, he told himself for the tenth time that morning. Then he started back to work on the stack of messages, letters, and internal Bureau memos and directives that had built up in his absence. So far, it was just a bunch of junk, but it gave him something to do until Yancey gave him an assignment.

Sullivan shuffled methodically through the mess on his desk, placing the sheets of paper in several piles. Each pile had a different purpose—papers to be filed, phone calls to be returned. This was a clean start just like he'd promised his dad—and he was going to do it right this time, he told himself. He stopped working for a moment and glanced over at the agent at the next desk. My new partner, Sullivan thought as he looked over at the older man, another Bureau precaution, Sullivan guessed. He hadn't been assigned to work with the oldest agent in the Dallas office by accident. He was there to help keep him in line.

"You alive or dead?" Sullivan said, but the man didn't move. His feet were up on the desktop, the brim of his gray felt hat pulled down over his eyes.

"That's my secret." Agent Grissum's face was puffy with years of unprocessed alcohol and nicotine and other assorted toxins. His eyelids drooped wearily, almost permanently covering the dark gray eyes hidden underneath them, making it impossible most of the time to tell whether he was awake or asleep.

Sullivan shrugged his shoulders and returned to his job of sorting through the papers on his new desk. "What do you think Yancey'll give us?"

"You always talk this much?" Grissum said.

"I'm just excited, I guess," Sullivan said.

"Yeah, they told me you were a real go-getter."

"What else did they say?" Sullivan asked.

"Not much." Grissum shrugged just one shoulder as he answered the younger agent.

"They tell you I wrote a letter to D.C. asking questions about the Cassidy report and to keep an eye on me?"

Grissum said nothing, not even bothering to lift a shoulder this time.

"Anyway, I'm ready to do my job now," Sullivan said.

"You wrote a letter to D.C.," Grissum said, laughing sarcastically. "Smart career decision."

Sullivan returned to his work again, collecting his phone messages into one big stack and then sorting them into two piles, ones to return immediately and those that could wait. "Oh, shit!" he said out loud as his eyes focused on his final unanswered phone message.

Grissum looked over at Sullivan. "Now what?" the older agent asked.

"I don't know," Sullivan said. "Just something I thought was over."

"Let it stay 'over' then," Grissum said sagely and returned wearily to looking at the underside of his hat brim.

Sullivan stared down at the phone message for several seconds, measuring Grissum's advice against his own feelings, and his thoughts returned back to that earlier day in November of 1963 when it had all begun.

Sullivan reached down for his telephone and dialed the number on the message slip. As he waited for his call to be answered, he could hear Grissum sighing in disgust at his decision.

"I said let it stay over," the older agent said with surprising intensity.

A recording answered the phone at the number Sullivan had dialed. "I'm sorry, but you have reached a disconnected number," a taped operator's voice said and the young agent looked back down at the date on the phone message. It was over three months old! He slammed the receiver down. Why the hell wasn't it forwarded to him in New Orleans? Sullivan thought angrily. It was just luck that he had seen it at all. If he hadn't been given the transfer, he probably never would have even gotten it.

"You better let me know what it is," Grissum said, but he didn't bother to turn and look at Sullivan this time. "Yancey told me that I'm supposed to keep an eye on you. So it'll just save me from having to go through your desk later."

"It's Strode's landlady. She told me that a Dallas police car showed up at Strode's rooming house almost immediately after the shooting," Sullivan said, eager to talk about it to someone. And as he spoke, Sullivan remembered the fear and uncertainty in the woman's voice when he'd given her his phone number on that day long ago.

"I shouldn't have asked," Grissum said, sighing deeply. "I thought you promised them you'd be a good boy if they let you come back here," Grissum said, punctuating the "they" with an almost imperceptible movement of his shoulder back toward Yancey's glass-paneled office at the rear of the room.

"I did, but . . ." Sullivan looked down at the phone message again before he finished what he had to say, and he felt himself being moved back almost against his will into the mystery of what had really happened on that day in November of 1963. "But the message says she's in trouble," Sullivan said. "I've got to help her."

A transatlantic flight can be a sad and lonely time. And Suzanne awoke several hours outside New York, feeling the full impact of her decision to make the flight without her husband. It was a few minutes after three in the morning, eastern time, when she opened her eyes from a fitful sleep and saw the darkened first-class compartment around her. The only noise as she stared straight ahead into the darkness was the hypnotic drone of the airplane's powerful engines. Something in her dreams had frightened her. It was the same series of images and feeling that had been robbing her of sleep for months, but that she refused to remember clearly when she was awake.

Her children were asleep, their little bodies spread awkwardly one on either side of her. They were huddled inside the rough gray airline blankets, their little hands tugging the rough wool up close to their faces. Her son's mouth was open wide and he was snoring gently, his body curled up into a tight ball, reminding Suzanne of how he must have looked when she'd carried him inside of her not that many years before. And her daughter with her sweetly delicate face, her thin almost transparent eyelids trembling with her own childhood dreams, lay on Suzanne's other side. Erin's thinly stockinged feet appeared beneath the edge of the airplane blanket, exposing the little girl to the cold air of the first-class cabin, and Suzanne instinctively moved her own blanket from her legs to cover them.

New York to Rome, Suzanne thought. Ten hours in the air and even with the sun rushing up to meet the plane, as it hurdled eastward across the Atlantic, there is inevitably this time, when even the V.I.P. seats of the first-class section are dark and lonely and you can suddenly become aware of how gray and bleak the ocean must be beneath the plane, and how dark and infinite the sky is around you, and just how terribly spent and cramped and hollow your own body can feel without enough of the right kind of sleep.

Maybe a commercial flight was a mistake, Suzanne thought, as she watched her children's restless bodies moving beneath the thin airline blankets. She could have taken a government plane or Konstantine would have gladly sent a fleet of private aircraft to whisk her across the water to Athens, but she had made the decision to take a regular flight—an act of independence, she'd told herself. She laughed softly at herself now as she thought of her reasoning. Oh, Suzanne, what a terribly strong and independent woman you are, she said, mocking herself. Taking a commercial flight from New York to Rome, leaving the man that you've been married to almost all of your adult life to stay on the private island of one of the richest men in the world—the protection of one strong man to the next with only a brief plane flight with four Secret Service agents on board watching her every move in between. Oh, how very independent. Suzanne laughed at herself again. And how terribly selfish and stupid and arrogant and . . . She left off calling herself names then and swept the window curtain aside as if it was the curtain that she was angry at, not herself. She looked out the window, and seeing the seemingly endless cold gray night just beyond the thin metal skin of the airplane, she felt even more tired and sad and alone. Was there a reason for any of this? Was there a reason for anything that had happened to her and to her family since that day in Dallas? Or had it all been just a lot of senseless chasing after power and glory? All the danger? The bone-wearing tension of constantly waiting for another horrible moment like that one instant, when she had turned and seen her husband's head exploded in a flash of blood and then the warm sticky redness pouring over the front of her dress and onto her hands and . . . She put her hand up to her mouth then, as if to stifle a scream that was starting deep inside of her. That was her secret, the thing that was buried inside her and that she relived each night now as she slept, the secret that normally she refused to let herself see when she was awake. That was the power of the night, she thought. It forced you to see those things that you had tried to leave only to your dreams. She had to stop this, she told herself angrily, and she forced herself then to focus her attention once again out the window on to the night sky. No clouds, no stars, too high in the air to see the water beneath her and too low to see the heavens, she thought, just somewhere in between, waking from a bad dream, alone now with her fears, with her uncertainties. That was one of the hardest lessons of all for her to learn about being alive, she realized then, to learn that no matter how much you loved someone else, how terribly separate and ultimately alone you each really were. She had faced that realization with all its power for the first time during that long night in Dallas as Jack lay balanced between this world and the next, but she had pushed it aside when he had come back to her. But here it was again, refusing to go away, and she would have to deal with it, she thought, but not now, not up here, not while she was cold and her body cramped and needing sleep. Now she just wished that she was safely back in her husband's arms somewhere, at the Cape maybe, or in Palm Beach or in the capital, anywhere, just with him and not alone.

She kept looking out the window at the great vacant deadness of the dark night sky that spread out endlessly around the small, frail, commercial aircraft that was flying her farther away every moment from where she wanted to be, flying her toward a strange city and a strange man and a strange wrong time ahead for her and for her family. But you have to learn, she told herself, you have to learn sometime in your life how to be alone. Maybe she could use the painful time ahead to teach herself that lesson and to find out a little of who she really was when she was no longer safe behind the big gates at Hyannis in a warm bed with her husband's strong arms around her—who she was when she was alone with only Suzanne and no one else—just Suzanne.

CHAPTER
18

Costello described the photograph in detail to his boss as the two men walked down the long rows of wooden crates and cardboard boxes stacked on the floor of the warehouse. Then he went through the rest of his meeting with Garrett. As he talked, he struggled to keep up with the much smaller but quicker man at his side.

The two men felt almost safe in the cavernous room filled with sacks of flour and rice and barrels of molasses, the walls of cardboard boxes muffling the sounds of their conversation. A bug or tap of any kind was almost impossible in the enormous high-ceilinged room, but nevertheless Costello spoke quickly and in low tense tones, as he always did when they met. It was an old habit, born of earlier days, before they had owned warehouse buildings and stacks of cargo boxes to hide their words.

"You should see the papers Cassidy's people laid on us," Costello said. They had only been walking for a few moments, but the strain of moving his ponderous body was already beginning to show in the short, gasping series of breaths that he was struggling to take now between each of his words. "Interrogatories, all this crap about bank accounts, real-estate holdings, everything," Costello showed the other man with his hands how many inches of paper had been served on them.

"We don't answer any of that," DeSavio said, wiggling the index finger of his right hand back and forth in Costello's face, as an admonition to him not to comply with the Justice Department's latest demands. "Paper," DeSavio said, spitting the word out to show his distaste for it. "The government believes in paper," he added with disgust. "Nothing of true value can be kept on paper," the little man said then. He touched the side of his head as a reminder to Costello. DeSavio had never written a debt, or a profit, or a credit down on paper in his life. If it was of true value, he believed, he would remember it, and so far, as both his friends and enemies had learned, his confidence in himself had been justified.

They paused for a moment, while Costello fought to regain his breath. His heavy face was sweating freely in the humid air of the warehouse. The New Orleans harbor and the fresh air of the Gulf were only a few yards away, but the warehouse doors were closed and locked to give the two men the privacy that their business demanded, and the air in the building was rapidly growing damp and thick. DeSavio reached up and adjusted his heavily framed dark glasses as he watched Costello fight painfully for breath. Steam had collected on the surface of the glasses and DeSavio removed an expensive silk hand-kerchief from his pocket and carefully polished it away. Finally the big man began moving again, waddling even more slowly this time, his enormous stomach protruding far out in front of him, as he managed to begin making his way slowly down the long row of packing cases.

"I'm more concerned about the photograph," DeSavio said, replacing his glasses onto the bridge of his nose. The two men continued walking together then, moving slowly down the long rows of stacked boxes, never moving in a straight line for long, but erratically turning left or right down long dark aisles to avoid any possibility of surveillance. As they walked, Costello explained again the details surrounding the delivery of the photograph. When he was done, he removed a handkerchief from the back pocket of his pants. His big, round face was dripping with sweat and under his darkly stained suit his expensive silk shirt was pressed flat to his body.

"This man, Lopez, Lopata, or whatever the hell it is that he calls himself now, worries me," DeSavio said and then paused to let Costello catch his breath again.

Costello didn't answer. He just stood in a small circle of sunlight coming in through one of the high windows of the warehouse building, and he breathed heavily in and out for several seconds. DeSavio waited, fighting not to let the distaste that he felt toward the grossly overweight man show in his face, but despite his efforts the little man felt the disgust grow inside himself, an intense hatred first for Costello, but then for the Justice Department lawyers, who had been pursuing him for the last several years, and for the Attorney General, who had been directing the case against him. And finally the hatred that DeSavio felt became almost overpowering as he thought about President Cassidy himself—the man ultimately responsible for all his troubles. He couldn't let his feelings rule him though, no matter how justified they were, he thought. He had to think it all through clearly. He couldn't let it become too personal, he told himself. He had to treat it just like any other piece of business.

"This man Lopata knows too much. He has too much power," DeSavio said, remembering the photocopied pages from Strode's diary that Lopata had sent to them a few months earlier. DeSavio stopped talking then and stood in the little patch of sunlight with Costello for a moment, trying to think it all through carefully, but his anger kept intruding, making it difficult to think clearly. The truth was that he wanted them all dead. They pushed him too hard. They should all die and then he could have peace. "I want a list," he said finally, and Costello nodded, understanding.

"We're going to have to close it all down," DeSavio said. "It's become too dangerous."

"And the woman?" Costello said.

"I will speak with her," DeSavio answered. "She'll understand. It's the only way now. What we need is a list of those that must be silenced. This man Lopata first, but then everyone!" DeSavio said, punctuating his decision with an angry sweep of his hand. "I'll deal with the woman."

"The truth is just as dangerous for our enemies as it is for us," Costello said.

"That's true." DeSavio smiled at the cleverness of the original plan and how well it was holding up even under the new circumstances. "And that danger is precisely why we will be able to accomplish it with very little risk to us. No one in authority will push too hard, because once they look closely, they'll see that we're doing their business as well as our own." DeSavio paused then before adding in triumph, "There is no one that will want us stopped, no one at all."

They had agreed never to meet again—never. But here they were, in the same room, sitting in the same chairs, with the same small formal cups of espresso and the short plain glasses of mineral water standing in front of both of them, conducting business in precisely the same manner that they would have in Havana before the revolution, or almost as they would have in Madrid or Barcelona, before the explorers had found the New World. They were each wearing almost the same clothes that they had on that other time they had met face to face. DeSavio wore another neatly tailored cream-colored silk suit, and the woman was dressed again in the black of her perpetual mourning. Even the topic under discussion was precisely the same as it had been at that earlier meeting—the assassination of the President of the United States.

"If we do nothing," DeSavio said and then spread his arms out, the palms of his hands turned upward, "I believe this man Lopata will succeed. I believe that he will truly find a way to kill Cassidy this time, but it will be done carelessly, with no precautions. He's lost all sense of his own safety, and that means that he will be caught or killed, and then the authorities will find their way back to us."

Everything was the same as that other night, the woman thought as she listened, the night she had asked DeSavio if it could be done and he had answered so swiftly, with such certainty that it had startled her. He must have guessed in advance why he had been summoned and he had his own reasons for wanting to see it done, but still the absoluteness of his answer had shocked her. It was only later that she had learned why he had been so confident. It was too late by then, though. It had all been set into motion, and from that moment forward it had taken on a life of its own, separate from her and unstoppable.

They had agreed never to meet again, and, if it had all gone well, there would have never been a reason for them to have to come face to face for a second time. The money was to be paid by a simple deposit in a bank that they had both agreed upon. The actual plans would be made by DeSavio and his people, and the execution of those plans would be left to others, but all had not gone well—and here they were again, meeting for a second time and talking secretly about the same subject they had on that earlier night—should President Cassidy live, or should he die?

The woman sat up painfully straight-backed and proper, with her long, age-spotted fingers folded on the top of the big desk that had been her husband's. She listened while the slightly hunchbacked man continued talking. DeSavio told her only what he thought she should know, speaking slowly and clearly with just the slightest trace of condescension. The woman looked at him carefully, watching his face for any sign of betrayal, but it was difficult to watch him for very long without being distracted by the misshapen features of his face. His head was small and disturbingly elongated, giving the appearance of some kind of a small predatory animal. And even at night in the darkened room he wore thick, heavily framed dark glasses with a faint greenish tint to them that hid his eyes. As he spoke small bubbles of saliva occasionally formed in the corners of his mouth, and at nervous intervals his small sharp tongue would dart out and swab away at the little curls of spit. It was all the woman could do to focus her attention on him and listen to his words without losing herself in the grotesqueness of his appearance, but she forced herself to listen to every word, follow every argument, as the man explained why he had broken their agreement and had asked to see her again.

When he had finished she remained quiet, thinking over the terrible proposition he had offered her. As she tried to think it through, her eyes moved slowly around the dimly lit room that had been her husband's office. The room was a strange blend of French and Cuban furnishings, as were many of the other homes of the Cuban emigrants who had escaped to New Orleans after Castro had come to power in their country. This room showed signs of having once been a little richer, a little better appointed than the houses of her friends, its furniture and fabrics and gold-framed paintings more expensive than the others. It was growing a little weary now though, she thought, a little tired and aged and a little threadbare, but the woman didn't really care. It wasn't a matter of money. Her husband's family had owned many acres of good growing land in Cuba before Castro and they had been wise enough to transfer their profits from those lands to banks on the mainland before the revolution. Now all that money was hers, but nothing had been changed in the room since she had begun sitting in her husband's chair behind the big desk, she thought proudly. The big blue and white and red flag of liberation still dominated the wall across from her, and the rows of dusty framed photographs still displayed her husband, first in earlier days in Cuba and then later in America, smiling, handsome, shaking hands with politicians and local dignitaries, and still the one large photograph in the place of honor above the stone fireplace just as her husband had left it that showed Don Martine shaking hands with President Cassidy himself. It was that photograph that Sylvia Martine had looked at throughout that earlier evening, when she had spoken for the first time to the ugly misshapen little man who sat with her now. The last few photographs showed her proud determined husband in his uniform preparing to return to his country under the flag of liberation. There were no photographs though of his final hours, she thought now, no heroic pictures of the ride in the small boat across the Gulf with the other men who believed as he did, or of his wading ashore at the place the Americans called the Bay of Pigs, or of his last few desperate hours dying slowly on the beach with a Communist bullet in his chest. The woman wondered, as her gaze moved back to the photograph that showed the two handsome men shaking hands, whether her husband had watched the skies for the American planes that the other man had promised, watched for the planes not to save him, but just to let him know at the end that his life had been given for something and that he had truly died helping to free the country of his birth. But the skies had been empty when he died. She knew that with certainty, because they had been empty all that night and all the next day and every day thereafter. Mrs. Martine brought herself back to the present then, her memories too painful to deal with any longer. She lowered her gaze from the photographs on the wall to the man in the cream-colored silk suit and darkly tinted glasses. "I still pray for Cassidy to die," she said with an intensity that stirred even the man in front of her, a man who had lived all his life with hatred and revenge and who believed in the necessity of both.

"As do I," DeSavio said finally, as if he were exchanging a courtesy.

She was careful not to say anything more. In dealing with people like this it was important not to show all of your emotion, she thought. She looked again at DeSavio's animallike face. Would her husband have done business with such a man? she asked herself. But she knew the answer. He would have done business with the devil himself if it meant returning to a free Cuba. Well, my beloved husband, that part of the journey was not left to you, she thought. The devil was left for me to deal with and not for you. For surely, if this small ugly man sitting in front of her waiting for her answer was not the devil himself alive on this earth, then certainly he was his agent and ally and closest and dearest friend.

"I, too, pray for Cassidy to die," DeSavio whispered. "But not this way. We can't let this man Lopata continue. Things have changed too much. He's become dangerous to us both," the little man hissed through his tightly drawn lips.

Mrs. Martine said nothing. Perhaps he isn't the devil at all, she smiled to herself. Unless, in the end, the devil is ruled by nothing more than selfish practicalities and fear. Her desire to see Cassidy dead, murdered, just as he'd murdered her husband, didn't bend with the changing circumstances, didn't change even if her own life and safety were threatened—it only grew stronger. Maybe, if the devil was in this room, it was in her. "So you want him stopped then?" she said, and DeSavio nodded yes. "There are others as well," he said, and Mrs. Martine shook her head at the terrible irony at what DeSavio was proposing now.

"We've made a list," he said, and he handed a sheet of paper across the desk toward her. "It's a short list." She took the paper in her hands and looked down at the names written on it. They were written in two columns and filled the page. She turned the paper over and there were more names on the back of it as well. Some of the names written on the paper were her friends, some she had only heard of or read about, some were unfamiliar to her, but all of them she guessed had been involved in some way with the plan to kill Cassidy. "These people die and Cassidy lives," she said bitterly and thrust the list back angrily toward DeSavio.

"It has to be."

"And if it's not?" Mrs. Martine said.

DeSavio was silent then and in the silence the woman finally understood fully the purpose of his visit. He hadn't come to ask her permission as she thought, but to tell her of a decision that had already been made without her.

"It has already begun," DeSavio said, pointing at one of the names on the sheet of paper that lay on the desktop. "When it is complete," DeSavio said, glancing down at the front page of his list, "only then will we be truly safe."

"Well, I guess I'm just going to have to trust somebody," Sullivan said and looked over at the part of Grissum's tired, heavily lined face that was visible below the brim of his lowered gray felt hat.

The senior agent made a pained sound when he heard Sullivan's naïve words, but Grissum's lips barely moved as he let the anguished sound escape from deep inside his body.

"Look, Sullivan, if you need someone to trust, do me a favor, find someone else, would you?"

Sullivan had been working with the veteran agent for only a few days, but he had already memorized Grissum's familiar reply, his answer to everything. "Yeah, I know," Sullivan interrupted him, "you've only got a few years to retirement. But face it, you're all I got." There was Denise, Sullivan thought, but he'd already made a decision after he'd returned from Tampico, to keep her out of it. He had made a mistake taking a woman to Mexico in the first place. It had been too dangerous and he had been damn glad that he'd sent her home before visiting Room 409 of the Mirador Hotel.

The agent with the blond crewcut looked over at the aging man huddled up in the passenger seat next to him. Grissum's head and shoulders were wreathed in smoke from a freshly lit cigarette that he left dangling untended from the corner of his mouth. "No, I've decided," Sullivan said, "I'm going to make you a hero."

"I've been a hero," Grissum said through the thick cloud of cigarette smoke. "Check my jacket."

"I have."

"Look, kid, first of all, you can't trust me. I'm the last goddamned person on earth that you can trust." Grissum kept his eyes pointed straight out the car's windshield, down the long empty strip of dark gray cement that led from downtown Dallas to their destination north of the city.

"I don't have anyone else," Sullivan said then.

"You don't have me either," Grissum said. "I'm the one that the Bureau assigned to watch you, remember? What do you think? It's a coincidence? Suddenly the Bureau's gone soft on a jerk like you? They give you a transfer back to Dallas and you get a partner who's a hundred and fifty years old, with a pension to lose if he lets you step out of line just once. You make them nervous, Sullivan. They probably just decided that you're safer to them flying around out here in Lizard Shit, Texas"—Grissum lifted a nicotine-stained hand to point out the window at the seemingly endless vista of dry, dusty brown desert that bordered the road—"than you would be back in Washington with all those politicians and reporters you might shoot your mouth off to. And to be damn sure you didn't make any more trouble, Yancey told me to report to him every goddamned thing that you do that isn't right by the book. So, do us both a favor and leave me out of your crusade," Grissum said, the layers of years of self-disgust thick in his voice as he finished what he had to say.

Sullivan suddenly slammed on the brakes, and the Chevy fishtailed off the highway. He'd almost passed the turnoff that he'd been looking for—Midland, Texas. It was easy enough to do, Sullivan thought, as the Chevy exited into a crossroads town with a business district that consisted of a general store and three gas stations set down in the center of a flat piece of dusty Texas badlands that stretched out uninterrupted, except for a few scrub cactus, toward the horizon line in every direction.

"Let me guess, First and A," Grissum said without reading the street signs mounted above the town's only traffic light.

There was a small cluster of pre–World War Two homes on a symmetrical crisscross of dusty residential streets behind the town's general store and Sullivan pointed the car toward them, knocking his speed down low enough so that Grissum could read the street signs and an occasional address. "Catch a number for me, would you?" Sullivan said. "We're looking for 612."

Grissum's head seemed to move slightly toward his side window then.

"I did read your personnel file, by the way," Sullivan said. "It tells a different story than you do."

"Don't let that fool you," Grissum said and then removed the cigarette from his lips and held it up toward Sullivan. A long dead gray ash hung precariously on the very tip of the unfiltered cigarette butt. "You see that,"

Grissum said, pointing at the cigarette ash. "It's a lot less burnt-out than I am." Grissum flicked the cigarette just once with one of his yellow soiled fingers, but so expertly that the ash rose in the air for a moment before diving down and crashing onto the floor of the car, disintegrating into a thousand specks of gray dust. "That's me," Grissum said looking down at the ashes scattered on the floorboard of the car. Grissum's graphic demonstration seemed to impress Sullivan, but the young agent shook it off after only a few brief moments. "That was you, you mean," Sullivan said then.

"I'm telling you, you're making a mistake," Grissum said. "I won't go down the line with you."

But Sullivan ignored the senior agent's half-mumbled warning. "You're going to go out in a blaze of glory, Grissum," he said.

Grissum's face remained ingloriously puffy and impassive, as he replaced the smoking butt of the cigarette back into the corner of his mouth.

Sullivan slowed down the government car in front of a small one-story house with the number 612 tacked above its front door. "For starters, this woman we're going to see now. She says that the police black-and-white she saw last November tapped its horn twice outside Strode's window, like a signal," Sullivan said, the excitement returning to his voice as he began to think again about the mysterious events of that day. Sullivan glanced over at Grissum to see if the senior agent was listening, but it was impossible to tell. "Anyway, when I tried to question her about it, the Dallas police wouldn't let me see her. The Dallas police!" Sullivan said it again for emphasis, but there was still no way for him to tell if Grissum was getting any of it. "They let it slip to me though," Sullivan went on, "that she was staying at her sister's. I put it in my report before I left for New Orleans, but as far as I can tell nobody ever followed up on it."

Grissum turned his head and looked out the car window at the dreary one-story house they had parked in front of. "Her sister's house, right?" Grissum said sarcastically, but Sullivan had already hopped out of the car and was headed for the front walk.

"Jesus, you're a jerk, Sullivan," Grissum grunted as he slowly moved out of the passenger door.

Sullivan moved briskly up the narrow path. A brass cowbell hung from a piece of rawhide near the front door, and Sullivan reached up and rang it energetically. Grissum looked at the noisily ringing bell in disgust.

The sun was blazing hot, but there was a narrow strip of shade under the roofline of the house, and as he waited for someone to answer the door, Grissum slipped back under the protection of the single shady spot. A few seconds later, a man appeared at the side of the house directly behind him. The man was in his sixties, dressed in a white undershirt and faded jeans, and he held a hunting rifle in both hands in front of him. The barrel of the rifle was pointed squarely at Grissum's back.

"Don't move," Sullivan ordered Grissum, as soon as the younger agent saw the rifle.

"What?"

"I said, don't move," Sullivan said again, and then he raised his own hands in the air to show the man with the rifle that they were empty.

"Who are you?" the man said.

"Oh, Jesus," Grissum said, catching on now.

"FBI agents. My name is Sullivan. This is Agent Grissum."

"How do I know that?" the man said suspiciously.

"I've got a card," Sullivan said, dropping one hand slowly toward his inside coat pocket.

"Be careful," Grissum whispered, but Sullivan completed the move and extended his open wallet toward the armed man. "Are you Mr. Foley?" Sullivan said, as he waited for him to check his identification card.

"Yes," the man said. Satisfied, he let the barrel of the rifle relax down toward the ground. "I'm sorry," he said, but his face was still puzzled. "Are you here about Katherine?" he asked then.

"Katherine Riordan, your sister-in-law. Yes," Sullivan said and then waited.

"You don't know, do you?"

"Know what?"

"Right down there." The man used the barrel of his hunting rifle to point down the road that the two FBI agents had just traveled. "A car hit her on the road back of Greeley's store," he added then, letting the rifle barrel drop back down toward the ground again.

"A car?" Sullivan said, not quite understanding.

"A hit-and-run car. She was walking right out there." The man motioned only with his head this time. "And this car just hit her and kept on going. Nothing like that ever happened around here before."

"When?" Sullivan asked.

"It's been almost a month now."

"And the police haven't found the driver?" Sullivan asked, as an anxious sick feeling began to spread through his stomach.

"No, sir," the man said. "They haven't. It was funny the way it happened, too."

"What do you mean?"

"I'll show you," the man said, and then he turned and started for the front door of his house. "It's all in the newspaper. I saved the article. The driver must have been drunk, or something, I guess. The sheriff said it was almost like the driver wanted to do it. You see, he could tell, from the way they found her body, that the driver had to come right up on the sidewalk to hit her. She was dead before the ambulance got there."

Garrett didn't let the phone ring more than once before he removed himself from the privacy of his bed and hurried across the room to answer it.

He was completely nude, and from where she was lying, propped up on her elbows in the four-poster bed, Leigh could see the soft white frailty of his naked body. She looked at it for several seconds and then sighed, wishing that she felt something when she saw him naked like that.

Garrett pressed the phone receiver up against his chest so that whoever was on the other end of it wouldn't be able to hear him as he hissed at her. "I need those," he said, pointing at the cotton undershorts that were lying on the chair by the bed. Leigh reached for the black lace bed jacket that she'd left on the floor beside her, pushing the rounded globes of her breasts forward provocatively for Garrett to see in the soft light of the bedroom. She stood then as she slipped into the low-cut lace top, turning her body just enough to let the lawyer see the firm mound of brownish-red pubic hair between her legs for a moment before the lace jacket dropped down and covered it. She knew how good she must look, posed there in the half light, her legs spread slightly apart, wearing only the flimsy see-through top, but Garrett wasn't interested.

He was gesturing wildly for her to hand him a pencil and paper from the writing desk. It must be serious she decided then—Garrett was normally like a little boy, docile and pliable to her will, unable to resist her body, even for a moment, when she seduced him with it.

"Yes, Mr. Costello, I understand." She could hear Garrett talking into the receiver and she paused for a moment after she'd handed him a notepad, studying the lawyer's anxious movements. She was too experienced she thought, and she had been around too many blocks not to recognize this for what it was. It was just a temporary gig, but it was one that she needed to hang on to very badly. It wasn't much, she thought, but she couldn't let herself lose it, because that's all there was for her now. And as Garrett turned his body away from her and completed the call, she forced herself to respond to the urgent, all-business mood that she knew he would be in when he hung up the phone.

When he was finished, he turned back to her, his face as serious as she knew it would be. "Here, write this down," he said, and then he flung a series of instructions at her, speaking quickly, as if he feared that if he forgot even a syllable of the instructions his very life might be over.

She took it all down intently and obediently, wondering if Garrett would want to make love later or if they were finished for the night, not that she really cared, but it gave her something more interesting to think about than the instructions for transfers of funds from a bank in Miami to a series of personal accounts in Mexico and then to a final destination in the Bahamas that Garrett was rattling on about from his own sketchy phone notes. Then suddenly it hit her, Jesus, she was dumb. This was all something that she didn't want to know about, wasn't it, probably part of that deep dangerous maze that the FBI agent had warned her about. Oh shit, she thought, how dumb could she be? What was the purpose of payments of this size, made in this complicated way? What the hell was Garrett getting her mixed up in?

"Type that up," he said, pointing at the instructions that he had just dictated. "No copies, no carbons, nothing." The fear in his voice was unmistakable.

"Now?"

"Yeah, now!" He yelled at her, suddenly angry. Then without saying anything more he turned away from her and entered the apartment's small bathroom. A few seconds later she could hear the water from the shower running. He was getting ready to go out again that night.

Her thoughts flashed back to the young blond FBI agent, but she dismissed her plan of going to see him and telling him the rest of what she knew almost as quickly as it came to her. Shit, I wish I had the guts, though, she taunted herself.

"Hurry with that goddamned typing, will you," Garrett yelled, sticking his head out of the bathroom door and she hustled out to the typewriter waiting on the writing table in the living room.

Several minutes later Garrett came out of the bathroom. He was fully dressed now in one of his many rumpled, lightweight, white linen suits that all looked the same to her. He walked directly to the writing table where she was seated. He had sprinkled himself liberally with lilac water, but she was certain that she could still smell the dark aroma of fear beneath the sweet cloud that followed him across the room. After he read her freshly typed sheets of paper, he removed his own handwritten notes that she had been working from and carried them to the fireplace. He stood with his back to her as he watched them burn. Now the only traces of the intricate instructions they had contained were the sheets of typed paper that Garrett folded and fitted carefully into the inside pocket of his suit coat before he walked to the front door of his apartment. Of course, whoever it was who had been on the other end of the phone conversation knew about them and now, Leigh Hodges knew too, she thought anxiously.

After Garrett left to do whatever it was that he had to do that night, she went into the bedroom and lay back down in the big brass bed and listened to the rain fall outside in the narrow, dark, winding French Quarter streets that held Garrett now. She hadn't even realized that it had been raining, she thought, until Garrett had opened the door of his apartment and without saying anything more to her had walked outside. But of course, it's always raining in New Orleans this time of night, she reminded herself, as she lay back in the brass bed, her lace top hiking up above her hips and exposing the mound of reddish-brown hair between her legs again. She closed her eyes and visualized the blond FBI agent named Sullivan, the one she'd had a drink with a few months before, and she let her hand drop down and touch herself as she thought about him. She began rubbing herself softly at first and then harder with a deepening rhythm, but it was no good. She felt too frightened, too confused. She was too damn tired and there were too many complicated thoughts running through her mind to let herself go completely and indulge in such simple pleasures anymore, and she opened her eyes and reached for the pack of cigarettes lying on the end table next to her.

She lay in the big brass bed then and listened to the dripping rain. She lit a cigarette and let its smoke curl up to the ceiling and join the big, spreading yellow stain on the ceiling right above her that had probably been made, she thought as she looked up at it, by other scared and nervous men and women, who had lain on that bed in other earlier days and wondered what their fate would be, just as she did now.

CHAPTER
19

St. Patrick's Cathedral, a few minutes
before dawn on a glorious holiday morning, with New York City's first shafts
of sunlight beginning to filter in from above and energize the colors in its
high stained-glass windows and illuminate the arched walls and the high
ceiling of the church's magnificent interior—there were few places on earth
that Frank O'Connor would normally rather be on a fresh clear morning in
early September, at the start of a new political year. But his joy that morning,
as he stepped through the cathedral's massive rear doors, was spoiled by the
purpose of his early morning visit.

O'Connor could see the President kneeling at the front of the church with
a tall white-robed priest standing above him. The remainder of the cavernous
interior was empty, except for the figures of the Secret Service agents, half
hidden in the shadows of the old building. None of the agents that O'Connor
could see were kneeling, but some of them were probably praying just the
same, he guessed, as he looked at their grimly determined faces, praying that
they would be able to do their jobs effectively that day and prevent what some
feared might easily become another day of tragedy.

O'Connor began making his way slowly down the long central aisle of the
high-ceilinged cathedral, a small lone figure, his hat respectfully in hand, a
bright red carnation nearly the size of a small cantaloupe displayed jauntily
in the buttonhole of his freshly pressed brown suit and his serious Irish face
set firm and hard with the purposeful look of a man on an important mission.

He paused a few rows from the front of the church and knelt briefly, his
cupped hand making the sign of the cross, before he permitted himself to

slide into the long wooden pew in back of the President's kneeling figure. O'Connor waited patiently then, his hands folded tensely in his lap, until the President had finished.

After several long minutes the tall white-robed priest touched the kneeling figure of the President lightly on the top of his head, completing his blessing, and Jack finally stood and turned toward O'Connor.

"Good morning, Frank," Cassidy said, smiling at his friend. "New suit?"

"No, I got it cleaned," O'Connor mumbled.

Jack nodded, still smiling. "It looks nice," he said as they started down the cathedral's long center aisle. "Coffee?"

O'Connor nodded and the two men followed the white-robed priest past the altar and down a darkened hallway that led finally to a small office at the very front of the church.

There was a pot of coffee standing on a hotplate in the small, simply decorated room, and the priest poured two steaming cups of the blackish-brown liquid and held them out to his guests. "Thank you, Father," both men said, almost in unison. O'Connor grasped his cup firmly in front of him with two hands, holding it close to him for its warmth and some early morning comfort.

"What is it, Frank?" the President said, sensing O'Connor's mood.

"I assume that you're still determined to go through with this?" O'Connor said. The President only looked up from his own mug of steaming coffee long enough to nod his head decisively.

"I suppose you could have picked a more dangerous place," O'Connor said, suddenly angry. "Although I can't say where it would be or when!" He lifted his eyes over the rim of his coffee cup and looked at the President through the rising steam portentously, trying to look like a wise old Irish sage.

"I have to, Frank. I don't have any choice," Cassidy reminded him. "Democratic candidates have walked in this city's Labor Day parade for over half a century."

"Yes," O'Connor said, lifting a finger from his coffee cup and pointing it at Jack. "That's exactly right, Democratic candidates," O'Connor underlined the word "candidates" with his voice and then, before going on, he glanced over at the nearby priest to make certain that he wasn't overheard speaking disrespectfully to the President. It had been an unwritten rule between Jack and his aides, since he'd been elected to the presidency, that they were always to speak their mind to him, but never in a way or at a time that someone could overhear them and misunderstand their candor as disrespect for the office that he held, but the priest had discreetly turned his back and moved politely toward a far corner of the room to let the two politicians do their business. It was hardly the first or last time that Democratic political decisions would be made before the silent, unquestioning presence of the Church, O'Connor thought as he glanced over at the white-robed back of the priest, who was respectfully pretending now not to overhear any of the private discussion.

"Frank, I owe it to Tim to do this, and, for that matter, after Atlantic City I probably owe it to Rance and to the whole damn Party," Cassidy said, trying to make his friend understand, but the President's words seemed only to make O'Connor angrier.

"Don't tell me that you owe it to Tim, because I know what Tim's been asking you to do. All he wants is for you to get started on the trip that you've been promising everyone you'll take and to leave the campaigning to him for now. There'll be plenty left for you to do in October. I know that's what Tim wants, because the Attorney General was on the phone to me this morning at five A.M. to tell me to get the hell down here and talk some sense into you." O'Connor checked himself again then, as he remembered where he was, but the tall, straight figure in white robes at the front of the room remained motionless. "For God's sake, Jack," O'Connor continued emotionally, "the parade route stretches through almost two miles of downtown Manhattan. The streets will be packed every step of the way by thousands of people, with high buildings on every side. And you're talking about walking right down Fifth Avenue like, like . . ." O'Connor sputtered slightly as his gift for words temporarily abandoned him. "There's no way on God's green earth that the New York City Police or the federal government or even the United States Army can guarantee to keep you safe out there, unless you start making some sense about this yourself." O'Connor pointed urgently out the church window with his coffee cup at the city's streets as he spoke.

"Frank," Jack said patiently, as if he were lecturing a backward child, "you know how I feel about these things, how I've always felt. If something's meant to happen, it will. It's that simple." Cassidy turned away from his friend then and added, "What happened in Dallas doesn't change that."

"Well, it should," O'Connor said quickly. "Damn it all, Jack, listen to me, you don't owe this to anyone. Certainly not to Tim, and I don't care what you've promised Gardner." In his urgency now, O'Connor no longer seemed even to care about where he was, or what words he used to make his point to the President.

"Frank," Cassidy said, in the voice that he used to close conversations, "I owe it to myself. If I want to have an effect on what happens during the next four years, I've got to earn it. And that means doing everything I can to ensure that we win this election—and if that includes walking in a parade and waving at a few people, then that's the way it has to be."

"Father, tell him, would you?" O'Connor, in his last extremity, finally called out for the help of the Church.

But it was too late. The President had already crossed the room to say his final thank-you to the priest. O'Connor knew by the decisive way that Cassidy held himself as he shook the priest's hand and then started for the back door of the private office and his waiting limousine that the President had made up his mind. He was going to walk with Gardner down the middle of New York's Fifth Avenue, just as he'd promised, and kick off the 1964 presidential campaign, no matter what O'Connor or anyone else said, and no matter what the risks were that might be waiting for him on the streets of New York.

Lopata used a train to travel in from the Cape. In Boston, he had to switch to a second line and the short, dark-haired man, dressed that morning in a pair of shapeless khaki trousers and a dark blue windbreaker, had time to stop at the newsstand and buy several New York City newspapers.

On the trip from Boston to New York, he sat all alone by the window in one of the train's commuter cars and searched through each of the newspapers carefully. OFFICIAL KICKOFF OF PRESIDENTIAL CAMPAIGN one of the headlines read. Lopata scanned the story quickly and then followed it to the inside pages of the newspaper. He went back and read the article through again from start to finish. He read English slowly, and it took him several minutes to finish, but when he had completed it, he felt satisfied. The story confirmed what had been reported to him over the television set that he had watched in his motel room at the Cape the day before. President Cassidy was going to begin the Democratic presidential campaign by marching in the traditional Labor Day parade down New York's Fifth Avenue. Jesus, Cassidy was a fool, Lopata thought as he finished reading the newspaper article. He must think he's immortal. Lopata ripped the article from the newspaper and jammed it into his shirt pocket. There was someone watching him! Lopata could feel it. In a flash, he whirled his head around. The commuter car was almost empty on the morning of the Labor Day holiday, but there was a single man seated at the very back. The man was dressed in a light brown trench coat, his eyes fixed straight ahead, staring down the long train aisle at him, but then the man turned his head away and began looking out the window at the rows of little suburban houses passing by outside the train. The man was following him, Lopata thought in panic. So, this was their game, Lopata thought. It was all a trap. The confirmation that he'd received of the deposit into the bank account in Nassau had just been their way of bringing him out into the open. DeSavio's people had been watching the airports and train stations in Boston, waiting for him to show himself. Lopata stood and hurried into the next car. He sat facing the rear of the compartment, watching the connecting door at the back of the car to see if the other man would follow.

The minutes went by slowly, but no one appeared at the entrance to the nearly empty commuter car that Lopata sat in now. Slowly he began to relax. Maybe it was just his imagination, he thought. It couldn't really have been the same man that he had seen in Mexico. That was impossible. He had to calm down. He was so close to his goal, he couldn't afford to panic now.

Without taking his attention from the rear of the train, Lopata removed the newspaper story from his shirt pocket. He unfolded it and spread it out in front of him. At the bottom of the article was a map of the parade route that Cassidy would take that morning. Lopata studied the map for several minutes, nervously glancing up every few seconds at the doorway at the end of the aisle to make certain that the man in the light brown trench coat didn't reappear. Finally, Lopata removed a pencil from his jacket pocket and placed a heavy black X on the map. He looked up suddenly, thinking that he sensed someone near him, but the aisle that led to the next car was still empty. Trying to relax, he forced himself to look back down at the map of the parade route and at the black cross that he had drawn on it, confirming his choice one last time. Then he carefully refolded the map and replaced it into his shirt pocket. He looked up at the doorway in front of him again, but it was still empty. This was crazy. He had to hold himself together. Everything was as he'd planned it. The first half of the money was safely deposited into his account in Nassau, enough money to make him a rich man, and Cassidy was doing his part too, by walking right into his trap. Lopata smiled as he thought about it. The train was pulling into a small suburban station and Lopata looked up at the clock mounted above the station platform. In a little less than two hours, Lopata thought, as he looked at the time on the station clock—in less than two hours now, it would all be over.

Jack felt a tentative touch on his shoulder as he stepped out of the limousine. He turned back to see O'Connor's face. It showed a troubled mix of excitement and apprehension. O'Connor was the last person that Tim should have sent to try to stop him today, Jack thought. It went against the very nature of the old Irish politician's own instincts. Jack smiled then at the predicament written so clearly on his friend's face. They were only a few yards from the platform where the pre-parade speeches were to be made, and they could hear the band playing loudly now. The air was charged with the political energy that they both had been born to be a part of, Jack thought to himself. There was no way that O'Connor would be able to change his plans now.

"We can almost see Granderman's apartment from here," Cassidy said, as he looked away from O'Connor's troubled face and up toward the branches of the trees that overhung the park's temporary grandstands.

"Jack, at least do this much, would you please?" O'Connor said dutifully, although he could feel his own heart beginning to pump faster as he thought about the audacity of kicking this campaign off right here in Granderman's own backyard. "Shorten the route. That's all I'm asking. Most of the crowd will be bunched up between here and about Forty-second or Forty-third. Just walk the first mile or so of the route. Let the television cameras get their pictures, but cut the distance down. I talked to Tanner this morning and he thought that would be all right," O'Connor said, referring now to the President's head of security.

"You have been busy this morning, haven't you?" the President said.

"Yes, I have, and, damn it, Jack, listen to me. Tanner thinks it's a good idea. He says that we can have a car waiting for you at the corner of Forty-third or wherever you say. But he thinks you should keep the entire appearance to under an hour. He thinks that would significantly reduce the risk to your personal safety—damn it, Jack, the farther you walk, the more dangerous it is. I'll see to the car personally," O'Connor continued. "It's good politics too," the older man said, returning to more comfortable ground. "The longer you're out there, the smaller the crowds get, you know that, and you sure as hell don't need anybody taking a picture of you waving to an empty street corner."

Cassidy smiled then, but it was possible that his arguments had begun to make an impact, O'Connor thought as he watched the President's face. "You know the rules," O'Connor said. "Always leave them wanting more," he added then, sensing that his friend might be weakening.

Cassidy nodded. O'Connor was right about that. "Have a car at the corner of Forty-second—we'll see how it's going then," he said.

"I'll see to it myself," O'Connor said, breaking into a smile for the first time that morning.

As their limousine followed the motorcycle escort around to the rear of the bandstand toward the parade's assembly point, the President could see the first of the crowd spilling out on to the pathway in front of them and he could hear the band loudly playing the opening chords of "Happy Days Are Here Again."

"Enjoy it, Frank. You may not see anything like this for a while," the President said to his friend.

"What does that mean?" O'Connor asked. The limousine pulled to a stop a few yards behind the grandstand then, and Secret Service agents began hustling from several different directions to surround the figure of the President, as he appeared from the back seat of the long black limousine.

"How's your Gaelic?" Cassidy said without turning back toward his friend.

"My Gaelic? My Gaelic's always good," O'Connor said. "Meaning?"

"Meaning, if Tim wants me out of the way for a while, maybe it's time we make that trip that I've been promising you," Cassidy said, and he smiled at O'Connor one last time before he started toward the first of the Gardner staff people, who were pushing their way through the ring of Secret Service agents toward him. O'Connor watched as the President shook hands with several members of the Vice President's staff, and then, smoothing his tie down with one hand against his shirt front, Cassidy began making his way toward the speaker's platform.

"Is that a promise?" O'Connor called after him, but with all the noise Cassidy couldn't hear him and he disappeared into the crowd without answering.

O'Connor continued watching as Cassidy moved to his place on the platform. There would be a series of short speeches before the parade began, followed then by the traditional walk down Fifth Avenue. O'Connor looked around him at the cool, early fall morning in Central Park, at the band members dressed in their red, white, and blue uniforms playing the familiar melody, at the crowd beginning to fill up the nearby bleachers, at the temporary stage draped in cascading folds of red, white, and blue bunting. He took in a few deep breaths of the glorious air of the politically supercharged morning. He would love to stay and hear the speeches. They would be good, old-fashioned, kettle-thumping American political speeches this morning, he thought, calls to action, full of love of country and party. O'Connor loved speeches like that. He loved the way that the crowds responded from their guts, particularly a New York City crowd, with tears and applause and cheers from deep inside their political souls, but he sighed as he remembered what he'd promised Tim the night before. If he couldn't stop Jack from making the walk down Fifth Avenue with Gardner and the others, he would do what he could to keep the President's route as short as possible. O'Connor turned back to the limousine and opened its back door. He instructed the driver to proceed to the corner of Forty-second Street and Fifth Avenue, and the limousine began working its way back through the crowd.

As the commuter train moved slowly along past the outskirts of the city toward Grand Central, Lopata reviewed his plan over and over again, thinking through every detail of it, until he was satisfied that it was burned permanently into his memory. He stood and walked down the empty aisle to the men's toilet at the end of the car. With him he carried a single suitcase. Alone inside the small room, he locked the door behind him and removed his jacket and placed it on a hook above the door. Then, as he fought to keep his balance on the floor of the slowing train, he placed his suitcase onto the narrow counter next to the sink. Inside the case, lying on top of his clothes, was his holstered weapon. The wooden butt of his long-barreled .38 revolver was plainly visible, protruding through the opening of its highly polished black leather holster. He removed the .38 from the shiny leather pouch and slid back the pistol's breech, checking for the hundredth time in the last two days to make sure that it was fully loaded and ready. He slid the long-barreled weapon back into its holster and, leaving the heavy brass button open on the leather flap that held the weapon in place, he slid the holster up over his left arm and buckled it across his chest. He jerked the heel of his left hand up and slapped the butt of the pistol, firmly seating the weapon deep into his armpit. Finally he closed the suitcase and left it lying across the sink of the little bathroom. There was nothing of value left in it anyway, he thought, and he decided to leave it behind. He turned then and removed his jacket from the hook on the wall. It was heavy with his passport and wallet; it also held Strode's diary, sewn carefully into its lining, and he checked to make doubly certain that everything was there just as he wanted it. Then he put his windbreaker back on, covering the bulging leather holster, and zipped the jacket up tight to his neck.

The train came to a stop and Lopata walked out of the bathroom and on to the station platform without hesitating. There was a man standing about fifty yards away at the far end of the platform, blocking the exit doors to the lobby. It was the same man in the khaki-colored raincoat that Lopata had seen on the train earlier that morning. Lopata's eyes searched the rest of the platform. It was practically empty, except for the two men in heavy topcoats moving quickly down the narrow walkway behind him. They were headed right for him, Lopata realized suddenly. It was a trap! He'd been right. DeSavio had only brought him out of hiding to kill him, Lopata thought in a flash, but then there was no more time to think, only to act, and he turned and started down the platform toward the exit, where the man in the khaki coat was standing blocking the doors to the main terminal building.

Lopata reached up and touched his jacket at the spot where the Smith & Wesson .38 was tucked beneath his armpit. His fingers moved up and touched the zipper of his jacket. Should he use his weapon? He could hear running footsteps approaching behind him on the station platform, and without needing to look he could sense that the men behind him were closing on him fast. He began to run. The station platform was nearly empty, but ahead of him loomed the man in the khaki overcoat barring his exit into the crowded Grand Central lobby. The man was raising his hand as if to stop him, but Lopata didn't hesitate. He lowered his head and rammed his shoulder hard into the man's chest, knocking him backward into the opening to the lobby. A woman screamed. There was a knife in the man's hand and its long silver blade was dulled with blood. Lopata looked down at his own arm. The dark blue cloth at his sleeve was torn open, and blood was seeping into the fabric from beneath the opening in the fabric. Lopata reached down with the fingers of his other hand and gripped his wrist near the cut in his sleeve. The men running behind him were almost upon him now and to avoid them he lurched into the crowded terminal lobby. He heard a police whistle coming from somewhere in the distance and he forced his staggering running pace to a steadier walking stride, trying not to attract attention. There was a door to the street less than a hundred yards away across the sea of people that moved through the busy terminal. He pushed his way through the crowd. Soon he was at the exit doors and then out onto the street. There was a uniformed policeman directing traffic at the corner, but his back was turned to him. Lopata jumped into the intersection against a red light, dodged between oncoming cars, and crossed to the far side of the street. He moved on then, still not looking behind him, his pace fast and steady, but not daring to run. He held his arm tightly with the fingers of his other hand as he moved along.

The sidewalks were jammed with people on their day off, families, children, groups of teenagers and young adults. There were vendors selling food and balloons and pennants. It was like a carnival, Lopata thought. He turned a corner and fought with himself to remember the details of the map that he had memorized only a few minutes earlier. Above him now was a street sign. He read the words on it—Fifth Avenue! His heart leaped. He forced his memory back to the details of the map again. He was very close; only a few blocks separated him from Cassidy now. Lopata looked behind him toward Grand Central. There was no sign of danger. He looked up Fifth Avenue as he hurried on toward the spot where he had marked the X on the map. Nothing could stop him now, he told himself, and he began to feel the wild thrill of the hunt beginning to churn inside of him.

* * *

"Frank, we might have a problem." It was Tanner, and the security chief's voice sounded urgent.

O'Connor was in the back seat of the limousine that was moving slowly back across town. "A problem? What kind of a problem?" O'Connor said, snapping to attention. When the telephone in the back seat of the limousine had lit up, he had answered it lazily, thinking about the trip to Ireland that might soon be ahead of him, but the security chief's voice had shaken him back to the moment.

"Don't get excited," Tanner continued. "Where are you?"

O'Connor looked out the window. The plan had been to swing out around the parade route and take Seventh Avenue down to Forty-second and then cut back to Fifth, but the limousine had come to a dead stop in heavy traffic between Sixth and Seventh on Central Park South. O'Connor repeated his location for Tanner.

"Okay," Tanner said. "We're stepping in on this. I want you to pull the President out of the parade."

"He may not . . ." O'Connor began, but Tanner's tense, efficient voice cut him off. "If he doesn't, my people are under instructions to carry him off," Tanner said. "Frank, if I don't contact him first you tell him that, all right?" the security chief added.

"What's going on?" O'Connor snapped.

"Is that agreed?" Tanner's voice was insistent.

"Yes, of course," O'Connor said. "But just tell me what's happening."

"It's probably nothing," Tanner said. "But we got a report that there may be a kid with an explosive device somewhere on the route. Something about the war. We don't have any details, it's just a tip. Like I say, it's probably nothing, but we can't take the chance. I want him out of that parade route at Forty-sixth, if you can get to him."

"He's not expecting me until Forty-second."

"I don't care, pull him out as quickly as you can get to him, even if you have to use an armlock on him to do it."

"I understand, but I'm not so sure that I can. We're bogged down here," O'Connor said tensely, looking out the window at the thick jam of traffic that surrounded the limousine.

"I'll radio your escort to use their lights and sirens. They'll get you through," Tanner answered sharply.

O'Connor looked out the window of the limousine again. It was stopped dead in traffic several blocks from the new rendezvous point. "We don't have an escort. The motorcycles that we had stayed with the President. It's just us out here, and right now we're stuck—you better have somebody else do it," O'Connor said. He could feel the fears that he had shared with Tim that morning beginning to flare up inside him again.

"Believe me, I'm trying, but right now, Frank, you may be my best bet. I can have an escort waiting for you at Forty-sixth and lead you right out to the airport. He'll listen to you," Tanner said. "But I've got to have you at Forty-sixth right now," Tanner continued. "Let me talk to your driver."

Forgetting for the moment to use the button built in to the base of the phone, O'Connor knocked frantically on the glass screen that separated him from the front seat of the limousine. The driver picked up the receiver instantly.

"This is Tanner," the security chief said, an even deeper sense of urgency in his voice now. "I'm going to get you an escort, but I need you at the corner of Forty-sixth and Fifth Avenue as soon as you can get there. Use your horn, use whatever you've got, but you get there! Do you understand?"

"Yes, sir," the driver responded. He tried to accelerate the long black car across Central Park South, toward Seventh then, sounding his horn in a long steady blare and turning the limousine into the outside lane of oncoming traffic, but he had to cut back as a city bus began coming at him, giving no ground. He swung the limousine to the far inside lane then, but it was clogged by cars stalled at a red light. O'Connor rapped on the glass again. "Look," he yelled at the driver. "I'm going to get out and . . ." O'Connor started, but suddenly one of the limousine's wheels lurched up on to the sidewalk, its horn sounding in a steady shriek, clearing the way. "Not now, you're not!" the driver shouted back at O'Connor through the glass and the limousine slid by the parked cars and then bumped back into the intersection against the red light. O'Connor could hear horns sounding frantically all around him and cars screeching to a stop only a few short yards away as the limousine swerved into Seventh Avenue, weaving its way across the intersection through the oncoming traffic and then began speeding down Seventh toward the rendezvous point.

Lopata hurried on across another street. The sidewalk was growing even more crowded. He looked up at a sign. He was on Fifth Avenue, moving up from Forty-fourth toward Forty-fifth. Right on schedule, he thought.

He stopped and backed into a shop entrance, standing under its tarp for a moment and trying to catch his breath. He was still safe. There was only a holiday crowd spread out along the street behind him. If anyone had followed him, he had eluded them for the moment. Slowly, he released his left arm from the tourniquetlike grip that he had applied to it. The wrist of his jacket was blood soaked, and he could tell now that the cut was on the top of the arm, running from his wrist back almost to his elbow. He could feel the pain from it now too. The opening in his flesh burned and the amount of blood soaking out of his arm into his jacket frightened him, but he knew from experience that the cut wasn't deep. He looked up Fifth Avenue toward the spot where earlier he had marked the X on the map. He could still do it. The pain in his arm only made him more determined. The odds were greater now, but that was how it should be, he decided. In the end, it should be him, only him, against everything, his single will pitted against the will of the entire world, if necessary. He didn't care what happened to him once it was accomplished. All he cared about was . . . He began to feel slightly light-headed and the strange feeling in his head made it difficult to finish his thought. He must act, he decided, nothing more, just act. He began to move ahead then and, with each heartbeat drumming loudly in his ears, he continued on up Fifth Avenue toward the spot where all of his energy was focused. The bleeding from his wound refused to stop, so he rested his hand up in the side pocket of his windbreaker, using the jacket like a sling to cushion his damaged arm. He could feel the firm metal outline of his long-barreled .38 revolver beneath his jacket as he moved along and the power of the hard metal object helped give him the strength to continue. Only his revolver and the place on the map where he'd put the X had meaning to him now. They were the only real things in his world, he told himself over and over, and the street and its people around him began to blur, as he moved along it, the corners of his vision narrowing, the colors around him dulling and the shapes losing their focus. Fifth Avenue had become like a long blurred tunnel, dreamlike, peopled by silly carnival shapes and distorted figures, the sounds of their laughter far away and wavering like bizarre music coming from another world. He crossed another street. The crowds were even thicker now, and he marshaled all of his remaining forces of will to keep his own body straight and walk and act and look like everyone else, not to attract attention, and to move the entire painful length of the tunnel to where his goal lay in front of him.

He could hear a band playing and the crowd gathered at the edge of the street was stirring, but the noises only moved in and out of his awareness, as he tried to focus his attention on the street where he knew Cassidy would be appearing at any moment, but ahead of him was a protective line of New York City policemen dressed in their traditional dark blue uniforms. Fear flared up in his stomach. He turned and looked behind him. He was half certain that the faces of the men from the train station were following close behind him now too, but he couldn't be certain. He pushed on deeper into the crowd. He tried to look at faces. There would be other enemies everywhere. Police in plain clothes, FBI, Secret Service, more of DeSavio's people, it would be impossible to tell which ones they were. They were all his enemies down here near the end of the tunnel, he told himself, and then he glanced behind him, more pursuers. All the faces that surrounded him now hated him, they all wanted to kill him! He could feel their hate and his head began to fill with fear. He wanted to pull out his weapon and fire at them, but not yet, he told himself. Get to Cassidy first, then start the killing. Take as many as you can, but first get to Cassidy!

He half ran, half walked across a final street corner. The sign told him that he had made it. He used all of his last reserves of strength to see clearly, hear everything around him, see the crowd, smell the steam of hot dogs coming from the vendors' push carts, feel the coolness in the midmorning air. He needed all of his senses for the final confrontation. The music from the band was very loud. "Seventy-six trombones led the big parade," someone near him sang along with the music, and the big brass-band sound filled Lopata's ears as it moved by him on the street only a few yards away. He pushed forward, knocking into people at random, moving through the thick crowd toward the edge of the street. Ahead of him he could see men dressed in dark business suits, walking behind the band. The men were waving at the crowd, smiling. They were moving by him too quickly, the band music fading away down the street behind him. Was he too late? He managed to push his way to the very edge of the street. There was a rope now that barred his way. It was stretched between temporary wooden barricades and it separated the crowd on the sidewalk from the parade route and the marching figures moving by in the center of the avenue. There were more policemen too, their dark-blue-uniformed backs turned to him, blocking his way.

He studied the walking men's faces. It was all right. They were all too old—old politicians' faces. One face was particularly familiar, a smiling old face above a vivid crimson sash.

Up the street now another band was marching toward him. The marching band was less than a half block away, just up Fifth Avenue, and the crowd at the sides of the street near it were beginning to erupt, the young women jumping up and down, the men smiling and laughing and calling out as they pressed forward toward another group of marching men. This must be it! Lopata froze in his tracks and strained to see the faces of the group of marchers. Jesus! It was him. It was happening. It was Cassidy himself! He was actually living through the moment, Lopata realized suddenly, the moment that he had dreamed about over and over so many times during the last two years. There was no mistaking the reality of the cocky, lying devil of a man who was strutting his big fleshy body down Fifth Avenue toward him. God, how he hated those familiar phony movements, Lopata thought, as he watched the man wave to the crowd and then pretend to smile, as he strutted like some kind of a king, back and forth from one side of the street to the other. He thinks that he's so much better than everyone else. Well, he isn't. He is nothing! Lopata's thoughts came to him, so fast now that they just seemed to flash by and merge into just one overpowering feeling of intense hatred. He could feel the hate in his stomach, inside his head, everywhere. He could even taste its sharp bitterness in his mouth. As he watched, Cassidy continued to walk down the broad boulevard, tickertape spilling around him, the band playing so loudly that it was impossible to hear any other sound as it passed directly in front of the corner where Lopata stood. Cassidy was surrounded by other men, more fucking lying American politicians and federal agents, Lopata thought. It was a pity that they couldn't all die this day too, but he would have to leave that work for others to finish, he decided, and, with precise strides, he moved to the very edge of the rope barricade that separated him from the intersection of Fifth Avenue and Forty-seventh Street, the very spot where two hours earlier he had placed an X on the map of the parade route. All was going exactly as he'd planned it, he thought then.

Cassidy was just approaching the intersection as Lopata removed his injured hand from the pocket of his windbreaker and let it drop down at his side.

There was no pain now, only numbness, and Lopata flexed the injured hand several times, preparing it for the task ahead.

He reached up with his other hand then and began to unzip his windbreaker, slowly at first, sliding the metal teeth down only a few inches and then a few more. It all had to be timed perfectly, he told himself, and he stepped carefully over the rope barricade, moving silently, so that he attracted no unnecessary attention as he pushed quietly toward the middle of the intersection. He looked ahead then to where the line of blue-uniformed police officers still barred his way to Cassidy. He gauged the distance between them and determined precisely where he wanted to stand just at the moment that Cassidy reached the midpoint of the intersection. He would duck low right between the two uniformed figures that stood in front of him now, then withdraw the weapon at the last possible second and fire at least one clean shot down the narrow alley formed by the spacing between the bodies of the uniformed figures. He had only one last moment to get it all straight in his mind. The group of marching men were only a few yards from him and Lopata looked up to where Cassidy was slowly strolling along. He knew that he had to be very precise now. No mistakes. Lopata started his final movements, but then suddenly Cassidy stopped. He stood for a moment only a few steps from the middle of the intersection. He hadn't moved the last, few expected feet toward him and Lopata's view of his body was still partially blocked by the bulky figures of the police officers who stood in his way. What was happening? He could just see the side of Cassidy's head, leaning over, listening to one of his men who had been walking alongside him. Did they know about him? Did they know? Was everyone looking at him? Lopata thought wildly, and he dropped his arm back to his side. Did they see the gun? Was it his hand? Had they spotted the blood? The sidewalk was clearing around him. He was discovered! His gun must be visible now outside of his jacket. He must move his arm up and grasp the cold metal zipper with his fingers and hide it again. Or was it already too late? No, it was something else. There was some kind of a disturbance coming from the side street. Lopata tried to remember the map, tried to recreate how the streets fit together. There was a long black limousine pulling into the intersection at Forty-sixth Street and the police were letting it through. It was sounding its horn, breaking into Lopata's awareness as it wove recklessly up Fifth Avenue to only a few yards from where he stood. Then the door to the limousine was thrown open and a man leaped out of its back seat, a dumpy, red-faced man in a brown suit. The man was running, a funny little half run, half walk toward the intersection where Cassidy was standing. Something was horribly wrong. What was it? Cassidy looked up then and said something to the running man and they both laughed. Then, still smiling, Cassidy turned and waved at the crowd on the far side of the intersection, directing his attention almost to the precise spot where Lopata stood. Lopata darted forward into the place that he had chosen earlier, between the figures of the two uniformed policemen. As he ducked down onto one knee, he reached up to his windbreaker and unzipped it in one fluid move. His hand continued on then and easily moved aside the covering flap on his leather shoulder holster and he could feel the solid weight of his .38 revolver slide butt first into the heel of his hand.

Behind him a woman was screaming, but the band's high brass notes were drowning out the sound, and the police officers in front of him were still turned into the intersection, returning Cassidy's wave. Secret Service agents were walking back and forth at the edges of Lopata's vision, but there was that one slim, open alley of fire between him and Cassidy now that he had guessed would be there, a short slender opening just like the line of fire at a carnival shooting gallery. The distance between the two men was less than thirty yards, and Cassidy's smiling gaze was attracted to his darting movement. Lopata knelt at the far side of the intersection and as they locked with Cassidy's his eyes were set hard, dead-bright with anger and resolve. His hand was inside his windbreaker, his fingers grasping the long-barreled .38, but before he could withdraw his weapon from its holster, an explosion rocked Fifth Avenue behind Cassidy, shattering windows and showering the street with stone and glass, sending fragments and debris rocketing into the street.

CHAPTER
20

The Mediterranean was an azure-blue dream. The air was hot and still and soundless. If there were birds, or rippling wind-swept water, or rustling sand moving nearby, their vibrations were lost in the vast quiet. From the uppermost deck of the great yacht that Konstantine Mykanios called *The Voyager*, Suzanne looked out across the peaceful island harbor through the polished copper railings that curved in front of her. She could see the faraway ruins of an ancient white stone temple slowly turning to dust on the barren hillside that overlooked what had become during the last century the private island of the Mykanios family. She lay across the thick white towels and bright blue cushions that had been arranged for her on the deck of *The Voyager*. With the Greek sun baking down on her, she began to believe that she could actually see the hot dry air moving above the island, picking up particles of stone and dust one by one from the surface of the old ruins and distributing them democratically on the fine white sand beach at the mouth of the island's perfect crescent of a harbor.

Suzanne was alone, lying on the ship's high deck in a quiet sealed-off area, so private that not even the servants could disturb her solitude. Her children were sleeping, buried in their afternoon naps several decks below. So Suzanne had removed the top of her low-cut bathing suit and her long dark hair was up and hidden beneath a light silk scarf that she had tied around the top of her head, leaving her face and her shoulders and the back of her neck free to the cooling breezes of the Mediterranean. Rivulets of sweat were dropping slowly from her scalp over the nape of her exposed neck and down to her shoulders. Her eyes were hidden and resting behind big circles of dark glasses that she had bought in Rome only the day before. Her body was darkly oiled and she could smell the oil bubbling against her skin, as the hot Greek sun burned her legs and stomach and chest to a burnished golden brown luster.

Slowly she turned her gaze from the island in the distance to look across the Mediterranean toward where a speedboat was cutting a white wake in the blue water from the shore below the main house. It was headed toward *The Voyager*. Konstantine wasn't due to arrive until later that day, but she'd seen the flurry of activity a few minutes before when the helicopter had set down on the gray cement pad at the far side of the shimmering, white marble Arabian Nights' dream of a house on the hillside overlooking the harbor, and she'd guessed that he'd been able to get away from Athens a few hours earlier than he had expected.

She pushed her body up and rested the palms of her hands against the polished wooden deck, her arms straight and locked in back of her. She let her naked breasts and shoulders feel one more last lick of the hot Greek sun, while she breathed in deeply and fully on the sea air, finally letting her slender body relax more than it had been able to in months. Then she reached out for the top of her bathing suit and placed it on over her shoulders, tying it in the back with both her hands straining to reach the frail cloth string that held it in place. She stood then and walked to the railing and waved at the motorboat as it roared into focus just a few yards from the side of the big ship.

Konstantine was on deck, his strong, deeply tanned face and lustrous dark black hair standing out dramatically above an immaculately tailored white suit coat.

Suzanne smiled down at him as he waved back at her, but he didn't return the smile. Instead, his face remained gravely serious and full of concern. And in that moment as she stood at the high railing and looked at the apprehension etched into Konstantine's face, the feelings of calm and well-being that had begun to regenerate in Suzanne's body over the last few peaceful days in Greece began to disappear. What could it be? she wondered. Probably nothing, just her imagination, she thought as she knelt and removed a long black and white silk robe from the back of a deck chair next to her and slipped the light robe on over her shoulders, enjoying the way that the cool silky fabric rested on her mildly sunburned skin. She tied the sash securely at her waist, tucking its top up close to her neck. She smiled at her own exaggerated preparations. This was the first time that she had seen Konstantine in almost a year, the first time she had ever seen him without the presence of her husband. It was important that he not misunderstand why she'd come, she thought. It was important, too, that she not forget why she'd come, she reminded herself then.

Her sandals were resting on the deck beneath her and she kicked her feet into them and hurried to the ladder that led down to the big yacht's lower decks. Almost at once, a white-jacketed servant appeared below her and helped her down the last few steps and onto the main deck.

Konstantine was already on board, waiting for her. When she arrived, he paused for a moment, removing the square-cut sunglasses that he often wore and showing Suzanne the seriousness in his bold dark eyes. He looked directly at her for several long seconds before he spoke. "Something's happened," he said finally.

Immediately after the sound of the explosion, Lopata turned and began pushing his way back toward the sidewalk, and as he did, his revolver stayed hidden under his dark blue windbreaker. He had never removed it, he realized, as he fought his way back through the crowd. People were moving in every direction around him, trying to sort out what had happened only a few seconds earlier. Lopata glanced behind him, straining for a look back down the street to where the sounds of the explosions had come from. There was a faint whiff of smoke and burnt chemicals in the air, and the sounds of sirens in the distance, beginning to move toward the intersection. Most of the people near him were running, some shouting out in confusion and, as Lopata started to move away from the chaotic street corner with them, he thought he could hear one of the police officers following closely behind him, but when he turned again to look, he could see the officers running across Forty-seventh Street toward the sound of the explosion. Lopata could see the figures of several Secret Service agents, too, sweeping into the intersection and forming a circle around the President. As Lopata watched, they moved the President back toward the waiting limousine and thrust him inside its rear seat. The agents ran alongside the limousine clearing its way to the near side of the intersection, and within seconds, the limousine that contained the President was moving against traffic across Forty-Seventh toward the East River. Cassidy had escaped again, Lopata thought. The explosion, whatever the hell had caused it, had been far up Fifth Avenue, maybe as much as a half block behind the President. Cassidy was safe; the smug bastard had probably not even had his famous hair messed this time, Lopata thought. Another moment and . . . But Lopata was too angry to finish his thought, and he turned away from the intersection and began moving back through the crowd. There was a woman in a bright summer dress blocking the sidewalk in front of him and he pushed at her hard with the flat of his open hand and she staggered out of his way. He could hear a man's voice calling out to him then and Lopata whirled away in a flash, his hand up inside of his coat and onto the butt of his weapon. The man stood frozen in fear, as Lopata glared at him for several long seconds. Finally, his hand still inside his jacket, he turned back toward Forty-second Street. His hand and the arm that had held the pistol were trembling uncontrollably now and he could feel himself sweating heavily. He stopped and rested against a glass display window. The crowd surged past him for several seconds, a blur of noise and color. There was a nervous shaking in his arms and hands and even in his legs that wouldn't stop. He reached down and zipped his windbreaker back up tight to his neck, as if he meant to strap himself up inside it and use the garment to keep himself from falling apart. The pain in his wrist, where the knife blade had sliced through his flesh, was beginning to throb again. He thought about heading toward Grand Central, but he couldn't go back there, he decided finally. DeSavio's people would be waiting for him. He had miscalculated. He had hoped that DeSavio would let him live, if he could complete the business with Cassidy once and for all, but he'd been wrong. DeSavio wanted him dead now more than he wanted Cassidy to die. He's more frightened of me, Lopata realized, more frightened of what I could tell the authorities. Lopata stood for a moment, letting the full impact of that realization sink in. It had all been happening so fast since he'd left the Cape that he hadn't fully understood until that very moment the precise truth of what was happening to him. He was truly alone now, with powerful forces pitted against him that wanted him to die. There was no place that he would be safe.

Lopata finally took a few hesitant steps away from the plate-glass window, and a single strange thought began to dance at the edge of his mind. He was wrong. There might be one place that he could go, one place where the power of the men in New Orleans or the law-enforcement agencies of the United States government couldn't touch him. There was one place where he might be safe. But did he dare?

Lopata pulled the map out of his pocket once more, searching for the bus station. He found a nearly empty block on it that led west through Broadway, and then he began to run at full speed toward Times Square. His hand and arm were aching deeply with the pain of his knife wound, but despite it, he began to experience a strange exhilaration. Yes, he did dare, he told himself. It was perfect—a place where they would never look for him in a million years, because they would never believe that he had the courage to actually go there.

"There was a problem here." It was Jack's voice, half buried in static on the other end of the long-distance line. Suzanne was standing in the big downstairs library of the Mykanios home. From the open library doors she could see the elegantly dressed guests beginning to arrive for the party that Konstantine had planned for her that evening.

"Yes, we heard. Are you all right?" she asked urgently.

"Yes, I'm just fine," Jack said, fighting to be heard over the transatlantic wire. "A policeman was hurt and three or four other people, but no one seriously. Everything is all right," he said and then repeated it again for emphasis. "Everything is fine, believe me."

Suzanne felt herself begin to relax. "It was a bomb?" She said the unfamiliar word into Konstantine's telephone and her question traveled in an instant the five thousand miles across the Atlantic that separated her from her husband.

"Yes, it was," Jack answered, crisply and unemotionally, as if he were briefing a group of his advisers. "An explosive device of some kind. The FBI is still trying to reconstruct what happened, but it wasn't serious, Suzanne, believe me. The explosion wasn't large enough to—" Jack hesitated only slightly before he finished what he had begun to say. "To kill anyone."

"Thank God," Suzanne breathed the words of relief out and as she did, she could see Konstantine's powerful figure crossing from the front of the house across the garden toward the open terrace doors that led to the library. He was dressed for the evening in a white dinner jacket, styled with boldly cut, double-breasted lapels that accentuated the width and strength of his broad shoulders perfectly. Suzanne nodded that everything was all right and then forced herself to look away from him and return her attention to the telephone.

"They think that they have the person responsible," Jack said. "It was a student, a young man." There was a sadness in the President's voice now that was even apparent over the long-distance wire.

"There was no connection to . . ." Suzanne began, but then guessing his wife's question, Jack interrupted her with the answer before she could finish. "No," he said with finality. "Absolutely not. There was no connection what-soever between what happened here today and what happened in Dallas."

Suzanne remained silent then, not wanting to continue, until she was certain that she could not be overheard. She looked up to see if Konstantine was still standing at the open terrace doors and when she saw that he was, she nodded to him again. He nodded back and, understanding, he moved away from the open door and returned across the lushly flowering grounds toward the front of his home to greet the arriving guests.

"You're not coming here, are you?" Suzanne said into the telephone then.

There was a long silence on the long-distance line from New York, followed by Jack's simple reply. "No," he said finally. "It would be a bad idea," he added, after a few more seconds of silence had gone by between them.

"You mean Rance and his staff people think it would be a bad idea," Suzanne said back to him angrily, and the static-filled long-distance silence between the two of them lengthened again.

"No, because I think it would be," Jack said coldly after a few seconds. "Tim's right here. We've been discussing it and . . ." Jack stopped then, not wanting to explain himself any further.

"I think Tim's just kicked me out of the campaign," he continued, his tone lighter and some of the humor returning to it. "Anyway, we've decided that I'm not needed here for the next few weeks. I'm probably doing more harm than good. What the ticket needs is clean track to run on, without Jack Cassidy around to steal all the headlines from it. Tim says that he's worried about my safety, but he's not fooling anybody. He and his new boss just want me out of the way." As she listened, Suzanne could imagine her husband smiling over at his brother in some hotel room in New York.

"Well, that's perfect," Suzanne said. "You should come here then."

Jack didn't say anything right away, but she knew what his answer would be before he spoke.

"I'm taking Jeffries up on his offer to visit him in Connemara. It's the right place for me now," Jack said.

"Is that what the polls show?" Suzanne said, without thinking, and then wished that she hadn't.

They were both quiet then. Strangely, Suzanne thought, after over twelve years of marriage there seemed to be nothing at all for them to say to each other.

"Suzanne, you have to understand," Jack said then. "Every move I make, every move that either of us makes now is front page news. Whether it's fair or not, Konstantine is still a very controversial person to a lot of people and I just can't be seen flying off in the middle of a campaign to some private Greek island and . . ."

It was Suzanne's turn to cut her husband's words off in midsentence. "Jack, we've been all through this," she said sharply, ending her husband's lecture.

"Yes, we have, and the answer is still the same, more so now than ever," he said and then lapsed into silence again. "The children are good and happy?" he said finally, before the latest of their silences became too painful to continue it any longer.

"Yes, they are. They're fine. It's beautiful here," Suzanne said and then turned her gaze out toward the ancient temple ruins on the hillside above Konstantine's island home. "Jack, I'm not ready to leave here yet," she said suddenly and the words even seemed to surprise her. "I feel that I've just barely——" She stopped then and waited for her husband's reaction.

"Yes, I understand," Jack said, but his voice was growing colder and even more distant and Suzanne could feel his anger increasing in the long silence. "There's no need for you to. Perhaps in a few days . . ." But he didn't finish his thought, the static that had been building on the line was making it difficult to hear his words now. "Suzanne, I want to be with you, but," he continued when the interruption on the line quieted again. "Greece is just all wrong right now. Please try to understand that. I . . ." Jack's voice trailed off then and the static moved back in to swallow up the call.

When the static on the telephone line lessened for a brief moment, Suzanne could hear her husband's voice again. "I said that I'll call you from March House in a few days, no later than Friday," he said, his voice hard and intense as it fought to be heard over the transatlantic wire.

"Yes, of course," Suzanne answered, but the interference on the line was sweeping in again. "You're sure you're all right?" she said, needing the reassurance one more time.

"Yes, I'm fine. Everything's fine," Jack said quickly, ducking his words in between the interruptions on the line.

"Good night, Jack, I . . ." Suzanne began, but before she could finish telling her husband that she loved him, she heard the telephone connection break away into final unpenetrable static and her husband's voice disappear across the Atlantic.

Suzanne stood for several more seconds, hearing only the annoying crackling on the telephone that she held tensely in her hand and, as she waited for the interference to clear, she looked back out toward the open door to the garden. Konstantine had returned and he was standing quietly, watching her with his bold dark black eyes. He stood beside one of the ornate Corinthian columns of white marble that formed the entrance to the garden. She could see now that he was dressed all in white, white dinner jacket, white silk shirt, and pale white tie, with only a single burst of color near the center of his chest, where someone had pinned a bright red island flower. He had a champagne glass in one hand, but he wasn't drinking from it. He was holding it close to his chest, forgotten, as he looked through the open doorway at her, and it was impossible for Suzanne to tell how long he had been standing there, or what he might have overheard.

Leigh looked at herself in the three-way mirror. She slowly ran her open hand down from her waist along the hard curve of her body to her thigh. She pretended to be smoothing the dress down in front, but all she really wanted to do was feel herself, touch her own body, reaffirm to herself how full and tight and warm her own flesh felt. This was still something she had left after all the years and she knew that the store clerks and the few customers still left in the exclusive little French Quarter shop were well aware of her and how good she looked in the tight-fitting gold sheath dress. The dress was cut low at the top and showed off her body beautifully. It wasn't a classy dress, but then she wasn't that classy a woman either, she thought as she looked at herself in the shop's three-way mirror again. But the dress was expensive, and with her in it, exciting as hell, and she wanted it badly.

Garrett sat behind her, watching her every move. She turned back to him now and lifted the dress on the side, revealing the entire length of her leg past her tan line and showing him the full curve of her hip, until it was interrupted by the matching gold lamé underpants.

"Do you think it's too much?" Leigh said, trying not to smile at the look on Garrett's face. He was so excited from watching her body that for a moment he couldn't even answer the question.

The saleswoman standing above him was busy pretending not to notice the little game of seduction that was going on between her two prospective buyers, and as the saleswoman moved away, Leigh tucked her finger under the matching gold lamé underpants, pretending to flick them down to cover herself, but in the process she held the elastic edge of the tightly cut fabric away from her for a moment, showing even more soft white flesh.

"No, it looks great," the lawyer managed. He was a little breathless from watching his secretary try on a string of provocative dresses for almost the last hour. Every guy who'd been in the place had to be turned on, he thought, as he looked up the long creamy-white expanse of her thigh.

"Do you think it's too expensive?" she asked, walking slowly over the few steps to where Garrett was sitting watching her.

"It is expensive," the lawyer said, his eyes fixed ahead of him at the soft bulge covered in dazzling gold lamé fabric between his secretary's legs. His mouth was dry and his heart was pounding as she turned back to the mirror, moving her body tantalizingly in front of him. She pretended to be trying to get a better view of herself in the three-way mirror by dipping her body down in back close to his face. "I want to look good for your clients," she said. "Do you think this would look good on a yacht? I don't think I've ever been to a party on a yacht before," she said.

"Uh-uh," was all Garrett could manage.

"Why do you think they invited us? They've never asked you out there before, have they?"

"I don't know," Garrett said. "Maybe I'm getting more important to them."

"And they really asked for me to come?" Leigh said, turning back to Garrett.

"Uh-uh. They asked for you special," Garrett said.

"Will Mr. DeSavio be there himself?" Leigh asked and Garrett nodded his head. "I think so," he answered.

"A Mafia party," Leigh whispered, smiling a little private smile at Garrett and dipping down even closer to him and showing the lawyer the full white front of her chest in extreme close-up. "It gets me a little excited," she whispered provocatively and then added in the same tone, as she fingered the front of the expensive dress. "Do you want me to have it?"

"Yeah, I want you to have it," Garrett said smiling back to her and not even trying to disguise the double meaning in their words.

"Good," Leigh said, spinning quickly on her heel and disappearing into the privacy of one of the little dressing rooms at the rear of the shop.

The saleswoman reappeared behind Garrett then. "This would look wonderful on her," she said to the little lawyer. "And it would be perfect with the dress," she added, holding a gold necklace out toward him. Garrett reached out for the necklace and then stood and walked to the dressing room door that Leigh had disappeared through a few seconds earlier. "I'll see if she likes it," he said, turning back toward the saleswoman, but she had already returned to the front of the shop.

Garrett knocked and then entered the elegant little dressing room without waiting for an answer. The dressing room was small, but it had a chair and a table with a decanter of sherry and matching glasses standing on it. The room was surrounded on three sides with gilt-edged floor to ceiling mirrors. There was a strong smell of alcohol in the small space and Leigh was standing drinking thirstily from a glass of sherry as Garrett entered into the private little room. Her new dress was unzipped and loosened down the back revealing the naked rear of her body past her waist.

"The girl thought that you might like this," Garrett said, lifting the expensive necklace, so that Leigh could see its reflection in the mirror in front of her without needing to turn back into the small room. She smiled then and relaxed her shoulders, offering her bare white back to Garrett. The lawyer approached her from behind and then reached up to drape the gold necklace around her throat. His heart was pounding wildly. He could smell the mingling odors of perfume and sherry, and, with shaking hands, he barely managed to make the clasp on the necklace work. Then he pressed himself up against his secretary's body and lifted her long auburn hair away from her shoulders and began kissing the soft white exposed place at the nape of her neck. As he did, he could feel her reaching back and firmly grasping him with her open hand through his suit pants and then making a long full rubbing motion against the rough linen fabric. He undid the fly of his pants. Leigh smiled into the mirror at him and let her hand slide off the rough linen fabric and on to his protruding flesh, massaging him firmly with her palm and the slender fingers of her long cool hand.

Garrett's eyes were misting over and he was beginning to breathe deeply and regularly as he lifted up the back of Leigh's dress and used both of his hands to reach into the warmth beneath her new gold lamé underpants and slide the fabric down, exposing the firm round fullness of his secretary's lower body.

Leigh still held the antique glass half full of nut brown sherry in her hand, as she watched Garrett in the mirror fumbling with himself and trying frantically now to insert himself inside her from the rear. She coolly lifted the little glass of sherry to her lips and drank from it, while the little lawyer finally managed to push himself inside of her.

She looked across at her image in the mirror, as she admired the necklace that Garrett had placed around her neck a few minutes earlier. It was beautiful and far more expensive than even the dress had been and she wanted it badly now too.

Suddenly there was a slight muffled sound on the dressing room door and Garrett withdrew himself reluctantly from inside her. The saleswoman! he thought, suddenly feeling frightened and embarrassed. But as he waited, his heart pounding, there was no further sound from the other side of the dressing room door. If the saleswoman had returned, she had quickly withdrawn again.

Leigh turned her body and slowly undid the clasp on the gold necklace and, holding one end of it between the fingers and thumb of her right hand, she used her left hand to lift her skirt back up in the front, then she slowly lowered the gold necklace down like a dangling snake, until it slithered, glittering golden into the soft reddish-brown pubic hair between her legs. Garrett dropped immediately down to his knees in front of her then, the golden necklace only a few inches from him.

"What do you think?" she said then in a husky voice and moved her body, gold necklace and all, so that it was almost touching Garrett's face. Unable to restrain himself any longer, the lawyer began passionately kissing the center of his secretary's body. He moved his hands up then, so that his palms fully grasped her buttocks, his palms flat against the lush curve of their underside.

Leigh smiled and moved into a firmer position next to the figure of the kneeling lawyer. She reached down with her hands then and placed her long fingers on the back of his head, forcing his face up as far as it would go between her legs. Men are such children, she thought as she removed the hand that still held the necklace from the back of Garrett's head and dropped the glittering golden string on to the table next to the glass decanter of sherry. A Mafia party, she thought, and the danger and excitement made her shiver almost as much as the things that Garrett was doing to her now. There would be rich, powerful men there and maybe it was time for her to move on, she added to herself as she touched Garrett's head lightly with her extended fingers. Maybe she'd find what it was that she was looking for at the party. And if she found it, she would take it, she decided. She would have what she wanted. There was nothing she couldn't get from a man, when she really went after it, she decided, nothing.

Sullivan was watching television with Denise. They had the sofa bed pulled out and they were lying under and over a tangle of sheets and blankets in the little furnished apartment that Sullivan had rented a few blocks from the Bureau's Dallas office.

Denise was lying back against an arrangement of soft pillows, her eyes closed in contentment. She was breathing deeply and rhythmically, her breasts rising and falling under a blue-and-silver T-shirt that said DALLAS COWBOYS—NUMBER ONE across the front of it. If she'd thought about it at that moment though, she would have disagreed. The Cowboys weren't number one—James O'Malley Sullivan was.

He was sitting next to her, his own pillows arranged so that he could see the portable television set that stood on top of his bookcase. Sullivan had pulled his shorts back on, but his big hand was still moving slowly up and back along the outside curves of Denise's leg. His mind was equally divided between the cool, silky way that her leg felt under his hand and the last few minutes of "The Fugitive" episode that was being played out on the little portable television set in front of him. "Shit," he said when his telephone rang and he had to reach over to the end table to pick it up. "Yes," he said into the receiver, not bothering to disguise his annoyance at the interruption of his privacy.

"Hello, my friend," the voice on the other end of the line said. Sullivan could feel the pleasant torpor that his own body had slipped into over the last few hours being jolted away by the intensity coming from the man's voice.

Denise could sense Sullivan's sudden uneasiness, and she raised herself up on the pullout bed and turned to him. "Jim, what is it?" Sullivan held up his hand, palm out toward her, to silence her. She kept her body raised up against the back of the sofa bed, watching Sullivan and listening carefully.

"Who is this?" Sullivan asked. The shirt that he'd worn to work that day lay wrapped somewhere in the tangle of bedclothes beneath him and Denise could see the muscles tighten under the bare skin of his shoulders and chest as he waited for an answer.

"We still have business," the voice on the telephone said, and in its strangely unnatural, very formal use of the English language, Sullivan sensed a deep uneasiness.

"We do?" Sullivan said slowly, trying to give himself time to think. "Have we met?"

Denise moved forward on the pull-down bed and turned the sound off on the television set, but the black-and-white screen still showed the Fugitive running between buildings, half lost on the deserted, darkened back streets of some imaginary American small town.

"Oh, yes," the voice on the telephone said, and with the sound of the television off the voice was loud enough that Denise could hear it as well. "In Monterey a few months ago," the voice continued.

"Mexico," Sullivan said, suddenly understanding and seeing again in his mind's eye the running figure dressed all in black that had tried to sell him a copy of Strode's diary in Mexico, but then had disappeared, leaving only the clue of Room 409 in the Tampico hotel room behind—the clue that had led to the dead end of the final bloodstained corpse.

"Yes, it's good to hear from you again," Sullivan said. Maybe what he'd found in Room 409 of the Mirador wasn't a final dead end after all, he thought.

The voice on the telephone laughed at Sullivan's pretense of casualness. "Yes, I'm certain that it is," the voice said. "Old friends shouldn't lose touch with each other in a world like this."

"How can I help you?"

"No, my friend, it is still I who can help you," the strangely formal voice said.

"For a price," Sullivan said.

"For a price," the voice repeated the basis of the relationship he was proposing in a tone just as flat as Sullivan's had been. "But last time the money part of our arrangement seemed to be a problem for you."

"Your information was a little disappointing as well," Sullivan said.

"I know the value of what I gave to you," the voice snapped.

"All we found in Room 409 of the Mirador Hotel was a—" Sullivan began, but the man's voice cut him off before he could finish.

"The man that you are looking for is a butcher," the voice said.

Denise could hear the man's words from where she sat next to Sullivan, and she reached over and placed her hand on his leg. Sullivan turned to her, looking into her eyes to let her know that it was going to be all right. "You sound close," Sullivan said. "I'd like to talk to you, see you face to face." At the suggestion of a meeting, Denise's hand tightened in fear on Sullivan's bare leg.

There was only silence on the other end of the telephone line for several long seconds then.

"That's the way we work it up here," Sullivan said sharply, sensing the contact's uncertainty. "If you want me to hit the Bureau up for some money,

I've got to know what I'm buying. Face to face, you tell me what you've got, and what you want for it, and I tell you if I think it's worth it."

There was more silence. For a moment, Sullivan was afraid that he'd lost him. "That's the only way it happens," the agent said with finality and then held his breath to hear the other man's decision.

"When?" the voice said slowly.

"Right now," Sullivan said, pressing hard. He could sense the other man's desperation now. He was probably in serious need of money, Sullivan guessed, and the Bureau was his only hope of getting any fast. "You tell me where and I'll be there," Sullivan said quickly, trying not to give the contact time to think.

"Alone," the voice said.

"If that's the way you want it," Sullivan shot back.

"With cash," the voice said.

"Not this time. There's no way that I can get cash tonight," Sullivan said, praying that this wouldn't blow it. "Look, we're in the States now. We're going to play by American rules. That means, if you want cash, give me a reason to go to the Bureau for it. If it's any good, I'll do my best for you," Sullivan said.

"It'll be good," the voice said, and Sullivan could feel himself beginning to relax again. He had him. Sullivan reached for a pad of paper and a pencil to take down the directions to their meeting place.

Sullivan drove out a lonely stretch of deserted Texas highway, past all the chili joints, and package stores, and two-pump gas stations to the very outskirts of metropolitan Dallas. It was nearly midnight when he passed the Dallas city limits. Occasionally another set of speeding headlights would flash by him headed back toward the center of the city, but very little else moved nearby, either coming or going, as the road narrowed from six lanes of super highway down to four and then two, except once or twice he thought that he had seen a hint of something that might be a pair of headlights far back down the road. Probably my imagination, he thought, but I might as well be certain, and he slowed his car and waited, but nothing approached in the darkness on the road behind him and he guessed then that he'd been right. It was nothing. Denise had wanted him to call someone else for backup, but he decided against it. He didn't want Yancey to know what he was doing until he had something a little more solid. Anyway, this guy, whoever he was, was an informant. He wanted money not trouble, Sullivan reasoned, but the memory of the flash of headlights far back down the road still haunted him, and he stepped back down hard on his accelerator and the government car moved forward even faster down the dark Texas road toward its destination. Sullivan checked his rearview mirror every minute or so, but there was still nothing. If there was a car back there, it had switched its headlights off and was driving nearly blind. It couldn't keep that up for long, Sullivan decided, and he stepped down even harder on the accelerator and pushed his own car on into the night.

He could see ahead of him now the shadowy outline of an abandoned amusement park. The big round circle of an empty Ferris wheel, outlined against the cloudless Texas sky, stood above the other low shapes in the abandoned park. This was the place.

Sullivan pulled his car off the highway then and found the side road that led to the dirt parking area at the front of the old park. He continued from there on foot, past the closed-down ticket booths to what had been the amusement park's main entrance. The entrance was locked and Sullivan stood for a moment and looked inside. The night was hot and silent. In the distance there was only the constant noise of crickets and the soft swish of an occasional car passing at high speed on the nearby highway.

Sullivan continued counterclockwise around the perimeter of the closed-up park, following the outline of the high wire fence that surrounded it. A few seconds later, he found the break in the fence just where the voice on the telephone had told him he would find it. Sullivan passed easily through the opening and entered the grounds of the abandoned park.

The grounds were pitch black, darker even than the parking lot had been, and Sullivan had forgotten to bring a flashlight and he could see only the bright white pieces of litter lying on the park's dirt floor; the discarded popcorn boxes and old crumpled peanut bags scattered in the dirt around him glowed like luminescent stone markers in the darkness. He began moving very slowly around the perimeter of the park then, continuing his counterclockwise course away from its front entrance, just as he'd been told, but he stayed close to the wire fence where he could see the empty parking lot only a few feet away. As he moved by the rows of boarded-up wooden structures papered over with torn and sun-faded signs advertising the park's past attractions, he almost began to believe that he could hear the sounds of carnival music in the distance and the noise of the daytime crowds, and the call of the barkers beckoning to him as he passed, but suddenly a figure appeared out of the shadows and stood squarely in Sullivan's path, interrupting his fantasy. The agent's hand shot up inside his coat for his holstered gun, but then Sullivan could see that the figure was standing with his own hands above his head, and, in the faint light from the nearby highway, Sullivan could tell that the figure's hands were empty.

"Hello," Sullivan called out and as he did the agent dropped his hand away from his weapon, but he left his coat unbuttoned so that he could reach back for it easily, if he needed it.

The figure nodded at Sullivan, but then it moved farther back into the shadows. And as he watched, Sullivan remembered the heavy awkward movements of the bulky body that had raced from the Church of Miracles in Monterey a few months before. "I think we've met before?" Sullivan called out toward the shadows where the figure was hidden now.

"We have."

Sullivan stayed quiet, waiting for the figure to make the next move, but there was only more silence. "You told me to come here!" Sullivan called out.

"Yes, we have business," the voice said, and then suddenly a car rocketed by on the highway behind him, its headlights flashing in the night, and the figure dove back even deeper into the shadows of the boarded-up refreshment stand that protected him from Sullivan's view. Before he could hide himself completely though, Sullivan caught a hint of the man's face in the headlights of the passing car. The features were heavy and broad with dark black bristles of unshaven beard accentuating the jawline. It was the same man that he had seen at the Church of Miracles in Monterey. Sullivan was certain of it.

"We've got some business to finish!" Sullivan called out, afraid that the man might run away at any moment. The agent thought again of his holstered weapon. He could use it to fire a warning shot if the man made a run for it, he decided, but the man in the shadows held his ground and, after another brief moment of silence, he began to speak again. "I need money," the man said, and the voice couldn't disguise its desperation any longer.

"In exchange for what?" Sullivan could sense the edge of panic in the shadow figure's voice and the young agent grew more confident that he could control the situation this time.

"There was a woman murdered in Monterey," the shadow figure said.

"Room 409, Mirador Hotel," Sullivan shot back, and he took a step toward the dark corner of the wooden structure that hid the man from his view. "Did you kill her?" Sullivan called out into the darkness. Then he edged forward another few steps.

"No," the figure hissed angrily. "He did."

Sullivan stayed quiet then, using the silence to move slowly forward even closer toward the dark corner where the man crouched in the shadows.

"That bastard she was sleeping with, he killed her!" the man hissed, but when Sullivan didn't answer, the crouching figure shouted out in fear. "Where are you?"

"Right here," Sullivan answered calmly and continued pressing forward slowly step by step toward him.

"Stay where you are," the man said, but his voice had no authority.

"You want the rest of your money, don't you?" Sullivan answered quietly.

"More," the figure in the shadows said. "Much more now."

"For what?" Sullivan said, and then he snapped around the corner of the little wooden stand that had protected the shadow figure from view, finally coming face to face with it. The figure reacted by taking a step backward and disappearing even deeper into the shadows, but it didn't turn and run, as Sullivan had feared that it might. The figure just froze tensely a few short yards from him. "For the name of the person who murdered her," it whispered.

"Why would I care?" Sullivan pressed.

The figure delayed for only a short beat before answering, and in that short moment of delay Sullivan felt his own heart stop. "Because he's the same man that you're looking for," the figure in the shadows said then.

"How do you know that . . ." Sullivan began, but before he could finish his question, a set of headlights flashed by, illuminating the man's face. This time, though, the lights were much closer, almost on top of them, and there were the sounds of a powerful car engine, and then the corner that had been buried in shadowy darkness was suddenly as bright as an artificial dawn.

The heavyset man crouching in front of Sullivan shouted at him. "I said come alone!"

Sullivan turned back toward the sound of the car engine then, and as he did all he could see was a set of headlights closing on him at high speed. He reached for his shoulder holster and his .45 fell heavily into his hand. He pointed the weapon at the front of the speeding car and fired. One of the oncoming car's headlights shattered with the impact of Sullivan's first round, but the other light kept coming straight toward him.

Sullivan turned away from the oncoming headlight and began running toward the center of the park. He could see the heavyset figure of his informant running awkwardly several yards in front of him, but after a few steps, the man ducked down a narrow back alley formed by a short row of temporary wooden buildings. Sullivan followed him. The man began to stumble on his thick legs and Sullivan closed the gap between them quickly and dove forward, managing to tackle the running figure low around the ankles and knock him to the ground. The car, with its single remaining headlight still blazing into the darkness, hurtled by the narrow opening to the alley and continued on down the row of little wooden stands, knocking a long line of the temporary structures noisily to the ground and splintering them into the earth with its heavy tires.

Sullivan grabbed the fallen man by his shirt front and lifted him toward him. "Who is that out there?" Sullivan shouted into the man's face and gestured back toward the hurtling car with his .45.

"I . . . I don't know."

"Is it the guy from the hotel?" Sullivan was shaking the man by his shirt front now, but there was no answer. "Talk to me!" Sullivan yelled savagely at him. "The pages you showed me in Tampico were from a diary. Where is it now?" Sullivan could hear the hurtling car shrieking to a halt several yards past the opening to the narrow back alley, and then the car lurched into reverse and splintered more of the soft, dry, rotten wood of the temporary structures as it reversed its way back toward the place where Sullivan and the frightened man were hidden. The agent realized that in another few seconds the car would come roaring down the short alley toward them. Sullivan began shaking the man violently then, but the shirt that he held him by ripped in his hands and the man's face was frozen in fear. "Tell me, you son of a bitch!" Sullivan shouted at him, as the sounds of the lurching car grew louder and more violent.

"I . . . I don't know," the man managed. "It wasn't even my idea. It was hers. We only had time to copy a few pages. Then we had to put it back before we finished it. I was afraid of him, very afraid."

"The man's name," Sullivan commanded. The single headlight swung into the opening to the alley then and lit the ground directly behind the two men. Sullivan could hear a car door opening, but he refused to turn around and face the sound. All his energy was focused on one thing now, getting an answer to his question. "I want his name!" he shouted again, shaking the frightened man's head and shoulders violently for an answer. "I'll get you your goddamned money, just tell me his name," Sullivan shouted.

"I don't know," the man stammered. "He had forged identity papers. I can tell you the name on them, but that's all I know."

Sullivan wasn't certain that he believed him, but he knew that they were out of time. The car was within only a few yards of them now and he released the man's shirt and let him drop back down onto the dirt of the alley. He ducked his own shoulder toward the ground and began rolling away from the light that spilled out from the car's remaining headlight as a gunshot flashed in the darkness from the mouth of the alley.

Sullivan forced himself to stay low as he'd been trained and continue to roll his body away from the patch of illumination made by the vehicle's single headlight. Just as his knee dug into the hard earth below him and he was forcing his body to make its second rolling move away from the oncoming light, a second bullet tore into the dirt where his body had been just a moment before. Then more bullets, followed by the sound of a rapidly propelled, hard metal object cutting deeply into human flesh. Once you'd heard that sound, you could never forget it, Sullivan thought, and then after it came the wild cry of pain from the man lying behind him.

Sullivan continued to roll until his body slammed into one of the temporary wooden structures behind him. He popped up onto one knee, his revolver extended in front of him with both hands. The car was hurtling down the narrow opening straight at him, the light from its single headlight bucking up and down over the uneven ground, illuminating first the slumped and lifeless body lying in back of Sullivan and then suddenly, Sullivan's own body. The young agent hesitated only long enough to steady the extended weapon and sight it on the hurtling car before he fired his revolver twice, not at the car's headlights this time, but up at its front windshield. The bullets shattered the glass and the car swerved, seemingly out of control, first headed at Sullivan and then swinging violently away from him and smashing its heavy metal grillwork against the body of the Mexican man lying behind him and squashing it violently against the back wall of the alley. As the car pulled past the smashed body it seemed to be looking for Sullivan, but the agent stayed low, out of its line of sight. The car lurched to a stop, its headlight spotlighting the wall just above Sullivan's head. There was a moment of intense quiet. In the silence, the Mexican's body slipped down along the wall and slowly crumpled into the dirt of the alley.

Sullivan fired his weapon at the windshield of the stopped car, and glass blew out toward its passenger compartment, but within a split second it started moving backward, its heavy tires chewing up dirt and rock as they reversed themselves in the soft earth.

Sullivan's second shot bit into the metal that covered the engine of the speeding car, but the vehicle continued on toward the end of the alley and then disappeared around the corner. An instant later all Sullivan could see was a blur of movement as the car rocketed back across the opening in front of him and then out of sight.

The agent stood and ran the few steps to where the dead body of the Mexican man lay squashed and broken and smeared with blood in the dirt below him. Sullivan knelt by the man's body only for a moment, confirming what he knew had to be true—the man was no longer alive to answer his questions.

Sullivan stood then and ran toward the mouth of the alley, his .45 held high in his right hand, pointed at the sky. He was still doing everything by the book, he realized as he ran, and he only lowered his revolver into firing position again when he reached the end of the alley and saw the car's red taillights flashing in the distance as it cleared the break in the wire fence. It was impossible to see the vehicle's license plates, or to even guess at the car's make or model, and it was too far away to shoot at with any accuracy. Sullivan's training told him to just let it go now, but his emotions said to do something—anything. He knelt and fired several stray rounds in anger at the departing taillights. The shots just sailed off harmlessly into the darkness, but firing them made Sullivan feel a little better.

CHAPTER
21

Jack looked down for a long time at the photograph on the front page of the American edition of the *London Herald Tribune*. The photo showed a badly blurred image of Suzanne lying on the white sand beach of Konstantine's island. Suzanne's shoulders were turned away from the camera and the picture had been taken from a great distance, probably with a telephoto lens, Jack guessed, but Suzanne appeared to be wearing only the bottom half of a low-cut bikini as she relaxed on the private beach. She was alone, but Konstantine's majestic Greek home loomed above her in the photograph, giving the impression of a watchful possessive presence that was not her husband. The picture was captioned slyly: "American First Lady—A Long Way From Home."

Jack realized that he had been staring at the photograph and that the others at breakfast in the banquet hall of March House were watching him to see his reaction. Jack smiled to himself then and tossed the newspaper down on the polished wooden surface of the formal banquet table and reached for the cup full of steaming American coffee that sat in front of him. The sideboard that lined one wall of the high-ceilinged banquet hall was laid out with a magnificent array of gleaming silver containers holding sausages, eggs, and oatmeal, and dozens of other deliciously fragrant Irish breakfast specialties, but for the moment Jack was making do with just the single cup of coffee and the front section of the London newspaper.

"I didn't know that the British went in for pictures like this," Jack said, tapping the newspaper's front page and keeping the smile fixed on his face as he looked up at his host. "It looks like an American movie magazine."

Jeffries's big, slightly evil-looking old man's face broke into a wide smile under his full gray-white beard. "I'm afraid, Jack, they can't make up their minds over here if you and Suzanne are heads of state or film stars," Jeffries said and then laughed, a deep melodic roll of laughter.

"In a few months we'll be neither one. I'll be back to being just another out-of-work politician looking for a job," Jack said and then glanced up as Frank O'Connor entered the great high-ceilinged dining hall. "Frank, good morning."

"What a perfectly glorious morning," O'Connor said. He was dressed in a shaggy Irish tweed suit and a bright green tie with little shamrocks painted on it. He crossed the room and stepped to the row of leaded-glass windows at the rear of the dining hall. He opened one of the windows wide and looked out at the long expanse of rolling green hills that rose up in front of Jeffries's Connemara estate. A rainstorm had greeted the President and his party on their way from Dublin to March House and it had ended only a few short hours before dawn, and the green hillside was still glistening with moisture. At the very crest of the hill, O'Connor could see a single rider mounted on a powerful charging chestnut-colored horse. O'Connor watched the horse and rider, marveling at their beauty and skill, as they seemed to fly across the hillside and then disappear into a thicket of trees in the distance. Just outside the window, rainwater was still dripping from the slanted roof of the old house down onto the thick leaded glass of the window. After a few seconds, O'Connor opened the window even wider, letting a few drops of the rainwater fall onto the sleeve of his tweed coat and darken it. He breathed in deeply, drinking in the cool, rain-freshened air. "Ireland," he sighed, a slight trembling in his voice as he spoke the beloved word.

O'Connor turned away from the window then and started down the row of steaming silver dishes on the banquet hall's long side table. It was several minutes before he moved back to the dining table, balancing two overflowing plates of food precariously in front of him. As he sat down, he noticed Jack smiling over at him.

"A poor politician has to eat when he can," O'Connor said, returning Jack's smile. Cassidy pushed the British newspaper out toward him then and O'Connor looked down at it, as he reached for the silver teapot that stood on the table and poured himself a brimming cupful of Irish tea. "Anything about the election in there?" O'Connor said, instead of responding to the big photograph of Suzanne that dominated the newspaper's front page. "There's something on the Italian elections I think," Jack said, baiting his friend.

O'Connor made a sound to show that he wasn't impressed. "I mean the real election."

"Poor Frank," Jack said to Jeffries. "He has two passionate loves in this world—Ireland and American politics—and to have one, I'm afraid, I'm depriving him of the other."

"It's a pleasure, Jack," O'Connor said, and then the older man looked back out the leaded-glass windows. "Do you think I'd trade this morning for some stuffy, smoke-filled room somewhere?"

Jack smiled again. "It would depend on who was running."

"You're probably right," O'Connor said and then started in on his food and the British newspaper simultaneously.

The President reached for his coffee cup again. "Is Allen coming down?"

"I passed his door," O'Connor answered between forkfuls of food. "And there was no sign of stirrin'." O'Connor paused for a moment, switching his attention back from his food to the newspaper again and beginning to flip through the London paper with a passion equal to his earlier attack on the silver dishes on the serving table. "Is there anything of interest in here?"

"Only an editorial that says the obvious," Jack said. Then, carrying his cup and saucer nestled in both hands in front of him, he walked to the windows at the far side of the room and looked out at the Irish countryside. The horse and rider that O'Connor had seen earlier had reappeared from the thicket of trees at the top of the hill and were making their way in a powerful controlled gallop down the gentle hillside toward March House. Jack watched as they came into view over the final slope of the green hillside and then the rider urged the big chestnut stallion up and over the stone fence at the front of the estate without breaking stride. Jack felt himself filled with admiration for the skill being displayed before him.

"And what is it that's so damn obvious to the British press?" O'Connor said, returning Cassidy's attention to the interior of the high-ceilinged banquet hall.

"Oh, just that . . ." But Jack paused then and watched the horse and rider slow their pace as they crossed directly in front of the manor house and turned toward the path that led to the stables. "Only that my little display of whatever-it-was-that-you-want-to-call-it at the convention didn't do either me or the Party any good," Cassidy said, but his voice sounded distracted and his eyes followed the beautiful riding figure as it first slowed the powerful horse to a steady trotting rhythm, then stepped slowly down the path toward the stables.

"I call it politics," O'Connor said, pushing the newspaper away. "Real politics, something the Brits don't know very damn much about, I'm afraid."

"They think that I may have cost Rance the election," Cassidy said, returning to his place at the head of the banquet table. "But then Frank's right, what do the British know about American politics, anyway?"

O'Connor looked up at his friend carefully. He knew Jack well enough to understand that, despite the smile, the sting of Suzanne's photograph on the newspaper's front page and the biting words of the editorial had hurt Jack deeply.

"You have to remember, Jack," Jeffries said from across the table, "Governor Granderman is a very appealing figure to most Europeans. He's an attractive and cultured man. In a lot of ways, he's far easier for them to identify with than your man from East Texas. If the election were held over here, Marshall Granderman would probably be the next President of the United States," Jeffries added confidently.

"Well, I'll tell you," O'Connor said, "he might just be anyway. Tim's got his work cut out for him over the next two months, and Gardner's damn lucky to have him on the ticket."

Jack stood then and restlessly paced back to the far side of the dining hall. He moved up against the open window, looking out past the path to the stables. Something about the grace and speed of the chestnut-colored horse and its skilled rider had touched him, but they had disappeared from view now. Cassidy turned back into the room, the disappointment visible on his face. O'Connor looked up at his eyes. He knew his friend. He was not the kind of man who backed away from a fight, yet here he was three thousand miles away from the fray. He was also a man who loved his family above all things, and he was separated from them now by circumstances and by his own pride. This must be a very hard time for him, O'Connor thought, and then he moved back from his breakfast plate and twisted his chair away from the long banquet table. He could look directly at his friend now and he wanted to say something to him to make the sadness he could see growing in Jack's face go away, but O'Connor could think of nothing that would really help, and a feeling of powerlessness spread through him. "Jack . . ." O'Connor began falteringly, without knowing what he was going to say, but then he stopped short as the door to the great hall opened and a figure appeared and stepped resolutely into the room. The figure was dressed in riding clothes of pure black. The riding jacket and pants were tailored to fit perfectly, and below the tight breeches the rider wore knee-length leather boots that had been polished to a high black gloss. It was unmistakably the rider that both men had seen earlier on the hillside above March House. Entering the room still wearing a traditional black riding cap, the rider reached up and removed it. Long light brown hair tumbled down then over the rider's shoulders.

"Gentlemen, let me introduce my daughter," Jeffries said proudly.

"I'm payin' for it. I should be the first one to try it out, right?" said the big man that they called The Rose. Then he laughed loudly as he pushed his body up against the young blond girl who was leaning across the bar. The girl was wearing an expensive cocktail dress, but it was lifted up in the back, exposing the bright red silk pants that she wore under it.

The Rose signaled then for the little Oriental girl kneeling below him to continue with her work. A small group had formed around them, talking and drinking, calling out crude jokes at the blond girl, who was leaning forward over the side of the bar, her skirt lifted up in the back and her red silk underpants gathered in the middle to expose a firm, round, fleshy working area for the Oriental girl kneeling below her to decorate with the metal tips of the long tattooing needle that she held in her hand. The Oriental girl was wearing only a pair of skin-tight orange stretch pants herself, and her small brown breasts were bare. There were several bills, hundreds and fifties, protruding from the waistband of her pants and several more bills were stuffed down the front of the cocktail dress of the young blond girl. The kneeling Oriental girl's needle dug into the other girl's flesh several more times then and the bright red petals of a flowering rose began to take shape on the surface of the clear white skin.

Behind the group that had gathered around the blond girl draped over the bar, couples danced in the semidarkness of the room below decks of *The Pleasure Queen*. A woman with long dark hair had lowered the top of her dress and had pressed her body up close to the front of the man she was dancing with, while another man was lost between two other half-naked women, dancing close to both of them, his hands up beneath the line of their dresses as he pushed them both close to his body. In the shadows, another couple was thrashing around on a couch in the far back corner of the room.

The man they called The Rose took a long drink from the glass of scotch that he was holding in one hand before he turned from the bar and looked out over the drunken sex-filled party in progress in the darkened room. "Ever been to a party like this one?" he asked the tall, auburn-haired woman standing next to him.

"I didn't expect it to be like this," Leigh Hodges managed, but as soon as she used that much of her energy to answer him, she began to feel sick. The room seemed to be moving back and forth before her eyes, and the floor beneath her began to dip and sway dramatically. She blinked her eyes several times, trying to bring the room back into focus, but it was no use. She could barely see what was going on around her anymore. She was hopelessly drunk, but it felt different than it usually did—much more powerful, she thought. The darkened room below deck of *The Pleasure Queen* was just a blurred pornographic dream to her now. It didn't make her feel aroused, only very drunk and now sick. She held out her empty glass to the man standing next to her, but The Rose only stared down blankly at it. "I tol' you I got some in my cabin," he said, pointing down the dark passageway that led to the very rear of the ship.

Leigh felt too sick to say anything, so instead she used her index finger, extending it above the glass and wiggling it back and forth to say no for her. She'd been saying no to men ever since the party had started, she thought, through the blur that had become the inside of her head.

"Hey, Garrett," the big man called out toward where the lawyer was standing near the bar watching the tattooing needles of the Oriental girl at work. "Your broad here wants another drink!"

Garrett started moving slowly through the semidarkness toward Leigh. The slow uncoordinated swaying movement of the lawyer's body made it clear that he had been drinking heavily, too. When she saw Garrett weaving unsteadily in her direction, Leigh held out her glass, bottom up, to show him that she was empty.

Garrett poured her a full glass of scotch from the bottle that he carried, but as he poured the drink his eyes were on the face of the big man standing next to her. "I don't think she's ever . . ." But it was clear that The Rose wasn't listening to him, so Garrett stopped talking and joined the big man in looking around at the drunken party in progress around them. "You know, she's just a secretary and all . . ." Garrett added apologetically to nobody in particular.

The big man only grunted a laugh then and lowered his eyes to look at Garrett's secretary more closely. Leigh was bent forward, her head bobbing on her drunken neck as she stared down at the amber-colored liquid in the glass that she held, but The Rose was looking only at the tops of her breasts, which appeared to be just about ready to pour out of the top of the tight gold sheath dress that she wore.

Leigh forced her head up then, looking first at the big man and then at Garrett. She looked like hell, Garrett thought. Her reddish-brown hair, which had been curled fashionably at the top of her head at the start of the party, was down around her face in a series of separate disjointed tendrils. Her full, overpainted, red-smeared mouth was hanging slightly open, and the rest of her face was showing all of its years.

"She's a sloppy drunk," The Rose said, and Garrett only smiled back, his face full of embarrassment. But Leigh heard what the big man had said, and in slow motion she moved her head around to look at his face. "There's something in my drink," she said, raising the glass up toward The Rose, as if to show it to him, but her hand and arm were too weak to complete the motion and after a half second of being suspended in the air between them, the glass plunged back down toward her side, spilling brown liquid across the front of her dress.

"Oh, shit," she mumbled, her head falling back down to inspect the damage. "Something bad in my drink," she added clumsily.

"Right baby," the big man said, laughing at her.

Just then a small cheer erupted behind Garrett and he turned back to look. The girl at the bar had her tattoo now and she was showing it to the small crowd that had gathered around her by bending over and waving her hips seductively back and forth, so that they all could see the bright red rose that was now permanently etched into her flesh.

"Who's next?" called out the little bare-chested Oriental girl who had done the work.

The Rose removed a hundred-dollar bill from a thick roll that he carried in his pants pocket and held it out in front of him, making the Oriental girl walk the few steps to him to get it. The girl stood silently in front of him for a moment with her small, tight, darkly nippled breasts almost touching his stomach, but The Rose did nothing. There was a tarantula etched in black-and-red ink crawling across the top of the girl's breasts and The Rose reached up and flicked the edge of the hundred-dollar-bill across the tarantula's belly. Then with his other hand he opened the front of the girl's pants and stuffed the bill down deep between her legs. The Oriental girl smiled confidently and then repeated her question. "Who's next?"

The Rose reached out with his big hand and pushed Leigh toward the bar. "It's on me!" the big man said.

Garrett took a small step forward as if to protest, but then he did nothing. "Why not?" the lawyer said, forcing a smile onto the little frightened features of his own face.

"Sure, why the fuck not?" Leigh mumbled and then looked at the blur of faces that were gathering around her now.

"Where are we going to put it?" the Oriental girl asked as she took Leigh by the arm and began moving her toward the bar.

"She's got great tits," someone said, and the Oriental girl bent back down and opened the black box that stood below the bar and began changing needles on the curved instrument that she had used only a few minutes before on the young blond girl.

"Yeah, I got great tits," Leigh slurred as she looked down at her front where her body was beginning to spill out of the shimmering gold cocktail dress that she'd gotten in the Quarter. "Exclusive party," she said angrily and looked up at Garrett's frightened face. She moved drunkenly toward him then, upsetting one of the bar stools and sending it tumbling to the ground. "You said this was going to be a big fucking deal," she said and then motioned with her drink out toward the people gathered around her in the lower salon of *The Pleasure Queen*. "Fucking gangsters," she slurred and then sipped at her drink. "This is shit," she said, pointing to the drink. "The bastard's put something in my drink," she slurred, but before Garrett could answer her, he felt a hand on his shoulder.

Garrett looked up into the eyes of The Rose. "It's time for you to leave," the big man said, bending forward and whispering the words in a voice that only Garrett could hear. The little lawyer felt a rush of fear fill his stomach and chest.

Garrett bent down and looked into Leigh's face. "I'm sorry," he managed sadly and their eyes locked for a moment, but only Garrett guessed what was going to happen to them now. Leigh could see the sorrow and the fear in his eyes, but she said nothing. Instead, she turned to the group of men that had gathered around her, making a sign with her thumb and finger to show how small she wanted the disfigurement of her body to be. "Littl' jus' a tiny littl'," she slurred, and at the moment that he heard her Garrett felt the hand tighten on his shoulder.

The lawyer nodded, accepting the inevitable, and he walked quietly with the big man out of the main salon. Behind him he could hear the Oriental girl's voice. "She's got a good ass, too," the girl said and Garrett turned to see someone lifting Leigh's skirt and showing the men crowded around her the tops of her white legs bulging out below the tight gold lamé underpants that matched her dress, but then The Rose's hand jabbed him in the back and Garrett staggered forward toward the stairs that led to the main deck of *The Pleasure Queen*.

Leigh wanted to protest, to pull away and find someplace to sleep, but she felt too weak to resist the hands that were pulling at her dress and too far lost in the hazy mist of alcohol to do anything. She might just as well finish it now and then sleep. Oh, Christ, I could sleep forever, she thought, or maybe she said it out loud. She couldn't be sure which any longer.

"What's it going to say?" the Oriental girl asked, holding Leigh's dress up with one hand and then slowly, teasingly beginning to pull down the matching gold-colored underwear with the other. Leigh did nothing in protest, only continuing to stand drunkenly, helplessly, in front of the small crowd of men and women around her. She began to lose her balance, but she reached out to steady herself on the edge of the bar. A man standing behind her gave her a fresh drink and she took it gratefully, trying to smile a thank you to him, but only making her face into a loosely twisted parody of what she had hoped that it would look like. "Is this going to hurt?" she asked nobody in particular and then took a big drink of the fresh scotch. It tasted as strangely bitter as the others had, and through the thickening mist that was covering her eyes she could see the man's face laughing in distorted slow motion in front of her. The taste in her mouth and the misty distorted laughing face made her feel even sicker than she had before. She sat down heavily on the bar stool then. The Oriental girl raised a metal device in her hand and a long silver needle lit by the light above the bar gleamed from the end of it.

"A dagger," a man's voice said, and through the blur Leigh could see the inside cover of the black box that held the rows of silver needles. Samples of the Oriental girl's work were displayed on small cutouts of tissue paper and Leigh could see a many-horned monster, an evil-looking red-and-black devil's face, and a sharp pointed dagger dripping big cartoon drops of blood. A man's finger was pointed at the dagger. God, they were going to put that on her body, forever, Leigh thought with terror.

The Oriental girl reached up and opened the top of Leigh's dress. Looking back up at the faces clustered around her, Leigh tried to smile, but it was hopeless. The faces closest to her now seemed to be all men's faces. Men, Leigh thought through the blur of faces that surrounded her. Men are like children. There's nothing I can't have from them, if I—nothing . . . But her thoughts became only a confused jumble then and she stopped thinking about anything in particular. Instead, she just slumped forward and let her breasts droop heavily down, sagging over the gold-lamé fabric of the expensive dress that she'd gotten just for the party. She barely felt the needle take its first bite into her flesh.

It was cooler on deck and very dark. Someone had turned off the bright string of colored bulbs that had lit the deck of the yacht when the party had first begun, but the city lights of New Orleans were visible in the far distance, a very faint yellowish glow reflecting in the dark water.

The deck appeared empty and silent. The only sounds now were the lapping of the Gulf waters against the side of the ship and the muffled sounds of the party going on below deck. The Rose directed Garrett to the gangplank that led down to one of the waiting motor boats that had been used at the beginning of the evening to bring the guests on board. There were two men standing in the prow of the small boat. They were just waiting there all alone in the darkness, Garrett thought, and the realization terrified him. It had all been set up from the very first, he realized then.

"I thought Mr. DeSavio was coming to the party," the little lawyer said, the terror showing in his voice. "I should say something to him."

"Nah," The Rose said, smiling at the little man in the white suit. "This was just a little party for some of Mr. DeSavio's employees. You know, keep-the-troops-happy kind of thing."

"Mr. Costello?" Garrett stammered then.

"Unh-unh," The Rose said, shaking his head. "They're both in Miami. Some kind of a hotel opening or somethin'. It's just us employees out here tonight." The big man had moved only a few feet from Garrett now, blocking the lawyer's route back to the deck of the ship. There was nowhere left for Garrett to go now but down the gangplank to the waiting motor launch and the two men waiting for him on its darkened deck.

"The girl?" Garrett said, but he knew the answer without having to ask.

"Don't worry, we'll take care of her too," The Rose said, laughing down cruelly at the lawyer's frightened face.

"Well, at least you got yourself a real crime to work on now—that should make you happy," Grissum said. He and Sullivan were just walking out of Yancey's office and Grissum was headed straight for the coffee table at the far side of the main bay of the FBI's Dallas office with Sullivan following only a few steps behind. "I've got more than that," Sullivan said eagerly. And then he paused for a moment, thinking about it. "I guess," he added uncertainly, but then he didn't finish, and his young, unlined face began to show the confusion that he felt about what it was that he really did have.

As Grissum approached the coffee table, he puffed hungrily at the last of the tiny slip of a cigarette that he held in the corner of his mouth, letting ashes cascade onto the front of his suit coat and then tumble down onto the worn gray carpet beneath him. Grissum removed a crumpled pack of Camels from his shirt pocket then and lit a fresh cigarette with the glowing tip of his old cigarette butt.

Grissum poured steaming coffee into Styrofoam cups and handed one across to Sullivan. The two men walked together then to their desks at the far side of the long room and sat down.

"So, you get everything you wanted in there?" Grissum said, pointing with his Styrofoam cup toward Yancey's glassed-in cubical at the back of the room.

"No," Sullivan said.

"Good. I'd be worried if you were too happy," Grissum said, settling into place with his feet up on his desktop and his head wreathed in cigarette smoke. But Sullivan wasn't listening. There was an envelope on his desk and he opened it quickly. Inside was a copy of a teletype from the Mexican police.

"Yancey said you can investigate the murder of that spic out at the fairgrounds. I thought that would make you happy," Grissum said and then drank first from his coffee and then puffed deeply on his fresh cigarette.

"It checked out," Sullivan said, reading the telex once through quickly.

"What checked out?"

Grissum bent forward just enough to reach his own mail and begin flipping through it with a single lazy hand.

"The guy who got killed two nights ago. He's from Tampico, all right. A local pimp named Rene Ortiz," Sullivan said, reading from the Mexican police report.

"A dead Mexican pimp," Grissum mumbled. "This could be a big case," he added, without removing the burning cigarette from his mouth. "I don't understand why Yancey didn't give you the priority on this thing that you asked for."

Sullivan set the telex down on his desktop then and turned to Grissum. "Yancey seemed more worried about me talking to the newspapers than he was about catching the guy who shot Ortiz."

"Now you're catching on," Grissum said, giving up on his own mail and slumping back into his chair.

"The girl, the whore, I guess," Sullivan corrected himself, "the whore who got herself killed in Tampico probably worked for this guy Ortiz. The way I have it figured, they heard that I was in Monterey looking for a suspect in the Cassidy shooting and somehow they knew about this guy who had Strode's diary. So they put two and two together and copied a few pages of the diary and tried to sell it to me, but the guy found out and he killed the girl before I could get to her."

"And then what?" Grissum said. "Your phantom second gunman follows this pimp back here to Dallas and kills him too?"

"Maybe," Sullivan said.

"Why?"

"Because he was afraid that this guy, Ortiz, would come to me or somebody else in the Bureau and tell us what he knew!" Sullivan said.

"Which probably wasn't much," Grissum said.

"Maybe," Sullivan shot back. "But we don't really know what Ortiz knew."

"And now you never will," Grissum said with finality. "You're right back where you started from, looking for some phantom gunman with no real leads worth a damn to point you in the right direction."

"I guess you're right," Sullivan said sadly after he'd thought about it for a few seconds.

"But let me guess," Grissum said. "You're just going to keep tryin' anyway, aren't you?"

"Yeah, I guess so," Sullivan said and then smiled brightly at Grissum. "With you on my side, how can I lose?"

"Easy," Grissum said and then sipped at his coffee and puffed on his little unfiltered cigarette in rapid succession.

"I've got another theory though, of what could have really been going on out there last Tuesday night. Do you want to hear it?" Sullivan said, pointing out of the office-building window in the direction of the amusement park at the outskirts of Dallas, where a man had been murdered only two short nights before.

"You know, Sullivan, I like your first theory. It was simple, a dead end, but simple—but now you've got another angle," Grissum said. "And I'm lookin' at you and what I see scares me. I've seen the look you've got in other guys' eyes before, not that any of those guys are still around to have theories and angles anymore, but I know it's no use telling you that, because you're just going to run me through your new theory, anyway, aren't you?"

Sullivan barely listened to Grissum's speech. "Uh-uh," the younger agent said. "Here's my other theory. If there really was a conspiracy to murder Cassidy and it failed, whoever it was that was in charge of that conspiracy is scared now. And the best way to cover himself is to end it completely, kill everybody connected to it, witnesses, the other conspirators, everybody, so that the trail can never lead back to him. Look at this." Sullivan picked a file off his desk. "A lawyer named Garrett and his secretary that I interviewed in New Orleans. They're both missing. I'm sure they were connected to it somehow, and now they're probably dead too."

"What are you telling me?" Grissum said. "If your theory about the assassination attempt is right, they'd have to kill a dozen people."

"More," Sullivan said quickly. "Maybe thirty, forty people. Maybe even more than that. I don't know."

Grissum was silent for a moment then. His face, beneath the thick wreath of cigarette smoke, looked puzzled. "I don't get it," he said finally. "How does that tie to what happened to your Mexican pimp?"

"That car out there two nights ago," Sullivan said, pointing back toward the ouskirts of Dallas again. "I think it could have been following me when I went to meet Ortiz. What I'm getting at is, maybe, whoever it was that was in that car wasn't as interested in getting Ortiz, as he was in getting me. I think I could have been the real target out there, not Ortiz. Maybe I'm the one that they really wanted."

Mallory heard the telephone ring and began groping around for his glasses. As he did, he upset the little glass of water that he always left on his nightstand during the night. The phone rang more insistently, louder and angrier this time. Mallory knew who was on the other end of the line now. It was the Vice President. The young aide gave up searching for his glasses and after a few fumbling failed tries at it, he managed to get the telephone off its hook and move it up close to his ear.

"Yes," he said, but there was no answer. Oh, God, he thought, he knew what that meant too. He stood then and managed to cross the unfamiliar room in the dark, bumping into hotel furniture as he moved to the door and unlocked it just in time for Gardner to push it open and stride past him into the room. "Dark in here," Gardner said, and he reached up and turned on the overhead light, flooding the room in harsh electric brightness, nearly blinding Mallory.

The Vice President was barefoot, dressed only in a pair of bright yellow silk pajamas. He was carrying a rolled-up sheaf of computer paper in one big hand and he crossed to the bed that Mallory had just vacated and let the long green-and-white roll of paper accordion out across almost the entire width of the hotel's double bed.

"We're goin' lose this election unless we do something damn soon!" Gardner thundered. As he listened, Mallory walked over to the nightstand and groped around on it for a few seconds, looking frantically again for his glasses. Finally, he came across one of the slender metal stems of their wire frames. The lens were wet from the spilled water and he had to hastily clean them on the tail of his pajama tops before he put them on. Mallory's eyes still hadn't fully adjusted to the light, but he felt better now that Gardner's face and body were no longer just a big blurred yellow shape. The aide glanced at his wristwatch. It was 2:30 in the morning, Pacific time. His day had started in Chicago at a breakfast meeting for union officials at 5:30 A.M., central time. His wake-up call had been at 4:45, or was that yesterday morning? Mallory wasn't sure any longer.

"Look at this!" Gardner said, pointing at one number in a sea of numbers organized in a seemingly endless series of neat rows on the surface of the printout. Mallory tried to look, but before he could focus on it, Gardner's big hand moved to another number and then another. "And this!" Gardner said. "And this one is goddamned unbelievable!" He thumped the back of his hand against the long sheet of computer paper to make his point.

"I'm going to lose this election unless something happens and happens fast," Gardner said, pushing the printout deeper into the layers of rumpled sheets and blankets on his aide's bed.

He reached then for Mallory's copy of the thick bound report that had accompanied the printout. It was a summary of the findings of thousands of interviews with voters all over the country. " 'The overriding issue of this election in the minds of the American people is leadership,' " Gardner began to read out loud from the report's summary page, but then he stopped and looked away from the thick book and up at Mallory instead. "Leadership?" Gardner said. "Can you believe it?" he added angrily. "I'm running behind Marshall Granderman on the issue of 'leadership,' of all damn things. Who the hell do they think has been running this country for the last ten months?" he said. "It sure as hell hasn't been Jack Cassidy—and the only damn thing that Marshall Granderman ever led was the line to his granddaddy's money."

Gardner handed the big bound report to Mallory. "Leadership isn't what this campaign is really suffering from," Gardner said then. "What the Democratic Party is really hurtin' from is a great big case of Cassidy disease and an epidemic of it broke out right there at the convention on national television for all the world to see. They think Cassidy's pulling my strings like I'm a damn puppet—look for yourself." Gardner gestured angrily at the report in Mallory's hands to punctuate his words.

Gardner reached out then to remove the stream of computer paper from Mallory's bed.

"I'll tell you this, Bill," Gardner said, sweeping the long curl of the printout off the bed and onto the floor. "If I'm going to lose the election, it's not going to be because of what I didn't do, it's goin' to be on account of what I do." As he spoke, Gardner began rearranging Mallory's pillows, making a comfortable place for himself on the top of his aide's bed. "I can't be just Cassidy's boy anymore. The son of a bitch is four thousand miles away and the voters still can't forget about him," Gardner added, as he settled into place, his back propped up against the headboard of the bed. The Vice President leaned back and folded his hands behind his neck, the heels of his size-eleven bedroom slippers resting in the middle of Mallory's bedcovers, toes pointed at the ceiling. He looked ready to stay the night. Mallory glanced at the clock on the nightstand next to the Vice President, making certain that he had the time right. He did: 2:43 A.M. "You want some coffee sent up, or something?" the young aide asked.

"I've only got five and a half more weeks. Five and a half more weeks to turn a sick campaign into a healthy one. All I have to do is figure out what the remedy is for Cassidy disease. From here on in, this has got to be my campaign, and what I've got to have, to make that happen, Bill, is an issue," Gardner said, pointing at Mallory, who was standing in the middle of the room now, looking down at the nice warm bed that he'd vacated only a few moments before. "An issue that'll let everybody know, everybody in this whole damn country finally understand, who the boss is now," Gardner said, his own eyes still fixed on the ceiling.

Mallory nodded his agreement, but the rest of his body was busy finding a chair and sinking down wearily into it. "Yes, sir, we'll come up with one, sir," he said.

"You're goddamned right we will, and when we've got it, we're goin' squeeze it." Gardner held his big hands out in front of him then and twisted them together as if he was wringing the neck of some great invisible beast, squeezing it into submission with just his own powerful hands. "We're goin' squeeze it until we turn it into more votes than all the money that Marshall Granderman, and Jack Cassidy, and their daddies, and granddaddies all put together could buy for themselves, even in their wildest dreams!"

"Vietnam is the rat hole that America's going to sink in!" Jack was trapped in a corner of the main salon of March House by a young man from Galway. The young man was a poet and he had refused to wear anything but a shaggy,

Irish, woolen sweater, even to a formal reception given for the President of the United States. The poet and his sweater had been caught in the morning's first rain and smelled now faintly like a wet sheep, Jack thought, as the young man, his face bright red from anger and too much wine, kept him pinned tightly in a corner.

As he listened, Jack's eye traveled past the shaggy figure of the young poet. Through the windows behind him, Jack could see the long parade of Rolls-Royces and other expensive cars in the circular front drive of March House, where horse-drawn carriages had stood less than a half century before. The chauffeur-driven limousines were waiting for March House's reception guests to depart, which, given the circumstances, Jack thought, I hope is pretty damn soon. Jeffries had invited his neighbors and a politician or two all the way from Dublin, and several of the writers and artists who lived nearby to a reception in honor of the President. Until a few minutes earlier and the approach of the young poet who had him trapped now, it had all seemed a very long way from the problems of Washington, Jack added to himself wistfully, but the poet continued to press his attack, poking a rough finger toward the President's chest to make his point. The Secret Service man standing closest to the President began to push forward toward him, but before he could take another step, Diane Jeffries moved in front of the young man and lightly touched his arm. She bent toward him then and whispered a phrase in Gaelic in the poet's ear and as she did, she skillfully turned him toward the door where her father was waiting. The poet found himself almost lifted through the door by Jeffries's powerful handshake, and in one motion he was led out the front door of March House and to his waiting car.

Diane turned back to the President with a smile. Jack returned it, his face showing the admiration that he felt for the graceful way that this young woman had handled the potentially difficult situation. "Thank you," Jack said.

"It wouldn't do for the best poet in Connemara to be arrested for assaulting the President," she smiled back, politely acknowledging the President's gratitude. "But," she said, the smile disappearing from her face, "what he was saying was absolutely right. I just didn't like the way that he was saying it to you, that's all. He was doing more harm than good for a just cause," she added and then stepped away from Cassidy.

The President watched her go. She was tall and athletically built, and she moved across the high-domed main salon of March House toward the doors to the garden with enormous confidence and grace.

Outside on the lawn a small ensemble was playing Irish folk music and the President continued to watch as the tall young woman crossed the garden to stand by the musicians.

Left alone for a moment, Jack started across the salon toward the garden. He moved outside then and joined the group that had gathered, listening to the mournful music being played by the little band of folk musicians. Diane

Jeffries's slender figure was only a few feet away, and as the musicians finished she looked over at his face and smiled.

"I think the only thing even remotely like it is American bluegrass," Cassidy said as he applauded the music. "And, yes, I do think our young friend from Galway was at least partly right about Indochina," he added, returning her smile.

She said nothing for a moment, choosing instead to turn her head so that her eyes looked directly into his. "Yes, American bluegrass or country music," she said finally.

"Would you like to walk?" Jack asked, indicating the winding stone path that led off from the garden toward the farther reaches of the Jeffries country home. Jack could feel the eyes of the reception guests on him and on the tall young woman at his side as they turned from the garden and started down the path that led away from the main house. He looked down then at Diane's face, and her expression told him that she could feel the attention focusing on them as well, but they both chose not to mention it. Instead, Jack asked, "Do you spend most of your time here, or in America?"

"New York mostly," she said. "I'm studying to be an actress." They were at the edge of the garden now. Just ahead of them, the path began curving down, out of the view of March House. Soon they would be alone, out of sight of her father's estate and its afternoon guests.

"I enjoyed watching you ride yesterday morning," Jack said.

"I ride every morning. Would you like to join me sometime?" she asked as she reached the top of the path.

"Perhaps," Jack answered casually.

They walked on in silence then for a moment, until they had both disappeared behind the bend in the winding stone path.

"You know, we met once before," he said, and she turned back to him as he spoke. "You were only about . . ."

"Thirteen," she said, finishing his thought.

Cassidy laughed. "You remember?"

"Of course," she said. "I remember it exactly. It was in California. You were a first-term Senator and I was a little girl home on a holiday from a fancy Swiss boarding school. I thought that you were the most handsome man that I'd ever seen, but I was just a little girl."

"And now?"

"And now," she said, returning his confident look with one of her own, "you're the President of the United States, and I'm a grown woman."

The two riders flew into the wooded thicket, the powerful flanks of their horses cutting through the dense underbrush. Diane's horse reached the edge of the woods first. Directly ahead of her was almost a mile of sloping lush countryside, before the soft green turf reached the sunlit ribbon of water that cut the heart of the valley. Before she urged her horse down into the gentle river valley, she paused at the crest of the hill and breathed in deeply on the moist air. She was dressed in her formal riding clothes, a closely-tailored brown tweed jacket and black vest over a rich white silk blouse, knee-length boots polished to a high luster, and skin-tight cream-colored riding breeches that showed off the full curves of her legs and hips. She could hear Jack's horse behind her now as it emerged from the dense patch of trees at the very top of the hill. She glanced behind her just long enough to catch Jack's eye and to smile playfully at him. He was moving his horse slowly and with less experience than she had, as horse and rider pushed their way through the last few feet of foliage and into the start of the open country at the top of the hill. Jack smiled back at her and as he did, she turned away from him and in a flash she was gone, urging her own mount down the emerald-green hillside toward the narrow, sparkling band of water at the base of the hill.

As she raced along, the morning wind chilled her face and blew her long brown hair back in a light fan shape behind her. She held a small whip in her right hand, but she used it sparingly, letting the powerful chestnut horse speed along with just the force of the free, open downhill run, his powerful sweating flanks finding their own natural running rhythm beneath her. It was early morning and as she flew down the hillside seated high on the powerfully charging horse, Diane could smell the day's first fresh breeze coming up from the river below and the faint smell of the heather drifting in from the forest at the far side of the narrow valley. It had rained the night before and there was still a faint drizzle in the air, but its blowing dampness felt cool against her skin. At first, she could hear the rhythmic sounds of Jack's horse moving closely behind her, but then the noise dropped away and there was only the sound of the rushing wind whistling in her ears and she could see in a blur of brown and silver the rock-filled stream at the base of the valley coming closer. It was almost upon her now and, as she approached the low ground, she realized that she no longer had full control over the powerful animal that she rode. She was frightened, but it felt wonderful, too, and she let herself be swept along with the powerful force, whose back she clung to with all her strength, until she felt that she was melting into the rhythmic movements of its body, with the wind rushing faster and faster around her, and the animal's hooves pounding louder and louder on the earth. Then, suddenly, she felt the wild soaring lift into free space, as the big beast rose up and above the rock-filled stream at the very heart of the valley, and she was in the air weightless for a measureless moment of suspended time, before her mount's hooves blasted back onto the ground, kicking up splashes of silver water into the air around her and jolting the center of her body down firmly into the leather saddle. Then she was lifted back up into the air again, free of the saddle, her head and shoulders extended straight upward toward the sky. On the next downward movement of her body, she forced her knees to tighten around the bulging flanks of the beautiful animal and let it begin to climb toward the dark woods at the far side of the valley. They were still moving fast, but Diane could feel herself regaining control of her mount, as it slowed against the upward pull of the hillside, and the valley began to rise in front of it at a steep angle. She used her knees to urge the horse forward and soon they were crashing into the branches of the trees at the top of the hill, and she had to duck her body low, lining her own head and shoulders up with the sloping head and neck of her mount, the tops of her shoulders brushing against the tree limbs and the horse beneath her slowing to avoid the great gnarled trunks of the old trees growing in its path. As she clutched tightly to the horse's neck, she could smell the frothy loamy smell of animal sweat mixing with the other forest smells. Suddenly her horse jolted to a stop and Diane found herself thrown forward, losing her grasp on the reins, and her body began lifting forward into the air. Her feet came free of the stirrups easily and she brushed forward along the chestnut's heavily muscled, sweat-drenched neck and then she felt herself sliding down onto the thick padding of drying leaves that cushioned the forest floor. She had made her body spin in a deft spiral and she hit the ground first with her shoulder and then bounced quickly onto her side and her eyes flooded with sunlight. Through an opening above her in the overhanging trees, she could see blue sky and a hint of a rainbow formed by the sunlight through the misting morning air. The wind was knocked from her chest and stomach and the sunlight was momentarily overpowering, as her lungs labored to refill her body with air, but she knew that she would be all right. She'd survived much worse falls many times, and, as she lay on the soft ground, she could hear her horse crashing on through the thicket and then stopping and circling back in its confusion, and soon she could hear the sounds of the other horse and its rider approaching behind her.

She could see Jack sliding down off his mount then and standing above her for a moment. Diane laughed softly to let him know that she wasn't hurt. Then she lifted herself up, resting her weight on her elbows to see his face more clearly and to confirm to herself that he was really there and that this moment was truly happening. His handsome face filled almost her entire field of vision now, but still it was almost impossible for her to know with certainty whether the moment was reality or a dream.

Jack's face was relaxed but serious as he bent down toward her. And as he came closer, his body momentarily blocked her view of the overhanging trees and even of the beautiful rainbow-tinted sky above her. Diane relaxed her own body then, letting her knees in the tight black riding breeches fall softly open to him, so that his hips fit perfectly into the gentle opening and then she arched back onto the tender bed of drying leaves that lay on the forest floor and let him press his body down firmly on top of hers. She lay beneath him then, her long hair spread back across the floor of the forest behind her in a multishaded display of spreading light- and darker-colored tentacles that seemed to reach from the top of her head into the deep rich mystery of the forest itself.

Jack kissed her tenderly on the lips, and instead of closing her eyes, she looked up past his handsome face and studied for a brief moment the vague luminescent edges of the rainbow that glowed in the sky above him. She could feel the misting rain on her face, but she wasn't at all cold. The man she had loved from a distance since she was a very young girl was holding her very tightly and then he was kissing her again. Together they removed her high, lustrous black-leather riding boots, slipping them down from her legs and calves and quickly she undid her belt buckle. Tucking her thumbs beneath the rear of her skin-tight riding breeches she slid the pants and the small slip of silk underwear that she'd worn that morning down beneath her knees before she lay back down on her side on the soft, moss-covered ground. She could smell the rich, loamy Irish earth close to her face now, as slowly, seductively, she lifted her knees toward her stomach and curled her body up in the back, offering herself to the man lying next to her. In the distance, she could hear her riderless horse crashing around noisily, lost deep in the thicket of the dense Irish forest that surrounded her.

CHAPTER
22

"Sir, I think we're being fired on!" Private First Class Donald R. Logan of Bakersfield, California, was a long way from home. The face of the officer that he reported the ambush to was that of his father. He knew now that he was caught in the middle of the same recurring dream that had haunted him since basic training. PFC Logan knew, too, that the dream was ending, as it always did at just this point, but he wanted desperately to finish it and to find out once and for all what happened next, but already he could feel the rough hands on his shoulders and the O.D.'s voice calling out to him, waking him from his sleep and robbing him of his dream. "All right soldier, let's go," the lieutenant's voice was calling him back to reality and his dream was lost again. "It's 0400, soldier," the O.D. continued rousing him. His voice was better than some, Logan thought sleepily, but it was insistent and the young soldier knew that there was no use resisting it. "Yes, sir," Logan mumbled and rolled over. The lieutenant waited for more. He'd awakened too many young PFCs for guard duty to believe anything they said until they were on their feet and moving around the barracks under their own steam. Logan was still clutching his blanket and trying to pull it up to cover his shoulders from the chilly morning air. That was a bad sign. "On your feet," the lieutenant said sharply, and finally the young soldier lying beneath him began to respond. Slowly at first, but then sensing the futility of it, the young PFC from California got to his feet and stood for a moment before the officer of the day. He didn't salute. It wasn't expected here in the darkness of the barracks before dawn with the other soldiers in the company still asleep, but Logan stood up straight at semi-attention, the front of his G.I. shorts open, his bare feet on the cold wooden floor.

"Five minutes, Logan," the O.D. said and then left, returning to the warmth of the squad room.

Logan turned slowly to his locker. He opened it and leaned against the metal door for several seconds, letting the cobwebs inside his head clear away. When he was ready, he let go of his support and reached into the locker. He looked briefly at the picture of the girl that he kept on the top shelf. He did that every morning. It was a small color picture, one of those high-school pocket pictures taken originally for the yearbook, but it was Logan's strongest link to home and he looked at it once in the morning and then again at night before he went to sleep—sort of like a religion, he thought, and then he smiled as he slid the picture back onto its place on the metal shelf.

He dressed slowly then. This was only his second month in Saigon, but he knew the Army well enough already to know that the O.D. was full of shit about "five minutes." What the fuck were they going to do to him if he was a few minutes late onto the perimeter, anyway, send him to Vietnam? Too late, he was already here, Logan smiled grimly as he thought about that and then he knelt and made his bunk, tucking in the sheets and rough green blanket and folding the extra olive-drab blanket at the foot—all regulation. He put his boots on last, being careful not to ruin the high black shine that he had given them the night before. Guard duty was the only time anyone gave you shit for not polishing your shoes anymore, Logan thought as he stood and then gave the toes of his boots a final extra buff by lifting each in turn and polishing their toes against the back of his fatigue pants. He reached up then and ran his hand across his chin. He'd shaved the night before so that he would have an extra few minutes to himself in the morning. He reached for his fatigue shirt and put it on, tucking its long ends into his pants as he turned back to his locker and removed his web belt and steel pot.

It was really no different than being in the States, he thought as he closed his locker and started down the long line of bunk beds to the squad room. The lieutenant saw him coming and started down the bay toward him. He had his keys with him. While Logan waited, the O.D. knelt and unlocked the big metal trunk that held the ammunition. He handed a full clip up to Logan and the PFC took it and went through the motions of checking it while the lieutenant relocked the metal trunk that contained the rest of the ammo.

"Okay?" the O.D. asked and Logan managed his second "Yes, sir" of the day. You think they'd trust us with unlocked ammunition boxes, the young PFC thought, looking down the row of bunks at the restless sleeping bodies of the rest of his company. They're more worried about us shooting each other than they are about the enemy getting us, he added to himself as he watched the lieutenant unlock the rifle rack. Logan stepped forward then and removed his M-1 from the rack. "Thank you, sir," he said as he loosened the sling and moved the rifle up to his shoulders. An infantryman's best friend, his drill sergeant had told him over and over, but that was a lie, an infantryman's best friend was his bed, Logan thought as he looked sleepily back down the main aisle of the barracks at his empty lower bunk.

Logan moved outside then and waited at a relaxed parade rest for the others to join him. As he waited, he looked up at the sky and around at the compound the South Vietnamese government had given the United States Army to house its advisers. Advisers? Logan always smiled when he thought of himself as an adviser. What was that, like a counselor? He'd hated his counselor in high school. The guy had a crewcut like something out of the fifties and he was the boys' vice principal. What a raving asshole that guy was, Logan thought as he waited. Counselor, adviser, probably the same kind of crap. But then he went back to just counting the days left on his tour that was his normal way of making time pass. The squad was formed now and the lieutenant turned it over to Corporal Cerrone. Good, thanks, Lieutenant, Logan thought as he watched the O.D.'s uniformed back returning into the warmth of the barracks. It's your fucking job, but just turn it over to Cerrone. The guy's a fucking psycho, but just give us over to him and go get another cup of coffee, you bastard—but Cerrone was issuing orders now and Logan followed them without even having to think. He executed a left face and marched into the predawn darkness.

His post was on the perimeter, just inside the wire gate that separated the American installation from one of the long, low, marshy fields at the outskirts of Saigon. He'd been alone for about ten minutes when he first realized there was someone out there in the darkness with him. It was probably a local kid, Logan thought. Guys were always coming off guard duty saying they saw or heard something out there, particularly in this section that faced the city. Shit, there were people living out there less than a hundred yards away, families, dogs, kids, you had to expect some activity, but there it was again and he quieted his own thoughts to listen to a second sound at the edge of his sector. Then a third. The sounds were closer now. Logan had a light. Each guard was issued a handheld flashlight, but he'd never used his before. He reached for it now and detached it from his web belt. As he did, he heard a series of running noises, like men hustling across the dark mud clearing in front of him. "Halt, who goes there?" he called out reflexively. The words sounded wrong to him as soon as he'd said them. Where had he gotten them? Were they from an old World War II movie? He'd never been trained on this part of it, not exactly. He started to call out again, this time using the password he'd been given by Cerrone, but he didn't. He didn't want the guard in the next sector to hear him. He had to live with these guys and he didn't need them thinking that he . . . What was that? There was a sudden flurry of soft sounds in the high grass that bordered the road just outside the fence. Then silence. Then movement again, as if something or somebody had raised themselves up and begun making a motion of some kind. Fuck this, Logan thought. Fuck what anybody thinks. He lowered his M-1 from his shoulder and undid the safety catch. He'd fire a warning shot, he decided, but there was a movement nearby now, just outside the wire fence. Something spinning in the grass, like a dancing many-headed snake spinning wickedly in the dry grass. A grenade! No, it was too big. A Russian version of the Claymore . . . The sky above the U.S. Army Adviser compound was suddenly bright yellow like day had just cracked through and exploded the night away forever. Then there was the noise of running men in the soft dry grass everywhere on the perimeter. Logan saw no faces, fired no warning shot. Instead, he felt his body lifted powerfully off the ground, one leg kicking up high over his head, and in the same moment, his neck jerking violently backward after it. He did have one final overwhelming feeling though. He could feel inside himself now just what an enormously private thing dying was, but there was no time for him to turn the feeling into a final thought.

Tim Cassidy was speaking in Detroit, or Cleveland, or maybe it was an auditorium in East Lansing or Columbus, when he got the news. The October crowds in the Midwest were all starting to look pretty much the same to him. He had just finished making his set speech in a college auditorium that was too hot and not completely full and at the edges of the crowd were the hecklers and the signs that said GRANDERMAN on them. Two young men held up a poster that showed a little cartoon puppet figure with Gardner's face, dancing on a string held by an evil-looking giant. The evil-looking giant had the face of Jack Cassidy. Tim was standing at the side of the podium waving and smiling at the crowd's applause as the high-school band played a loud rendition of "On Wisconsin." I must be in Milwaukee, Cassidy thought, when Dave Jennings leaned over and whispered in his ear, "Gardner wants you back in Washington."

Cassidy whispered back without taking his eyes from the crowd or changing his expression, "Now?"

"The message says pronto," Jennings whispered to him.

"Then pronto it is," Cassidy said and gave one last smiling wave at the crowd and then headed for the exit.

There was a limousine waiting for him just outside and Cassidy ducked his lean body down athletically into its back seat. Jennings was already waiting for him inside.

"We've canceled the rest of your schedule for today and for tomorrow morning," Jennings said, and Tim saw the images he'd had of another series of speeches in rented halls in Cincinnati or Dayton or St. Paul melt away before his eyes.

"What's up?" Cassidy asked as the limousine began to pull slowly through the crowd of students that lined the road.

"I don't know. I talked to Mallory. All he said was to get you back to Washington as soon as possible. Gardner's called a secret meeting of the Security Council. It's in session now."

"How did Mallory sound?" Cassidy said.

"Harassed."

"Uh-uh, so what else is new?" Cassidy said, smiling and waving out the window at the crowd that stood along the narrow side street that led away from the auditorium.

"Don't look so happy," Jennings said. "We've told the press that you've caught a severe cold. So, for God's sake, when we go by the photographers up here, look miserable, would you?" Jennings pointed at the gate that led to the main road, where the reporters and photographers were gathering for a last look at the candidate.

"Why all the mystery?" Cassidy said.

Jennings shrugged his shoulders. "You want my personal guess?"

"As long as you're right," Cassidy said smiling, but being careful now not to let the crowd that pressed in close to the window of the limousine see the relaxed expression on his face.

"I think Gardner's got something and he's going to play it for all it's worth. He's been looking for an issue to run with for the last month—somebody, somewhere probably just gave it to him."

"Yale graduates are much more cynical than they were ten years ago," Cassidy said, looking at Jennings's sharp young face.

The aide shrugged his shoulders again, meaning he couldn't help that. "I notice you didn't tell me that I was wrong though," he said.

"I didn't say that you were right either," Cassidy said briskly, and then he turned his attention back toward the crowd at the windows.

"Look at these faces," Tim said. "It's not like four years ago, is it?"

"I wouldn't know. I was still at New Haven, remember?"

"How could I forget, you're always reminding everyone," Cassidy said. And then he smiled again, but his eyes were still on the crowd. "There's a different feeling now, there's no real excitement. They don't jump," he added then, trying to smile once more, but his voice sounded strangely sad and puzzled by what he saw. "Four years ago, all Jack would have to do is come near them and . . ." Cassidy didn't finish, just letting his voice trail off in disappointment.

"It's not you," Jennings said. "Everything's different now."

Tim smiled and shook his head in disagreement. "I'm not Jack," he said slowly, thoughtfully. "I never will be." He looked out at the crowd again. "There are candidates that the voters jump up and down for and then there are all the rest of us," Tim said, smiling back at his aide, but then he corrected himself quickly. "I'm sorry, Dave, maybe I'm wrong. Maybe when it's your turn, they'll jump for you, too. I don't know. All I know is that, for me, they don't jump. I'm still just the younger brother."

"Oh, Jesus, there's some photographers up here," Jennings said, pointing to the corner of the auditorium where a small pack of reporters waited for the limousine to pass. "Stop smiling and look sick, for God's sake."

"How's this," Cassidy said, rubbing his nose absently with the back of his hand.

"Terrible," Jennings said. "Don't you have a handkerchief or something?"

"Cassidys aren't supposed to get sick," he said.

"Well, they are today. Here," Jennings said and reluctantly reached into his breast pocket and removed his carefully folded white display handkerchief and handed it to the candidate. The young aide reached forward and pushed the button that lowered the glass window that divided the limousine's back compartment from its driver. "Slow it down in front of these cameras," Jennings ordered.

Cassidy looked solemn and then pretended to blow his nose into his aide's clean white handkerchief. The move was perfectly timed for the cameras gathered at the school's front gates and dozens of shutters clicked and film whirred, as the photographers got their pictures. The image of the vice-presidential candidate fighting his cold was guaranteed to be prominently displayed on the evening news and in the morning newspapers.

"How was that?" Cassidy said, looking over the no longer fresh handkerchief at Jennings.

"You should take better care of yourself," the aide said as the limousine began to speed up again and passed through the college gates toward the airport and the waiting campaign plane that was already warmed up and ready to return Cassidy and his staff to the nation's capital.

Tim smiled as he removed the handkerchief from his face and held it up in front of him. "What do I do with this now?" he said, giving the handkerchief another light pass across his nose.

Jennings looked at it with displeasure. "Keep it, it's a gift."

"It's monogrammed," Cassidy said, smiling broadly now that he was safely out of camera range and holding up the handkerchief so that the big block DAJ could be seen on the edge of the once clean square of white linen.

"No, that's okay, you keep it, you'll need it. Vice presidents are always having to come down with unexpected illnesses."

President Cassidy set the telephone down and broke the transatlantic connection to the White House.

Above Cassidy stood O'Connor and seated directly across from the President was Rozier, but both men felt powerless to help the President now. They could see the deep sadness in their boss's face and sense the feelings of finality and resignation in the movements of his body as he hung up the phone and ended the call.

"A compound of American military advisers was attacked by superior Viet Cong forces at dawn Saigon time," Cassidy said sadly, his eyes refusing to look at the faces of his assistants as he spoke. "Thirty-one American military personnel were killed and eight American civilians. One was a woman. There are numerous other injuries. The Viet Cong losses were minimal." Cassidy reviewed the facts that he had just received for his staff. He knew that they had overheard his conversation and were probably aware of most of what he had to tell them, but Cassidy needed to say the words anyway. "The Vice President has the Security Council in emergency session. Their recommendation is to execute retaliatory air strikes against three North Vietnamese targets." Cassidy paused for several seconds before he added in a deeply troubled voice, "I approved their recommendation. Four American destroyers that have been stationed outside North Vietnamese territorial waters will be directed to move within three miles of the coastline, or closer if necessary, in direct support of South Vietnamese commando raids, which will be timed to coincide with the air strikes. If fired on, the destroyers will be under order to fire back," Cassidy said.

"Gardner's got his war," Rozier said quietly.

"No," Cassidy said firmly. "This is intended as a single set of retaliatory actions. We are not implementing an overall change in policy. This was my direct order," Cassidy said. "The Vice President is going on television within the hour to communicate to the American people that this is a single limited response and not a change of our overall policy in Southeast Asia."

"Not yet, anyway," Rozier said.

"What?" Cassidy snapped.

"I mean, it's not a change of policy until after the election. Then Gardner will be able to do whatever he wants," Rozier said.

"What's Tim's reaction?" O'Connor interrupted, before the dialogue between the President and his press secretary broke into an open angry argument.

The President swung his gaze toward the face of his old friend. "He's not there yet, Frank. He was campaigning and he's in transit back to Washington now." Cassidy paused. "But it doesn't matter. Some kind of action had to be taken. The targets that the Security Council have chosen are purely military. It's the right decision," Cassidy said, but his face betrayed his uncertainty. "We'll be leaving for Washington in the morning," Cassidy added then.

"Yes, sir," Rozier said in a flat monotone, not wanting to anger the President any further than he already had.

"We're going to ask Congress for a resolution approving our actions and authorizing whatever action might be required in the future," Cassidy said. "I guess my exile is over," he added, smiling bitterly. He formed his fingers into a tight fist then, as if he were struggling to contain some unseen opponent that was fighting its way from his grasp.

"He's won," Rozier said.

"What?" Cassidy's irritation was obvious again as he turned back to his press secretary.

"I said that Gardner's won the election," Rozier said, making himself clear.

Cassidy didn't answer for a moment, and then his only reply was to nod his head once decisively, signaling his agreement. "Yes, Allen, I think you're right about that. If the Vice President handles the next few days as I'm confident that he can, the American people will support him. Rance will have his presidency then. And if he wants it, he may have his war as well." Cassidy let his clenched hand slowly relax. As it did, he could almost feel the final strands of power that he'd fought so hard to hold on to beginning to unravel, and he knew that the transition of authority from his hands to Gardner's that had begun in Dallas less than a year before was now very close to being complete.

What was it about the file that bothered him so much? Sullivan sat in Denise's bedroom, his feet propped up on the edge of her bed. He had Strode's FBI file in his hands and he was reading it for the third time in the last hour. Okay, Sullivan said to himself, start it over, be methodical, read every line, question every word of it, challenge every assumption. Do it right this time. And he flipped back to the very beginning of the file again. "Strode, Arthur Allen—69477896RA" he read. God, he'd read one line and already he could feel the uneasy feeling in his stomach beginning again. What the hell was it?

"I'm taking the kids, I'll be back in about two hours," Denise said, sticking her head in the bedroom door.

"Uh-uh," Sullivan answered her, without looking up. Then he could feel her coming close and bending over him, kissing him lightly on the top of the head.

"Are you reading that damned thing again?" Denise said, pointing at the file, but she didn't wait for an answer. "I'll be back a little after noon. Will you still be here?"

"No, I'm just going to take a look at this and then clear out," Sullivan said, gesturing at the file. "I don't want to be here when Kit gets back. It's bad for your reputation."

Denise shrugged her shoulders to show that she didn't care what her roommate thought of her lovelife. "Where do you think Kit was all night, at a prayer meeting?"

"Have a good time," Sullivan mumbled vaguely, returning his attention to the file.

"A good time at the dentist?" Denise asked, slightly puzzled, and then Sullivan could hear the sounds of her rounding up her kids and herding them out the door. "I'll call!" Sullivan shouted just before he heard the front door close behind her.

Sullivan went back to work, and then he was lost in the ugly, confused, and very sad life of the man who'd died in Dallas eleven months earlier. Sullivan stopped reading only when he heard a sound in Denise's living room. Startled, he stood up and dropped the file down onto the floor below the bed, out of sight.

The door of Denise's bedroom opened slowly. "Yes," Sullivan said, but it was too late. Kit was standing in the doorway, looking across at him. Suddenly he realized that he was wearing only a pair of pale blue boxer undershorts.

"Oh," Kit said, but she didn't do anything about taking her eyes off Sullivan's half-naked body.

"Denise took the kids to the dentist," Sullivan said.

Kit only continued looking boldly across the bedroom at Sullivan's exposed chest and legs.

"You want some coffee?" she asked.

"Yeah," Sullivan said gratefully, and finally Kit turned slowly and walked back out into the living room.

Sullivan reached down first for his pants and then his shirt, both of which he'd thrown over Denise's end table the night before. Then he returned the Strode file to the FBI lock bag and replaced it in the jewelry box in the dark corner of the top shelf of Denise's closet. He'd changed his mind about destroying the file, at least until he'd figured out what it was that troubled him so much about it. He had offered to take the file someplace else several times though, but Denise seemed to like having it there and he didn't have a better place for it, so it had stayed. Probably a mistake, Sullivan thought, but just one of many in his life that he hadn't quite gotten around to correcting yet. Kit was already seated at the couch, her long legs up and resting on the coffee table where two cups of steaming black coffee were sitting.

"Instant," she said pointing at the coffee.

"I should get going," Sullivan said.

Kit only smiled at him. Then she used the fingers of her right hand to casually comb out her long dark hair. Sullivan sat down across from her and watched.

They were both silent for a few seconds, Kit looking directly into Sullivan's eyes. Feeling awkward, Sullivan moved forward and picked up his cup of coffee. As he did he could see the long length of Kit's legs exposed below the line of her dress. They were uncrossed and relaxed, the heels of her feet resting squarely on the tabletop directly in front of him. Her loose dress was pulled up nearly to her thighs and her legs were spread comfortably apart. She was wearing nothing under the soft, loosely fitting dress; Sullivan could see that clearly and as he looked, Kit opened her legs farther, letting Sullivan know that what he was seeing was no accident. He looked up into her face. She was smiling provocatively at him. Her features were almost perfect, Sullivan thought, beautiful, dark, almond-shaped eyes, classic aquiline nose, and smooth white skin. She raised her knee then and let her dress fall back even farther toward her thigh.

"How was your date?" Sullivan said. His feelings were a strange mix of embarrassment and excitement, a confused feeling that he couldn't remember ever having felt before.

"He was a great big disappointment," Kit said, drawing the words out and giving each of them special intimate significance.

Well, this is the moment of truth, Sullivan thought, as he watched Kit move provocatively on the couch only a few feet from him. There was no mistaking her actions now. He either was, or he was not the kind of a person who made a move on his girlfriend's roommate, and, as he took another cautious look between Kit's long, smooth legs, he had no idea what the answer was going to be. Where the hell is her underwear, anyway? he thought angrily, and he forced his eyes back onto his coffee cup. He felt mostly confused now. There was so much that he didn't know about women and some of it he didn't want to know, he decided. "Got to get going," he said abruptly and then stood up. He looked back down at Kit, but only at her face this time. The moment had passed anyway, he realized then. Denise's roommate was standing herself now and her dress had fallen back down around her knees. "Okay." She smiled at him and suddenly everything seemed back to normal. Maybe it had all just been his imagination anyway, Sullivan thought as he started for the door. What a jerk I am, he added to himself, but then he stopped and turned back and took one final look. Kit had already withdrawn her attention from him and she was crossing the room toward the telephone. Sullivan had a feeling, though, that it hadn't been any mistake, and whoever it was that Kit was calling now was a very lucky man. And as he started out the door and down the narrow cement pathway toward his car, Sullivan felt more than a little jealous.

Jack woke in the middle of the night with the wrong woman sleeping next to him. A storm was pounding the Irish countryside, and outside the windows of his room he could see the sudden violent flashes of lightning and then a few seconds later he could hear the explosions of thunder. It reminded him of his dream. Vaguely frightened, he reached out to touch Suzanne's shoulder and to draw her close to him for comfort, but it was the wrong shoulder, and Jack remembered now where he was and who he was with and why. He slid out of bed and reached for his robe and then, being careful not to awaken the woman sleeping in the bed beside him, he moved to the door.

The great hall of March House was dark, but Jack managed to descend the staircase and to find the book-lined library that opened just off the front landing. It was his favorite of all the rooms of the manor house and he settled into a deep leather chair next to the stone fireplace that dominated the far end of the library. He sat alone then and watched the rain beat against the leaded-glass windows of the old wood-paneled room. Occasionally a great crackling explosion of rolling Irish thunder would rocket through the sky and illuminate the darkness that lay just outside the window. He could scarcely hear the knock on the library door over the fury of the lashing wind and rain outside, but he stood when he saw the towering figure of his host filling the doorway.

"May I come in?" Jeffries said. The big man was dressed in a light gray robe and he was holding a single white wax candle in a brass candle holder in one hand. The effect was ghostlike and slightly ominous. "Of course," Jack said, and Jeffries entered the room, not pausing at the door to turn on the electric light, but instead placing his candlestick on a table near the window, keeping the room in a flickering semidarkness of erratic light and occasional shadows.

A roll of thunder moved across the sky above March House and Jack shuddered with its unexpected impact and power. Both men were silent then. It was Jack who spoke first, needing to explain his discomfort. "The thunder . . ." he said and then paused, unable to finish what he had wanted to say.

"It sounds like bombs exploding," Jeffries said, completing Jack's thought in his deep-throated, rumbling way, and Jack nodded his head.

"Everyone's asleep?" Jack said, motioning past the open door that led to the great hall.

"Yes, I saw Allen on my way down though," Jeffries said, smiling. "He was having one of the servants bring in some extra blankets and a quart of brandy."

Jeffries sat down in a medieval claw-armed chair that stood directly across from Jack. The candle on the table behind the older man shone down and illuminated his enormous bearded face. In the light from the candle, Jack could see the crosswork of deep lines that ran from the corners of the older man's eyes in an intricate pattern, like the webbing of an industrious and imaginative spider. And as Jack looked into Jeffries's face, he could see, too, the source of the compelling green eyes of Diane Jeffries, but Jack turned away then, not wanting to see any more. "The only way that I could get Allen to come at all was to tell him that we might stop in Paris on our way home. He and Suzanne both love . . ." Jack said, but at the mention of his wife's name, Cassidy's body began to tense and his voice trailed off before he could finish.

"How is she?" Jeffries asked.

"Oh, the last year has been difficult for us both," Jack confessed into the darkness of the high-ceilinged, book-lined room. The light from the single candle didn't quite reach his face and he was beginning now to find it easier to talk to his old friend in the darkness.

"And your father, we haven't really talked about him either," Jeffries said, and then the older man stood and walked to the bar at the far side of the room and poured brandy into large, bowl-shaped snifters.

Jack didn't answer right away. Instead, he watched as Jeffries carried the two snifters across the room and handed one to him. Jack drank the rich amber liquid and let its warmth and strength seep into his body. "Thank you," Jack said after he'd finished. "God, I didn't know how tired I was," he added with a great sigh as he felt the energy of the drink beginning to punch holes into the heavy fatigue that cloaked his body. He put his feet up on the leather footrest in front of him then and let his head and eyes tilt up toward the ceiling. "Was he ever frightened?" Jack said into the darkness. "Ever really uncertain? I've never seen him that way, you know."

"Your father?" The older man stood and walked to the darkened window and looked out at the storm raging against the Irish countryside before he answered, as if the wind and the rain and the great forces of nature being played out in front of him reminded him of Jack's father and helped him to form his answer. "I suppose that I could tell you what I've told the others, the journalists and the biographers, who've come to see me about him."

"No, please don't," Jack said. "Unless it's true."

"Energy and courage and daring," Jeffries said, drawing each word out to accentuate their meanings. "Like you," he added. "But don't ask me to compare the two of you and don't do it yourself. What it means to be a man," Jeffries stopped then and corrected himself. "To be a person, is entirely different, in different times, in different places," he said and then laughed. His voice, when he began again, was softer, lighter, as if it came from a different part of himself. "I should know, I've made over sixty movies now, some good, some bad, but all about the same thing. You'd think someone would take me seriously after all those miles of film—particularly my own godson," the big bearded man said from his place near the window.

"I do," Jack said. "He frightened me sometimes," Jack confessed into the tall brandy tumbler that he lifted toward his face as he spoke.

"Oh, he scared himself," Jeffries said, returning to the chair across from Jack. "That's something else he helped teach me. I think people are mostly mysteries, even to themselves," Jeffries stopped then and corrected himself again. He wanted to be very certain of what he was saying to the younger man now, as if there was a duty to pass on to him the few precious things that he'd managed to learn in all his years of living. "Maybe mostly to themselves," he said. "And if they have any courage—and your father has a lot more than most—they keep experimenting, trying on different parts of themselves, acting them out, seeing if they fit, how they feel, what they can learn from them. That's how they grow, how they learn who and what they really are. You do that, Jack. I've seen you."

"Do I?" Cassidy said. "Yes, I guess I do," he added, his face growing more serious. "I suppose that means that I'm not certain of who I am yet."

"I suppose it does," Jeffries said.

"And I make mistakes," Jack said very softly.

"Yes, you do," Jeffries said.

"It's not as simple as you make it sound," Jack said. "The man who's President of the United States can't make too many. He can't be too uncertain."

Jeffries shrugged his shoulders. "Maybe not, I've never been a President, but Presidents are men, too, and men have the right to grow and change, but I know it's difficult to do that without making mistakes, big mistakes sometimes."

"Did my father?" Jack asked again.

"Yes, I think so, but then he thought that I did as well."

Jack waited to hear more.

"It took your father a long time to learn the one thing that I thought was really important," Jeffries said. "In fact, I'm not sure he ever has," he added with a short laugh. "I hope that you do."

"What was that?"

Jeffries paused before answering. "That nothing good can ever come from something bad. For me, that's all there really is to know, that we can't justify even the smallest act of injustice, because we hope, or even if we believe that it will lead in the end to a greater good," Jeffries stopped then. "But, of course, that's why I'm an artist and not a politician or a businessman. The decisions I make are much easier."

Jack looked over at his friend and smiled. "I see," he said. "Sixty movies and no tough choices," Jack said.

Jeffries returned the smile. "One or two," he said. "You've avoided my question though. How sick is your father?" he asked.

"Very," Jack said, trying not to let his emotion show.

"And you feel that you've failed him, failed your family, your country, failed yourself, too?"

"I'm not sure," Jack said. "Do you think that what we're doing in Vietnam is wrong, John? That it was naïve of me, whatever my motives, to think that something good might ultimately come from it? Is that what you're trying to say to me?"

"Yes," Jeffries said. "I do. I think it's wrong and it shouldn't have been begun." Both men were quiet then. "Maybe coming here was a bad idea," Jeffries said finally.

Jack shook his head. "No. It wasn't. You see, I really had no place else to go," he said, and then he paused. "Are you angry, John?"

"About what?"

"Diane."

Jeffries let a clatter of thunder pass away outside the window before he tried to answer. "Other people's mistakes always make me angry," he said. "Mine, on the other hand, are easily explained by the extraordinary circumstances that I find myself in."

Jack smiled, "Yes, mine too. My failures are easily explained away."

"Failure, yes, I know the word," Jeffries said grandly. "I've been a failure many times, and a success, and then a failure again." He stopped for a moment. "I am mostly a success now, but I hope to be a failure at least one more time before I die."

"John," Cassidy said. "Those times before when you were a failure. How did you stop being one? How did you find your way back to being a success again?"

"I don't know, Jack, I always trusted what I felt, I guess," Jeffries said, tossing the thought off as if that part weren't of much importance. "I just did the simplest thing first. The thing that I was surest of, had a drink," Jeffries said, and he held up his glass. "Took a walk in a place I loved." He motioned out the window at the grounds of March House, and then he dropped his casual air and said in a more direct voice, "Talked to someone I loved. Tried to correct the wrong that I'd done, if I could."

Jack was silent then for several long seconds. "Sounds easy enough when you say it," he said finally.

Jeffries laughed. "Oh, but it wasn't, and it won't be for you either, but do it. Call her. I know you, Jack, and that's where it starts for you, with your family. The rest will come—start with the simplest thing first, the thing that you're the most certain of. Call her and tell her you've been a damn fool, even if you haven't been."

Jack shook his head no. "That part's easy, John. I have been."

The two men smiled at each other then. "I suppose tonight, all this, will be in you memoirs," Jack said.

"It would make a fine chapter wouldn't it? The night I counseled the President on love and war and other related matters." Jeffries laughed. "But I'm a movie maker, not a writer, and it would make a damn bad movie— too much talk."

"Thank you," Jack said, motioning with his brandy glass toward his friend.

"Your father and I have a few similar arrangements," Jeffries said. "Mostly though, for all my fancy speeches, it's not been me that's had to protect your father, but your father that has been kind enough through the years to not repeat a few things that he's known about me," Jeffries said, smiling and nodding a respectful thank you for the courtesy toward his old friend's eldest son.

Suzanne paused in the hallway just outside of Konstantine's room. Behind the ornate metal door in front of her were Konstantine's personal quarters, his reception area, his private office, his library and study, then his dressing area, and at the very far end of the east wing was Konstantine's private bedroom.

Suzanne had to be very certain of what it was that she wanted before she entered those rooms. She stood in the hallway for several long seconds and let the breeze from the sea blow across the courtyard and cool her sunburned skin as she tried to force her thoughts and feelings into some kind of a final pattern. But she wasn't able to make any real sense out of all the conflicting feelings that moved inside her before the high, intricately carved metal door opened and Konstantine stood at the threshold.

"I hadn't expected you," he said, and then he stepped aside.

The reception area held rows of telexes and various other business machines, but the machines were quiet now and the secretary's desk at the center of the room was vacant. They were alone.

Suzanne followed Konstantine through the reception area and into his private office. "Would you like a drink?" He turned back to her and looked into her eyes. Up close, it always surprised Suzanne how taut and unlined his skin was and how full of energy his eyes seemed for a man that she knew to be almost twenty years older than she was.

"Yes, I'd like something very strong and very Greek," she said to his offer, and they passed quickly then into his private study. The study adjoined his office through a tall rounded wooden archway, sealed off by tall mahogany doors. The room was decorated in rich leathers and heavy, darkly burnished wood paneling. It looked like Konstantine himself, Suzanne thought, as she heard him closing the tall wooden doors behind her. She turned back to him then and watched as he crossed the room toward the bar at the far side of the room. He was dressed in silk that night, as he often was, a light-green silk shirt open at the throat to show a gold medallion that he wore around his neck. He wore thick, rope-soled sandals that added an extra inch to his height, but as he approached her across the thick white carpeting of his private study their eyes were almost perfectly level.

There was a single window in the study and through it she could see a pale white moon dropping beams of light across the gently moving surface of the Mediterranean. It truly was one of the most beautiful places in the world, she thought, as she looked down at the water and listened to it lapping up softly against the shoreline.

Konstantine had poured two tall glasses of ouzo, and he handed one across to her now. "Very Greek, very strong," he said as she took the drink.

They touched glasses and then they drank their first sips of the fire-hot liquid, slowly, solemnly, watching each other's eyes carefully over the rims of their cut-crystal glasses.

Suzanne felt uncomfortable being watched so intently by his dark powerful eyes, and she turned away from him and sat down on a long low couch that ran beneath the room's single window. From there, she could see only a few yards away from her the door to the final set of rooms of the private east-wing complex.

"Did you enjoy the party?"

"I appreciate everything that you've done for me and for my family," Suzanne said, and the suddenness of the words and their formality stung Konstantine. He set his drink down then and moved across the room to sit only a few feet from her. Once he was seated, he leaned forward toward her, his head lower than hers, but his eyes raised and fixed once again on her face. "There is so much more that I would like to do." As he spoke there was no mistaking the depth of his feelings toward her. But then, fearing that he'd let himself say too much, he added quickly, "It's been an honor," and his voice became very formal and very restrained.

"Jack called," she said.

He nodded, showing that he understood her message, even the unspoken part. He slid back in his chair, increasing the distance between them, and raised his head and eyes up level with hers again. He unclasped his powerful hands slowly, feeling surprised as he did at just how tightly he had been holding them gripped together in front of him.

"Jack asked me to join him in Paris on Sunday. From there we're to return to Washington."

"Neutral ground, how diplomatic," Konstantine said, reaching for his drink and not even trying to disguise the bitterness in his voice now.

Suzanne smiled. "No, not really. If he had wanted absolute neutrality, he would have suggested Brussels. Paris means a victory for me," she said, smiling gently.

"Yes, of course," Konstantine said. "I see, or Geneva."

Both of them smiled at each other then, but there was very little warmth in Konstantine's face, as he fought with the deep disappointment that he felt at Suzanne's announcement. "I had hoped . . ." he started, but Suzanne refused to let him say something that either of them might regret later. "We'll only be in Paris for a few days. Jack's agreed to be home for the last month of the campaign."

"The campaign, of course. I understand perfectly," Konstantine said.

"Jack said that he's dreading getting back and campaigning again, but the truth is there's nothing that he'd rather be doing," she said.

"And you? What do you want?" Konstantine asked, his eyes finding hers again. "Do you know?"

"Yes, I want to be with my husband," Suzanne said with equal directness, and then she stood up, showing the full length of her elegant body to the man sitting only a few short feet away from her. "But thank you for all that you've done," she added and extended her hand, holding his tightly, while his eyes rested on her face. He began then to slowly increase the pressure on her extended hand, beginning to draw her closer to him, while his eyes remained firmly fixed on her face.

Suzanne returned his gaze, feeling hypnotized by the man's enormous power and magnetism and energy that was, for the moment, focused entirely on her. She could feel her body drawing close to him and then swaying slightly forward and back, as Konstantine's hand slid toward her wrist. His strong fingers touched the soft underside of her arm, and his hand locked tightly around her forearm and began to pull her toward him. Their eyes met and she felt that she could sense both his body and his soul pulling her toward him, but slowly she withdrew her arm from his grasp and managed to step back from him. He took a step forward toward her, and for a moment Suzanne was afraid that he wasn't going to let her go, but then he stopped and looked away from her, forcing himself to look out the window behind her at the hot Greek night. She could hear the soft wind from the Mediterranean blowing restlessly in the scrub pines that surrounded Konstantine's home.

"Suzanne," he said sharply, "do you think for a moment that a man like your husband isn't involved, that there aren't other . . ."

Suzanne wouldn't let him finish. "My husband and I love each other," she said, making certain that her answer made it impossible for him to continue. "That's more important to me than anything else."

Jack found Diane at the stables as he knew he would. He watched her from a distance, wondering what he was going to say to her and how he would say it. She was dressed for her morning ride and, as he stood at a distance and watched her, Jack couldn't help but admire her strong, youthful beauty. She was waiting for the grooms to finish saddling her horse and as they worked she stood and gently patted its soft brown muzzle. It was a few minutes past dawn in Connemara. At first light in another country, American planes had bombed Asian harbors and supply depots and Jack knew that as carefully as those targets had been selected for their military significance that innocent people had died that morning, died at his command. He had been up very early talking on the telephone to Washington, taking every precaution to limit the response, but he knew that it couldn't be contained entirely and he'd wanted to be outside in the open air at first light in Connemara, not indoors with the telephone and the dispatches that were arriving regularly now and beginning to pile up in the downstairs library that he had made his office.

The rain had stopped, but the earth on the path that led to the stables was soft and he could feel his shoes sinking deep into the wet ground as he walked the final few yards to the open stable doors.

"Good morning," she said, without even turning around to see him. She didn't need to. She knew the sound of his steps on the stable path by heart now.

"Good morning," Jack answered and she turned slowly, her hand still resting for reassurance on her horse's soft mane. "You're not riding this morning," she said as she turned and saw that Jack was dressed in only a sport coat and slacks.

"No," he said, shaking his head. "Something's happened."

"I know," Diane said.

Jack looked across the pathway at her and suddenly he wanted to walk over to her and take her in his arms and hold her close to him, but he didn't. It would only make it more difficult for both of them. And so, instead, he motioned for her to follow him down the path toward the edge of the woods that surrounded her father's estate. As she moved from the stable door, she could hear the big chestnut-brown horse that she'd ridden since she was a child begin to move restlessly in its stall. "Something's bothering him this morning," she added then and smiled at Jack, but not very convincingly.

"You've heard, then?" Jack said, and she nodded.

"I've decided to go to Paris and then back to Washington," Jack said.

"I see," she answered. "When?"

"Tonight."

"That is soon," she said in a low soft voice as she walked up the pathway away from him, and then she stopped and looked back at March House.

"Well, I suppose I'll see you again somewhere—in California, maybe," she said, her face still turned away from him.

"Yes, I hope so," Jack said, but his voice admitted that it was unlikely.

She turned to him then. "Am I doing this right?" she blurted out suddenly. "I've never . . ."

"You're doing wonderfully," Jack said. "I'm the one who isn't . . ." He let his voice trail off then, and, instead of speaking, he walked the few steps to her and stood close to her and looked down at the luminous green eyes that he had grown accustomed to looking into over the last several days, but even as he did, he didn't reach out and touch her. He knew that they couldn't be seen that way together. He had to be careful, and he restrained himself, backing away so that it would appear that they were two friends on a morning walk, nothing more.

"Jack, I'll never tell anyone about us, never."

"I'm not worried about that," Jack said.

"What are you worried about then?" Diane said.

Jack paused for a moment before he answered. "Whether I did the right thing, I guess," he said finally. "And knowing that I didn't."

"Please don't apologize. That's not the way I want it to end." She drew a deep breath, using the time to find her courage. "I don't want you to mis-understand what I'm going to say and I don't want you to feel that you have to lie, so please don't say anything when I'm finished," she said and held up one delicate finger toward his lips as if to seal them. "But I'll always love you," she said quickly, and then she swept past him, so that there was no time for him to say anything in return.

She walked very fast down the path that led to the stables. Her chestnut-brown horse was saddled and waiting, and she mounted the powerful stallion in one graceful swinging move.

"Will I see you at lunch?" she called out to Jack in a loud steady voice.

Jack nodded at her and then she led the beautiful stallion past him and down the path that led to the woods. A few seconds later she was racing over the rolling, emerald-colored Irish hillside toward the thick forest in the dis-tance.

CHAPTER
23

The campaign ended for Jack pretty much the way that it had begun—in New York City, with his family in a big suite at the Waldorf and a late dinner from a room-service cart. There had been a final rally and speech in Times Square and he was tired from the final frantic weeks of campaigning. His health was better though. The headaches that had been so debilitating only a few months before were less frequent now, but they did still recur under extended periods of stress. He was far from back to normal yet. The long hard campaign that he'd just completed had proven that to him. In the end, Gardner had needed almost every minute of his time and he'd complied, doing everything that the Vice President had asked and sometimes more. Jack's voice was rough and scratched, too, from the weeks of traveling and speaking, but the campaign was over now and there was nothing left to be done except to finally get some rest, and then sit back and watch the votes come in and be counted.

The chicken on his room-service plate was growing cold, but he was too tired to deal with it. He used his fork instead, to pick at little pieces of potato salad and aim them vaguely at his mouth, but finally he gave up on that as well, and just poured himself a fresh glass of wine and let his body slump back into the hotel chair. As he did, Tim lightly tossed a small metal object across the table and let it land near Jack's plate. "These things are turning up all over the country. What do you think?" Tim said. Despite his smile, Tim's face showed the deep weariness of the last few crowded months of campaigning even more emphatically than did the President's.

Jack reached out and picked up the little object that Tim had tossed over

315

to him. It was a campaign button, and Jack smiled as he read its printed message: CASSIDY AND CASSIDY IN 1968.

"Forget it," he said. "Even if I do get the nomination, I'm not going to pick you as my Vice President. You're too close to Rance now. I couldn't trust you."

"That's not the way I read it," Tim said, pointing at the button in Jack's hand. "It's Cassidy," he said, pointing at himself first, "and Cassidy," he added, only then pointing at his older brother and giving him the second spot.

"You're both wrong," Suzanne said, reaching for the button in her husband's hand and holding it to her own chest. "But I'm sorry, Tim," she said, smiling over at her brother-in-law. "I'm not going to pick you either," Suzanne paused then. She felt tired too, but relieved that tonight was the last night of the campaign. Whatever happened now, soon she and Jack could go back to living something close to a normal life again. "I'm going to pick Kay," Suzanne said, turning to her sister-in-law.

"Cassidy and Cassidy," Kay said, laughing.

"Or, Cassidy and Cassidy," Suzanne said, trying the button on Kay and putting her at the top of the imaginary ticket.

"Or Erin and John, Jr.," Kay laughed and then added, "I think we're all a little punchy from too many nights on the road."

"I'm glad the show's closing," Suzanne said.

"Ours is closing," Jack said and then added, lifting his wineglass toward his brother, "but Tim's is just beginning."

"I hope so," Tim said.

"It is," Jack said confidently.

"They still weren't leaping out there tonight," Tim said, motioning out in the direction of Times Square.

"What do you mean?" Kay asked, but Tim didn't answer right away, his thoughts somewhere else. "Oh," he said finally, realizing that the others were waiting for him to finish. "Nothing. It's just that it wasn't like 1960, that's all."

"The crowds, you mean?" Suzanne said to Tim, but Jack had to answer for his brother, whose tired thoughts had drifted away from the table again. "No, Tim's right. They turn out and they're curious and I think in the last analysis they'll vote for us, but it's different. There's not as much . . ." Jack couldn't seem to find just the right word. "Confidence, joy, whatever. There's a different feeling to it now."

"Too much has happened," Suzanne said, with a trace of sadness in her voice. "Too much has happened to us and to the country. We can't expect it to be the same."

"God, was it just a year ago that we were in Dallas?" Kay said.

"Not quite a year," Tim said.

"It barely seems possible," Suzanne said. "So much has changed."

"We can't let what happened in Dallas change the direction of the country though," Jack said with a flickering of sudden anger. Then he added quickly, in a lighter tone, "But that's Tim's concern now."

"I'm afraid that things already have changed," Tim said quietly. "The country is cynical now. They just don't believe that anything is possible for us as a country anymore."

Suzanne shifted around in her chair. She knew what her husband was thinking, that he was blaming himself. She stood and walked to a chair that stood across the room from the informal dinner table. "Jack, you did everything that Rance asked you to do. Everything that could have been expected of you. We all did," she said, sweeping her hand out toward Tim and Kay. "Whatever happens tomorrow, you can't blame yourself."

"I'm not so certain," Jack said.

The room was quiet then, as the mood of the four deeply tired people swung rapidly away from the feelings of relief and humor of a few minutes earlier to a brief gloom.

"I have a confession to make," Tim said after a few seconds of the heavy silence. "I've been sent here to undertake a serious and delicate undercover mission." Tim's voice was lighter and full of humor again.

"Your friend, Gardner, sent you," Jack said, the beginning of a smile returning to his own face.

"Uh-uh," Tim said, nodding, and then he looked around dramatically at his wife and at his sister-in-law before he continued. "I've been sent here to discuss your future, Jack," he said and then paused. "I'm supposed to find out if you would be willing to take some kind of a post in the new administration."

Jack laughed then.

"The truth is Rance is certain that you want to be his Secretary of State, and he doesn't know how to tell you no," Tim said.

"So, you've been sent to do it for him," Jack said, still chuckling slightly.

"Yes."

"Well, tell me then."

"No," Tim said. "No, you can't be the Secretary of State."

"Well, I guess that settles it," Jack said. "Is the vice presidency taken?"

"Yes, by a rising young star," Tim said. "At least until Gardner's people can find a way to get rid of him."

"I've tried, and it's damn near impossible," Kay Cassidy joined in.

"So have I," Jack said. "And you're right. He's tenacious as hell." Jack turned back to his brother then. "Well, what's left, Tim?"

"There is one real possibility," Tim said, his face growing serious.

"No," Jack said waving his hand in front of him to ward off his brother's words. "Not tonight, Tim."

"You can't tell me that you haven't thought about it," Tim said, and when Jack didn't respond right away, he went on. "You might consider an ambassadorship."

"Ireland," Jack said smiling.

"France," Suzanne said.

"No, the United Nations," Tim said, his voice full of excitement. "With full Cabinet status. I've talked to Rance about it."

Jack didn't answer for a moment. Tim could tell from his brother's face that the idea was tempting. "And what did Mr. Gardner say when you mentioned it to him?" Jack asked.

"I told you, I'm on a secret mission," Tim said.

Jack looked at his wife then. "Have you and Suzanne been talking about this?"

"No, I didn't have the nerve. I think Suzanne wants you to go off and write your memoirs or something," Tim said, smiling at his sister-in-law.

Suzanne nodded her agreement. "In a quiet little village somewhere."

"What do you think, Jack?" Tim said, turning his attention back to his brother.

"I don't know, Tim. I'll think about it," Jack said evasively.

"Wait a minute," Suzanne said, not willing to let Jack get away with his vague answer. "I've seen that look in your eyes before. Just what is it that you do have in mind?"

"We'll talk about it later," he said. "Tim, I appreciate the concern, but I think it's best that, whatever I do now, I maintain my independence from the new administration. Remember?" He picked up a little red-white-and-blue CASSIDY AND CASSIDY IN 1968 button then and flashed it at his brother. "You never know what might happen over the next four years."

"Oh, I see," Tim said. "It's all right for me to be trapped in the record of Mr. Gardner's new administration, but not for the older brother."

"Something like that," Jack smiled.

Suzanne took her husband's hand then and walked with him into the bedroom of the hotel suite, leaving Tim and Kay alone at the dinner table.

"He's planning something, isn't he?" Kay said after Jack had left the room.

Tim nodded in agreement.

"Do you have any idea what it is?" Kay asked.

"No, but I'm certain that he'll let us know, when he's ready to."

They would carry Texas and with it the election. Gardner was positive of it. It wasn't the polls or what he saw in the newspaper articles or on television. It was what he felt in his chest and in his gut. He could feel it coming.

He stood and looked out over that small part of the great, vast Lone Star state that he could see from the front porch of his ranch, and then up at the clear Texas night sky. At that moment, the night seemed almost as bright as daylight, and as he stood and watched the moon move along close to the earth, seeming for those few brief seconds almost close enough to touch, he remembered other Texas night skies that he had looked up into when he was a boy, and then again when he was a young man, looked up into and dreamed of doing great things, of becoming a great man. And now, looking up at this sky on this night, the eve of that greatness was truly before him. Ransom

W. Gardner, the schoolteacher's son from East Texas, was about to be elected President of the United States. He closed his eyes and let himself feel the moment fully. God, he loved this country and this state, he thought, as he opened his eyes again to look at the vast Texas sky. There wasn't another man alive who could have done what he was about to do, to whip Marshall Granderman, whose family was rich enough to own this part of Texas if they wanted to. He let himself feel the thrill of that thought for several private seconds, but then, no longer able to contain the feelings that were bursting inside of him, he exploded. "Bill!" he shouted, and Mallory came running from the living room of the ranch house to the long porch at the front of the home where Gardner stood.

"I want people in here tonight," Gardner said.

"Yes, sir," Mallory said. "It's late though," he added.

"I don't care. I want people to talk to tonight. There's a motel chock full of reporters less than twenty minutes down that road," Gardner said, pointing out into the night, past the front gates of his ranch.

"Yes, sir, I know," Mallory said.

"Call 'em. Tell 'em I'll talk all night if they want. Invite 'em on up here. We'll drink bourbon together and I'll tell 'em all about the United States of America that I intend to build over the next four years. We'll make a little history together tonight and they kin tell their grandkids about it thirty years from now. Call 'em!" Gardner said. "I can't sleep, not on a night like this," he went on, waving his arms in a broad gesture at the sky. "Remember this night, Bill," he instructed his aide then, but Gardner's eyes remained fixed on the distant stars. "This is the beginnin' of it. When you come to write your history books about all we've done and all we're goin' do, remember tonight, because this is the true beginnin' of it, right here and now. The true start of a great new America, and you were right here at the birth of it."

"Yes, sir," Mallory said. "I'll remember tonight."

Cuba—he could smell it across the water, hot and fetid, its west coast overgrown with thick sun-ripened foliage.

Lopata stayed buried deep in the hook that was formed by the stern of the little motor launch, where he could watch the two-man crew that he'd found in Miami. They had been willing to take him across the Gulf in their fishing boat and land him at this deserted jungle beach—for a price.

The smell of the island filled Lopata with memories of other earlier days —days before it had become Castro's island. But before he could drift too far into the past, Lopata snapped himself back to the little boat and the two men who had agreed to take him to the Cuban shore. He fingered the holster of his long-barreled .38 pistol, reminding the bearded man working closest to him that he had it. These men couldn't be trusted; he had decided that in Miami. They were frightened to make the last few miles of the trip inside Cuba's territorial waters and they had good reason for their fears, Lopata thought, eying the two men as the launch approached the shoreline in the dark. But they would be paid well when they finished the dangerous journey and landed him near Santa de Carine.

The launch began to slow. Lopata looked up to see the man on the bridge above him easing the ship's controls down, and he could feel the engine shifting down into a slower but more powerful gear. Lopata stood and looked out at the darkened Gulf waters that stretched out around the side of the boat. What little moon there was that night was hidden in dense gray clouds and he could see less than a hundred feet in any direction. This was the time of maximum danger. Once he was ashore he would be all right. The papers that he'd bought in Miami were good enough to pass casual inspection, and he knew the island well. He'd been born there and there would be people willing to help him until he decided what he should do next. But the next few minutes were crucial.

Lopata could see the beach coming up in front of him. The tiny sliver of a moon had found an opening in the sky full of clouds. Lopata felt his heart leap. The feeling of joy surprised him. He hadn't realized how happy he would be to see his homeland again. He stood at the bow and watched the beach ahead of him as it approached in the uneven pace of the launch. It was strange, Lopata thought, but Castro's Cuba was the only place he felt safe now. The one place that the people who searched for him couldn't go easily, not the American government, not the men who worked for DeSavio—the one comfortable place in the world for him, despite that pig Castro, or maybe because of him. Lopata smiled at the realization. He would use Castro's Cuba to protect himself, Castro's soldiers to protect him from his enemies, and maybe, if he could think of a way to arrange it, Castro's banks to receive his money.

"Are we in Cuba now?" he called out to the bearded man in the rough gray workshirt, and as he did Lopata motioned out at the murky gray midnight sea that surrounded the launch.

"*Sí*," the man said, pointing due east, but the sliver of moon had returned behind the thick clouds again and the outline of the Cuban coastline was no longer visible through the dark night. "We must be very careful," the bearded man said, his voice full of fear. "There are patrols."

Lopata laughed contemptuously in reply and then turned back toward the island and stood with his knees pressed against the side of the launch. He undid the zipper of his shapeless khaki pants and, as the bearded man looked on in disbelief, Lopata urinated out to sea in the direction of Havana, where Castro and his most trusted soldiers slept that night.

The numbers in the neat little parallel columns seemed to be growing all by themselves. It was like some kind of horrible second-rate science-fiction movie, Longwood thought. Hollywood would have called it *The Issue That Ate the Republican Party*. Longwood smiled wearily at his private joke and then refolded the printout and tossed it on the empty airplane seat next to him. The Senator was flying home late on the final night before the election. He'd been in eighteen states in the last five days and he was tired, his coat off, a tall drink in his hand. He looked out the window of his chartered jet at the clouds and the dark sky and imagined that the mountains and deserts of Arizona were already visible below him, but all he could really see outside the window for the moment was dark empty sky.

He looked at the printout lying across the seat beside him. He was grateful to be alone at the end of a very long day. If some of Granderman's people had been with him, he probably would have said his bad joke out loud and he could guess how it would have gone over, like some of the other things he'd said in public and in private over the last few months probably, Longwood decided, and then he took a long sip of his drink. Well, the hell with it. He'd done his best, and if it wasn't good enough he could live with it, but, God, they had come close and there was still a chance, a small one perhaps, but a chance. They'd have won it too, if that damn Vietnam Cong force hadn't chosen October 5, 1964, to murder thirty-six American soldiers. God, that was the irony—in the crisis the American people had turned back to the administration. They'd supported Cassidy and Gardner, rather than seeing that it was precisely the policies of the Democrats that had led to that disaster out there in Southeast Asia and that if Gardner won the election there would be worse to come. He'd made his case though, Longwood told himself. The people had heard him out, and if tomorrow they choose another four years of the Democrats, so be it.

Longwood looked up as Tom Stone, his campaign manager, pretended to knock on the metal bulkhead that separated the candidate's private compartment in the rear of the plane from the front of the aircraft, but the half knock was only a courtesy and Stone slid the thin gray curtain back and joined him without waiting for an answer. He slid into place in the double airplane seat directly facing Longwood without any further formalities.

Stone threw his legs up wearily on the empty seat next to the candidate and let the heels of his shoes crunch down disrespectfully on the thick computer printout under his feet.

Rather than say anything then, Stone took a long drink from the big glass of scotch and ice that he carried with him. "Don't blame yourself, Bill," the campaign manager said, but he didn't look at Longwood as he spoke.

"How bad do you think it will be?" Longwood said, without even bothering to check first at the opening to the private rear compartment to see if there was a reporter or a junior staff person standing nearby who might hear the gloomy assessment of their position.

Stone shrugged his shoulders. "It's not over," he said and took another drink of his scotch. When he looked up from his drink, Longwood's dark blue eyes were focused directly on his face and the Senator's expression was clearly ordering him to cut out the bullshit and level with him.

"Seven or eight points, no worse," Stone said in response, and Longwood turned his hard gaze away from him then. There was no more competent and realistic national politician in the Republican Party as far as Longwood was concerned, and the candidate only nodded his head and accepted what had become—over the final weeks of the campaign—the inevitable.

"Granderman worked damn hard," Longwood said wearily, remembering the grueling, seemingly endless months of campaigning that were behind them now. "Harder than I thought he was capable of," Longwood added with respect.

"Yes, he did," Stone said. "The country just wasn't buying it. They didn't see a nickel's worth of the difference between what Granderman was saying and what Cassidy and Gardner were already giving them. It was just the same old worn-out New Deal policies. So why change? You were the only one saying anything new out there, Bill," Stone said, gesturing out the airplane window at the country going by beneath the airplane.

Longwood nodded his head again, accepting Stone's words as a compliment. "I did what I thought had to be done," he said. "I think, at the very least, I influenced administration policy. I don't think that Gardner can do everything that he'd like to do now. For one thing, he's either going to have to fight this damn war or get out of it," Longwood said and then breathed out deeply. "At least that's something."

"It's a hell of a lot," Stone said, using the very lowest ranges of his deep, authoritarian voice to drive the point home to his friend. "Bill, without you the last three months wouldn't have been worth a damn to this country, but with you, it's a start."

"Perhaps," the Senator from Arizona said, and then he closed his eyes and listened to the low droning sound of the airplane's engines outside the window. He was too tired to take credit for very much that night. "God, I used to love flying," he said after a few minutes. "But I don't want to fly again now for a month."

"The job's not done yet," Stone said firmly, and then he moved his heavy, middle-aged body forward and toward the aisle so that he was looking directly at Longwood. "Nineteen sixty-eight begins tomorrow."

Longwood opened his eyes and stared across the narrow aisle at his campaign manager, hoping to find a clue to how the man could generate that kind of enthusiasm after the ordeal they'd both been through during the last few months, but all Longwood saw was Stone's short, brush-cut, gray hair and his heavyset middle-aged face. "Tom, for such a good politician, you're sure lousy at predictions. The only thing that starts tomorrow is November 8, 1964," Longwood said and then closed his eyes.

"Bill, we've been given a very precious gift and we can't waste it," Stone continued undeterred, his voice even more insistent than it had been. "The last three months have given us a chance to get all the kinks out of our little traveling circus here," Stone said, motioning with his glass of scotch up toward the front of the plane, where the rest of Longwood's campaign people were seated. And then Stone pointed a carefully manicured finger out at the candidate himself. "And the last three months have given you a chance to make a fool out of yourself once or twice at Marshall Granderman's expense, and not at your own. No one in this country will blame you for what's going to happen tomorrow. This was Marshall Granderman's campaign and he's finished in national politics now. For you, though, it could be just a dress rehearsal for 1968, but you're going to have to make that happen."

"You may be right, Tom, but all I really want right this moment is a good night's sleep."

"Bill, there's a flood of conservative feeling out there," Stone said, gesturing out below the plane again as he spoke. "And it's just waiting to be tapped. If you don't do it, it could be lost for another generation." Stone swept his hand out dramatically to make his point, but the campaign manager's grand gesture went unseen by Longwood, who had closed his eyes again and returned to visualizing not the White House, but his own Phoenix home.

After Stone had finished, Longwood only nodded again. "Tom, it's a good speech. In fact, it's one that I've given myself more than once, and I don't disagree with any of it—but I'm just saying, 'Not tonight.' Until at least this time tomorrow, I'm a candidate for the vice presidency of the United States on a ticket headed by Marshall Granderman, and until the voters settle that issue, once and for all, I just don't want to talk about any of this, all right?" Longwood sipped tentatively at his drink, which had now become more melted ice than a ten-year-old scotch.

"Okay, just promise me, though, that you'll think about it—that's all," Stone said and then kept his body forward, refusing to turn away from Longwood until the candidate gave him an answer.

"God, you are relentless," Longwood said finally. "All right, if that's the only way that you'll let me get any sleep, I promise that I will think about running . . ."

"Becoming," Stone cut Longwood off.

"Okay, fine, I'll think about becoming the President of the United States in the year of our Lord, nineteen hundred and sixty-eight. Satisfied?"

"No, Bill, I'm not satisfied at all," Stone said. "And I won't be until it actually happens and there are millions of Americans, who feel the same way I do, but I'll shut up for a while now and let you get some sleep."

"That'll do," Longwood said, setting his watered-down drink aside and then loosening his tie and letting the all-too-familiar drone of the big chartered airplane's engines lull him into what now seemed like only a temporary rest.

They could see the shoreline now, low and shadowy under the moonless sky, with the dense jungle growing right down to the waterline. Lopata stared nervously at the beach, his gaze darting from one end of the small cove that the launch was headed for to the other. Something was wrong. He could sense it. His body tensed as the man on the bridge above him cut the engine of their craft and let them drift toward the shore.

"We don't go any farther," the bearded man closest to Lopata said defiantly in Spanish. Lopata looked out at the shoreline again. It was still over a hundred yards away and the waves near the sides of the little boat were high and powerful. Lopata shook his head no. Their agreement was that he was to be taken ashore, not dumped in the surf a hundred yards from the coast. This wasn't Santa de Carine anyway, Lopata realized suddenly. They were several miles north of where he'd ordered them to land. "Where are we?"

"It is safer," the bearded man said. "There are patrols."

Lopata considered reaching for his revolver. It would settle the dispute, but the man could be right. It might be safer to wade ashore than to risk bringing the boat piloted by two frightened men in any closer to the coast at gunpoint. Lopata looked down at the water below him at the side of the boat. It was rough and choppy, surf slopping up over the edge of the little craft.

"It is very shallow, *señor*," the bearded man said.

Lopata thought of the last of his money and of the diary. They were both wrapped in oil paper and packed in a flight bag that he'd bought in Miami, but he couldn't risk getting either of them ruined by a miscalculation as he fought his way ashore in the treacherous surf.

"No," Lopata said and pointed ahead to a spot closer to the shoreline where two large rocks emerged from below the water and framed the entrance to the cove. As he looked, the sky exploded in bright golden light. He jerked his eyes up toward the bridge of the little ship. The sky above it was as bright as daylight. The man on the bridge had fired a flare and it was still spreading light as it lazily dropped back out of the night sky. Somewhere nearby, Lopata could hear the engines of a powerful boat closing in on them—then a warning shot. The man on the bridge had disappeared from view, but his flare gun still lay in full view where he'd dropped it at the side of the ship's wheel. Lopata looked quickly back down toward the lower deck. The bearded man was diving for cover behind the wall of the main cabin. There was still time to withdraw his weapon and perhaps fire a clear shot at the man's back, but Lopata decided against it. He'd been betrayed. These two men had probably sold him to Castro's people for a few dollars, but it wouldn't be smart to try to kill them, not now, not with his body outlined in the light of the flare. So, very slowly, Lopata turned back toward the sound of the approaching patrol boat. The flare had descended into the waves now, but its bright light had been replaced by a searchlight that lit up the deck of the little fishing boat around Lopata with a flood of bright yellow light. There was another gunshot, but Lopata guessed that it wasn't intended to hit him, but only as a warning.

In Spanish, a loudspeaker ordered him to drop the pistol that he held high in one hand now. Then the loudspeaker repeated the order in English. Lopata could see that there were two patrol boats closing on him, and one of them was very close. He had been a fool to think that he could come back here, he thought, as he stood frozen on the deck of the little launch. Lopata knew that government soldiers had their rifles pointed at him at that very moment. He dropped the pistol onto the deck of the ship and kept his hands high in the air in the full blinding glare of the searchlight.

Below him, wedged into the bow of the little fishing boat, Lopata could see the blue vinyl flight bag that he had carried with him since he'd left Dallas—his insurance policy he'd called it. Lopata looked down at the flight bag as the first of the government patrol boats closed on him. He could lift the bag with his foot, Lopata thought, and kick it over the side into the dark, choppy gulf waters below the little fishing boat. It might even be possible to do it without being seen from the deck of the approaching patrol boats. But should he do it? He edged his foot out until it was touching the handle of the bag, and he calculated the new odds that he faced. Arrested alone, by Castro's soldiers, without the diary, he was just a man returning illegally to his home, but he knew that there were those in Havana who would remember him from before the Revolution and who would guess at his true sympathies. He could easily be shot. With the diary, though, there might be a better chance, but he couldn't be certain.

One of the patrol boats was alongside now and the crew had thrown a rope around the fishing boat. Lopata felt the deck of the boat tremble as the first of Castro's soldiers leaped on board. He looked back down at the flight bag. It was now or never. There were things in Strode's diary that were very dangerous to him, particularly in the hands of Castro's people, but he was nothing to them. His testimony coupled with Strode's words, though, would be political dynamite in America and would be very useful to the new Cuba. He could tell a story dangerous to Castro's enemies, including the Cassidys themselves, a story of who had really conspired to murder the President of the United States and more important how and why—a story almost no one else left alive could tell. He unhooked his foot from around the plastic strap and left the blue bag alone at his feet for the soldiers to find. Within seconds the government soldiers were upon him, rifles pointed at his stomach and chest. He and the diary were both prisoners of the Cuban Revolutionary Government.

"You votin' today?" Sullivan asked. The voice of the Irish kid from Pennsylvania was beginning to take on a little touch of Texas twang.

"Is Summers running for anything?" Grissum said.

"Unh-unh. He doesn't have to, he owns the Bureau."

"I don't have to worry about it then," Grissum said.

"I am," Sullivan said. They were in one of the Bureau's no-frills, cream-colored cars, headed for an address in West Dallas on a routine security check. As always, Sullivan was at the wheel.

"You'll get over it," Grissum managed and Sullivan smiled at his partner. He knew that Grissum thought of him—that he was a political fanatic. "I didn't vote four years ago, but I want to make sure and do it this time, though," Sullivan said. "Do you know where I'm supposed to go or anything?"

Grissum used his thumb to slip the brim of his hat back, so that he could see the younger man's face clearly when he delivered the news to him. "Where'd you register?" Grissum asked, guessing the answer even before he asked it.

"Oh, shit!" Sullivan said. "I didn't know I was supposed to."

"You are," Grissum said. "You know, Sullivan, if you're going to try and save the world, you're going to have to learn the rules."

"I guess that means I can't vote."

"Guess so," Grissum mumbled, and he curled his body up in the passenger seat to try to get a little rest on what was left of the trip to West Dallas. "Fucking shame," he added, closing the discussion once and for all.

Lopata watched the metal tailgate close in front of him. Then he heard a padlock click loudly into place. A sour smell filled the rear of the crowded tarpaulin-covered military truck. Lopata tried to shift his face away from the rotten smell toward the opening at the back of the vehicle, but his wrist was handcuffed to one of the truck's interior supporting bars, and he couldn't move without feeling the steel of the cuffs biting into his flesh.

Lopata could feel the truck starting up again. There was no way to know why they'd stopped or why the tailgate had been lowered, maybe to give the men in the rear of the truck some air, he thought. If that had been the purpose though, it had been a failure. The foul smells of too many unwashed men crowded into too small a space still filled his nostrils.

The truck had been traveling all night and Lopata's body was wound in with the bodies of the other prisoners, all of them twisting and turning with every violent movement of the old army vehicle along the unpaved Cuban backroads. Occasionally during the long trip Lopata's body was flung up into the air and hurtled into the tangle of other handcuffed prisoners who were lined up around the walls of the truck bed or thrown back against the metal sides of the old Russian army vehicle, until his shoulders and ribs were bruised from the constant pounding. In the night, a man near him had thrown up, vomiting in the tight quarters onto his clothes and onto the floor of the truck beneath him, and during the hours before dawn, the vomit had soaked into Lopata's own clothing and into the clothes of the other men lying with him in the cold darkness.

As the first light of dawn began to filter in below the canvas tarp that covered the rear of the truck, Lopata hoped desperately that the trip that had started in the small seacoast jail near where he had been arrested was coming to an end. Even if all that was waiting for him at their destination was a firing squad, Lopata thought, the pain and horror of the long journey had to end soon.

Finally the truck began to slow. Lopata fought his way through the tangle of sweaty manacled prisoners and peered through the narrow opening below the canvas tarpaulin. He could see the outline of several low Quonset-hut-like buildings and around the perimeter of these squat gray buildings rose a high wire fence. The fence was capped with spiraling rolls of sharp barbed wire—Muiriel Prison. Lopata had guessed his destination during the night, and now his feeling was confirmed.

The truck slowed at the prison's main gate and Lopata could see his driver exchanging words with a uniformed guard. Then flashlights shone into the rear of the truck, illuminating the grim faces that had been assembled at the various stops on the journey up the coast. Lopata tried to raise his hands against the powerful light, but his wrist only strained against the metal shackles that bound him to the side of the vehicle.

The flashlights moved away and the truck began to roll slowly inside the prison gates and Lopata watched as the gates closed and locked behind him. He was a prisoner now in one of Castro's most feared prisons, without a trial, without being charged, without even being given a chance to use the money and Strode's diary to bargain for his freedom.

The truck rumbled down narrow dusty pathways past rows of the low barrackslike buildings, all with their windows barred and heavy iron locks on their doors. Soldiers in khaki uniforms lounged on the front steps of the locked barracks or in the shadows between the buildings. The soldiers had rifles slung across their shoulders or pistols in shiny leather holsters at their hips. The men's uniforms and their manner were familiar to Lopata. They reminded him of the days in Havana immediately after Castro had come to power. Although he wouldn't let it show on his face, Lopata was desperately frightened. He hadn't stayed in Havana for long after Castro had come to power. He had known what was coming for the new Premier's enemies, and he had the same feeling now. Justice in Castro's Cuba would be swift and final.

The truck stopped suddenly in front of a squat sprawling series of low buildings. The few temporary buildings that they had passed were at the very center of the camp, separated from the other buildings by a wide dirt clearing.

There was more waiting then, as one by one the men who had ridden with him during the night were led inside the first of the low buildings.

Several hours went by. More than once, Lopata thought that he could hear the sound of rifles firing in the distance. Even though he strained his ears to hear the sound, each time it was repeated he couldn't be certain of what it was. One thing that he was certain of though; none of the men who left the rear of the truck had returned.

Lopata waited until several hours after dawn for his turn to come. Finally his handcuffs were unlocked. The rear of the vehicle was almost empty as the soldiers pulled Lopata down on to the ground. He could feel a pistol barrel being pushed into his back and he stumbled along on knotted legs up the short path and into the building where the others had gone before him.

Inside the building a young Cuban man in clean starched khakis sat behind a metal desk. The insignias on the collar of the young man's uniform indicated that he was a captain in the Revolutionary Army, and the small black-and-white plate on his desk had the word COMMANDANT imprinted on it.

Lopata stood staring straight ahead at the front of the room until the commandant signaled for him to approach his desk. The building's interior space was long and narrow and badly lit and it wasn't until Lopata was halfway across it that he saw a soldier standing in the shadows behind the young man at the desk. Lopata stopped a few feet in front of the two men.

The commandant examined Lopata carefully. Then he unbuttoned the flap on the shiny black leather holster that he wore at his hip and removed his pistol from it. Lopata recognized the make and model of the Russian-made pistol. "Leave!" the commandant ordered with a flick of his pistol barrel at the guard standing in the shadows at the side of the room.

With a second wave of his gun barrel, he gestured for Lopata to sit in the single folding metal chair that faced the desk.

Lopata moved across the room to the metal chair and awkwardly managed to sit down with his manacled hands still clasped behind him, the steel of the handcuffs cutting into his flesh with every movement of his body. As he sat down, he could hear the door closing behind him. They were alone now.

There was a long silence. In the tense, soundless space of time, Lopata could see only the open wide mouth of the commandant's pistol. It was held in a relaxed hand, but the barrel was dropped and pointed directly at Lopata's stomach. To Lopata, the man behind the desk had no face, no features, just a uniform with a pistol barrel protruding dangerously from it. Lopata could feel his entire body being possessed by a numbing fear. He thought again of the sound of explosions that he had heard earlier while he'd waited outside in the back of the truck. Had they come from this pistol? He wanted to look around the place where he sat now, at the floor beneath the chair or at the wall behind his head. He wanted to see if there were signs of splattered blood, but his eyes refused to leave the barrel of the gun even for a moment, because he feared in that instant it would explode and the muzzle would flash with bright red-yellow flame. He kept his eyes trained only on it while the young commandant studied him in their mutual silence.

Lopata's own long-barreled .38 pistol lay in front of the young lieutenant. The shells had been removed from its chamber and lay alongside it. On the table next to the weapon was Lopata's blue vinyl flight bag, its contents scattered on the desktop, with Strode's diary lying at the very center of it, in front of the commandant.

In the distance, somewhere out on the dusty parade field, Lopata heard a rumbling sound like little pops of distant thunder. He looked up at the lieutenant's face. Its thin features were set hard as he stared grimly back across the desk. Apparently, Lopata thought, he was to get his trial, and his sentencing, and perhaps even his final punishment, now.

Kit could sense that something was wrong as she walked up the unlit front path to her apartment. She turned back to say something to her date, but he was already peeling out in his sports car, shooting up gravel and dirt under its spinning wheels as he pulled away. It was his way of showing his anger because she hadn't invited him in, Kit decided, as she watched the little red Porsche pull out of sight. Well, screw him anyway, she decided and turned back toward her front door. It wasn't worth it just to get a safe escort to your door to let all your standards down. If she started letting creeps like that take advantage of her, what the hell chance was there that she'd ever land anybody really worth having? She hurried up the path toward her apartment. Anyway, Denise and the kids would be back from the movie anytime now and there was no use getting started with something and then just having to stop. Maybe she should get her own place, she thought, as she fumbled in her purse for her key. But things were so expensive. She looked behind her then into the dark Dallas night. God, something was wrong. She could feel it in her bones, as her mother used to say. She found the key and forced it into the lock. "Thank God," she said out loud as she fell inside her darkened apartment. She relocked the door from the inside and double-locked it with the chain before she even reached up for the light.

She crossed the living room quickly and turned the television on loud for company. The newscaster's familiar voice made her feel better and she stood for a moment and listened, trying to breathe regularly again and regain the composure that she had lost on the trip up the path to her front door. The newscaster was announcing the first election returns from the East Coast, and the early indications were that a Texan was finally going to be elected President of the United States.

"Yoo, hee!" Kit did her own version of a rebel yell to relieve her tension. "Looks like we've got our first Texas President," she said out loud, making her voice as cheerful as she could, but there was still a strange uneasiness deep in the pit of her stomach. She left the television playing as she started into her bedroom to change clothes. Maybe she'd stay up and watch the election returns for a while, at least until Denise got home, she thought, as she reached around the door to her bedroom for the light switch before she walked inside.

There was a knock on the front door then, a scratching, muffled sound. The sound frightened her, but she turned to it and crossed the living room and stood by the front door. "Denise?" There was no answer. Kit walked to the window and moved the curtain aside. Oh, him, she thought, as she recognized the figure at the front door. What the hell did he want? She glanced at her watch as she moved back to the door. It was after eleven. She slid the chain lock aside and then undid the bolt lock. The door opened quickly then and a powerful black-gloved hand sealed off her mouth and nose. Her first scream was lost against the tightly pressed hand.

Oh, dear merciful God, Kit thought suddenly. She had always been afraid that something like this might happen to her, but now that it was really happening it seemed impossible. She had never guessed that it could be this way.

She started to scream again, but the powerful gloved hands tightened their hold, cracking bones at the base of her neck with their relentless strength. The sickening cracking sound filled Kit's mind with horror and then overwhelming pain. But even in her terror, she began to search her memory for the things that she had planned to do in such a moment. Don't fight back, she remembered from somewhere, and she tried to make her body go limp in the figure's powerful hands. She wouldn't struggle if he ripped her clothes away and began to rape her, she decided, her mind racing.

But it wasn't rape that the figure had come for that night, and Kit's relaxing neck and throat collapsed easily under the figure's powerful hands. Her neck snapped loudly, but she never heard the final noise, as blood rushed clumsily up and filled her brain with darkness.

The figure let the body slump to the floor then, and Kit's dress slid up, exposing pure white thighs and a small neat patch of dark black pubic hair. The figure knelt down next to her then and thrust first one gloved finger into her vagina and then a second extended finger. He moved the fingers of the gloved hand roughly in and out several times, but his face showed no emotion. The exercise was just part of the figure's carefully conceived plan, a cover for the police and medical examiners to ponder, and he moved his fingers in and out only long enough to open the vaginal canal. He walked across the living room and removed a wine bottle from its place on the dining-room table. He poured its contents onto the floor. Then he returned to the young girl's body and thrust the greenish-colored glass neck of the bottle up deep inside the opening that he had made between the girl's legs.

The figure stood and began searching the apartment in a thorough and highly professional manner. When he was finished with Kit's bedroom, he crossed the short hall and began the same procedure in Denise's bedroom. Finally, he found what he was looking for in a jewelry box in a far corner of her closet.

He used a set of skeleton keys to try the lock on the heavy fabric bag. Finally, one of them worked and the lock fell away. Inside the bag was a single manila file. The figure removed the file and glanced briefly at its contents. The name Strode, Arthur Allen, was typed neatly on its front tab. The figure folded the file and placed it in the inside pocket of his coat. Then he returned to the living room. He overturned chairs and pulled out drawers, spilling their contents on the floor, taking a few objects at random and placing them in his pocket as he worked his way through the living room to the dining room and kitchen. There would be more than enough for the police to ponder now, he thought, as he surveyed the chaos that he'd created in the small apartment.

Suddenly headlights flashed on the curtained living-room windows and the figure crossed the room quickly and moved the curtains aside just enough to see down the short path that led to the apartment's parking area. Somebody was coming!

Denise's daughter felt heavy in her arms and her little sleeping face was pressed up tightly against the softness of her chest. Without saying anything, Denise bent down and let her son reach into her purse for the key to the front door. She waited under the porch light with her daughter in her arms while her son fumbled with the key in the lock. "Come on," she said, and finally the key turned and the door opened several inches, but then caught against something. Denise stepped forward toward the partially opened door and called out for Kit. Inside she could hear the television playing loudly. Her daughter was getting unbearably heavy, and she called out again. Denise turned her body and leaned against the door, but it still refused to open wide enough to let her pass. What the hell was it? "Kit!" she called out again, but there was no answer, just the sound of the television set coming from the living room. She could guess what Kit was doing up in there. She turned back to the driveway, looking for Kit's date's car, but she didn't see it.

"Wait here," she said and set her daughter down on her feet. The little girl looked up sleepily at her mother, not understanding. "I'm going to try to get in the back," Denise said. "Let me, Mom," her son said, but Denise had already turned and started around the side of the building. She could hear her son's footsteps behind her. "No! You wait with your sister right here," she said then, pointing back angrily at the front doorstep.

Denise felt a little frightened as she walked around the side of the apartment in the dark. She came first to Kit's window and considered knocking on it for a moment, but then she didn't. That would be kind of rude, she thought, and instead she continued on to her own room. The screen was off and the window was open. Denise froze in fear. She turned then and looked behind her. The apartment's grounds were dark and silent.

In a panic, she scrambled up onto the window ledge and slid inside. Even in the darkness she could see that her bedroom was a shambles. She stood for a moment in the darkened room, her legs shaking in fear, her heart pounding wildly. She could hear the faint muffled sounds of the television set in the apartment's living room. "Kit!" Denise called out, but there was no answer. "Kit!" She rushed through the darkness of the bedroom, stepping over tangles of her clothes and other belongings until she hurtled headlong into the hallway and finally into the living room. She saw Kit then, her body lying wedged up against the front door, her head at a strange, unnatural angle.

Denise began to scream, but then, remembering her children, she managed to control her fear, and she stood silently looking down at Kit's mutilated body. Behind her on the loudly playing television set, Denise could hear a newscaster declaring that Ransom W. Gardner from the state of Texas had just been elected the thirty-sixth President of the United States.

PART FOUR

September 1967—November 1967

CHAPTER
24

A large crowd of reporters and cameramen waited on the Capitol steps for the most celebrated member of the Senate Class of 1966 to return to Washington and begin the second year of his new term as the Junior Senator from the State of Massachusetts. Promptly at 8 A.M., eastern standard time, just as it had been announced, a long black limousine pulled up in front of the Capitol and John Trewlaney Cassidy, looking tanned and healthy, stepped out of its back seat.

"Welcome back," a reporter called from the rear of the crowd.

"Thank you, Larry," Cassidy acknowledged the reporter, with a big smile and a wave of his hand. Questions began coming then from every direction.

This is a hell of a lot different from the polite, orderly presidential press conferences of a few years earlier, Cassidy thought, as he looked around the Capitol steps at the reporters who surrounded him. They all seemed to be shouting questions at once, clamoring to get his attention. It had been almost a year since the voters of his home state had returned him to the Senate, but during that time Cassidy had chosen to remain quiet about several important issues. It was apparent though, from the excitement caused by his return to Washington after Congress's summer recess, that the nation's reporters were hoping that the new Senate year would bring with it a more vocal Jack Cassidy.

"How does it feel to be back?" someone shouted.

"I'm very happy to be back in Washington and so is my family. We've been away too long," Jack said. Then he added, "Although there are those who would probably disagree with that."

"Don't you think there are enough Cassidys in Washington already?" asked

335

a young reporter who had managed to elbow his way to the front of the crowd. And then he stared boldly at Cassidy, waiting for his answer.

Jack smiled at him for a moment, timing out his reply for the proper effect. "No," he said finally. "No, I don't, and apparently neither did the voters of the State of Massachusetts."

He started into the crowd of reporters then and began to make his way up the white marble steps that led to the Senate rotunda.

"Senator, have you been satisfied with the support that the administration has given you since you've left the White House?" a reporter shouted up the steps at him. Cassidy stopped and turned back to face the questioner. "Vice President Cassidy has been a big supporter of mine," Jack answered, still smiling.

"But the President has seemed less than enthusiastic about your return to Washington. Do you have any comment about that?"

"President Gardner has far more to worry about than Junior Senators from New England," Cassidy said before continuing up the marble steps toward the Senate building.

"How has it been serving as the Junior Senator, when your younger brother is the Senior Senator from Massachusetts?"

Jack stopped again and turned back to the crowd of reporters for a second time. "I feel that Senator Cassidy and I should be able to continue to work very closely together." He smiled.

"Are you going to continue to support the administration's Southeast Asia policies?" The smile faded from Cassidy's face, and he paused for several seconds before he tried to answer. The crowd quieted and Jack could hear the sound of television cameras whirring nearby as the film crews waited to capture his answer for the evening news.

"I intend to continue to support the administration in every way that I can," Cassidy said, as he had since his surprise entry into the Massachusetts Senate race the year before. Despite his caution, the differences between his own and President Gardner's Southeast Asia policies had begun to be apparent to the public.

"What does that mean?" someone called out to him, but he didn't say anything further. He pressed his way through the remainder of the crowd and up the remaining steps of the Capitol building. There was more to say, much more, but now wasn't the place or the time. He was just a Junior Senator returning to the Capitol for the new term, a good soldier in the administration's congressional army, and he would leave it that way for now.

"Do you plan to run for President in 1968?" The question that had followed him almost from the first moment that he'd left the White House was shouted up the stone steps at him as he tried to walk away. Cassidy continued on up the steps toward the rotunda, without turning back to give the reporters and their television cameras the same practiced reply that he had grown tired of hearing himself give over the last three years, but inside his head he formulated the familiar answer that he'd responded with so many times before. I have no political plans or intentions at this time, other than to serve a full term in the United States Senate, he told himself again, but even as he did, he wasn't certain if he even believed it himself anymore.

There were photographs spread out covering almost every inch of the President's desk. There were pictures of schools, a variety of crude manufacturing plants, airstrips, dams, and bridges, and seemingly endless jungle trails filled with soldiers, and supplies, and truck convoys.

Behind the President's desk and blocking out the Oval Office windows were a pair of multicolored terrain maps resting on twin wooden easels. During the meeting that had just ended, the men who had been seated in a tight semicircle around the President's desk would occasionally stand and walk to one of the maps and carefully check a location on it, but the President had only turned to the map once during the entire day-long meeting. He hadn't needed to. He knew the geography of Vietnam by heart. It was burned into his memory. He knew almost all of the strange Asian names of each of its towns right down to the tiniest villages. He knew where and how the rivers ran, and precisely how and when they changed course during the rainy season. He knew the jungle trails and the major highways and he knew whether they were paved or dirt, and approximately how wide each of them was, and what their capacity was for transporting supplies and for moving troops. He knew where the seaports were and what the tonnage "in" and "out" was on a seasonal basis. He knew the populations of the villages and what percentage of the people were said to be civilian and what percentage reported as military. He knew, too, where the civilians lived in reference to the major roads, manufacturing plants, and storage facilities, where the schools were, the hospitals. Ransom W. Gardner of East Texas knew more about this tiny Southeast Asian country than he did about his own home state.

The President was alone now. The men who had filled his office during the day and early evening, bending over the maps and photographs, pointing at the strategic spots, asking each other questions and reading reports since early that morning, were all gone. The last one to leave had been the Secretary of Defense. Secretary Forbes had remained over the conference table, making last-minute notes on the final listing of bombing targets for the following week, long after the others had left the room, but finally he, too, had gone, leaving the President with the final typed list with the Secretary's notes in black ink along the margin, the list that specified where, when, and how American planes, piloted by American pilots, would drop American bombs on the people of this other country located half a world away.

Gardner looked down at the final list of targets. It had been compiled with precision and compassion. Enormous care had been taken to balance the need to protect the enemy's civilian population with the need to destroy its capacity to wage an effective war. The list required only one last thing to set the events that it called for into operation.

As the President looked down at the list for what had to be at least the hundredth time that day, the page began to blur before his eyes and his head began to throb with pain. He dropped the single sheet of paper onto his desktop and removed his wire-frame glasses and twirled them for a moment between his thumb and forefinger. Then he let the glasses drop onto the desk as well. He remembered that he hadn't eaten anything in hours, but his stomach was churning and he was afraid that he wouldn't be able to eat even if he tried.

He moved his chair in a half circle to look out his office window at the lights of the Capitol behind him, but the high easeled maps blocked his view. All he could see was Southeast Asia. Suddenly he felt trapped, alone in an oppressive room, and a wave of fear began spreading through him, starting deep in his stomach and then spreading quickly up to his chest and head. He whirled around in his desk chair. Other empty chairs, vacated less than an hour earlier by his advisers, stood everywhere in the room, barring his way to the door. He was a prisoner at his own desk, trapped by chairs and easels and photographs and papers and maps. He tried to breathe in deeply to regain his composure, but the strong smell of cigarette ashes and stale cigar butts that littered the ashtrays of his office filled his lungs. He could feel himself choking. He loosened his tie from around his throat and he began gasping for air. There was a long row of buttons mounted on a wooden panel on the underside of his desk. He reached out and pushed one of the buttons several times, and within seconds a servant entered the room.

The President forced his voice to remain calm as he asked for a diet soda and a bottle of aspirin. He watched then as the white-jacketed servant left the office. He would be all right, Gardner told himself, with the aspirin he would feel better soon. It would be all right this time, but he had to start taking better care of himself. He reached down for his wire-frame glasses and stretched the frame back, hooking their stems carefully over each ear. He started through the list again, but the words no longer made any real sense to him. He reached up with a reluctant hand and wrote at the bottom of the page: "Approved, President Ransom W. Gardner, September 10, 1967."

He slid the paper away from his body and let the pen drop from his hand. He turned to the map behind him and looked again at the places with the strange Asian names that he and his advisers had chosen for destruction. Great things, he repeated to himself. I came to the presidency to do great things.

"Come here often, stranger?" Sullivan recognized the voice, but it had been a long time. He turned and was shocked at what he saw—shocked and very pleased. Denise looked terrific. Her face was thin and lightly tanned and she was dressed stylishly in a red wool dress that stopped several inches above her knees. Her hair was cut short and brushed back playfully from her face, like the models in the fashion magazines, Sullivan thought. Gold earrings in the shape of a circle and cross, the peace sign of the antiwar movement, dangled from her ears, and another peace medallion hung on a gold chain from her neck. Sullivan followed the necklace down to the low-cut front of her dress, where her lightly freckled chest appeared above the bright red fabric. "Denise?"

"Thank you," Denise said, and Sullivan became aware of the fact that he was staring at her, staring and blinking his eyes a little to make certain that he was seeing what he thought he was seeing.

"I do look good, don't I?" Denise said, smiling confidently.

How long had it been? Sullivan's mind raced to remember, but he gave up counting months when they passed a year and began approaching a second one. He felt too embarrassed to go any further.

"It's good to see you," Denise said and reached out and touched the top of his hand.

Sullivan nodded back. "Me too."

Sullivan slid down off his bar stool. "Should we find a table?"

"I don't think there are any," Denise said, looking around at the floor of the crowded singles' bar. It was full of young Texas men and women in a noisy, Monday, after-work mood.

As she turned from Sullivan to survey the crowded festive room, he let his gaze slide down Denise's back to her waist and hips. The red wool dress clung tightly to her body.

"Fifteen pounds and holding, since you saw me last," Denise said as she turned back and found Sullivan still looking at her admiringly.

"Jesus, sit down," Sullivan said, standing up to offer Denise the bar stool. Denise slipped by him then, letting her body brush lightly against his.

"You know, usually I don't like all the hippie stuff and things," Sullivan said, looking down at the peace earrings and then at Denise's short skirt that moved up well above her knees as she sat down in front of him.

Denise only laughed. "Jim, I'm not a hippie," she said. "I'm just against the war, aren't you?"

Sullivan didn't answer right away. "I don't know," he said. "The government's probably doing the right thing. I guess," he added, without any real conviction in his voice.

"And the dress is just the style now," Denise said. And then, looking out at the sea of young men and women crowded into the little singles' bar, she smiled and added, "Even in Dallas."

"I know," Sullivan said, feeling even more embarrassed than he had before. He could see Denise looking now at his dark gray suit and shiny narrow tie. The crowd shifted and someone bumped his shoulder and Sullivan had to step up close to Denise to keep his footing. He looked at her face only inches away from his. After a moment had passed between them, Denise began moving her head from side to side, making an exaggerated search for something.

"What is it?" Sullivan asked.

"I'm just looking for a wedding ring on you," Denise said, her head still bobbing around, inspecting Sullivan's hand.

"Who, me?" Sullivan said, sounding surprised. "No, nothing," he added, holding up his left hand so that she could see the empty ring finger.

"Me, too," Denise said, holding up the empty fingers on her own left hand. "My divorce is finally final though."

"Well, what? Congratulations?" Sullivan said, his awkwardness continuing. "About the divorce, I mean."

"Thank you." Denise smiled. "I've got a new job too, and a new apartment," she added.

"Jesus, new woman, huh?"

"I'm trying," Denise said, looking away from Sullivan, her smile turning shy. "I really am trying," she added in a low, sincere voice.

They were both quiet for a while then, not knowing what to say to each other. "Jim," Denise said finally, "why did you stop calling?"

"I felt guilty, I guess," he said, shifting his gaze away from her in embarrassment.

"About what happened to Kit?" Denise said. "Jim, there was nothing for you to be guilty about. There were five robberies and God knows how many assaults in that apartment complex last year. That's why I moved, that and . . ." Denise couldn't finish and her voice broke off.

"That and the old apartment reminded you of Kit," Sullivan said. "You did the right thing."

"Yeah, I know I did," Denise said. "But God, that was no reason for you to stop calling."

Sullivan shrugged his shoulders. "I read the police reports. I felt bad that you had to lie."

"Jim, I didn't lie," Denise said. "They just didn't ask."

"You mean, the police didn't ask?" Sullivan stopped for a moment, looking around the crowded bar to make certain that no one could overhear him. When he began again, he dropped the level of his voice to a confidential half whisper. "They didn't ask if you had any stolen FBI files hidden in your apartment?"

"Bad police work, huh?" Denise said, smiling gently. "Jim, what happened to Kit was just a terrible accident. It could have happened to anyone. It didn't have anything to do with you, or your file. So please don't blame yourself. That's not fair to either of us."

Sullivan set his beer down. "Walk?" Denise gathered up her purse and followed Sullivan's lead through the maze of bodies in the crowded bar.

Alone on the street, they began walking west toward the center of the city. After they'd continued on in silence for several seconds, Sullivan finally turned back to her. "I shouldn't tell you this," Sullivan said, "but I figure you have a right to know." He paused then, weighing what he felt that he had to say to her against the rule never to disclose confidential Bureau information to an outsider. "Right after it happened, I told my bureau chief about the file," he said. "And he reviewed the police reports on it. He even did a little investigating on his own."

"And?" Denise asked.

"And nothing," Sullivan said. "He couldn't find any connection to Strode's file, or to me, or to anything else connected to the Bureau."

"See, what did I tell you?" Denise said, but Sullivan's face still didn't look satisfied. "What is it?" Denise asked.

Sullivan shrugged his shoulders again. "Nothing. It was just a robbery, I guess. The Bureau came to the same conclusion as the police did, that's all there is to it."

"That's not all," Denise insisted. "What aren't you telling me?"

"Well, it's just that whoever it was, Kit probably let him in to the apartment herself. I would have thought she'd be more careful than that," Sullivan said. "It's still an open case, too," he added. "They never did find the guy who did it."

"Is that so unusual?"

"No," Sullivan admitted. "I don't know. The other part that bothers me, I guess, is that whoever it was took the jewelry box with Strode's file in it. I just don't know why anybody would do that."

"Mistake," Denise said, shrugging her shoulders. "He could have thought there was something more valuable in it—and when he found out he was wrong, he probably just burned the file without even reading it."

"Maybe so."

"What is it, really?" Denise stopped and took Sullivan by the arm, not allowing him to go any further without really talking to her. Sullivan stopped then and looked down for the first time directly at Denise's pale blue eyes. There was more strength and intelligence in them than he remembered, he thought, as he looked at her up close again. "It's just that I'm not really very good at any of this. I was kidding myself when I thought I could make a difference on something as big as what happened to Cassidy," Sullivan said, shrugging his shoulders helplessly. "Realizing that about myself has changed me a little, I guess. Anyway, I made a little deal with Yancey. Nothing formal or anything, but we understand each other all right. I stop worrying about cases that I'm not assigned to and . . ." Sullivan paused then, embarrassed about the rest of it. "And I get my own section."

"Congratulations," Denise said.

"Well, it hasn't happened yet." Sullivan held his hand out toward Denise to slow her down. "A slot has to open up first and that could be a while still, but I've held to my part of the bargain—and in a couple of more months, a year at the most . . ." Sullivan let his voice trail off then. "It would be small, probably only five or six agents at first, but I'd be pretty young to get it," he added a moment later. "And it could lead to a real career in the Bureau for me. That's something I've always wanted."

"Your parents will be happy," Denise said.

"Yeah, they are. It's for the best." Sullivan nodded in agreement. "I mean, if half of what I was working on was right, if there really was a conspiracy or something, it would be so damn big, so many powerful people—" Sullivan stopped then. "Who the hell did I think I was, anyway?" He turned away from Denise and started walking again, west toward the very center of the city. Suddenly he realized that Dealey Plaza itself was less than a block directly in front of him.

Denise stood for a second, looking at him walk away before she called out to him. "I don't believe you!"

Sullivan stopped when he heard her, and he turned back and watched as Denise took a few running steps, closing the distance between them. "I don't believe you really think that about yourself," she said as she caught up with him. "I think, deep down, with or without your big promotion, you're still as crazy as ever." Denise paused. "You just need someone to remind you, that's all."

"You do, huh?" Sullivan said, trying to remain stern, but finding Denise's smile irresistible. "How are your kids?" Sullivan asked.

"Horrible," Denise said, laughing at her own honesty.

"Is Danny still kicking up a storm at all your boyfriends?"

"I don't have any boyfriends, not really," she said, her light blue eyes open and honest.

"Me neither," Sullivan said, returning her look. "Or girlfriends either," he added. "I've kind of turned into a loner in a lot of ways, I guess. Maybe it's Texas," he said. He looked away from her then, feeling embarrassed by his confession. Where he came from a man was expected to have friends, to be "one of the boys." Sullivan wasn't, and he hadn't been since at least November of 1963, but he'd never admitted it to anyone else before.

"But I guess it's just lonely at the top, right?" he said with a false smile. Denise could see the embarrassment and pain and disappointment in his eyes. She reached out toward him then and laid her hand on top of his. "Jim, let's be friends again."

He started to answer her, but the words caught in his throat, so he just nodded his head instead. "Uh-uh," he managed finally. "Yes, definitely," he said and then looked away shyly.

"So what did the big bad Bureau of Investigation do to you for stealing their file?" Denise said, taking the broad-shouldered agent by the arm and leading him back up the street.

"Not much. That's when Yancey sat me down and offered me his deal. They take care of their own, or so they say," Sullivan said. Then he added, a little sadly, "I just had to promise in blood that I'd be a good boy, that's all."

"And have you been?"

Sullivan shrugged his broad shoulders, but Denise was holding on to him so tightly that the powerful movement failed to dislodge her grasp, and they continued on together down the Dallas street toward Dealey Plaza in the distance.

* * *

On the night that they returned to the capital after the summer recess, Jack and Suzanne had dinner alone in the house that they'd rented in Georgetown. They'd spent the last year commuting back and forth from Boston to Washington, staying in hotels or at Tim's home outside Washington, but over the summer Suzanne had found a place for them. It was less than a mile from their first home that they'd lived in after the war, when Jack had come to Washington as a first-term Congressman from Boston.

Their new brick-fronted home was at the crest of a slight hill, and from their dining room, through the lightly misting rain that was falling that night, they could see the lights of Washington spread out below them.

"It really is a beautiful city, isn't it?" Suzanne said, and Jack nodded his agreement. "Are you happy to be back?" he asked, and Suzanne only smiled, the answer apparent in the peaceful beauty of her face. She looked particularly radiant that night, Jack thought, as he looked across the small dining-room table at his wife's shining dark brown eyes. "It must be the lights from the city," he said out loud, smiling at her.

"What must be?" she asked.

"Nothing," Jack said.

"Do you know how many invitations I had to turn down in order to arrange a private dinner alone with you, Senator?" Suzanne asked.

"Do you miss them?" Jack said.

"No, not at all," Suzanne answered. "This is one of the nicest nights I've had in a very long time."

They sat for a moment and Jack poured a cup of coffee and held the container toward her, but she shook her head no. "It's a whole new life for us, isn't it?" he said, sipping tentatively at the hot coffee.

Suzanne reached out and placed her hand on top of her husband's. "I've always loved Georgetown." She turned her gaze from her husband's to look out the window at the view of the city lights twinkling through the drifting rain. "It reminds me of when we were first married."

"And when we were young," Jack said.

"Younger," Suzanne corrected him. "You want to know a secret? I like being a Senator's wife, too," she said. "It's like having a second chance at life somehow, a different one, but maybe even a better one—who knows?" She paused then, thinking about the day that she'd spent alone. "I went walking today, after lunch," she said. "It may sound silly. It was so simple. I just put on a coat and walked right out the front door and down Jackson, all the way to the river. I walked all by myself for almost an hour. It felt wonderful. It felt like the whole city, the people, the buildings, the trees, and even the air were all created just for me and nobody else." She paused then and looked at her husband. "I never felt like that when we were in the White House. I always felt like the city belonged to everyone else but me, and that I belonged to the city somehow, a little like one of the monuments, always on display, always open to the public. After a while it was almost impossible for me to know what was really important."

"And now?" Jack asked.

"Oh, and now I know," Suzanne said. She stopped then and breathed in deeply. "The whole day and I didn't see one reporter."

"No, the reporters were all busy tracking me down, I think," Jack said.

"Being a Senator's wife is good for you, isn't it?" Jack added then, studying his wife's relaxed face as the firelight played across it. "I don't know when I've seen you looking more beautiful. It has more proportion for you somehow than being the First Lady."

Suzanne smiled, agreeing with her husband's words.

"You're such a snob," Jack said, laughing gently at her. "What other woman in the world would be so damn exclusive that she would prefer being a Senator's wife to being the First Lady of the United States? Only you."

"What is it, Jack?" Suzanne pressed, sensing that there was something that her husband was holding back.

"The war?" Suzanne said, guessing now.

Jack nodded his head. "I feel like I'm a prisoner of it sometimes," he said, as he felt his wife's fingers press against his hand. "There's so much that I want to say publicly, but I feel that I can't." Jack stopped then, not wanting to go over it all again.

"What are you going to do?" Suzanne asked.

"I love being here with you," her husband said quietly, not answering Suzanne's question.

"I see. You're going to be mysterious even with me," Suzanne said. "Well, I can be mysterious, too." She looked away from him.

"I do like being a Senator's wife," she said, before her husband could ask her what she had meant by her secretive answer. "It's more real somehow. Not that I would expect you to fully understand. It's hard work making me into a real Cassidy, isn't it?"

"I've given up trying," Jack said. "I think we're just going to have to take each other the way we are," he said, finishing the last of his coffee and beginning to push his way back from the table. "Shall we go straight to bed," he added, reaching out his hand for hers, his meaning unmistakable.

"Yes, as long as you understand that kind of thing has consequences," she said, gesturing back toward their bedroom. And there was something in the way that she'd said the words and in the enigmatic smile that spread across her face that made Jack realize that there was something else going on.

"What is it?" he said, looking at her for clues.

"I told you, Jack," she said. "I feel thirty years old today, maybe even twenty-five," she added, secure with her secret. "I love Georgetown," she said, delaying her news even more. "I think we're going to be very happy here, don't you?" Suzanne said, smiling at her husband and drawing out her power over him as fully as she dared. "All of us," she said then, finally snapping out the punchline, after a short pause, like a good comedienne.

"Oh, my God!" the Junior Senator from Massachusetts said. "You're going to have a baby." He blurted out the words and then immediately felt a little foolish and a little in awe of the woman who sat across from him now, her eyes shining with happiness. "We're going to have a child."

Thirty-three months was a very long time to stay alive at Muiriel Prison; dysentery killed almost as many prisoners as suicide and murder and the official executions combined. He was one of the lucky ones. Lopata lay on his bunk in the dark, looking up at the wooden slats and coiled metal springs of the bunk bed above him, and he laughed at the thought. Lucky one? He was alive, but he was too weak even to roll his body onto its side. He lay flat on the hard prison bed and tried to force his stomach muscles to relax against the pressure of the wave of stomach cramps that had awakened him a few minutes earlier, but the peace lasted only for a few seconds before he had to raise his body with the next wave of cramping. And then he was on his feet, working his way down the line of beds to the door at the rear of the barracks. A few yards behind the barracks a canvas tarpaulin had been stretched around a series of open pits dug in the hard Cuban soil of Muiriel. Lopata half walked, half ran to the latrine, unbuttoning his pants as he threw the flap on the canvas tarp aside. The smell inside the latrine was overpowering and he moved only as close to the edge of the first hole as he dared. Then, letting his pants drop below his knees, he squatted down in the darkness. The dysentery and fever that he had managed to avoid for so long had finally caught up with him. Flies buzzed around his face as his body wretched in agony over the filthy open pit. He hadn't slept through the night in weeks. The dysentery brought with it severe dehydration, and Lopata lightly touched the skin of his arm as he rested for a moment between his body's painful wretching spasms, and the skin felt as dry as old parchment to his touch. A few moments later, he cleaned himself as best he could with a small slip of oily paper that he had managed to scrounge earlier in the day. Then he dropped the paper into the filthy pit behind him, being very careful not to turn and look at the open latrine hole even in the darkness. He knew that the sight of its contents coupled with the nauseating smells coming from it trapped in the hot, motionless night air of the enclosed area would make him feel even sicker. Instead he fixed his gaze on the olive-drab canvas that surrounded the latrine and pulled his pants back up, buttoning them slowly with his weary, dehydrated fingers. The pants buttoned easily over his waist, and the prison clothes, an army shirt and pants without insignias that he'd been given that first morning, hung down loosely over his emaciated body.

This couldn't go on, Lopata thought, as he shuffled toward the canvas flap that served as a door to the latrine. He was getting weaker by the day now, but the medical care at Muiriel was almost nonexistent, and only the very weakest prisoners were even permitted to stay behind in the barracks, while the others went off on work details. He would be dead in another few months at the very most, he decided as he touched the fevered skin of his arm again.

Lopata paused on the low cement step that led back into the barracks for a few seconds before he walked inside. As he thought about it now, Lopata wished that he had been shot that first morning, taken into the high weeds at the end of the parade field at the rear of the commandant's office and shot just like so many others that he had seen in Muiriel since that first day. But something had stopped the commandant from doing it. He had stared at Lopata's face for a long time after the prisoner had finished telling his story. And then, while Lopata waited, a statement had been typed up containing everything that Lopata had said during the interrogation and Lopata had signed it. Nothing in the commandant's manner had betrayed whether he believed the contents of the statement or not, but finally he had taken both the statement and the red leather diary that had been Strode's and dropped them into the manila file marked with Lopata's name. He'd called for the guard and Lopata's life had been spared, but for what? To die in the narrow lower bunk in Barracks 9 that had been his home ever since? Had he told the story the right way? he asked himself as he had so many times before. Should he have told only the truth? Or should he have pretended to know more? Pretended to have actually been one of the planners of Cassidy's execution? But they wouldn't have believed that. Should he have given the names of those who had recruited him? Maybe even gone back to the very beginning and told the commandant about the conversations he'd had with Strode, that first time they'd met during their early training? There was so much more he could tell them, if he only had another chance. He could tell them about the lawyer in New Orleans, and about the woman who had been General Martine's widow, and all the rest of it. The story he could reveal to the world would rock the American government and end the Cassidy family's power forever. That was his only hope now, the only thing that helped him to stay alive—that somehow Havana would come to an understanding of his value to their cause. But for all he knew the diary and his signed statement could still be locked away inside the commandant's desk. All he could be certain of was that he was alive, but for how long? How much longer could he stay alive on such slender hope? But there was something else, he reminded himself grimly. There was still Cassidy to live for. As long as Cassidy was alive there was a reason for him to continue to live as well.

The television screen showed an old, low stone wall. American Marines squatted behind it in the bloodstained dirt of what had once been a vegetable garden. Gunfire was coming in from the rice field on the other side of the walled garden and from somewhere in the thick jungle beyond. Suddenly a mortar blast destroyed a portion of the protective wall, and then machine-gun fire began to erupt from the little bamboo hut behind them, and the Marines were trapped between two lines of fire. The handheld cameras focused on the face of one young Marine. He was looking down at the face of the dead soldier he held in his arms, cradling the man's body at an angle and displaying it directly to the television camera. The young Marine was crying as he looked into the face of his dead comrade.

From where she stood at the doorway of the den of her home in the Virginia hills, Kay Cassidy could see the tears making a clear path in the dirt-streaked cheeks of the young soldier, but the handheld camera moved away from the face of the crying boy then, trying to find the source of the automatic-weapons fire, and a newsman's voice could barely be heard over the sounds of the loudly crackling gunfire. "There's a new danger now, from behind us!" the reporter said and then there was a long pause, followed by the sounds of running, while the camera showed a shifting, uneven rhythm of pictures, first the ground, then the sky, then the movement down toward the ground again. "There seems to be a new danger in every direction," the newsman's voice came through between heavy ragged breaths. "Some element in the village that A Company believed that it was protecting has now opened fire on it. For the moment, we're trapped between two lines of fire, one from the enemy, one from the village itself. We've become prisoners in something that we don't understand!" There was more gunfire then, and the film report ended a few seconds later with the camera shutting off abruptly and the picture stopping without any warning or explanation.

Kay Cassidy caught her breath as the anchorman came on the screen from the network's New York studio and attempted to give some kind of meaning to the piece of film that she'd just seen. But Kay didn't listen. Below her she could see the unsteady movement of her husband's head and shoulders. She looked down at Tim's face then. He was seated on the far end of the couch, and, as she watched, he brought the unsteady movement of his body under control. His expression, which had been filled with sadness, became grim and defiant and angry, but his eyes remained red and still brimming with undried tears.

CHAPTER
25

Far ahead Jack could see Tim's slim figure skiing down the snow-covered mountain. Dressed in a bright red wool sweater, his brother was cutting in and out of the trees and rocks at breakneck speed.

Jack laughed and let out a breath of frosty air just as Tim disappeared behind a bend in the ski trail hundreds of yards beneath him. There was no chance of catching him now, and Jack slowed his own pace and began traversing the trail at a sharper angle, kicking up drifts of clean white snow as he dug the edge of his skis into the hillside at a steeper angle, slowing his descent into the valley below. Jack began to make out the shapes and colors of the tall pine trees at the edge of the trail now. They had been only a bright blur of green before, as he skimmed along the surface of the snow in pursuit of his younger brother. And now, too, he could smell the fresh, clear, pine-scented air. It was late October in Sun Valley, and an early snowfall had covered the ski resort just before the family had arrived for a few days of vacation together. It had snowed again early that morning and several inches of thick white powder lay on the ground. And Jack enjoyed traversing it slower than his brother had, moving from side to side down the hill until he came to a final scoop of land and the sweeping curve in the wide, snow-covered ski trail that his brother had disappeared behind a few minutes earlier.

Tim was waiting for him at the edge of the trail. He stood with his back to the mountain looking out over the snow-covered valley. The little town of Sun Valley was just barely visible beneath him, a series of tiny black specks in the far distance.

When he saw his brother, Jack dipped his knees and shifted his weight gracefully, coming to a stop just a few inches behind him and kicking up snow onto Tim's ski pants.

Tim turned back to him. "A little slow coming down that last set of hills," he chided his older brother.

"Hills?" Jack breathed in deeply several times. "Sheer cliff is more like it," he said, motioning with his ski pole back up the steep mountain trail. One set of tracks wove smoothly back and forth from one side of the open space to the other, traversing both the width and length of the snow-covered hillside, leaving behind a gracefully beautiful pattern of descent, while the other showed a direct slicing pattern, moving dangerously in a fast almost straight line down the sharp incline. It wasn't hard to tell which brother had left which set of tracks. "You could have gotten killed coming down that thing," Jack said, looking at the long drop-off at the side of the trail, where Tim's tracks had come perilously close to the edge several times during his descent.

"Washington seems a million miles away," Tim said, ignoring his brother's warning. He turned to look back out at the long expanse of untouched snow on the remainder of the trail below them and then out at the long stretch of open, snow-covered fields sprinkled with more white powder at the base of the mountain.

Although the two brothers had been together for the last several days, they had scrupulously avoided talking politics, each waiting for the relaxation of the holiday to recharge their spirits before they began discussing the difficult choices they both faced when they returned to the nation's capital.

"It's been hard on you, hasn't it?" Jack said. "Harder even than either of us guessed that it might be."

Tim only shrugged his shoulders.

"In some ways being Vice President has been the easiest job I've ever had," Tim said.

"Meaning that you hate it," Jack said, and Tim laughed then at how well his brother knew him.

Both men turned at the sound of voices on the ski trail behind them. Tim's wife and oldest son, Michael, were skiing into view, laughing and moving by close enough to Jack to kick snow up over his legs before they sped off quickly down the hill toward the valley below.

Tim laughed and, pretending to be angry, he loosened the ski pole from his right hand and scooped up a hurried ball of snow and threw it at his wife's rapidly moving figure, missing her only by inches.

The two men stood together for a moment watching the departing figures slip away down the curve of the hillside.

"How's the President holding up under the pressure?" Jack said.

"I wouldn't know," Tim answered. "I haven't been alone with Rance in weeks."

"He certainly looks like hell," Jack said. "They shouldn't let him go on television looking the way he does sometimes," he continued, but Tim had moved away, back toward the rim of the mountain again, and Jack lifted and turned his skis and let himself glide across the surface of the snow back to the spot at the edge of the trail where his brother was standing. Both men stood quietly, waiting until Kay and Michael curved back into sight on the ski trail below them. Tim waved down at his wife as soon as she came into view and she jerked her head up and smiled back at him, slowing momentarily, but then skiing off at an even faster pace.

"God, she's even crazier than you are," Jack said, watching Kay Cassidy's figure speeding down the hill with what seemed to him very little regard for her own safety. Seconds later she was followed down the snow-covered hillside by the racing figure of her oldest son. "They both are!" Jack added in amazement.

"I've made a decision," Tim said. He was still looking out at the ski slope and at the beautiful snow-covered valley beyond, but his voice was set hard and full of determination.

"I've been wanting to talk to you about it for a long time now," Tim said. "I've decided that I'm not going to run for reelection next year."

Jack's first reaction to the dramatic announcement was laughter. "What makes you think that Rance will ask you, anyway?"

Tim smiled, shrugging his shoulders in response. "Well, I hadn't thought much about that, but I suppose he might not," Tim said.

"Rance may not need you anymore," Jack said, as he began to realize how serious his brother really was.

"I'll tell you honestly, Jack, that would be fine by me," Tim said, looking up directly at his brother's eyes. "If things continue as they have, I don't think he'll be reelected with or without me, and I'd rather not be part of a disaster."

Jack stayed quiet, standing behind him, shifting his weight on his skis to stay balanced at the edge of the mountainside.

"I'm useless to him anyway," Tim said, turning his head and shoulders back toward his older brother. "Sometimes I think that he enjoys treating me the way he does. I'm very serious when I say that weeks go by and I don't see him, except in Cabinet meetings, and then my advice is ignored. Every last word that I say or write has to be cleared by his office, my appointments are screened by his staff people, and my schedule has to be approved in writing a week in advance. There's a combined State and Defense Department trip planned for Saigon right before Thanksgiving. I've asked him several times to let me go on it, but the answer is always the same. He says that he can't risk having anything happen to me, but the truth is he's just so damned afraid that I'm going to contradict administration policy on the war that he doesn't trust me to go, and frankly, Jack, it's all that I can do not to speak my mind. He's right, I am dangerous to him."

"I understand," Jack said.

"Jack," Tim started, but then he paused before saying what he had wanted to say to his brother for months. "Jack, I think if you tried, you could take the nomination away from him."

Jack laughed again. "I thought that we just lived through all that."

"I'm serious," Tim said. "There's something happening in this country." He gestured down the valley toward the open countryside below them. "The feelings are so deep, I don't think the old political rules are going to hold this time."

Jack smiled at his younger brother. "Tim, you never have."

They were both quiet then. It was Jack who broke the tense silence. "Tim, please try to understand what I'm going to say. I do understand your feelings and I share most of them with you—the anger, the frustration, the futility of the war, and Rance's refusal to reconsider our commitment to it—but I can't speak out about it directly, not now. For the first time in years, probably since Dallas, my life is starting to make some sense to me again. I feel useful in the Senate. So much of what we've all worked for is beginning to really happen now. Maybe I'm not as powerful or as glamorous a figure to the world as I was when I was President, but I'm a good Senator and we're doing good work. Whatever you and I might believe is wrong in Southeast Asia, the administration's domestic policies are important and I'm an essential part of making those programs into law. Suzanne and I are happy, too, and the opportunity to become President again is still very much in my grasp." Jack paused again then. "But not next year. Not in 1968," he said again for emphasis, and then he took a deep breath before he continued. "I came dangerously close to making that mistake three years ago, and I'm not going to make it now," he said firmly. "Rance Gardner, for all his faults, is the President of the United States and he's the leader of the Democratic Party— and until he's damn good and ready to step aside all by himself, I'm going to support him to the limits that my conscience and my judgment permit me to, and I hope when you've had an opportunity to think about this some more, that you'll decide to do the same."

Tim was quiet then, weighing his brother's words. "What if you're wrong, Jack? What if it's a fight you can't stay out of? What if the country won't let you stay out of it? You may be the only person who can do it, the only one with enough pure political muscle to knock Rance out of the presidency—and by God, Jack, I think it has to be done."

Jack shook his head back and forth several times. "No," he said firmly. "Tim, this will all take its course, you'll see. I know how much it has to hurt you . . ."

Tim wouldn't let him finish. "Someone has to do it," he said, interrupting his brother.

"Meaning you."

"Meaning, someone. I don't know," Tim said. "Jack, the truth is that I'm considering not even waiting until next year to leave the administration. I'm considering resigning in the next few months and going after the nomination myself."

Jack only nodded his head then, his expression faintly sad and faraway. "I think it would be a mistake."

"Jack, I just don't believe in business as usual anymore," Tim said. "Too much is happening. Too many people are dying out there," Tim pointed with the lift of his ski pole out past the snow-covered mountains and valleys of Idaho.

The unhappiness that his younger brother felt showed deeply in his face as he spoke, and Jack couldn't remember a time that he felt more separated from him. He tried to look back down at the valley below them again, but suddenly, Washington and its problems felt a lot closer than it had only a few minutes before.

"I guess, in the last analysis, I can't stop you, can I?" Jack said.

"No, you can't," Tim said. "It's going to have to be my decision."

"Well, what do you think I should do?" Sullivan said, holding up the letter again for Grissum to see, but it was easy to guess what Grissum would say when he finally got around to answering. That was the beauty of talking to him. Grissum only had one answer for all questions: No. It made being with him easy, Sullivan thought, as he looked over at the veteran agent's face. He had to admit it. He did miss the old bastard though. They were no longer partners, probably because Yancey had decided that he didn't need daily watching anymore, not after he'd kept his nose clean and played it the Bureau's way for so long now, but this letter could change all that. Sullivan fingered the envelope nervously.

"You see that trash can over there." Grissum pointed with the glowing tip of his cigarette toward a corner of the restaurant.

"Uh-uh."

"I think you should fold that letter up into a little paper airplane and sail it straight into it. That would show me a lot, Sullivan."

Sullivan laughed and put the letter back into his coat pocket. They weren't partners and they weren't friends; Grissum had made both points very clear to Sullivan on more than one occasion over the last few months, but still the older agent was one of the few people in Dallas that he liked being with, even now.

"It's no wonder you sleep through the afternoon," Sullivan said as he watched Grissum take a short quick shot from his little pint bottle of rye and then replace it inside his coat pocket.

"If you're really asking me about that letter," Grissum said, ignoring Sullivan's comment, "I think you better write back and tell them you just made a mistake and send Yancey a copy of it. That way it's in your god-damned file." Grissum paused before adding, "You know how many people have been in to talk to him, anyway. You're not exactly going to be the first."

Sullivan laughed again. "Yeah, thanks, good advice," he said sarcastically, after he'd stopped laughing. "You know, Grissum, nobody wears hats like that anymore," Sullivan said, lifting the fork up that he had been using to eat his lunch with and pointing it at Grissum's long-brimmed, gray felt hat.

"Summers does," Grissum mumbled.

"Not to lunch," Sullivan said.

"How the hell would you know? Your red-hot law-enforcement career is dying out here in the Lone Star State at just about the same rate as mine did," Grissum said.

"Yeah, maybe, but for different reasons," Sullivan said, admitting the truth of what Grissum had said. Then he went back to his plate of chili relleños, tacos, and refried beans. Over the last year, Sullivan had become a Mexican food addict. He knew and had dragged Grissum along to every out-of-the-way chili joint within twenty miles of downtown Dallas. This one was in a little suburb east of the city. It was a single, small, crowded room with a long mirror-backed counter and a few mismatched tables and chairs separating the counter from a half dozen imitation red leather booths, one of which Sullivan and Grissum were sitting in now.

"You sure you don't want something?" Sullivan said, reaching past Grissum's reclining figure for the napkin-draped plastic basket of flour tortillas and then removing three of them with his long fingers and curling them into a container in the palm of his hand.

"God, no!" Grissum said, his eyes peeking painfully out beneath the brim of his hat and watching Sullivan pile refried beans into the folded tortillas. "That shit burns," Grissum added, pointing with disgust at Sullivan's handful of Mexican food.

"Yeah, and that shit you drink doesn't?" Sullivan said, still shoveling piles of beans and rice into the reinforced layers of thin white tortillas and then folding the finished product into a thick, cylindrical Mexican sandwich.

Grissum turned away in disgust and took another sip of his beer.

"You gonna tell Yancey about the letter?" Sullivan said. A thin red-brown sauce dripped on to his fingers as he moved the tortilla sandwich away from his mouth.

"Shit, why bother? Chances are he already knows," Grissum said. "But I'll probably tell him anyway, just to remind him of whose side I'm on," the older agent added, after he'd had a chance to think about it a little longer.

"There's not a damn thing that Yancey can do about it," Sullivan said defiantly. "If I go, I'll do it on my own time, and anyway, he's got no authority to stop me."

It was Grissum's turn to laugh. "Don't kid yourself," he said wearily.

"Anyway, I think I'm going to go ahead and do it," Sullivan said, setting his dripping hand down on the plate in front of him for a moment and reaching with his other hand for a fistful of paper napkins.

"I might even do it on Bureau time," Sullivan said. "I've got an open file, an unsolved homicide—and I think it connects."

"Your famous dead-Mexican-pimp case?" Grissum asked, his face showing some concern.

"Yeah, what else?" Sullivan said. "That pimp knew something that connected up to the guy I saw in Dealey Plaza right after Cassidy was shot. I'm sure of that much, and somebody put Ortiz away before he could talk to me."

"I thought your theory was that they were after you that night, not him. Make up your mind," Grissum said.

"It could have been either way," Sullivan said. "Or both, for that matter. The result's the same—somebody didn't want me or anybody else to find out what really happened to Cassidy."

"Don't do this," Grissum said, with a lot more heat than Sullivan was used to hearing from him.

"The Bureau gave you a goddamned break. Now be smart enough to take it, or . . ." Grissum added with surprising intensity, but he suddenly realized that he had said more than he'd meant to.

"Or what? What the hell are you saying?" Sullivan asked angrily, but as he finished he noticed that the music in the jukebox behind him had stopped and that he'd spoken so loudly that some of the other customers nearby were turning to look at him. Still Grissum didn't answer, so Sullivan angrily pressed on. "I asked you a goddamned question," he said in an even louder voice.

"Nothin'," Grissum mumbled. "I just thought you were getting smart, that's all. I guess I was wrong."

"If nothing else, it will be an experience. I mean, who wouldn't want to talk to Leonard Green, the man who shot Strode. The son of a bitch is part of history, right?" Sullivan said, lowering his voice.

"I wouldn't," Grissum said, his own feelings on the issue back under the safe double protection of his hat brim and the floating cascade of smoke from a newly lit cigarette.

"I mean, other than you, who wouldn't want to talk to him?" Sullivan said, forcing a laugh to keep himself halfway calm. "I put in this request a good two years ago. It got held up by every piece of governmental bureaucratic bullshit known to mankind, but it finally came through. And I didn't go looking for it either. I'd forgotten I'd even asked for it, and then out of the blue it just arrives. Some clerk at the Federal Department of Prisons just sent it out. I checked with them, the delays were all because of the federal court here in Dallas that had Green up for trial and some internal holdups at the Department of Prisons itself. Nobody at Justice or the Bureau even knows about it as far as I can tell—at least they never filed a protest."

"It's your funeral," Grissum said in a flat voice. Then he added, "Half the big-shot law-enforcement men in the country have been in to talk to Green. What makes you think you'll get anything new out of him?"

"Maybe he doesn't trust big-shot lawmen," Sullivan said. "Maybe he's even scared of them. I've been reading what he's been sayin' to the press. He's got a lot more that he knows than he's given out so far. He just needs the right person to say it to."

"And you're the one?" Grissum said, his voice laced with sarcasm.

"Maybe."

"The guy's in a goddamned federal prison—what's he got to be scared of?" Grissum asked then.

Sullivan laughed and reached for his beer. The food that he'd so carefully prepared had been forgotten in his excitement and was starting to cool now on his plate and harden back into its congealed origins. "Maybe he's afraid of being in a federal prison," Sullivan said. "And I'm starting to understand the way he feels."

"What's that supposed to mean?" Grissum said. He was quiet then, the part of his expression that Sullivan could see beneath the brim of his hat fixed in disgust.

"Look," Sullivan said, reaching into his shirt pocket. "I made up a list of people I've got to talk to first." He tried to hand a piece of lined, yellow legal-size paper across the table to Grissum, but the older agent reached out with the rim of his beer glass and flicked the paper aside.

"Don't show me your goddamned list, Sullivan," he said. "And don't ask me to bullshit around Dallas with you for the next two months while you talk to all these assholes who saw gunmen in the shadows and Commie agents buying Strode drinks in 1953, because I'm not into that kind of crap."

"Okay," Sullivan said, and then he went back to his cooling plateful of Mexican food, but it didn't look as good to him as it had only a few minutes earlier.

"Tell me this, though," Grissum said then.

"Uh-uh."

"If you really go ahead and see this guy, Green, what are you going to ask him? I mean, what's the sixty-four-thousand-dollar question?"

"That's easy," Sullivan said, without hesitating: "I'll ask him who paid him to kill Strode, because whoever that was, ten to one it was the same guy who paid Strode to assassinate Cassidy."

Grissum shook his head in disbelief. He lifted his beer glass slowly and formally in the direction of the young agent and took a big drink from it, as if to toast Sullivan a permanent and official good-bye.

The woman dropped the first of the photographs across the desk toward Costello. The big man bent over, his belly straining against the edge of his belt as he reached forward to slide the photograph back toward himself. The black-and-white picture showed a man in profile sitting behind an open window. The man's face was desperately thin, his eyes sunken dark holes buried deep in his skull.

"It's him, isn't it?" Costello said, and Mrs. Martine nodded her head. She slid several more photographs back across the table then, returning them to Costello. She had seen enough. He took them one by one in his fat, ring-laden fingers and examined them in the faint light of the private office that opened off the central courtyard of Mrs. Martine's New Orleans home.

The photographs showed a variety of views of the same man. He was pictured against long rows of decaying barracks buildings, or from a distance standing or walking along the dirty open spaces of a Cuban prison. Costello tossed the photographs back onto the desktop after he had finished inspecting them. "Three years," the fat man said. "Almost three fucking years. We thought he was dead."

"How did you get these?" the woman said, pointing at the photographs that Costello had brought to show her that morning.

"He looks like he's lost a lot of weight," Costello said, ignoring her question, as she'd assumed that he would. Then he inspected the photographs one last time before he returned them to the envelope from which he had removed them only a few minutes earlier. "But it's him. There's no doubt about that."

"He's so thin he could be sick," the woman said, and Costello only smiled.

"Not sick enough," Costello said, resealing the envelope. "I hope the son of a bitch has the plague," he added as he dropped the envelope of photographs back into his briefcase.

The woman folded her once-elegant but now extravagantly wrinkled hands across the front of her long black dress, clenching her fingers tightly together to help her control her emotions as she continued to negotiate with the grossly overweight man. It was a discipline that she'd taught herself over the years since Don Martine's death and she'd learned it well. Costello could detect in her face none of the distaste that she felt for him. Mrs. Martine was certain of that, but she was less certain of what he had been sent by DeSavio to ask her for that night.

"He was a fool to think that he could go back to Cuba at all," Costello said, and Mrs. Martine nodded her agreement.

"What does he call himself now?"

"Lopata, still the same, Antonio Lopata. We believe that he had forged identity papers on him when he was arrested," the big man said. "So he had no chance to call himself anything else this time."

"And the diary?"

Costello laughed abruptly. "That's the real question, isn't it—the god-damned diary? If he was captured with the diary in his possession, Castro himself could have it by now. These men," he said, pointing at the envelope in his briefcase to remind Mrs. Martine of the faces of the Cuban officers in the photographs that she had just seen, "soldiers, who run a prison like this, wouldn't they be some of the most loyal to the Revolution?"

"Loyal, perhaps," the woman said, choosing her words carefully. "But not the wisest necessarily. They may not understand the value of something like his diary, or they may not believe that it is truly what it seems to be. They may have no idea what to do with it."

"Why would he go back there in the first place?" Costello asked.

"Because he's arrogant and he's a fool," the woman said, beginning to understand what had happened. "And he probably believed that he could use Havana to protect himself. He underestimated the new government. I suppose he thought that he would be safe, but he couldn't have realized just how much Cuba has changed. There is no one left there who can be trusted anymore."

"No one?" Costello asked pointedly, and Mrs. Martine waited then to hear the rest. "No one that perhaps you know, who could be trusted at least enough to do one simple thing?"

She understood now why DeSavio had sent this man to see her. In the three years since she had sat in this same room with Costello's boss and he had presented her with his short list, much progress had been made. DeSavio's people had moved slowly but surely, spreading their activities out over time, as they often did to help them cover the pattern of events. Of the names on that original list only a handful still remained alive, but of all the names none was more important to their safety than the man in the photographs. But now DeSavio had learned that he was out of even his powerful reach, and he was asking for her help to complete the job that he and his people had failed to accomplish themselves.

"We believe now that you must do something," Costello said.

In the silence that followed, Mrs. Martine studied the man's round, expressionless face. He was being very careful not to say directly that even his and DeSavio's enormous power didn't extend into the walls of Muiriel Prison, but that her power might. This man, Lopata, had been right about that much of it, she thought. He was safer in Cuba than almost anywhere else he could have chosen, safer at least from DeSavio and his people—but perhaps not from her.

"It's impossible to know just what's in that diary," Costello said. "But without a living witness to support its allegations, whatever it says will be much less dangerous to us. We believe that, without a witness, the diary could easily be dismissed as just the ravings of a lunatic. It would become practically worthless then to Castro or to whoever it is that has it now," Costello went on, using a wave of his thick hand to complete his thought. "Is there anyone left in Cuba that you can still trust enough to help us?"

The question hung in the air between them for several seconds. In the silence, Mrs. Martine clenched her hands that she held in her lap hidden beneath the desk so tightly that the knuckles showed white and bloodless and the single golden band that she wore on her left hand to remind her of why she lived the way that she did now, cut into flesh with the intense pressure. Her face though, above the high-collared black lace dress that she wore, was still an emotionless mask. Finally, she nodded. "Yes, I think so," she said, making her voice sound the words slowly, solemnly, like the death sentence that she knew them to be.

CHAPTER

26

Sullivan started at the top of his hand-written list. His counselor in high school was right about him, he thought, as he reviewed the long list of people that he wanted to talk to before he met with Leo Green. He was a plodder, just like his counselor had told him. Make a list, push everyone on it methodically, until they agreed to a meeting, laboriously write out all the questions in advance. Then later, after the meeting, write out all the answers that you were given, check and recheck what you've learned against the rest of what you had—a plodder, methodical, dull, straight-ahead, but in the end usually effective.

It had been easy enough to find out the name of the police dispatcher who had been broadcasting radio calls to the Dallas patrol cars on November 22, 1963, but it had been hard as hell to get her to agree to see him. It was only after half a dozen phone calls that she'd finally told him the name of the beer bar that she went to after work. It was going to be a tough interview, Sullivan thought as he pushed his way inside the bar's front doors. A lot of time had passed since the events had occurred that he wanted to question the dispatcher about.

It was a cowboy bar, like a couple of hundred others on the fringes of downtown Dallas, and the locals with their store-bought cowboy hats, fancy western shirts, clean shiny boots, and too-new blue jeans eyed Sullivan suspiciously as he walked into the room wearing his charcoal-colored Ivy League suit and pointed-toe, highly polished black dress shoes. He passed by the dimly lit pool tables toward a corner table, but the bartender called to him before he could settle into the dark faraway booth. "What do you want, Tex?" A couple of the locals snickered.

As Sullivan walked back to the long bar at the front of the room, he felt like a cross between the lone stranger who'd just come into town and the dude from the East. The place's décor was strictly Dallas beer bar, a few tables and chairs, two worn pool tables, a jukebox pouring out mournful country sounds, and an ancient collection of mutely lit beer signs glowing and rotating in the stale darkness. As he completed his quick survey of the room, a big, bleached blond in a red satin cowboy shirt cranked her bar stool around to face him. "You Sullivan?"

He nodded and the woman waited for him to order and gather up his bottle of Lone Star before she led him back to the table in the far dark corner of the room.

Sullivan watched her walk, her legs and hips stuffed into a pair of brand-new blue jeans that were at least two sizes too small for her. She walked slowly and seemed to let him watch as much as he wanted to, and at the key time of her descent into the chair at the corner table, she did an exaggerated push out toward him with her buttocks, before dipping her body down and settling it into place.

"You're Ginny Cole?" She nodded her bleached-blond head, and Sullivan reached into his inside pocket for his wallet and identification card.

"Put that shit away," the big woman said, pointing at Sullivan's FBI card, and then she began looking around the room nervously to see if they were being watched by any of the locals.

"I've got friends in here," she said. "People I work with."

"You afraid of the Dallas police?" Sullivan smiled at the blond woman's obvious discomfort, and she shifted her gaze back to his smiling face. "Look, I don't have to be here with you."

"So, why are you?" Sullivan said, starting to pour his Lone Star into his glass, but a closer look at it changed his mind and he set it aside and drank straight from the long-necked bottle instead.

"The FBI asks me to do something, I do it," the blond woman said simply.

Sullivan almost laughed. "That makes you about the only one in the state of Texas then."

The woman shrugged her shoulders, and as she did her face moved into the yellow glow from a nearby beer sign. She was a good ten years older than he'd guessed at first, Sullivan thought, as he looked at the layers of pink makeup caked over the crosswork of deepening lines etched into the flesh at the corners of her eyes.

"I'm very interested," Sullivan said, pushing his own face across the table toward her. "I mean, I've talked to maybe a couple of a dozen Dallas cops in the last few years, and most of them treated me like I had a disease."

"I'm not a Dallas cop," the big blond woman said. "I'm an employee of the state of Texas, strictly civil service, like you," she added then.

"Meaning what?" Was it possible that this woman was really going to say something to him?

"Meaning . . ." she started, but then she suddenly began pushing her way back from the table. She stood and wiggled her hand deep into the front pocket of her too-tight jeans, bringing out a fistful of change. Then she walked to the brightly lit jukebox. The machine had stopped a few minutes earlier and the room had quieted. She trickled change into the metal slot and, working from memory, she punched a sequence of square plastic buttons. Soon the room was full of western sounds again, blaring out of the tinny speaker mounted on the wall above the jukebox. Satisfied, she returned slowly across the room toward Sullivan. Every man in the room with a good angle to watch her walk followed her movements back to the dark corner table.

"Meanin', I guess," she said as she slowly squatted down again into the seat across from him, "that I'm not part of the private club and so I don't owe nobody nothin'. And so I do what I want to do, when I want to do it." She smiled for the first time at Sullivan then.

"Were you on duty on November 22, 1963, the day Cassidy was shot?" Sullivan asked.

"You know I was," the big blond woman said, touching her lips together, so that the thick layers of very red lipstick stuck together and then slowly separated.

"I was in a patrol car that afternoon," Sullivan said. "Less than an hour after it happened, I heard a call go out. It was for a short, dark-skinned man. The report said: 'A Latin, in a blue plaid shirt.' Did you make that call?"

"If it was on the radio that afternoon, I made it," the big woman said, leaning forward now and letting the front of her tight satin cowboy shirt spill out over the top of the beer-stained table that separated Sullivan from her.

"It was," Sullivan said.

"Then it was my call," the woman said.

"You don't remember it though?"

"Unh-unh," the woman said, shrugging her wide shoulders under the bright satin shirt.

"How would a call like that originate?" Sullivan asked.

"Lots of ways," the blond dispatcher said. "An officer could have called it in. It could have come from someone in the squad room, a written request maybe."

"But you don't remember a call for a man in a blue plaid . . ."

"Look, no," she said, cutting Sullivan off. "There was a hell of a lot going on that afternoon. I remember a lot of it, most of it probably, but not that. If I made the call, I probably only made it once, or I would remember."

Sullivan sat back deep in his chair then and sipped thoughtfully at his beer. "Thanks," he said with a touch of disappointment.

The woman relaxed back into her own chair then and chugged down what was left in her beer glass with one long swallow. "You could check it out in the log, I guess."

"The log? What log?" Sullivan said, sitting back up in his chair and leaning across the table toward her again.

"Every call gets written down. What it was, where it originated, the units that responded to it, everything."

Sullivan felt a new wave of excitement start inside him then. Of course, a log, he thought. God, he was a plodder. "Where does the log go after you're done with it?"

"Well, normally it goes to the chief dispatcher, but that day everything went to just one place."

"What do you mean?" This was the first break that he'd had in this case in a hell of a long time.

"Well, after it was all over, after all the screw-ups and everything, a committee got formed. It was supposed to investigate what happened. An Internal Review Committee they called it," the big blond woman said. "It wasn't exactly the Department's finest hour."

"No, it wasn't."

"Anyway, everything—all the reports, logs, even written notes—all of it went to the committee."

"I never heard about any committee," Sullivan said.

"Nobody has. It was all just bullshit," the blond woman said. "There was never a report or anything, at least not as far as I know, there wasn't. It was just a place to clean up all the Department's garbage, if you know what I mean."

"Who was on the committee?"

"That's why it was so much bullshit," the blond woman said. "The same people were on the committee who did the screwing up in the first place."

"Such as?" Sullivan prompted.

"Well, such as mainly Deputy Chief of Police Jacob Boyer, the son of a bitch. It was Boyer's committee. He ran it, everything went to him."

"Including your log?" Sullivan said, remembering as he did the unpleasant, beefy-faced deputy police chief he had met on that famous weekend four years earlier.

"Everything, and that's why it's such bullshit," the big blond woman said. "If anybody was in charge that weekend, it was Boyer. He was there in the squad room calling the shots from Friday morning, right on through until the shit started to settle down a little later that next week. If there were screw-ups, he was the one responsible for them. And I'll tell you this, too— if anybody hated Cassidy enough to help him get shot, it was Boyer."

"What are you saying? Was Boyer an honest cop?"

The blond woman shrugged her shoulders. "Not as bad as some." She glanced around to make certain that no one could overhear her.

"But he wasn't totally clean?"

"How the hell would I know?" she said. "I just hear things," she added, letting Sullivan know that she didn't want to talk about it anymore.

"Could Boyer have been the one who gave you the call for the man in a plaid shirt, or could he have been the one who wound up canceling it?"

"Sure." The blond woman paused then and thought about it some more. "In fact, it would be real possible that he did, particularly pulling a call that I'd already made once. That's something only he would have bothered about. I mean, if anybody would have." Sullivan was quiet then, reviewing his own memories of Boyer, his mind racing with the possibilities. Boyer could be the key to everything that happened in Dallas that weekend, he decided finally.

"What you're doing is dangerous as hell!" O'Connor said, and Tim didn't bother to deny it. He knew that his friend was right.

"If Gardner finds out that you've been meeting with Rothman, he'll go through the roof," the old Irish politician continued.

"Once," Cassidy said then. "I met with Rothman once," he added, swinging his glass out at the interior of the Vice President's private dining room and then toward the capital buildings that were displayed just beyond the window of the executive office building.

"And just what the hell did you tell him when he asked you to resign and run against Gardner for the nomination?" O'Connor asked bluntly. "Did you tell him all those student radicals that think he's God, half of whom, by the way, are too young to vote anyway, will throw their political support to you?"

"I'm still here, aren't I?" Tim said, indicating the walls of the White House executive offices with his glass of ice tea.

"That's not an answer," O'Connor said gruffly.

"I'm not Rothman's or anybody else's first choice, Frank. We both know that," Tim said sharply. "All he wanted is for me to convince Jack to see him, that's all, talk to him."

"Well, maybe you missed it, but your brother already has a job."

"We don't always get all the regional news down here." Tim smiled.

"That's God's truth," O'Connor said. "And that probably explains why you don't seem to understand that Jack promised the people of Massachusetts, way up there in faraway New England, that if they'd vote for him, he would serve at least one full term in the United States Senate doing the job that they elected him to do. You may have forgotten, but things can get a little rough out there in those regional elections even for ex-Presidents. Sometimes the voters go so far as to ask if you're serious about doing the job that you're asking them to give you," O'Connor said in a voice that he was fighting to keep under control. "And Senate terms, in case you've forgotten that, too, Tim, are six years in length. That doesn't make Jack eligible for another job until nineteen hundred and seventy-two, which happens to be very neat and tidy for him and for all the rest of us." O'Connor pointed his finger across the lunch table at the Vice President then. "Because, God willing, a man from Jack's own party will continue to hold that position until just that precise date. A man by the way, that your brother publicly endorsed for the job and campaigned very hard for."

Cassidy nodded at O'Connor, indicating that he understood, and when the old Irish politician continued his voice was softer, more conciliatory. "Tim, I know how you feel, but five very short years from now, Jack will only be fifty-five years old, still a very young man. Fifty-five is an age when most men first begin to even think seriously about running for the presidency. And all he has to do between now and then is just behave himself and he'll have the united endorsement of the entire Democratic Party. Now, that doesn't make him a sure thing in 1972. I know that. There's no such thing as a certainty in this business, but I'll tell you this." O'Connor paused to emphasize how strongly he felt about what he had to say next. "He'll be as goddamned close to having a lock on the presidency as any man in my lifetime, and that's nothing to throw away now on some half-baked crusade against the war stirred up by Rothman and his radical friends."

Tim didn't try to say anything right away. He understood O'Connor's position. He'd heard the arguments over and over during the last few months. He'd even made some of them himself, when he'd met with Rothman, and with others, but there was still so much else that it left unanswered. "Maybe politics just isn't reasonable anymore, Frank," he said finally. "Maybe everything we've been taught, all the old rules, maybe they just won't work this time, not with what's happening in the world today."

"You sound like Rothman talking."

"Do I?" Tim said and then thought about it. "Yes, I guess I do," he added finally. "But I just can't help thinking that somehow next year might be different, that 1968 might be a year like no other in our history, and if it is, we have to be a part of it, move with it, or we'll be swept aside by the changes, just the way I believe that this administration will be."

"Rothman's not a politician. He's a professor, for God's sake." O'Connor's voice left no doubt about the value he placed on the political advice of college professors, even ones with large and enthusiastic followings.

"It's not Rothman. It's what I see out there myself. What I feel," Tim answered.

"Tim, for God's sake," O'Connor implored the younger man, "Jack can't win now. In the final analysis it's really that damn simple. We've been over the numbers a thousand times and it's just not there, Timothy. And that's really the only thing that matters, when all is said and done. If your father taught you nothing else, I know he taught you that much, didn't he? If you're going to play, play to win," O'Connor pressed. "And right now winning is impossible."

"More important than throwing away another ten thousand American lives, Frank? Another twenty thousand?" Tim said impulsively.

"I'm not going to answer that," O'Connor shot back angrily. "And if you believe it's that simple then you should resign."

Tim was quiet then, but O'Connor could see in his face how deeply he had been stung by his words. "You asked me a question earlier," Tim said finally. "I didn't answer you then, but I'm going to now, with the understanding that what I'm about to say will go no further than this room. You asked me what I said to Rothman when he asked me to resign and to challenge Gardner for the nomination." The Vice President paused then. "I didn't tell him no, Frank," Tim said finally.

O'Connor looked stunned. "If either you or Jack moved now for the nomination against a President from your own Party, even one as unpopular as Rance Gardner, you'd have the entire weight of history against you. It would only result in ending not only your own political future, but it could split the Party for years to come," O'Connor said.

"I didn't tell Rothman no, Frank," Tim said again. "I told him that I'd think about it."

"Good God," O'Connor said. "You're playing an even more dangerous game than I thought."

"I know, Frank," the Vice President said. "But it's begun now and I'm part of it, and I don't see that I have any choice but to play it out and see where it leads."

"It might be starting to come together a little," Sullivan said. "I've got a little more digging to do before I see Green, but I'm telling you, it's beginning to make a little sense to me now. One guy I'd really like to talk to is this guy Boyer, though, and I need to see his files, too. He's got everything, the dispatcher's log, all the field reports—but I can't get to him without some backing from somebody, and it sure as hell isn't going to be Yancey. I've got to find another angle. I'm finally getting close to some real answers. I can feel it and I have you to thank for it. I was just letting the whole thing slip away until I saw you again, but now I'm back on top of it."

Denise stayed quiet then, refusing to take any credit for Sullivan's renewed enthusiasm. "Well, anyway, I've decided to give it one more try, and then lay it all out for them in Washington, and if that doesn't work, I'm going to go in and talk to the Vice President himself. What do you think?"

Denise laughed. They were in the living room of her new apartment in a high-rise building in North Dallas. Below her window and across the network of interconnecting expressways, Denise could see the lights of the new suburban shopping center where she worked now. "I think that's two tries," she said, smiling.

"Yeah, but don't you see, it's starting to add up. And if what I say makes sense, they've got to listen . . ." He stopped then and walked to the tall floor-to-ceiling window where Denise was standing looking out at the view of the Dallas suburb and its expressways. He suddenly realized that he'd been rattling on nonstop about "the case" again for several minutes. "I really like the way the place looks," Sullivan said, changing the subject by turning back into the room and surveying Denise's new apartment. It was clean, bright, and modern, the way Denise herself looked now, Sullivan thought. The furniture in the spacious living room was a combination of simple straight-edged designs and bright psychedelic colors. Framed posters of Jimi Hendrix and Mick Jagger decorated the far wall. Sullivan's gaze stopped when he reached the door that led from the living room to Denise's bedroom. This was the one room that he hadn't been invited to enter during the half dozen or so weeks since he'd run into her again at the singles' bar in downtown Dallas—punishment for not calling in over a year and probably a fair one, Sullivan decided, as he looked a little sadly at the closed bedroom door.

Denise turned from the window and sat down in a low, white-vinyl beanbag chair a few feet from where Sullivan was standing. Sullivan had never seen anything like the chair before. "What's that thing got in it?" he asked, but the chair didn't hold Sullivan's attention for long and Denise laughed as she watched Sullivan's eyes move from the chair and begin to follow her miniskirt up to where its fabric stopped several inches above her knees. "Just friends, remember?"

"I can't help it," Sullivan said, forcing himself to lift his eyes back to Denise's face and eyes. "Miniskirts are a great invention," he added after he thought about it some more. Then he took a hurried drink from his beer. The fad had sure come along at the right time for her, Sullivan thought as he took another look. When he'd first met Denise, she was strictly a sweater-and-skirt girl, with her full front filling out her tight sweaters and her round, but slightly heavy lower body safely covered by long loosely fitting skirts. But now, fifteen or twenty pounds lighter, her legs were truly worth showing off and she was right in fashion with the short-short skirts of the fall of 1967.

"I hope you're wearing something under that," Sullivan said, grinning broadly and gesturing with his beer bottle back to Denise's very short skirt.

Denise only laughed at his question. "You're damn right, I'm wearing something," she said and then stopped. "With friends like you around, I should wear chain metal."

"Don't," Sullivan said quietly, but he didn't follow up on it.

Denise crossed her legs tightly in front of her body then in the white beanbag chair, closing off the best part of Sullivan's view and letting him know exactly where he stood with her for now. Men who don't call for a year, don't even get any free looks, was Denise's time-tested policy—and she didn't feel like changing it, just because it was the "anything goes" sixties. She'd wear the clothes, she decided, and buy the furniture, but her sex life now was going to stay strictly where it had begun, smack in the middle of the nineteen fifties.

"Well, anyway," Sullivan said a little sadly, "after I see Green, if it goes the way I hope, I might make a trip to Washington and talk to somebody back there in person. I've given up on Yancey."

"What do you think Green's going to say to you that he hasn't already said to the press?"

"I want to try my whole theory out on him, see what he does," Sullivan said. "I want to lay out the stuff about a second gunman in Dealey Plaza that day, the cop car at Strode's boardinghouse, the pilot they found buried in Louisiana a week later, Boyer, the whole thing—" Sullivan stopped then. He realized from the look on Denise's face that he was letting himself get carried away again. "I'm sorry," he said.

Denise set her drink down on the floor next to the white vinyl chair. "You know, Jim? The thing I like most about you is the same thing that sometimes I don't like at all."

"Yeah, what's that?" Sullivan said, looking away and pretending not to care, but inside his heart was pounding in anticipation.

"You can get so damn wrapped up in things," Denise said.

"Is that bad?" Sullivan said.

"It can make being with you very hard sometimes," Denise said. "You're special though," she added. "Who would have ever thought that I'd find someone like you working for the Bureau," she said, and then she smiled at her own sense of surprise. "When I was working for that lawyer, do you know how many cops and government guys I'd gone out with before you? And since then, too. I thought for a while there that maybe I had an addiction to them, like a drug or something."

Sullivan held up his hand, stopping her. The subject of who Denise dated was something that he never let her talk about. "There's nothing wrong with working for the government. It's just a little slow to understand sometimes, that's all. It's cautious," Sullivan said defensively. In the silence that followed, he was forced to think about himself for a few seconds, think about his life and where he was headed, something that he hated to do. "Not special," he said finally, to break the silence and the flood of confusing thoughts that he was beginning to have about himself. "I'm not special at all," he said. "I just told myself some things when I was a kid, made some decisions about how I wanted to be when I grew up, how I wanted to live. And it's always been important to me to try and remember those things, that's all."

"Truth, justice, and the American way?" Denise laughed, and Sullivan looked away from her in embarrassment.

Denise smiled at him then. "See, you are special," she said softly.

"No," Sullivan insisted. He was starting to feel very embarrassed. He wasn't used to talking about himself and what he felt to anybody.

"You really don't understand, do you?" Denise said, studying Sullivan's clean-shaven, square-jawed young face. "Jim, everybody decides things like that when they're a kid, but nobody ever really does it. Nobody even tries after a while. Just you, that's why you're so special," she said.

Sullivan didn't know what to say.

"Look at me," Denise said. "I promised myself that I'd marry a lawyer or a doctor maybe and live in a big house with a lot of kids and never have to work. And I didn't get any of it and probably never will." She shrugged her shoulders then and smiled at her own failures. "I've got an apartment with rent I can't afford, two half-screwed-up kids. I work my ass off trying to do a job that's probably too tough for me to ever be any good at, and instead of a doctor, I've got what?" She smiled at Sullivan again, but he was still too embarrassed and confused to have any answers for her. "I've got a good friend," she said. And then she added, with more than a touch of sadness, "Just a friend, who used to make love to me. See, nobody gets to be the way they wanted."

As she spoke, Denise let her legs uncross, and when she did her dress moved up even farther, showing a hint of white cotton underwear with little red cartoon hearts embroidered on them.

"You know, I've never seen your bedroom," Sullivan said, pointing back with his beer bottle toward the door at the far end of the long psychedelically decorated living room. "Are your friends ever invited in there?" he asked hopefully.

"Unh-unh," Denise said, "but you are." She stood up then, reaching out for Sullivan's hand, and led him across the room.

Sullivan stood for a moment and watched the young family playing together at the swings on the other side of the park. The FBI agent watched them all laughing—the father, no older than he was, the mother, her long blond hair tied back from her face, leaning over to catch her daughter as she slid down the little metal slide into her arms.

Sullivan crossed the grassy stretch of park to the brown dirt area that surrounded the play equipment and stood a few feet away from the man. The young father refused to look up at first, but Sullivan continued standing near him, until he could no longer be ignored.

"Remember me?" Sullivan said.

The young man's eyes studied Sullivan carefully. After several long seconds there was only a flicker of recognition in them, nothing more.

"I'm the FBI agent that you and your partner drove to Arthur Strode's rooming house . . ."

"Oh, yeah," the young father said, interrupting Sullivan. "I'm with my family," he said. "It's my day off."

"I phoned the station," Sullivan called out to the police officer. "I got nothing from you or your partner . . ."

The young police officer whirled back toward Sullivan angrily. "I said, it's my day off!"

"Billy, what is it?" the young officer's wife called out anxiously. She was kneeling by the foot of the slide now, holding both of their children in her arms and looking up past her husband at the tall blond stranger who had interrupted their morning.

"Talk to me," Sullivan said before the young man could turn and answer his wife's question. Then Sullivan looked down at the kneeling woman and smiled. "I'm sorry, Mrs. Everett, I work with your husband. I just need to talk to him for a minute," he said politely, and then he repeated in a softer undertone that only the police officer standing closer to him could hear: "Talk to me, Everett."

The officer's wife stood and nodded her head that it was okay. Sullivan could see now that she was pregnant. Three kids, Sullivan thought, and I bet this guy's younger than I am. Sullivan turned then, still thinking about it, and started walking toward a narrow path that led around the outside of the nearly empty midmorning park. Soon Sullivan could hear the police officer's reluctant footsteps behind him. Sullivan slowed his pace and let the younger man catch up with him.

"Mrs. Riordan, remember her? Strode's landlady. Anyway, she's dead," Sullivan said bluntly. The young patrolman's face responded to the old news with surprise, but he said nothing.

"She was killed by a hit-and-run driver. You didn't know that, did you? The driver had to come right up on the sidewalk to do the job," Sullivan said, but the only sound in return was the crunching of the dry gravel under the other man's feet as he moved along the cinder path.

"She was staying with her sister-in-law in a town north of here called Midland," Sullivan said. "Do you know the place?"

Still there was only a hard silence from the other man. So Sullivan continued, but he let the anger show clearly in his voice now. "Population five hundred and something. If they ever had a hit-and-run there before, nobody remembers it." Sullivan paused then, before adding with disgust, "There's evidence that after it hit her, the car backed up and rolled over her a second time."

"What do you want from me?" the young police officer said finally, and then he stopped walking and turned to face Sullivan.

"You're a cop . . ." Sullivan started, but before he could finish, Everett turned on his heel and began walking back toward the play area where he'd left his wife and family.

"I said, 'You're a cop.' Doesn't that mean anything down here?"

The young patrolman stopped in his tracks and turned defiantly back to Sullivan. "It means one hell of a lot."

"Look, I just want to make sure that you know what the facts are, because I want to ask you some questions," Sullivan said, closing the distance between them. "I don't want to make things rough on you, but every time I start taking a close look at what happened that day three years ago, I don't like it. Mrs. Riordan isn't the only one. I don't know how the hell many people connected with it are dead now," Sullivan added, and when he did the young patrolman's face tightened noticeably.

"Yeah, I know," Everett said.

Sullivan nodded. "So, you're worried too? Maybe you think like I do, that your department dropped the ball on the investigation about a hundred and fifteen different ways?"

Instead of answering, Everett slowly turned away and began walking down the path again.

"I asked you a question," Sullivan said.

"And I don't know the answer to it," Everett said. "I'm not a detective. I'm a third-year patrolman with . . ."

"I know what you are," Sullivan interrupted him. "Did you file a report?"

"Sure."

"And what did it say about what we found at Strode's?"

"The truth, everything."

"That a Dallas black-and-white stopped outside his rooming house a half hour before it should have been there?"

"It said that his landlady thought she might have seen one, yeah."

"And what happened?"

"What do you mean, what happened? We filed a goddamn report."

"Where did it go?" Sullivan was nearly shouting at the younger man now.

"Where they all went," Everett said. "To Boyer. He was in charge of the investigation."

"Was that standard?"

"Standard? Standard for what? Standard for when the President of the United States comes to town and nearly gets his goddamned head blown off? Who the hell knows?" The young man dug the heels of his heavy shoes deep in the dry rock and cinder of the dirt track and spun his body away from Sullivan.

"One more question," Sullivan said, but the young man had already begun to walk away again, returning to the spot at the end of the grassy park where he'd left his family.

"Who do you think was in that black-and-white that went to Strode's rooming house?" Sullivan called out and then jogged down the path after Everett. "Could it have been Towne?"

"I don't think it was a black-and-white," Everett said.

"Yeah, but if it was, could it have been Ray Towne?" Sullivan pressed.

Everett shrugged his shoulders, but his pace didn't slow. "Sure. But it could have been half a dozen other guys, too."

"A half a dozen other guys didn't catch up with Strode that day, only Towne! A half a dozen other guys weren't Boyer's special handpicked number-one boy! A half a dozen other guys didn't have a connection to Leo Green, and half a dozen other guys didn't just happen to stumble onto Strode and wind up getting into a shootout with him. Just Officer Raymond Towne!" Sullivan let it all spill out of him now. He could see the shock on the young patrolman's face. "Yeah, that's right. People have been talking to me. A lot of people, cops, people at Green's old club, I even talked to his brother, who's running the place now. They all had a lot to say. Now it's your turn."

The young patrolman hesitated for a moment, but he stayed quiet, so Sullivan continued pouring out some of the new facts that he'd been able to learn over the last few weeks of hard digging. "Green and Towne go way back, don't they? Even before November of 1963. In fact, Green told half the cops in Dallas that if Towne ever came into his club again, he'd kill him. Something about some money Officer Towne was supposed to have taken from him for protecting his club and the girls Green was running out of it, but then Towne didn't keep his end of the bargain, or so the story goes. So Green broadcasts to anyone that will listen that he's going to kill Towne. Towne's boss, Deputy Police Chief Boyer, was getting some of that money, too, but Green didn't go around talking about shooting Boyer, just Towne. Why was that?"

Everett shrugged his shoulders then. "Green was pissed off. He wasn't thinking right."

"I asked you if you think that could have been Towne at Strode's rooming house."

Everett stayed quiet for a while. "I heard it could have been," he said finally, not looking at Sullivan.

"From who?"

Everett held up his hand palm out to show that he was finished now.

"If you won't talk, I'll go to your partner. Where is he?"

"Get fucked!"

"It's easy to check," Sullivan called back angrily.

"Then check at the fucking morgue!" the young cop snapped.

"Jesus," Sullivan breathed out, finally understanding and feeling like a first-class bastard for pushing so hard.

"Look, Mr. G-man, cops get killed. It happens," the off-duty patrolman said before Sullivan could apologize. "It doesn't mean any big federal conspiracy is going on." Everett stopped talking then, his shoulders slumped forward as he looked down at the gray-brown cinder track below him. When he started talking again, his voice was lower, calmer, the fight and anger gone out of it. "It was a freak thing. Barry was off duty. He tried to break up some kind of a fight or something in a bar that he used to go to. Later, coming home, he wound up with a knife in him. He was dead before the ambulance got there. It wasn't supposed to happen, but it happened."

But the FBI agent watched as the young cop turned and walked back over to the play area to rejoin his wife and kids.

"Shit," Sullivan said out loud, but to nobody in particular, as he watched the young patrolman walk away. It wasn't a coincidence, Sullivan thought. It just couldn't be—everybody connected to what had happened in Dallas that day was being systematically murdered.

CHAPTER
27

The federal prison in Dallas was new and still reasonably clean. The air conditioning worked and the building had wide, freshly painted corridors, big well-lit rec rooms, and private visiting rooms filled with new furniture. As Sullivan waited he looked around at the freshly painted walls. If he ever broke any laws he'd make certain that they were federal ones—not state, he decided. And then the hall door unlocked and Green came into the room.

It was painfully obvious from Sullivan's first glance at Strode's executioner that Leo Green's life sentence in federal prison was going to be a very short one. Green's body had the slumped, hollowed-out look of a man whose insides were being rapidly eaten away, and his skin had a sickly grayish-yellow tinge. He was dressed in a wrinkled, khaki-colored uniform, with the name GREEN stenciled in black ink on a strip of tape above his left breast pocket.

He stood weakly at the doorway for several seconds, letting his body sag under the badly fitting uniform until the attendant who had accompanied him left the room and relocked the door. So this was the man, Sullivan said to himself, feeling more pity than anything else, this was the man who had changed history in the basement corridor of the Dallas police station four years before. Sullivan had caught only a brief glimpse of him then, but this was not the man of the photographs and the famous news film, a stocky, dark-haired man stepping aggressively forward and firing at Strode's stomach at point-blank range. The image was frozen in Sullivan's mind, and the man standing in front of him seemed like an entirely different person. God, had it only been four years? Sullivan watched Green move unsteadily across the

371

room and then slump down into the gray-metal folding chair across from him. The short trip from his cell to the visiting room had left him out of breath and Green kept his head down, making a series of shuddering, gasping sounds.

"You okay?" Sullivan said.

Green laughed at the young FBI agent—the laughter short and rasping, even more painful to listen to than the breathing had been.

"You want some water or something?" Sullivan asked. Green shook his head no.

"I want to get some rest is all," he said, not looking at Sullivan any longer, but letting his head and shoulders slump back down toward the floor. The newspapers had said that he was sick, but Sullivan hadn't realized until now just how serious Green's condition really was. How long could a man like this last, six months? A year?

"So, what do you want?" Green managed in a hoarse, throaty voice interrupted by sharp intakes of breath between almost every word.

"Why did you agree to see me?" Sullivan's reply surprised the older man enough for him to look up again and study Sullivan's face carefully for a moment.

"Agree? You're the one with all the power, not me, government man."

"You could have said that you were sick—you've done it before," Sullivan said.

At Sullivan's words, Green let his head slump down toward the floor again, gasping for a breath that wouldn't come. "Maybe I'm looking for an honest man," he managed finally.

"I'd like to be," Sullivan said.

Green paused, gathering his strength before he tried to answer. "You're working at the wrong job then, kid."

"Maybe not," Sullivan said stubbornly.

"Sure, you're right," Green said, gasping out another painful half laugh. "Anything can happen these days, I guess."

"Life's crazy, right? Like the songs say," Sullivan said, and Green nodded his head slowly.

"If you found your honest man, what would you tell him?" Sullivan pressed. "The truth?"

"I don't know, I might. There's nothin' anybody can do to me now," Green said, pointing a hairy finger at his own dying chest and gut.

"A newspaper reporter did a story about how they'd injected you with cancer cells so that you'd die and take your secrets with you," Sullivan said, surprising himself as he spoke. When he'd written out the questions for the interview in advance, he hadn't intended to say anything like that, but there was something about Green's attitude that made him risk it.

Green raised his eyes to look more closely at Sullivan as he answered him this time. "Yeah, I read that, too. I sure as shit wish the story'd said who the 'they' were, though," Green said, wheezing a small laugh as he thought about it. "God, maybe," he added then, as an afterthought.

"Joseph DeSavio is my guess," Sullivan said flatly.

Green stopped laughing when he heard the Mafia boss's name. "DeSavio. He's not God."

"For you, maybe close enough," Sullivan said.

Green was quiet then, his harsh, erratic breathing the only noise in the shiny-clean prison visiting room.

"Some people say he owns you. That he's owned you for a long time," Sullivan said.

Green was breathing so hard now that he could only manage to shrug his shoulders under the loosely fitting prison shirt in reply.

"And people tell me, too, that if you care about anything in this world, it's your brother Al; that you've lived with him since you were a kid. That he brought you up after your mother died, but the way I hear it Al's not too smart, and without you around to help him, he just scrapes by. And people tell me that you were sick long before you ever came in here," Sullivan continued. "Sick enough that you were afraid that you weren't going to live to do the one thing you wanted to make sure got done—that your brother got taken care of. And that if DeSavio needed someone to do him a big favor, like gun someone down for him in public, and then take a prison term for it, you were the perfect guy. At least you knew that if you did DeSavio his favor, no matter what happened to you, your brother would have it good the rest of his life. DeSavio would see to that. And there was a chance with the kind of power that DeSavio has down here that he could get you paroled in a few years. And if you lived that long, when you got out there'd be more money waiting for you than you could have ever made nickel-and-diming around Dallas for the rest of your life, however the hell long that was going to be."

Green remained quiet, except for the heavy labored sounds of his breathing.

"The word I got was that you and the cop Strode killed that day had a bad beef going. I hear you even told people that you were going to kill Towne, if you ever got the chance."

Green only shrugged his shoulders again.

"I thought you liked cops," Sullivan said.

"I've got a temper, that's the way I am."

"Yeah, but a cop?" Sullivan said. "Nobody goes around talking about shooting a cop, unless there's a reason."

Green still sat with his head down, saying nothing. Suddenly angry, Sullivan lashed out at him. "We're wasting each other's time here," Sullivan said. "Why don't I just go ahead and tell you what happened on November 22, 1963. What do you say?"

When Green didn't respond, Sullivan continued. "There were two shooters that day, not just one. The other one was a little dark-haired guy in a blue plaid shirt. I happen to know that, because I nearly tripped over him in the parking lot right behind Dealey Plaza a couple of minutes after the shots were fired. The two shooters had plenty of backup too, cars, a plane to take them out of the state, faked I.D. cards. It was a planned hit, organized, professional. I've seen them before, never on anyone as important as the President of the United States, but there's a pattern to them. My guess is that this one came out of New Orleans, and that means your pal DeSavio. Now, I'm going to start guessing a little, but it's educated guessing. I think it was Ray Towne's job to eliminate at least one of the shooters, maybe both. The stakes were too high on this one to let the trigger men go on living for very long. Once they were both dead, the links back to DeSavio would be almost impossible to trace. So, Towne is waiting for Strode at his rooming house before anyone else even has the word on him. Maybe Strode's been told that Towne's patrol car is going to be his transportation out of the city or at least as far as the pickup point for the other shooter, the guy in the blue plaid shirt. What better way to clear downtown Dallas that day than in the back seat of a Dallas black-and-white? But the truth is that it was just a setup. Towne was really there to kill him, clean and simple. It was a perfect way to eliminate a guy like Strode, a nut killed resisting arrest, end of story—but something went wrong.

"Jump in here whenever you want to," Sullivan said to Green, but still the older man stayed silent and Sullivan continued, piecing together all the bits and pieces and fragments of information that he had picked up in Dallas and New Orleans and Mexico over the last four years, and throwing them all out at Green now in the wild hope that it would convince the dying man to confirm what to Sullivan was so far mostly just suspicion and guesswork. "But like I said, something went wrong. Strode got smart or maybe just lucky, and it's Officer Towne who gets killed. But there was a backup. There's always a backup plan in professional jobs like this one, and my guess is that you were it that day," Sullivan said, pointing a finger at Green. "You were in it all along, but the original plan was for you to finish Towne off, not Strode. If it all had gone the way it was supposed to, you would have waited a week or so after the shooting, let it all cool down a little, maybe even give Towne enough time to be a hero for a while, and then one day you would come along and settle your old score with him. But when Strode did your job for you and finished Towne, you were ordered to go in after Strode instead. It wasn't as neat and clean as it could have been the other way, because you'd worked out all the details in advance on your cover story for killing Towne, but it was going to have to do. Strode had to be kept quiet, and you were the best thing DeSavio had left to get the job done for him. So they cooked up a new story for you. How you were a big Cassidy fan and you were pissed off at Strode for taking a shot at him, a little thin, but what the hell, a lot of people were pissed off at Strode and maybe they could sell you as just crazy enough to actually do it. You were a regular around the police station, everybody's pal, free drinks at your club for cops. It was a good-enough cover story for how you got into the station that night, but the truth is that you had more going for you than a few old friends and some luck, because it wasn't just you and Towne who were on DeSavio's payroll, but so was at least one other cop. Someone with enough authority that he could make damn sure that you got into the police station untouched that night and then make sure you got close enough to Strode that you could do your job. My guess is that other cop was Deputy Police Chief Boyer."

Green stayed quiet for a long time after Sullivan had finished. The older man just kept looking at the floor and breathing deeply and painfully in and out. "Take me to Washington or somewhere safe," Green said finally, his eyes still on the floor. "Get me the hell out of Dallas and I'll talk to you."

Sullivan stared down at the thinning grayish-black hair on the top of Green's head. "Why?" the FBI agent said after several more seconds had gone by.

"Do it, and I'll tell you the whole fucking story," Green blurted out then. "I don't give a shit about any of it anymore, but get me the hell out of Dallas!"

Green's head shot up then and his eyes began darting around, as if whatever it was that he was afraid of was lurking in the corners of the freshly painted room. "They own the fucking city," Green said. "Maybe it's in the food, I don't know. Or maybe it's like the guy said, and it's in the goddamned air that they pump into my cell, or the fucking water, but something's killing me. Get me the fuck out of here and we'll do some business," Green said wildly, his eyes still moving restlessly around the room, as if he were searching for its secrets. Sullivan looked at him, wondering if maybe Green really was crazy. Crazy enough to have killed Strode for the very reasons listed in the Bureau's final report and nothing more. And crazy enough now to make up some wild story to get himself out of Dallas and try to save himself from the slow, ugly death that no one could really save him from. Sullivan wasn't certain which way it was with Green, but he had to know. "Who are you telling me the 'they' is, that's trying to kill you?" Sullivan asked.

Green was quieter now, concentrating again on his own strained breathing. His head and shoulders had slumped back down toward the floor as he spoke. "You're guessing pretty good," he said.

"It was DeSavio's operation, wasn't it?" Sullivan said. "Nothing that big comes out of this area, unless it has his personal blessing, but who was the client? Or was it DeSavio himself? He hated Cassidy as much as anybody."

Green didn't answer him this time. Sullivan glanced down at his watch. His time with Green was almost over. "I need something in writing," Sullivan pressed him now, but Green only laughed his painful half laugh.

"Look, you've got to give me something. I'm just a goddamned junior agent. I'm not John J. Summers, for God's sake. I can't work miracles."

After Sullivan finished, the room was quiet again. Both men could hear the bailiff coming toward the heavy metal door to the visiting room, and the sound increased Sullivan's feeling of urgency. "You've got to trust somebody, sometime, or you're going to die in here. Maybe I'm as close as you're going to get to an honest man," Sullivan said.

Green lifted his head and looked the younger agent over carefully.

"I'll tell you this much, government man," Green said. "You've got some of it right, but there's one hell of a lot more that you don't know. There was a conspiracy to kill Cassidy, all right, and by the time it was over, it was so wide, so deep that it would fill up a page and a half of indictments. Strode, Towne, me, we were just the tip of the fucking iceberg, the part that you could see on the surface, while all the real players were buried safely out of sight—and they're getting safer all the time."

"What do you mean by that?" Sullivan said, but Green didn't answer. Both men could hear the key turning in the visiting-room door itself now. "Get me out of here," Green said in a low hoarse whisper. "And I'll give it all to you. And I'll tell it in a way that'll make it stick, names, dates, places, no more guesses. I'll nail it all fucking right down for you." Green finished just as the guard entered the room, and, after a few seconds of regathering his strength, the prisoner stood up and passed by Sullivan without saying anything more.

"I'll try," Sullivan said, as Green shuffled by him, and then Sullivan could hear the heavy metal door opening and then closing behind him as the prisoner was returned to his cell.

The bodies were stacking up like in a war, Sullivan thought. What was it the television people were calling it in Vietnam? "Body count," that's right. Well, he had his own goddamn body count going on right here in Dallas, except nobody else was taking the trouble to keep score.

He walked slowly along the cemetery path, looking at the rows and rows of markers stretching out in neat lines on both sides of the road. Near him an automatic sprinkler sprayed out pulsing streams of water over a patch of newly planted green lawn. Sullivan removed the little card that the guard at the cemetery gate had given him and reread the designation written hastily on it: "CBX-147." Sullivan looked down at the stone pin buried deep in the moist brown earth at the edge of the path. Only the top of the marker was visible and the letters CBU were painted in black letters on its gray stone surface. Sullivan moved ahead to the row marked CBX, and then he started down the long strip of soft earth, his route flanked on both sides by twin lines of neat bronze markers and occasional headstones of uniform size and shape.

When he finally reached the spot in row CBX marked 147, there was no headstone, just a hint of a small rectangular brass marker.

Sullivan knelt down and scraped dirt off the metal plate. There were ants thriving in the crevices formed by the letters and numbers cut deep into the surface of the marker, and dozens of the insects hurried away in every direction as Sullivan uncovered their hiding place.

This was the second grave that Sullivan had visited in less than four hours. The first grave that Sullivan had stopped by earlier that morning had read: MR. & MRS. ADRIANA DELLA-ROSA. Several weeks before, Sullivan had interviewed the Della-Rosas at the small grocery store that they ran in West Dallas. They would probably still have been operating that store today, Sullivan thought angrily, if they hadn't had the bad luck of locating their business across the street from the exact spot where Arthur Strode had gunned down Police Officer Raymond Towne in the early afternoon of November 22, 1963, and the even worse bad luck of having seen not one but two men run away from the scene. One of those men, Mr. Della-Rosa had told reporters that night and then later repeated to Sullivan, was short and dark and had been wearing a blue plaid shirt, and with those words, Sullivan guessed now, Mr. Della-Rosa had secured both his and his wife's death warrants.

The Della-Rosas had lived long and Sullivan hoped for their sakes, full lives, but the grave that Sullivan looked at now was the final resting place of a very young man, younger even than Sullivan himself. The marker read: WILLIAM TYLER EVERETT, FEBRUARY 12, 1943—NOVEMBER 6, 1967." Sullivan's thoughts wandered back to the young patrolman he had questioned in the Dallas park only the week before, and then, as hard as he tried to force the image from his head, Sullivan could see again the young man playing with his children at the swings of the nearly empty play area that morning. But as the image expanded to include the young man's young, pretty, and pregnant wife, Sullivan refused to look at it any longer. He stood up quickly instead, and he pushed dirt and leaves back over the marker with his foot.

Sullivan walked back toward the cemetery path at the end of the row of markers, feeling the ground soft and spongy beneath the soles of his highly polished black dress shoes. In the distance, he could hear the rhythmic whisking sound of the mechanical sprinklers watering the cemetery grass. There hadn't been any real reason to come here, Sullivan thought to himself, or to visit the Della-Rosas' twin graves that morning. But he had needed to see them for himself—and now he had, and so what? The Della-Rosas were really dead and buried and so was the young Dallas cop named William Everett, and his partner before him, and Strode's landlady and . . . Sullivan stopped himself. The list was too long to continue to repeat to himself over and over as he had been for days. He had to take some real action. But what could he do? There was Yancey. There were the Bureau people in Washington. But he had tried with both before and failed. There were the Cassidy people themselves. Hadn't Tim Cassidy told them to ask, if they needed help? Well, he needed help now. There was a way to get to him. There had to be. He had some people in Washington he could call. God, but he might as well kiss off his career in the Bureau after that. But the hell with his own career, he decided. As soon as he made the decision though, he could feel a sadness and a deep sense of loss surging up inside him for the things that he'd worked for and dreamed of all his life.

CHAPTER
28

The services at Ben Cassidy's grave were as private as they could possibly be for a man who had been prominent in the public affairs of his country for over a half a century and whose sons had become Senators, the Vice President, and the President of the United States. The ceremony, restricted to only his family and a few of his closest friends, had been one of the Cassidy patriarch's final requests.

The funeral had been held in St. Patrick's Cathedral in New York and the famous and powerful and the abundance of the press that they attracted had all attended, but the burial service had been held in a little chapel near the Cassidy home in Hyannis.

After the burial, there had been a reception at the Cassidy home, but while it was still in progress the two oldest brothers had managed to slip away and return the few miles to the site of their father's grave. The sun had almost set when they finished their private prayers and started back through the stone markers of the little New England graveyard toward their waiting limousine. It was late fall and a stiff wind was coming up from the nearby sea, blowing cold, bitter air into the faces of the two men, and their eyes were soon red and raw from the whipping wind and from the tears that they'd shed earlier in the day. They were silent, too, and talked out, but they wanted to be together, and as they approached the waiting limousine, they realized almost simultaneously that despite the discomfort of the cold, they weren't yet ready to rejoin the others and end their quiet private time together. It was Jack who raised his arm to signal the driver to wait for them and then both brothers continued walking silently on side by side down the lonely path.

378

"Can you stay another day?"

"No, I don't think so," Tim said. "I have some commitments."

Jack nodded his understanding. They continued in silence then, turning away from the road and descending back into the uneven rows of ancient stone markers that filled the old churchyard. Behind them, the slowly moving limousine came to a stop by the side of the narrow cemetery road.

"I'm going to miss him terribly," Tim said as the two men continued on away from the road, moving even more deeply into the irregular sea of stone markers that surrounded them.

Jack nodded his agreement and then kept his head down, looking at the hard November ground beneath his feet.

"Too much death," Tim said, but he didn't finish his thought. "Jack, I've spoken to Rothman again," Tim tried again a few moments later, but then he stopped for a second time. His face and eyes showed the great difficulty that he was having trying to find just the right words to express the depth of the secret that he had been hiding from his brother for the last several days, but when he continued the words seemed to just break from him and explode into the cold air. "Jack, I'm convinced now that it has to be done."

Jack searched his mind for something new to say to help his brother now, but there was so little that they hadn't already said to each other about the dramatically opposing positions each held.

"I've prepared a letter," Tim said, avoiding his brother's eyes. "All that remains is for me to sign and date it."

"But you wanted to talk to me first," Jack said, and Tim nodded.

"Have you spoken to the President?" Jack asked, the anger and disappointment heavy in his voice.

"I've tried," Tim said.

"But he doesn't know that you're actually considering a resignation, does he?"

"No," Tim said, and then he corrected himself. "Jack, I don't know for certain what Rance thinks anymore, but truthfully, I believe that he might welcome it. I've made one request of him during the entire three years that I've served in his administration, and it's been denied."

"To accompany the Secretary of Defense to Saigon next week," Jack said.

"He owes me that much."

"Tim, that's not sufficient reason to consider . . ."

"Of course not," Tim angrily cut his brother off in midsentence. "It's just a small part of the problem. The real issue is that I can't continue in good conscience to serve in an administration whose policies I'm deeply opposed to. It's that simple."

The two men walked on in silence through the lonely churchyard.

"What do you want me to say?" Jack said, his voice laced with anger. "That I approve? Well, I don't. I don't approve at all."

Tim looked up into Jack's eyes then, as the cold November wind blew his brother's hair straight back from his face. Jack's expression still showed the pain that he felt at the loss of their father, and Tim hesitated to go further. "I want you to tell me now, Jack, not what's smart, not what's good politics, but what you think is right," Tim said. But as Jack started to answer, Tim held up his hand to stop him. "Not what's right a year from now, or a month, or for the next election, or for the greater good of the Party, or for my own future, or for yours, but what's the right thing for me to do now, today," Tim looked into his brother's eyes then, challenging him, but Jack could say nothing. Finally, he turned away.

"Can you wait, Tim?" Jack said.

Tim looked back at his brother. There was one thing worth waiting for, one thing that would alter the decision that he had made, and both men knew what that one thing was. "Jack, if you don't go after the nomination, I will," Tim said decisively. "I don't care what rules I break, what traditions I ignore, or who I anger doing it. I'll run against the President, because I think that it has to be done. Do you understand?"

Jack nodded his understanding at his younger brother. They had stopped walking and they stood now under a once mighty, but now barren oak tree, its naked branches hanging low, arching over and framing the two men against the rolling New England hillside. Jack realized that they were lost in the unruly maze of headstones in the New England churchyard, their father's fresh grave hidden somewhere behind them among all the others. It was almost night and the headlights of the waiting limousine far back down the road cast a very faint white illumination on the figures of the two men. The wind was cold and neither man was wearing a topcoat and, as they stood silently together for a long moment, they each felt the great rushing wind pouring in from the Atlantic against their faces and cutting through their wool suits to touch their skin.

"I can wait," Tim said quietly. "But I can't wait for long."

Jack held out his hand toward his brother's. "I think Dad would understand if we went in now," he said, and their hands touched briefly and then locked tightly together, forming a bridge over the cold earth of the wind-chilled churchyard.

Allen Rozier waited at the corner table that he normally sat in, when he had lunch at La Caravelle. He ordered a drink but sipped at it sparingly when it came, as his attention remained focused on the front entrance to the restaurant. There was no mistaking the man that he was waiting for when he arrived. He was dressed in a long camel's-hair topcoat, expensive and neatly tailored. The Revolution has been generous to some of its supporters, Rozier thought as he watched the man approach his table.

"Señor Estanza," Rozier said and then stood up and moved forward to shake the hand of the white-haired man. Estanza bowed slightly in reply, using only a graceful subtle motion of his head and shoulders, saying nothing. Impressed with his quiet dignity, Rozier waited for the older man to sit down before returning to his own seat.

Rozier watched as the elderly man ordered his drink—a dry vermouth with no ice. Although Estanza's snow-white hair and his grayish lined skin gave away his age, the man's movements and his brilliant dark black eyes could easily have belonged to a much younger man. He was no ordinary opponent, and he was going to have to be careful dealing with him, Rozier decided. "Señor Estanza," he said, "before we begin, I want to be very certain that we understand each other. I am here in my capacity as a private citizen and only because I am personally curious about the subjects that we discussed over the telephone, but I believe that it is imperative for you to fully understand before we go any further that I do not officially represent the United States government in this matter nor do I speak for the Cassidy family." Rozier had prepared the somewhat long opening statement in advance, knowing that Estanza was likely to somehow try to tape-record the conversation.

"I do understand, Mr. Rozier. You made that very clear to me over the telephone," the elderly man said, in a slow, rather formal manner, with only the faintest hint of an accent. "I, on the other hand, do formally represent the official government of my country."

"I understand that as well," Rozier said, and then he paused while the waiter returned to the table and set down the vermouth.

After the waiter had left, Estanza solemnly lifted the small glass to his lips and sipped delicately at it and then set it down precisely in the middle of the table in front of him. He was a very careful man, Rozier thought as he watched him, careful and what else? Dangerous? Perhaps, he decided—careful and dangerous.

"I also want you to understand, Mr. Rozier," Estanza said, "that my government has not yet made any formal attempt to contact the American government about this matter. We may, however, find it necessary in the future to make our requests through normal diplomatic channels."

Rozier nodded. "So you haven't spoken to the State Department about it yet?"

"Not yet," Estanza said. "But we are not promising that we won't."

"I see," Rozier said cautiously.

Estanza smiled then. "You are wondering why we have chosen to speak to the Cassidy family before we have discussed the matter officially with your State Department."

"Perhaps," Rozier said, even though the elderly Cuban diplomat had guessed his thoughts precisely.

"You see, the information we have is quite harmful to the United States government," Estanza said confidently. "But it is even more damning to your friends, the Cassidys, much more so."

Both men were quiet, each measuring the other. In the silence, the word *blackmail* began to sound in Rozier's mind. It was of course what he'd expected after he'd had an opportunity to think about the telephone call that he'd taken earlier in the week from Señor Estanza, during which the diplomat had hinted at the purpose of the meeting, but Rozier had hoped that he was wrong.

"My government believes that it might be in its best interests to speak with the Cassidy family about our information, before we either release the information to the world press or discuss it with the administration," Estanza said, reaching slowly into his inside coat pocket and withdrawing a slender gold cigarette case.

The elderly man offered the open case to Rozier. Allen looked down at the row of slim, exquisitely made French cigarettes in the gold case carefully before shaking his head. Rozier wasn't smoking any longer, and he wanted only to inspect the little gold box for a recording device, but as he looked down at the neat row of slender foreign cigarettes, he realized how hopelessly out of place he was in this world of spies and diplomats and blackmail. He was a newspaperman and maybe a press secretary, but he didn't know a hidden recorder from a pack of Lucky Strikes.

"Well, as I've said, I'm not in a position to speak for the Cassidy family," Rozier said. "But, personally, I believe that your government's decision not to go to the press was wise. So many of these kinds of things have turned out not to be accurate. It could have had embarrassing results for everyone," Rozier said, as he watched the elderly man's exaggeratedly delicate movements with the cigarette and then with a slim gold lighter that he withdrew from the waist pocket of his suit coat.

"Yes," Señor Estanza said, smiling, but without agreeing with Rozier, and then the Cuban finished lighting the cigarette that he held between his extended fingertips. A small cloud of perfume-tinged tobacco smoke curled above the table between the two men then, adding, Rozier thought as he inhaled on it secondhand, to the carefully constructed atmosphere of delicate haziness of the negotiations that Estanza was attempting to establish between them.

"I can't go to the Cassidy family with mere hints and speculation. The demands on their time are enormous," Rozier said sharply, attempting to cut through the cloud of mystery and vague threat that Estanza had been carefully attempting to create.

"I quite agree," the elderly man said. "However, the matter that we're speaking about now is not speculative, Mr. Rozier. It is fact, and it is of enormous importance."

"We shall see."

"No, Mr. Rozier," Estanza said slowly. "The information that my government has in its possession is accurate, and it is quite damning to the American government and, as I have said, even more damning to the Cassidy family. There is no doubt about that," Estanza said dramatically. "All that remains to be determined is what my government will choose to do with that information."

Rozier was suddenly frightened by whatever it was that the diplomat and his government had in its possession, but he tried hard not to let his fear show for even an instant. "Are you in a position to tell me how this information was acquired?" Rozier shot back, feeling a little surprised at how well he was, at least for the moment, playing the other man's game.

"Perhaps, but not at this time," the elderly man said, and then he puffed deeply on the slender cigarette, filling the air with perfumed smoke again.

"What are you in a position to tell me now?" Rozier said, relying on his natural skills as a reporter and interviewer to move ahead in the dangerous game with the more experienced man.

"That my government is prepared, under certain circumstances, to deliver the original of these documents along with a further crucial piece of supporting evidence either to the American government," Estanza said and then paused before adding pointedly, "or, if you would prefer, we could deliver these items of evidence directly to the Cassidy family itself."

He was being used to blackmail not only the Cassidy family, but the American government as well, Rozier realized suddenly. "Señor Estanza, I must reiterate my position here," he said again. "I am only an interested private citizen. I have not contacted anyone in the United States government about this or anyone in the Cassidy family either, and I may not in the future."

"We are willing to take that risk," Estanza said, smiling confidently. He was either a superb actor or a man very certain that what he had to offer was of enormous value, Rozier thought, as he watched the other man's confident face.

"What I am about to give you," Estanza said, reaching for his attaché case, "are copies of several pages from a diary kept by Arthur Strode during the months prior to the attempt that he made on the life of President Cassidy in Dallas four years ago." Estanza paused then to let the dramatic importance of what he was saying have its effect on Rozier. "The diary itself is highly detailed, and it tells a quite different story of why Mr. Strode acted as he did than does the official explanation arrived at by your government's law-enforcement agencies—quite different. These pages should suggest to you a few of these differences. And there are other more significant differences contained in the remainder of the material which we have in our possession. Senator Cassidy will recognize their importance as soon as he is made aware of them." Estanza set a long manila envelope down on the tabletop in front of Rozier. The reporter eyed the envelope, and it took all of his will power not to reach out for it and open it immediately.

"Arthur Strode apparently kept the diary as his own insurance policy, as you will see," Estanza said, pointing at the envelope with his burning cigarette. "He did not fully trust the people that he was working for, with good reason as it turned out," Estanza added. "As you know, Mr. Rozier, there are individuals within your country and elsewhere, who, for their own political reasons, would like the world to believe that the assassination attempt on President Cassidy's life was in some way sponsored by or even planned directly by my government or by Communist forces operating inside your country that were sympathetic to my government. This lie has done enormous damage to the relationship between our two countries, but as you will see, nothing could be further from the truth."

Rozier noted the first signs of anger in the elderly man as he spoke of those "individuals," but Rozier couldn't be certain if the anger was real or simply feigned by a consummate actor, an actor experienced in the playing of many such scenes of political intrigue.

"You, Mr. Rozier, are known to be a good and close friend of former President Cassidy and his brother, a confidant. You are also known by my government to be a fair and honest man, with a high regard for the truth. It is with that understanding that my government has instructed me to give you this," Estanza said, touching the envelope lightly and directing it toward Rozier.

"You mentioned 'certain circumstances' under which the originals of the entire diary would be delivered over to the American government. What kind of circumstances?" Rozier said, still refusing to touch the envelope that sat only a few inches from him now.

"We will speak of that when you, or whoever it is that you choose to contact concerning this matter, have become convinced of the importance and authenticity of what we have to offer," Estanza said. "I can assure you that our request will be reasonable and in the best interests of both of our governments, and that nothing you do will be in any way harmful to your country. On the contrary it will be quite beneficial. What I have just given you," Estanza said, gesturing with his burning cigarette toward the long manila envelope and then dropping his voice down to an even lower and more confidential tone, "will permit our two countries to resume normal financial and political relations that were to a certain extent interrupted by the ugly and unfortunate rumors begun at the time of the events in Dallas. These pages are, of course, merely copies. The original is a little over sixty-four pages in length, handwritten. We can conclusively prove its author to be Arthur Strode. That will be easy enough for you to prove to your satisfaction as well by the use of your own handwriting experts. We, however, have certain additional proof of its authenticity. And we are also willing, at the appropriate time, to turn over to you that additional proof."

"The Cassidy family is not in a position to grant concessions on behalf of the American government," Rozier said, dropping his mask of experienced negotiator of political intrigue and letting some of his true anger show for a brief moment as he spoke, but Estanza only shrugged his narrow shoulders. "Senator Cassidy is certainly one of the most powerful men in the United States. We believe that, should he choose to, he could help enormously in effecting the policy changes toward our country that we believe are now necessary. We also believe, as do many in your own country, that Senator Cassidy may very well become President Cassidy again soon. But, Mr. Rozier, truly that determination is not for either you or I to make," he said. "I would suggest that our role here is much more limited. We are middlemen in this transaction only. Perhaps we should leave the determinations of the value to be received by each party to the principals themselves."

"And you speak for Premier Castro?" Rozier said, but Estanza didn't answer his question.

"We believe that when Senator Cassidy is made aware of these materials he will want to be certain that they not become public knowledge, and that he will be willing to utilize his considerable influence within your government to ensure that they are not released to the world press. To say anything further at this time is not in either our best interest or in yours, Mr. Rozier."

Rozier still refused to reach out and touch the envelope. Once he took possession of these materials, it was difficult to know where it could end. What was it that could be so damaging? Should he contact Jack first before he went any further? Tim? Ask their advice? No, Rozier decided it would be a mistake to involve either of them without reviewing and authenticating the contents of the envelope himself. It would risk their reputations unnecessarily. The so-called Strode diary was probably a fake, and in all likelihood he would never have to involve either Jack or Tim in it at all. This entire meeting could easily be a trap of some kind engineered by the Russians or by Castro, and he'd be damned if he would be an accomplice in leading Jack into it, without knowing a hell of a lot more than he knew now. He reached out and placed his hand on the manila envelope and slid it across the table toward his side of the table, then placed it quickly in his leather briefcase.

"Mr. Estanza, I appreciate your bringing these matters to me," he said and smiled. For the first time, he could see a flicker of doubt cross Estanza's darkly confident eyes. Rozier pressed the advantage. "I want to be very clear," Rozier said. "I am promising nothing in return for an opportunity to review these documents."

"I understand."

"And you will make our understanding known to Premier Castro," Rozier said, his heart pounding fast now.

"Of course," Estanza said, nodding his head slightly and then drinking from his glass of vermouth, finally betraying a hint of his own nerves at playing the high-stakes game.

"You said earlier, Mr. Estanza," Rozier continued, "that in addition to authenticating the handwriting on these documents, you had available to you another manner of proving that these papers were actually written by Arthur Strode. I should know what that other evidence is now, so that I can properly evaluate the entire situation."

"There is a reference throughout the diary to a second gunman that was to be present in Dallas that afternoon. I assume that you are familiar with that theory popularized by some members of the press."

"Of course," Rozier said.

"Yes, good," Estanza replied coolly, his confidence returning as he played his trump card. "There is such a man, and we have him in our custody at this time. He will verify the truth of almost everything contained in the diary. And . . ." Estanza paused briefly then and reached down to retrieve his cigarette case from the tabletop. As Rozier watched the elegant older man's careful movements, he wondered if what he was really doing was shutting off the recording device that Rozier suspected was hidden somewhere in the thin gold case.

"This other man, who was present in Dallas that afternoon, is of course part of what we are offering to your government."

"His testimony," Rozier said and then felt foolishly naïve as soon as he'd heard his own words.

"His testimony or his death," Estanza said coldly. "Whichever serves the purposes of our governments and the Cassidy family most effectively."

The auditorium was erupting in violence. It had been burning like a slow fuse throughout the Vice President's speech, and now students were spilling out into the aisles and pressing up chaotically at the edges of the stage where Tim Cassidy stood protected by only a thin line of campus police and Secret Service agents.

"Murderer! Murderer! Murderer!" The chanting came at first from a small group of students at the back of the room, but soon the chant was taken up by others in the audience and the sound of their voices seemed to come from everywhere in the auditorium. Objects began hurtling through the air then, smashing around Cassidy's lectern. A heavy metal bottle opener violently cracked the plastic screen just below his head, but the young Vice President refused to move from his position at the center of the auditorium's stage. He stood his ground and looked at the violent scene being played out in front of him, his own feelings a jumble of regret and sadness and anger. He bent forward toward the microphone several times, trying to speak, but each time his words were lost in the noise and chaos that filled the room.

Dave Jennings crossed the stage and grabbed him by the arm. "Tim, it's no use!" he said, yelling the words directly into the Vice President's ear. "Let's get out of here!"

A few of the students were approaching the stage now, and one of them held a container in his hands. Cassidy watched while the student splashed a dark red bloodlike liquid on the uniforms of the campus police.

Another group of students surged forward then, trying to reach the lectern, and the noise and tumult in the auditorium reached a fever pitch.

Two Secret Service agents ran up beside the Vice President, and Cassidy turned to them. "I want to finish," he said, motioning toward the shattered plastic lectern in front of him and then gripping it tightly in both hands.

"It's out of control!" Jennings shouted at him and pointed at the line of campus police that was beginning to lose ground against the angry surge of students. Only then did the Vice President reluctantly loosen his grip on the lectern and start slowly for the back of the stage.

The stage door opened as Cassidy approached it, and a cold blast of Midwest wind and snow blew in against the Vice President's face. The icy wind bit into his flesh, but there were more students outside and at his appearance a chorus of angry noise descended on him and then snowballs began landing on the protective line of police that moved ahead of the Vice President trying to create a safe channel through the unruly crowd to his waiting limousine.

A snowball smacked into Jennings's shoulder. "Shit!" the young aide said. "There was something in that one," he said, looking down at his neat tan topcoat that now showed a dark wet splatter mark on its carefully tailored fabric. "This wasn't in the job description," Jennings said, but Cassidy's face remained grim and stern and vaguely puzzled as he surveyed the angry faces that surrounded him.

Suddenly, a long-haired man ducked through the protective ring of security people. Out of the corner of his eye Tim could see the blur of the dull gray color of the man's shirt and then the quick cutting movement of his hand. There was an object in the man's hand and, remembering Dallas, Cassidy looked at it in horror, but then the security officers jumped between them and the man was forced back into the crowd. The object that he'd held in his hand dropped into the snow as he was moved away, but before Cassidy's eyes could focus on it. Then more Secret Service agents closed around the Vice President and roughly pushed him into the back seat of his limousine.

Cassidy looked down at the front of his dark pin-striped suit. It was splashed with a jagged crimson stain. Was he bleeding? The dark red line started at his right shoulder and ran diagonally across the front of his jacket, almost the entire length of his suit coat. He hadn't been hurt he realized finally, but the long-haired student had left his mark in vivid red ink for all to see. Suddenly, Tim could feel the limousine speeding through the crowd that blocked its way to the university's front gates.

Cassidy looked out the window of his rapidly moving vehicle to see the narrow campus street packed with more angry, chanting students, some carrying signs of protest, others throwing snowballs or rocks at his limousine. As Cassidy looked up at the faces packing the roadside, he was suddenly reminded of another ride in another long, black limousine down crowded streets. On that day long before though, there had been Americans holding candles of hope in their hands, lighting the darkness as he passed by. He remembered the love and support in the people's eyes that night. How long ago had that night been? Cassidy thought sadly as he looked out the window of his limousine at these faces. Why had it changed so dramatically? What terrible thing had been unleashed in the streets of his country since that night?

Tim reached up and flicked the little button down that activated the limousine's intercom system. "Stop the car!"

"Jesus, Tim, what are you doing?" Jennings said.

"I'm going to talk to them. They don't understand," Cassidy said and started to open the limousine door as it slowed to a stop on the icy road.

"You can't," Jennings shouted and as he did, the two Secret Service agents riding in the back of the limousine with them moved toward the Vice President as if to restrain him, but Cassidy challenged them angrily. He looked directly into their faces, commanding them to leave him alone, and the two dark-suited agents froze in place.

"This isn't the time," Jennings shouted again, but the Vice President was determined. "At least take off the goddamned coat. It looks like you've been shot," Jennings said, seeing now that it was too late to stop him from stepping out onto the road to face the students.

Tim pulled off his stained coat and threw it on the floor of the limousine before he got out of the car onto the roadside. It was cold and snow was falling all around him, but he barely noticed. He moved to the front of the vehicle and leaped up on its hood.

He stood in the cold air for a moment with the snow falling around him, waiting for the crowd to quiet before he began speaking. As he waited in his shirtsleeves in the driving snow, he noticed a dark crimson stain splashed in a jagged pattern across his white shirtfront as well. Ignoring it, he began speaking to the crowd. His words deviated from the prepared text he had planned to deliver that afternoon, the one that the White House had approved in advance, and in its place he began for the first time in years to say publicly what he believed and how he truly felt.

" 'I will go to Saigon!' Good God, I never thought I'd accuse a Cassidy of soundin' like Eisenhower, but there it is!" Gardner shouted at the television screens mounted in front of him in the study of the presidential retreat at Camp David, seventy secluded miles deep into the mountain and forest country of Maryland.

All three networks were carrying the report of Cassidy's dramatic speech given in the snow from the hood of the vice-presidential limousine as their lead story on the evening news, and a flashing series of images of the young Vice President were displayed on the television screens set up against the far wall of Gardner's study: Cassidy standing at the podium before an auditorium of angry protesters and then the plastic teleprompter shield suddenly shattering in front of him; Cassidy again, being led through the crowd and into the rear of his limousine; Cassidy standing on the hood of the limousine in his shirt-sleeves oblivious to the cold, the snow falling around him, his shirt splashed with a dark red bloodlike stain.

"Who cleared his speech?" Gardner said, turning to Mazeloff, who was seated at one of the long, formal leather couches that stood in front of the President's desk. "Get it for me, I want to see it. Then I want to talk to him!"

"Sir, there's nothing in it," Mazeloff said.

"Nothing in it? What the hell do you mean! You saw it!" Gardner said, pointing at the trio of television screens at the far end of the room. " 'I will go to Vietnam!' 'I will tell the President of the United States what to do!' You call that nothing?"

"He didn't exactly say that, sir," Mazeloff said, but Gardner barely heard him. The television screens had begun playing out news footage of the war, and Gardner's attention was focused exclusively on it now. Mazeloff summoned some more courage and continued. "Sir, none of what the Vice President said out there this afternoon was in the prepared text," Mazeloff said, raising his voice above the low hum of the voices from the television monitors. "We went through the copy of his speech his office gave us with a fine-tooth comb."

When he finished, Mazeloff waited for a reply, but the President watched each of the three network news broadcasts through to their first commercial breaks before he reached forward and used the dials built into a panel below his desk to cut off the sound. Only then did he turn his attention to Mazeloff, looking down through his metal-framed spectacles with great intensity at the neatly dressed little man seated in front of him, but still saying nothing.

"What are we going to do?" Mazeloff looked away from the President's face and turned his own gaze up toward the log-cabin roof of the mountain retreat, as if he expected to hear shells fired by faraway reporters exploding on the roof of the mountain cabin at any minute.

"Do you want me to deny it, tell the press that in the excitement of the moment the Vice President misspoke?" Mazeloff said. "I think that might be best."

"The first thing I want," Gardner said, pressing a button on his desk, "is to make certain that the Vice President has nothing more to say about any of this, until . . ." Gardner stopped then as Mallory appeared at the door to the President's private study. "Bill," the President continued, "tell the Vice President that I want to meet with him first thing Monday morning." Gardner turned back to Mazeloff. "For the moment, Ted, we have no comment on the Vice President's speech or on his announcement," the President continued calmly. A small smile was starting now at the corners of his mouth. "There's an old expression that we have back home," he said to his press secretary. "Maybe it's just what the Vice President needs a taste of right now," Gardner said. "In Texas, it's called giving the man enough rope to hang himself. 'Cept here there might be enough rope to hang a man and his brother at the same time."

"We have the same saying in California," Mazeloff said, smiling at the President, but the first of the networks had resumed their news coverage and Gardner's attention had already returned to the pictures on the television screens.

Allen Rozier pushed back from the desk of his New York apartment and removed his reading glasses. He dropped the heavy glasses into the scattering of papers spread out in front of him on the desktop.

Throughout the weekend he had read and reread the half dozen photocopied pages of meandering, confused ramblings that had been given to him by the Cuban diplomat. It was late Sunday night, almost sixty hours since his meeting with Castro's ambassador, and Rozier was convinced now that the papers might actually be authentic. There was a good chance, he thought, that they could really be the words of Arthur Strode, written in the weeks preceding the attempt on the President's life, and if they were, they began to suggest a shockingly different story about the shooting than did the FBI's final report.

Rozier had read the blurred, badly copied sheets of paper several times, checking them as best he could against other reports of the events leading up to that day in Dallas four years earlier. The materials that Estanza had given to him also contained written opinions from two Cuban handwriting experts confirming that the work was Strode's. Of course that would have to be checked independently, but Rozier was convinced that the papers he had might actually be part of the real thing, and if they were, the nagging question now was what the hell was he going to do about it?

Rozier stood and walked slowly across the room. He reached up to draw back the long draperies that covered the floor-to-ceiling windows at the far side of his apartment's living room. Below him were the lights of New York City. He stood for a moment and looked down at the river and then up to the outline of the U.N. Building in the distance. Suddenly his telephone rang, jolting his attention back toward his desk. He crossed the room quickly then and picked up the phone.

"Allen, Dave said you called." Tim Cassidy was on the other end of the line.

"Are you all right?" Rozier said. He hadn't spoken to the Vice President since Cassidy's now-famous speech from the hood of his limousine to the angry students of a small college in Ohio.

"I'm fine," Cassidy said. "The President has asked to see me first thing tomorrow morning."

"It's one way to get some time with him," Rozier said.

"Yes," Tim said abruptly.

Rozier paused then, not certain of what he was going to say next. In the silence, he reached out and fingered the materials on his desk, and then he picked up the notes that he'd made from his review of the Cuban papers.

His notes were a seemingly endless series of questions, some answered, but most not. Who? What? Where? When? How? the notes asked over and over. Once a journalist, always a journalist, Rozier thought, smiling to himself as he looked down at his pages of carefully prepared comments.

"Allen, what is it?" It was late in Washington, too, Rozier thought, as he listened to the irritation in the Vice President's voice.

"Tim, it's important." Cassidy quieted as he noted the uncharacteristic note of urgency in his friend's voice. "I need to talk to you," Rozier went on, still fingering the stacks of paper on his desktop and continuing to choose his words very carefully.

"Yes, of course," Cassidy said, equally aware of the possibility of their conversation being taped or overheard.

"Can you come to New York?" Rozier said. "I have some things that I need to show you in private."

"It would be difficult right now, but if you think that it's necessary, we could set something up."

"I do," Rozier said flatly and didn't try to explain any further. He knew that there were few people on earth that Tim would trust enough to make the trip without any clue as to why he needed to see him, but using the phone for something like this or even to hint at what he wanted to show him was out of the question.

"It may have to wait until next week, though," Cassidy said.

"You think the President may actually let you make the trip to Saigon?"

"Yes, I think he might," Cassidy said. "He's either called me in tomorrow morning to approve the trip or to fire me, and I guess I won't know which until he tells me himself."

"Yes, I see," Rozier said as he thought through the Vice President's request that their meeting wait until Tim's hoped for return from Southeast Asia. Well, Strode's diary had waited this long, almost four years, it could certainly wait another week. There was no immediate danger; this second gunman, if he even existed, was safely locked away inside a Cuban prison, and there was still a good chance that the diary and the pages he'd been given were phony, anyway. The extra time might even give him an opportunity to find a handwriting expert that he could trust and have him check the materials before he brought Tim into it. And God knows Tim had enough to worry about for now anyway. Maybe a week of cooling off on it would be the best thing for everybody, he decided finally. "If you do make the trip, can I be the first on your list when you get back?" Rozier said, trying to make his voice sound lighter and more confident than he truly felt.

"Of course," Tim said, but Rozier could tell from the faraway sound of his friend's voice that he was barely focusing on the telephone conversation. His thoughts, Rozier guessed, were focused on his meeting with the President and his chances of being granted permission to accompany Secretary Forbes to Southeast Asia later in the week.

"It all depends on what the President has to say to me tomorrow morning," Cassidy said then.

"I understand," Rozier answered.

"Either way, I'll call you."

"Thank you, Tim," Rozier said. "Good-night."

"Good-night, Allen."

Rozier hung up the phone. His first emotion was relief; he'd done all that he could for now, and he closed his eyes for a moment, but the relief lasted only for a few seconds. His apartment was deathly quiet, and in the silence he began looking around at the shadows on the walls of his study and then reacting to the noises that he imagined he heard in the hallway outside the room. Had he made a mistake? Should he have told Tim about the diary over the phone? Or should he have risked flying to Washington with it and discussing it with Tim at the White House that very night? No, what could one more week possibly matter now? Suddenly he felt very tired and unsure of himself and then very frightened. He moved back to his desk and scooped up the pages of Strode's diary and his own notes and crossed the room. It wasn't just the Cassidy family who wouldn't want this material made public knowledge. There were other powerful and dangerous people who would be willing to stop at nothing to keep the story contained in Strode's writing from being released. If the papers were really what they purported to be, there was one hell of a lot of risk now, for himself and for everybody connected to it. He dropped the pages onto a small side table and reached up and removed the plaque that covered a small metal safe that was built into the wall of his study. When he had worked the combination of numbers, he nervously yanked on the metal bar that opened the safe, but it didn't budge. He looked behind him. He was certain for that split second that he could hear a noise in the hallway outside his study, but as he stood and listened the noise, if it had ever really been there, began to fade away. He tried to calm himself then, but it was no use. He fumbled with the safe's knob again and this time, after he'd finished with the tumblers, the handle moved in response to the heel of his hand. With his heart pounding in his ears, he crammed the papers deep into the safe. He closed the swinging metal door and spun the black plastic tumbler, locking the double-walled stainless-steel safe. Jesus, he whispered to himself, as he turned back into the room, he wasn't cut out for this kind of cloak-and-dagger stuff. He was just a journalist, but he was in it now, and there would be no getting out until everyone whose name was in Strode's diary had played out his part in this dangerous game to the very end. He was deeply in that game himself now and it was a very dangerous place to be, he realized, as he watched the lights and shadows playing erratically and frighteningly around him on the darkened wall of his study.

CHAPTER

29

Sullivan stepped into a crowded reception area filled with activity. He crossed slowly to the front desk as men and women moved hurriedly around him.

"My name's Sullivan. I have an appointment to see Mr. Shore," he said to the receptionist, but she shook her head indicating that she couldn't hear him over the other noise and confusion in the room. He bent forward and repeated his message almost directly into the woman's ear and only then did she nod her understanding. Sullivan straightened up and took a puzzled look around. This was Washington all right, he thought to himself, the puzzled look on his face turning into a faint smile. It hadn't changed much, a little crazier if anything, that was all.

The gray-haired receptionist returned his smile as she reached for her phone to ring Shore's office. "You didn't see the news this morning?" she said to the young FBI agent, as she waited for someone on the other end of the line to answer her call.

"No," Sullivan said and he shook his head to be certain that he was understood.

"What's going on?" he asked, but the receptionist had reached someone now and she was busy talking into her phone, explaining that "Mr. Sullivan is here to see Mr. Shore," and Sullivan's thoughts returned to the morning that he'd just spent in his hotel room going over the many strands of the complicated web of facts and theories and suspicions that he had come to Washington to talk to Cassidy about, but then looking around at the noisy confusion in the Vice President's reception area, Sullivan began to doubt that he would actually have a chance to see him, at least not today.

"It's nuts, isn't it?" Tom Shore said, as he threaded his way through the chaotic reception area to where Sullivan was standing by the front desk. "God! I'm sorry, I forgot. What with all the flap and everything," Shore said and then flashed a quick smile that radiated energy and excitement. Sullivan couldn't remember when he'd seen a smile quite as enthusiastic. It certainly hadn't been around the Bureau.

"Well, can we reschedule?" Shore said, already beginning to backtrack toward the long busy hallway behind him. As Shore turned to Sullivan to say something, another aide flung open the front door to the reception area and called out loudly, "Battle stations everyone! Here comes the press!" And a small army of reporters followed the assistant into the already crowded reception area. "Oh, God! I've got to get out of here," Shore said, as he took another half step and began to lose himself back down the hall toward the staff offices.

"Look, this is important!" Sullivan said angrily. Unasked, he followed Shore down the private corridor. The two men walked toward an office near the end of the long, straight hallway then. "We're preparing something for the press now," Shore explained over his shoulder to Sullivan. He pointed at Sullivan's briefcase, as the two men finally ducked into the comparative safety of a small side office near the end of the hall. "Do you have something that I can read?" Shore said. "And then I can get back to you?" The phone next to him began to ring insistently, but the young aide showed no sign of responding to it.

Sullivan began to fumble in his briefcase, his big hand coming across the thick, unruly file that he'd brought with him from Dallas. It was hardly a standard Bureau file, he realized, as he rummaged through the disorganized mass of papers. By itself it would be useless, he decided. He had to talk to Cassidy, explain it to him, or it would just be a waste of everybody's time. Sullivan snapped his head up and looked at Shore. "God damn it! I've got to see him myself. It has to do with people's safety!"

Shore looked surprised by Sullivan's unexpected outburst. Some guys just can't take the pressure, his expression said, as he tried to decide what he was going to do with the uncooperative FBI agent. "Safety?" Shore said. "I didn't understand that from what Kent Barker said to me over the phone. I mean, shouldn't this go through channels then?"

"Look, I was on assignment in Dallas on the day President Cassidy was shot. Your boss told me personally that I was to see him if I needed something. Well, I need something now. It's important."

"But this is such a bad time," Shore said, pointing at the phone that was still ringing on the desktop. "You can see that, can't you?"

Sullivan reached back into his briefcase and managed to locate the hand-written summary of his findings he'd prepared in his hotel room the night before.

"Please give him these," Sullivan said, thrusting the sheaf of notes at Shore. "And I could wait somewhere, until he's ready to see me."

Shore reached up and took the papers. He started to say something, but then changed his mind. "I can't make any promises, but I'll do what I can. I'll talk to Dave Jennings. Maybe he'll clear it. Wait here."

Sullivan sank down into a chair in front of Shore's desk. "What's all the excitement about, anyway?" he said just before Shore ducked out the door, and the assistant turned back to him, almost laughing at the question. "You mean, you don't know?"

"Unh-unh."

"We just got the word, the President's finally letting us go to Saigon!" Shore said, his voice filled with triumph, and then he ducked out the door.

Sullivan stayed seated, looking for several seconds at the door that Shore had used to leave the room. The young FBI agent shook his head slowly in disbelief, remembering Shore's eager face as he announced that he was being permitted to go to Saigon. *I think I'm crazy, but these people are the ones who are really goddamn nuts,* Sullivan thought, as he glanced over at the phone ringing on Shore's crowded desk. *What the hell is so great about going to Vietnam, anyway?*

"Mr. Vice President," Jennings said tentatively.

The Vice President was in his shirtsleeves, stacking files into a series of leather travel bags. He looked up from his work and glanced over his shoulder. "Yes, Dave," Cassidy said briskly and then returned to his packing.

"There's an FBI agent named Jim Sullivan. He's with Tom Shore. Tom thinks that you should see him. He says that it's a matter of personal safety. I know sir, that it's . . ." Jennings began, but Cassidy cut him off before he could finish. "Whose safety?" Cassidy snapped at the younger man and then turned from his packing to face his aide.

"I think your brother's, sir," Jennings said. "Apparently he was one of the agents in Dallas four years ago and he says that you told him if he ever needed anything that he was to contact you," Jennings continued.

"And Summers doesn't know he's here, I take it," Cassidy said sharply.

"I don't think anybody knows he's here. He and Tom apparently have a mutual friend, an assistant at Justice that Tom went to Princeton with. He's the one who called Tom about it."

"That's four careers down the drain for one request—must be important." Cassidy smiled, seeing how nervous Jennings was and trying to relieve the younger man's concern. "You did the right thing bringing it to me, Dave. An FBI man from Princeton?" Cassidy said then, pretending to misunderstand, as he weighed what he should do about the unorthodox request.

"No, sir," Jennings said. "I don't think he's . . ."

Cassidy held up his hand, cutting Jennings off. "Does he understand the time pressure that we're under?" Cassidy said, looking back up at his aide's surprised face.

"Yes, sir," Jennings said. "Shore told him."

"Good, then let him know that he only has five minutes, all right?"

"Yes, sir."

After his aide left the room, Cassidy returned to his desk. He picked up a file almost at random and flipped through it as he waited. He closed the file only when he heard the sound of the door to his office opening. Tim turned then and looked across the room at a tall blond man dressed in a charcoal-gray suit that fit him too tightly across his broad shoulders. The man stood uncomfortably at the door for several seconds, not knowing what to do next.

Cassidy extended his hand. "Agent Sullivan?"

"Yes, sir," the tall blond man answered and then, awkwardly, he began to make his way across the room toward the Vice President.

Tim sat at his desk for several minutes after the FBI agent had left. Cassidy was already running late on a crowded schedule that would end with dinner at Jack and Suzanne's home in Georgetown later that night, followed by an early morning helicopter ride to Andrews Air Force Base, and then the first leg of a flight halfway across the world to Southeast Asia. He could imagine the mood that he would find his brother in after this morning's announcement of the trip to Saigon. Oh, well, he'd just have to handle Jack as best he could when the time came. For now, there was the problem of what to do with the information that this FBI agent had just given to him. Could there be anything to it? He sat at his desk, going over and over in his mind the things that the young agent had told him. The Vice President reached up and grasped the thick file that the agent had left for him to read. Papers spilled out of it, notes, copies of reports, newspaper clippings. Cassidy removed a copy of one of the reports. It was dated in the early spring of 1964, when Tim was still the Attorney General. The report was an internal FBI document from Agent Sullivan to his superior in the Dallas Bureau. Tim scanned its contents briefly. It was as the agent had indicated. Sullivan had reported his theories of the assassination to his superiors at least as early as March of 1964.

Cassidy had no doubt that this report had been passed along to Director Summers in Washington. Summers had covered up Sullivan's findings. But why? Did they consider Sullivan's theories to be wrong, or so unproven as to be worthless, or was it because they were afraid that they might be right? If the agent's story could be believed, it did at least confirm one thing. The Bureau apparently did have a file on Strode prior to November of 1963, and Summers had lied about that, probably to make the Bureau look a little less incompetent in its failure to stop Strode from firing the shots at the President that weekend. But if he'd lied about the Strode file, he could be covering up other things as well. He had to look into this, Tim decided, but when? There wasn't time now. There was barely time to think it through properly. The buzzer on his intercom rang and he reached for the phone. "I need another minute," he said.

The Vice President hung up the phone and looked down at the FBI agent's thick file. Well, there was nothing else to do, he decided then; he would just have to take the damn thing with him to Saigon and read all of it himself. He looked again at its sheer size and at its disorganized contents. God, it was going to be a chore though, he thought.

If he had a chance, he'd mention it to Jack at dinner, but he knew that his brother's mind would be on other things and he could guess Jack's response. He reached down for one of the big leather briefcases that stood in a row by the wall behind his desk. All but one of the briefcases were already bulging with materials that he needed to read before he arrived in Saigon on Wednesday morning. Forget sleeping, Cassidy thought, as he began to place the FBI file into his case, but before he could his hand caught the rough edge of a piece of sketch paper that protruded from the side of the file. Cassidy withdrew the heavy paper and set it on top of the other documents, and his heart skipped a beat. On the sheet of rough paper was an artist's sketch of a man's face. Beneath the sketch someone had written the words: "Second Gunman, Dallas, November 22, 1963."

They came for Lopata in the middle of the night, shadow figures moving in the darkness above his bunk. Lopata called out for help as strong hands gripped his shoulders and lifted him onto the floor. He could feel the point of a hard metal bayonet cutting into his back, pushing him toward the door. He called out in fear, but none of the other prisoners stirred. They were all too afraid for their own safety.

In the moonlight outside the barracks Lopata could see the faces of the men who had come for him. They were familiar ones, soldiers of the prison, faces that he saw everyday, but they seemed particularly grim that night as they moved him down the dirt path between the rows of low barracks buildings. In the distance, Lopata could hear the surf of Muiriel pounding on the rock beach that lay a few hundred yards outside the prison camp's barbed-wire fence. A rough hand took Lopata's shoulder and grasped it hard, pushing him out toward the parade field in the center of the compound. Lopata didn't resist. He just let his body stagger out into the high grass field. Coming back from the latrine late at night, many months before, Lopata had seen a prisoner executed at the far edge of the parade field by the wire fence that he could see in front of him. Was he to be shot himself now? The small band of men continued on the entire length of the moonlit parade field toward a small wooden shed at the far end. The door to the dilapidated wooden building was open and Lopata was pushed inside and the door locked behind him. So, his execution would be in the morning, he guessed then, feeling relieved for a moment, but almost instantly then the overpowering fear that he'd felt earlier returned with nearly the same intensity. Suddenly the door opened again and the soldiers returned. With them this time was a tall, thin man carrying a black leather bag. Lopata recognized the man as the doctor from the nearby village.

Lopata stood silently and then, at the doctor's command, he removed his shirt and unbuttoned his prison work pants, letting them drop down below his knees.

The doctor reached into his bag and removed a syringe filled with a yellow-green liquid. He gestured for Lopata to turn his body and lower his underpants. Lopata did as he was told and an instant later, he felt the hot sting of the syringe's long needle and then a burning liquid sweeping through his veins. For an instant he feared that he had been poisoned, executed by a fatal injection, but his heart continued to beat and he turned his body slowly back into the room. The doctor had a small brown envelope in his hands and as Lopata watched he tossed it down on the bed. A few tablets spilled out of the unsealed packet. Pills to slow the dysentery—Lopata knew the precious white tablets well. He had seen them traded in the prison's black market for enormous sums, but now he was being given an entire packet for himself. But why? Before Lopata could ask him, the doctor was quickly escorted out of the room by the soldiers.

Lopata hurriedly pulled his clothes back on and then went to the bed and grasped the precious little packet in his hands. He took two of the pills immediately, swallowing them down without water. Then he counted out the remaining contents of the envelope. There were enough, if he was given a chance to use them, to check the dysentery and at least let some of his strength return. He placed the pills into his shirt pocket and lay down across the single woolen blanket.

He pulled the blanket over his belly, but he knew that it was no use to try to sleep. He was still too frightened. Outside the locked door he could hear the doctor and the soldiers departing into the night. Why had they brought him to this place? Why had they brought the doctor in to see him? What did it all mean? As he huddled under the thin wool blanket and felt the cold wind rushing up from the sea, Lopata alternated between thoughts of hope and images of the firing squad that he feared waited for him at dawn.

He must think of something else. There had to be something else that he could hold on to, something that would save him from becoming forever lost in his fear. And then he saw it, and the sobering energy of hatred filled him, calming him, as his emotions focused not on his own life or death, but on the death of another man—and through the night Lopata clung desperately to the single image of the final inevitable moment of confrontation that he had dreamed about for so long. Somehow, he told himself, he must leave Muiriel alive. He must stand before Cassidy again, face to face, and become his executioner.

CHAPTER
30

At dawn the guard came and when the cell door was opened Lopata looked closely at the man's face. He thought that the guard's expression would tell him what was to happen now, but the old man's blank eyes were impossible to read. The guard moved aside and let the prisoner step out into the early morning daylight. There was a cold chill in the air and Lopata's weakened body shivered against it underneath his thin prison clothes. As soon as his eyes adjusted to the light, Lopata looked immediately out at the long grass parade field in front of him, to see if there were any preparations for an execution. He saw nothing out of the ordinary, but his brief feeling of relief was quickly ended by the sight of an army vehicle speeding toward him across the parade field.

The prisoner strained his eyes to see what was in it, but the olive-green canvas tarp that stretched over the back of the vehicle blocked the rear of the truck from view. What the hell is going to happen now? Lopata thought, the fear growing even stronger inside of him.

The truck pulled to a stop, but the tarp remained down. Two uniformed soldiers that Lopata had never seen before were seated in the cab. The soldier in the passenger side stepped out onto the dirt path at the edge of the parade field and walked back the few yards to stand in front of him. The tall soldier's uniformed body blocked the faint warmth of the faraway sun's morning rays, and, looking up at the single silver lieutenant's bar on the soldier's starched khaki collar, Lopata's body began to shiver in cold and fear.

The lieutenant addressed him by using the name of his birth, not the name Lopata, which he had given to the commandant on that first night in Muiriel and by which he had been known in the prison camp ever since. So they knew. His true identity alone could signal his death, he thought. He said nothing in response, fearing to admit the truth.

The tall lieutenant slapped Lopata twice across the cheeks. Neither blow drew blood, but the prisoner's cheeks were stung raw in the cold air and his eyes blurred. Behind him he could feel the prison guard pushing him toward the rear of the truck. Lopata stumbled past the lieutenant's towering figure to the back of the Russian-made vehicle and the stiff, mud-splattered canvas that covered it. Without prompting Lopata stepped up then into the cargo area of the military truck.

The old prison guard followed behind him and Lopata felt the man locking a metal handcuff onto his wrist and attaching the other steel cuff to one of the interior supporting bars of the cargo bed's metal frame.

The lieutenant peered into the rear of the truck then to make certain that everything was as he wanted it to be. Satisfied, he returned to the truck's cab. Lopata could hear the vehicle's door slamming and then the labored whining of the engine being forced to restart on the cold morning. The old prison guard sat down on one of the wooden benches that were bolted into the sidewalls of the truck's rear cargo area directly across from Lopata's manacled figure.

The two men eyed each other warily as the engine finally caught and held, and then Lopata's weary body felt the slow painful shifting of heavy gears and the jolting forward as the Russian truck started back across the parade field.

The truck turned a corner and passed the commandant's office. Lopata watched the single isolated Quonset hut fade from view behind him, lost at the end of the muddy main street of the prison camp. Within seconds, the truck was passing the main gate and then miraculously they were beyond it and Lopata could see the camp retreating behind him through the opening in the soiled green tarp. The low outline of the buildings grew even smaller in the distance, becoming only a series of flat, faraway shapes surrounded by a high barbed-wire fence with a stretch of rocky coastline behind it, and the truck began to climb away from the coast toward the mountain roads that led into the heart of the island. Then suddenly, the truck rounded a curve and the camp was gone completely!

Lopata felt a flood of hope sweep through him. If he was to be shot now, it was to be in secret, perhaps on the winding, untraveled mountain road ahead of them that led to the center of the island, but something told him that he wasn't to be shot at all, that the Revolution had found another use for him.

"Where are we going?" Lopata called out to the guard.

The old man turned his head toward him before he answered. "Havana," the guard said.

Lopata's stomach grew hot with excitement. He was being taken to the capital. Maybe to see Castro himself! They had finally understood his value to them.

"Havana," Lopata said out loud, and repeating the word made him happier than anything that he'd experienced in a very long time.

The truck continued working its way up into the hills behind the prison, but all Lopata could think of was that single word—Havana. He thought of what he must do once he got there. What he must say. Soon he had lost track of time or precisely where he was. He knew only vaguely that he was somewhere deep in the rocky, lonely, hill country between Muiriel and the capital. There were no towns or signposts to mark his way, only endless steep mountain curves, but there was so much else to think about.

The first bullet sliced through the truck's front windshield and struck the young Cuban lieutenant sitting in the passenger seat. The military truck had just passed a sharp curve in the mountain road—a perfect place for an ambush, Lopata realized, as he looked out at the rocky barren terrain that surrounded the vehicle. But an ambush by who? Why? His mind whirled, trying to understand what was going on, but it was all happening too quickly for him to make any sense of it. There was no way to even distinguish the second round from the others that came then in a rapid volley. It was clear to Lopata only that the truck was under attack from both the front and the rear. A bullet cut through the thin tarpaulin just above Lopata's head. He strained at his cuffs, trying to lower himself to the floor of the truck, but the steel only bit painfully into his wrists. He could barely move his body to protect himself from the bullets that were tearing into the tarpaulin now only inches from his head. Lopata looked across the aisle toward the face of the old prison guard. Strangely, the old man's expression did not look at all surprised; his face was calm and dead-eyed. He had lowered his body down balanced on one knee below the protective metal line of the interior wall of the truck, and his rifle was in his hands now, its long barrel pointed not out at the roadside where the shots were coming from, but across the rear of the truck directly at Lopata's chest.

The Vice President's plane landed briefly at an Air Force base in Australia to refuel, but at the Vice President's orders it didn't lay over for the night. Instead, it pushed on for Vietnam after a little over an hour on the ground. The visit to Saigon was brief enough as it was, and Tim had determined that he would make use of every possible moment.

He slept for the first few hours outside Melbourne, but the sleep was very light and dream-filled. Finally he just lay with his eyes open, staring at the ceiling of the small sleeping compartment with his consciousness somewhere between dreaming and waking. His body was tired and drained of strength and he remembered the last few days before he'd left Washington as just a blur of activity as he and his staff had prepared and scheduled the trip as quickly as possible, racing against the fear that at any moment Gardner might find a reason to cancel the visit. But he hadn't and here he was, Cassidy thought, or almost, anyway. At that moment, he could feel only the swift movement of the aircraft through space and he could hear only the steady mechanical drone of its engines. There had only been time for a brief dinner with Jack's family before he'd left Washington. And throughout the meal he and Jack had barely talked, and his older brother's displeasure had been apparent. Without saying it directly, Jack had let Tim know that he believed the visit to Saigon was a mistake, a decision that would only raise the country's expectations and then disappoint it bitterly in the end. Maybe he was right, Tim thought now. His part of it had all been put together so quickly, rushed into, really, in his haste to do something, anything to end the feelings of frustration that had built up in him over the last few years of serving in Gardner's administration. And now he was going to Saigon with no overall strategy and no power. There would be no announcements of policy changes, no surprise moves when he returned to Washington. Gardner had granted him nothing but the permission to make the trip. His entire schedule had been prearranged by the President's staff, and all of his statements would have to be cleared with the administration before they were released. They had built a very tight box around him, with no way out of it during the visit, or when he returned. It was, in reality, he realized now, a carefully constructed political trap—and he'd walked right into it. By making the trip without any ability to make changes, he was essentially underwriting existing administration policy. But, damn it, wasn't it better than just staying in Washington and doing nothing? Or maybe it wasn't. He wasn't really sure anymore.

He'd had only a brief opportunity at dinner to mention the visit that he'd had with Agent Sullivan, and Jack's reaction had been pretty much as he'd expected on that subject as well. His brother had dismissed Sullivan's story as probably being without substance, just another half-baked theory about Dallas by a junior agent, who in all likelihood had some kind of a personal motive for going against the Bureau. But Jack hadn't objected when Tim had told him that he was going to check Sullivan and his story out very thoroughly anyway on his return.

So much to do when he returned to Washington, Tim thought, and, suddenly gripped by a despair that he rarely felt, he sat up in the small closed-in space at the rear of the airplane and slowly pivoted his legs around so that the bottoms of his feet rested flat on the cold metal floor of the aircraft. Jack was right about the trip, he decided finally. He was powerless. Nothing could be gained by his visit, only more disappointment, more anger and frustration in the country. Gardner already knew everything that he would say to him on his return, and the President would ignore his arguments—as he had since the beginning.

Feeling powerless, Tim reached over and angrily pulled aside the curtain that covered the small porthole next to him. He saw dark sky and faint bright stars and then he saw his own image partially reflected in the plastic airplane window. Behind the image of his face he could see reflected infinite black night and small pinpricks of white-yellow stars. In the strange double reflection, it was as if he was merely a shadow of something, a minor reflection in an illusory foreground with the great, vast, powerful universe everywhere around him.

When the prison guard aimed his rifle toward him Lopata didn't hesitate. He kicked forward with both legs and jolted the barrel of the rifle with the toe of his boot. The barrel veered off at an angle and then exploded and the bullet tore through the top of the dirty green tarp, leaving a ragged tear in the canvas just inches above Lopata's head.

A moment later the truck slammed to a stop, throwing the guard forward violently against the metal wall that separated the rear of the truck from the driver's compartment. Gunfire began ripping more holes in the protective tarp. Lopata fell forward with one arm stretched out painfully behind him, restrained by the metal handcuff that linked him to the frame of the truck, but he managed to bring the weight of his body across the guard's arms, pinning the rifle between them.

With another burst of gunfire ripping through the air above their heads, Lopata reached for the handle of the bayonet locked in its sheath on the guard's belt. The military sheath unsnapped easily, and Lopata withdrew the long metal blade from its resting place. The guard dropped his grip from the rifle then and began clawing frantically for the bayonet. His hands were cut by the sharp edges of the heavy blade as he tried to hold back the force of the driving piece of steel, but Lopata thrust the blade up through his bleeding hands and plunged it deep into the guard's stomach. The heavy bayonet made a loud thumping sound as it pushed into the old man's hollow stomach cavity. Lopata fell forward then, using the force of his falling body to jerk the metal blade toward the guard's abdomen. Blood and intestines poured out and soaked warmly over Lopata's hand and clothes, but he only glared angrily into the old man's eyes until the guard's body slumped lifeless to the floor beneath him.

Outside the tarp, Lopata could hear the running footsteps of the driver. In another moment he would be at the opening at the rear of the truck. Lopata rolled his body back in the direction of his manacled hand, uncovering the guard's rifle that lay on the floor beneath him. He clutched the stock of the rifle with his free hand and aimed it at the opening to the tarp, his finger reaching for the trigger of the weapon. The guard had already locked a round into the chamber and the weapon was ready to fire, and when the driver's face appeared at the small opening, Lopata fired at it without hesitation. The driver fell backward into the road, his face blown open by the heavy round fired at nearly point-blank range. Lopata dropped the rifle to the floor and turned back to the body of the guard. He edged forward and removed the key to the handcuff from the guard's uniform pocket. The little key was still wet from the guard's blood, but Lopata managed to fit it into the lock on the metal cuff and release himself. He fell flat to the floor as the heavy steel cuff dropped away from his wrist, and then he reached out for the guard's rifle. A full clip protruded from the rifle's firing mechanism with, Lopata guessed, only one round expended—that would mean that he had at least eight, perhaps as many as nine rounds left in the Russian-made rifle.

He edged forward and peered over the lip of the truck's tailgate, and a bullet whined off the metal inches away from his face. How the hell many of them were there out there? And who were they? Had they been sent to free him? Or to kill him? The questions rocketed through Lopata's head as he peered out through the narrow crack at the base of the truck's tailgate. He could see the vehicle's driver sprawled in the dirt of the narrow mountain road beneath him. There was no mistaking the awkward, meaningless position of death, Lopata thought, as he looked at the man's fallen body.

Lopata lay on the floor of the military truck at an angle to the protective line of the tailgate with the guard's rifle resting securely in the hollow of his shoulder. Through the narrow opening at the base of the vehicle he could see the mountain road behind him. There was at least one other person out there, he thought, and at least one other somewhere at the front of the truck. They couldn't wait out there forever though, he decided, not after attacking a government vehicle on a road between Muiriel and Havana, however deserted it was for the moment. He considered calling out to the men who had ambushed the truck. Maybe they were friends, maybe they'd been sent to help him to escape. But he had no friends. His only value to anyone now was to Castro and to the Revolution. No, whoever it was that was out there had been sent to murder him before he could be removed to safety in Havana. Lopata looked back at the body of the guard. The old man had been part of it, Lopata decided as he thought it all through, and he could guess now who had arranged it. He waited grimly behind the tailgate of the Russian truck, watching the road for any sign of movement, while the rest of his mind began planning the details of his revenge.

The American Vice President was brought to a dimly lit back room normally reserved for banquets and small parties at the rear of the La Caravelle Hotel in Saigon. The darkness and the movement of air, swept along by an arrangement of three large paddle-armed ceiling fans, gave the room an illusion of coolness even on a hot Saigon night.

Despite the heat, it was still raining outside and Tim could hear the rain splashing into puddles in Saigon's muddy back streets. Jennings was with him and one other aide, but no military or embassy people. The group of people waiting in the room were all Western reporters, handpicked by Jennings earlier in the day. The assistant had agreed to deliver up the Vice President to an informal press gathering after Cassidy attended a reception at the American embassy. But it was after midnight now and as the hours had gone by and the levels on the bottles of hotel scotch had grown lower, the reporters' hopes of actually seeing the Vice President that night had grown dimmer.

Cassidy smiled at the faces that surrounded him. They all seemed to be talking at once, asking him questions before he could even remove his raincoat and settle into a chair at the long banquet table in the center of the room.

"How was the reception?" a reporter called out.

"Have you ever been to an embassy reception?" Cassidy bantered with him.

"No," another reporter sitting down the table from the Vice President answered. "Not as an invited guest, anyway."

"I have—too many," another reporter said with a laugh.

Cassidy joined in the laughter. "Yes, so have I," he said. "It's a vice-presidential specialty."

A reporter standing near Cassidy held up a bottle of scotch toward the Vice President and Cassidy nodded his head and a half dozen glasses were quickly offered to him. "Trying to get me drunk?" Cassidy said, smiling at the offered glasses. Then he reached out and selected one that looked slightly cleaner than some of the others, and a reporter at his elbow poured the glass full to the rim.

"Come on now, I haven't had much sleep," Cassidy said, looking suspiciously at the glass tumbler filled with scotch.

"Truth serum," another reporter said from across the banquet table.

"You don't need this," Cassidy said, pushing away the glass of whiskey. "I'll answer your questions as best I can. That's why I'm here," he said, his lean face growing more serious.

There was another chorus of questions, the voices in the room so loud that they managed to drown out the sounds of the rain falling outside the hotel window.

"Did you really learn anything today?" a young German reporter asked, leaning his body angrily across the table directly toward Cassidy as he spoke.

"Yes," the Vice President answered calmly, returning the reporter's angry accusing stare with a milder but equally direct look of his own. "Yes, I did."

The reporter began reading in a heavily sarcastic voice from a preprinted press handout of the schedule for Cassidy's first full day in Saigon. " 'Airport—Review of Troops and Greetings; Ride to Embassy; Morning—Embassy Reception; Meeting—American Military Staff; Lunch—American Embassy; Briefing—Embassy Staff.' " When he was done the expression on the reporter's face left no doubt of his own disgust at how the time had been spent.

"Tomorrow," Jennings said, moving through the crowd behind Cassidy and finding a place for himself at the banquet table near the Vice President's side, "we're going on . . ."

"A tour of a handpicked rural village," another reporter finished Jennings's sentence for him.

"Why don't you just go to Disneyland instead?" another voice called from the back of the room.

Cassidy didn't try to answer yet. It was late and he knew that the reporters had been waiting a long time for him to arrive, and they needed to blow off some steam. As he listened to their sarcasm he removed his dinner jacket and hung it over the back of his chair. Then he tried to relax by placing one foot up on the seat of the empty chair next to him, and once he was reasonably comfortable he took a small sip from the tall glass of scotch. He reached up after his drink and undid his black silk bow tie and let its ends hang down carelessly over his white silk shirt front. There was as much to learn in this room as there was at the formal briefings that he'd just come from, probably more, he thought, as he looked from one reporter to the next.

A photographer pushed forward and tried to take a picture of him, off guard, relaxed, drinking scotch, the crisscrossing pattern of lines that streamed out from the corners of his eyes more deeply cut and dramatically pronounced than the public normally saw them, but Jennings reached out and waved the photographer off. Photos were off limits that night, only conversation—that had been part of the ground rules set down earlier in the day.

"What's your impression of my trip so far?" Cassidy said, picking out the face of a small, handsome, gray-haired woman at the back of the room whom he recognized from the formal press briefing he'd given that morning.

The woman didn't hesitate. Her accent as she replied was unmistakably British, and Cassidy listened carefully to her cool, unhurried assessment of his trip. "I believe, Mr. Vice President," she said with some formality, "that you are being shown only what your American military people here want you to see, nothing more."

"You're getting less real information than if you stayed home and watched the nightly news," an American reporter added then in a far less respectful tone.

Cassidy nodded at the British journalist, meaning for her to continue, but before she could, she was interrupted again by the young German reporter sitting across the table from the Vice President. His voice now was even more insistent than it had been earlier. "This whole trip is a farce," he said emphatically. "You already know what you're going to tell the American people when you return and you knew it before you ever came out here. Gardner's press people are working on it for you right now, and you'll be back in Washington by Monday morning and damn well read it for them."

"There are a number of us who believe that you're only here to buy the administration more time," the British journalist said in agreement, using her own coolly defiant style and reserved tone rather than anger to make her point. Cassidy looked across the room at her then. He felt stung by her words, by all the reporters' words. They were lashing out at him a little more than usual that night, he thought. Jack was right. They were angry at the false expectations that they, too believed had been raised by the trip. Maybe it was the deep fatigue that he felt or just a culmination of the several long months of stress that he had endured, but a general sense of failure and frustration was beginning to sweep over him. Those at the table that night could see it clearly as it settled into his deeply lined face and in the slump of his body, and they eagerly kept pounding on him, hoping for a breakthrough of some kind.

"What are you going to say?" the German reporter insisted. "That with just a few more troops, a few more planes . . ." But even the young German's determined voice couldn't finish its questions, as other voices broke in to drown it out, and Cassidy had to hold out a weary hand to quiet the room.

"Are you prepared to tell the American people the truth yet?" Bud Frazier, an old friend of Cassidy's from Frazier's days of covering the 1960 presidential campaign, moved forward then and asked his questions from point-blank range only a few feet from where Cassidy sat.

"Bud," the Vice President said, looking up at Frazier's usually friendly, heavyset face. "I'm prepared to tell the American people the truth of what I find out here," Cassidy said, but even as he said it, his own voice sounded suddenly hollow. He'd heard himself say these things too many times before, he thought, and then had found them swallowed up and lost by the actions of the rest of the administration.

"Well, you sure as hell won't find the truth in a pacified village selected by Langston and his staff," the German reporter snapped.

"You may be right," Cassidy said and then turned to Jennings. "What are we scheduled to see tomorrow, Dave?"

"Khe Dang," Jennings said, without needing to refer to the schedule that the embassy people had given him earlier in the day.

"Khe Dang!" the German said derisively. "They've poured troops into that area for weeks getting ready for this visit, but as soon as your helicopter lifts off the ground tomorrow morning it will go right back to being what it was a month ago—a Viet Cong stronghold. The whole pacification thing is an American military lie, and you're playing right into the deceit by going out there tomorrow and giving it your blessing."

Cassidy looked up at Frazier's familiar face. Its expression and a short emphatic nod confirmed its agreement with the young German's words.

"I've heard all this," Cassidy snapped angrily. He felt tired and confused. He'd come all this way and still there seemed to be nothing that he could do to make a difference.

"Well, then why don't you do something about it, see for yourself." It was the British journalist's voice, swift and defiant, much of the distance removed from it now. She was issuing a challenge directly to the American Vice President. "I'm doing a story on the so-called pacified villages of South Vietnam. If you weren't here, I'd be traveling to a place less than two hours north of Saigon tomorrow, a village called Jah Whe. It's listed by your military as 'pacified,' as are most of the villages within several miles of it. If you're serious about wanting to find the truth, go there with me tomorrow, talk to the people, see what you find. The military can hardly object to your traveling in an area that they've declared secure for months now." The British woman unrolled a small map from a briefcase full of notes and papers that rested against the leg of her chair. Using a pair of half-empty whiskey bottles to tack down the ends, she spread the map out on the table in front of Cassidy. It was a military map, marked in red, green, and yellow, like an American stoplight, signaling the military's assessment of the comparative safety to Westerners, or the so-called pacification of each of the villages in South Vietnam.

"Look at this," the reporter said. "Were you shown something like it today, when you were briefed by the military people?" she asked.

Cassidy nodded his head, his eyes fixed on the map's multicolored surface.

"Well, one of the stories I'm working on is that you, right along with the rest of the American people, are being brainwashed into believing in what is in reality a totally failed program."

The challenge was unmistakable and the room quieted to hear Cassidy's reply.

"There," she said, pointing with her glass of scotch at a spot on the map north of Saigon. "Jah Whe."

Cassidy leaned forward to see more clearly. The soft light of the room fell on the American map, setting off its surface colors with a strange luminescence. The area around Jah Whe glowed out a warm, safe, moss-green color. But under the faintly pinkish Oriental light and after hearing the words of the journalists, the Vice President thought the greenish color looked faintly shimmering now, like a mirage.

Jennings moved up behind Cassidy. He recognized the signs that the Vice President was accepting a challenge. He'd seen them many times before, and now they were written all over the young Vice President's face.

"This map looks to me like the American funny papers," the German reporter said. "I've been here," he said, rapping the table on the spot the map marked as safe. The German was close enough to the Vice President now that Cassidy could smell the cloud of alcohol that escaped from the young reporter's mouth each time that he spoke. "And here," he added, swinging his finger out to touch another green spot on the map. "And here," he added, his pace quickening. "And none of them are secure for Westerners. There's nothing special about Jah Whe. Pick any one you like," he added, sweeping his hand out at the abundance of green dots that the American military had painted on the areas representing the towns and villages of South Vietnam to demonstrate the apparent spreading success of their efforts. "All I'm saying is, don't let Langston and the others pick it for you."

Cassidy was tired. He hadn't really slept in almost three days; his eyes were bloodshot, the lines in his face far deeper and harsher than usual. He moved away from the group of reporters and stepped to the window. He stood for a moment and looked out at the glistening Saigon street at the rear of the hotel. American soldiers and olive-drab American Army vehicles had closed off the street and surrounded the building since early that afternoon, protecting him or sealing him off from those things that they didn't want him to see, Cassidy wasn't sure which.

The Vice President turned back into the room to face the expectant faces of the others grouped around the long banquet table with the military map still glowing on it. The multicolored map, braced by the twin whiskey bottles and with its softly luminescent shadings of green and red and cautionary yellow, seemed to be challenging Cassidy as he looked across the room at it now.

"It's entirely out of the question," Jennings said, attempting to cut off the conversation before the Vice President acted impetuously.

"Can we do that, Dave?" Cassidy asked, and then, without waiting for an answer, he continued, directing his words at the British journalist who had proposed the trip. "If we can set it up, I'll do it," Cassidy said, meeting the challenge. "And just to keep me honest I think that you and Mr. Frazier and Mr. . . ." Cassidy paused then and directed his attention toward the young German reporter, whose name he didn't know.

"Diechter." The German supplied his name in a cautious voice, as he studied Cassidy, looking for the trick.

"Mr. Vice President, we can't," Jennings said, the concern showing openly on his face.

Cassidy stood up then and removed his formal black dress coat from the back of the chair. His scotch remained on the table in front of him, almost untouched.

"You know you're going to make my staff pretty damn mad," Cassidy said as he looked around the room at the reporters. "They haven't had any sleep as it is, and now . . ." Cassidy looked at Jennings, making his words into an order for the young assistant. "And now, they're going to be up all night again figuring out how to get this done."

"Yes, sir," Jennings said reluctantly.

"As for me," Cassidy said, throwing his dress coat over his shoulder with a jauntiness that he didn't really feel and then heading for the room's rear door, "I'm going to get a few hours sleep."

Soon the gunfire ended and it was silent in the little mountain pass that led from the prison at Muiriel to the island's capital city. The silence seemed to last forever, but still Lopata lay hidden and immobile behind the metal tailgate of the Russian truck. He would wait for an eternity, if that's what it took to survive, he told himself, as he listened to the ominous silence.

There was a stirring at the roadside—then the crouching shape of a man approaching the rear of the vehicle step by step. Was this man the only one left alive, or were there others? Lopata watched the man cautiously move toward the truck. The man came closer and closer, but Lopata forced himself not to shoot. Within seconds though, the man's shadow passed over Lopata's face and then the man's pistol was directly above his head, pointing in at the rear of the vehicle, and Lopata could wait no longer. He fired his rifle. It was pointed squarely at the man's heart. The man's weapon was an American automatic and it sent out a wild spray of gunfire, blasting the inside of the truck with erratic explosions of ricocheting bullets sparking metal pieces off the rear compartment. Then silence.

The man had fallen backward onto the roadside, his body only a few feet from the uniformed body of the driver. Lopata could see both bodies clearly through the crack beneath the tailgate of the Russian-made vehicle. There could easily be more men waiting in the rocks at the sides of the road, he thought then. And his eyes scanned the rocky hillside above him.

He waited in the hot tarpaulin-covered rear of the truck longer than most men would have believed possible. Hours went by without a sign of life anywhere around him. They could all be dead, he thought, or they might have fled, fearing discovery by the Cuban army. Or, Lopata thought, they could still be waiting for me to show myself, just as I'm waiting for them. His body was sweating freely in the heat and stillness of the canvas-covered vehicle, and the beads of sweat rolled down and burned his eyes. His legs and arms stiffened painfully, cramped in the awkward position as he lay on the metal floor, but still he didn't move.

Only after several more hours of the painful waiting did he creep slowly out of the back of the truck, his legs and arms clinging to the metal tailgate, until he could lower himself down into the dirt of the road, hidden behind the truck's thick Russian tires. He waited then with the bodies of the two dead men lying in the dirt only a few feet from him. He waited until the hot Cuban sun had sunk out of sight below the line of the rocky hillside that framed the mountain road on the west. Only then, in the cooler, shadowy half light of the end of the day, did he begin inching forward, sliding on his stomach over the uneven ground. He moved along on his chest and belly until he reached the metal grille at the front of the military vehicle. He could see two more bodies now, lying on the road in front of him. They had apparently been shot during the first exchange of gunfire, Lopata thought. One of the bodies appeared to be still alive. The movement of the man's chest as he fought for breath was weak but unmistakable. Lopata emerged carefully from beneath the front grille of the truck. As he stood up, dirt clung to the red stain on his shirt front made by the blood of the guard, who had tried to murder him hours earlier.

He approached the wounded man cautiously. When he was close enough to fire a round from his rifle into the wounded man's head with little chance of missing, he fired.

It was deadly quiet then in the little mountain pass between Muiriel and Havana, as if the birds and other small living things that lived nearby had fled in fear. Only Lopata remained and he stood for a moment with the rifle in his hands, the front of his shirt dark red with dirt and another man's blood. He surveyed the deserted, sunless piece of ground that he stood alone on now, with the bodies of six dead men scattered around him in the dirt as his only company. Just as I promised, he whispered only to himself, I have survived!

CHAPTER
31

Lopata returned to the running board of the Russian-made truck and sank down onto it. The exhilaration that he'd felt only a few minutes earlier, when he'd first realized that he'd survived the ambush, was gone now, replaced by deep fatigue. Gone, too, was the pumping adrenaline that had filled his veins for the last few hours, masking the symptoms of the dysentery from his consciousness. His hands and legs were trembling and his stomach and bowels began to churn. A few seconds later the sweating started again, and when he touched the skin of his arm, it was burning hot. He fumbled in his shirt pocket and removed the envelope of pills and swallowed two of them. He stood then and walked over and looked down at the first of the men lying dead in the curve of the road. Lopata couldn't be certain, but he thought he recognized the dead man. He went methodically through the pockets of his clothes then. He found nothing that confirmed his suspicions of who the man was or who it had been that had sent him, but Lopata didn't need any more evidence. He could guess the truth now, and his mind quickly conceived a plan to protect himself. If he were to die out here, he would die, or so it would appear. He returned to the rear of the vehicle and carried its driver with him, placing the dead man back into the cab of the truck. Then he returned to the roadside and lifted the body of one of the Cuban men who had died in the attack, and he carried the body back to the rear of the vehicle.

Lopata removed the man's shirt and pants, then his shoes, socks, and even his underwear. They were all smeared with blood, but without hesitating Lopata dressed himself in the dead man's clothes. Then he carefully redressed

411

the man in his own discarded prison uniform. He lifted the dead man's newly dressed body up and handcuffed it into position in the rear of the truck.

The dead man was small and dark, close to Lopata in appearance, but Lopata used the man's own rifle to fire a bullet directly into his face. Lopata stopped then and studied the damage. Still not satisfied, he fired a second round. There would be no one who could identify this man now, Lopata thought with grim satisfaction, as he looked at the smashed and bloody remains of the man's features.

Lopata stepped out of the rear of the truck and removed the reserve gas can from its canvas straps. He splashed gasoline first onto the slumped bloody figure of the man wearing his prison clothes and then onto the canvas tarp.

After he'd finished, Lopata ran to the front of the truck. When he opened the door of the truck's cab, he saw a large metal box. It was lying on the floor of the vehicle, near the feet of the dead lieutenant, whose body remained seated upright in the cab's passenger seat. Lopata reached down and picked up the box. It was locked, but he threw it on the ground and then used the lieutenant's pistol to explode the metal padlock. Inside the box was his blue vinyl flight bag. With anxious fingers, Lopata ripped the bag open. His long-barreled .38 pistol fell from it, the pistol's cartridges sprinkling the ground near his feet. Lopata knelt down and scooped up the cartridges. Then he searched carefully through the other contents of the metal box until he found a single manila file. Lopata recognized it even before he opened it. It was his own prison file, the one he had seen on the commandant's desk that first day at Muiriel. Among its contents was Strode's diary! And below the diary was a stack of yellowed, partially blurred documents. Lopata inspected them quickly. They were the original and two additional copies of the signed statement that he had given to the commandant on his first night in Muiriel. There was a copy of the diary as well. Copies? Did that mean there were others? Probably copies of both his statement and the diary had already been sent to Havana. That was why his life had been spared, but there wasn't time to think about that now, he decided, and he stuffed the file hurriedly into the flight bag. Then he replaced the metal box into the cab of the truck. He had everything that he'd brought into Cuba with him except the stack of American bills wrapped in oil paper. Someone had kept the money but had left the gun and the diary. They will both be useful though, he thought. He reached down then and released the metal hand brake and moved the heavy truck gears into neutral. The truck began rolling backward with its own weight toward the edge of the narrow mountain road.

He barely had time to leap free of the cab and ignite the gas-soaked canvas tarpaulin with a pack of matches that he'd found on the body of the driver. He had meant to set fire directly to the handcuffed man lying in the rear of the vehicle who was wearing his prison clothes, but there wasn't time.

Lopata watched as the flaming truck rolled over the edge and then fell clear of the mountainside, tumbling slowly through space, until it exploded into even brighter flames on the rocks at the base of the cliff.

* * *

Tim Cassidy awoke reluctantly in the darkness before dawn. Above his bed stood Dave Jennings, who looked as if he hadn't slept in days.

As soon as Cassidy's head had cleared enough to remember who and where he was, he looked up at his aide's tired eyes and asked, "Did you manage it?"

"Jah Whe?" Jennings asked back. "Yes. In the last five hours I've managed to change your itinerary and piss off most of the American and South Vietnamese personnel in Saigon. I've had quite a night."

Cassidy nodded a thank you and then managed to swing his body around and get both feet onto the thick carpet of the VIP suite on the top floor of the American embassy in Saigon.

"Anything from the President?"

"No, he wouldn't know yet. It just got done," Jennings said wearily. "But give him another forty or fifty minutes," Jennings added, glancing down at his own watch.

"It's not the President that I'm the most worried about, anyway," Cassidy said, smiling only slightly.

"Your brother?"

Tim nodded that Jennings had guessed right.

"Maybe nobody will tell him and he'll never find out," Jennings said, pretending to be serious.

"Yes, that's probably my best hope," Tim said sarcastically. He paused before adding, "Dave, I don't want you going with me this morning, you need some sleep." Cassidy stood and walked slowly toward the suite's bathroom.

"No, that's all right," Jennings said. "I made the arrangements. It will all go smoother if I'm there."

"You look terrible," Cassidy called out to him.

"Yeah, thanks," Jennings said, crossing the darkened bedroom to open the draperies that covered the windows overlooking the embassy's grounds.

"How much time do we have?" Cassidy asked through the partly open bathroom door.

"We're already a half hour behind schedule," Jennings said, without needing to check his watch again.

"That's not bad," Cassidy said. "Coffee?" Cassidy asked as he stepped out of the gray silk pajama bottoms that he'd slept in and bent down naked to begin running the water for his shower. The water came out sparse and cold against the Vice President's outstretched hand.

"Tea," Jennings called back to him.

"No, coffee."

"I'm warning you," Jennings answered.

"I don't care, coffee." Cassidy stepped gingerly into the sprinkle of cool water then and closed the shower curtain behind him. He was alone now for one of the few precious moments of his waking day and he closed his eyes and relaxed as best he could under the steady flow of cool water. He soaped his body hard, trying to rub some life back into it, but it remained deeply tired from the long days of traveling and lack of sleep. After what seemed to him only a few seconds of solitude, his aide's voice interrupted him, reminding the Vice President again of his lack of time as Cassidy rinsed away the film of soap that stubbornly clung to his body in the tropical climate as best he could and then shut off the sparse flow of tepid water.

Jennings held a towel out over the shower curtain and Cassidy took it, burying his face in it for a moment and breathing in deeply in the darkness made by the rich warm fabric of the thick embassy towel before beginning to vigorously dry the rest of his body with it.

"Jah Whe," Cassidy said then through the shower curtain, meaning for Jennings to begin briefing him on the day ahead.

"The Army insists on having some of their people go along," Jennings said.

"God, I hope so," Cassidy responded with mock fear. "Hopefully guys with guns, no generals."

"One general," Jennings corrected him.

"Which one?"

"Langston."

"Fine," Cassidy called back. "He looks young enough to still actually do a little fighting, if he has to."

"They've had helicopters going in most of the night," Jennings said. "I'll tell you this, if Jah Whe wasn't pacified six hours ago, it sure as hell will be by the time we get there."

"Pacified or destroyed," Cassidy said.

Jennings paused then before adding in a more serious tone. "It's still a bad idea, Tim, and as soon as the President hears about it, he's going to be angry as hell."

"Maybe so," Cassidy said thoughtfully, still rubbing his body with the thick embassy towel. "You heard those reporters last night, though. None of them believed that I was out here doing anything but grandstanding. And I'll tell you, David, I was beginning to forget why I was here myself. This morning's trip should help. The President will understand after I've had an opportunity to explain it to him."

Jennings only laughed then. "Sure," he said as Cassidy stepped out of the shower enclosure, the embassy towel wrapped around his narrow waist.

"General Langston sent over some khakis," Jennings said. Cassidy had disdained pseudo-military clothes, staying instead with his own stateside uniform of business suit, white shirt, and tie, which gave way to just a shirt with rolled-up sleeves and loosened tie by the heat of midafternoon, but with a long helicopter ride and hours in a jungle village ahead of him, he reached out for the bundle in Jennings's hand and tore its brown paper wrapping away. On top of the clothes was a shiny black leather holster with a forty-five caliber side arm seated in it. Cassidy looked up at Jennings's face. "It looks like Langston sent over something else," the Vice President said.

Jennings nodded back. "It's just the Army's subtle way of telling you that you're being a damn fool," Jennings said. "As for me, I prefer the more direct approach. You're being a damn fool, Mr. Vice President," Jennings said and then reached out for the holster and weapon. "Should I take it back?"

"Yes, I think so," Cassidy said.

"It might look pretty good on the six o'clock news. Give you some of that John Wayne vote that you've been losing out on."

"I'll leave that to Longwood."

"I'll go see about the coffee," Jennings said, carrying the weapon awkwardly in both hands out in front of him, as he started for the door.

"I want the coffee," Cassidy said. "But you don't have to shoot anybody to get it for me."

"A man does what he has to do," Jennings said dramatically, in his best hero's voice.

Cassidy watched the door close behind his assistant before he smiled and nodded his agreement.

Sullivan hadn't told anyone the flight that he was taking and he didn't expect anyone to meet him at the airport, but as he entered the crowded passenger lounge he found himself looking around at the nearby faces, half hoping that someone might be there anyway. He almost didn't recognize Denise when he saw her though. He was just attracted to the vivacious freckled face, the stylishly cut red-blond hair, and the high, tight mini-dress that she was wearing, this one bright valentine-red, with knee-length, very shiny, black vinyl boots and a matching black vinyl purse dropping down on a long gold metal chain that reached below her waist. Sullivan couldn't believe how terrific she looked and that she was waiting for him.

Since he'd seen Cassidy on Monday morning, Sullivan had spent his time in Washington keeping a low profile. During the days he'd worked halfheartedly on a case he had used to cover the real reason for his trip to the capital and at night he'd tried to stay out of the way of anyone who might have asked him what he was really doing in Washington. He hadn't realized, until that very moment, when he saw Denise standing in front of him, just how much he was looking forward to the vacation back home in Philadelphia with Denise and his family that he'd managed to piece together by tacking two weeks' leave on right after the Thanksgiving holiday. "God, it's good to see you," Sullivan said, taking Denise in his arms.

"I took a chance and came."

"I'm glad you did. You look wonderful." Sullivan stepped back from her, still holding the tops of her shoulders in his hands.

"It's this city," Denise said. "I love it here."

"Dad's been showing you around historic old Philadelphia, huh?" Sullivan said, and he started toward the terminal's exit. Then Sullivan slung his single, hang-up bag over his shoulder and they threaded their way through the Thanksgiving weekend crowd.

"He's been great," Denise said.

"I'm sorry I couldn't get in earlier."

"That's okay," Denise said, looping an arm around Sullivan's waist. "It worked out fine. I think they even like my kids. They're babysitting them now." Denise smiled and then added, "Your mom says Danny is a lot like you, when you were that age."

"Oh, God," Sullivan groaned, and they stepped outside. "Where's the car?" Denise pointed at the overflowing parking lot across the busy terminal street.

"The Thanksgiving crowds are getting bad already," Sullivan said absently as they waited for the streetlight to change. "Everyone's going home for the holiday."

"Like us," Denise said, and Sullivan drew her closer with his free arm. "But how are you, Mr. Washington, D.C.?" She reached up and playfully reshaped the knot on Sullivan's narrow black tie to show how important he must think he was now.

"I'm sorry I didn't call," Sullivan said. "I didn't want to talk about it on the phone, but I saw the Vice President." The light changed and students and holiday travelers pushed around them to cross the street to the parking lot.

"How did he look?"

"Look?" Sullivan hadn't thought about how the man had looked before. "I don't know. He's kind of short, I guess," Sullivan said.

"I read that," Denise said. When they reached the parking lot, Denise pointed toward the very rear of the overflowing airport lot.

"Anyway, I saw him and I told him my story and . . ." Sullivan paused, and as he did Denise could feel the tension releasing from his body. "And he didn't think I was nuts."

"I don't think you're nuts either," Denise said, reaching up on her toes to kiss the FBI agent on the cheek.

They walked on in silence for several seconds then. "I've got your dad's car," Denise said.

"The Buick?" Sullivan said.

"I guess so," Denise answered uncertainly.

"Is it a little bigger than a bus and drives like a heavy Army tank?" Sullivan smiled.

"That's the one," Denise said, returning Sullivan's smile. "Look at you," Denise added, lightly touching the side of Sullivan's face. "You really are feeling better, aren't you?"

"Yup," Sullivan said casually. "I gave Cassidy my whole damn file, everything. It's his problem now and he definitely didn't think I was crazy, I could tell." Sullivan paused then before adding, "He doesn't think I'm right or anything either, but he said he'd look into it. And he wants to see me again, after he gets back from Vietnam. All I know is, it's okay and I haven't felt this good in a long time. He told me not to worry, that it was all under control. The Vice President of the United States!" Sullivan smiled broadly before looking down at Denise's face. "I really do think it's all going to be all right now."

"I'm glad. I'm really happy for you," Denise said. "But do you know what would make me even happier?"

"Name it."

"If you drove that beast back to your dad's house," Denise said, pointing at the big yellow Buick parked along the wire fence at the back of the parking lot.

Sullivan held out his hand then and Denise dropped his father's key ring into his palm.

"I told you, I come from a very old and wealthy Philadelphia family," Sullivan said as he walked over and unlocked the trunk of the ancient Buick that his father had driven since Sullivan was in high school. "We're just a little eccentric, that's all." He threw his bag into the trunk and then lightly tossed his nearly empty briefcase in after it. Life was starting to make some sense to him again, he thought as he turned back to Denise.

"Happy Thanksgiving," she said.

"Happy Thanksgiving," he said in return.

The chopper stayed low and Cassidy could see the lush green tops of the jungle trees as the military craft passed from the outskirts of Saigon into the Vietnamese countryside. On either side of the chopper and to its front and rear were accompanying helicopter gunships, and behind the Vice President's craft was the single crowded press helicopter.

The six aircraft flew in formation at only a few hundred feet above the jungle landscape of South Vietnam. Occasionally one of the escort ships would dip down beneath Cassidy's craft and survey the ground below the Vice President's route, or one would push up above the formation and search the airspace above them for enemy aircraft. As the Vice President watched the gunships' careful searching movements, he found himself becoming very aware of the fact that he was in a war zone.

The Army had finally insisted on two generals accompanying Cassidy to Jah Whe, not just one, and they sat on either side of him and attempted to fill him with information about the area during the entire first hour of the flight. The three men were the only occupants in the rear of the military aircraft. Up front was the pilot and the remainder of the ship's small crew.

As they moved along, Cassidy could see the top of the jungle spread out like a thick green carpet below the aircraft, and as he looked more closely, he could see the small brown lines of the narrow paths cut by villagers in the lush jungle terrain. The trails seemed barely wide enough for a single man to move along, the Vice President thought, but the intelligence reports insisted that vast amounts of personnel and supplies were moving into South Vietnam over just such narrow trails and that a vast network of them led from Hanoi in the north almost to the doorstep of Saigon itself. Cassidy looked behind him to see the press helicopter and wondered if Jennings was getting any sleep back there in the trail craft, but he could guess the answer. No one slept surrounded by a dozen journalists as they flew over a war zone.

The craft began rising then and Cassidy looked ahead. Over the next set of hills was Jah Whe he realized then, as just ahead of the craft the jungle stopped abruptly before a broad marshy plain planted in rice fields, with peasants kneeling, working in the wet ground. Cassidy was close enough to them to see the white of their peasant shirts standing out against the brown and green background of the rice fields. Then a hillside rose up in front of the chopper and obscured the landscape for a moment and the helicopters rose vertically in precise formation and glided above the crest of the hill. What the hell was he doing out here anyway? Cassidy thought as he turned back to look at the strange picture of the peasants kneeling in the wet brown earth below the formation of helicopters again. In the distance there was a faint rumbling sound like low thunder, but as Cassidy craned his neck from his kneeling position and glanced up, he could see that the morning sky was a clear pale blue with just a few faint wisps of clouds and in the east a bright white-yellow sun. This was a very beautiful country, Cassidy thought and then he heard the thunderlike sound again, this time closer and even more ominous, and he turned back to look at the lean, hard face of General Langston. The young general was seated only a few feet behind him, but before either man could say anything, the ominous booming sound repeated itself, its concussions rattling the inside of the craft. Cassidy looked past Langston to the gunship that was visible outside the window of their own chopper. The escort helicopter was rocking in a violent, erratic side-to-side motion. And then suddenly the craft's blades began rotating at crazy disjointed angles, as it plummeted out of the sky and exploded in flames against the barren hillside.

The gunship on Cassidy's left dropped down out of sight and then seconds later reappeared suddenly, popping up into view on the other side of the Vice President's craft, where the other escort helicopter had been only moments before.

There was gunfire all around them now, automatic-weapons fire repeating like strings of firecrackers and leaving orange-yellow traces in the air as the bullets passed close to their craft, and gray-black explosions of smoke appeared in the once-clear air from the heavier ground fire.

Adrenaline and fear pumped through Cassidy's body, leaving little room for any other thoughts except for his own survival. He moved back to the far wall of the craft and looked down at the jungle terrain behind the crest of the hill that they had just passed. He could see the source of the fire. In the jungle below him, a webbing of tiny trails opened into a small clearing. The clearing had been shielded from view by the crest of the hill until the precise moment that the formation of American helicopters had been directly over-head. A skillfully conceived ambush. He could see one of the escort gunships diving down now and firing into the jungle clearing. The gunship's fire was being returned from several positions concentrated around the hillside, but none of the enemy was visible to the Vice President.

Cassidy looked behind his own craft. The press chopper that had been directly behind him was lost in the thick smoke-filled air. The cloud of black smoke spread and began pouring in around him. Cassidy's lungs burned with each lungful of the acrid air that he inhaled. Chatter was coming in over the pilot's radio, static-filled words from the command center in Saigon demanding to know what was happening. As Cassidy listened he could feel his pilot pulling the craft up and away from the danger of the incoming rounds, but suddenly Tim could feel the chopper's blades clipping against something hard and metallic. The craft tilted at a sharp angle then and Tim could see the big olive-green belly of one of the escort choppers directly above him. The blades of his helicopter had torn a great gash in its metal side and the heavy chopper was falling through the sky on top of his own aircraft. Then, strangely, Cassidy felt himself being lifted powerfully up into the air for a brief moment, as the two helicopters slammed together in midair, exploding into hot orange flames, and Tim was surrounded by heat and flashing bright orange-and-yellow colors. He tried to breathe, but there was only heat and smoke. The flaming aircraft began tumbling wildly out of control then, turning over and over slowly in the air and crashing into a final shower of bright yellow flames, into the dense green jungle foliage of Vietnam.

PART FIVE

November 1967—March 1968

CHAPTER

32

Therewas a standard procedure that had
been established for waking the President during the night. It had been
prepared by the presidential staff during President Gardner's first week in
office, as early as January of 1965, and copies of it had been placed in black
three-ring binders and given to each member of his immediate staff. But
when the news of the events in Jah Whe reached the White House in the
early morning hours of November 26, 1967, those carefully laid-down formal
procedures were forgotten. A phone call went directly from the Situation
Room, located deep in the basement offices below the White House's executive
offices, to presidential assistant William Mallory, and then Mallory placed a
call to the private number that rang the telephone by the President's bed.
There was no preliminary confirmation of the decision with anyone, no checks
or counterchecks. Mallory knew that there was no other possible decision to
be made, and he made the call without hesitation.

Gardner awoke quickly from a light sleep. He hadn't slept well in months,
and he almost welcomed the urgent ringing sound and the insistent flashing
of the phone light by his bedside signaling that an emergency call was coming
through. Gardner glanced at the clock by his bed. It was a little after three
o'clock in the morning.

"Mr. President," Mallory said slowly, his voice betraying the news he had
to report. The assistant paused for a moment and gave Gardner a chance to
come fully awake. There could be no mistakes, no chances at miscommuni-
cation, Mallory told himself as he waited.

When Mallory spoke, his report was as clear and as complete as it could be under the circumstances. Gardner's first reaction was anger, but the anger flashed by quickly and the President was left with only a deep, numbing sadness. Later he would think back to that moment and how he'd felt at the news, and the enormity of the sadness would always surprise him. He knew, too, as he sat alone in the darkness of the White House, that as President he couldn't long afford the luxury of his own emotions. The news that he'd just received would have so many political and personal ramifications that he couldn't possibly begin to grasp them yet. And he knew that he had to quickly force himself to begin considering each of the many decisions that needed to be made now. His mind began to grope for the exact date and time— November 25, no the twenty-sixth now, three eighteen in the morning, eastern time, he thought looking at the glowing greenish-yellow numbers on the face of his bedside clock again.

"What time did it happen?" Gardner asked then in a flat, emotionless voice, interrupting the steady flow of facts that Mallory was busy feeding him over the open phone line. There was a short pause then, as Mallory checked his notes. "One thirty-three our time, sir."

Gardner looked back down at the somberly glowing face of his bedside clock. He was transfixed by time. It seemed the only thing of importance to him now, an anchor of fact and reality to grab on to and to hold against the swirling currents of his own emotions.

"Does his brother know yet?" Gardner asked. As he spoke, he was surprised to find that his throat was choked with emotion.

"Probably not, sir. The information was only received here a few minutes ago."

Gardner paused then, still fighting to sort out the rush of thoughts and feelings that crowded in on him, each clamoring for his immediate attention.

"Is there any possibility that the information we have is incorrect?"

"None, sir. We're still waiting for a final confirmation from I Corps in Saigon, but it's only a formality." Mallory paused, and Gardner could hear a deep, unsteady intake of breath on the other end of the line, as if the reality of what he had reported had begun to make an impact on his aide as well. "There's no doubt, sir," Mallory added, his voice no longer even attempting to disguise the emotion that he felt.

"I want to speak to Senator Cassidy," the President said sharply. Gardner knew that the phone call would be perhaps the most difficult one of his life, but he issued the order without any hesitation and as soon as he did, it made him feel a little better for the moment to simply begin to take some kind of action.

"Yes, sir," Mallory answered, his voice crisply efficient again. "Of course. Do you want to be fully briefed first, sir?"

"No." Gardner shook his head at the telephone and, as he looked down, the President was surprised to find that the receiver was shaking slightly in his own unsteady hand. "No," he said again. "I want to talk to him im-

mediately. Then I want a meeting of the Security Council called in . . ."
—the President looked at the clock by his bedside again—"one hour."

He set the phone down and waited, and he didn't turn on either his overhead light or even his smaller bedside lamp. All alone, then, in the darkness and privacy of his bedroom at the White House, he remembered a line of a prayer from his childhood—a short bleak prayer for the dead, full of stern, simple, Baptist words of consolation for the living, and he repeated those words now, first to himself and then out loud in a low, thick, western voice, his only audience a tall, ornately framed oil painting of General Washington glowing out of the darkness from the far wall of his bedroom. Gardner was trying to remember the rest of the words to the prayer when the phone by his bedside rang back. The noise startled him and he felt his nerves jump at the sound, but his hand shot out immediately and picked up the receiver.

As he spoke, Gardner kept his eyes on the portrait of his country's first President in the gold-framed painting on the bedroom wall above him. "Jack," Gardner said slowly, "I have some terrible news."

Suzanne pressed one hand tight to the side of her abdomen where she could feel the baby inside her as she listened to her husband talk in tense clipped sentences into the bedside telephone. Tears were running freely down her cheeks and her body was rocking back and forth slowly, rhythmically, soothing her unborn child, her hands spread wide open, palms pressed flat against her sides.

Jack's tense fingers still held the telephone tightly to his ear in the darkened bedroom, but there was no longer anyone on the other end of the line. The conversation had ended, the news reported, their lives irretrievably changed for all time, and still her husband held the dead phone line in his hand and looked off into the empty space above their bed. Suzanne leaned over and buried her head in his shoulder, and she could hear the telephone finally settle down into its place. Her husband's hand came up and lightly caressed the side of her face. She could sense, from the heavy, unnatural breathing coming from deep in his body, the enormous emotion that he held inside himself now. "I have to call Kay," he said, his voice so thick and unnatural and unrecognizable that Suzanne pulled away from his hand and looked into his face, almost fearing that it was a stranger who held her in his arms. Her husband's face bore a look of pain and sadness that she had never seen on it before and she prayed that she would never live to see again.

"God, Jack," she whispered, and then they held each other and pressed the baby that they had given life to together tightly between their bodies one last time before Jack withdrew from her embrace.

"Are you all right?" he whispered thickly, and her sobbing quieted and she looked up at his strong, handsome, but deeply saddened face and eyes.

"Yes," she said, but she left unspoken the single thought that at that moment truly dominated her, and she pressed her hand against the swelling flesh of her belly, thinking that the child inside her would never know her husband's brother now.

James Sullivan, Sr., was always the first one up in the Sullivan household, a residue of thirty-five straight years of factory gates before dawn, interrupted only by four years in a U.S. Navy minesweeper in the Pacific during the war. Thirty-five long, hard years that had left him in retirement with his once-strong, broad-shouldered body spreading and softening and riddled with arthritis. Dressed in his gray plaid cotton bathrobe and brown bedroom slippers, he moved slowly out of the second-floor bedroom he shared with his wife of almost forty years. He walked down the short hall past Jim Jr.'s room to the little center staircase that led to the living room of the home he'd bought after the war. The home had been in the far western suburbs of Philadelphia then, but as Philadelphia had sprawled out far past what anyone had dreamed of in 1946, the neighborhood was now considered part of the city itself.

Today was a special day, he thought, as he paused in the darkened upstairs hallway outside his bedroom for a moment. James Jr. was home for the long Thanksgiving weekend and he was sleeping only a few feet away in the same bed that he'd slept in when he was a boy. His father looked proudly down the short hall at the door of his son's room and smiled—an FBI agent, he thought, no factory gates for him, no waking before dawn for his only son and no hours of painful manual labor. He passed by the room that had been Jim's sister's, before she had married and moved away. Inside it this morning slept Jim Jr.'s girl and her two children, his father reminded himself as he glanced at the final bedroom door. It was no good waking them now. They were here for a rest, even Jim Jr.'s girl worked at something or the other, he remembered then. Times change, he thought, and he walked downstairs to begin his morning ritual.

The newspaper in this workingman's neighborhood was already at the doorstep and James Sr. scooped it off his front doorstep, stepping out onto his front porch with it tucked under his arm. It was cool in the late November morning in the few minutes after dawn, and James Sr. looked down the block where he had lived since the houses had been built right after the war, and as he stood there feeling the cool chill of the Pennsylvania morning, he could almost see his son again, riding his bicycle up the tree-lined street, or playing ball with the kids in the autumn leaves of the adjoining front yards. God, those were good days, he said to himself, as he lingered on his front steps and surveyed the familiar street again. He'd survived a depression and fought a war and worked hard almost every day of his life, but it was worth it. He'd done his job and raised good kids and today one of them was back to be with him again.

It was warmer inside and neatly comfortable. Maybe he and his son would go for a walk together after breakfast, he thought then, down the block past the old grammar school, maybe all the way to the high school, and they could talk about the old days and about the future, too, James Sr. added to himself, as he remembered Jimmy's girl and her two kids sleeping upstairs in his daughter's old room. He set the newspaper down on the little stand by his easy chair and crossed the room to the television set. He turned it on low and only a test pattern lit up the small, rounded, black-and-white screen, and then a muffled humming sound came from the fabric-covered speaker below it.

James Sr. fixed his coffee carefully and toasted two pieces of white bread in the chrome-colored toaster that stood on the kitchen table. He buttered the toast lightly and cut the slices in half down the middle the way that he always did and carried them on a small plastic plate along with a cup of the hot black coffee back into his living room and set the plate and cup down on the television tray next to his chair.

The test pattern flashed off then and James Sr. anticipated the familiar opening for the "Today" show. He watched it every morning now, since he'd retired. He liked being alone in a quiet house with Frank McGee and Barbara Walters. By the time that his wife was awake and downstairs he was ready to give her the news of the world.

But the introduction he had expected didn't appear on the screen. Instead, the picture leaped to a reporter in a downtown New York television studio. As the reporter began to talk, James Sr. sat up in his chair and concentrated all of his attention on the little television set in front of him, and as he listened he felt an anxious mix of excitement and fear. The feeling reminded him of that Sunday afternoon in December of 1941 when the radio's regular programming had been unexpectedly interrupted. It was happening again now, just like that other time. He could feel it inside himself. Pearl Harbor, James Sr. substituted inside his head, as the reporter on the television set said the unfamiliar name "Jah Whe." Sneak attack, Jim Sr. said to himself as the reporter said, "The Vice President of the United States, Timothy Cleary Cassidy, has been killed." December 7, 1941, he told himself, as the television screen filled with pictures of a burning helicopter seen from the air and the events that had occurred during the early morning hours of November 26, 1967, were reported to him. Pearl Harbor, Jah Whe, "sneak attack," "unprovoked criminal act," December 7, November 26, "a day that will live in infamy," the reporter's words and James Sr.'s memories merged, until he could barely distinguish one from the other. And then Jim Sr. remembered his own family sleeping above him on the second floor of his house and particularly his young son, three years younger than he'd been himself on December 7, 1941. There was nothing to do now but to wake him. He had to know, he decided, and reluctantly he stood, on his slightly arthritic legs, and with the sounds of the broadcast continuing behind him, he walked to the stairs of his home and then up them to the second floor. "President Gardner's to address the nation," he could hear the reporter from the New York studio saying, and James Sr. remembered another President on another day then speaking to the country. He could imagine the words that this President would say. There would be a real war now, his son's war, as that earlier war had been his war and the war before that, his father's.

When he reached the second-floor hall he moved very quietly by the first door on his left, the room that his son's girlfriend slept in that morning. Should he awaken Jim's girl and tell her the news? He'd leave that decision to Jim. He walked to his son's room instead and knocked lightly on the door, and then slowly he edged the door back and looked inside, just as he had so many times during the years that his son had been growing up in that room. He'd awakened him on so many mornings in just this way, he thought, for school or for football practices in the early fall, or for his paper route, or for a family camping trip, and now, this morning, to tell him that his country was about to be at war.

"Jimmy," James Sullivan, Sr., whispered into the darkness of the small room—but unlike all the other times, when Jim Jr. had been growing up, there wasn't just one blond head on the pillow right below the collection of red-and-white Phillies' pennants and next to the worn desk with the row of black-bound encyclopedias lined up against the wall behind it. But now there were two heads, one blond and cut short and neat, the other reddish-blond and dropping down in small curls over soft, lightly freckled white shoulders.

James Sr. was startled at first, feeling for a moment that his son must be in some kind of trouble, and the older man froze in the doorway, not recognizing what he saw in his son's room for several seconds. Then, finally understanding, he turned and tried to tiptoe out of the room without being noticed, but at that moment the floorboards creaked and he knew that he would be detected. He looked back over his shoulder at the little bed by the window. Jim Jr.'s eyes were wide open now and he was staring across the room directly at his father's face.

"Jim, son, excuse me," the older man said haltingly. "Something's happened."

Jim Jr. sat up in bed, exposing his powerful arms and shoulders above the sheets. The girl lying next to him was awake now, too, although she was pretending not to be, her body slowly sinking down and trying to disappear beneath the blankets of Jim Jr.'s childhood bed.

"Vice President Cassidy was killed last night in Vietnam. The President's going to be on television in a few minutes." Jim Sr. blurted out the words and then stepped back toward the hall. "Anyway, I thought you'd want to hear him," he added, still backtracking toward the door and being careful not to let his gaze drift over to the descending reddish-blond head that was still sliding down slowly along the side of his son's naked body. "I thought you'd want to know," he finished, and then he tried to step back into the hall and close the door, but he couldn't. Instead, he bumped into the figure of his wife, who was standing in the doorway behind him.

"Jim, what is it?" Out of the corner of his eye, Jim Sr. could see the tousled red-blond head finally managing to disappear out of sight beneath the blankets, leaving a telltale second shape bulging up in the bedcovers right next to his son. He could guess from his wife's face that she had seen it, too. "Times change," he said as he took Mrs. Sullivan by the elbow and led her back down the hall away from James Jr.'s childhood room.

It felt strange to Jack to visit the White House through the south visitors' gate. He leaned forward in the back seat of the limousine and acknowledged the Marine guard at the gate with a single curt nod of his head. The guard, grim-faced, returned the nod with a brisk salute.

Jack leaned back then and watched the south side of the White House coming up in front of him and listened to the gravel of the driveway crunch under the tires of the big car. It was still dark in the nation's capital, but most of the lights at the front of the White House were brightly lit against the cold dark morning and when the limousine rounded the final curve in the drive, Jack could see the lights from the East Wing conference room where the Security Council would soon be meeting in emergency session. He had intended to join them, but now suddenly, looking at the brightly lit windows that ran along the east wall of the White House, he decided against it. Jack reached over then and touched the little silver button that activated the limousine's intercom. "Not the East Wing," Cassidy said and then paused. "The Executive Offices," he instructed the driver a few seconds later.

"Yes, sir," the driver responded and then accelerated the limousine out and around the small cluster of other long, dark limousines that were bunched up near the high ornate steps that lead ultimately to the big formal conference room where soon the President and the others would be meeting.

Jack could see Cabinet members and key congressional leaders exiting from their limousines and moving briskly up the white Colonial steps and he couldn't help feeling grimly proud then, as he watched the various diverse components of the American government hurriedly and efficiently being assembled to deal with the crisis. A big part of him wanted to join them, as Gardner had requested him to do, but he let his decision stand, and a few seconds later the limousine stopped in front of the low shape of the darkly quiet Executive Offices. There were no lights on at all on this side of the White House. Cassidy leaned forward and, without waiting for the driver to open the car door for him, he opened it himself and stepped out into the dark, icy November air that surrounded the White House in the hour before dawn. The wind from the river whipped Jack's face as he stood for a moment and looked across the gravel drive to the entrance of the Executive Offices. Two Marine guards in their dress blue uniforms, displaying bright red sashes across their chests, the cold wind rippling their uniforms, stood at attention on either side of the building's front entrance.

Jack ran his eye along the row of office windows that faced out toward him until his gaze rested on the office of the Vice President. The lights were off and the office windows dark. What else had he expected? Jack bowed his head slightly against the wind and placed both his hands deep into the pockets of his suit coat and crossed the driveway to the building's front entrance. And as he walked along against the wind, he could feel the cold burning at the places below his eyes where the tears had fallen during the short drive from Georgetown, and he could feel the hard wind cutting easily through the simple wool business suit that he wore. In the back of his mind, he made a note to begin wearing a topcoat on mornings like this. He was too old now to try to brave cold mornings with only a suit coat. That kind of thing was good for the photographers when he was young, but it was foolish now to pretend that he was anything but what he was, and he no longer felt like a young man.

Inside the office building the halls were deserted. One of the Marine guards went ahead of him down the long carpetless hallway, and their twin footsteps tapped in unison along the deserted corridors until they reached the vice-presidential offices.

The guard opened the door to the reception area and Jack followed him through it and down the narrow unlit back hall that led directly to the Vice President's private office. After the guard unlocked the final door, he turned back to face the morning visitor.

"Thank you," Jack said. "That's all I need." The guard saluted briskly and returned to the hall. Jack could hear the heels of his military shoes tapping smartly in the hallway for several seconds, but then the sound faded away.

After a few moments of standing in the silent darkness, Jack crossed the room and switched on the single floor lamp that stood by the side of what had been his brother's desk.

The light displayed a room full of files and papers and books, some stacked in neat piles, but most left loose, lying at haphazard angles to each other on the desk and tables and even some lying on the office floor. And as Jack looked around at the room, it seemed to him a living thing, frozen for a second in time, waiting only for Tim to return and bring it back into life and motion.

Jack walked around and stood behind his brother's desk and looked out at the office from what would have been Tim's vantage point. On the wall directly in front of him were a series of photographs. The first and largest was a picture of Tim kneeling with his family on the long rolling green lawn of his home in the Virginia hills—Tim, Kay, all the kids, even their family dog, were all smiling out at the camera, with their big, two-story, Colonial-style home in the background. Next to that was a picture of Kay in her wedding dress, and standing with her and wearing an uncomfortable-looking dinner jacket and a youthful smile was the twenty-three-year-old Tim. Next to the wedding picture was a photograph of Jack, a little over ten short years later, taking his oath of office. It was the words of the oath that he'd taken that day that flooded back to him now, and, instead of a prayer for his brother, Jack silently began to repeat the presidential oath of office to himself. I, John

Trewlaney Cassidy, do solemnly swear . . . when a rapping sound on the office door interrupted him and he looked up to see the real President of the United States entering the room.

"Jack," Gardner said, and Cassidy looked across the room at the face of the tall man who stood in the doorway. The President's first instinct seemed to be to reach up and switch on the overhead light and flood the room with artificial electric brightness, and one of his large hands immediately fluttered nervously up part way to the wall switch, but then, seeing Cassidy's face illuminated only in the soft pool of light from the single floor lamp by the desk, he changed his mind and his hand moved slowly away from the switch and fell clumsily back to the side of his body. Gardner entered the room and sat down in one of the twin leather chairs in front of the Vice President's desk.

"It's a terrible tragedy, Jack," the President said quietly. As he spoke, his face and eyes were darkly somber.

Cassidy nodded his head at the older man, accepting his words.

"Information is starting to come in on exactly what happened out there. The Security Council is meetin' on it right now. When you're ready, if you want to join us, I'd like to have you there. That is, if you want . . ." Gardner let his voice trail off into uncertainty then.

"No, I don't think so," Cassidy said, his own voice determined and steady. His eyes were red and raw and he looked years older to the President than the last time Gardner had seen him, but Jack's jaw was tightly clenched and his face looked hard and determined.

"Would you prefer a private briefing?" the President asked, and Cassidy nodded his head that he would.

"I understand," Gardner said. "Any time you're ready, I'll arrange it."

"Thank you," Cassidy said. The two men sat in silence then. Outside the window the capital was creeping slowly toward dawn, but there were no real signs of it yet, except for the deepening darkness that the city always seemed to descend into right before the first sunlight.

"Jack," Gardner said, "the Vice President ignored the advice of the embassy, I Corps, everyone. He had no business being in that area. It was a last-minute change of plans."

"Is there any indication that the attack was specifically directed at the Vice President?"

"No. There couldn't have been time. That route was selected only at the last moment, but there were helicopters going into Jah Whe most of the night. The activity apparently attracted the ambush. I'm afraid, Jack, it was just chance that it was your brother's craft that was attacked," the President said sadly.

Cassidy nodded his head.

"Jack, I'm sorry we couldn't protect him out there, but, damn it, he shouldn't have done it." Gardner's own sense of outrage and frustration showed as he spoke, but then he looked away from the younger man and added in a less emotional voice, "I really do think it would be best if you attended the Security Council meeting, however briefly. We're considering some very important options."

"Options? What options?" Cassidy asked the question with a suddenness that jolted the President.

"Appropriate action," Gardner said. "In all likelihood, we're going to have to ask Congress for a formal Declaration of War now," Gardner said. "Additionally, we may decide to call up a portion of our reserve forces and place them on active duty."

"How many?"

"We're considering activating four hundred thousand Army and Air Force reserve personnel, maybe more. And . . ." Gardner stopped as he saw the look of disapproval begin to spread across the younger man's face.

"And?" Cassidy prompted angrily.

"And an appropriate immediate military response of some kind," Gardner said.

"Increased bombing?" Cassidy said.

"Perhaps."

"Mining the harbors?" Cassidy went on. "Limited nuclear weapons?" Cassidy's voice escalated in tone and anger, as he proposed each of the familiar military options that he and Gardner had discussed with each other so many times before.

"Jack," Gardner said, his voice a throaty half whisper. "I'm very sorry that we have to talk about these things now, but . . ." He didn't finish. Instead, he spread his big hands out from his body in a display of how helpless he felt to deal with the problem any other way.

"No, Rance, I think it's best that we do," Cassidy said. "I think it's important that we each know where the other stands now."

Gardner didn't answer right away, but when he began talking again, his voice was louder, steadier, his confidence returning. It was an ugly business, he thought, negotiating with a man whose brother had just been killed, but it had to be done.

"I've asked the networks for airtime to address the country this morning, ten o'clock eastern time," the President said. "I had planned to announce the decisions that the Security Council and I determine to be appropriate at this morning's meeting, but I could consider delaying the final decisions until later in the day, if that would make it easier for you to join us. I want you to know though, Jack, that whether you decide to attend the meeting or not, those decisions will be made," the President said, in a flat, hard voice.

"If you ask Congress for a formal Declaration of War, I'll fight you every step of the way," Cassidy said. "And on a call-up of the reserves as well. You should know that, too, Rance. So that there are no misunderstandings between us."

There it was, Gardner thought. It was all in the open now. The split between the two men was final and irrevocable. "Jack, we're expectin' all hell to break loose when the country finds out what's happened. I'm going to need your support now more than I ever have," the President said in a voice far milder and more conciliatory than he truly felt, while inside he began to seethe with anger. "We're placin' federal troops on alert up and down the eastern seaboard right now. There's goin' be some very angry people out there in those streets," Gardner said, letting one of his big hands flutter up and point out the Vice President's window at the streets of the nation's capital and beyond. "You know damn well there are forces in the country that will try and use what happened last night for their own purposes, and you'll be playing right into their hands if you don't . . ."

Cassidy cut the President off. "Rance, I'm not going to let you make my brother's legacy an act of war," Cassidy said and then tried to continue, but he couldn't. Instead, he stood up behind his brother's desk and turned his body sharply away from the President.

"Jack, I understand and respect your personal feelings," Gardner said. "But you know as well as I do how big the stakes are now. As a nation we just can't let this happen and not take some kind of action. When you've had enough time to think it all through, I'm certain that you'll feel differently about it. In the meantime, Jack, please don't say anything publicly. You'll only make matters worse," the President said. "I need the support of the entire country today. There can be no exceptions."

Cassidy stood with his body outlined against the dark office windows behind him. "I can't be silent any longer, particularly not today," he said.

"Jack, I think you're emotional right now. When you've had a little . . ."

Cassidy turned back into the room then, but he didn't look down at the President; instead his eyes focused on the photographs of Tim and his family mounted on the far wall of the office.

"Tim wanted peace, not war. That's why he went to Saigon. That's why he died," Cassidy said. "I'm not going to let the country forget that, and I'm not going to ask for a revenge for this death that he would have opposed himself."

Gardner nodded his head silently at the other man. He wanted to leave him now, leave him to his private grief, but he couldn't. They were not private men and their decisions, whether they were based on public or private concerns, had public ramifications that couldn't be ignored.

"Jack," Gardner said, wishing that he didn't have to continue to press his point, "please come to the meeting, at least listen to what the Joint Chiefs have to say. Speak your own mind, if you want, but don't leave it like this. There are considerations you're not aware of. There are substantial enemy troop buildups around Saigon. We expect a massive enemy offensive at any time now."

"And my brother's death is a convenient time for you to get the troops that you need to deal with it."

Gardner refused to answer the accusation.

"The answer is no," Cassidy continued. "I will not permit my brother's death to become an excuse for an escalation of this war. If, in your judgment and in the judgment of the Security Council, an increased level of military commitment to South Vietnam is required, then tell the country that, but don't use Tim's death as an excuse for it. I won't let you!" he said, still angry. "Rance, try to understand this," Cassidy added. "For me, it's very clear now. I know how Tim felt about the war and I can't permit his death to be used by you or by anyone else as an excuse to widen or prolong it. It's become that simple for me."

"But it's not that simple," Gardner said sharply. "Your brother was the Vice President of the United States. He was killed by enemy troops, and, as the President, I have to do something about that."

"And, as his brother, I have to try to stop you."

"You're wrong, Jack. And you know it. You've sat where I'm sittin' now, weighing options, balancing competing values, vital interests. You know damn well that it's not as easy as you're tryin' to make it sound," Gardner went on angrily then, being far less careful of what he said than he normally was. "Presidents, leaders have to do things that other people don't even have to consider, and sometimes those things seem wrong even to us, wrong and ugly and hard, but they have to be done just the same. You, better than anyone, know that. That's what this job is all about. That's why those people out there have a President in the first place. So, that they can make their idealistic speeches, and carry on nobly, and talk about all the terrible things that we do, and then go home with their consciences satisfied, go back to their safe, comfortable homes—homes made safe by the very things that we've done for them. It's the secret bargain, Jack. We do the things for them that they want done, but that they don't have the nerve or the stomach or the guts to do for themselves," Gardner said, the strain of the years of making those decisions showing all too clearly in his face as he finished. "You know that I'm right, Jack, and in time you'll regret anything that you do to try and stop me today, because despite all the fancy speeches, and peace marches, and demonstrations, down deep, action is truly what the country wants and what it needs to keep it safe now." He stopped and looked across the room with weary, dark-circled eyes at the younger man.

Cassidy listened carefully, not fighting against the words or their meanings. He wasn't sure that they were wrong. He'd had the same thoughts, himself, many times over the years of his public service, the same feelings, and he'd acted on them often—but that morning in the cold November darkness they no longer mattered to him. What mattered was that his brother was dead and that he couldn't let his memorial be a greater war.

"I'll be with my family the rest of the day." As Cassidy said these words, he was struck by their correctness. This was a time to be with Kay and Suzanne and the children, not in some smoke-filled East Wing conference room.

"Yes, of course," Gardner said solemnly.

"Allen Rozier will be in charge of liaison with the White House concerning details of the funeral," Cassidy said, his voice returning to a businesslike tone. "I don't expect any difficulties between us on arrangements. The decisions should be Kay's."

Gardner nodded his agreement. "Please, Jack," he said then, his voice nearly pleading with Cassidy as he spoke. "Consider very carefully what you say and do now. The decisions that I announce today will not have been arrived at lightly," the President said solemnly. "The whole world will be watching us."

"Then we must be very careful of how we act," Cassidy said and then fell silent again.

"I can arrange to have a helicopter take you to . . ." Gardner began, but Cassidy waved off the offer before it could be completed. "No," Cassidy said. "I'm going out to see Kay and the children and I'd just as soon drive. Suzanne's with her now."

"Please give her my deepest sympathy," Gardner said. "I'd like to come out there and see her myself later in the morning. If that'll be all right."

"Of course," Jack said and then started to move past him, but he paused by a chair that stood at the side of his brother's desk. On it was piled books and files and papers and among the jumble rested an old brown leather football. Jack looked down at the football's scuffed leather surface for several seconds. Jack liked footballs. He liked their weight, and the way they felt when he rolled them in his hands, and the peculiar way that somehow, despite their awkward shape, when thrown correctly they seemed to defy the laws of gravity and nature and glide gracefully through the air to their target. He could rarely resist picking one up whenever he saw one, but that morning he let Tim's football lie untouched, half buried in the mound of papers and files that surrounded it.

The President had stood himself now and was looking over at Jack, watching him very closely. "I'm sorry about what's happened between us, Jack," Gardner said then, his voice full of real sadness. "I suppose it was inevitable, though."

Cassidy was quiet for a moment before he spoke. "I suppose it was," he said.

There was nothing more to say to each other then, and Cassidy waited for the President to leave the room first. Within seconds Jack could hear the tap-tap sound of Gardner's long strides in the carpetless office corridor.

Cassidy walked to the door to his brother's office, but instead of leaving, he turned back into the room to look at it one last time the way that it was, the way that his brother had left it, and as he did, Jack's eyes were attracted to the big grandfather clock that stood against the far wall. It read a few minutes before five o'clock in the morning. My brother has been dead for less than four hours, Jack thought, and already the rest of us, the survivors, are fighting over his ashes.

Jack moved his gaze then, and outside the window of his brother's office he could see a few early winter snowflakes dropping softly on the long, dark green surface of the White House lawn.

CHAPTER
33

The sounds of champagne corks popping, laughter, and shouts of happiness filtered in through the open terrace doors where Sylvia Martine stood watching the party that was in progress behind the high, moss-covered stone walls that enclosed the courtyard of her New Orleans home. Her family and friends, like many other people all over the world, were celebrating the news of Tim Cassidy's death.

Her son, a handsome, young dark-skinned man with a gleaming pompadour of shiny black hair swept straight back from his face, was approaching her across the long stone courtyard. He held a champagne glass in each hand. When she saw him, he held one of the glasses out to her and smiled broadly, revealing a double row of even white teeth. She shook her head no, acknowledging the young man's smile by lifting her own glass of champagne to show him that she didn't need another, but she didn't return his smile or even look into his eyes as she gestured toward him with her glass. And then she turned abruptly away from him, signaling that she wanted to be left alone. He looked so much like his father, it was almost impossible to look at him sometimes, and she could feel the pain filling her heart again. Even today, she thought sadly, even today I can feel nothing but pain.

When she finally turned back to the open terrace doors her son was gone. She stayed watching the crowd for several minutes more, but no one else dared approach her, although the garden at the rear of the house was overflowing with friends and relatives. They had begun arriving early that morning, almost immediately after the news of the Vice President's death had been carried in local news reports.

She turned away from the doors to the terrace and walked back inside the house. On the wall of the room that had been her husband's study was a long series of photographs. She stopped by one of them and looked up at it. It was a brightly colored picture of her husband that had been taken six years earlier, one month before he'd died. Don Martine was standing before a microphone. Behind him was the flag of the free Cuban republic rippling open in a light breeze, displaying proudly its field of blue and white and bright red. Next to her husband was another man, an American politician, and the politician was smiling at Don Martine, a false politician's smile, she thought as she looked at it now. In the photograph next to it, the politician's hand was extended to shake her husband's extended hand. The politician was President Cassidy, and behind him stood his brother.

"Know the pain," Sylvia Martine said in a deadly quiet voice, her lips and teeth and mouth releasing the sounds of the words toward the photographed image of John Cassidy, her neck and head making the darting movement a deadly snake might make as it struck forward toward its prey.

She heard a champagne cork burst outside her terrace doors somewhere in the overgrown foliage of the garden courtyard, and a voice called out *"Viva Cuba! Viva liberte!"* And then other voices joined in, laughing and singing joyfully. She turned away from the photographs and walked across the room to sit in the big chair behind the desk that had been her husband's.

She listened then to the sounds coming in from the courtyard, but she wasn't drawn to them. Instead, she reached forward onto the massive wooden surface of the desk that had been her husband's and touched a button built into its front panel, and seconds later a neatly dressed young Cuban woman entered the room.

"I will go to the cemetery this morning. Please have the car brought around to the side," Mrs. Martine said, and the dark-haired secretary left the room to do as she had been told.

Mrs. Martine stood and crossed the room to the wall of photographs again. Yes, this was the one that she wanted to see this morning, she thought, as she looked at the picture of Don Martine and Cassidy's now-dead brother. The picture had been taken the night after the rally in Miami. As she studied the photograph her feelings moved from a grim kind of satisfaction to a numbing deadness that finally overcame the other emotions she'd felt since the news of Tim Cassidy's death.

A few minutes later, without letting her guests know, she left her home by a side door and entered the darkened rear seat of a long, black Cadillac limousine.

The limousine started down the front drive of her home and out its front gates, onto the Garden District street that was packed that morning with the cars of her guests, and then the limousine began making its way toward the cemetery outside the city that held the body of her husband.

There were people coming and going to and from the party on the narrow street in front of her home, but she sat alone in the limousine's rear seat and kept her eyes straight ahead, refusing to acknowledge their presence. She'd brought a black wool coat to cover her white dress and she clutched it to her with one hand at her throat. There was a black lace veil down over her face and she drove the entire way to the cemetery in silence, holding the coat pressed tightly to her body.

Senator Cassidy's car pulled down the long gravel drive of what had been his brother's home in the Virginia hills. It was almost dawn now and Jack kept his eyes out the side window of the limousine, watching the hills come into focus against a slate-gray sky until the limousine pulled to a stop at the front of the Cassidy's Virginia estate.

Kay Cassidy was standing alone on the white-painted Colonial portico that formed the front entrance to her home. It was a cold morning and the breeze from the hills above her home stirred around her, blowing bitterly against her face and ruffling the outline of her short-cut brown hair, but she stood very straight and still as she watched the limousine roll to a stop in front of her. Its rear doors opened and Jack started up the short path toward her. Kay seemed to look expectantly past him for a moment, as if she were waiting for another figure to emerge from the limousine's back seat, a shorter, leaner figure with a shock of rumpled light brown hair and electric, bright blue eyes, but no second figure appeared from inside the limousine, and then she knew that it was true. Until that moment, a corner of her mind had whispered to her that Jack would do something, that somehow he would sort through it all and find that it was just a terrible mistake of some kind, and then he would bring Tim back to her. But now she knew that wasn't going to happen and she had to admit to herself that she would never see that slender figure again and the finality of the loss rushed through her and filled her with a barely tolerable sadness. She took a small step toward Jack, and he moved forward to take her in his arms.

"Oh, Jack," Kay said, and she held herself tight against the dark wool suit coat that her brother-in-law wore that morning. She felt as if she wanted to stay hidden against his body forever, but she forced herself to raise her head away from the warmth of the dark wool coat and look up into his eyes. "Are you all right? I know how much you loved him," she asked, and Jack smiled down at her, moved by his sister-in-law's courage.

A few seconds later, they walked up the home's front steps together and entered the house. "How are the children?" Jack asked, as he held his sister-in-law tightly to his side.

"They're upstairs, Suzanne's with them," Kay said. "The White House has been calling every ten minutes. The President wants to talk to you."

Jack nodded his understanding as they stepped together inside the old Colonial home's front doors.

"It's a cold morning," Kay said, turning back to the high doors and closing them tightly against the grayness outside, and then they were both silent for a long moment, Kay's somber words echoing in the empty, high-ceilinged entry hall, while above them a crystal chandelier fought a losing battle to light and warm the room in the cold, dark morning. "I think they're holding the line open," she added and gestured toward the dining room where a telephone stood on a table by the door.

"It can wait," Jack said, and they walked back through the dining room of his brother's home and past the waiting telephone into the breakfast area that separated the big formal dining area from the kitchen built at the rear of the house. Kay sat down at the head of the breakfast table at the chair that had been her husband's, but her body was turned at an awkward angle away from the table, so that she was facing out toward the tall windows at the side of the room that displayed the long green backyard of her home.

It was a little past dawn now and she could see the first light beginning to illuminate the familiar objects on the grounds of her home as the mysterious sullen shapes of darkness were once again transformed by the morning light into a grouping of lawn furniture, and the outline of a child's swing, and in the distance an uneven row of white, leafless birch trees.

"Suzanne's still upstairs with the children. She's been wonderful," Kay said. But as she spoke, her eyes didn't leave the familiar shapes of her backyard, and her awkwardly twisted body didn't turn back to face her brother-in-law.

"I told the White House that Allen would work with them on the arrangements, if that's all right?" Jack said and his sister-in-law nodded her head. "I suppose there's a lot to do," she said vaguely, but then, as she thought about Allen and the pain and the loss that Tim's death would cause him, a new flood of sadness poured through her and showed in her face. "Poor Allen," she said.

On the table in front of Jack was a fresh pot of coffee in a tall silver container, steam rising slowly from it. When he saw it, Jack reached out and poured first a steaming cup for his sister-in-law and then poured a few inches into a small china cup for himself.

Kay left the coffee alone. She kept staring out the window of her home at its empty backyard.

"That's where we were," Kay said softly, unable to raise even a finger to indicate the place on the green hillside behind her home. "That's where Tim and I were when we learned about Dallas," she said, and then she turned back to face her brother-in-law. "We thought we'd lost you," Kay said. "But then it was all right . . . That's what I thought this morning," she went on, "when the White House first called. That somehow it would be like it had been then. That he'd come home with you, but when I saw you get out of the car alone," she said, pointing out to where Jack's car and driver still remained waiting in the driveway of her home, "I knew then that it wasn't going to happen that way this time. That this was different." Kay was crying now, but softly, almost noiselessly.

Jack could only nod his head at her to continue talking.

"At that moment, Jack," Kay said, her eyes still fixed on the spot on the back lawn of her home where she and Tim had stood on that November day in 1963, "at that moment, I think that he would have died for you, if that would have helped. He believed in you that much," she said. "Loved you that much, and, Jack . . ." Kay paused then, wanting her brother-in-law to understand precisely what she had to say. "Whatever has happened between you over the last few months," she said, turning back to him, "nothing has really changed. I'm certain that he would want you to know that now."

"I do," Jack answered. Then he stood and crossed to the window that looked out over the rolling green hills that bordered his brother's Virginia estate.

"You know what the only thing is that I'm afraid of, Jack?" Her brother-in-law turned back to listen. "No, not afraid of," Kay corrected herself. "There's nothing left to be afraid of anymore. But I guess that I'm just very sad now that no one will ever really know what he could have become. None of them, not his country, not you, not even his own children. They'll never know now, just how great his love was for all of them."

Jack placed his hand on Kay's shoulder. He could feel her body trembling slightly, but she wasn't crying any longer, and as he looked down at her, Jack could see that she was fighting desperately to contain the terrible loss that she felt. "But I know," Kay said, with a sudden mixture of sadness and pride, "I know what he was and what he could have become." She turned again to try to look once more at the grounds at the rear of her home where on another day news of another tragedy had reached her, but Jack's body blocked her view.

"I should take that call," Jack said then, gesturing toward the telephone in the next room.

"Yes, of course," Kay said, composing herself. "I'll go tell Suzanne that you're here."

"Kay," Jack said, stopping her before she could leave the room. "I understand what you've told me, and there's something that you need to know as well." He paused then, finding the words. "I was wrong. I should have been the one who was out there last night, not Tim," Jack said. "But all that's changed now. I promise you, Kay. I won't let Tim's death be for nothing."

"I know," Kay said. "I know that you won't."

"It's Cassidy's doing!"

The President's address to the nation had just ended and Gardner's words had been somber and restrained. There had been none of the calls to action or of rallying the country to war that James Sullivan, Sr., had expected, and the anger and confusion that he felt at the President's cautiously solemn speech were registered on his face, as the television screen switched away from the Oval Office and began showing one of the many antiwar riots that were beginning to break out in cities all over the country.

"I don't understand," James Sr. said. "What's going to happen now?"

"He said that there would be an 'appropriate military response,' " his son answered quietly.

"I know, but what the hell does that mean? Are we at war or aren't we?"

"We're not," his son said then, his voice firm and decisive.

"It's Cassidy, I know it is!" James Sr. exploded in anger again. "He's holding the President back, tying his hands somehow. He wants to make a damn martyr out of his brother, rather than do what has to be done now."

"Which is what?" Sullivan said, his own anger showing in the tight, determined way that he challenged his father's words.

"I'll tell you this, if the Democrats don't have the guts for it . . ." But then James Sr., a lifelong Democrat, couldn't quite bring himself to finish the difficult thought. "Jim, aren't you going to call in?"

"No," Sullivan snapped. "Why the hell should I?"

"I'll tell you why," his father answered him. "Because your country might need you, that's why."

"You mean it might want to use me," Sullivan said, standing up as he spoke, and moving toward the front door of his father's home.

"You're no better than they are," his father said, without thinking, and then he pointed at the television screen where pictures from a handheld television camera were showing the chaos caused by a group of war protesters on a small college campus somewhere in northern New England.

"Maybe they're right," Sullivan said then.

"What do you mean?" his father said, barely under control.

"Maybe that," Sullivan said, pointing at the turbulence on the television screen, "maybe that's the only way that anyone can hear you in this country anymore."

James Sr. looked closely at his son and, as he did, the older man no longer felt anger, but just sadness and a sense of both his own and his son's deep confusion. There was something changed about Jim, something that he didn't begin to understand. What was it? What had changed his son so dramatically?

"You're right about one thing, though," Sullivan said. "Tim Cassidy was the best of them. The others . . . I don't know. I . . ." He stopped then, searching for words that would match his emotions. "He was the only real hope for any of us, and now he's dead. God knows what will happen to us without him."

His father just looked blankly across the room at him, failing to understand.

"I'm sorry, it's just that . . ." Sullivan began, but he couldn't finish what he had to say. He turned away from his father and started for the door. "I'm going for a walk."

"Wait, Jim, I'll go with you," his father called out to him, but it was too late. His son had already entered the hall and a brief second later James Sr. could hear the sound of the front door slamming closed.

* * *

They were making a second boarding call for his bus now, but Lopata didn't make a move toward the door that led to the main terminal. He stayed seated at the dirty gold-flecked Formica table in the brightly lit bar off the terminal lobby and watched the television screen mounted against the far wall of the room. He was drinking beer and his blue vinyl flight bag was pushed up under the small round table near his feet. There had been a small packet of American money in the pocket of the clothing that he had exchanged with the dead man in the hills above Havana, and the dead man's money and some luck had brought Lopata from Cuba to Miami in a little less than thirty-six hours. There had even been enough money left over to buy a bus ticket to New Orleans, but the dollar that he'd just spent on the beer in the bus terminal bar was the last of it. He was back in the States now, safe from Castro and his people, but he was broke. No money, no identification papers, nothing—nothing, except a small fortune in a bank in the Bahamas—a fortune that he didn't dare touch, he thought angrily, because if he did, DeSavio's people could find out and they would know that he was still alive and come looking for him. He couldn't even risk a telephone call. Any move at the money now and he could be discovered. Lopata lifted the glass bottle from the table and drank from it. He thought of the man whose dead body he had dressed in his own prison clothes and left to be discovered in the hills above Havana. If I do nothing for a while, they will believe that I am dead. A few months, a year at the most, and it will be safe, he thought. Meanwhile I will survive, he told himself proudly—I will survive.

His health was even a little better, he thought, fingering the packet of pills in his shirt pocket.

Lopata reached for his beer again to salute himself, when he heard the final boarding call for his bus, but still he didn't move toward the door. He was enjoying watching the drama being played out on the television screen in front of him too much. The screen showed the night sky above Honolulu as the television cameras searched for the first glimpse of the big Air Force plane that held the remains of the country's Vice President. The glowing lights of the American naval base at Pearl Harbor were visible in the background.

Cassidy's body had been flown out of Saigon and had arrived in New Zealand, and now the big Air Force plane was descending into Honolulu for refueling before it made its final long-distance flight across the Pacific and back to Washington.

Then the television screen showed the streets of Miami. There was a very different mood in downtown Miami. It wasn't the somber, respectful silence of the mourners at the airport in Honolulu. Antiwar rioting was breaking out on the streets of Miami, as it was in much of the rest of the country, and Lopata watched as the television screen in front of him showed a fire erupting in a series of old buildings located less than a mile from the bus station where he sat at that very moment. The first of the fires had probably been set by someone in the crowd of people who moved restlessly against the police barricade that had been set up in front of the building, he thought, and a feeling of excitement began rising inside him. There were pictures of the crowd and of looters breaking into shop windows and of groups of angry war protesters taunting the police. A car was overturned and began burning out of control, and Lopata could feel the strong tug of the violence that he saw on the television screen and he longed to be part of it. He pushed his beer bottle aside and walked over to the counter where he'd bought his ticket earlier in the evening and asked the clerk to exchange it for one the next morning. Then, he used one of the station's lockers to store his flight bag.

Feeling liberated, he walked outside into the steamy Miami night. From the street in front of the bus station, he could hear the sounds of the rioting and he could see the flames leaping in the air from the old buildings only a few blocks away. Then he could smell the smoke and he could hear the sounds of approaching sirens. His heart began to beat rapidly and he could feel the blood moving in his veins faster and faster. He ran across the street, avoiding cars with quick moves to his right and left, running toward the sounds of the sirens. Soon he could smell the smoke and hear even more loudly the sounds of other people, and he ran even faster toward the flames.

The White House was under attack. Temporary walls of sandbags and rolls of military barbed wire stood around its grounds, while federal troops in full battle gear stayed at the ready, waiting at several strategic spots around its perimeter. Rocks, bottles, and paper cups filled with dirt or urine had been hurtled over its protective walls, thrown by the angry crowds that had formed along Pennsylvania Avenue. Tear gas had been used hours before to push back a charge of young people who had attacked the south lawn, but faint traces of the poison gas still hung in the leaves of the trees and clung to the battle uniforms of the soldiers.

Through the windows of the Oval Office the President could see flames in the night sky, and he could smell the smoke from the fires that blazed in the streets of the nation's capital, and occasionally he could even hear the faint sound of gunfire in the far distance.

"God, if I could only make them understand," Gardner said through tightly clenched lips. He was standing facing the tall windows behind his desk, one hand clutching his other wrist, locking his arms tightly behind his body. Out the window he could see sandbags being stacked in front of the fence on the south lawn, and he could see the shadowy outline of federal troops patrolling the grounds, ensuring that the rioting crowds that were destroying other parts of the city didn't penetrate the perimeter of the White House itself.

"Sir, the helicopter is ready. We can leave anytime you want now, sir." Mazeloff had entered the room behind the President and stood now on the other side of Gardner's desk. He'd heard the President's remark about wanting to make the American people understand, but he'd chosen not to acknowledge it. Gardner hadn't wanted an answer, Mazeloff reasoned. He'd been around the President long enough to know most of the time what he really wanted, and the press secretary guessed that all Gardner wanted now was to stand by the window and look at the flames in the night sky over the nation's capital and to say whatever came into his head without being contradicted or questioned by anyone. So Mazeloff remained quiet and waited for the President to speak again.

"I can't fight a ghost," Gardner said and then turned from the window and returned the few short steps to his desk. "The ghost of Tim Cassidy," he said, breathing the words out as lightly and as lacking in substance as the spirit that they symbolized to him. He stood for a long moment by his desk chair before he sank wearily into it. "I don't have any choice. I have to do something. I can't . . ." Gardner stopped talking then and lifted the immaculately typed document that lay in front of him at the very center of his desk. "Executive Order 47983," the brilliantly white sheet of paper read: "By Order of the President of the United States, Ransom W. Gardner."

"It's less than half the response that the Joint Chiefs requested, sir," Mazeloff said, but Gardner acted as if he hadn't heard. He just remained seated at his desk, the unsigned executive order lying in front of him. "A ghost," he said very softly into the dimly lit room. "Look at that," he added, his voice picking up power again, as he turned back to the window and pointed toward the orange glow in the night sky above Washington. "That's how they celebrate him."

"Sir," Mazeloff said after a suitable period of doing what the President had requested and looking out the window at the light from the fires of protest in downtown Washington. "I really believe that we should go to Camp David. There's nothing more we can do here."

A small tear hung in the corner of the President's eye as he looked out of the window of his office at the barricaded White House grounds. It was impossible even for Gardner, himself, to tell whether the tear was caused by a hint of the smoke and gas filtering in below the windows, or if it came only from the deep sadness that he felt now. But either way, he managed to brush it away skillfully before he turned back into the room to face Mazeloff—and it remained forever his secret. "No, the President should be in the capital on a night like this," he said sadly, but with very little real conviction in his voice. He reached out to pick up a drink that stood in front of him, but his hand slid weakly toward the base of the glass and rested with its palm flat on the desktop. Gardner looked down at the hand then, as if it were as unrelated to him as the executive order that lay still unsigned on the desk next to it.

Mazeloff heard the weakness in the President's response. With a little more waiting, he decided, with a little more patience, he could coax Gardner safely onto a helicopter and then to the peace and safety of Camp David. Mazeloff wondered what Washington would look like from the air on a night like this, with fires burning from the downtown streets and the White House barricaded and surrounded by troops. He began formulating it then, as he listened to the President's deeply tired voice continue, into a chapter for the memoirs that he was planning to write after he left the White House staff.

"Do you remember, Ted," Gardner said, "that night at the ranch, right before dawn, the morning of the election?"

Mazeloff nodded his head that he did, although he'd been a thousand miles away in New York City that night, and he went on formulating the chapter of his memoirs in his head, while his eyes pretended to focus intently on the weary figure of the President, slumped behind his desk.

"Do you remember how clear it was that night? And the stars . . ." Gardner's voice was full of the rich power of remembering now. "I thought then just for a little while that maybe I could see forever," he said and then forced his deeply wrinkled face into what turned out to be only a parody of a smile. "Out there tonight," Gardner said sadly, turning only his neck and head toward the window where the night sky should have been, "I can't even see the sky."

Mazeloff nodded in agreement, but he chose to say nothing. He wasn't even certain what it was that the President wanted to hear from him now, and so silence seemed the wisest course.

Gardner turned back into the room then and looked down at the unsigned executive order on the desktop in front of him.

"You know, Ted, back there this morning," the President said—and the thought that it had only been that morning seemed incredible—"when I met with Cassidy, I think he was only bluffing, don't you?"

"Yes, sir." Mazeloff nodded. "Cassidy's been quiet all day."

"He was bluffing," Gardner said insistently. "He's got nowhere else to go. In the end he has to support me. I'm the President and he's a politician, an ambitious politician. In the end he has nowhere to go, but to support me— don't you think so, Ted? Isn't that right?" the President urged. "Well, I don't bluff," Gardner added angrily then, but he refused to look directly now at the unsigned executive order that lay on his desktop, mocking his words. "I lose some, I get beat sometimes, but I, by God, don't get bluffed down."

Mazeloff nodded his head in agreement again.

"This is our chance," Gardner said. "This is the moment when the American people will finally understand the need for real action," Gardner said, going over it again for at least the hundredth time that day. "Those"—the President pointed vaguely out in the direction of the demonstrators gathered in front of the White House—"those are not the people," he said, but the strength had gone out of his voice. "If Cassidy breaks with me over this, there's nowhere for him to go. He's dead." Gardner paused then, struck by the inappropriateness of his own phrase on this night, but he repeated the word anyway, so that there would be no mistaking how strongly he felt about it. "Dead," he said again. "He should've known, I don't bluff."

Mazeloff remained quiet. He knew now that Gardner had decided not to sign the order and that he was only looking for a way to justify the decision in his own mind. "It's Cassidy's fault, sir," Mazeloff said. "He's bluffing, but you can't risk it without his support. It would divide the Party and destroy the support for the war that you've been able to put together in Congress. There'll be another time, one that doesn't belong to the Cassidys. It may be too late then, but it's the way it has to be now, isn't it, sir?"

Gardner nodded. "It's Cassidy's fault," he said and then reached out and crumpled the unsigned executive order in his big hand and dropped it into a waste-paper basket beneath his desk.

Both men were quiet for several long seconds then. In the silence, Gardner could feel an overwhelming fatigue begin to settle into his legs and arms and spread up into his back and shoulders. "God, I'm tired, Ted," he said finally. "Is there a chopper ready, did you say?"

"Yes, sir," Mazeloff said. A trip in the presidential helicopter through the night sky with the capital in flames below them—it could be the highlight of his book. He could write it by contrasting it with the night during the War of 1812 when the British had burned Washington and forced President Madison to flee the capital and hide in Baltimore. Now, a hundred and fifty years later, a second President was being forced to leave the city, this time, though, by his own citizens.

"The helicopter's waiting, sir," Mazeloff said.

"I wish I could sleep on those damn things," Gardner said. "Never could sleep on them, too goddamn noisy." He stood up then and moved slowly past his desk toward the door. Before he left the room, he took a final look around at the Oval Office, and in that moment he felt as if in some way he were leaving it forever. Papers and maps were still scattered on the table by the far wall and on the sides of his desk were tall piles of even more papers and files. God, it had been a hard day, Gardner thought. Maybe the longest and hardest of his presidency, and now it was ending almost twenty-four full hours after it had begun with Mallory's early morning telephone call. And nothing had been accomplished really; the only decision of any magnitude lay canceled in the presidential wastebasket. Was he doing the right thing? It was impossible to know for certain, he told himself, as he had so many times before. It was possible only to try to do his best. He was struck then by the simplemindedness of his own thoughts of consolation. The message that he gave himself hadn't changed much since he was a schoolboy, he decided. Do your best and move on—but it didn't change the enormous sadness that filled him, as he looked again at the books and papers and maps lying almost everywhere in the historic room that he was leaving now.

"It comes down ultimately to the ability to govern, doesn't it?" he said dramatically, and Mazeloff's attention snapped back to him, debating again, as he watched Gardner's deeply lined face, what it was that the President wanted to hear in reply.

There were faintly ominous sounds of sirens in the far distance, somewhere on the capital streets. It may have been Mazeloff's imagination, but it seemed to him that the street sounds might be getting closer. But the President didn't seem to even hear them. He seemed too far lost now in his own memory and in vague speculation about the future to fully sense the moment. "The ability to lead," Gardner said forcefully, but then he let his body slump forward, as if he were giving up. Finally, he turned and followed Mazeloff out the door toward the waiting helicopter.

The small dark-haired man occasionally caught a fleeting glimpse of his own reflection in the glass of a store window, and, as he passed, he would glance over and see a flash of the weakened body still dressed in some loosely fitting peasant clothes that he had bought before he'd left Cuba. And the image of what he looked like now only made him move even more swiftly down the Miami streets toward each new center of danger and excitement that lay in front of him.

Lopata felt like a jungle animal, let loose from captivity as he moved along at the edges of the surging crowds, and he began to experience a wonderful intoxication.

He loved the free-flowing openness of the streets that night, the lawlessness, the freedom of moving anonymously at the edges of the crowds and just sampling the chaos, but always managing to keep his own body safely out of harm, as he watched others taunting the police or hurling objects at store windows. He cheered wildly when a group of rioters near him charged a police line with rocks and sticks. It was all like a great fantasy spectacle to him, a wonderful black dream of life gone wild, and he was free to move through it as he chose without any restrictions, any sense of rules or laws, and he gloried in it all, the chaos, the running people, the fires breaking out on the streets around him, the fear in the faces of the police, but most of all in the feel of red-hot anger let loose in the air. There was no order, no meaning, only wild destruction and excitement and he ran back and forth from one cluster of action to another, drinking it all in, until he stopped finally, nearly exhausted, to catch his breath at an intersection filled with people. From where he stood at the rear of the crowd, he could hear the sounds of destruction and he could smell the smoke from the fire in the cheap wood-framed building across the street that had attracted the people that he stood with now, and he could see the flames leaping in the air toward the cloudy, moonless sky. It was like a carnival, he thought happily, a great black carnival of destruction.

When he was rested, he turned from the flames and continued on down the streets. He stopped after a few minutes though and hurled a rock through an already smashed plate-glass window into what was left of a broken television screen. He laughed at the destruction. Standing in front of the broken shop window and looking in at the broken television screen, he felt more powerful than he had in a very long time, at least since that day in Dallas. A free animal, he reminded himself, as he caught a glimpse of his own face in the jagged sheet of glass that still remained inside the broken television set, and, as he looked back at himself, his dark eyes seemed to burn as brightly as the flames that burst out of the destruction and chaos of the streets reflected behind him. His image in the jagged sheet of broken glass reminded him of something. What was it? he asked himself, and then it came to him. The pictures of the devil in his mother's Bible, when he was a child—uncontrollable evil. Lopata smiled at the thought, remembering how as a boy he had always admired that face of evil in his mother's precious book. Now, he decided proudly, he looked out in triumph from just such a face himself.

He was attracted then by a bright fiery light rising into the night sky behind him, and immediately he began moving down the crowded street toward it. As he ran, he skillfully avoided the figures dashing in and out of the shadows of the nearby buildings and moving rapidly by him, until soon he found himself at the edge of another crowd. It had come together across the street from a wall of flame that had engulfed nearly an entire block of old buildings. The night sky above it was bright orange with flames, but as he watched the fire out of the corner of his eye, he saw a figure advancing toward him and then he felt a sudden powerful jolting of his body, as something very strong squeezed his wrist and then jerked his arm up into the middle of his back.

Lopata swore angrily in Spanish and began to twist his body, violently, trying to get away from the vicelike hold, but the powerful grip only tightened on him. He felt his body being spun around then and pushed toward a vehicle that was parked on the street in front of him. The rear of the vehicle was open, but before he was thrust inside of it, his arms were propped up against its cold metal side and his legs were spread out behind him. Rough hands searched his body, starting at his ankles and reaching finally the area behind his neck.

Lopata could hear nearby voices shouting at him, and then objects were being thrown in his direction, lighted cigarettes, a half-full can of beer that thudded heavily against the side of the vehicle just above his head. When he turned to look, he could see that a small crowd had gathered around him. For a moment he felt like a hero, a celebrity, but within seconds he was pushed into the open rear door of the vehicle. After a few stumbling steps into the darkness he lost his balance and fell forward onto his hands and knees, slamming against the hard metal floor, and he heard the door close behind him and then lock. He realized then that he was in the custody of the City of Miami's police department.

CHAPTER
34

The Sullivan family, like most of the rest of the country, stayed huddled around their television set throughout the Thanksgiving weekend. Even Denise's children sat quietly for long periods of time, transfixed by what they saw on the little black-and-white screen in front of them.

A film crew had been in the trail helicopter behind the Vice President's craft and it had captured the entire scene—the strafing bullets like streaks of angry light rocketing up from the ground, then the craft jolting upward and its powerfully rotating blades catching the steel underbelly of the big American gunship that flew above it, and finally the seemingly endless slow-motion-like descent through the smoke-filled air into the Vietnamese hillside. The short piece of film was shown over and over again along with the networks' coverage of the other related events of the news-filled weekend.

The Vice President's body had been moved from the jungle clearing north of Saigon to the nation's capital with astonishing speed. Early Saturday morning, Tim Cassidy's wife and children bravely stepped forward across the windy landing field to greet their father's plane.

The little screen in front of Sullivan showed Jack and Suzanne Cassidy now. They were waiting on the edge of the tarmac as the airplane that bore the Vice President's body broke down out of the clouds and glided to a slow, ceremonial stop on the cement runway in front of them. The wire fence that surrounded the airport held back a vast crowd of people, a few holding single glowing candles as a reminder of another early morning vigil four years earlier, but in the sky above them shone the flickering light of several larger flames, and the glow of those other fires easily overpowered that from the small candles—an entire section of downtown Washington was on fire, and the light from its destructive power lit the capital's sky like an angry artificial dawn.

The television cameras showed the Cassidy family in close-up then. Tim Cassidy's own children were dressed that morning in blacks and dark grays —the little boys in somber black suits, the girls in dark gray dresses—as they followed their mother across the runway toward the big, fat-bellied military plane that held their father's body.

A few seconds later, Jack and Suzanne Cassidy stepped out onto the tarmac and crossed the few feet of windswept cement airstrip to where Kay Cassidy and her children stood waiting for the cargo doors of the aircraft to open and the casket bearing the Vice President to appear. Soon, the bomb-bay doors of the aircraft slowly opened and the hydraulic platform began its slow, heavy descent. It bore a single flag-draped casket and when it had reached the ground, not the family, but a Marine honor guard took possession of the simple coffin.

Sullivan watched carefully, as the wind blew fiercely at the head and face of Jack Cassidy. Cassidy's eyes were blurred and filled with sadness, but he didn't shed a single tear for the cameras. Sullivan wondered how he would react in such a moment and what enormous forces of control and discipline guided this other man now, but the answers were impossible for him to guess at.

There were several hours of television coverage then of the long slow procession down Pennsylvania Avenue to the Rotunda, where the body of the Vice President was to lie in state until the funeral on Monday morning. The streets of the capital were packed with mourners, and a police line had been established along the procession route to keep onlookers at a distance, but occasionally a television camera would pick up a hint of the President or a Cassidy family member behind the bulletproof glass of their limousines, as they passed slowly down the crowded streets.

Throughout Saturday afternoon and into the evening and then again all day Sunday, the television coverage stayed with the events in the Rotunda as mourners passed by the flag-draped coffin that lay in the center of the high-domed ceremonial room of the Senate building.

The networks cut away from the scene at the Capitol only to show pictures of the continuing violence in the streets of Chicago and Los Angeles and Miami and even in parts of downtown Washington. But always the coverage returned to the flag-draped casket in the center of the formal high-domed room and the long lines of mourners filing slowly by the closed coffin to pay their final respects to the Vice President.

On Monday morning, the Sullivan family—along with almost every other family in the country—sat in front of their television set and watched as the Cassidy family appeared before them again.

The church service was simple and brief, and the last of the speakers was Senator Cassidy. He stood at the church's high pulpit, his face showing the depth of the tragedy that he had endured. The Sullivan family sat silently and watched as he spoke eloquently of his brother and his brother's dreams for the country and for the world. He chose also that day to talk of the future, and then, as the cameras found the faces of Tim Cassidy's wife and children, Sullivan could hear Denise beginning to cry.

As his speech reached its climax, Cassidy spoke of the need for peace, but as Sullivan listened he reminded himself that it had been this man who had led his country toward war. Cassidy spoke then of coming together as a nation and Sullivan could hear Denise crying even harder, but Sullivan could think only of all the anger and the divisions that this other man had caused in his own political party and in the politics of his nation.

Sullivan sat forward as Cassidy finished his speech. The Senator's eyes appeared to be filled with tears, but the fullness of his pain was still in check, refusing even now to show itself fully to the television cameras and to the world. Sullivan looked closely at the screen, narrowing his own eyes, trying to see through to the truth somewhere inside this other man, and as he did, he could hear the sounds of Denise still sobbing quietly—but what was the real truth of this man who spoke so gracefully less than five short days after his own brother's death? Wasn't he the very man who on other days grasped for power, compromised openly with ideals, sold out other people's lives in the pragmatism of the political games that he played, and even ordered other people to their deaths for what he determined at that moment to be in the best interests of his country? Could such a man truly be trusted? The question was very real to Sullivan. He had to know the answer to it, but he felt terribly confused.

In anger, Sullivan slammed his body back into the chair that he sat in, and the impact made a loud exploding sound. He was aware that the noise drew the attention of the others in the room to him, but he continued to only stare straight ahead at the television screen. What are you, you son of a bitch? he asked the image on the screen angrily, but only inside his own thoughts. And what am I and my family to you really? Are you any damn different than any of the rest of them? If I go to you and tell you the things that I suspect, what happens to me then? Underneath those tailored suits and graceful movements and carefully crafted words, what kind of man are you really? I've got to know before I put my life into your hands.

Lopata didn't sleep during the night, and he was wide awake when the sunlight began streaming in through the high windows above him.

After the Miami police had taken him into custody he had been placed in an overcrowded holding cell at police headquarters in downtown Miami, but as the weekend wore on and the little holding cell became more and more crowded, he was moved along with a truckload of other prisoners to a large public auditorium on the outskirts of the city.

By Monday morning the auditorium was also filled to overflowing with people arrested during the long weekend in what the press was now calling the Thanksgiving Riots, and more prisoners were arriving by the hour. Police vans continued to pull up into the parking lot outside the auditorium and unload the new prisoners. Most of the prisoners were young, some students at the local universities or on vacation in the Miami area during the Thanksgiving school break. There were some businessmen and housewives in the strange mixed crowd, and a few blacks and Hispanics from the rioting in the city's poorer areas, but the vast majority of the crowd was white, middle-class, and very young. During the night there had been singing and antiwar chanting among the students and even in the private dark corners some lovemaking, but now the crowd was much quieter, subdued by the long night and the lack of sleep and the realization that seemed to come again with the shafts of sunlight through the auditorium's wire-reinforced windows that they were all still under police arrest.

Around the outside of the auditorium were bleacher seats and above them a balcony. Police guards holding rifles patrolled the balcony, looking down at the crowded auditorium floor from above. The auditorium was an unlikely place for a prison, Lopata thought, as his eyes roved around the high-ceilinged facility. It had apparently been prepared for a basketball game, not a jail, and a royal-blue-and-white banner draped down from the balcony exclaimed in big bold print: GO KNIGHTS!

He lay back against the cold cement wall and watched the floor of the auditorium. Some prisoners milled around aimlessly, while a few began the rhythmic chant of the night before. But the words "Stop the War" had somehow lost their power in the cold daylight, and soon the chanting faded away.

Lopata surveyed the scene with a practiced prison eye, as he weighed the odds of escape. There were only four exits. The ones on each wall of the lower floor were heavily guarded and all the windows on both the lower and upper floors were covered with a thick metal screening. There would be more guards outside in the parking lot that surrounded the building, but probably not many. Still, escape would be very difficult, almost impossible, Lopata thought, and what would happen if he were questioned? He had no identity papers and he could be in serious trouble. If he were referred to the federal authorities, his true identity might even be discovered. His only option, he decided, was to wait and see how the police were going to try to handle such a large number of prisoners. There would be mistakes, opportunities. He would just have to be very careful. If he was patient, he would have his chance.

Sullivan watched the funeral through to the final long procession of limousines to the grave. A big hole had been dug in the frozen ground of Arlington Cemetery, and they put Timothy Cleary Cassidy's body into it. A movie actor who had been the man's friend in life said some final noble words at the gravesite, and a long string of famous people stepped forward and took handfuls of dirt and scattered them on the top of the lowered casket. Next President Gardner and his wife passed the grave, followed by Senator Cassidy and the rest of the family, and then finally, Kay and her children came forward and said their last good-byes.

The television coverage drifted off then to commentators standing under distant trees, looking down over the long sweep of the cemetery toward the site of Tim Cassidy's newly dug grave. And soon the studio announcers back in New York began summing up the events of the long, grim Thanksgiving weekend, as tapes were replayed of the crash, the President's speech, the plane that had brought the Vice President's body back to the capital, the Cassidy family at the airport, the procession to the Rotunda, the mourners passing by the casket, the funeral, the speeches, and then pictures of the burial, and Sullivan sat in front of the television in his family's living room far into the night watching it all again, hoping somewhere in all the news coverage to find a clue that would help him decide what he should do next. Even his father had given in and gone upstairs to bed around midnight, but Sullivan still stayed and watched.

The networks occasionally interrupted their summary of events in Washington to show the antiwar demonstrations still in progress in a few of the nation's other cities, but by late Monday night the country's mood seemed to have slowly begun to change from shock and anger to a somber peaceful resignation. And finally, even Sullivan dozed in front of the television set, his head falling forward to his chest like that of a tired little boy. Denise found him like that, sleeping uneasily, his head bobbing up and down against his chest, and she watched him sleep for a little while, smiling at his boyishness, before she laid a gentle hand on his shoulder.

He woke suddenly, jerking his head back up into position, and tried to focus on the television set in front of him. "What is it?" he asked sleepily.

"Come to bed," Denise whispered.

"I can't . . ." he said, but he didn't finish his sentence. Instead, he only nodded toward the television screen, as his only explanation.

"It'll all be on tomorrow," Denise said, but Sullivan continued sitting, staring blankly at the screen.

"I moved my things into your room," Denise said. "We're not fooling anybody."

"No, I guess not."

Denise flicked the television off and the living room went dark. She reached down and took Sullivan by the hand and stood him up.

"Jim, come on," she urged him, tugging at his hand. "We'll talk about it upstairs." And the two young people found each other in the darkness and crossed the room with their arms, which they'd wrapped tightly around each other, as their only support and guidance.

Neither of them spoke again until they were upstairs and safely inside Sullivan's room. The light was off in the little bedroom, but Sullivan could see the arrangement of mattresses and pillows that Denise had devised so that they could sleep comfortably next to each other in his narrow boyhood bed.

Sullivan undressed slowly in the dark then and left his clothes over his desk chair, as he had so many times before when he was growing up.

He moved into bed next to Denise and her eyes were open wide, looking directly at him as he climbed in next to her.

"You okay?"

Sullivan only shrugged his shoulders, trying to make the movement reassuring, but when he completed it, he knew that he'd failed. He could see it in Denise's face and in her eyes that were still turned expectantly toward him.

"Jim, why don't you at least tell your dad about some of it?" she said. "He's so worried about you."

Sullivan shook his head. "No, I can't," he said. "He doesn't understand. He thinks it should be World War Three or something," he added. "Personally I'm happy as hell Gardner decided not to declare war, or call up the reserves, or whatever the hell it is my dad wants him to do, and I don't care if it's Cassidy or who it is that's keeping him from doing it."

"So am I," Denise whispered.

"My dad doesn't understand," Sullivan said. "How could he? He had a nice simple war to fight. Good guys and bad guys. I've got . . ." Sullivan stopped then. "Shit, I don't know what I've got, but I know that he wouldn't understand. Anyway, I just can't drag anybody else into it. I feel bad enough that I got you into it. You and Kit . . ." As soon as he realized what he'd said, he stopped and turned his body away from Denise.

"What do you mean, me and Kit?" she asked, but she could feel the fear beginning deep in her own heart, and she could guess then what the answer had to be. "You still think that Kit's death had something to do with Cassidy, don't you?" she said softly into the darkness of the little room.

"I don't know, I'm just confused, I guess," Sullivan said. "It's just that I don't know what the hell I'm going to do next. Without the Vice President, I just don't know where to turn now."

"Oh, Jim," Denise said, placing her hand on his naked shoulder, while she tried to work up the courage to say what she truly felt.

"Uh-uh."

"Why don't you just quit?" she said finally. "Why don't you just quit the Bureau?"

"Quit?" Sullivan said, as if he were trying to get it straight, but he'd heard and understood. "I've never quit anything in my life," he said finally.

He was quiet then for a long time, and Denise thought she could see tears in his eyes. "I'm not smart enough to think it all through," he said sadly. "I just know that I don't want to quit," he added very softly then, and, as he did, his voice was hoarse, thick with emotion. "Or get fired either. I just want to do my job. I just want to help."

Denise put her arms around him and pulled his head close to her.

"But maybe I should," he said suddenly then. He was angry now, and he pulled away from Denise's embrace. "Maybe I could go sign up for the war, make my dad happy," he added, smiling grimly at the possibility. "But I probably wouldn't be any better at that, than I am . . ." He stopped talking then and began shaking his head back and forth, hoping somehow that he would find an answer, but nothing came to him. "Not that I'll have a choice," he said finally, and Denise waited to hear what was at the true heart of his fears now. "Not when they find the file I gave Cassidy. They'll come after me then."

"What do you mean?" Denise asked finally.

Sullivan only laughed, a cold, bitter laugh. "Don't you see? The Bureau has a big investment in its final report on Dallas. It may be the most important thing that it's ever done, and Summers has put the entire credibility of his precious Bureau behind it. So, if he knew that I jeopardized that credibility by going over his head to see the Vice President, he'd probably kill me, I guess."

Sullivan had meant for his words to be funny, but as soon as he'd said them, he knew that they hadn't been. "I don't mean kill me," he said quickly then, trying to soften the impact of what he'd said, but the deadly phrase still hung in the air of the small bedroom, unerasable in its power.

"Don't you?" Denise said.

Sullivan looked up at her in the darkness. "I guess I'm not really sure what I mean," he said sadly.

"You could go see Senator Cassidy, lay it all out for him," Denise said.

"I'm not sure he wants to know," Sullivan said. And then, seeing the confused look on Denise's face, he continued trying to explain the feelings that had been growing inside him during the last few days. "I mean, he was the President, the only man in the country with the real power to override Summers, or anybody else who was standing in his way of finding out the truth about Dallas," Sullivan said. "And he didn't do a damn thing about it. He barely seemed to care about the investigation while it was going on, and when the Bureau put out its final report, he just accepted it, without even raising the most basic questions."

"I'm sure he thought that was the best thing for the country," Denise said.

"Or the best thing for Jack Cassidy," Sullivan responded angrily. "But either way, it's pretty clear to me that it's not the truth he's after. It's something else."

Sullivan stopped her and waited a moment before he tried it a different way. "Cassidy's a politician and he wants to be President again and I think that's more important to him than just about anything else. And if what I have to say about the case, even if it's true, doesn't fit what he needs to help him get elected, then it's of no value to him. I'm of no value to him. He's different from his brother. Look at the war. He thinks it's wrong, but he doesn't say anything. He doesn't challenge Gardner about it, because he's afraid he'll lose his precious power if he does. It would be the same with Dallas. It's not the truth that's important to these people; it's power."

"Jim, I just don't think," Denise began, but Sullivan interrupted her before she could finish.

"You don't think what? That Cassidy wouldn't lie to the country, if he thought he should? You think he or Gardner or Summers or any of the rest of them wouldn't go on television and tell us that black was white, if it suited their purposes? That's how the game is played. That's what I've learned at the Bureau, that's what they've all taught me. So, I guess what I'm saying is, sure I could go over Summers's head and see Cassidy now, just like I did his brother, and tell him what I know and what I suspect. I could do it, except for one thing . . ." Sullivan said. "I don't think I can trust him."

The crowd of prisoners in the Miami auditorium grew more restless as the morning wore on. The sun was higher in the sky now and wide shafts of sunlight were beginning to flood in through the auditorium's wire-mesh windows, making the crowded room unpleasantly hot and bright.

The first thing Lopata noticed was that the police guards who patrolled the auditorium's exits and balconies were the same as they had been the night before when he'd first arrived and they were beginning to look worn out by their lack of sleep. Their uniforms were growing disheveled and their faces tired and unshaven. And then there was the matter of food. There hadn't been any. Nothing had been served during the night and there was still no breakfast. And since dawn, long impatient lines had formed at the auditorium's two small bathrooms. All of these problems, though, only made Lopata's spirits rise. It was becoming increasingly obvious to him that the police didn't have the proper facilities to hold this many people. The jails had been full to overflowing during the weekend; Lopata had seen that firsthand. They would have to start turning people loose soon or they could face a disaster.

Finally, in the late afternoon, a sound system was set up on the auditorium's balcony, and the slow processing of the prisoners began. Names were called and people threaded their way through the crowd to a narrow door near the very back of the auditorium.

As he waited, Lopata thought about what he would say when it was his turn. He hadn't been formally booked or even officially charged with any crime, but he'd given his name as "Antonio Lopata" when he'd been arrested. Maybe that was a mistake. It was unlikely that anyone was still looking for Antonio Lopata of Miami, Florida, but he couldn't be certain, and without identity papers anything could happen to him.

Big boxes of doughnuts were being passed out now. Lopata couldn't even bring himself to look at the food, but a young girl with dirty blond hair sitting near him had taken several of the doughnuts and she was eating them greedily. The sweet smell of the food made Lopata's stomach begin to churn. He reached up for the envelope of pills in his shirt pocket, but then he remembered that he'd taken the last of them during the night. Lopata could feel the rage rising inside him and he stared angrily at the girl's face, looking at the reddish line of pimples that ran across her chin and at the faint line of light-colored hair that formed a slight blondish mustache above her mouth. He wanted to strike out at the fat, ugly, greedy girl eating the sweet food so close to him that its smell filled his stomach, but he knew that if he did, he could be in even more trouble than he was already, and he fought with all of his willpower to control his emotions.

"Lopata, Antonio!" The name sounded over the loudspeaker, interrupting his thoughts of violence, and he stood and worked his way across the auditorium to the guard at the exit door.

"Which one are you?"

"Lopata."

"I should have known," the guard said, smiling with superiority and glancing down at his list. He stepped aside then and let Lopata into a short hall, where a second uniformed police officer impatiently motioned him into a cramped back office. Inside the small office, a man in street clothes sat behind a desk stacked high with papers and files, and at the back of the room was a shirtsleeved man, standing behind some police camera equipment. Below the camera was a card table piled high with more stacks of manila files. The guard motioned for Lopata to stand up against the far wall and face the camera. When he hesitated slightly, he felt the sharp thrust of the policeman's baton in the center of his back. Lopata staggered forward and stood up in front of the white screen that was mounted on the wall opposite the camera.

"Antonio Lopata?" the man behind the desk said, as the first camera flash caught the short dark-haired man square in the face.

"Yes," Lopata said, blinking at the overpowering flash of white light.

"To the side," the photographer said and Lopata shuffled sullenly into profile.

"You're one of the lucky ones, Lopata," the man behind the desk continued. He kept his head down as he spoke and shuffled through dozens of loose papers and files that lay in disarray on the desktop in front of him. "I'm going to tell you a secret," the man said in a phony conspiratorial whisper. "I don't even know who the hell your arresting officer was," he said then, shuffling a few more papers aimlessly around before finally looking up at Lopata again. "In fact, I don't even know what the hell it was that you did. That makes you Mr. Lucky, I guess," the man behind the desk said, the disgust thick in his voice. "Like ninety-nine percent of the other creeps in there," he added and jerked a dirty thumb in the direction of the floor of the auditorium that Lopata had just left.

"Other side," the photographer called out and Lopata shuffled around and faced the room directly.

"You don't happen to remember who it was that arrested you, do you?"

Lopata stayed silent as the white light flashed again.

"No, I didn't think so," the plainclothes officer said.

"Step over to the desk," the photographer ordered. There was fingerprinting equipment spread out on the edge of the crowded desk and Lopata walked over and stood in front of it.

"Maybe you remember why you got arrested?" the plainclothes officer said as the photographer jerked Lopata's right hand up and forced his thumb onto the pad of black ink that stood open on the desktop.

"I didn't do anything," Lopata said, as the photographer rolled first his thumb and then the other fingers of his right hand from side to side on a piece of cardboard marked: LOPATA, ANTONIO, leaving the unique imprint of the grooves and ridges laced into the tips of his fingers behind in smudged black ink on the white surface of the card. The photographer pointed at the short stack of brown paper towels then and Lopata reached for one and began wiping the excess ink off his thumb and fingers.

"So, like I said, I guess it's your lucky day," the plainclothes officer said. Then picking up a pen, he asked, "What's your address?"

Lopata finished with the brown paper towel and then reached into the pocket of his windbreaker. "I'm on my way to New Orleans," he said, tossing his bus ticket down on the desk. The man behind the desk looked down at the bus ticket and his face even seemed to lose its scowl for a brief moment. "You got an I.D.?"

Lopata reached into his pants pocket and removed a key. "My stuff is all at a locker at the bus station. I could get it and be on the next bus to New Orleans."

"Okay," the man said, without even needing to think it over. A ticket out of the jurisdiction was as good a solution as any, and better than some of the others that he was getting as he worked his way through the overwhelming mass of prisoners. "New Orleans'll be a good place for you. There's a truck outside. When it's full, it's going downtown. Get on it," he ordered.

Lopata dropped the ink-stained paper towel in the trash can below him and scooped up the key and the bus ticket. As he turned for the door, he could see that the photographer was already back in place behind his camera, getting ready for his next subject. Instant justice, Lopata thought. He was breathing easier now, as he headed back into the hallway. It had been a hell of a lot simpler than he had feared that it might be.

"Lopata!" He froze when he heard his name. "What's in New Orleans?"

Lopata didn't hesitate. "Business," he said, looking back into the room and returning the police officer's stare with a cold hard look of his own.

"You a businessman?"

"Uh-uh." Lopata turned and walked outside into the short, dark hallway that led to the parking lot where the police van was waiting to return him to downtown Miami. He did have business in New Orleans he thought. Important business.

CHAPTER
35

On Tuesday morning after the long Thanksgiving weekend, the telephone in the Sullivan dining room rang early. Jim Sullivan, Sr., had barely settled down in front of the television set with his toast and coffee, and he had to force himself up and cross the living room to take the call. It was his son's boss in Dallas. The FBI!

Mr. Sullivan set the phone down and hurried up the stairs to his son's room. He started to open the familiar door out of habit, but then, remembering himself, he knocked on it instead.

"Jim, it's your boss." He used an excited stage whisper to reach his son through the closed door, and a few seconds later Jim Jr. shuffled into the hall wearing only his underwear and picked up the receiver of the extension phone. "Yes."

"Jim." Sullivan was struck by Yancey's attempt at informality. The two men hadn't spoken face to face in months, and even then their conversation had been tense and strained.

"Uh-uh," Sullivan said sleepily into the upstairs hall phone.

"Jim, I'm sorry. I've got to ask you to go to Washington. They need to see you right away."

"Jesus, I had two weeks. It's only Tuesday," Sullivan said, feeling more than a little angry about the typical Bureau power play.

"I know. Hollis promised that they'd keep it short," Yancey said. "But it's got to happen now. The Air Force probably has something going out today. If not, take a commercial flight."

"Yes, sir," Sullivan said. "Do you have any idea what it's about?"

"None," Yancey said sharply, and Sullivan guessed that he was lying. Supervisors always get to lie, he thought. It was for the best interests of the soldiers, Sullivan added angrily to himself, but "Yes, sir," was all he said out loud into the phone, and then Yancey ended the call.

Sullivan stood in the hallway for a few seconds, trying to decide if he should go back to bed and get a little more sleep before he began calling around to find a flight back to Washington, or if he should go downstairs and get started right away. He could hear his father's television in the living room, more of the Cassidy stuff. The hell with that, Sullivan decided. He was sick of hearing about it, and he turned back toward his bedroom.

Denise was lying peacefully in a corner of the bed, and when Sullivan wiggled into the narrow space next to her, she rolled over and let him wrap his long body around hers.

"Bad news," Sullivan said. "They want me back in Washington."

"What for?" Denise asked.

"Probably a firing squad."

"Do you think they found out about you and Vice President Cassidy?" Denise's voice was full of fear as she remembered the terrifying things they had talked about the night before.

"Probably," Sullivan said. "Somebody has to come across the file I gave him sooner or later, and when they do . . ." Sullivan didn't finish his sentence.

Jack's sailboat was just a small dot on the eastern horizon, and from her place by the upstairs window of their home at Hyannis, Suzanne could barely see it any longer. She glanced up at the darkening sky above the Atlantic. It was growing late and the air was becoming threatening.

"Maybe someone should go out and get him," Suzanne said.

"It'll be all right." Allen Rozier stood behind her, his voice a soothing monotone, although secretly he felt almost as uncertain as Suzanne did. "Jack's a good sailor. He won't do anything foolish."

"He's been out there all day," Suzanne said, her eyes still fixed on the small black dot in the distance.

"He just needs to be alone right now," Rozier said.

Suzanne turned from the window. Her arms were crossed in front of her, her hands resting on her elbows, as if to form a protective shield for the baby that she carried inside her body. "I know, Allen, but I just wish that he didn't. I wish that he wanted to be with me now."

"He will soon." Rozier crossed the room and stood at the window next to her.

"Can you stay?" Suzanne said, as her eyes returned to the window and the outline of her husband's sailboat far out on the horizon.

"No, I'm afraid, I can't. I need to be back in Washington."

"What's he going to do?" Suzanne said then, her eyes still on the faraway outline of her husband's sailboat in the distance.

"What do you want him to do?" Rozier asked her back.

"I don't know." Suzanne shrugged her shoulders. "Not that it matters. God knows, in the end he won't listen to me anyway."

"I don't think that's true."

Suzanne turned to him. "Don't you, Allen? Don't you really? You know Jack. In the end he'll do whatever he, and only he, thinks best."

Rozier said nothing. In the silence, he thought of the report he'd prepared over the weekend, which he'd been considering giving to Jack sometime during his visit to Hyannis—the report containing a summary of his meeting with Estanza and the materials that the Cuban had given him to review. The report lay now undelivered in Rozier's suitcase in the guest room of the Hyannis Port home. Clearly now wasn't the time to deal with him about it he decided, as he glanced back out at the small dot on the eastern horizon that he knew to be Jack's old single-masted sailboat—the boat that Jack and his brother had sailed in so many times together since their childhood.

He had to lay it all out for him soon, but he could delay talking to him about it for a little while longer, Rozier thought, at least until the worst of Jack's grief had passed. The Cubans certainly couldn't expect an answer immediately now anyway, not after all that had happened.

"What is it, Allen?" Suzanne said, her voice full of alarm.

Rozier looked away from her then, embarrassed. He hadn't realized that he'd let his concern show so openly on his face. He was going to have to be more careful, he thought. "Oh, nothing," he said quickly. "I just have some things that I need to talk to Jack about, but I guess they'll have to wait for a few days."

They were both quiet then. Across the sand in front of the Cassidy home there was the steady sound of surf pounding up on the Atlantic beach. It seemed to be gaining in force and frequency as the nighttime approached.

"Damn it, I wish he'd come in," Suzanne said, turning anxiously back toward the window.

"Suzanne, what will you do if he decides to enter the primaries now?" Rozier said, asking the question that had been on both of their minds all morning.

Suzanne was tense and motionless as she thought about the answer to her friend's question. "Everything I can to make certain that he wins," she said finally.

Rozier smiled. "So, he's made a Cassidy out of you at last."

Suzanne turned back to him. "Yes, I guess so," she said, returning Rozier's smile with a small smile of her own. "As much as I can ever be, anyway."

Behind her, Rozier could see Jack's sailboat returning slowly toward shore. "Why don't you go tell him that then?" Rozier said, motioning back toward the window.

Suzanne paused for only a short moment before turning back into the room. A pink wool sweater was thrown over the back of a nearby chair and Suzanne reached down for it and wrapped it around her shoulders. She flashed a smile at Rozier before moving past him toward the door.

Rozier walked to the upstairs window. Soon he could see Suzanne striding across the front lawn of her home toward the darkened Atlantic beach in the distance.

Rozier watched as she crossed the road and waited on the narrow sandy beach for her husband's sailboat to arrive at the small windswept dock at the shoreline.

Sullivan got an Air Force jet out of Philadelphia and it brought him into the capital in the late afternoon. The pilot, an old reserve colonel who was using the flight to pick up the hours that he needed to keep his rating, promised him a spot on the return flight the next morning. Sullivan thanked him, but didn't mention to him that by morning he might not have a job that permitted him to hitch rides on government aircraft anymore. In fact, Sullivan thought, by morning he could be on his way to join Leo Green at that fancy federal prison building in downtown Dallas.

Washington was still in mourning on the Tuesday after the Vice President's funeral, and Sullivan watched its streets slowly slide by from the front seat of the colonel's Air Force vehicle. The federal buildings displayed American flags flying at half mast.

The ride took him right to the Bureau's headquarters at the Department of Justice, and Sullivan mounted the familiar steps and then walked the old halls, wondering if this would be the last time that he would see this beautiful, historic building that he loved as an FBI agent.

Hollis's secretary seemed happy to see him. "Oh, good," she said, looking up at Sullivan from her work. "You're the last."

"The last what?" Sullivan said, trying to smile, but he knew as soon as he'd flashed it at her that it hadn't come out right.

"They're down the hall," the secretary said, pointing out the door that Sullivan had just entered toward the big formal conference room at the end of the corridor. "Do you know where it is?"

"I used to live here," Sullivan said, backtracking toward the hallway. Used to live here? Sullivan repeated his words to himself as he hustled down the hall toward the big conference-room door at the end of it. What a dumb thing to say. He paused in front of the door to the conference room, standing just long enough to square his coat and tie into place. Then he reached out and firmly grasped the heavy brass doorknob and pushed his way inside. Oh, Jesus, it was worse than he'd thought. Sitting at the end of the long table at the very back of the room was the Director himself! What the hell was Summers doing sitting in on a meeting with a junior agent? A cold wave of fear began spreading through Sullivan's body. It doesn't take the Director of the whole damn Bureau to fire one little junior agent. It had to be something else, but what?

Sullivan recognized most of the other faces that bordered the long conference-room table. Quite a lineup, Sullivan thought, as he looked down the row of grim faces to where the Director sat stoically at the head of the table, his hands folded neatly on the tabletop in front of him. And as Sullivan looked across the room at him, Summers seemed to nod imperceptibly in his direction, but the movement was so slight that Sullivan couldn't be sure. Oh, God, what the hell do I do now? He compromised on a half cough, half nod as he dropped his head and ducked down into the first empty chair that he could find.

"Sorry to interrupt your vacation," Hollis said, seeing Sullivan's obvious discomfort, "but it is important." Hollis's eyes met Sullivan's as the handsome, gray-haired Assistant Director spoke, but Sullivan could find no clues there, no expectation, no offer of friendship or disapproval, just good bureaucratic eyes, Sullivan thought, as he looked back down the long conference-room table directly at his former boss.

Hollis moved around the room and pulled down a white textured screen that was mounted on the wall at the far end of the conference table. Sullivan noticed for the first time then that there was a slide projector on the table near where Hollis had been sitting, and next to it was a sixteen-millimeter film projector. Before returning to his seat, Hollis turned off the conference room's overhead light. He turned to Summers. "Are you ready, sir?"

The Director's only reply was another slight nod of his head.

"Over the last couple of years," Hollis began, as he crossed the room in the dark to return to his place at the conference table, "there have been some questions raised about the Bureau's final report on the events that occurred in Dallas on November 22, 1963." Hollis reached down and switched on the film projector, and the machine began to cast a ray of white light through the darkened room, illuminating the textured screen on the far wall.

As Hollis spoke, Sullivan's mind raced. What the hell was going to happen now? What were they going to show him? Films of the assassination attempt? He'd seen them a thousand times, the open car coming slowly into the plaza, the President lifting his hand to wave at the crowd, and then the sudden jolting of his body backward against the limousine's rear seat. They raised a lot of questions, questions that the Bureau's final report had failed to answer, but they proved nothing conclusively one way or the other about the possibility of a second gunman, or any of the other mysteries of that day, as far as he was concerned, Sullivan thought. And why show it to him now? What the hell was going on?

"Some of these questions you've raised yourself in your reports," Hollis said, looking across the table at the young agent. "And your own investigation, although highly unorthodox, has certainly been resourceful and relentless," he added.

Sullivan was even more puzzled now. Maybe they hadn't brought him here to fire him after all.

"As I understand it," Hollis said and then he shook his head, as if to indicate his own confusion about Sullivan's theories of the case—"and I'll have to admit I don't really follow all your ideas, but as I understand it, your investigation has focused on the possibility that there was a second gunman in Dealey Plaza that day, a man you believe you actually saw in the parking area at the far side of the plaza. But this man apparently showed you some counterfeit Secret Service credentials, so you let him go. This man!" Hollis reached over and jammed a slide into the projector that stood on the desk in front of him, and the Bureau's sketch of the dark-haired second gunman suddenly leaped onto the screen.

"Yes, sir," Sullivan said, his eyes fixed on the big blowup of the face of the man that he had been tracking on and off for the last four years. It didn't necessarily mean that they'd recovered the material he'd given to Cassidy, Sullivan decided, as he quickly thought it through. Washington would have kept at least one copy of the sketch in their master file.

Hollis continued. "I believe your theory is that there was some kind of a link between this man and the Dallas police."

"I heard a police call right after the shooting, before they even had Strode . . ." Sullivan stopped trying to explain, when he saw the look of displeasure on Hollis's face. Well, one of the mysteries was answered, the young agent told himself. They hadn't brought him here to do any talking —only listening.

"Yes," Hollis said, and then he paused while Sullivan slid back in his seat and waited for him to continue.

In the silence that followed, Sullivan tried to get a look out of the corner of his eye at Summers. The Director's face was immobile, set hard and firm into an expression that refused to give even a hint of what was going to happen next.

"You apparently followed a lead of some kind down to Mexico," Hollis began again.

"There were four deaths connected to that lead," Sullivan said, unable to keep quiet any longer. If he was going to go down, he was going to go down swinging. "Two men who flew a plane out of Dallas a few hours after the shooting, and then a prostitute who was murdered in Mexico, and later a man who . . ."

"We know that you've become personally committed to all of this," Hollis said then. "But I think what we have to show you today will clear everything up once and for all." He reached down then and clicked the slide projector's cartridge into place again. Immediately the sketch of the second gunman disappeared and a second image took its place. The screen at the end of the room showed a blowup of a grainy black-and-white photograph now, a photograph of a dark-haired man shown in profile standing behind a barred window. There was a faint curl of cigarette smoke escaping from the man's nose and mouth, making the man's identity mysteriously obscure, but Hollis quickly snapped the metal handle of the slide projector again and another image appeared. In the second photograph the man had turned his head toward the camera and his image was free of cigarette smoke.

"That's him!" Sullivan said. The face was older than he remembered it. The flesh was deeply lined and the eyes sunken deep into a gaunt face, but

Sullivan was struck by the intensity of his feelings about his identity. "Jesus, that's him!" he repeated.

"Yes. Good, we thought so," Hollis said, and then he snapped three more photographs methodically into place one after another, pausing just long enough between each image to be certain that Sullivan could have no doubt about what he was being shown each time.

"Where is he?" Sullivan said in his excitement. "We can bring the son of a bitch in on the faked Secret Service credentials for a start . . ."

"No, we can't," Hollis said, cutting Sullivan off in midsentence. And he flicked the slide projector switch off and the screen at the end of the long conference room went blank. Hollis reached over then and activated the power switch on the film projector next to it.

The screen filled with a rapid series of continually moving black-and-white pictures. Probably from a handheld camera, Sullivan guessed, as he watched the first few seconds of the amateurish film begin. The opening scene showed a deep, rocky mountain gorge, and the handheld camera panned unsteadily down the austere setting for several seconds before coming to rest on the remnants of a military truck smashed at the base of an outcropping of rock about halfway down the steep mountain cavern. The truck looked to be a Russian vehicle, Sullivan thought, but the terrain was not as he imagined Russia to be, and as he wondered to himself why he was being shown this strange piece of film, the camera began moving in slowly to show the charred remains of three badly burned human bodies. The three burned corpses had been placed in a neat row on the ground several feet from the wreck of the truck. The camera lingered on each body in turn, showing long close-ups of charred and brutalized flesh.

As Sullivan watched the screen intently, Hollis reached for the file in front of him and began to read out loud from one of Sullivan's initial reports on the Dallas investigation. Sullivan recognized the words as his own, even as his eyes stayed on the screen lit up bright with the image of the final badly burned corpse.

" 'My primary concerns are twofold,' " Hollis read Sullivan's own earlier words. " 'First, that this second gunman may have escaped justice and, second, that he may present an ongoing threat to the safety of President Cassidy and his family,' " Hollis finished reading and then he looked across the table at Sullivan. "You've found the man that you've been looking for," Hollis added, jerking a thumb up toward the movie screen behind him and the charred body that it displayed. "He died trying to escape from a Cuban prison camp a little less than one week ago. As you can see, he didn't escape justice, and he is no longer a threat to Senator Cassidy or to anyone else. Your case is closed now."

"How can you be sure that's him?" Sullivan said, pointing at the image of the unrecognizably charred body on the screen.

"We're sure," Hollis said. "The details are in here," he added then, sliding a file folder down the table toward Sullivan. "There's a copy of a very thorough report in there from the Cuban government itself. That's your man, and he's dead," Hollis said, a tone of absolute finality in his voice.

Sullivan could see Summers standing now. "We'll leave the details to you," the Director said, nodding at Hollis. "Good day, Agent Sullivan," Summers added, and then, without even glancing at anyone else in the room, the Director moved toward the door at the rear of the conference room. Hollis stood and hurried to open the door for the Director, and Summers acknowledged the courtesy with only a brief nod of his head before he walked outside. What now? Sullivan thought, as he watched the other Bureau officials follow Summers and file slowly from the room, leaving him alone with Hollis. This was the end of the public portion of the meeting, the part that would go into the participants' personal files, and if necessary, be testified to some day in court or before a congressional review committee—the part that would protect Summers, and the Bureau, and the rest of them, if the issue of their handling of his reports was ever brought into the open somehow. But Sullivan had a hunch that the public part of this meeting had been just preliminary and that the real reason for calling him to Washington was going to be disclosed only now, in the second and more private part of the meeting.

Sullivan reached out and began to open the file that Hollis had given him, but the Assistant Director's voice stopped him before he could. "Jim, we want you to read the file, satisfy yourself completely on this thing, but we're not going to let you take the file or any of its contents out of this room, nor will you ever see it again. You're going to have to review it here, satisfy yourself, and then, that's the end of it. If you ever mention any of this again to anyone, we'll deny it."

Sullivan was feeling both confused and angry now. What was all this shit? This guy was either tied to the shooting or he wasn't. "What do you mean, you'll deny it?"

"Just that," Hollis said. His voice had a very hard edge now, as did his face and eyes. "After you walk out of here, none of this exists. The film, the pictures, the file, our little discussion this afternoon, none of it!" Sullivan looked up at the screen when Hollis had finished talking. The film had ended now, the screen blank. It was just as Hollis had said. It was as if none of it had ever happened. Sullivan opened the file that Hollis had given to him then and, as Hollis reached up and snapped the conference-room lights back on, they illuminated the names "Lopez, Antonio (a.k.a. Lopata, Antonio; Cirello, Antonio)." There were other aliases as well, but Sullivan kept looking at the code number typed below the list of names. Suddenly, Sullivan's heart began pounding wildly. Something was wrong. He could feel it. He couldn't focus on what it was yet, but its impact on him was immediate and powerful. He forced himself to concentrate on the names and code number again and as he did, his stomach and the inside of his head began rolling with waves of fear. What the hell was it? He remembered now that Hollis was watching every move that he made and he tried as hard as he could to keep his face from showing his true feelings, and he finally managed to withdraw his eyes from the heading on the file and begin reading hurriedly through the rest of its contents.

"You can see what we mean," Hollis said, as Sullivan continued reading. "He was just a drifter, a petty criminal, a nobody. Born in Cuba, but as far as we can tell no connection with Castro or with the Revolution. No politics really. He turns up in Miami later on and either out of commitment or just for the money, he volunteers to train with the Cuban freedom fighters, but long before the big day comes, he disappears. He goes AWOL well before any of the shooting starts. It turns out he has no real taste for violence—look at his record," Hollis said, stepping forward and flipping a few pages of the file for Sullivan's benefit. "No firearms with any of it—shoplifting, bad checks. He's a goddamned lightweight, Jim," Hollis added. "Anyway, the group he trained with got the hell shot out of it at the Bay of Pigs."

"General Martine?" Sullivan asked, reading the unfamiliar name out of the file.

"Martine was his commanding officer," Hollis said. "At least until our boy goes AWOL, which is what? Less than a week after he first hired on for the job. Martine himself died in the invasion. He was, I guess—still is," Hollis corrected himself, "a big hero in the Cuban exile community down in New Orleans."

"New Orleans?" Sullivan said thoughtfully.

"Right, New Orleans. There and Miami, that's where most of these people live now," Hollis said in a calm, assured voice, as though he was confident that Sullivan would understand and go along, if he just took the time to listen carefully to the explanation that he was being given now. "We've got to look at the big picture on all this, Jim. Our job is fighting Communists. I'm sure I don't have to remind you of that. And the Cuban community in Miami and New Orleans are our friends in that fight, some of our very best friends as it happens, and we have absolutely no desire to start making trouble for them for no good reason. And believe me, this guy, Lopez, or whatever he called himself, is nothing to rattle anybody's cage over. His connection to the 'good guys' down there in New Orleans is minor, but believe me, if, and I said if, he had anything even remotely to do with Strode, or if he really was the guy you saw in Dealey Plaza that day, the press would make one hell of a lot of trouble for everybody about it. There'd be stories trying to link the assassination attempt to the freedom fighters, and, damn it, that's just what the Communists want." Hollis was angry now and Sullivan felt compelled to look up from the file and watch him closely as he finished. "We can't let our friends down there be embarrassed by this bastard. He's just not worth it."

"To say nothing of embarrassing the Bureau," Sullivan said.

"That's right," Hollis shot back. "The Bureau's published its findings on Dallas—and, for the good of the entire country, it's imperative that no one starts reopening it now, especially not for some minor-league punk like this." Hollis pointed at the file that stood open in front of Sullivan.

Hollis walked slowly back around the conference table then and settled into his place across from Sullivan. "Jim, this guy Lopez may have been in Dealey Plaza that day. It's possible. He might even have some kind of connection to Strode, but the important thing now is that he's dead. And that's just exactly where the American government wants him to be," the Deputy Director said. "Dead."

Sullivan looked down at the contents of the file again. He felt very confused. The story he was being told was logical and clear and obviously the way the Bureau wanted it to come out, but something about it still nagged at the back of his head. If only he had some time, he thought. It was all happening too fast for him to understand what it was that was bothering him. It would come to him though, he thought, if he just had a little more time to figure out what it was.

"After he goes AWOL from Martine," Hollis continued explaining, not giving Sullivan any time to think, "he just floats. Tampa, Coral Gables, San Juan, Baton Rouge. He's a bum. You say he was in Dallas." Hollis shrugged his shoulders. "Could be. Maybe he even knew Strode. Who the hell cares? Look at his record, Jim, he's not the stuff of big-time political intrigue. If you think Dallas was a professional conspiracy of some kind, this guy blows your whole theory. No one would hire a punk like this to do anything even halfway important—much less choose him to assassinate the President of the United States. Look at his record. It speaks for itself."

Sullivan continued reading. Hollis was right. This was not the kind of a guy someone as smart as DeSavio, or anyone else for that matter, would hire for a job of that size.

"But he could be very embarrassing," Hollis added, interrupting Sullivan's thoughts.

"Why the file?" Sullivan said, finally setting it back down on the conference table.

"We've got one on everybody connected to the Cuban freedom fighters," Hollis said. "They were being trained on U.S. soil in military operations. We had to know about them."

"Trained by American personnel, American Marines, the CIA," Sullivan said out loud and Hollis nodded his head that he was right. "Yes, a lot of the stuff we have on him and on the others is from Central Intelligence. They did the initial check on all these guys."

"How did he die?" Sullivan asked, his mind racing to sort through the torrent of facts coming at him so quickly now that it was impossible to make any real sense out of them.

"He was arrested about three years ago for trying to get back into Cuba illegally, probably to see his family or to do some business. Who knows? Anyway, he was in a place called Muiriel Prison on the west coast of Cuba until about a week ago, when he died in an accident. We're not sure of the exact date yet, but it was probably last Tuesday the twenty-fourth, or Wednesday, the twenty-fifth. He was being transported as part of a work party and his truck crashed in the mountains," Hollis said. And then he paused before adding with a touch of finality, "We have no real reason to link him to the Cassidy thing, but we wanted you to see this. So that you could get straight about it."

Hollis began closing up the projectors then and replacing the film and slide cartridge into the cases, signaling that as far as the Bureau was concerned the matter was over now.

Sullivan stayed quiet, looking first at the file and then up at Hollis's confidently composed bureaucratic face. Something was very wrong. Sullivan knew it. If only he had a little more time, he could put it all together, ask the right questions. For all Hollis's outward coolness, Sullivan knew that he was lying to him now. There was a lot of truth mixed up with the lies— that was the Bureau's way. Sullivan just didn't know which parts were the lies, and which parts the truth, and if it even mattered anymore. The bad guy was dead. Wasn't that all that really mattered? Sullivan looked up at the empty white screen, where a few seconds earlier the image of the charred and blackened body of Antonio Lopata had been displayed. Unless they were lying about that, too.

"Jim, we consider this whole issue ended now," Hollis said, without looking up from his work of repacking the film and slide equipment. "And we assume that you do, too. This man doesn't pose a threat to Cassidy or to anybody else anymore, if he ever did," Hollis said. Then he paused and looked straight at Sullivan. "And he sure as hell didn't escape anybody's justice—ours, yours, or anybody else's. He's dead," Hollis said, removing the Bureau file from the desk and locking it into his briefcase with the other materials. "And we walk out of here clean."

"How did we get all this stuff?" Sullivan asked, almost before Hollis could finish. The young agent was afraid that if he let the room grow silent for even a moment that he'd lose his nerve.

"Agent Sullivan," Hollis began. "You're an FBI agent. You could be a good one someday. The Bureau takes care of its own, remember that, but we need something from you, too. There are some parts of this story that for security reasons we can't let you know about, and so you're just going to have to trust the Bureau on it, that's all." Hollis was silent then. "But let me give you a hypothetical. Let's say . . ." Hollis paused then, his face taking on a clever turn, as if he were enjoying his pretense of answering Sullivan's question with a hypothetical set of facts, a hypothetical story, that both men knew perfectly well was the real truth of how the Bureau had gotten the photographs of the dead bodies lying in the hills above Havana. "Let's say the American intelligence community, the Bureau, the CIA, is willing to, under certain circumstances, accept information from every conceivable source. And sometimes that might even require taking materials from sources that can do things that government agencies can't always do themselves, maybe things that aren't strictly within their authority. So, maybe it keeps contacts, contacts with people like General Martine's widow, people like that, powerful anti-Communists who don't always have to worry about the strict letter of the law. And let's suppose, hypothetically, of course, that sometimes these people either know something or find something out that they believe we'd be interested in, and when they do they let us know. It's that simple," Hollis said, spreading his hands out and smiling at the younger man.

Sullivan took a deep breath then and gathered his courage. "Sir, I know the investment that the Bureau has in the Cassidy Report and I know how important it is to the country that the Bureau's credibility is preserved, but one hell of a lot of people have died since that day, and all of them were linked in some way or another to what happened in Dallas. Maybe . . ."

Hollis raised his hand palm out to silence him and the junior agent obeyed the command instantly.

"I'm only going to say this once, Jim, and I want you clear on it," the senior man said, his tone efficient but almost matter-of-fact in its certainty. "If, after today, you insist on pushing this thing in any form, inside or outside the Bureau, the Bureau can't guarantee your safety." Hollis stood then and, without saying another word, he walked past Sullivan and out the conference-room door.

Sullivan sat alone for several minutes in the deathly quiet room, trying to understand what had just happened to him. His hands were trembling slightly and his heart was pounding. Finally it came to him with stunning clarity, and he realized—that his life had just been threatened by the Federal Bureau of Investigation.

CHAPTER
36

R ozier sat at a quiet table in the back room of a little restaurant near Forty-fifth and Broadway. The restaurant was a short cab ride from the meeting place that Estanza had suggested when he'd called Rozier and asked to see him again.

The dinner dishes had long since been cleared away and the other diners and even the after-theater people had moved on. Out front in the main room the busboys were beginning to clean the floors and stack the chairs on the tabletops. It was a long time since he'd closed a place all by himself, Rozier thought with a small smile. He was nursing his third cup of black coffee now and the caffeine was mixing with his own adrenaline and making his heart beat uncomfortably fast. Finally, he pushed the cup away and glanced at his watch. He was still early.

Estanza had been very precise about the place and time for their meeting. He had also been definite about keeping the meeting a secret. Rozier had done as he'd been told, but now he was beginning to regret it. He felt frightened. With the decision that he'd reached in Hyannis a couple of weeks earlier not to talk to Jack about any of it, yet, he was still the only one who knew about the Cuban claim that they had a man locked up in one of their prisons, a man whom they said could prove that he had been part of a plot to assassinate the President of the United States. That put him smack in the middle of very high-level blackmail, and that could be a very dangerous place to be, Rozier thought. Who was this man that the Cubans were holding? he asked himself then. And why was he so damaging to the American government? And to the Cassidy family? Or maybe he didn't really want to know.

Maybe it would be safer that way. Why the hell was he doing this anyway? He wasn't James Bond. He couldn't play cloak-and-dagger all by himself with the Cuban government and hope to survive. What he really wanted now was a drink, but he didn't dare. He had to be as sharp as possible when he met with Estanza. He glanced at his watch again. It was two minutes later than it had been the last time that he'd checked. He hadn't told Jack or anybody else about the diary pages that he'd been given for very good reasons, he reminded himself for the tenth time in the last hour. He was still far from convinced that the Cuban government wasn't just laying a clever trap of some kind by using the pages from Strode's diary as bait and attempting to draw Jack into it. And as long as he stood between Jack and the Cubans, the less the chances were that Jack himself could be seriously harmed. He should at least be reasonably certain of the authenticity of the pages from the diary before he pulled Jack into it, particularly while his friend was still emotional and vulnerable from Tim's death. And the handwriting expert that Rozier had given copies of a portion of the documents to, still hadn't reported back to him. No, Rozier told himself he'd done the right thing by keeping his meeting with Estanza a secret so far.

Rozier reached down and removed a notebook and a pen from his attaché case. He bent over the pad of paper for several minutes, detailing his first meeting with Estanza and then the circumstances that surrounded this second meeting. When he was finished, he folded the sheets of paper into an envelope and sealed it. He wrote "Senator John Cassidy" across the front of the envelope and then stopped. He felt vaguely foolish. What was the purpose of all this? The Cubans hadn't arranged this meeting to kill him or to kidnap him. He wasn't living in a spy novel. This was New York City in 1967. There was a candle on the table and Rozier studied the flame for several seconds, considering burning the letter. Instead, below Jack's name, he wrote his own address. That way if something did go wrong the letter would find its way to Jack, but more likely he'd just have a good laugh at himself when it arrived in tomorrow's mail. He glanced at his watch again; it was time to go.

Outside on Forty-fifth it was cold and windy and dark. The streets were empty, but a lone cab turned the corner at Broadway and Rozier flagged it down.

There was a mailbox at the end of the street and before the taxi pulled past the intersection, he asked the driver to stop. Rozier found a stamp in his wallet and placed it on the envelope. Then he slid out of the cab and dropped the letter into the mailbox. He ducked back into the cab then and gave the driver instructions to his real destination.

On the short drive toward the river, Rozier was struck again by the majesty of the city, as he always was whenever he saw the New York streets late at night swept clean of people and traffic. That night the city was particularly beautiful, too, Rozier thought as he looked around at the brightly colored Christmas decorations displayed along the nearly empty streets. The ride had a soothing effect on him, and by the end of it he was feeling a little better than he had been earlier. What was there to worry about, anyway? he told himself. But the answers rose to the surface too easily, and when the cab began to slow near the U.N. building, Rozier moved forward in the back seat and stared anxiously out the window at the dark and empty riverside park that was his destination.

"Are you sure?" the cab driver said, looking up at Rozier's reflection in the rearview mirror.

"Yes." Rozier handed the driver a bill and slid his heavy body toward the door without waiting for his change. If this was going to be the end of it, he might as well go out with a big tip, he thought, laughing at himself, and then he started down the dark tree-lined path that led to the river's edge. Behind him, he could hear the taxi pulling away into the night and he knew then that he was alone. He looked around at the dark places at the sides of the path where anything could be hiding. This is it, he told himself then. If I get out of tonight in one piece, it's the end of this kind of thing for me. From here on in, I leave this kind of stuff to the CIA and the rest of them, and I go back to being a journalist with a typewriter and a nice, clean office somewhere. But even as he thought it, he noticed that the way the blood was surging through him at that moment made him feel very alive. He looked around again then, memorizing it all, eager to tell Jack about it at the very first opportunity.

At the end of the path the breeze from the river caught him full in the face and he pulled his trench coat up even higher around his neck.

Señor Estanza was already there waiting for him. He was sitting on a wooden bench by the low cement wall that separated the little park from the sloping edge of the river. When he saw Rozier approaching, the elderly man stood up with some difficulty and extended a gloved hand toward him.

"Good evening, Mr. Rozier," the gray-haired Cuban said, bowing his head slightly toward the younger man.

"Good evening," Rozier said. "Should we walk?" He gestured back toward the bright lights of the U.N. building.

"No, if you don't mind," the elderly gentleman said. "It will be all right."

Rozier glanced around him then. Estanza's meaning was clear. They weren't alone. But Rozier couldn't see any of the Cuban's people, although he could sense their presence now, close by, watching them both.

Estanza smiled gently, as he noticed Rozier looking around nervously at the trees and the dark shadowy places that surrounded them. "Please forgive me, Mr. Rozier. I prefer not to do business in this manner as well," the elderly gray-haired man said. "But I fear that we both live in a world not entirely of our own making."

Rozier stepped down the path to join Estanza on the wooden bench. Both men sat facing out, away from each other, looking at the night lights of the city of New York reflecting off the surface of the water.

"Please convey to Senator Cassidy my government's profoundest sympathy for the great tragedy that has befallen his family," the gray-haired man said.

"It was a tremendous loss for us all," Rozier said.

Estanza nodded.

"My government needs to know, Mr. Rozier, if you have had an opportunity to pass the documents that we gave you at our last meeting along to the Cassidy family."

Rozier smiled at the directness of the question, but he knew that he had to be careful now and not say anything that could implicate the Cassidy family. At the same time, he had to delay Estanza from taking his story to the press, at least for now. "I have reviewed the materials that you gave to me at our last meeting," he said. "But I would like some additional time now in order to have the documents reviewed and verified by handwriting experts before I decide what I should do next."

"How much time?" Estanza said.

"Three or four weeks, maybe more. With the holidays, it will be difficult," Rozier said. "But I'll do the best that I can."

"Much time has been lost already."

"These are difficult decisions," Rozier said. "I'm sure you agree that we both need to be absolutely certain of each step that we take."

Estanza paused then, as if he was considering the request. Finally, he simply nodded his head. "I am going to proceed through this evening," he said, "on the assumption that you have verified a portion of the information that I gave you at our last meeting and that, so far, you have found it to be reliable, at least to your own satisfaction, but that you are using extreme caution for the moment in order to protect the Cassidy family from any needless risk."

Rozier nodded his head, admitting nothing.

"Perhaps that is as it should be," Estanza said. Then he paused for a moment and withdrew a small envelope with his gloved hand from the pocket of his immaculately tailored camel-hair topcoat. He held the envelope out toward Rozier. "It is my government's belief that both you and Senator Cassidy will be interested in this."

Rozier took the envelope gingerly. "And what will I learn when I review this new information?" Rozier said, holding the envelope carefully out in front of him.

"You will learn that the man we spoke of earlier is dead."

Rozier stayed quiet, trying to understand. A few river birds flapped across the surface of the water below the park. "Dead?" Rozier said. And the softly spoken word seemed to echo off the shiny black surface of the river and stir ominously in the overhanging tree branches that arched above the heads of the two men.

"Murdered," Estanza said. "We were worried that something like that might happen, but in attempting to move him to a safer location in Havana the vehicle that he was being transported in was attacked. In the fighting, the truck went over a cliff, several men were killed, including, as you will see," Estanza said, pointing at the envelope, "this man, who called himself Antonio Lopata."

Rozier nodded and placed the envelope deep into the pocket of his trench coat. "Why tell me?" Rozier asked. "I don't understand."

Estanza smiled again. He liked Rozier, his intelligence and his directness made dealing with him less complicated and time consuming than dealing with the professional diplomats that Estanza was used to. That was one of the reasons Estanza had chosen to approach him in the first place. Speed was important in such delicate matters. "We considered not telling anyone," Estanza said. "But we decided that would be a mistake. You need to trust us, as does Senator Cassidy. In the end, you would have found out anyway, and we prefer that you learn the truth from us now."

"And we may have known already," Rozier said.

Estanza moved his head and shoulders in agreement. "That is always a possibility," he said. "And of course, it was a consideration. The people responsible for Señor Lopata's death may have found it advantageous to communicate the fact to your government, to your FBI, or to your Central Intelligence Agency. Senator Cassidy could have learned of it from them, or . . ." Estanza paused dramatically then. "It is, of course, possible that Senator Cassidy himself ordered the death of Señor Lopata." Estanza's voice was strangely matter-of-fact as he made the accusation and he paused only long enough to glance at Rozier's face. Rozier returned his brief emotionless look with a cold, hard stare of his own, hoping that the anger that he felt at the accusation didn't show in his expression.

"We want you to trust us," Estanza continued. "Some of what we had to trade when we spoke a few weeks ago is gone now, but much remains," Estanza said. "We still have this man's detailed written statement. You will find a copy of it in the envelope that I've just given to you."

"And the diary that he claimed to be Strode's?"

"We have spoken enough already," Estanza said. "We believe that the items that we have in our possession are more than enough to permit us to still find a mutual understanding, but my government believes that it is now time for Senator Cassidy to indicate to us his willingness to proceed further before we discuss the details of our arrangement with you or with anyone else."

"As I've said, I need sufficient time to authenticate the materials you've already given to me."

Estanza gracefully shrugged his slender, well-tailored shoulders again. "There is much at stake here, Mr. Rozier. Do not underestimate the urgency of Senator Cassidy's position. If you have truly chosen to not yet speak to him of these matters, I must warn you once again of the gravity of the risk you are taking. Believe me, Mr. Rozier, even though Señor Lopata is no longer alive, the information that we have in our possession is still quite sufficient to destroy Senator Cassidy's political career forever."

"That's the risk that I'll have to take," Rozier said, his voice confident, but his heart pounding with fear and uncertainty.

"If I may offer you some advice, Mr. Rozier—from one older and perhaps more experienced in these matters. It is sometimes best to remain simply a messenger in affairs of this magnitude. The fewer decisions you make yourself and the less risk you assume personally, always becomes the wisest course. You see, Mr. Rozier, my experience with politicians has been that when politics and friendship come into conflict, often times, politicians choose to ignore their friends."

"Meaning?" Rozier shot back angrily.

"I only mean to suggest," Estanza said, lightly shifting a gloved hand to punctuate his remarks. "That many men have died already in this affair, and in all probability many more will as well. I would hope that neither you or I will become one of them."

"You think Jack—Senator Cassidy," Rozier corrected himself. "You think that Senator Cassidy could have ordered the death of this man Lopata?"

"In matters of assassination, it is wise to always suspect those who have the most to gain, at least until proven otherwise. As you yourself can quite obviously see, Mr. Rozier, Senator Cassidy had the most to gain in this regard."

"There are others as well," Rozier said. "A man like that involved so deeply in American and Cuban politics would make many enemies."

"Perhaps," Estanza said. "But I would move quickly nonetheless. Unfortunately, Mr. Rozier, you have become the man in the middle here—the only man between my government and Senator Cassidy. This is something we did not wish to have happen for such an extended period of time, and we hope that it is a situation which is ended soon. In my experience, Mr. Rozier, in matters of this kind, the middle is the most dangerous place to be."

The journalist didn't answer immediately; he continued looking thoughtfully out at the river. "For the moment, I'll stay in the middle," he said finally.

Estanza smiled broadly now. "I admire your loyalty, Mr. Rozier. It is one thing that the modern world often lacks. But please move quickly. The fact is, Señor Lopata is dead; who succeeded in eliminating him is almost irrelevant, but my government still has certain goals that are of the utmost importance to it, and we will continue to pursue those goals with whatever means we have at our disposal. Señor Lopata's death just give us one less tool to work with, that's all." Estanza spread his gloved hands out, palms up, to demonstrate how simple it all was to him.

"It's been a pleasure, Mr. Rozier," Estanza said. The gray-haired man pointed at the envelope in Rozier's pocket again then. "As I've said, in my judgment, Mr. Rozier, you should consider giving Senator Cassidy the materials and removing yourself from this affair as soon as possible. If you wish to do that, you need only mention one name to Senator Cassidy, and I believe that he will then be more than willing to take the matter from your hands immediately," he said, dropping his voice to a confidential whisper. As he spoke, Rozier had the feeling that the man was sincerely trying to help him now. "That name is 'St. Christopher's Island.' Please remember that, Mr. Rozier. If it becomes too uncomfortable in the middle for you, that one name, spoken to Senator Cassidy in connection with my government's knowledge of it, should be sufficient to remove you from this awkward and delicate role that you find yourself in. There are things here that only Senator Cassidy can appreciate and understand, things that I'm certain you know nothing of, and, for your own safety, you should want to leave it at that."

Neither man said anything for a moment. Finally Estanza lifted a gloved hand toward the shadows behind them. "Would you like someone to walk with you? The streets can be dangerous this time of night."

"No," Rozier said and then stood.

"I'll be in contact," Estanza said as Rozier walked away.

The journalist moved back through the small riverfront park, his head down, his right hand thrust into the pocket of his trench coat, touching the envelope that the Cuban had given to him. As he walked slowly along, Rozier's mind whirled. What was that last part about? St. Christopher's Island? For my own safety? What was he saying? That the matters the Cubans believed they had to trade were so politically powerful that if he knew too much about them, he was in danger himself? In danger from whom? From the American government? From Jack? That was ridiculous, Rozier thought then, but as he walked back down the remainder of the darkened pathway alone, toward the lights in the distance, for that moment almost anything seemed possible.

Tom Stone liked coming to Phoenix. Sooner or later, his job took him to almost every part of the country, and when he traveled to Phoenix with other political pros, the others would often make fun of it, laugh at the desert-colored Indian weavings on the airport walls, or make jokes about the cowboy hats and string ties that the businessmen wore and smile condescendingly at the women's less-than-fashionable dresses, just the way that some of the other so-called "political pros" laughed at the regional peculiarities of Portland or Milwaukee or Macon, Georgia. But he never joined in that laughter. The people and their differences, that was why he was in politics in the first place, he reminded himself, as he looked around at the unique western stamp of the crowded late afternoon Arizona airport. If the people in Phoenix thought and voted just like the people in Washington, D.C., there would be no reason for a politician to ever need his skills. But the people didn't, and they never would, and that meant he would never be out of a job.

Stone passed out of the terminal and found his rental car. He headed west toward Scottsdale. Stone used the surface streets as he drove, not the freeways, and he watched the people. He loved looking at people, watching them walk and interact and talk to each other. That was another reason that he was in this business, he told himself, as he looked out at the Phoenix sidewalks full of simple, straightforward western people. There were hardly any hippies, or long-haired kids protesting the war, or any of the other craziness that was infecting cities that Stone had just come from, or that was splashed all over the papers and TV these days. And there were more people like this, more places like Phoenix in this country than there were hippies and crazies—that was what Stone was here to explain.

The highway was beginning to be bordered by exclusive fenced communities and above him off to the left of the highway, Stone could see the hillside that the Longwood family had lived on since almost the beginning of the century. It looked back over the new growth and development at the outskirts of Phoenix to the east and then off into what was still the wide, great, vast challenge of the Arizona desert to the west. Achievement and challenge, like the man himself, Stone thought, and he stepped hard on the accelerator of his rented car when he saw the hillside appear in front of him.

Arizona was just the kind of place that would create a Bill Longwood, Stone thought as he started up the private drive that led to the Longwood home, a man who had the strength of character and the courage to bring some sense back to this confused and fragmented country that they both loved, a man who wouldn't back down from doing the right thing, when someone like Cassidy put the heat on him the way Gardner had. It was common knowledge among Washington insiders now, what had happened when Cassidy's brother had been killed. Gardner had wanted a formal Declaration of War and an immediate call-up of the reserves, but Cassidy had forced him to back down. That kind of leadership couldn't go on forever, or America would lose its place in the world—and that was exactly the reason for his trip. Longwood must see it now, too. He must see that something had to be done. Maybe it was a godsend that Longwood had lost the nomination to Granderman four years before, Stone thought. Because this is when the country needs him the most. And it's the very time when he might just be able to really be elected. As the high metal gates at the top of the drive opened, Stone drove his rented Ford up onto the flat ground at the top of the mesa that held the Longwood home.

Bill Longwood, the man himself, was standing at the side of the path that led to the main house. He was dressed in blue jeans and a simple faded denim workshirt. He waved at Stone, and the political manager looked across the long roll of front lawn planted in cactus and bright desert flowers at the man that he'd come two thousand miles to visit.

As Stone slowed his car in the circular drive his eyes met those of his host. Longwood smiled and then energetically flashed a thumbs-up signal to Stone. The meaning of the signal between the two old friends was unmistakable. Stone's excitement and optimism were not misplaced. He and the Republican Party both had themselves a candidate for the presidency of the United States in 1968—a candidate who could win!

" 'Reassessing'!" Gardner slammed the newspaper that he'd been reading down on his desktop, but, as if by black magic, the photograph of Jack Cassidy still landed face up, staring out at him from the newspaper's front page.

"Is that what he calls it?" Gardner thundered. Sitting across the desk from him in the Oval Office, Mazeloff smiled a tight-lipped little smile that communicated his own distaste for what was becoming more and more each day now an obvious power grab by Cassidy and his people. Mazeloff said nothing that could set Gardner off though. Any mention of the maneuvering that Cassidy was doing to defeat a sitting President for the nomination of his own party had to come from the President himself.

"He's running," Gardner said flatly. "He met with Rothman at least twice last week, and they've both got their people roaming all over New Hampshire. He's done everything up there but open an office and pay the goddamn filing fee! He's running all right, and he has been—ever since his brother was killed. He may be trying to use that as an excuse, but the truth is, he would have done it anyway. He just can't stand to see us in charge of what he seems to think is his own personal damn country!" Gardner said. He looked at the faces of the men gathered around him in the Oval Office that morning for a political strategy meeting. The holidays were over now, a new year had begun, and the first presidential primary was a little more than two months off. And the President's face showed deeply the worry and concern that Cassidy's undeclared campaign was already beginning to cause him. He looked twenty years older than when he'd first taken the job, Mazeloff thought, glancing over at the big man sitting behind the executive desk in the Oval Office. There were those who said that even if he won reelection in 1968, Gardner would never be able to serve out his term.

"Bill," the President said, pointing at Mallory, who was sitting at the far side of the room, his chair slightly separated from the others. Mallory's head was down, his tie uncharacteristically undone, and when he looked up at the President, Mazeloff noticed a strange deeply fatigued expression on the assistant's face. God, he's not a boy anymore either, is he? Mazeloff realized suddenly, as he moved his gaze across the room from the President to look at Mallory. Jesus, I wonder what I look like myself these days, Mazeloff thought then.

"Bill, I want you to go on up to New Hampshire and see for yourself. Talk to our people. See if there's any chance on God's green earth that Cassidy would dare take us on up there and do us any real damage."

Mallory said nothing. He just looked at the President, as if he meant to communicate something to him, but then his eyes swept the other faces in the room and he stopped. The decision was long overdue. The New Hampshire primary was barely eight short weeks away now and the undeclared, but very real write-in movement on Cassidy's behalf was in full swing, better organized than the President's own reelection campaign. "Yes, sir," he said finally, rather than whatever it was that he had really meant to say. Then he began flipping through the crowded note-filled steno pad that he held in his lap, until he found a clean half page, and then he bent down over the notebook, jotting down more instructions to himself.

"Need that done soon, end of the week, no later," Gardner said in the string of short phrases and half breaths that had become his way of communicating to those around him over the last several weeks.

"Yes, sir," Mallory said again, but with little conviction in his voice.

The small group of advisers was silent then, as if the decision to send Mallory to New Hampshire to explore Gardner's position in the nation's first primary was the best that this roomful of highly paid political experts could come up with to help save Gardner's rapidly slipping political popularity.

Mazeloff couldn't believe it. He'd been with the President for years and he'd never seen a political meeting like this one that wasn't filled with energy and enthusiasm, most of it flowing from Gardner himself and igniting the others into a flurry of ideas and activity. But the meeting had just begun and already there was silence. "Maybe you should consider going up there yourself in a few weeks," Mazeloff said. He waited for a response from the others, but there wasn't any.

"I can't go now. There'd only be trouble," the President said. "Demonstrations, peace marches."

"If we could only get a break in the war," Mazeloff agreed dutifully, as he saw that there was no hope in firing the President into action that morning. And all the heads in the room nodded their agreement, except for Gardner's. The big man just stayed slumped in his desk chair, his eyes looking at nothing in particular. Slowly though, he began to realize that all the eyes at the long conference table were focused on him, and it was rapidly becoming apparent to everyone that the President was no longer following the conversation in the room. "I have another meeting in a moment," the President said then. "Let's resume this later, after Bill returns with his report." Gardner stopped then, leaving the awkward silence to fill the room again.

Slowly, uncertainly, each man sitting around the President's desk stood and shuffled papers or ground out cigarettes in the Oval Office ashtrays, each procrastinating and making very certain that the President really meant to adjourn the strange, unfocused meeting so abruptly, without even discussing the long checklist of pressing political issues that each of the advisers had come to the meeting prepared to discuss. What had they decided? Mazeloff thought to himself. Mallory is to go to New Hampshire and report back on what? He found it hard to get it straight even now, seconds after the President had issued the order. Jesus, it was all so unclear, but apparently that was going to be it. Gardner failed even to stand as this first political meeting in months began slowly to disperse and his advisers headed for the door of the Oval Office as confused and directionless as they'd started out that morning. Gardner did manage to raise his head and half catch the eye of one or two of the departing advisers, but then he turned away from each of them quickly and returned in his embarrassment to looking back at his desktop or just down at the tightly interlaced fingers of his big hands that rested on his lap.

"Sir," Mallory said, interrupting Gardner's faraway look.

"Yes, Bill," the President said.

"I need to talk to you," Mallory said, but Gardner shook his head no. "Can't it wait?"

Mallory paused uncertainly before answering. "Yes, sir," he said finally, seeing the fatigue in the other man's face. "But I did prepare this," Mallory continued, and he laid a neatly typed envelope down on Gardner's desktop directly in front of the President.

Gardner looked down at the long, clean, white envelope with a feeling of very real sadness in his heart. The President knew what it contained without opening it. He had received dozens of them from his staff people and government appointees over the last few months, but of course, this one was different. Bill Mallory had been with him, close to him, for a very long time. Like a son, Gardner began to say to himself, but he cut off the overly sentimental thought before he would really have to complete it. He couldn't afford personal feelings now, not about this. He was the President and he had a job to do.

"I'd still like you to make that trip up to New Hampshire for me," the President said. Although he hadn't wanted it to sound the way it had, his words came out as if he were pleading with the younger man now, asking for a personal favor. "Forget it," the President said then, feeling embarrassed and waving his hand up to cover the space between himself and the younger man.

"Of course," Mallory began.

The President wouldn't let him finish. "No, forget it. It's not necessary. I may cancel the trip anyway. It was a bad idea. I don't know. But you go ahead. I understand." Gardner's speech was rambling, and he refused to look at his assistant as he spoke. "You did a good job. I'm grateful. I wish you well," Gardner said, and then he stopped talking altogether and the Oval Office was filled with silence.

Mallory hadn't meant for it to happen this way. He'd been with the man for over ten years; a big chunk of both their lives was ending now and the man behind the desk refused even to meet his eyes as they spoke. "Thank you, sir," Mallory said, but the President didn't respond.

After Mallory was gone, and the door firmly closed behind him, Gardner opened his top desk drawer and pushed Mallory's unopened letter deep inside it. Then he closed the drawer again, so that there was no chance of seeing the plain, white envelope with "President Ransom W. Gardner" typed neatly on it.

"You've been sick," Grissum said, sliding his desk chair back and standing up.

"Who me?" Sullivan said from behind the mound of paperwork on his own desk.

"You've been a model agent ever since you got back from seeing your father at Thanksgiving," Grissum said. "Somebody put the fear of God into you?"

"Something like that," Sullivan mumbled.

"I've got nothin' to report to Yancey anymore," Grissum said and shuffled off toward the elevators. It was quitting time and the older agent moved with the crowd of other agents toward the exits, leaving Sullivan behind at his desk. Grissum couldn't be more wrong, Sullivan thought, but he was pleased that how he really felt didn't show to the other agent. Sure, he was scared, scared and hurt by what he'd been told by Hollis when he'd been called in to the capital. But mainly he was angry, and out of his anger had grown a strategy on how to handle the Bureau and maybe save his own neck in the process. And not letting Grissum or anybody else know his true feelings was an essential part of that strategy.

They can't guarantee my safety, shit! Who the hell were these guys to threaten him? But then a little of the fear returned again, as he remembered the answer to his question—these men were some of the most powerful people in the country, probably the world! That's who they were. The better question was, who the hell did he think he was to rock their boat? He was Jim Sullivan of the Pennsylvania Sullivans; that's who, he thought quickly then, answering his own question with a half laugh. And they can go screw themselves, he added, but still only to himself. I'll show Grissum who the hell's been sick, Sullivan thought impulsively, and he reached down and opened his lower desk drawer and dug out the notes he'd made on the plane coming back from his meeting with Hollis in D.C. In them was everything that he could remember about the file that Hollis had shown him for the man the Bureau knew as Antonio Lopez. Sullivan spread the notes out in front of him and reread them for at least the tenth time in the last month. He looked again at the Bureau control number that had been typed on the front cover of the file, then at each of the aliases of the man, who'd called himself "Lopez-Lopata-Cirello-Garcia" and half a dozen other names over the last several years. Sullivan wondered then what that would be like—no family, no friends, no job, or home, not even a name. Shit, it might be enough to make anybody crazy, but not crazy enough to start taking shots at the President, not unless there was something very wrong with you to start with. Anyway, there was no real proof the guy had ever shot at anybody. In fact, his file indicated that he might not even know how to fire a weapon and certainly not very well. What the hell had it been that had set the alarm bell off inside his head, when he'd first seen the file then? It wasn't this guy Lopez-Lopata's record. Like Hollis said, his record was strictly lightweight, definitely not the stuff of top-level political conspiracies or even a violent criminal, just a minor-league petty thief.

He wrote the file number down on a sheet of paper then and began mixing it over and over with the first initials of each of the aliases of the mystery man's name, as if it was a code to be broken. Then he wrote the control number backwards, leaving a space between each digit. He stared down then at the numbers—nothing. Shit! He pushed the notebook away and reached for one of the files on his desk that he was supposed to be working on and opened it, but he could get no further with it than the file cover. Burnleigh, Austin, James—8794333AK. He looked down at it again and then quickly snatched up another file off his desk and then another. Of course—that was it! He hurriedly compared all the control numbers on each of the files on his desk to the file number that he had for Lopez-Lopata. The answer hit him with such stunning ease then that he almost sat up in his desk chair and shouted it out loud. All Bureau files had nine-digit control numbers—seven arabics and two alphas. Every damn file that he'd ever seen was the same, all but two—Strode's file and the file that Hollis had shown him for Lopez-Lopata! It was easy to miss, he thought as he looked again at the control number in his notes for the Lopez-Lopata file—69477987RA. It was just an extra arabic, eight digits before the two alpha delineations at the end of the control number. It was the same thing that he'd seen, but not understood, or even realized that he'd seen in the Strode file. It had just looked wrong to him then, nothing he could place easily, but it had sent off a warning signal, and it had nagged at him ever since. Only now did he realize what it was: a single, extra, damned digit. But what did it mean? Was it a coincidence of some kind? Maybe just a mistake? Was that possible? A coincidence that an extra number turned up on the files of two men who just happened to be present in Dealey Plaza that day? No, that was too much to believe, Sullivan decided. There was a reason for it. There had to be, but what was it? He tried to remember the exact number on Strode's file, but he couldn't bring it back. Too many years had passed and too many Bureau files had moved by his desk since then. He was certain, though, that he was right. It had eight control numbers. Could someone else have been investigating Strode and Lopata? Someone with enough power to designate internal Bureau numbers? Whoever had issued that number to Strode had to have done it before, not after, November 22, 1963. Jesus, he was certain of at least that much, because he'd seen the strange control number on Strode's file himself on the night of the shooting. So, the number on Strode's file had to have been issued at some time prior to the assassination attempt. That could mean that there was a link of some kind between Strode and Lopata before the shooting—a link that the Bureau knew something about. Hollis had said that the Lopata file had been initiated when the CIA had begun background checks on anti-Castro soldiers being trained for an invasion of Cuba. Maybe that was it, Sullivan thought then. CIA—maybe that was the connection. Maybe the extra digit indicated a file containing CIA input of some kind. Sullivan thought back then through the few contacts that he'd had with the Central Intelligence Agency during the last few years. There was one possibility. Sullivan scratched the name on a piece of paper and half walked, half ran to the file room. The same young woman who had manned that station four years earlier, when he'd first requested the Strode file, looked at him from the last of her day's work. "Just doing a final couple of things," he said. "I hate to, but . . ." Sullivan pushed the late request for a file across the counter toward her.

As the file clerk reached for his request slip, another thought flashed through Sullivan's mind. Maybe the link is Cuba, anti-Castro stuff, "freedom fighters," or something like that, and he reached down then and hurriedly scratched a second name onto the request slip. He waited impatiently for the clerk to return from sorting through the walls of files in the long room that tunneled back behind her desk.

"What are you working on, anyway?" the clerk asked as she delivered the two files he'd requested across the counter to him.

"Nothing much. Just some draft-resister junk," Sullivan lied.

"Hippies?"

Sullivan nodded toward her absently as he glanced down and checked out the tabs on the two files that he'd requested. His heart sank, seven arabics, two alphas on both files, standard stuff. It was hardly a definitive test, but Sullivan had a feeling now that Cuba and CIA weren't the links. It had to be something else that joined the two men—but he knew he was close. The Bureau had reason for issuing those two irregular control numbers to the Strode and Lopez-Lopata files and to no others. He was just going to have to figure out what it was.

Sullivan tucked the files under his arm. They were useless to him now, but he thought he'd better at least make a show of needing them or someone might get suspicious. He was in enough trouble already. He thanked the clerk and started back toward his desk, but then he stopped suddenly and turned back to her. Who would know better? It could get me killed though, he thought, remembering what Hollis had said to him. He hesitated for a moment then, looking at the file clerk's face, saying nothing. What the hell, he decided finally. Not knowing might get me killed, too.

"You ever see a file designation like these?" Sullivan scratched two numbers at random, each containing the extra control number, and shoved them in front of her.

"What do you mean?" The clerk looked down at the numbers and shrugged her shoulders in confusion.

"I mean, if I requested some files and all I had were these numbers, what would you do?"

"I'd go look for them, I guess," she said, still not understanding, but she could see that Sullivan was waiting for more. "And if I had them and there wasn't a hold on them or something I'd give them to you."

Sullivan was still silent, waiting.

"I don't get it. What's the trick?" the girl said and then a small smile started across her face. Maybe this was Sullivan's way of flirting with her, she thought. "I'd just give you what you want," she said, smiling a little more broadly now.

Sullivan nodded a polite acknowledgment of her double meaning, but pressed on past it. "No, I mean, aren't there too many numbers here?" He pointed down at his imaginary control numbers again.

"I'd just ignore the last number, I guess," the girl said looking down at the pad. "Anything over seven numbers and two letters, I just wouldn't worry about it. That's none of my business."

"You'd just read the first seven numbers?" Sullivan said, trying to understand.

"Yeah, sure, what else am I supposed to do?" The girl was truly puzzled now.

"Does that happen?" Sullivan asked.

"Does what happen?" the girl said. "Look, what is this, a security check or something?"

"No, I'm just wondering if you've ever seen a file or a request or anything for a file with more than the normal seven digits on it, that's all." Sullivan tried to make his voice sound casual, but his mind was racing.

"No," the girl said flatly and turned away. "And anyway, even if I did, it's none of my business. Those numbers come out of Washington. If there's anything more on them than just the normal seven digits that's their concern, not mine. Probably not yours either," she added.

"You're right," Sullivan said. He couldn't afford to have anyone else pissed off at him right then.

"Hey!" she said sharply and Sullivan stopped backtracking. "You forgot your files."

"Oh, yeah," Sullivan said, stepping gingerly back toward her and reaching down for the files that he'd made her pull for him. "Thank you." He smiled and backed up toward his desk with the two useless files tucked foolishly under his arm.

He was going to solve this thing, with or without the Bureau's help, he thought then. There was a way to figure out why the Strode file and the file for this guy Lopata or whatever the hell his name was, both had been issued the same special control numbers, and he was going to come up with it. Sullivan was certain that when he did the case would break wide open. In the end they'd be grateful. He was betting on it. And the stakes, he reminded himself grimly, had become his own life.

CHAPTER
37

Rozier sat in one of the many windowless, underground rooms built deep below the White House. Around him were the files, documents, books, papers, and even the clothes that Tim Cassidy had taken with him to Vietnam.

Since the Vice President's death, much of Rozier's time had been spent in this somber little room, trying to disentangle Tim Cassidy's life and work from the government that he had served in one capacity or another for nearly the last twenty years of his life. It was a tedious and thankless job, but they were nearing the end of it. The suitcases and other materials that the Vice President had taken with him on his final trip had been held up by the military in Saigon and had only arrived in Washington the day before, two months to the day after the Vice President's death, but this was the last of it. Rozier studied the stacks of files mounded on the desk in front of him and then at the boxes full of personal possessions piled up into the corners of the little room.

"Another late night?" Gene Norrie, the presidential staff man who had been assigned to work with Rozier in sorting out Cassidy's things, joined Rozier in looking around at the cramped room piled high with files and papers and overflowing cardboard boxes.

"I think we got through the worst of it last night though," Rozier said, and then he glanced down at the preliminary accounting prepared by Norrie's office. He hoped that there wouldn't be any controversy about any of the items tonight. Rozier didn't feel like fighting about any of it. He was tired and he could feel the sadness and loss welling up inside him as soon as he opened the first file and looked down at the familiar hurriedly scrawled handwriting. How many times had he seen Tim's handwriting in all the years . . . Rozier forced himself to stop the flow of memories that were beginning to pour over him then, and mechanically he continued reviewing the file's contents. It was a SEATO file—clearly government property. There would be no dispute about this one at least, he thought gratefully. Rozier checked its number against the typed list on the desktop in front of him. When he found the matching control number on the list, Rozier initialed the space next to it and placed the file on top of the stack on the far side of the desk closest to Norrie.

Rozier reached down for the next file, but it was too thick and unruly to pick up with one hand. He stood up and took the heavy file in both hands and set it down on the desk in front of him. Rozier glanced at the number stamped on its cover and then checked it against the government accounting: FILE 8845-PERSONAL. Rozier thumbed quickly through the file's contents. Unorganized papers spilled out of it. It certainly wasn't a standard government file, that was obvious enough, but what the hell was it? It didn't look to him like one of Tim's personal files either, although that had apparently been the government's preliminary classification. Rozier looked at the contents more closely. The file contained mostly handwritten notes on sheets of lined white paper, but none of it was in Tim's handwriting. Rozier was getting good at recognizing the handwriting of most of the Cassidy staff people too, but this was a mystery. He glanced up at Norrie. The presidential assistant was too busy to notice. He was hard at work cataloguing the thick stack of government files on Southeast Asia that Tim had been reviewing during the last few days before he'd left for Saigon and then had taken with him on the trip to Vietnam. Many of them contained highly sensitive material, and Rozier knew how eager Norrie was to get them back to the vice-presidential offices.

Rozier looked back down at the file in his hands and began reading its contents. Good God! It was assassination material, he realized suddenly. But whose? Why did Tim have it? And why in God's name had he taken it with him to Saigon? Rozier's mind was filled with questions. He glanced back up at Norrie again, but he was still reviewing the Top Secret Southeast Asian files.

Rozier flipped through a few more pages of the mysterious file. Jesus, there were copies of internal FBI reports buried in it. What the hell was Tim doing with something like this? Could there be a link to the Cuban materials that Estanza had given to him? There was only one way to find out, Rozier decided—get this file out of here and back to his apartment where he could review its contents thoroughly in private. There had to be a way to do that.

Norrie finished stacking the files that he'd been working with and looked up at Rozier. "As I understand the ground rules, there's not going to be any trouble over files marked with government control numbers, right?" Norrie said, setting his hand down on top of the sensitive stack of SEATO and Southeast Asian files on the desk in front of him.

Rozier nodded his head in agreement, while at the same time his hand closed the cover of the mystery file, so that Norrie wouldn't get a glimpse of its contents.

"I think it's obvious that we're not going to finish all this tonight," Norrie said. "But if it's all right with you, I'd like to make sure that at least a few of these things get back to the vice-presidential offices, just as soon as possible," Norrie said, pointing at the stack of critical Top Secret files that lay on the desk in front of him.

"Take them with you tonight if you like," Rozier said, forcing his voice to sound as casual as he could.

"Do you want to see them?"

Rozier smiled. "I can see them," he said, dropping his gaze a fraction of an inch from Norrie's face to the tall stack of files lying on the desk in front of the presidential assistant.

"Thanks," Norrie said. "I wasn't looking forward to being up all night again." The staff man's middle-aged face was showing the strain of working the extra job of sorting through Cassidy's files and papers on top of his already busy White House schedule.

Rozier nodded amiably again, assuring the overworked presidential assistant that he wouldn't stand in his way.

"I'll sign a receipt for these," Norrie said, and he touched a button on the desktop. Within seconds there was a sharp knock on the door and a secretary entered the room. "Type this up for my signature and for Mr. Rozier's, would you? Mark it, 'Receipt' at the top. After we've signed it, Mr. Rozier will want a copy for his files, and the original should go upstairs to my office."

The secretary took the list and headed for the door, but she stopped when Norrie called out to her. "And have Administration send someone over to carry these files up to the executive offices, would you? We'll put them in my office for now."

The secretary nodded to show that she understood and then hurried out of the room. After she left, Norrie glanced over at Rozier. "You want to take anything with you tonight? The clothes maybe, or some of the personal things?" The presidential assistant had gotten everything that he hoped to get from Rozier that night and he was obviously in an expansive mood.

Rozier only smiled. "I don't think so. Anything I take, I'd just have to carry myself."

"No, no," the staff man said generously. "I can have our people help you with it. Do you have a car upstairs?"

Rozier nodded his head. "Well, thank you. Maybe some of the easier things then, things that we're not going to put into storage. The photographs, the clothes, maybe a file or two." Rozier let his hand move down and lightly touch the cover of the mysterious FBI file that stood on the desktop in front of him then, but, as he made the seemingly graceful movement, he could feel his heart beginning to pound fast and hard.

Rozier stood and lifted an empty cardboard box off the floor. "Thank you, Gene," he said. "I'll start putting a few things together. It'll make it easier on us tomorrow night. Maybe we can wrap it all up in one more session."

"God, I hope so," Norrie said. "You go ahead. I'm going to call my wife. Let her know that I might be home before dawn for a change."

"Aren't you going to tell me first who the President's chosen as his new Vice President?" Rozier smiled across the room at the overworked presidential assistant. Gardner had been taking his time making his selection of a Vice President, but the rumor in Washington was that he was almost ready to announce a replacement now.

"Who says he's picked anybody yet?" Norrie said, giving Rozier the standard White House reply.

"Gene, we're both working overtime for something. Is it Putnam?"

Norrie paused. "Off the record?"

"Off the record," Rozier agreed to the expected ground rule.

Norrie nodded his head sharply once, signaling that Rozier had guessed right. The presidential assistant turned to the door then, without saying anything out loud that could be quoted later, but his meaning was unmistakable. Senator Putnam of Minnesota was to be Gardner's new Vice President.

Rozier waited until the door had closed behind the presidential assistant; then he went to work. Hurriedly he reached down and picked up the mysterious FBI file and placed it into the cardboard box on the floor below him. On top of the file he placed several of Tim's books and personal photographs.

He sat down then and prepared his own handwritten receipt, itemizing the materials in the neatly packed cardboard box. Rozier knew that there should be a final check of the FBI file by Norrie or some other administration official before it was removed from the White House. And that by taking it with full knowledge that it contained FBI reports, he wasn't just violating his arrangement with the White House, he was probably violating federal law as well. He looked up to see Norrie reentering the room, and as he did Rozier felt his own heart skip a beat. What he was doing had to be a crime! But he glanced over at Norrie confidently, hoping that his feelings didn't show. "Your wife happy?"

"Yes," Norrie said. "Do you have what you want?" he asked, crossing the room and pointing at the neatly packed cardboard box on the desktop in front of Rozier.

The presidential assistant looked briefly at Rozier's handwritten receipt, and as Rozier's heart began beating even more rapidly Norrie shuffled through the box, counting the files and comparing their numbers with those on Rozier's receipt, but not opening any of them to inspect their contents directly. Finally satisfied, he initialed the receipt at the bottom.

"You don't mind a handwritten receipt for now, do you?" Rozier said, holding to his poker face. "It's so damned late. We can have it typed up tomorrow."

"No, that's fine," Norrie said.

Two Marine guards entered the little basement room and Norrie pointed out the boxes of inventoried files that he wanted moved up to the vice-presidential offices. "And when you're done with that, put this box in Mr. Rozier's car," he said, pointing at the cardboard carton sitting on the table in the middle of the little windowless room.

Norrie smiled over at Rozier then. "Thank you, Allen. It should move pretty fast now, don't you think?"

Oh, it's moving fast enough, Rozier thought. If it moves any faster, I could be in Leavenworth by tomorrow night.

God, what had he done? He was supposed to help the White House sort through Tim's things and he'd wound up stealing a secret government file. The doubts were followed by an enormous rush of fear as Rozier drove the Washington streets back to his hotel. He glanced at the clock on the dashboard. It was after two in the morning. The sign for the hotel's parking garage loomed up in front of him. He took one final glance into his rearview mirror before he let his rented car dip down into the subterranean parking structure. God, it is quiet down here, he thought. There was a parking place between two cement pillars in a far dark corner and Rozier pulled his car to a stop in the vacant spot. He sat for a moment in the dimly lit underground garage. The things I do for the Cassidys, he laughed nervously to himself, as he reached into the cardboard box on the seat next to him and hurriedly shifted the stolen file containing the FBI reports into his own briefcase. He took a deep breath and locked the car before starting his way across the shadowy parking structure to the bank of elevators at the far side of the underground lot. A set of headlights suddenly illuminated his path. Rozier began moving more quickly toward the elevator. The single car pulled by and stopped and Rozier reached up and hit the elevator button. He could hear the car door slamming closed behind him just as the elevator doors slid open. Rozier jumped inside without hesitating, and immediately reached out and pushed the button to close the elevator behind him.

Breathing hard, he waited for what seemed an eternity as the metal doors slowly moved together and then locked into place. The other car was nothing, he told himself, just another late-arriving guest. But he could still feel his heart pounding with fear inside his chest.

When the elevator opened into the lobby, he went to the office of the night manager. A copy of the Cuban materials that Estanza had given him to review were locked in the hotel safe. It was just a hunch, but Rozier wanted to have the Cuban information with him when he reviewed the FBI file. There just might be a connection.

After the night manager returned with the package, Rozier stuffed it deep into his briefcase along with the stolen FBI file. Once he was safely inside his room, he closed the drapes and double-locked the door. Then he unloaded the materials from his briefcase onto the big table in the living room of his suite and separated out the contents of the stolen FBI file from the Cuban materials, making two tall unruly stacks of papers on the tabletop. He looked down at the mounds of paper and sighed at the enormity of the task ahead of him. It would take the entire night just to sort through all of it, and trying to make some sense out of it could take days. And then what? He'd probably take it all to Jack, but not yet, not until he knew a little better what he had. After all, even Senators can be found guilty of breaking federal secrecy laws, he reminded himself.

Rozier took a fresh pad of paper from his briefcase and laid out several ballpoint pens on the table in front of him. Then he reached for the first document, but as he did something wedged in the stack of FBI documents caught his eye and he pulled a single piece of paper from the middle of the thick stack. The sheet he selected was folded in half and Rozier had to open it and smooth its corners down before he could get a good look at what it was. His heart seemed to stop for a moment then, as his eyes slowly began to focus on it. He was looking down at a charcoal sketch of a man's face. Rozier turned the sketch over; it was stamped with a date and an FBI identification number.

His heart still beating in fear and excitement, Rozier quickly sorted through the material Estanza had given him. His fingers finally came across the photograph of the dead man the Cubans had been holding in one of their prisons—the man whose statements the Cubans said could prove that he had been part of a conspiracy to murder the President of the United States. Oh, my God, Rozier thought as he looked at the two pictures side by side. The man in the Cuban photograph and the one in the FBI sketch were the same man!

"You arranged this, didn't you?" Grissum said.

"What?" Sullivan asked, playing dumb, but he knew what Grissum meant, and, when the older agent just stayed quiet and waited for his answer, Sullivan finally gave it to him. "Yeah, maybe. I figured you liked this kind of an assignment."

Grissum's face let Sullivan know that he didn't believe him. The older agent knew there was another reason and, if he just waited long enough, he'd learn what it was. The two men were sitting in Sullivan's car, parked on a hillside overlooking an abandoned farmhouse several miles outside Dallas. They were in their fifth day of what was turning out to be a dull investigation of a group of long-haired draft dodgers. The Bureau wasn't interested in just the young draft dodgers, though. The government wanted to arrest their leader, a civil-liberties lawyer named Shapiro, and Yancey had a tip that if someone waited long enough, Shapiro would show up at the farmhouse. Yancey had picked Sullivan for the job and Sullivan had asked for Grissum to accompany him. This was their third day of waiting. There was a lake nearby and the two FBI agents dressed each morning like fishermen and loaded down their cars with fishing gear. Then they drove out to the hillside outside Dallas that overlooked the farmhouse and waited, watching the valley below through long-range binoculars. It was a dull, slightly silly case, Sullivan thought, but it was perfect for what he really had in mind. It gave him a chance to get Grissum alone and talk to him. There was a tried-and-true method in the Bureau for finding out things that your superiors didn't want you to know. All you had to do was ask an "old hand" about it, or even better, ask every old-timer that you knew, until you could piece together the real answer. But since everyone in the Bureau, old-timer or not, would barely talk to Sullivan anymore about anything, much less about Bureau secrets, there was only one person left for him to ask—Grissum.

And Grissum didn't seem to really mind that he'd arranged to have him assigned to the case, Sullivan thought, as he looked over at the older agent. Stakeouts were Grissum's specialty. He could sit for hours, almost immobile, his hat brim tipped down, seemingly covering his eyes, his legs propped up on something comfortable, even the dashboard of a car would do, with his head wreathed in a great cloud of cigarette smoke, and all the time watching a suspect's house, or car, or apartment, or whatever, for anything suspicious. Grissum rarely even used his binoculars when he was on a stakeout, or listening devices, or any equipment at all. All he used to get the job done was his squinting dark gray eyes.

"Draft resister, shit!" Sullivan said, looking over at his partner. It was late in the day and the fish that they'd bought at a local bait store earlier in the week and placed in their borrowed ice chest were starting to smell up the inside of the car and make Sullivan even more unhappy. "I mean, I'm not in Vietnam either, but I'm the good guy because I'm in the Bureau, right?" Sullivan went on. "And that means I don't have to go get myself shot at. But they're the bad guys, because they don't want to go over there and get killed. Look at them," Sullivan pointed down the hill where in the distance now some of the long-haired young men were visible in the open grassy area in front of the little farmhouse. "How bad do those guys look to you?" Sullivan continued. "Do they look like criminals?"

As Sullivan spoke, Grissum barely stirred. There was a slightly contented look on the older agent's face. Shit, Sullivan thought as he glanced over at him, this is his idea of a great case.

"Hell, I don't want to go to Vietnam either." Sullivan went on pouring out his feelings to the older agent, even though he had no idea whether Grissum was really listening to him.

The older agent stayed in place as Sullivan talked, the lowest sliver of Grissum's dark gray eyes leveled on the clearing in front of the farmhouse below them where a few girls had appeared now to join the men. "Look at those bastards," Grissum said as he watched the young men and women mixing easily with each other in the valley below the road. "Shit, I didn't even get laid until I was twenty-two fucking years old." Sullivan looked over at the older agent and smiled.

"Look, I can't help it if you got a shitty war," Grissum said then, changing back to the earlier subject, "and I got lucky and got a good one."

Sullivan shrugged his shoulders. It was time now, he thought, while Grissum was in a talkative mood. "Can I ask you a question?" Sullivan said, trying to sound nonchalant.

"No," Grissum said, but Sullivan went ahead anyway. "I came across something the other day that I'd never seen before," Sullivan said.

"That doesn't surprise me," Grissum said with a bored tilt of his head toward Sullivan, but the older agent's eyes didn't leave the valley.

"I pulled a file on a guy." Sullivan paused for a second and tried to sound even more casual. "It had a crazy file number on it, too many digits, an extra number or something. It had eight numbers and two alphas. What do you think?"

Grissum stayed quiet, his eyes still following the movements of the young hippie kids playing in the fields below him.

"You ever heard of anything like that before?" Sullivan pressed. His voice had lost all of its easy quality now. He just wanted an answer to his question and he didn't even care anymore if Grissum knew just how much he wanted it.

Grissum slowly moved his hat brim up an extra half inch above his eyes before he turned to the younger agent. "Don't fuck with me, Sullivan," he said finally.

"Fuck with you? I'm not fucking with you. I'm asking you a goddamned technical question. Isn't that what veterans are supposed to do, train the new guys in Bureau procedure and things?" Sullivan was rambling on now in an unconvincing voice, trying to cover his embarrassment at getting caught trying to sneak one by the older agent. Shit, he should have known better, Sullivan told himself. "I just asked. I mean, you've been around a long time, I thought maybe you came across something like that, sometime," he added, feeling even more foolish.

Grissum stayed quiet then.

"I talked to some people about it," Sullivan lied. "They'd heard somewhere that sometimes Washington does things like that, sticks an extra number or an alpha or something onto a file for their own reasons back there. You ever heard of that?"

Grissum turned his face toward Sullivan and the young agent looked away, feeling even more embarrassed. "You're still screwing around with that thing with Cassidy, aren't you?"

Sullivan considered lying again, but then he decided the hell with it. He was rotten at it anyway. "A little," he said finally. "I've got a theory I'm working on, that's all. Want to hear it?"

"No," Grissum said flatly. He turned away from Sullivan to study the hippies again.

"I knew you'd say that," Sullivan said and then paused to get his thoughts together. His latest theories on "the case" were starting to burst inside him and he had to talk to somebody about them or he was afraid he might lose them. It was just going to have to be Grissum. "My theory is that there are files back in Washington that the big boys don't want any of the rest of us to know anything about," he began explaining in an excited voice. "Files on political secrets and stuff, but the bigshots know it's not logical for there not to be any files at all on say, some guy who defected to Russia or fought at the Bay of Pigs or something, like Strode. So, maybe they run two files, or three, or whatever, on a guy like that. All the rest of the world gets to see is a dummy file, with just a lot of bullshit in it, but the bigshots add another control number to this dummy file to let the right people know that the file they're looking at isn't the real file at all. That extra number tells people like Yancey, or Hollis, or whoever, that there's another file somewhere back in Washington with a hell of a lot more information in it. So, if the wrong people get hold of it somehow, they can't tell anything's wrong, but for anybody who knows the secret, it's simple. They just look at the control number and they know there's more information somewhere. Or . . ." Sullivan paused to catch his breath. "Or," he said again, "maybe they've got a whole second file on the guy back in Summers's private vault or something. And the file we're looking at out here in the sticks, or the file they give to a congressional investigating committee, or to the press or something is total bullshit, all lies from top to bottom, and it just feeds the rest of the world some cover story they want us to swallow for their own protection." Sullivan finished, out of breath. This was the first time that he'd heard his theory out loud and it didn't sound half bad to him. Strode and Lopez-Lopata, and God knows who else, had two identities, each contained in separate files, a phony one for the agents in the field and all the small-fry in the Bureau and for the press, while all the time the real information was being kept secret in a second file someplace. It just so happened that in Strode's case, the fact that the Bureau had any kind of file on him at all—even though it was full of false and misleading information would have made the Bureau look bad. That's why Yancey had tried to hide it after the President had been shot. But if his theory was right, Sullivan thought, the file he'd taken out of Yancey's desk that night was only a cover for a second real file kept somewhere else, probably in D.C., that had all the really serious stuff in it, the secrets that could truly rock the Bureau if they were ever disclosed. The existence of that second file, though, was probably only known to a few people at most. In fact, the whole truth might only be known by a couple of people, maybe only Summers and the President or the head of the CIA or something like that, Sullivan thought, but he didn't say anything more. He could tell from the look on Grissum's face that it had been a mistake to talk to him about it in the first place.

"Going around accusing the Bureau of crimes puts you in about the same category as those assholes down there," Grissum said, pointing down at the hippies in the grassy field in front of the farmhouse. "And I think they're shit!" Grissum said, trying to close the conversation once and for all.

The young agent felt angry and hurt by Grissum's attitude, and to cover his feelings he took a long deep breath. He remembered the film that Hollis had shown him. What did any of it matter anyway? Maybe he had stumbled onto something with this file-number crap, but who really cared? This guy Lopata was dead now. What did it matter that the Bureau may have been hiding something from the public about him? If they had been, they had their reasons, and they were probably good ones, and what business was it of his anyway?

"You're right. It doesn't matter," Sullivan said. "None of it matters. If you're still reporting stuff to Yancey, let him know I don't give a shit about anything anymore," Sullivan said, his own weariness and anger exploding out into words, but Grissum still said nothing, and so Sullivan just went back to doing the job he was getting paid for and watching the hippies in the grassy valley below the road.

The woman would be easy, Lopata thought, as he stared straight ahead into the fog that was rolling up in thick waves from the harbor and encircling the block of warehouse buildings across the street from where he stood. The woman would be easy, but the man was a professional and he would be very difficult. A sudden stream of light cut through the fog then and almost touched Lopata's hiding figure, but the illumination finally dispersed in the thick New Orleans fog, just inches before it reached him.

Lopata could hear the sound of a car engine, expensive and heavy, and he could guess that the man he had been watching, day and night for the last several weeks, was safely resting behind the thick metal plating of his big black limousine. That was all right, Lopata thought, tonight was not the night, or tomorrow night either, but soon. Very soon he would have a plan and the plan would be executed, but it would be difficult with such a man, perhaps even more difficult than it will be with Cassidy. The light from DeSavio's limousine began to move out into the street in front of the darkened shapes of the warehouse buildings behind it.

Lopata had spent most of the nights since he'd arrived in New Orleans watching DeSavio's office, just looking up at the outline of the big cement building and imagining how it could be done. He knew each of the man's cars now and the exterior details of his office and his home. During the days, Lopata worked at a job that he'd found in a French Quarter lunch counter or walked the streets of the neighborhoods where DeSavio lived, and he would pause briefly in front of the high stone walls that surrounded the man's estate or in front of one of his warehouse buildings.

The dark black limousine passed within a few feet of him now, with the man himself sitting behind thick bulletproof glass. Almost close enough to reach out and touch, Lopata thought, but DeSavio's head didn't even turn to notice the single lone figure shrouded in the fog and shadows standing only a few short feet away from him. The woman will be easy, Lopata thought again, as he watched the heavy, bulletproof limousine pull past him and down the street and disappear into the dense New Orleans fog, but the man will be very difficult.

* * *

Sullivan found it in the middle of an otherwise uneventful February afternoon. The office was almost empty, just a few stray agents catching up on their written reports, a few Texas-size files being slapped from the paddles of one lazy ceiling fan to another, no supervisors, no Grissum, no break in their case on Shapiro, just another hot, dull Friday afternoon.

The funny part about it, Sullivan thought when he found it, was that he hadn't even been looking. He'd meant what he'd said to Grissum, and he'd done nothing on the Cassidy case for almost two weeks. And when it happened, Sullivan was just playing the time-honored Bureau game of matching faces. During the weeks before, he'd used a telephoto lens to photograph each of the kids at the farmhouse in the hills. And then, on that particular Friday afternoon, he'd spread each of their pictures out in a wide semicircle around the outside of his desk. The goal was to try to find a face from the farmhouse that matched one in the books he'd checked out from Records that morning. A little more information about the identity of one of the kids at the farmhouse might speed the search for Shapiro. Anyway, that was Sullivan's theory, and the search filled a lot of slow afternoons at the office. Grissum was at the lake now on Mondays, Wednesdays, and Fridays, and Sullivan took the stakeout on Tuesdays and Thursdays. On the off days each stayed at the office and looked at faces. One hell of a lot of manpower to track down one poor little long-haired hippie lawyer, Sullivan thought, but of course, this hippie lawyer had made the mistake, after he'd been arrested for breaking into the Bureau's offices in Chicago and burning some FBI draft-resister files, of dressing up like Summers and doing an impersonation of the Director for the television cameras. It was a pretty good imitation too, Sullivan thought as he remembered it now. So, this wasn't just some draft-resisting hippie anymore, this was Public Enemy Number Eight that Sullivan was closing in on. If the war goes on another year and if he keeps working on his Summers impression, this guy Shapiro could become Public Enemy Number Three or Four, Sullivan thought.

Sullivan reshuffled the photographs, setting the snapshots of the six permanent residents of what Grissum was now calling Sunnybrook Farm out across the top of his desk. At the center, he placed a single clear picture of Shapiro taken in Chicago before the lawyer had gone underground. Sullivan reached for another stack of files. Off to the left side of his desk was a tall stack of Bureau files and on his other side was a pile of photographs of the visitors at "Sunnybrook," the kids who floated through for a night or a weekend and then floated away again. There wasn't room to spread all their photographs out on the desktop, and . . . Shit, here's a match, Sullivan realized suddenly. Where did I see this girl before? The thin manila FBI file in his hand was open to a picture of an overweight young girl with long, dirty-blond hair. Sullivan reached down for the pack of photos of the "Sunnybrook Irregulars." He flicked through the dozens of photographs of long-haired, unwashed young men and women until he found the one that he wanted. He flipped the snapshot over. The time and date that it was taken was shown on the back: February 6, 1968, less than a week before. There were a couple of other shots of the same young woman, all taken within a few days of each other. One picture showed her leaning up against the side of the farmhouse, another with some other young people while she was holding a guitar and singing, another smoking what was probably marijuana. If the war goes another year, maybe she can make the top ten too, Sullivan thought, and he moved the thin FBI file over in front of him. The girl's name was Melinda Howard, born in Syracuse, New York, December 10, 1948. That made her all of nineteen, Sullivan thought, doing the math quickly in his head.

He reached down then and pulled up the thick Shapiro file from its resting place on the floor below his desk. Inside was a chronology of all the dates and places where the Bureau believed Shapiro had been since he'd gone "underground" in late 1966. Sullivan began checking Shapiro's history then against the notes he'd made from the girl's file. No matches, nothing. Dead end. No prize today, Sullivan thought finally, as he closed up the Shapiro file and set it back down on the floor with the others. He could almost hear the quitting-time buzzer going off inside his head then. Time's up, the buzzer seemed to be signaling. He'd done enough for one day. Shit, he'd done enough of this kind of work to last a lifetime. He looked down at his watch then. He'd told Denise that he'd sneak out early for the long weekend and pick her up at work. Maybe they could . . . Sullivan stopped suddenly. Christ, he thought, it was back, he was seeing the guy in his daydreams again! He'd almost shut the girl's file without focusing on the man sitting next to her in one of the candid photos contained in the file, almost but not quite. Shit, it was him—or it was his goddamned twin brother. It was the bastard in the blue plaid shirt that he'd run into in Dealey Plaza that day. Sullivan flipped the photograph over with nervous fingers. No, it couldn't be. The photograph was marked NOVEMBER 30, 1967, MIAMI, FLORIDA. The Thanksgiving Riots, Sullivan thought, looking down again at the photograph. The Bureau had apparently taken candid pictures in Miami of the detainees that the local police had arrested and held during the rioting. This was exactly the way the system was supposed to work, Sullivan thought. Although he couldn't remember it ever having worked for him before—at least not this well. The Bureau took tens of thousands of photographs at every illegal assembly, every riot, every leftist meeting or grouping of suspected radicals that it could infiltrate. It wasn't as effective as an arrest and a formal booking with fingerprints and official photographs, but it was one of Summers's favorite devices, a perfectly legal way of keeping tabs on the radical movement without interfering with their civil rights. This couldn't be him though, Sullivan thought. He remembered precisely that the picture of Lopez dead in Cuba that Hollis had shown him had been taken on November 24 or 25, 1967. So this couldn't be the same man, alive and well and in a Miami detention center almost a week later.

Sullivan stared down at the photograph again. It looked like it had been taken in a tightly packed high-school gym or auditorium of some kind. There was this girl from "Sunnybrook," her long dirty-blond hair, stringing down over the side of her face, her mouth open wide, as if she was talking loudly or maybe singing. But it was the man next to her that Sullivan couldn't take his eyes off now. He was much thinner than he had been in the photographs that Hollis had shown him in D.C., but Sullivan was certain that it was the same man he'd seen in Dealey Plaza four years before.

The young agent leaped to his feet then and walked quickly through the sea of empty Friday afternoon desks to the file room. When he got to the counter, he scratched out a request: "All information on the Thanksgiving Riots—November 1967—Miami Area," and he handed it to the Records clerk.

Less than an hour later he found the name "Lopata, Antonio" in a long list of those "Arrested and Held" during the nights of November 26–29, 1967. He'd been right. It was him! This bastard Lopata was alive and in the United States, after the date that the Bureau had reported him dead!

Sullivan sat looking at the name for several seconds. He felt stunned, betrayed, and frightened all at once. It could just be a screw-up, Sullivan thought. If Lopata was in Miami on the 26th, Hollis could have the wrong dates on the Cuban photographs, but it still didn't make any sense. The precise dates weren't that important, anyway, he realized suddenly. Hollis had said that Lopata had been in a Cuban prison camp for the entire three years prior to his death and then he had died in Cuba, while still in government custody. If that was true, it meant that he couldn't have been in Miami anytime after November of 1964. So something had to be wrong somewhere. Sullivan looked back down at the file and read the notation indicating a cross-reference to a local file being kept by the Miami Police Department. Did he dare call? The police in Miami could have instructions to contact someone in the Bureau before responding to any inquiries about Lopata, Sullivan thought, but he had to know. He had to know what had happened to the man that he'd been seeing in his dreams for the last four years.

The clerk in Police Records in Miami was reluctant, but after a little effort the power of the Bureau prevailed and Sullivan managed to convince him to pull the file that they had on "Lopata, Antonio" and read him the contents over the phone. "It's a thin file," the clerk said. "There's only one entry."

"Read it," Sullivan ordered.

"Detained, Miami City Jail and Orion Civic Auditorium, November 26–30, 1967, released November 30, 1967," the clerk read over the phone. "That's it," the clerk said then. "There's not even a charge. There's a photograph, a set of prints, and a description, though," he added. "Do you want me to describe him?"

"Yes."

As Sullivan listened to the clerk in Miami describe the man who had been arrested and held in late November of 1967, he knew with certainty that the information that the Bureau had given him was wrong. The man he'd seen in Dealey Plaza hadn't died in Cuba on November 24, 1967. And he could still be alive somewhere, even now!

Another secret meeting—Rozier had never noticed before what a great town Washington was for them. The city was dotted with dark, intimate little bars and restaurants, most of them with private corner booths, and park benches hidden under the shadowy branches of ancient trees, and hundreds of obscure motels located on the outskirts of town. The city was built for spies and informants and "unnamed sources," he thought. Rozier had chosen a little roadside bar off the Beltway a few miles from Chevy Chase for his latest secret meeting, with his own "unnamed source," but there were a thousand other spots that he could have chosen just as easily.

Sanders was a small, unpretentious man and Rozier was so busy watching the crowd and trying to guess the secret business of each of the groupings that he barely noticed his presence, until the quiet little man in the humble gray suit was suddenly standing right next to him.

"Good evening, Allen," the little man said, and Rozier began hurriedly clearing a place for him at the end of the bar.

"Do you think we should talk here?" Sanders said uncertainly.

Rozier only nodded his head that it would be all right. "I take it you've finished," Rozier said.

"Yes, it was quite easy, really," the little man answered, holding out his briefcase, clutched tightly in both hands, toward Rozier. "Like I said, it was just a matter of getting to it. I'm sorry that it took so long."

"And?" Rozier said, eager to hear the quiet little man's decision.

Rather than answer him immediately though, Sanders took a few more nervous glances back over his shoulder. "Are you sure you want to talk about it here?" Sanders asked again, his voice even more nervous, and Rozier could see that it was useless now. The bar had been a mistake. Sanders was half frozen in fear. It would be difficult to get anything much out of him in here that was useful, and Sanders's answers were too important not to do it right. Rozier reached into his pocket and threw a few bills onto the bar, enough to pay for the drinks that he'd been nursing since earlier that afternoon, and then he led the small man outside to his parked car.

Sanders seemed to relax once they were alone with the windows of Rozier's car rolled up and the doors tightly locked. "I treated it just like a Department matter," the little man said as he handed the file toward Rozier. "I mean, I didn't use Justice letterhead or anything, but I used the exact same procedures that I would have if the request had come in through regular channels."

It took some guts for Sanders to do what he had, Rozier thought then. He had worked under Tim at Justice during the early sixties and his loyalty to the Cassidy family was strong, but Rozier still appreciated his taking the risk. Using government facilities for a private request, particularly one as dangerous as this one, could get Sanders into serious trouble and Rozier knew it.

Rozier opened the file cover then. The first page was titled "Handwriting Analysis and Report—Arthur Allen Strode." Bill Sanders was one of the best handwriting experts in the country, maybe the best. Rozier flipped directly to the report's last page and read its summary and conclusion. "You're certain?" Rozier said a few seconds later.

The little handwriting expert nodded his head rapidly several times then. "Yes," he said. "The copies of the pages from the diary that you gave me matched precisely with handwriting samples of Strode's taken from our files, samples that were verified by the FBI during the initial investigations into the shooting back in late 1963 and 1964. The pages you gave me are copies from a diary kept by Arthur Strode, there's no doubt in my mind."

Rozier took a moment to let the impact of Sanders's words sink in. Okay, he told himself. This is the last piece of the puzzle. I've done all I can alone. Jack has to be told about it now, and he has to be told as soon as possible.

CHAPTER
38

The second gunman was alive! Thinking about it kept Sullivan from being able to sleep. Sullivan looked at the clock on the nightstand next to him—three thirty in the morning. Shit, he might as well get up, he decided, and he eased his way out of the double bed, careful not to awaken Denise.

Sullivan walked down the hall to the kitchen then. He knew that he had to do something. But what? He had solid proof that this man Lopata hadn't been killed in Cuba, at least not on the date he'd been told or anywhere close to it. The Bureau could just be wrong about the dates somehow, or . . . Sullivan hated to think about the other possibility, but he knew that he had to. The Bureau could have been intentionally deceiving him. But if they were, why? Why lie to him? The answer to that one came easily—to keep him from threatening the credibility of their precious Assassination Report.

Sullivan started his coffee and then stood looking out the kitchen window, waiting for the water on Denise's stove to boil. It was still dark outside and as he stared sleepily out the window, Sullivan could barely make out the shapes of the buildings that surrounded the high-rise apartment. What the hell was he going to do now? Maybe it was time to go see Cassidy, lay it all out for him. Maybe there was some way that a man like Cassidy could use his power to make some sense out of all of it. The trouble with that idea, Sullivan reminded himself, was that if the Bureau was trying to hide something, maybe Cassidy was, too. And if the Bureau found out that he had even tried to see Cassidy, he was finished. Anyway he asked himself then, even if I trusted Cassidy, and thought I could get away with it, do I have enough proof? Have I done all I can do here? There was something else that he'd wanted to do just before he went to see Tim Cassidy last November. What the hell was it?—Boyer. That was it. Deputy Police Chief Jacob Boyer, the man whose name kept turning up everywhere you looked in Dallas on the weekend of November 22, 1963. I'll go talk to the son of a bitch, Sullivan decided impulsively. Maybe he'll give me something that'll be worth risking taking directly to Cassidy. At least it would give him something definite to do, however crazy, rather than just sitting around endlessly asking himself questions that he had no real answers for.

Less than an hour later, Sullivan was on the road, headed north out of Dallas. Denise had still been asleep when he'd left her apartment. He'd written her a note and hoped that she'd understand, but he knew that she probably wouldn't. They'd both been looking forward to the holiday weekend together for a long time. He had to do something though, he reminded himself. He couldn't just wait around Dallas and do nothing, not now, not after he knew that this guy Lopata could still be alive somewhere. Anyway, he'd be back before late afternoon, he thought, as he reached over and checked the map that lay open on the car seat next to him.

The address that Sullivan had for Boyer was in a place called Clear Lake, about a hundred miles north of Dallas. Sullivan could imagine a beat-up trailer parked at the edge of some polluted pond of water that the real-estate developers were trying to pass off as a real lake. Something like that is the way all retired law-enforcement people wind up in the end, he thought.

As he headed his car down the Texas superhighway, he remembered back to the night that he'd met Boyer, the night that Strode had been executed by Leo Green right there in the basement of the Dallas police headquarters. Sullivan hadn't liked Boyer much then, but he had never dreamed that over four years later he'd be half convinced that he was one of the keys to a conspiracy to murder the President of the United States.

The highway to Clear Lake began to rise off the hot flatlands of north-central Texas into a gentle set of low rolling mountains and then, as the air began to cool and take on a clean freshness that Sullivan hadn't expected, pine trees began to appear at the sides of the winding mountain road. Maybe Clear Lake was going to be all right after all, Sullivan thought, as the road leveled off onto the high mountain plateau.

A side road led to a gate-guarded community and as Sullivan showed the uniformed guard his FBI credentials, he looked closely at the man's face. It had to be Boyer, Sullivan thought, as he carefully studied the guard's features, but Sullivan was wrong again. The retired deputy police chief was an official resident of this little exclusive community, not an employee, and less than a mile down the road Sullivan found the mailbox marked BOYER. From the main road, all Sullivan could see was a thick grove of trees, but after he wound his way down the long gravel drive and pulled to a stop, he could see Boyer's house. It was at the very top of a long, green hillside and he could see now that it was a modern, two-story, wood-and-glass hunting lodge, not the trailer on a rented lot he'd imagined. Behind the house and around a long sweep of green lawn, Sullivan could see down to a wide panorama of Clear Lake itself, and the water in the lake looked very clear and very blue and very expensive. Sullivan could feel his stomach tightening into a knot. Something was wrong.

He reached over and removed his keys from the ignition and unlocked the glove compartment. Inside, packed in a black leather shoulder holster, was a Bureau-issue, short-barreled .38 special. Sullivan hesitated for a moment, but finally he removed the holstered weapon from the dashboard compartment. He methodically checked the weapon as he had been trained, to be certain that it was loaded and operational. Then he replaced it into its holster. When he was finished, he opened his car door and stepped out onto the gravel path that led to Boyer's house. He removed his coat, buckled the holster into place around his shoulder, and put his suit coat back on. He returned to the driver's side of his car then, feeling the awkward weight of the weapon slapping against the side of his body. Sullivan didn't particularly like guns and he rarely wore one, and as he sat for a moment and looked down at Boyer's home below him, he wondered why he had suddenly felt the need for one now.

He noticed a woman starting down from the patio built at the side of the house. She was dressed in a long white satin robe, but the robe was open in the front and it was easy for Sullivan to make out the narrow bands of a short-cut black bikini under it.

"Mrs. Boyer?" Sullivan asked as the woman approached his car. The woman shook her head no, but she didn't explain further.

Remembering himself, Sullivan showed her his identification. "My name is Sullivan," he said as the woman looked closely at his card. "I need to talk to Mr. Boyer."

The woman had short hair bleached a white-blond color and teased into a high bubble on the top of her head. Dark glasses covered her eyes and gold high-heeled slippers made her appear taller than she really was. A pair of long earrings that Sullivan guessed were real diamonds completed her outfit for a morning in the sun. Sullivan took it all in, trying not to stare. She was about Boyer's age, Sullivan guessed, but she was hardly the dutiful overweight companion of the retired deputy police chief in his twilight years that Sullivan had expected.

"Shouldn't you have called or something?" the woman said, looking up from reading Sullivan's identification card. "It's real early."

She hadn't bothered to pull her bathrobe closed as she spoke and Sullivan could see the places where the black knit bikini stopped and her freckled, slightly aging, but deeply suntanned body began.

"I got on the road early this morning, and I didn't want to disturb anybody. I'm an old friend," Sullivan said, faking his old-friend smile.

"Jake won't be back until lunchtime," the woman said.

"This is a very nice place that you have here," Sullivan said.

"It's Jake's," the bikini woman said. Then she pointed at the high crest of a rock formation that appeared above the treetops about a mile farther down the side road that Sullivan had just traveled. "He goes up there most mornings," she said. "To hunt," she added, with a little touch of drama.

Sullivan turned and followed the direction that the woman was indicating in the air with her bright red fingernail. He paused then, half expecting to hear the sound of faraway gunfire, but he could hear nothing except for the faint sounds of the morning wind rippling off the lake surface at the bottom of the hill.

"If you want to try," the woman said, looking at Sullivan's lightweight wash-and-wear suit doubtfully, "you could go on up there."

"Maybe I will."

"I can tell you where he might be," the woman said and stepped forward toward Sullivan. She let her robe fall even more provocatively open in the front then, as she pointed to a spot near the crest of the hill where a single, gnarled oak tree stood outlined against the Texas sky. "He'd be right on the other side of that outcropping of rock."

"I think I'll give it a try," Sullivan said, and he restarted his engine. "I'm sorry to have bothered you so early."

"Be careful," the woman said, most of her low-cut-bikini-covered body clearly visible to the younger man now. "In that city suit, Jake's liable to take you for a deer or somethin', maybe even put a bullet in you by accident," she said. And then she smiled at Sullivan for the first time, as both of them thought about what a bullet hole would look like in Sullivan's lightweight tan suit.

"I'll be careful," Sullivan said as he started his car back down the gravel path that led to the main road.

At the end of the drive, Sullivan glanced in his rearview mirror. The woman was still standing in the same spot, watching him through her dark glasses. Her robe had finished undoing itself down the front and Sullivan could see her full body now, darkly tanned, and deeply wrinkled, hidden by only the two thin lines of her little black knit bikini. As Sullivan looked, a spark of early morning sunlight caught one of the stones that dangled down from her long diamond earrings.

Sullivan pulled the car out of the private drive and started down the main road. When he could no longer see the blond woman in his rearview mirror, he let his breath out and began to slowly relieve some of the tension that had built up inside him. That was a lot of woman to be keeping happy on a cop's retirement pay, he thought. It was a lot of woman to be keeping happy on any kind of pay, he added to himself then, as he drove up the hill toward Boyer's hunting grounds.

Sullivan heard a gunshot in the distance and he knew that he was getting close.

"Boyer!" he shouted, but there was no second explosion, only silence. So he pushed forward through the branches of the pine trees and finally emerged onto a narrow clearing that displayed a view directly down the tree-lined hillside of a thin slice of silver lake in the distance.

Sullivan looked hard down the hillside, but he could still see nothing but pine trees and sparkling water. He unbuttoned his suit coat and let it fall open, exposing his holstered weapon. Sullivan's fingers reached up and touched the holster's metal snap. He hesitated for a moment, finally opening the snap but leaving the weapon inside its shiny black leather pouch. He started down the hill toward the lake, the soles of his city shoes slipping along on the surface of rocks and mud and fallen leaves. Occasionally he would glance back to measure his progress against the old oak tree and the outcropping of rock at the crest of the hill near where he'd left his car, but mostly he just let his mind drift back to why he was out there, rethinking how it really all must have been on that November weekend four years earlier. He had the story pretty straight now, he thought. Suddenly though, he was looking directly into the big lead-colored openings of a double-barreled shotgun. Sullivan's eyes focused only on the circular twin barrels for several long seconds. He could feel an ice-cold fear start in the pit of his stomach and quickly spread up to clutch at his chest and throat. Only very slowly was he able to force his eyes to look above the twin metal openings to the beefy red face of the man holding the weapon. It was Boyer. Four years older, at least twenty pounds heavier, but it was unmistakably the same man that Sullivan had met that fateful night in Dallas four years before.

The big man was dressed in a red plaid hunting shirt, and the heavy, iron shotgun wasn't locked into his shoulder. Its wooden stock was down, resting against the side of his protruding stomach, but the gun's big double barrels were pointed directly at Sullivan's head.

"What the hell are you doing here?" Boyer said, cautiously eying the agent's open coat and the gun butt protruding from the holster strapped to Sullivan's shoulder.

Sullivan couldn't answer Boyer's question for a moment, and when he finally tried his voice was low and uncertain. "I'm an FBI agent; my name is Sullivan."

"I remember," Boyer said. The details of that night were probably as permanently burned into Boyer's mind as they were into his own, Sullivan thought, as he looked up at the big man's face and eyes. "Point that thing away from me, would you?"

Very slowly then and smiling broadly at Sullivan's fear, the retired deputy police chief pointed the shotgun toward the rocky ground beneath his own feet, but he continued watching Sullivan carefully and his arms and hands remained tense, ready to jump into action at the slightest movement of the agent toward his own weapon.

"I wanted to talk to you, and the woman at your place said you were up here," Sullivan said, as the twin metal barrels moved away from him. "Maybe I should have called," Sullivan added then.

Boyer only nodded a reply, but he looked at Sullivan's face closely. The fact that Sullivan hadn't called meant only one thing to the old lawman. This wasn't just a routine inquiry. It meant that Sullivan suspected him of something. That was a basic rule of investigation—surprise your suspect, don't give him time to think about how he is going to answer your questions. Boyer stared angrily at Sullivan then, letting him know now with his look that he knew why he was up there and why he hadn't called first. Finally, the retired police officer stepped past Sullivan and moved up the hillside, the way the young agent had just come, but as he did, he kept his head and eyes turned back toward Sullivan, still watching his every move.

Sullivan stayed frozen in place for several seconds, trying to catch his breath. He reached up and loosened his narrow tie from around his neck before he started up the hill after Boyer's bulky red-checkered figure.

Sullivan didn't say anything until he'd caught up to the ex-deputy police chief and was at his side. "What do you shoot up here?"

"You a hunter?" Boyer asked without turning his head to look over at the younger man.

"No, not really," Sullivan said. "Sometimes with my dad, but I'm not much at the killing part of it."

"Man in our line of work has to know how to kill," Boyer said, finally looking over at Sullivan and finding his eyes and looking deeply into them to let the younger man know just how serious he was.

"Yeah, I know," Sullivan said, and he dropped his own gaze back to Boyer's big shotgun. "I guess it could get down to that sometime."

"You stay at it long enough, it always does," Boyer said flatly.

"Well, I think if I had to . . ." Sullivan began.

But Boyer interrupted him before he could finish. "It's the thinking that kills you," he said, lifting the big shotgun back up into Sullivan's sight for emphasis. "You just gotta do it."

Both men could see the crest of the hill in front of them now. With a few more steps they would reach the sharply angled outcropping of rock that stood at its highest point.

"You've got a nice place," Sullivan said, gesturing over the crest of the hill toward where Boyer's lakefront home would soon be visible below them.

Boyer jerked his head back then and stared hard at the young agent. "Yeah," Boyer said, after his eyes searched Sullivan's face for several long seconds.

"Expensive," Sullivan said, returning Boyer's hard look with one of his own. The ex-cop turned away from Sullivan then, and without saying anything more Boyer walked quickly to the crest of the hill.

"I think someone in your department knew about the Cassidy assassination attempt in advance," Sullivan called up the last few feet of the hillside toward him then. "Knew about it and helped it get done."

"Fuck you," Boyer said, and he lifted the weight of his big shotgun up closer to his hip.

"I think it went like this," Sullivan said, ignoring both the shotgun and the look of rage on Boyer's face as he began telling the story that he'd been working on for the last four years, letting some of his pent-up anger and frustration stream out with his words. "Boyer, I think you're that someone. I think that's where you got the money to live in your big house. I think your job was to oversee everything that happened in Dallas that day. And that included making very sure that the two gunmen in Dealey Plaza got taken care of before they could talk to anybody else and lead them back to you and to the rest of the people really responsible. And Ray Towne was your boy, the one you assigned to do the 'dirty work,' while you just stayed safe and clean at police headquarters and built up a nice little 'cover story' for him. The primary plan was for Strode to be set up to look like he'd acted alone, but there were backup plans, too. All good operations have contingency plans, don't they, Boyer? It makes them harder to trace after they're executed, because the evidence always points in at least two different directions then, just like it does for this one. But the primary plan was for Strode to look like a lone assassin that day. He didn't know that, of course. He was just told that Towne would help get him and the other gunman out of the city, probably to an airport somewhere, but Strode got suspicious. And after the shots were fired in Dealey Plaza, he went back to his room and packed two things for himself before he let himself get into Towne's squad car, two things nobody else knew about—a diary that he'd been keeping on the entire operation and a gun. Towne picked him up then and drove him to the rendezvous point to meet the second gunman. My guess is that your primary plan was for the other gunman to help make certain that Towne took care of Strode at or near the rendezvous point. Two against one is always safer, right?

"But your neat little plan started to fall apart right there, didn't it? Strode had a gun on him that nobody else knew about and it was Officer Towne, not Arthur Strode, who lost the gun battle out there on the streets of south Dallas, while the second gunman just watched it all happen and then when he saw which way it went, the second gunman drove off in the same car that he'd used to clear Dealey Plaza. And you might not know this, but the second gunman drove off with Strode's diary that day too—a diary containing every detail about the conspiracy that Strode knew or could guess at. Anyway, it turned out that it was Towne, not Strode, who got shot down that afternoon. That was probably a little embarrassing for you, but you still had your backup plan. Like I said, all good security operations have a backup plan, right, Boyer? Every cop knows that."

As he talked, Sullivan didn't even care anymore if it was the smart thing to do or dangerously stupid, he just needed to say it to Boyer, just as he'd told part of it to Green, because Boyer, like Green, was the perfect audience. The retired deputy police chief was one of the few people left alive who knew that what he was saying was the truth or damn close to it, and Boyer stood silently, glaring at Sullivan while the agent poured out his theories to him.

"And while all the action was going on out there on the streets, you just sat back at police headquarters and pulled the strings, didn't you? Your part of it was to make sure the record would look good for the investigations that would follow. So you had to be ready with cover stories for both your primary and your backup plans, just in case. Creating a cover for the first part of your contingency plan was simple. Once the shooting started out there in south Dallas you figured that Towne might have a chance to not only get Strode, but the second gunman as well. And that would be all right by you, because both of them had to die sooner or later anyway, and just in case that was what wound up happening, you needed to have a plausible cover story for why Towne would have killed both of them. So you made sure that there were radio calls right after the shots were fired at the President for both Strode and for a guy matching the description of the second gunman. That way, just in case Towne did manage to shoot either one or both of them, there would be a good reason for it—shot attempting to escape. But you pulled the call on the guy in the blue plaid shirt when you found out what had happened to Towne. You knew then that the second gunman was probably going to clear Dallas safely, and your best bet was to have no trace of him at all in your records. You could go right back to your primary cover story then, that there had only been one 'shooter' in Dealey Plaza that day, not two, and just let the second gunman continue on with the rest of plan number one, which was to fly him out of Dallas and take him somewhere else, Mexico maybe or New Orleans, before he was eliminated by someone else. There would be others waiting for him at his destination and you knew that he would probably be taken care of by them. But the second gunman was smart enough to figure out that if Strode was expendable, he was, too. A pilot named Regan and a lightweight private detective named Case out of New Orleans screwed that part of it up, and their payoff was to get dropped into a Louisiana swamp a few days later.

"Meanwhile, Leo Green was the second part of your contingency plan— the Dallas part of it, wasn't he? He had always been your 'cleanup' man in Dallas. You had Green waiting to take care of the survivor of the shoot-out between Strode and Towne, but you'd expected Towne to do his job and be the one to come out of it alive. So you had Green all set up with a motive for putting Towne away a few weeks later, some bullshit beef that you put together between the two of them about payoffs and Green's nightclub, but then, when things got all screwed up in south Dallas and it turned out that it was Strode and not Towne that needed to be taken out, all you did was have Green switch targets—and somebody working for you just let Green waltz into that circus you were running in police headquarters that night and shoot Strode down right in front of everybody. The motive Green had for killing Strode wasn't as good as the setup for killing Towne, but it would have to do. Green was just made to look a little nuts and pissed off at Strode for trying to assassinate the President. I met Green. He was pretty sick, but I don't think he was crazy and I don't think he was the kind of a guy who ever went very far out on a limb, unless there was something in it for him. I don't know what you or somebody had on Green, but I know it was something big. He'd done DeSavio a lot of favors through the years and maybe one or two of those favors were serious enough that they could have gotten Green the death penalty if he didn't do exactly what you told him to do, and Green was willing to trade that something for a few years in federal prison for executing a public nuisance like Strode, particularly if, when Green walked out of prison in a few years there'd be a big bank account waiting for him and for the promise that whatever happened to him, his brother would be taken care of. But what Green didn't realize was the same thing you haven't figured out yet yourself, Boyer! And that's this—everybody connected to something this big has to die!" Sullivan quieted for a moment then and let the fact sink in on Boyer.

"Everybody," Sullivan said again, but he shouted it at Boyer this time. "Because whoever it is that's at the center of all this is smarter and more powerful than the rest of you put together, and he knows that he can't let there be anybody left anywhere in the whole damn chain of conspirators to point the way back to him.

"That's my story," Sullivan said, feeling himself starting to calm down again.

Boyer looked stunned by what he'd heard, and it took him a few seconds to recover. "If that's all true," he said finally, "why don't I just lift up this shotgun and blow your fucking head off? You and I both know that you couldn't even clear the holster on the thirty-eight or whatever the hell it is that you're wearing under your arm there, before I could pull the trigger on this thing." Boyer patted his shotgun gently with one hand as he spoke. "Ten to one you never even took the safety off on your piece before coming up here either," Boyer added confidently then.

"It's off," Sullivan said quietly, and then he met Boyer's gaze with a long steady look of his own. In the silence that followed, Sullivan could see the muscles in Boyer's arms clenching and unclenching, as if he were trying to make up his mind whether he should fire his shotgun or not. Sullivan considered reaching up and drawing his own weapon, but Boyer was right, it would be a race that he would probably lose. So he began talking instead. "But the real reason you're not going to shoot me is because you know I can't prove any of it," Sullivan said. "It took somebody pretty high up in the Department to get all the pieces to fit into place in Dallas that day and then to cover it up when it was over. Somebody who hated Cassidy and somebody who had a reputation for taking money to look the other way every once in a while. Somebody like you, Boyer, but I can't prove it. And nobody else can, either. It was all put together too well. All the players were just spokes in a lot of little wheels. None of them knew each other, or knew any other part of the story, except for their own little piece of it. You were the hub of the wheel in Dallas, and to stay safe all you had to do was to make sure that all the spokes of the one little wheel that led back to you got snipped off— Towne, Strode, how many more finally? Bill Everett, and before him, his partner—snip, snip, snip—until there was only you. But what you didn't think about was that there were wheels within wheels in this thing, Boyer. All you know about is Dallas, but there was New Orleans, too, and Mexico, and other places. Strode and this other guy had to be recruited, trained, moved into position, cover stories built—wheels within wheels, Boyer. You and I both know what that means, don't we? We both know who works that way." Sullivan paused before he spit the word out angrily at Boyer's face. "Mafia— you've been working for the goddamn Mafia, Boyer, whether you knew it or not, that's the kind of lawman you turned out to be, you son of a bitch! That's how you got your big house and your fat retirement!"

When Sullivan finished this time, Boyer began to raise the shotgun up to his shoulder, the barrels pointed at Sullivan's stomach and chest.

"Fuck you!" Sullivan lashed out the words with the enormous pent-up emotion of all the frustrated years of working out all the little pieces of the story, but his hand remained low at his sides, still making no movement toward his holstered weapon. "You're not going to shoot me, because you're not stupid. You know that I can't get to you, because you've known for a long time what I'm just finding out. Nobody wants this one solved. Nobody! Because down deep something stinks so bad in this thing that nobody wants to know the truth. Maybe not even me anymore," Sullivan said, dropping his head and arms in disgust. "I used to want to know," Sullivan said then. "But I'm not sure that I do anymore. Almost everybody connected to it is dead now, and you'll be dead, too, soon enough."

Sullivan managed to look back up at Boyer's face one last time. There was a real fear in the older man's eyes and Sullivan knew that somewhere along the way Boyer had figured that last part of it out for himself, too. "Wheels within wheels," Sullivan said again. "That's all you are to them, Boyer. When the time's right, they'll come for you, too. It won't be me they find out here," Sullivan turned and swept his hand back down the hillside to display Boyer's hunting grounds. "But you," Sullivan said, "you'll be the hunting accident, not me. I think it's about time now, too. There's no one left for you to clean up for them. Mr. and Mrs. Della-Rosa, Billy Everett, and all the rest, spokes in a wheel cut off one by one to protect the single man at the center—but it turns out that you're just a spoke in a wheel yourself, Boyer, a little spoke in somebody else's bigger wheel, and now it's time for them to cut you off, too!"

Sullivan wound up shouting it all up the hillside at Boyer's frightened face. It wasn't the way that Sullivan had planned it. He had come there to ask questions, not answer them, but there weren't really any questions left to ask, none that Boyer would give any real answers to anyway. Sullivan knew most of what had really happened without Boyer's help anyway, and some of what would happen next. He had almost as many answers as Boyer did. He had just wanted to say it to him, let him know that he really hadn't gotten away with any of it, and Sullivan had wanted to see his face when he told him the part about them coming for him, too, because that was as true as the rest of it, and both he and Boyer knew it. Once you started something like this, it didn't stop until it came full circle, Sullivan thought, and that circle was closing back in on Boyer now. Sullivan's only regret was that he couldn't penetrate right to the heart of the mystery and look into the eyes of the one who had started all this violence, look at that person's eyes in that final moment when they understood the truth of it too, just as he was looking into Boyer's tightened eyes now, but he wasn't going to get to do that, Sullivan thought. He was just a junior agent in a very big organization and looking at Boyer, as the full realization of his self-imposed death sentence passed over his face, was just going to have to be enough.

Sullivan stared up the hill at him and watched Boyer's grip on the shotgun weaken and its twin barrels tip back down and point toward the ground.

Finally, Boyer called to him, "I could have shot you, Sullivan, and no one, no one in the state of Texas, no one in your own agency, no one in the whole fucking world would have given a good goddamn!" Boyer said and then paused, feeling the weight of the big twin-barreled shotgun in his hands.

Sullivan thought about it for a second. "You're about right," he said. "Enjoy your big house," Sullivan added then, as he pushed by the ex-cop and started back down the other side of the hill toward his parked car. "I'll read about you in the papers," the agent said as he walked away.

Boyer called after him, "Unless I read about you first!"

Sullivan found his car and drove it back down the hill toward Dallas, but Boyer's final words kept ringing in his ears—and all he could see was the image of the big twin barrels of Boyer's shotgun pointed directly at him. Suddenly the weapon that he was wearing strapped to his own chest began to feel brutally heavy, weighing him down, making him feel like something that he had never wanted to become. He saw the young, frightened face of Billy Everett then, and the old lined face of Mrs. Della-Rosa, and then the face of Leigh Hodges and of the lawyer Garrett, all the other poor dead people. He slammed on his brakes and flung the car door open. He could see the lake through the trees at the side of the road and he ran toward it. When he was only a few yards from the edge of the water, he reached up and removed the heavy pistol from its shoulder holster. Without hesitating, he threw it out over the surface of the lake and watched it sink below the rippling silver-blue surface.

CHAPTER
39

Dressing in the dark before dawn in strange hotel rooms, a speech before breakfast, lunches, and dinners, and meetings with local politicians, standing in the snow in lonely shopping centers, campaign planes and long bus rides, rousing speeches and loud brass bands, seemingly endless hands to shake and hopeful eyes to look into, motorcades, reporters and television cameras, and thousands of repetitious questions to be answered, and occasionally a noisy, happy crowd to wave at and to draw love and energy from—Jack Cassidy was running for the presidency again.

"How does it feel, eight years later, to be back in New Hampshire doing it all over again?" a reporter asked him, as the candidate tried to work his way through the crowded lobby of his Manchester hotel.

Jack looked up at the familiar face of the reporter who had asked the question. "You tell me, Walt. You were here with me eight years ago, weren't you?" Cassidy said smiling. But not waiting for his own question to be answered, the candidate pressed on through the crowd toward the elevators at the rear of the lobby. "I think Yogi Berra said it best, 'Coming back is like déjà vu again,' " Jack said, and then he added with a smile, "but I don't think that he was talking about New Hampshire."

Another reporter called out, "So you can go home again?" There was an open elevator door waiting for Cassidy now, but for the moment the candidate chose not to enter it. Instead he turned back to the small group of reporters and other onlookers. "Yes, if you mean the White House."

"What you're doing is wrong," a woman's voice shouted at him, and Jack could see the television cameras hurriedly moving their lights and sound equipment in the direction the words had come from. "You're tearing the Democratic Party apart, just to make yourself President again!" The accusation cut into Jack and hurt him deeply. "The decision that I made to enter the primary here in New Hampshire was a very difficult one for me to make," he began, and as he attempted to answer the question, he could see the television cameras returning to focus on him again. He could feel the warmth of their lights of his face and chest and he could hear the soft steady whirring of their machine-fed strips of film. But when he spoke he didn't speak to the cameras; instead, he spoke directly to the woman at the rear of the crowd who had asked the question. He'd heard the accusation, or ones very similar to it, many times since he'd arrived in New Hampshire and announced that he was going to run against the President in the state's primary, but each time the question had been asked, he'd chosen to answer it as honestly as he could, because he knew that it was the issue that lay at the very heart of the election, and how the voters viewed it would determine if he or Gardner would succeed in New Hampshire, and which of them would win the Party's nomination for the presidency in 1968. "But in the last analysis I came to believe," he continued, "that an honest and complete discussion of the vital issues that lie before the nation can in the end not harm my Party, but can only serve to strengthen it." Cassidy continued to look directly through the crowd at the woman who had asked the question. "And so, I've chosen to run against the President at this time because I believe that many of the policies of the current administration are themselves damaging the Democratic Party and must be challenged," he added decisively. Then he waited for a moment, trying to determine if the woman wanted to respond, but she remained quiet and so, finally, Jack turned back for the waiting elevator.

God, that was a lot of work to try to quiet one person's voice against you, Jack thought, as the elevator doors closed behind him and the metal platform began its ascent toward the top floor of the hotel. But that was the way that New Hampshire had to be worked. You had to move slowly, work it county by county, town by town, neighborhood by neighborhood, even block by block. And finally, near the end, you had to work it face by face, voter by voter, particularly if what you're trying to do is win a primary against a seated President and fly in the face of two hundred years of political tradition. There were very few deals to be cut in New Hampshire, very few blocks of votes to be delivered; you had to come here and stand with and talk to the people and let them see you close up, hear your voice, answer their questions, let them "take the measure of you," as the New Englanders say. And as he thought about it, Jack could feel his confidence building. And that was his real edge here, he thought, as the elevator doors began to open onto the hotel's top floor. He was here with them and Gardner was not. The President had decided to stay in Washington and let his aides run the campaign in New Hampshire, and in the end, Jack thought, it won't be the polls or the television ads, or the politicians' endorsements, or what I say, or even the policies of the President, but the fact that I'm here and he's not that will settle the matter. And what that meant was that he was going to win this election.

As Jack stepped out of the elevator, he could see O'Connor waiting for him at the far end of the hall. There was a big smile spread all over the old Irish politician's face and under his arm he held a fat computer printout.

"We've got some new numbers, Jack," he said as the candidate stepped out of the elevator and began to make his way down the hall toward him.

"And?"

"And you're within five points of him," O'Connor said. "Five points of an incumbent with less than two weeks left in the campaign!"

"That's good progress," Jack said, carefully understating the excitement that he felt at the news.

" 'Progress'?" O'Connor said. "It's goddamned glorious, is what it is! And the 'undecided' has grown, too. It's back up to fifteen percent. That means it's moving our way. We've got him, Jack. We've got the son of a bitch!"

"It does look good," Jack said. Out of the corner of his eye he could see more staff people beginning to move down the hall toward him. He had only a half hour allotted between appearances to rest and to change clothes for the dinner that he was scheduled to attend that night back across town, and he wanted to be alone with Suzanne for as long as they could manage before they had to leave for it, so he stepped carefully past O'Connor and started toward his private room at the end of the hall. "Anything else?"

"Anything else?" O'Connor said, his voice incredulous. "I tell the man that he's just about to make history, do the impossible, perform a political miracle, and he asks me: 'Is there any . . .' "

"Frank," Cassidy said, cutting his friend off in midsentence, "I want a few minutes of privacy before dinner. I'm very pleased, believe me. But we haven't won it yet. There's still another twelve days to go, and a hell of a lot can happen between now and then. We both know that." Jack continued toward his room.

"Oh, one thing," O'Connor called after him. "Allen called from Washington. He says that he has to talk with you right away."

Jack stopped and turned back to his aide. "Did he say why?"

"No, just that he had to see you right away, and that it was urgent."

"Urgent?" Cassidy's voice showed his surprise. Rozier knew how tightly scheduled he was between now and the election, and Allen was not the kind of man who made a request like that unless it was absolutely vital. "Call him back and tell him I'll see him first thing in the morning," Jack said. What the hell could Allen want that was so damn important? And what was it going to cost him and the campaign? Jack could feel a strange uneasiness beginning to replace the optimism he'd felt only a few seconds earlier.

"You smell like fish," Denise said.

Slowly, Sullivan looked over at her. He'd been so lost in his own thoughts, he'd almost forgotten that she was there. "I'm on a stakeout," he said vaguely. He didn't notice when the puzzled look on Denise's face failed to go away.

Denise finally just laughed at the silliness of his answer, but then she couldn't resist. "Sounds pretty fishy to me," she said, smiling, and Sullivan reached for a pillow and tossed it at her. Denise ducked it easily and moved in toward him, pressing herself close, until she was half sitting and half lying on the white plastic beanbag couch next to him, but still his thoughts seemed to be drifting away from her. "It's back, isn't it?" she said softly then, finally understanding.

Sullivan lowered his eyes from the plaster-sprayed ceiling of her apartment and looked down at her lightly freckled face. "Sure," he said simply, after he'd found her face again. "You're right. It's back."

They were both quiet then, and in the silence Denise slid her soft body farther forward on top of his. Finally, responding to the sweetness of her weight, Sullivan moved his hand under the back of her short skirt and slipped his fingers inside the waistband of her underwear and pressed his open hand flat against the warmth of her flesh. He leaned over and kissed her softly on the top of the mess of red-blond curls that covered her head.

"This guy Lopata or Lopez, whatever the hell his name is, it turns out he isn't dead after all, or at least he wasn't as of late last November, when he was supposed to be."

As soon as he'd said it, he could feel Denise's body tighten under her light cotton dress. "I'm sorry," Sullivan said. He shared her feelings of powerlessness and fear, but there it was again, still following him. "It just happened. I was running something else, this stakeout that Grissum and I are on and . . ." Sullivan started to apologize, but before he could finish he seemed to run out of words, and so he just stopped.

"You're back with Grissum?" Denise said.

"Uh-uh, at my request," Sullivan said. Then, catching something in Denise's tone, he asked, "Why?"

"Oh, nothing," she said.

But Sullivan's detective instincts had taken over by then. "You went out with him, didn't you?" Sullivan said, as the truth of the sum of a lot of little hints and pieces of information that he'd picked up over the years finally added up.

Denise answered slowly, obviously embarrassed. "Yes, a couple of times," she admitted. "It was a long time and about twenty pounds ago." She patted her own leaner hip then just below where Sullivan was caressing her to remind them both of the weight that she had managed to lose over the last few years.

"You sleep with him?" Sullivan said. But when Denise didn't answer right away he began to feel foolish. He thrust his hand down deep between her legs then and held her hard, squeezing with his full hand pressed tightly against her. "I said, did you ever sleep with the guy?" Sullivan said.

Denise let out a small scream. "No! Your hands are like ice!" She laughed and his grip relaxed slightly then, but his fingers remained firmly in place between her legs. "It was years ago in the old apartment. All we did . . ." She could feel the hand beginning to slowly tighten. "All we did," she repeated, but faster and louder this time, "is hang around and drink and watch TV." The hand struck again and Denise screamed and laughed, as she blurted out the rest of it. "And we went to the movies once or twice!"

The hand relaxed but still stayed cupped firmly between her legs as a warning. "Is that it?" Sullivan said.

"Yeah, yeah," Denise managed, almost out of breath now. "Look, I wasn't exactly Miss Popularity in those days, you might remember. He came in a couple of times to see the lawyer that I was working for. He asked me out. I went." Getting courageous, she challenged Sullivan with a direct look and added, "I did go out with other people before you, you know?"

"I guessed, when I saw that you had kids," Sullivan said. "But Grissum . . ." He let his voice trail off in disgust to let Denise know how he felt.

Denise shrugged her shoulders. "He was a nice guy. I don't know why he bothered though. He never tried anything."

"What if he had?" Sullivan said, tightening his hand into striking position again.

"Jim, are you serious?" Denise said. There was something about Sullivan's look now and the way he had kept up the questions that was starting to worry her.

"No," Sullivan said. "It's just that . . ." His voice trailed off and then he started over again. "I don't know, I guess it was just sort of a surprise. I'm with the guy almost every day, and you . . ." Sullivan stopped again before saying the truth. "It just makes me feel like some kind of a jerk or something, that's all," he said sadly. Then he removed his hand from inside her underwear and looked back up toward the ceiling. As he did, he was truly surprised at the intensity of his own feelings. Jesus, it was just a date, he told himself, but the feelings still didn't disappear.

"Jim," Denise said firmly, "look at me." She took his head in her hands then and slowly Sullivan turned his eyes back to her. "It was nothing," she said meaningfully. "Nobody was anything until you."

She watched his face then. It was the closest that either of them had ever come to saying what they truly felt about each other. Denise could see the start of a tear in Sullivan's eye, and his face was serious and deeply touched like the face of a very dear little boy.

"I'm sorry," he said, his voice full of emotion. "So much has been happening to me, so much that I never counted on . . ." he said. "I just thought I had my life all figured out and I guess that I didn't."

"Thirty-year man?" Denise smiled.

Sullivan nodded his head in small uncertain movements.

"Kiss all the girls and make them cry?"

Sullivan nodded his head again, but the smile was spreading now from Denise's face to his own.

"Big, tough FBI man?" Denise said and then collapsed down to press her cheek against Sullivan's chest, putting her face as close to his heart as she could, until she could hear it pounding with life inside his heavily muscled chest.

"I was going to do it all and I was going to do it alone," Sullivan whispered, his heart beating even faster.

"And a silly, slightly overweight, curly-headed legal secretary with two crazy kids and an ex-husband wasn't in the plan, was it?" Denise said.

"Unh-unh," Sullivan said honestly through the small irregular opening in his throat, but then he added quickly, "You're not those things."

Denise smiled, but Sullivan couldn't see her, because the side of her face was still pressed tightly against his shirt front. "Most of them. Not silly, maybe," she said. She was wearing the gold earrings formed in the shape of the peace symbol and she reached up and touched one of them lightly before adding, "I'm trying not to be, anyway." She stopped then and raised her face up to eye level to look directly at Sullivan again.

"I'm not going to keep all those promises that I made to myself, am I?" Sullivan said, his expression very serious.

"Which ones?"

"I always told myself that I'd die a bachelor."

"I think you lied," Denise said softly and with just a touch of shyness.

"Yeah, I think I did, too," Sullivan whispered back hoarsely, before he let the beautiful woman lying on top of him kiss him. Strangely she kissed him first very tenderly on the eyes and only then on the mouth. Sullivan had never considered himself the kind of a person who would be kissed on the eyes, but, as he thought about it, he realized that he'd never felt happier in his entire life than he did at that moment.

"Jim," Denise said as she lifted her face slowly away from him.

"Yeah."

"Some of those promises that you made were worth keeping. Not the agent-with-a-girl-in-every-city ones, but the other ones—the truth-justice-and-American-way ones," Denise said, smiling down at him.

Sullivan nodded his head back in agreement.

"I'd like to help you keep those," she said.

"Thank you," Sullivan said, and he nodded his head in acceptance of her offer.

They were both quiet for a moment then. In the silence Denise untangled her body slowly from Sullivan's and then she stood up and returned to the chair across from him. "You have to do something about it now, don't you?"

"Yes," Sullivan said, "I do. The main reason I backed off before was because I thought this guy Lopata was dead, but if he isn't—that changes everything."

"You've got to see Cassidy, then."

Sullivan slowly nodded in agreement.

"How?"

"I don't know for sure, but I'll find a way," he said.

"You've given up on the Bureau?"

"And vice-versa, I think," Sullivan said, trying to sound casual about it, but inside it hurt to think about it. "I don't have any choice," he said, and then he paused for several long seconds before he told her the worst of it. "You see, I think now that the Bureau might be part of it," he said. "And that means I've got to find a way to get to Cassidy as soon as I can. I've got to warn him."

There were five photographs face up on the desktop in front of Jack. All five photos were of good quality, clear and sharply focused. Cassidy was looking at them now for the first time and he studied each picture carefully. It was a rare moment, Jack thought, when a man can look into the faces of other human beings who had conspired to murder him and had almost succeeded in doing it. It made his own flesh grow cold and the inside of his stomach twist with horror.

Jack looked at the woman's face first, lifting the closest of the shiny black-and-white photographs that Rozier had spread out across the hotel's desktop. The light from the lamp above it shimmered off its glossy surface and displayed a woman in late middle-age. The slightly dark cast of the woman's skin was apparent even in the black-and-white shadings of the photograph. The face was decidedly lean and its skin weathered and dry, but the eyes were still hard bright black and they seemed to be staring directly up into his own face.

Jack remembered that he had once met the woman and her husband. Looking down at the image of her face now, he remembered her husband's powerful handshake and he remembered, too, the blue-and-white-and-red flag displayed across the stage behind them and the wildly cheering crowd, as the woman had bent forward toward him and kissed him lightly on the cheek. He remembered then, in a new surge of memory, touching her elbow lightly to help her balance as she leaned close to him and the soft way that the silk of her dress felt to his hand and even the clean fresh smell of the flowers that the woman had worn in her dark hair that night. Less than two months later, Jack thought, her husband had died on a bloody Cuban beach in an invasion that, as President, he had known about in advance and had approved. In the end, though, he had also been the one who had issued the order that held American planes on the ground, while men like General Martine had died waiting for them to arrive. As he thought about it, Jack could look at the woman's face no longer. He turned instead to the second photograph. He had never met the man that they called the "Boss of Bosses" in the southeastern United States, the territory that included Miami and New Orleans and that some investigators believed spread all the way across Texas to include Houston and Dallas and maybe beyond. The face in the photograph was small and misshapen and strikingly ugly, the eyes lost behind heavy square-cut dark glasses, but Jack found it difficult to turn away.

"Unions that DeSavio controlled contributed over one hundred thousand dollars to your campaign in 1960," Rozier said from where he was standing at the far side of the New Hampshire hotel room.

"I guess he didn't think that he got his money's worth," Jack said, smiling grimly but still unable to look away from the powerfully cruel and ugly face in the photograph on the table below him.

"When Tim was Attorney General, he had a file this thick on Mr. DeSavio and his union," Rozier said, indicating with his thumb and forefinger a file several inches high. "It was no secret that the Justice Department was going to do whatever it could to get an indictment against him," Rozier continued. "They've moved slowly on it since Tim's left, but it has continued to move, which is probably a surprise to Mr. DeSavio," Rozier said. "It turns out that it wasn't just Jack and Tim Cassidy who wanted his operations stopped, it was the law and the American people, but I don't think DeSavio believed that four years ago."

Jack reached for the next photograph.

"That's a man called Costello," Rozier said. "He's DeSavio's number-one boy."

The photograph showed the face of a grossly overweight, middle-aged man. The skin of the big man's face looked very white and his eyes appeared to be mere slits half lost in the layers of loosely sagging flesh that surrounded them.

"You're becoming quite an expert," Cassidy said, trying to keep his tone light, as he glanced back over his shoulder at Rozier.

"I'm a reporter at heart, I guess," Rozier said, returning his friend's smile. "And this is a hell of a story, even though it may be one that I never get a chance to write."

Jack nodded and then turned back to the desk and took a final look down at the faces of the two men and one woman who had planned and arranged for his own violent death. Looking at the faces made a cold shiver move through his body, starting at the base of the spine and then spreading slowly up to the tip of his neck, and he delayed looking at the photos of the other two men for the moment.

"I think it was what the underworld call a 'hit,' Jack," Rozier continued coolly. "Bought and paid for by Mrs. Martine. She knew DeSavio from the old days in Havana. He owned gambling operations there, and it was common knowledge how much he hated you. They moved in some of the same circles in New Orleans in the early sixties. It would have been easy enough for her to approach either DeSavio or Costello about it." Rozier tried to keep his voice calm, almost nonchalant, as he explained the facts as he understood them from reviewing the Cuban material that Estanza had given to him. The information given to him was apparently only a small fraction of what the Cubans had in their possession, though, only a few pages from a quite lengthy diary and a few heavily edited copies of pages from the statement given by this man Lopata when he had been arrested by the Cuban authorities in late 1964. But with a lot of hard work, Rozier had been able to combine the information contained in the Cuban material with the contents of the FBI file that he'd found among Tim's things in Washington, and by doing some research of his own he pieced together a cohesive and what he believed to be credible picture of many of the events that had led up to the attempt on the President's life, a picture that had never appeared in the official FBI report. But there was still a great deal that he didn't understand. What was St. Christopher's Island? And why were the Cubans so certain that the information that they were still holding would be so politically damaging to Jack? And why didn't the FBI's final report on Dallas contain any reference at all to any of these matters? Rozier could only hope that Jack would be able to supply the rest of the answers, after he'd heard the story that Rozier was now ready to tell him.

"And this man?" Cassidy asked, picking up the fourth photograph. It showed a short, dark-haired man with a frighteningly thin face and penetrating dark black eyes. The man was standing in profile behind a barred window. He was smoking a cigarette and the smoke curled around him, obscuring his face in a mysterious veil.

"The materials that I've seen indicate that he was the second gunman in Dallas that day," Rozier said, his voice having difficulty disguising its true anger now. "He fired on the motorcade from in front somewhere, probably from what they've been calling the 'grassy knoll' at the far end of the plaza."

Cassidy nodded his head then, remembering. The shaded grassy area at the south end of Dealey Plaza was a very real place to him, and his memory of it came back to him clearly now.

"From what I can tell, he fired at least two shots, including in all probability the one that struck you in the head." Rozier lowered his voice as he said the words that he felt he had to say now, but when he'd finished he could tell that they had still hit Jack hard. He could see his friend's eyelids flutter and the muscles of his face tighten, as if he were reliving the moment and the sudden, hard jolt of pain that he must have felt when the bullet had exploded against his skull.

"He's in prison?" Cassidy said, needing to distract himself from the horrible memory by lifting the photograph and studying it carefully.

"No, sir, he's dead now," Rozier said. "Apparently he attempted to enter Cuba illegally sometime during the fall of 1964, but he was arrested and held in Muiriel Prison, on Cuba's west coast, until late last year." Rozier pointed at the photograph in Jack's hands then. "He attempted to use his knowledge of the conspiracy to assassinate you to gain his release. He gave a statement to his captors right after he was arrested. During my last meeting with Estanza, I was given a copy of a few selected sections of it to review. Apparently Lopata was smart enough to know that Castro could use the information that he could give him, particularly the part pointing at Mrs. Martine, to seriously damage the anti-Communist Cubans in this country and . . ." Rozier hesitated now.

"Yes," Jack said, urging his friend to explain the rest of it, however difficult it might be for both of them.

"And damaging to you," Rozier said finally.

"Did this man Estanza give you any clue as to precisely what that information might be?" Jack asked quietly.

"No, not exactly. There are big gaps in the materials that I've been given. The Cubans apparently didn't want me to see all the information that they have. They gave me only enough of Strode's diary to confirm that it was his handwriting, and I was given even less of the Lopata statement. So I'm not certain what it is that they believe will be so damaging to you personally, but when I met with this man, Estanza, he did mention a place called St. Christopher's Island. There was nothing in the materials I was given though that gave any clue as to what it has to do with any of the rest of it. He just said to tell you that they knew about St. Christopher's Island." Rozier shrugged his shoulders, indicating that it didn't make any sense to him. "I looked it up," he continued. "St. Christopher's Island is a small island off the coast of Florida. There's not much information on it. From what I can tell, it's controlled exclusively by the Navy, but there's no indication of . . ."

Cassidy held up his hand then, stopping Rozier in midsentence. "I know about St. Christopher's Island," Cassidy said, his voice cold and hard. He stood up then and walked to the window of the hotel room, his back toward Rozier.

Rozier stood near the desk behind him, waiting for his friend to explain, but the silence between them grew long and awkward, until it became apparent that Jack was not yet ready to say anything to him. Rozier reached down and began anxiously sorting through the files and papers on the surface of the desk, until he found the file that he had been looking for. "The Cubans claim that this second gunman had Strode's diary with him when he left Dallas," Rozier said, but still Cassidy didn't turn back from his place at the window or alter his gaze from its fixed position, looking out over the streets of New Hampshire. "As I say, they gave me a copy of a few pages of the diary," Rozier continued. "And I had a handwriting expert look at it. He's certain that it's Strode's handwriting. The entries are dated during the period leading right up to Dallas. There's even an entry the night of November twenty-first. It's incredible stuff, Jack. Even from what I've been able to put together from the bits and pieces they gave me, it appears that what the Cubans have tells an entirely different story about Dallas than the one contained in the final FBI report. Strode was far from being the lone mentally deranged assassin motivated by some vague pro-Communist sympathies that the official report concluded." Rozier's voice was racing as he continued to explain to Jack what he'd learned. "Both Strode and Lopata were recruited by DeSavio's people. Although he didn't realize it until it was too late, Strode was set up from the very first to make it appear as if he'd acted alone. He was made to look like a loner, mentally ill, a Communist, with a deep personal hatred for you. In other words, a perfect cover story, one that the American public would be all too eager to buy, but in reality every step Strode took from late 1962 on was choreographed by DeSavio and his people. Apparently, Strode wasn't as big a fool as they thought he was though. He seems to have kept notes on everything that happened to him, and if we can believe Estanza, the entire story of what really happened is set out in his diary." Rozier indicated the sample pages from Strode's diary spread out across the surface of the hotel desk below him, but still Cassidy didn't turn back into the room. He stayed at the window, his hands tensely clasped behind his back, his eyes looking out over the streets below him.

"And what Strode didn't know for certain," Rozier continued, "he made some very educated guesses about. He was born in the New Orleans French Quarter and he'd seen its 'underworld' in operation since he was a kid."

"Who has the actual diary now?" Cassidy asked.

"I'm not sure," Rozier said. "The first time that I spoke to Estanza, he indicated that his government did. It was part of what they were willing to trade, the diary and this man Lopata along with his written statement, but when I met with Estanza in New York this last time, he was evasive about it. I think all we can be certain of now is that even if somehow they've lost control of the original diary, they must at least have retained copies of it. Estanza seemed very confident of their position. At my last meeting with him, he gave me an envelope full of documents. Included in that package was a list of the political and economic changes between Cuba and the United States that Castro is demanding that you support in exchange for his government's silence in these matters."

Only then did Cassidy turn and walk back to the desk littered with files and papers and photographs.

"And so I'm being asked now to use whatever power I have, or that I may have in the future, to help force political concessions in favor of the Cuban government. And in exchange, Castro is willing to remain silent about the identity of the people really responsible for Dallas, and he's willing as well to suppress other information in his possession that he says is somehow politically damaging both to me and to the anti-Castro forces in this country."

"Yes, sir," Rozier said.

"And what about this FBI file? What do we know about it?" Cassidy said, letting the photograph that he had been holding drop from his hand back down onto the desktop.

"I don't think Tim could have had it very long," Rozier said. "I doubt that he could even have had time to read all of it." Rozier paused then, reviewing his thoughts. "It was apparently kept by an agent named Sullivan. I checked the logs in Tim's office. He met with a man named James Sullivan on the afternoon of November twenty-third of last year, right before Tim left for Saigon. My guess is that he must have received the file then. I wish to God that he'd said something to me about it, but he didn't," Rozier said sadly. "I guess there wasn't time."

"He mentioned it to me," Jack said.

"He did?" Rozier sounded surprised.

"Yes," Cassidy said. "Tim was going to look into it. We talked about it briefly before he left for Saigon. I didn't take it very seriously then. Obviously I should have." Cassidy's voice was full of disappointment.

"You couldn't have known," Rozier said.

"Does the Sullivan file reach the same conclusions as the information that's coming from the Cubans?" Cassidy asked, his voice crisp and businesslike again.

"Yes, pretty much," Rozier said. "I haven't been able to cross-check everything yet, but Sullivan was working on a theory of a second gunman too." Rozier bent down and shuffled through the papers on the desk again, until he came up with the FBI artist's sketch of the dark-haired man that Sullivan had seen in Dealey Plaza. "This is the man Sullivan was looking for. Drop twenty or thirty pounds off him and he could easily be the same man," Rozier said, setting the sketch down next to the picture of the man photographed in the Cuban prison camp. Cassidy compared the faces in the two pictures carefully as Rozier continued. "Sullivan's reports indicated that he was convinced that someone pretty high up in the Dallas Police Department was involved. Now that fits almost precisely with the story that Lopata told the Cuban authorities and with what Strode wrote in his diary. The rest of it fits together, too. Sullivan even managed to follow this second gunman's trail out of Dallas to Mexico, but finally it died out on him. No one seems to know where this man went then though, until he was arrested trying to enter Cuba almost a year later. I've read all three sources of information thoroughly," Rozier said. "The FBI file, the excerpts from Strode's diary, and the parts of the written statement Lopata gave to the Cuban prison officials that I was supplied with. Read together, they appear to show a complicated pattern of death and deception, one that's still continuing to this very day—and the entire pattern all with one purpose, to hide the identity of the people really responsible for the attempt on your life." Rozier pointed at the photographs on the desk in front of Cassidy then. "The people really responsible," he said again. "Joseph DeSavio, Anthony Costello, and Sylvia Martine."

Rozier was quiet then, and in the silence he reached for the charcoal sketch in the FBI materials. "It was a very complex operation, Jack. If there was a flaw, it was that they underestimated both Strode and his second gunman," Rozier said quietly.

Cassidy shook his head slowly back and forth. "No, Allen, there wasn't any flaw even there," Cassidy said. "These men were chosen for the job for a reason, a very specific and a very good reason," Jack said.

"What do you mean?" Rozier asked, not understanding, but when Cassidy didn't answer him right away, he went on. "Jack, I'd like your permission to see this through," he said. "I'd like your help in taking a look at the government's files on Lopata and on Strode. I want to see just what the Bureau and Central Intelligence had on both of them prior to November of 1963. My guess is that they had plenty and that's why Summers blocked Sullivan's attempts to investigate these issues properly. The Director just wasn't willing to risk having the Bureau look even partially responsible for what happened to you in Dallas. I think he was afraid that the press would attack the Bureau for knowing about Strode in advance and still not being able to protect you from him, but I think there's even more to it than that. I don't know just what it is yet, but I'd like to get to the bottom of it. I'd like to look into it all, Jack. I think we can really nail Summers on this."

Cassidy shook his head very slowly. "No, Allen, the government files won't tell you anything."

"How do you know?" Rozier was even more puzzled now. "Summers blocked Sullivan's reports before they got to either Tim or to you, didn't he?"

"Yes," Cassidy said. "Neither Tim nor I ever saw Sullivan's reports. I'm certain of that. Tim would have told me."

"Jack, that's a crime. Summers was trying to cover up his own department's incompetence by not letting anyone else see those reports."

"Allen, I'm afraid it's not that simple," Cassidy said decisively. "I appreciate all you've done, but I have to ask you to stop now. There's a great deal here that you don't know about. None of this can go any further," he said, pointing at the documents on the desk and issuing the order without any reservation in his voice. "Do you have a problem with that?"

Rozier felt hurt and a little angry. He moved slowly to a chair by the window and sat down. "Jesus, Jack," he said, the energy drained from him now. "I don't understand," he continued. "The political damage would be negligible. From what I can see, the Cubans are exaggerating the potential damage that it could do to you. I know that it doesn't look good that it was anti-Castro people and not Communists behind the attempt on your life. And it brings out the Bay of Pigs problem all over again, too, and I know none of that is good politics, but it's not that serious compared to what Summers has done. It just seems to me that there's a lot more here than some temporary political damage—even with the primary so close. But we could easily hold it until after . . ."

Cassidy raised his hand, cutting Rozier off. "Allen, I know how difficult this is for you, but you're just going to have to trust me for now. All I can say is that there is one hell of a lot going on that doesn't show up in any of what you've seen so far," Cassidy said, pointing at the stack of documents on the desk in front of Rozier. "And I want to leave it that way," Jack continued. "Any additional materials that may come into your possession, the remainder of the diary or the rest of this man Lopata's statement or whatever, I want you to pass them along to me immediately. Don't review them yourself. Is that understood?"

"Yes, sir," Rozier answered promptly.

"There is one thing that you can do though," Cassidy paused then. "I assume that you haven't spoken with Agent Sullivan yet."

"No, sir."

"The important thing now is to get to him. Find Sullivan and tell him that I need to speak with him as soon as possible, but as for the rest of it,

I'd like you to be absolutely quiet about it, not a word to anyone, not even to Agent Sullivan."

Rozier took a deep breath. He remembered Estanza's earlier words of warning to him now. "Be very careful, Mr. Rozier, the middle is a very dangerous place to be," the old diplomat had said. "Be careful"; it was a little late for that now, wasn't it? Rozier thought, laughing to himself. Was it careful to quit his job as a reporter for a major newspaper and hire on with a thirty-nine-year-old, second-term Senator who was going to try to become the next President of the United States? Was it careful to meet with Communist agents in the middle of the night and become the go-between in an attempt to blackmail the American government? Or to steal government files and smuggle them out of the White House? He had stopped being careful and started following his own instincts a long time before, and he knew the decisions that he made now wouldn't be any different. He trusted Jack Cassidy—end of story. "Of course," Rozier said, smiling at his friend. "Whatever you say."

"Good. I want you to talk to him as soon as possible then," Cassidy said. "I think Agent Sullivan could be in a great deal of danger."

After Rozier had left the room, Cassidy was alone with the photographs of the four men and one woman who had planned and almost accomplished his own murder.

He was late for a breakfast meeting downstairs in the hotel's ballroom, but his eyes refused to leave the photographs spread out across the desktop. He looked first into the faces of his two would-be executioners—Lopata and Strode. Flickers of madness danced out at him from their eyes and Jack looked away quickly. Their motives were clear and understandable to him, at least as understandable as madness can be to another human being. But he paused a little longer on the grotesquely twisted features of the little man called the "Boss of Bosses" in the southeastern United States and then again on the grossly overweight face of DeSavio's number-one lieutenant. If you looked deeply enough into evil and greed you find only fear, Cassidy decided. Fear and greed and madness, motives for murder as old as history, even if the victim was a king or a president. He understood all four of the men's faces, he told himself then, but it was the woman's who touched him the most deeply, and he turned to it last. The hate that he saw in the woman's eyes wasn't fueled by greed or fear or even madness, but from another emotion, one that was as old as human history too. It was moved by revenge. An eye for an eye, a tooth for a tooth, an oath of revenge for a dead husband, a promise made to herself to settle the score.

The phone rang then, but still Cassidy couldn't remove his gaze from the photograph, and after a few seconds, the ringing ended. What had motivated this woman who had commanded his death and begun all this violence? he wondered. But no, that was wrong, he decided then. She hadn't begun the violence. She, like so many others, had only continued it. The violence had begun much earlier. God knows exactly when, but somewhere buried back deep in time and in the history of her island, and Sylvia Martine had just added her name to the long list of people who had chosen to perpetuate it. His own name was on that list too, Jack realized then. He didn't like the thought, but its truth was undeniable. He had approved a military invasion of her country. He had ordered destruction and death for her people, and, by doing that, he had brought himself and his own nation into the ancient cycle of violence and death and revenge begun somewhere in an earlier time. He remembered now how he'd felt when he'd reached that decision. He'd ordered "American-sponsored" violence into the woman's country out of his great confidence that it was being done for the right reasons, and because he believed that he could control it, if and when he needed to. He would turn the killing off, he'd thought, just like an electric light switch, after there had been just the right amount of destruction and death, but only after the objectives that his country couldn't achieve politically were assured. And it would all come out for the best in the end. He would do just a little murder for the greater good of the world. Cassidy laughed at himself now. He wondered how many other powerful men had thought the same thought. Then Cassidy looked down at the face of the woman in the photograph again. Her dark eyes stared back up at him, mocking him, laughing at how naïve he'd been. The truth was, Jack thought, that violence, once it was unleashed, was beyond even the most powerful of men to control. And innocent people died as the cycle of violence swept along and it always seemed to return somehow and touch those who had helped continue it, as it had touched General Martine. It was an iron rule, wasn't it? But it was a rule that every generation, maybe every person, had to learn somehow for themselves, even presidents. There may be times when it was truly necessary for a leader to resort to violence, but it was never without its costs, never without its consequences. That's what Tim had been trying to teach him during those last months of his life, Jack thought then. Oh, dear Jesus, the violence that he'd brought his country into had come back to touch him, too, hadn't it? First in Cuba, and that violence had returned to touch him personally in Dallas, and then, another cycle of ancient violence in another part of the world that he had helped perpetuate had come back to touch him and his family in a little Southeast Asian village. An iron rule, Jack thought. He reached out and pushed the photographs away. He had been responsible for ordering violence and death more than once, he told himself sadly, and each time it had returned to touch him personally, as it always must.

"I owe you one," Sullivan said, but Grissum didn't answer. He just stayed in his stakeout position, his head and body immobile under his slouch hat and soiled khaki-colored fisherman's shirt. He obviously didn't want to talk about whatever was on the younger man's mind, but Sullivan felt compelled to continue anyway. He still couldn't really believe what Denise had told him the night before, but it was eating at him and he had to get it settled, before it drove him crazy.

"I didn't know that you went out with Denise," Sullivan said, and it sounded even more incredible to him when he finally said it out loud. "How come you never said anything?" he added angrily then.

"Huh?" Grissum said, moving his head imperceptibly toward Sullivan.

He obviously wasn't going to make this easy, Sullivan thought as he watched him. "Denise Richards," Sullivan said, pressing in on him. He wanted to get this cleared up with Grissum once and for all now.

"Oh, yeah," Grissum mumbled. But before he could explain any further, there was a sudden movement of activity in the valley; an old Volkswagen van was kicking up dust on the dirt road that led from the main highway down to the little farmhouse.

"This is it," Grissum said, and he moved up in his seat. In all the time I've been this guy's partner, I've never really been in action with him. And I sure as hell have never seen him move that fast before, Sullivan thought as he watched Grissum now. "How do you know?" the young agent asked, his mind clicking back to the immediate business before them.

"We got a tip," Grissum said.

Sullivan felt another wave of anger sweep over him then. Why hadn't Grissum said something? They'd been out there for over an hour together, plenty of time to tell him. Grissum was the senior man and Yancey routed all instructions through him, but damn it, Grissum should have told him there'd been a tip, Sullivan thought. What the hell was going on? "A tip?" Sullivan said, and an anxious feeling began deep in the pit of his stomach.

"Yeah, this morning," Grissum said, without taking his eyes off the speeding van in the valley below the road. "I would have told you, but you wanted to talk about all that other bullshit and . . ." Grissum didn't finish his sentence. The van had fishtailed to a dusty stop in front of the farmhouse. A man and a woman were getting out of it now, and Grissum reached down for the pair of binoculars that he'd left on the floor of the car.

Some of the regular members of the small "Sunnybrook Farm" community were beginning to gather to welcome the new arrivals, and Sullivan reached down for his own binoculars and joined Grissum in getting a better look. A second woman was crawling out of the back of the van, but Sullivan kept his glasses focused only on the man who had been the vehicle's driver. He was of medium height, dressed in faded jeans and a multicolored, tie-dyed T-shirt. He wore beads and sandals and his long hair and thick full beard were a blackish-gray color. It could be Shapiro, Sullivan thought, but with the long hair and beard covering his face it was impossible to tell for sure. The photographs that they had of the radical leader were all taken before he'd gone underground and they showed him clean shaven and usually wearing a coat and tie.

"Look, why don't I stay here and watch, and you can call Yancey and get some backups," Sullivan said, reminding Grissum of the procedure that they'd agreed on at the start of the stakeout. There was a bait shop less than a mile back down the road with a pay phone where they could easily make a call.

"No," Grissum said, dropping the glasses down from his face. The new arrivals had been hustled inside the farmhouse now and one of the regulars was already beginning to pull the van out of sight around to the back of the old structure.

"We're going down for him," Grissum said. Sullivan could barely believe his ears. Was this Grissum talking to him? Two-years-to-go-until-retirement Grissum?

"We don't even know for sure if it's him," Sullivan said. "That van had some kind of plates on it. Why don't we . . ."

"No," Grissum cut him off. "We're going in."

Sullivan hesitated. None of it felt right.

"I cleared it with Yancey this morning. This is the way he wants it," Grissum said, opening the car door and stepping out onto the tree-lined hillside.

"There's eight or ten people down there," Sullivan said, suddenly frightened. What the hell was it? His mind whirled with questions. He'd been in action before, but this was not the way that he'd imagined going down after Shapiro or whoever the hell it was that had just pulled up in that van. It was all moving too fast, no preparation, no backups, no time to think.

"They're just a bunch of hippie-dippies," Grissum said, leaning back in the passenger door, so that Sullivan could hear him. "If we screw around now we could lose them."

"Shit, I didn't know I had a hero for a partner," Sullivan said, as he moved reluctantly out of the car and slammed its door in frustration.

Sullivan walked to the rear of the car then, but Grissum already had the trunk door up and was reaching down to unsheath a special issue, Bureau double-gauge shotgun from its black leather carrying case. He cracked it open and checked the breech. Then, as Sullivan watched, he loaded it carefully with shells from the cartridge box that he kept in the trunk of the car. Watching the big, shiny, copper-based shells get shoved into the firing mechanism made Sullivan's stomach begin to move uneasily. Those babies could do a lot of damage, he thought.

"We really need those things?" Sullivan said, pointing at Grissum's big shotgun. After all, Sullivan thought, we're only going in against a bunch of draft-dodging kids and one middle-aged lawyer, who went around wearing beads and an earring.

"Yes," Grissum said. "The tip we got said Shapiro might be heavily armed."

There it was again; something felt wrong to Sullivan about the whole thing—tips, reports, private meetings with Yancey. What the hell else had been going on between Grissum and Yancey, that they had decided not to let him in on?

Grissum could see the confusion in Sullivan's face. "Check out what's going on?" Grissum said, pointing to the edge of the hillside. "I don't want that son of a bitch slipping out the back way on us, or something."

Sullivan hesitated, looking down at the second shotgun.

"I'll take care of that for you," Grissum said.

"Yeah," Sullivan nodded, grateful that he didn't have to fool with the heavy weapon and the big ugly shells at that moment. He walked around to the front of the car and looked down the tree-lined hillside. All looked calm below him at Sunnybrook Farm.

Grissum broke the quiet by slamming the heavy metal breech of the shotgun into place behind him.

"Everything okay down there?" Grissum approached Sullivan from the rear.

"Uh-uh," Sullivan said. "They're all inside."

"Don't fire until you see the whites of their eyes," Grissum said, handing Sullivan the heavy weapon.

Sullivan took it and lifted it with one hand. Even in his hand the big double-barreled shotgun felt wrong, too heavy and awkward. He switched it to his left hand then and let the barrel drop down toward the ground. With his right hand the young agent opened his jacket and started to withdraw his brand-new standard-issue handgun from the holster strapped beneath his armpit. The short-barreled handgun was an exact replica of the .38 police special that Sullivan had reported as "lost" only the week before, and Sullivan hadn't even found time to qualify with the shiny new replacement weapon yet. The shotgun had been Grissum's idea though, part of their cover, as outdoorsmen, he'd said. But Sullivan remembered thinking that it didn't make much sense. And he'd guessed then that Grissum just enjoyed having the heavy weapons, and that he checked them out whenever he had a chance, and so Sullivan had gone along. Now he wished that he hadn't.

"Use the fucking shotgun," Grissum said, as Sullivan started checking his new handgun.

"Okay, okay," Sullivan said, reholstering the smaller weapon and rezipping his jacket back over it. He couldn't afford any arguments with his partner now. "It just seems like a hell of a lot of firepower for what we've got down there," Sullivan said, pointing down the hillside. He returned the shotgun to his right hand, but he still held it only by its heavy wooden stock, its barrel pointed at the ground. Grissum's weapon was up at the ready, held firmly in two hands at an angle out across his chest, just the way you were supposed to do it, Sullivan thought. Down deep, Grissum was a pro, Sullivan decided, as he looked over at him. And then, remembering his own training, the younger agent imitated Grissum and moved the shotgun into its correct position with both hands out in front of his chest.

"We go down together to there," Grissum said, interrupting Sullivan's thoughts and pointing to a row of trees at the base of the hill. The treeline was less than fifty short yards from the farmhouse itself. "When I signal you," Grissum continued, "you cross that open area to the rear of the farmhouse. There's got to be an opening back there of some kind, a window, a door, something. I'm going in the front; when I do, you go in the back."

"What if there's no way in?"

"Make one," Grissum said and started down the hill. Sullivan followed after him. "How will I know when you're going in?" Sullivan whispered anxiously.

"You'll know," Grissum said, without looking back at the younger man. "I'll be the one yelling and screaming at the top of my fucking lungs."

Sullivan had to laugh. Grissum was scared too. He could hear it in his voice. The younger agent felt better just knowing that, and he began to relax just a little then. It was going to be okay, he told himself. It was natural to be scared, however the hell many times you did something like this. Jesus, after all, this one wasn't going to be too tough. It wasn't a bunch of hardcore killers waiting for them. Those kids down there were the ones who should be scared—not him. Sullivan watched Grissum moving carefully in his khaki shirt and pants down the tree-covered hillside in front of him then. He was grateful to the older agent. Grissum had taken the lead assignment and given Sullivan the easier backup job. There was a good long stretch of open ground between the safety of the tree-covered hillside and the front door of the old farmhouse. Grissum would have to cross it and then come in the front door against them alone. That job was going to be a lot tougher than just swinging around in back and coming in at them from the rear. A lot of senior agents would have done it the other way around and given the younger, inexperienced man the tougher assignment. Under all that crap on the surface, Grissum had some guts. He wasn't just the man who he'd seemed to be all those years. There was something more to him. He should have known there was, Sullivan decided. You didn't do this job for as long as Grissum had done it without there being something there. They'd reached the bottom of the hill now. Sullivan stayed inside the treeline, kneeling low. He watched Grissum for his signal. There would be no more words now, just the Bureau's standard prearranged hand signals.

The older agent was kneeling too, his eyes sweeping the open area between the rows of trees that hid him and the rickety old structure of the farmhouse in the middle of the open valley. Without looking away from his own destination, he waved one arm and signaled Sullivan to move out.

The younger agent didn't hesitate. He just let his training and his instincts take over then. Sullivan knew it was too late for any more thinking about it. It just had to be done. And staying low and letting his field of vision widen out so that he could see any dangers in the periphery, but at the same time still keeping his primary focus on the little patch of dirt that was his immediate goal at the rear corner of the old wooden structure, Sullivan crossed the open ground easily and quickly. He dove down into the dirt and hugged the earth with his elbows and stomach at exactly the spot that he'd chosen a few seconds before, and then he hooked the side of his body up tight against the back wall of the little farmhouse. When he was firmly in position, he arched his head back and let his eyes sweep around him in a full three-hundred-and-sixty-degree arc. He was safe.

He peered out at the spot in the treeline where Grissum was still kneeling. Sullivan grinned and flashed the senior man a thumbs-up sign. Grissum returned it.

Sullivan moved his attention to the rear of the farmhouse. That would be the last he'd see of Grissum, he thought, until the actual moment of contact with the suspects. He had to force himself to take a few long, deep, slow breaths, while his eyes scanned the rear of the building, looking for an opening. Sullivan was lying prone, his elbows propped up under him, the heavy shotgun slung across the inside of his arms, like a young Marine landing at Guadalcanal or wherever the hell they're landing at in Vietnam now, he thought, as his nostrils filled with the smell of the red Texas earth just inches below his nose.

Directly ahead of him there was an unlatched door flapping open in the light breeze, and the opening was smack in the middle of the rear of the farmhouse—right where he wanted it to be, a fucking piece of cake, Sullivan thought. Grissum must be psychic. Sullivan stood then and began moving slowly toward the flapping screen door. Where had he seen that door before? He could have sworn he'd seen it somewhere, but that was impossible, he'd never . . . He forced his mind to forget about it. He had to think now only about the job ahead of him. He moved his gaze from the strangely familiar screen door to the back wall of the farmhouse. There were no windows between him and the door, and he began moving a little quicker across the ground toward his objective. Imagine that bastard, Grissum, and Denise, he thought. Watching TV in the old apartment with Denise's crazy kids running around and Kit . . . And Kit . . . And . . .

Suddenly, Sullivan heard a noise behind him. Oh, sweet Jesus, he thought. I'm dead.

He turned. Grissum was there, standing behind him, the heavy shotgun up and rock hard against his shoulder, its barrels pointed straight at Sullivan's face.

No, that was all wrong, Sullivan thought in a flash. You were supposed to go in the front. I'm just covering here in the back. What was that other thought? Sullivan searched desperately for it again, as if it might save his life. Oh, Kit. Kit, of course. She'd opened the chain lock on the apartment that night. She'd never do that for a stranger, only someone . . . Grissum fired. The muzzle of his gun erupted bright orange. Sullivan could see the flash of fire in the chamber clearly. He'd never seen anything like that before. It fascinated him. No one had ever fired a gun at point-blank range at him before. No. Wrong. Once. Three years before in a North Dallas amusement park. Someone in a speeding car. Sullivan looked at the man's face behind the orange flash of light standing in front of him now. It was the same man, Sullivan knew that somehow. They hadn't just wanted Ortiz to die that night. They'd wanted to kill him, too! Grissum had been following him, his own partner. Sullivan realized it all clearly in that flash of a moment, and he even had time to think how funny it all was, if you thought about it that way— the poor dumb plodding junior agent torturing himself to think it all through and Yancey and Grissum ten steps ahead of him the whole time, before the round hit him, not in the face as he feared, but only in the chest. Oh Jesus, that's good, Sullivan thought. I was afraid of the face—the chest, that's okay. The impact only stunned him at first, like someone had thumped him hard across the heart with a baseball bat. As soon as he could, he lifted his own weapon, aimed it sloppily, and pulled the trigger. It clicked metallically, harmlessly on an empty chamber. Grissum and Yancey had thought of everything, Sullivan realized then, and the thumping feeling in his chest turned first to warmth and then to wetness and then for a brief flash he could feel the opening, shockingly big and wide and very ragged. He didn't want to look. He knew it would scare him and he didn t want to be frightened now. He wanted to be with Denise. He wanted to tell her how he felt about himself and about her, but it was Grissum who was closing in on him, his shotgun raised, still pointed at his face. He won't fire again, Sullivan thought. One wild shot in the confusion of an arrest, that could be an accident, but two at point-blank range—that had to be murder.

PART SIX

March 1968—June 1968

CHAPTER
40

There were three funeral services scheduled to be conducted that morning in the chapel on the hillside overlooking the federal cemetery in Dallas. The other bodies that were being buried that day had been flown in from Vietnam only the night before and as Jim and Nora Sullivan moved slowly out of the chapel's front door, following a few steps behind the gray metal casket that held their son, they passed within inches of another couple who stood waiting near the entrance for the services for their own child to begin. The sleeve of James Sullivan, Sr.'s, coat even brushed lightly across the shoulder of the other dead boy's father, but, embarrassed by his own grief, Mr. Sullivan refused to look up and see the sadness of the other man.

The services were being held in a federal cemetery, the final resting place of soldiers who had died in both World Wars, and Korea and now Southeast Asia, and each of their graves had been marked by a simple white cross. It seemed so big, James Sr. thought, as he looked out at row after row of the small white crosses. Surely little Jim's body will be forgotten here. He had wanted his son's body brought home and buried in the small Catholic cemetery near their own church where someday he and his wife would be buried, but the federal people who visited him had been so persuasive and it had all happened so quickly, so terribly suddenly. Maybe they were right, though, Jim Sr. thought now. Maybe his son belonged in a federal cemetery, a hero, just like those two other boys that they'd flown in from Vietnam the night before, but Jim Sr. wasn't sure.

Denise walked a few steps behind the Sullivans. She couldn't help noticing how old they looked now, years older than they had only a few months before, when she had stayed with them in Philadelphia—particularly James Sr., whose arthritis had bent him over at the waist and made his walk become a slow stiff hobble, as if all of the life was gone from his body.

At the gravesite there were more folding chairs than people to sit in them. Sullivan had very few friends in Dallas, and along with those whom he had worked with during the week, most of them hadn't bothered to come. His sister had flown in from Pennsylvania, but the plane flight was long and expensive and the rest of the family had stayed home. Yancey and Grissum were there though, both men sitting in the back row of folding metal chairs. The remainder of the small crowd consisted almost entirely of agents from the Bureau, too, Denise thought as she looked at the faces of those seated around her. That's one thing about working for the government, they can always come up with a suitable number of bodies for your funeral, she added to herself angrily, and then she slid into a seat by the far aisle, several yards away from the gray casket and the open grave that waited for it. She'd worn the little gold peace earrings that Jim had often laughed at her about, and during the ceremony the fingers of her right hand reached up several times and tugged anxiously on the little dangling gold hoops, but she didn't cry during the short prayer service, and when her turn came to pass by Sullivan's coffin and sprinkle dirt on it she refused. She only watched as James Sr. hobbled forward on sad, slow, stiffly formal legs and did his duty, dropping a small handful of dirt on top of the box that held his son. Then the others came forward shuffling in a slow line to join in the ceremony, but still Denise refused. Even as the last of the mourners moved by her toward the open grave, she stayed seated on the edge of her hard metal folding chair and stared grimly down at the hole in the earth that they'd dug for Jim to lie in.

After the last of the line had passed dutifully by the coffin, some of the others turned to her, waiting for her to act, but still she sat frozen in place, her eyes staring straight ahead.

Only after all the others had finally drifted away, moving up toward the road and the waiting cars, and even Mr. Sullivan had walked painfully away on his nearly dead legs, did Denise stand and move to the edge of Sullivan's grave. She looked down into the hole scooped out of the soft brown earth. The federal casket was lined with a thin, gray fabric and Denise shifted her gaze to it now. She had not been allowed to see Sullivan's body after the shooting, and the casket had been closed throughout the funeral service. So, as she looked down at the cloth-covered casket now, she imagined Sullivan lying inside the metal box, looking pretty much the way he'd looked the last time that she had seen him, with his unruly, short-cut, blond hair, his honest blue eyes and tough, square-jawed face. And she imagined his body as still straight, tall, and well-muscled, without the impact of the shotgun blast at close range having torn a hole in his chest and stomach. "Jim," she began to say out loud, hoping that somehow he would be able to hear her, but then she stopped, as a shadow crossed the gravesite below her. It was Yancey, his lean, hawklike face staring down at her and his slender figure standing close enough to block the sun from touching either her body or Sullivan's open grave.

"Leave me alone," Denise whispered in a hoarse, emotion-filled voice, but the tightly built, dark-suited man remained standing quietly only a few feet behind her, saying nothing.

Denise looked up at Yancey's eyes. They were steady, controlled, openly judging her. He was attempting to gauge what she knew or didn't know, she thought as she looked back up at his face, trying to discover, what, if anything, Sullivan had told her, making up his mind, she decided, if she, too, would have to die.

"The Bureau's very sorry about what happened," Yancey said, his eyes still searching her face for any clue.

"No, it's not," Denise said in a low but intensely angry voice.

Yancey's heavily lined face tightened, the muscles around his jawline standing out in hard straight lines as they clenched under the tight leathery skin of his face. He was judge and jury, Denise realized then, a court with no appeal, and Grissum was the executioner, but she said nothing out loud. She wasn't going to make it that easy for them. She wasn't going to let them know that she knew the truth. If they did decide to kill her, she wanted their decision to be filled with doubt. Maybe that way, she thought, someday they would have to face how truly monstrous they really were.

"It was a terrible accident," Yancey said, but his face remained impassive, still judging. Then, suddenly, for no reason at all, he seemed to become frightened and his eyes darted away from Denise's face and began searching back over his shoulder and then on either side of where they stood by Sullivan's open grave.

What had happened to Jim was no accident, Denise was convinced of that, and seeing Yancey's gaze broken by his sudden fear of being overheard, she began looking around then as well, hoping to find the television cameras or the reporters that the federal people who had planned the ceremony had promised Mr. Sullivan would be present at the hero's funeral for his son, but there were no television cameras in sight. Maybe they were up the hill at the services for the two dead boys from Vietnam, Denise thought, or maybe they were just busy somewhere else that morning.

"I'm certain that you're upset," Yancey said, his judging eyes returning to her face.

Denise wanted to say something to frighten Yancey, but something that didn't reveal her suspicions absolutely, something cutting and full of just enough suspicion to keep him on edge, and to unsettle him, and make him frightened about what he'd done, but she could think of nothing to say. She didn't know how to do these things, she thought then. These were men's games, ugly male power games full of murder, and calculation, and manipulation of innocent people. She didn't want to ever be any good at games like these, she decided. So she turned away from Yancey without saying anything more and walked past him, but as she moved away from the gravesite, she could still feel Yancey's judging eyes watching her every move.

She looked up at the path ahead of her. Suddenly she realized that to reach the road and the waiting cars, she would have to pass right through the middle of the group of FBI agents who stood blocking the path that led back to the short line of rented limousines that were parked at the side of the cemetery road. Denise looked ahead. Grissum was standing at the rear of the group. He was leaning lazily with one shoulder resting against a tree that stood at the very edge of the dirt path. The old agent was smoking a cigarette, his shoulders bent forward, the brim of his hat slouched down and covering his face in shadows. A sick fear filled Denise's stomach and the fear pumped quickly through her, moving into her arms and legs, weakening her to the point that she felt as if she didn't have the strength to lift one leg in front of the other—and she was afraid that at any moment she would stop, paralyzed in the middle of the cemetery path, maybe falling hopelessly to the ground in fear and weakness. Somehow instead though, she managed to command her body to move directly up the path, aiming herself boldly at the group of dark-suited men that blocked her way. For a moment she thought that they hadn't seen her and that her route to the upper road would be stopped, but at the last second the men's bodies seemed to just melt away and let her pass. Only Grissum's loomed in front of her now. Her heart clutched with fear, as she saw up close his heavily lidded eyes just visible under the long brim of his hat, but she refused to look away. She locked her gaze onto his and moved defiantly at him, and neither of them spoke a word as she approached to within only a few inches of his lazily held body, but finally Grissum moved slowly away, too.

Denise could see the stooped back of Jim Sr. and the saddened figure of Mrs. Sullivan in front of her then, and she quickened her pace to catch up with them. Mr. Sullivan helped his wife into the back seat of one of the rented limousines, and then he began fighting with his own crippled body, trying to push his way inside the vehicle to sit next to her. Denise took a few running steps and moved behind him and then gently reached forward and took his arm. He turned his old man's eyes to her. God, he'd aged a thousand years since she'd seen him last, she thought as she forced a small smile onto her face and tried to help the suddenly very old man into the unfamiliar back seat of the limousine. Funerals and weddings are the only times that people like us ever get to ride in these things, Denise thought, as she looked along the gleaming polished side of the long, black, chauffeur-driven vehicle. Her own two children were sitting in the front seat. They were dressed in their best clothes and, seeing them now, Denise realized that this was almost as she had imagined it would be for her wedding. Both her family and Jim's would be dressed up just like this and seated in rented Cadillac limousines. The only difference would be that Jim would be at her side now and not lying back there in a hole cut in the Texas earth, she thought with finality, realizing completely for the first time that her dream of a wedding and a life with the man she loved would never come true.

She glanced behind her to look at the gravesite one last time, but her view was blocked by the outline of two men standing next to the grave, their heads bent together in whispered conversation. It was Yancey and Grissum talking quietly to each other, blocking her view of Sullivan's final resting place.

Denise turned quickly away from the scene then and got into the back seat of the limousine, but what she had seen had frightened her. The image of the two men, their figures bent together over Sullivan's open grave, haunted her. She knew that Yancey had made his final judgment about her, and she was frightened of what that decision had been, but what frightened her even more was the overwhelming feeling of just how powerless she was to do anything at all—about any of it.

DeSavio was comfortable here. Even from the window of the rented room across the street from the old Italian restaurant called Pascale's located on the edge of the French Quarter, Lopata could see the easy movements of the ugly little man's hunched body, as he walked through the canopied passage from the restaurant's parking lot to its front door. Costello was with him, as always, and several of their men, but nothing was different from a dozen other visits that Lopata had watched the two men make here over the last several weeks, except that tonight there was a long-barreled hunting rifle with a telescopic sight propped up against the windowsill next to Lopata. It was impossible to get a clear shot at DeSavio now, though, not with Costello's bulky body in front of him and the other bodyguards on either side of the stoop-shouldered man. So Lopata left the rifle where it was, and this time he only watched as DeSavio moved safely into the restaurant.

Lopata turned to the telephone in his own small second-story rented room. This was the fourth Thursday evening in a row that he had watched DeSavio visit the restaurant. He knew the man's timing and movements perfectly. Tonight he would strike.

But not quite yet. Lopata forced himself not to pick up the phone and call the restaurant. Not yet, he told himself again, better to let the two men eat and drink and relax before he put his plan into motion; that way their guard would be down even further, their ability to react slowed—and Lopata wanted every edge. So, he stayed by the window and waited. In the restaurant's parking lot two young men lounged against DeSavio's car—a snow-white Rolls. As Lopata watched, he visualized DeSavio's blood splattered in a crimson explosion across the sides of the immaculately white car. If he could, he would do it just that way, he decided.

There were three other men inside the restaurant with DeSavio and Costello, and Lopata knew each of them by sight. He knew their builds, the speed of their reactions, whether they were right- or left-handed, the type of weapons that they carried, and which of them he would kill first, if the opportunity arose. There was one in particular that would be a pleasure, a Cuban, maybe a brother or a cousin to one of the pigs that DeSavio and the woman had sent for him in the hills above Havana. Yes, DeSavio first and, if there was time, the pig of a Cuban.

Finally, he could wait no longer, and Lopata moved from the window to the telephone in the rented room. He dialed the restaurant's number and waited.

"Mr. Costello," he said when the maître d' answered, and a few seconds later he heard the familiar voice on the other end of the line. "Who is this?" Costello's voice cut across the wire, its tone clearly angry at having his dinner interrupted.

"A friend," Lopata lied and then waited. There was a long silence. Then Costello asked his question again, this time slower and more thoughtfully. "Who?"

"An old employee," Lopata said. He could hear the fear beginning in Costello's voice and in his heavy labored breathing, and Lopata began to enjoy himself thoroughly as he listened. "I believe that you have been looking for me. I've been away," Lopata paused before adding dramatically, "in Cuba."

Costello knew who he was now. Lopata was certain of it. He could tell from the sounds of discomfort coming from the other end of the telephone line. Lopata knew, too, that the price he was paying for this moment was that his chances of ever reaching the money in the Nassau bank were being reduced to almost nothing, but it was worth it. Tonight would be worth almost any price, he thought as he continued listening to the other man's heavy, frightened breathing.

"Where are you now?" Costello said.

"Here in New Orleans," Lopata said. "And we still have unfinished business." Lopata reached up and patted the place inside his jacket where Strode's diary rested.

"Yes," Costello said, trying to buy himself time to think. "You have something that you were to deliver to us. Something that we've already paid for."

Lopata only laughed then.

"There are new terms," Lopata said. "Two hundred thousand dollars, cash, tonight."

"That's impossible."

"There are other buyers," Lopata said.

Costello was quiet then, only the painful sound of his heavily labored fat man's breathing coming over the telephone line for several long seconds. "Bourbon and St. Louis in an hour," Lopata said. "You have the money with you. You'll be given the diary."

"It's Mardi Gras," Costello said incredulously. "Bourbon will be a madhouse."

"One chance on this," Lopata said. "An hour." He hung up the phone and returned to the window of the little rented room across the street from the restaurant. As he waited, he checked his rifle again, making certain that it was loaded properly and that the firing mechanism would operate smoothly when the time came.

Costello came through the door of the restaurant first. He was followed closely by two of his men. Lopata's heart sank—one of the men following behind Costello was the Cuban. It's your lucky night, both of you, Lopata thought, as he brought the loaded rifle up to his shoulder and moved the crosshairs of its sights first onto the face of the young Cuban and then squarely onto Costello's big belly, which pushed up against the front of the fat man's expensive suit coat. Lopata pretended to squeeze off a round directly into the big man then, but he didn't waste a round on him. Costello was a pig, Lopata thought, but pig was not what he was hunting now, and he let Costello get into the big white Rolls and drive off into the night. He was followed by the Cuban and another of Costello's men in the long black Lincoln that the Cuban always drove. That left only one bodyguard inside the restaurant with DeSavio. Lopata laughed as he watched the black Lincoln move away only a few yards behind the white Rolls that held Costello. Your lucky night, he thought again, as the Lincoln sped away from the restaurant.

Lopata settled in to wait. The pig and the weasel, he thought to himself. Costello and DeSavio. DeSavio was the boss, the brains; without him, Costello would fall soon enough. Remove the head and the body will die. Lopata repeated the old saying to himself. Finally, DeSavio appeared at the door to the restaurant, just as Lopata knew he would. Costello had been dispatched to do the dirty work on Bourbon Street and DeSavio was practically alone, his body shielded for the moment from Lopata's powerful long-range rifle by the body of only one lone guard. Lopata waited. He could see DeSavio's head clearly and he sighted the crosshairs of the rifle on the place where the frames of the man's heavy, square-cut glasses came together right between his eyes.

A middle-aged Mardi Gras couple, the woman in costume with a fur wrap slung across her shoulders and the man in a badly fitting old-fashioned tuxedo, moved up the restaurant's front steps. For a moment, Lopata's scope showed a distorted picture of the four people—DeSavio, his bodyguard, and the foolish middle-aged couple, but Lopata waited patiently for the picture to untangle. As it did, he took his breath and held it, steadying the picture in his scope with expert precision, and then he began to squeeze the trigger of the weapon that would explode DeSavio's head into a dozen broken pieces. Lopata continued holding the single deep breath as he squeezed the trigger and then watched as the bullet exploded smack into the center of DeSavio's thickly framed glasses. Lopata knew then that the second and third shots were unnecessary, but it was wonderful to watch them do their destruction.

There was a party in progress in the Manchester hotel suite that had served as Cassidy campaign headquarters for the last several weeks, and a roar of approval greeted the candidate as he opened the door to the hotel room and stepped inside.

"You looked terrific!" O'Connor said, pointing at the television at the front of the room where only a few minutes earlier the roomful of happy campaign workers had watched Cassidy accept victory.

"Winning candidates always look terrific," Jack said, smiling as he edged his way slowly into the crowded room.

"How was it down there?" O'Connor shouted at him over the noise.

"A madhouse," Suzanne said, as she followed Jack into the hotel suite. It was late in her pregnancy, and that fact, despite her carefully designed clothes and the graceful way that she carried herself, was becoming more noticeable by the day.

"What do you expect?" O'Connor said. "We've beaten the President."

"By less than three percent of the vote," Cassidy reminded him. The others who had been with Jack and Suzanne downstairs began filing into the room then, forcing the candidate and his wife toward the bedroom door at the rear of the suite.

"That's not the point," O'Connor said. "The point is that you won."

"Did Gardner call?" Jack said, leaning toward O'Connor as he asked the question so that no one else could hear.

O'Connor shook his head, and his expression showed clearly how he felt about the breach of tradition.

"It wasn't by the book to run against a President from my own Party either," Jack reminded him.

"It is, if you win," O'Connor said. "Anyway, you rewrote the book tonight, Jack. They'll be talking about this one for a long time."

"Well, I think we better start talking about Indiana, don't you?" Cassidy said. "We have less than a month, now."

O'Connor nodded in agreement. "They won't make the same mistake twice either," the old politician said. "Gardner will campaign in Indiana, you can bet on that."

"And so will we," Jack said, sliding past O'Connor and entering the suite's back bedroom.

He was alone for the first time in days, and he crossed to the bedroom's window and looked out at the snow lightly falling on the streets of New Hampshire, the snow that the experts and historians would write had kept the voter turnout just low enough to permit him to beat an incumbent President from his own Party in the state's Democratic primary. Maybe God's on my side this time, Jack thought as he watched the snow float lazily past the window.

There was a sound behind him then and he turned back to see Suzanne standing at the door. "Are you coming out?"

"In a minute," he said, and Suzanne closed the door and crossed the room to stand with him. "Congratulations," she said.

"Thank you," he said and leaned forward, kissing her gently on the lips. They held each other for a moment then, saying nothing.

"I like it better this time," Suzanne said.

Jack nodded at her, as she separated from his embrace.

"I'm surer this time," Suzanne said, "more certain that it's right."

"I know," Jack said. "We're a wise old couple now, aren't we?" Jack said, smiling down at her.

"Not so old," Suzanne said, smiling, too, as she reached down and touched the side of her gently swelling body.

"How do you feel?"

"Fine. I think you forget just how tough I am, sometimes."

"I'll try not to," Jack said, still smiling, but he knew from experience that he and his wife's intimacy probably wouldn't last much longer, and his head turned instinctively to the door a split second before the knock sounded on it.

"Excuse me," O'Connor said, pushing only the top of his body inside the bedroom. "Allen's on the phone, he says that he has to talk with you."

Jack nodded and turned toward the table by the far wall. His private line was lit up and the candidate punched down at the plastic button, opening the line to Rozier in New York.

"Allen," Cassidy said, turning back into the room, but both Suzanne and O'Connor had already left and the hotel bedroom was empty again.

"I just heard," Rozier said. "Congratulations." Jack remained silent waiting to hear the real reason for the urgent call.

"Jack," Rozier started and then he paused again, and Cassidy could feel the other man's pain in the silence.

"I tried to contact Agent Sullivan," Rozier said.

"Allen, what is it?" Jack asked, suddenly alarmed.

"I couldn't."

"Why not?"

"He was shot, Jack. He was shot during an arrest of some radicals at a farmhouse near Dallas. I'm trying to put it all together, now," Rozier said, switching to his journalist's voice.

"Allen, are you okay?" Jack asked.

"No, not really," Rozier said, and Jack could tell from the sound of his friend's voice that he was still stalling.

"What happened?"

"He's dead, Jack," Rozier managed finally.

"Oh, God, I'm sorry," Cassidy said without even waiting to hear the rest, and then he felt an enormous sadness for the death of a man that he'd never even met.

"He was shot by another agent," Rozier continued after a few seconds. "His partner fired a shotgun into his chest at point-blank range. They took him to a hospital in Dallas, but he never recovered consciousness."

"Oh, my God," Jack said, and strange thoughts began to fill his mind. At first all he could think about were those moments in his own memory from the time that he had lain somewhere between death and life in a Dallas hospital, himself.

"Jack," Rozier interrupted him, bringing him back to his hotel suite in New Hampshire in March of 1968. "I tried to call Sullivan a few days ago," Rozier continued explaining. "I didn't reach him, but I made the call to the FBI office in Dallas. I think now that it could have been a mistake."

Rozier was being careful in his choice of words. Both men knew that the telephone line that they used now could easily be monitored by any one of a half dozen possibilities from the Republican National Committee to the KGB in Moscow. But Jack could guess what Rozier was really trying to say to him. Rozier was telling him that what had happened to Agent Sullivan in Dallas might not have been an accident at all, that Rozier believed that the Bureau might have murdered Sullivan to keep the truth of the assassination conspiracy from becoming public. And Allen doesn't even know how big the stakes really are in all this, Jack added to himself.

"Jack, what do you want me to do?" Cassidy heard something in his friend's voice now that he'd never heard before. He couldn't quite place it, but he guessed that it was probably fear.

Cassidy hesitated only for a short moment before he issued his instruction. It was time to do what he should have done a long time before. "Fly down to Washington," Cassidy said. "Tell Director Summers that I need to meet with him, immediately and in private. No one else is to know. Make whatever arrangements are required."

"Do I tell him why, Jack?"

"No, Allen, how can you? You don't know. You only think that you do." Rozier could hear the strength and control in Cassidy's voice returning and he imagined Jack's face now tensing with determination, as he fought to bring this crisis back under control. "I want to meet with him as soon as possible, do you understand?"

"No, not entirely," Rozier said.

"Good, we're going to leave it that way."

"You and Summers, that's one meeting that I'd like to listen in on," Rozier said, his journalistic instincts returning, but then he was certain that he could detect more than a small note of sadness in Jack's voice when he answered him.

"No, you wouldn't, Allen, believe me. There's very little good that's going to come out of our discussions, but they need to be held at once," Cassidy said. "In fact, I'm afraid that they're long overdue."

Mrs. Martine said a short prayer in the cemetery chapel outside New Orleans before walking down the narrow tree-lined path that led from the church to her husband's grave. A long black Cadillac limousine followed discreetly several yards behind her.

She came to Don Martine's grave every Sunday, directly after mass. The gravesite was the only place that she visited regularly and even here she remained surrounded by her bodyguards and family and friends. Every time she left her home there were many dangers for her, Communist agents, pro-

Castro people, men who had been her husband's enemies and who had now become her own.

She permitted herself only one brief moment of being alone during her visit, and that was the time when she crossed the last few yards of soft earth and knelt by the side of her husband's grave and spoke first to God and then to the spirit of Don Martine. This was a private moment, reserved only for her and for the invisible forces that she believed surrounded her. She would say a short prayer and leave a single flower at the base of the tall, gray marble headstone that rose up from Don Martine's burial site. In the summer she always left a rose, red or white, to memorialize the summer day upon which she had first met Don Martine. In the winter the rose would become a simple white lily or sometimes a pale violet chrysanthemum. But it was always just one, left resting against the gray marble headstone that showed, chiseled deep into its polished surface, the uniformed image of her husband's head and shoulders, glorious in death, with the dates of his short life cut in the marble beneath his image: JANUARY 23, 1918—APRIL 18, 1961.

Lopata watched her from the high ground hidden in the trees of the hillside littered with uneven stone and marble markers for the dead. Lopata waited patiently, until the men walking on either side of her turned and started back for the long black limousine that waited at the side of the cemetery road several yards from Don Martine's grave. Lopata had watched the ritual played out by the woman and her protectors every Sunday morning for the last three weeks, and he knew just when to lift the rifle that he had been holding from his lap up to his shoulder and precisely where and how to sight it on the figure of the woman kneeling in the damp morning cemetery grass below her husband's headstone.

As the woman knelt in front of her husband's grave, Lopata found her image easily and perfectly in the sights of his rifle.

There was a slight wind blowing east to west and the rifle, which he had purchased only a few days earlier on a French Quarter side street, pulled its fire slightly high and to the left, but Lopata had corrected for the weather and the rifle's own deficiencies by moving the sighting mechanism the proper number of clicks over and down while he had waited on the hillside for the woman to appear. He had fired the rifle only once, the afternoon before at a range outside the city, but he knew it well enough for a simple job like this one. The figure of the woman dressed all in black stood out dramatically against the light gray backdrop of her husband's headstone. Lopata smiled as he steadied his aim, finding the center of the woman's black lace veil precisely in his scope's crosshairs.

He waited, breathing regularly and deeply, letting the picture of the woman in his rifle's sights move up and down rhythmically with each deep intake of breath, as she placed the white flower that she held in her black-gloved hand on the ground above her husband's grave and then made the sign of the cross with practiced, slightly cupped fingers across her forehead and chest. When she had finished, Lopata moved the calibrated black crosshairs of his rifle's sights back perfectly into position, so that they intersected in the spot where the kneeling woman's long, black veil dropped down over the front of her face.

At the moment of sighting he had stopped his own breath and so the image of the woman remained steady and true even as he slowly, but very surely, squeezed the rifle's trigger. He knew how much resistance to expect and there was no need to move any other part of his body, except for the mere squeeze of that single finger, until the final resistance of the rifle's firing mechanism was overcome.

The two useless bodyguards standing by the limousine didn't even move at the first shot and Lopata had more than enough time to calmly resight his weapon onto the collapsing figure of the woman in black and fire two more rounds, first into her neck and then into her chest. The black lace of the veil that had covered her face was splashed with bright red blood, but the falling body itself looked lazily peaceful, Lopata thought, as it slumped toward the ground in front of her husband's grave.

There was even time, if he chose, for Lopata to fire at one of the men who dashed toward the body of the fallen woman, but he decided against it. It wasn't these men that he'd come for. It was the woman who'd sent the others to kill him in the hills above Havana, and that was done. Lopata turned away and, crouching, he fled through the overhanging tree branches, the rifle held at his side, his body hidden from view behind the clutter of high stone markers to the dead that covered the hillside. The woman had been easy, just as he'd known that she would be, and now his business in New Orleans was ended.

CHAPTER
41

There were no reporters in sight when the *Trewlaney Rose* pulled away from its moorings and out into the Chesapeake Bay. There were, of course, due to the prominence of its passengers, a few Secret Service men on its deck. There was a small crew on board, but down below in the main cabin there were only two men—the former President of the United States, John Trewlaney Cassidy of Massachusetts, and the man who had served him and five other Presidents as their Director of the Federal Bureau of Investigation—John James Summers.

Both men had created cover stories for the press to disguise their meeting that afternoon. Cassidy was supposedly in transit between his home in Hyannis and an appearance later that night at a campaign stop in Indiana, and Summers had told the press that he was spending the day having a routine medical checkup at Bethesda Naval Hospital.

Outside it was beginning to rain, but below decks the two powerful men were seated warm and safe in swiveling leather armchairs. They both sat in front of the large Plexiglas window, in the stern of the ship, through which they could watch the heavy winds kicking up enormous white spots on the surface of the sea and the rain wash in and slant against the transparent plastic screen that protected them from the weather.

On the tabletop in front of the two men were several manila files. Cassidy's hand rested on the thickest of these files, and, when he finally began to speak, his fingertips occasionally tapped on its surface to accentuate a point or to underline his emotion.

And Cassidy wasted little time getting down to business after the big yacht began pulling out to sea. "In late 1961," he began, his eyes fixed directly on the face of the man seated in front of him, "as President, I approved a secret plan. I know that you remember it, Mr. Director. It was called Crossbow." Cassidy could see Summers's body tense slightly at the word.

"It was a highly secret plan, the totality and purpose of which was known only to the two of us," Cassidy said, pointing at himself and Summers before adding, "and to the Attorney General and the Director of the Central Intelligence Agency at that time, Admiral Willisey. As you well remember, those in the Central Intelligence Agency and the FBI who were given authority to implement the plan, were treated strictly on a need-to-know basis. Since Admiral Willisey is now dead, as is Attorney General Cassidy, that means that only the two of us in this room remain alive with any personal knowledge of the overall operation. Do you remember Crossbow, Mr. Director?" Cassidy's expression was set hard and his eyes were still fixed on the Director's face.

Summers nodded his head slightly, but Cassidy refused to be satisfied and he continued waiting for his answer. "Yes," Summers said finally.

"It was a plan brought to me by you, Mr. Director," Cassidy said, and he raised a fingertip from the files on the table to point it at the older man. "Crossbow's purpose was, as you will remember, to create and train a small cadre of government assassins." Cassidy stopped talking then to let the full power of what he was saying sink in on the other man. In the silence, Cassidy studied the Director's face. It showed almost nothing. Whatever Summers felt still lay hidden behind the stoic mask of his face. In all their years of dealing with each other, Cassidy thought then, he had never seen that emotionless mask lifted for more than a brief moment at any one time. Jack wondered now if that would change after Summers had heard the rest of what he had to say to him that day. "Government assassins, who could be called upon by our government in the last extremity to alter the internal affairs of other governments by direct intervention." Cassidy hated the bureaucratic euphemisms and he quickly changed his words to directly state their true meaning. "By the assassination of the leaders of other countries," Cassidy corrected himself, saying the words in a flat voice, but his emotions could be seen in his face and in the play of his fingertips on the tops of the files lying on the table in front of him. "It was agreed that these assassins would never be used without a direct order from me, or from my successor in office, and only in the event that the President deemed such action absolutely necessary to eliminate an even greater loss of life or to protect a vital national interest. We all hoped and believed that no such event would ever arise, but at that time we deemed it to be in the best interests of the country to have such a capacity in the unlikely and extraordinary event that it was needed."

Summers nodded his head again then, acknowledging his understanding.

"The plan was placed into the very early stages of operation. As I understood the situation at the time, agents for this—no, let's call them what they were. Potential assassins were recruited by the Central Intelligence Agency, and these men were scheduled to enter into training in the tactics of political assassination. This training was to be undertaken at a location known only to a very few people, and a small, federally controlled island off the coast of south Florida was chosen as their training base. The island was called St. Christopher's Island," Cassidy said, and then he paused. "But as you know, Mr. Director," he continued a few seconds later, "at the urging of the Attorney General, I later rescinded all authority for Crossbow and ordered the program disbanded. Both you and Admiral Willisey were present at a meeting in the spring of 1962 in my office—and at that time you agreed to undertake the plan's absolute destruction. I have the minutes of that meeting, copies of which were sent to both you and to Admiral Willisey immediately following our meeting." Cassidy's fingertips continued their drumbeat on the cover of one of the files on the desk.

"But my orders to end the operation to recruit and train American political assassins on St. Christopher's Island weren't fully carried out until almost a year later, not until January of 1963, were they?" Cassidy looked at Summers long and hard for his answer, but this time the Director refused to say anything.

"All right," Cassidy continued angrily. "Hear me out: I know now that my order to disband Crossbow wasn't put into effect until almost a year after I issued it, and that the plan wasn't terminated even then, until after a small group of men were actually trained in the tactics of political assassination. I know it because I have proof," Cassidy said, and he opened the file that he had been tapping and reached for the sheets of paper containing copies of the excerpts from Strode's diary that the Cuban government had given to Rozier. Cassidy placed the papers face up on the tabletop directly in front of Summers. Then Cassidy reached into the file again and removed the copies of the pages from Lopata's statement to the Cuban authorities and laid them down next to the pages from the diary. "These papers are copies of portions of documents now in the possession of the Cuban government," Jack said. "They were given to Allen Rozier for transmittal to me by one of Castro's diplomats. Allen was also given a list of Cuban terms and conditions for that country to renew normal economic and political relations with the United States. After Allen had reviewed these documents and confirmed their authenticity as best he could, he passed them along to me." Cassidy paused for a moment then before continuing. "Allen knew that the materials were important but, of course, he couldn't have known the full extent of what he was bringing to me or just how powerful these documents really are, because he never knew about Crossbow or anything even remotely connected to it. And what Allen must have thought were just randomly selected pages from these materials were, in fact, carefully selected passages, which would be truly and completely meaningful only to someone intimately aware of the details of that entire operation. Someone like you or me, John," Cassidy said. And then he slid the papers even closer to Summers's side of the table. "And these documents confirm what I've feared for some time now," Jack continued. "That despite my order to terminate it, a small cadre of men were actually recruited for Crossbow, and these men were trained in assassination techniques by agents of our government, trained by members of the CIA and the Federal Bureau of Investigation in methods of political murder . . ." Cassidy's voice trembled with barely controlled rage and he stopped for a moment to calm himself before he went on. "I believe when we receive those documents in their entirety they will prove," he said finally, as he brought himself back under control, "that contacts with organized crime were used to help in the recruitment of the six men who met the profile that those in charge of Operation Crossbow had created for the job of assassin, and that members of organized crime were involved in the actual training of these men." Cassidy stopped briefly then to compose himself further before he continued. "A small base on St. Christopher's Island was established for the purpose, and the entire operation continued just as though no order to terminate it had ever been issued, and those six men were trained in the most highly sophisticated assassination techniques known anywhere in the world. These assassins were told that their targets had not yet been selected, but it was strongly hinted to them that Premier Castro was to be their number-one target. During the course of their training, these men were given elaborate and often contradictory cover identities. The CIA's files and the FBI's and all other known government and private files and data banks here and throughout the world were intentionally filled with false and misleading information about the true identity and background of each of them. Additionally, complicated cover stories were created for these potential assassins that linked them to the Communists, and bits and pieces of this erroneous information were intentionally scattered in files and computers throughout the world. Photographs of them taken in Russia or at Russian embassies with known Communist agents were falsified and placed in government files. Money that could be traced to Russian sources was deposited into bank accounts in their names, and photographs were taken of them at Communist rallies or meetings. Even false stories about them defecting to Russia or Cuba and then somehow returning to the West and engaging in pro-Communist activities were fabricated for them. It was an impossible trail of false leads and phony clues that would drive any government investigator or journalist, who might later try to string together the proof of who and what these people really were, into a deep, mysterious maze of falsified facts and erroneous cover stories. And of course, it was all done to hide one simple fact—that these men were really American agents taking direct orders from elements of the American intelligence community." Cassidy stopped then, but still Summers refused to say anything or even to acknowledge that he knew about the things that Cassidy was telling him now.

So Cassidy kept talking. "But then, in early 1963, something happened. The Attorney General began vigorously prosecuting the head of organized crime in the Miami area, a man named Joseph DeSavio, and in the course of that investigation he began getting very close to the truth about Crossbow, and those in charge of the renegade operation at St. Christopher's Island decided that it was time to finally terminate the plan. The resources, including the training facility, were destroyed, and the half dozen or so men, now thoroughly trained political assassins, were set loose by the American government. So Crossbow itself was finally ended, but these six men were its legacy to the world. Six highly skilled, professional assassins with cover stories for their true identities so complex and so well established that no one, not even those who had created them, would ever be able to fully unwrap their true identities and backgrounds again. And, if the United States government no longer had a use for these men, the underworld leaders of Miami and New Orleans, who had participated in their recruitment and training, did." Cassidy paused then momentarily before dramatically shifting his focus.

"One of the men, who died at the Bay of Pigs, was a General Martine." Cassidy could tell now from the subtle change in the expression on Summers's face that he was finally making an impact on him. "General Martine's widow blamed my administration . . . no, Mrs. Martine blamed me for the death of her husband. In her anger, she let it be known to the boss of organized crime in New Orleans, this same man, Joseph DeSavio, whom the Attorney General had under investigation at the time, that she would pay a substantial sum of money to have me murdered. Under most circumstances, I believe that even a man as ruthless as Mr. DeSavio would not undertake to assassinate a President of the United States at whatever price Mrs. Martine was willing to pay, because it would simply be too dangerous, but Mr. DeSavio was under tremendous legal pressure from the Attorney General, and he probably assumed that my death would remove those problems. But there was another, even more important reason that DeSavio agreed to risk undertaking to murder the President of the United States. You see, he knew precisely how it could be accomplished with almost no real risk of his associates ever being linked to the crime. Four of the six men who had been trained in political assassination at St. Christopher's Island died mysteriously during the period immediately following their release from training. It's my guess, although I could probably never prove it, that their deaths were ordered by those in charge of their recruitment and training so that these men could never embarrass the government agencies that they had worked for by later telling the true story of Operation Crossbow. But the remaining two men were known to DeSavio. That meant that he had within his control two men trained in political assassination by the American government, two men that the United States government had supplied with nearly foolproof cover identities linking them to the Communists. These are the two men." Cassidy reached into one of the files on the table and removed the photographs of Arthur Strode and Antonio Lopata and slid them across the table toward Summers.

"But here was the truly brilliant part," Cassidy said, pausing before completing his explanation. "I believe DeSavio knew that if they utilized these men to assassinate me, no one within the government would want to know the truth of what had really happened. Your bureau, the very government agency that would be in charge of investigating the assassination, would in fact have the most at stake in not uncovering the truth. Because if the public ever learned that the Bureau, itself, had worked with organized crime to create an elite cadre of political assassins and that the partnership had gotten so out of control that those assassins had murdered the President of the United States, the results would be disastrous for both you and the Bureau. DeSavio knew that, and so he counted on the FBI accepting the cover story that he would offer to it and then, perhaps, even actively helping him to keep the real truth from ever coming to the surface. Who was going to challenge these assassins' fabricated identities as defectors, Communist sympathizers, possible KGB agents? Certainly no one in the Bureau, certainly not you, John. And what about the Attorney General? DeSavio believed that my brother would never let the true story of St. Christopher's Island come out either. Even if Tim could somehow weave his way to the truth, it would in all probability be political suicide for him to disclose what had really happened within the government while he was the Attorney General, and disclosing the truth about Crossbow would certainly deeply stain the memory of me and my administration as well—and DeSavio guessed that Tim would never be willing to pay that price." Cassidy paused again then, but Summers still refused to respond. "It could end the Cassidy political dynasty forever. It was brilliant. DeSavio had a perfect assassination team hand-delivered to him by the United States government. And it would be a murder that no one in authority would ever really want solved, because the trail of responsibility would always run directly back to the highest elements of the American intelligence community. And since DeSavio knew that he would in all probability have the law-enforcement machinery of the United States on his side helping him to cover up the truth, he did what he might not have dared to do under any other circumstances—he accepted a commission to assassinate the President of the United States."

In the silence that followed, Summers barely glanced at the faces of the two men in the photographs on the table in front of him. So Cassidy moved forward and pushed the photographs to the very edge of the table, only inches away from the Director's emotionless face. "These men," Cassidy said, touching first the photograph of Strode and then the one of Lopata, "these two men were recruited and trained to act as assassins in some other country, but when it finally happened, it didn't happen somewhere else. It happened in the United States, and it happened probably with some justice, to the very man who approved the plan that began it all in the first place. It seems, Mr. Director," Cassidy said, pausing only briefly before stating his ultimate conclusion, "that in late 1961, I authorized a plan that resulted in an assassination attempt on my own life."

CHAPTER
42

Now came the poker game, Cassidy thought, looking at Summers's impassive face. Well, if it were to become a game to Summers, it would be a game that he made very certain that the Director lost, he decided.

Drinks were served below deck on the *Trewlaney Rose* and then dinner. The two men talked and inspected documents and the rain continued, slanting into the sea outside the window, as the craft churned quietly along the Maryland coast.

Summers read the pages from Strode's diary, and then the excerpts from the statement that Lopata had given to the Cuban officials, but he didn't need to read the reports from Agent Sullivan. He had copies of those in his own files back in Washington.

"Gardner didn't know any more than I did when I was President, did he?" Cassidy said, as the Director finished. "You kept it all from coming to us, didn't you, John? You stopped Sullivan's reports or anything else that got close to the real truth from reaching the Attorney General, or me, or President Gardner. The conclusion that Strode had acted alone out of sympathy for the Communists suited our purposes, too. So we let you do it. We accepted your version of events in Dallas without seriously questioning it. But you knew the truth all the time. You knew who Strode was as soon as he was arrested. You must have had a master file on him, and on Lopata, and the others, and you knew where to start looking for leads to the conspiracy within a few hours after his arrest. But you believed that, once the investigation led to Miami and New Orleans, the entire story of the Bureau's involvement in Crossbow and its failure to close down the operation after I ordered it to be disbanded would come out. And the result would be that the Bureau, that you've given your life to create, would be permanently damaged, maybe even ruined, and your job as its Director would in all probability be lost. So, you decided that the public should never learn the truth. Not even someone with as much power as you have, Mr. Director, could have withstood a scandal of that proportion. So you suppressed Agent Sullivan's reports, and probably others as well, and DeSavio's ingenious plan began to work out just the way he'd believed that it would. DeSavio had the FBI working for him, helping him to put the responsibility for the assassination solely on Strode and the falsified story that had been created for him that he was a Communist sympathizer or possibly even a Russian agent."

"Whatever I did, it was done to protect the country," Summers said quietly.

It was the first crack in his armor, Cassidy thought, and a small feeling of triumph started to grow inside him. "John, I'm certain that you believed that," Cassidy said. "I believe that you acted at all times as you thought you must, but . . ." Cassidy stopped then and drew a deep breath before he continued. He wasn't enjoying this, but he had to go on. "Any piece of evidence that didn't tie into the theory that Strode was insane, and a Communist, and working completely alone, was discredited by you and by the people working under your direction. In the end the Bureau issued a final report that contained conclusions that you knew were lies, but you convinced President Gardner to place his political credibility behind them. Only this man, Sullivan, kept pushing, kept digging for the truth, with the entire weight of the Bureau and the government of the United States against him." Cassidy's eyes found Summers's face. "I know that Agent Sullivan was shot down five days ago in Dallas. I know that he was shot at close range during an arrest of some suspected radicals, and I know that he was shot by a fellow FBI officer, but what I don't know, John, is what you're doing about it."

Summers's face was no longer impassive. It showed sadness now and defeat, but still the Director remained silent.

"John, I need to know," Cassidy said. "You can keep quiet about the rest if you believe that you must, but about Agent Sullivan, I need to know. Was there an order to kill Sullivan? Or did the cover-up just get out of control like all the rest of it did?"

Summers managed somehow to stay quiet, even in the face of what was nearly a direct accusation of murder.

"John, I know the difference," Cassidy said. "Believe me, if anyone else on earth does, I do. I know that you can't always stop the actions that you put into motion, no matter how powerful you are." Cassidy paused, and the room was absolutely silent. Only the insistent sound of the rain beating against the glass behind the two men and the pulse of the ocean against the side of the ship could be heard in the room below decks on the *Trewlaney Rose* as Jack waited for his answer. "I want to believe that you did your best," he began. "I want to believe that we all did. That this horror started from the very best of motives, but that it got out of control, as we should have known that it would have to in the end," Cassidy said, sweeping his hand out at the tableful of documents. "I want to believe that you never intentionally disobeyed my order to terminate Crossbow, but that somehow it just happened. And by the time you tried to stop it, it already had a life of its own, and that then it just continued, almost by itself. Maybe a subordinate ignored one of your orders or misunderstood it or overstepped his authority. Believe me, John, I understand how that kind of thing can happen. I want to believe that about Agent Sullivan's death, too, that it was somehow created only by initiating the cover-up, not by a direct order. And that no one could control it after that, and the violence, the deaths, the murders just fed on each other, until they reached Sullivan. Tell me, John, you owe me that much," Cassidy said, raising his voice for the first time to almost a shout. He slumped back into his chair and waited. There was nothing more to say. It was up to Summers now. And as he waited to hear the other man's final answer, Cassidy prayed that it was all truly more than just a game to the other man.

"I could never order the death of a member of the Federal Bureau of Investigation," the Director said, and looking at him and hearing his voice, it was impossible to question the sincerity of what he said.

"Thank you, John," Cassidy said. "I believe you."

Both men were quiet then, each weighing their options. It was Summers who spoke first. "The Cubans have all of this, I take it?" He indicated the files on the table in front of him with a tight movement of his hand.

"No, not all of it," Cassidy said. "The Cubans have the statement signed by the second man in Dallas that day, a man named Antonio Lopata, and it swears to much of what we've talked about this afternoon, but, as I believe you know, Lopata is dead now and most of the story that he sets out in his statement is practically untraceable, as is his true identity and background. Your department and the CIA saw to that. So, all the Cubans have is an unsubstantiated statement from a now dead man, and, in my judgment, that makes his statement practically worthless to them. They may still have the diary kept by Arthur Strode prior to Dallas, though, or at least copies of it, and it confirms portions of the overall story as well. But again, Strode is dead now and the contents of his diary, particularly the parts about his role in a conspiracy to assassinate me, are almost impossible to trace or to ever prove. No, John, only you and I know the complete truth. I believe that the Cubans needed at least one living witness to help them substantiate the documents that they have and they lost that last fall when this man Lopata died. What Castro has left in his possession now could prove politically embarrassing to both of us, but I think, if I take certain actions during the next few weeks, that it won't amount to much more than that in the end."

"What do they want for their silence?"

Cassidy moved forward and sorted through the papers on the desktop, until he came to the list of Cuban demands. He handed the sheet of paper to Summers. "I see," Summers said after he'd read carefully through the list of conditions that Jack was expected to support in exchange for Castro suppressing the documents from the world's press. "So, how do you propose to deal with them?" Summers said then, tossing the paper back onto the table in front of Cassidy.

"There's a great deal the Cubans don't know, and even more that they could never prove. I think that I can lessen their demands considerably and successfully negotiate with them on terms acceptable to me, but, as I said, it will require one final act on my part. Castro's entire strategy is based on his belief that I will do almost anything to prevent the fact that I approved a plan like Crossbow from becoming public knowledge during a presidential campaign. So I believe the only way for me to deal with him effectively now is to prove that he's wrong. And in order to accomplish that I'm going to release a statement to the press myself—a statement that sets out my full involvement in Crossbow, including my initial approval of it, the Attorney General's quite legitimate concerns about its consequences, and the order that I subsequently issued for its termination, but nothing of its link to the events in Dallas. The statement will also not concern itself with the Bureau's failure to implement Crossbow's termination or the Bureau's cover-up of that fact or its failure to investigate other aspects of the assassination attempt in order to protect its own secrets. The only person who might guess the truth is Allen, but I'll speak to him, and I trust his word and his loyalty absolutely. As for the Cubans, when I release a statement outlining my initial authorization of Crossbow, they should be ready to deal more reasonably. I believe that a public statement from me outlining everything that I personally did wrong should destroy Castro's ability to blackmail me almost entirely."

"And end your chances at the presidency," Summers responded flatly.

"Perhaps," Cassidy said, trying to keep his voice as light as possible. Cassidy looked at Summers's face. There was a trace of a smile on it. They were down to the real poker playing now, Cassidy thought. Summers didn't believe him. The Director saw it only as a bluff, but a bluff in order to gain what? The Director's face was patient, waiting for the rest of it. He had played games like these with Presidents and men who would be President many times before, his expression said, and in the end he'd always won. "I believe that I can get the Cubans to agree to remain silent in exchange for my support of a reasonable set of conditions that would begin to normalize relations between our two countries," Jack continued. "There are portions of their demands that are long overdue, and I'm willing to negotiate with them on that basis. Mrs. Martine is dead now and so is Joseph DeSavio. DeSavio's number-one lieutenant, Anthony Costello, is being prosecuted by the Justice Department on enough crimes to put him in prison for the rest of his life—tax evasion, jury tampering, racketeering. I no longer consider him a problem. Both Strode and Lopata are dead now as well."

Summers nodded his understanding, but he remained noncommittal. What the hell was Cassidy proposing? Was he really suggesting that the actual assassination conspiracy and the FBI role in covering it up not be disclosed? That the conspiracy of silence be continued?

Cassidy could see the uncertainty in Summers's face, so he went on. "John, in my judgment it comes down in the last analysis to a choice between suppressing the details of the assassination conspiracy on my life or destroying the belief that the country has in its government. If this entire story were to become public knowledge now, the nation's trust in its intelligence and law-enforcement agencies would be destroyed, and that would come at a time when our country is at war and is deeply divided internally. I'm just not willing to risk the credibility of our entire law-enforcement community—not when there is nothing to be gained by it." Cassidy looked down at the rubble of evidence scattered on the table in front of Summers. "So I'm going to have all of it—the photographs, files, reports, papers, even Strode's diary—I'm going to have everything that connects to what happened in Dallas five years ago sealed in the National Archives and not opened for a hundred years. Then it will become a story for the historians—not for today's press."

Summers kept looking across the table at Cassidy. He had dealt with men like Cassidy long enough to know there was always a price for everything, his expression said, and he was waiting now to hear what it was that Cassidy was going to demand in exchange for his protection of the Bureau and its secrets.

"John, your legacy to this country is the Bureau," Cassidy continued. "The country must have a respected federal law-enforcement agency, now perhaps more than ever. You've given the country that and I know that neither of us wants it destroyed. But I believe that the only way that it can be maintained is for these materials to be put away and for you to use your power to clean the Bureau out yourself. I want you to conduct a full inquiry into the failure of Crossbow to be terminated and into the death of Agent Sullivan, and I want the resignation or dismissal of the people responsible for both events."

Summers began to move his heavy body around awkwardly in his chair, his eyes darting nervously around the room.

"That's my only offer," Cassidy snapped angrily then. "I wish to God that the country could stand a public trial and a conviction of those involved, but I don't believe that it can right now, and I'm not willing to risk the security of the country on it."

Summers was quiet, weighing his options. Cassidy watched his face in the silence that followed. Jack knew that the Director was still trying to decide if he was only bluffing.

"I need time," the Director said finally. As he spoke, his face showed that he still believed that somehow he would find a way to win in the end. "I need to look into these allegations concerning the death of Agent Sullivan, and I need to find out precisely what happened with Crossbow," Summers said, looking defiantly across the table at Cassidy. "I'm not ready to respond to any of this yet. I'm going to need a few weeks, maybe longer, in order to conduct my own investigation into these matters."

Cassidy understood what Summers was doing. The Director still thought that it was all just a bluff, that he would never back up his threat to release the truth of his own involvement in Crossbow and jeopardize his return to the presidency. And without that initial admission Summers remained safe. The Director was going to try to wait him out. If he didn't release the statement, Summers would do nothing, and the status quo would be maintained. Summers's face returned to an impassive, Buddha-like mask, confidently waiting for the younger man to respond. There would be nothing more from him, Jack guessed, until he'd proven to him that he was serious about his threat.

"I understand your position," Cassidy said. "But I want you to understand me as well, John. I want your dignity and the dignity of the Bureau to be fully maintained. Under the circumstances that the country finds itself in at the moment, I believe that is absolutely imperative." Cassidy paused then, his eyes resting directly on Summers's face, as he added his final condition. "But after you've conducted your investigations and taken whatever action is appropriate to punish those directly involved, I want you to resign as the Director of the Bureau. If you don't, I will be forced to disclose everything to the President and demand that you be fired. And if he doesn't take immediate action, I'll disclose the information to the press, not just my own involvement, but all of it, and I'll begin an investigation in the Senate as to the Bureau's and your own personal failures in this matter. So don't force my hand, John. If you do, no one will win, not you, not me, not the Bureau, not the American people, no one."

"What the hell is that?" Mazeloff said, nearly jumping up out of his chair and splashing a few drops of whiskey on his carefully tailored shirt cuff as he did.

It was the Sunday after the New Hampshire primary, and a small group of presidential aides and advisers were gathered in Mazeloff's office to watch the President's first major address to the American people in several months. The prepared text of the President's speech had been meticulously crafted over the last several days by a half dozen speechwriters, and copies of it had been distributed in advance to the press. The announced subject of the talk was the necessity for increased American military assistance, including fifty thousand additional American combat soldiers, to be sent to the Republic of South Vietnam.

Mazeloff and the others were watching the speech on a small television monitor set up in the press secretary's office less than a hundred yards away from the Oval Office itself. There the President was seated behind his desk, his big hands folded on the desktop in front of him, his gold-framed spectacles off, letting his eyes gaze up just above the television camera in front of him where the teleprompter was located and the words of his speech rolled by slowly in bold black print, big enough, Mazeloff thought as he watched him, for the President to read without his glasses. The beginning had gone well. The President had read the carefully prepared words from the television screen, moving at his own pace, and he had seemed to be looking directly at the American people. It was all just as the media experts had counseled him, all except for the sheet of yellow legal-size paper that he had removed from his inside coat pocket a moment before and set on the desktop directly in front of him.

Oh, Jesus, is that what I think it is? Mazeloff said to himself, as he and the other presidential assistants began to huddle more closely around the television set in Mazeloff's office, taking renewed interest in the President's speech now. Mazeloff moved forward in his chair, feeling his body beginning to tense. He craned his neck forward, as if he might somehow be able to read the words scrawled on the sheet of paper off the little television screen in front of him.

"Are you holding out on me?" The press secretary turned to one of the President's speechwriters, who was seated nearby. "I've got to deal with those bastards." Mazeloff pointed toward the press room down the hall, where most of the White House press corps were gathered to watch the President's speech. "If he deviates from the text that I gave them by a goddamned semicolon, they'll have my head."

On the television screen, the President had moved on, continuing to slowly drawl out his prepared text. Mazeloff turned his attention back to him and listened.

"So far, so good," Mazeloff said a few seconds later, looking down at his watch, as the President continued reading the text of his speech in his mournful Texas voice. The words were a solemn reminder of the "high stakes" and "noble purpose" behind the decision to increase the nation's military commitment in Vietnam that the President would announce toward the very end of the speech. "He's halfway through the damn thing," Mazeloff added out loud, shuffling pages of the prepared text that lay in front of him, but even as Mazeloff spoke, the President's right hand moved up and touched the folded sheet of legal-size paper that lay on his desktop.

"What the hell is that thing, anyway?" one of the junior staff people seated with Mazeloff blurted out.

Mazeloff could guess what it was, but he didn't want to say it out loud, not now. He just held his breath and buried his eyes in the advance text, straining for the President to finish each phrase. Occasionally, as he listened to the painfully slow words, Mazeloff checked his watch or counted ahead to see how many pages of text remained, until the deliberate manner in which Gardner was reading the speech became sheer torture. Would the man ever finish? Two-thirds completed, God, Mazeloff thought, now almost three-quarters done. There was a chance they'd make it and then he could go in there and talk to him, calm him down, remind him of the . . . "Oh, God, there he goes again!" The little press secretary was half standing now, his hands on his knees, his slender body bent slightly forward at the waist, his eyes squinting down in expectation at the television screen. The President's right hand had reached up again and was touching the paper on his desk.

But the President seemed to change his mind once more and he returned his hands to the clasped position that the media consultants had instructed him to use to express his sincerity, and Mazeloff sank back down to a sitting position. "What the hell's he going to do?" Mazeloff said to no one in particular, and none of the others in the tense, crowded room turned back to him or attempted to answer his question.

Mazeloff abandoned the prepared text now and he no longer glanced nervously at his watch every few minutes. He only stared at the President on the television screen at the front of the room. They were in the home stretch, the final summing up only moments away. It's going to be all right, the press secretary thought hopefully. All he needs is some rest, a week at the ranch. I can get some of his friends in to remind him of how the votes really stack up come convention time, help remind him how meaningless what happened to him in New Hampshire really was, just a fluke. New Hampshire is Cassidy country anyway, meaningless. Wait until the primaries move west, Oregon, California, Cassidy doesn't have a prayer out there, even Indiana, that could still work out all right, if only . . . Oh God, what now? "That is why I have decided . . ."

"What the hell's he saying now?" Mazeloff said, and he began flipping frantically through the pages of the advance text of the President's speech as fast as he could. None of this is in there, he realized in horror as he reviewed the final sheets of text. None of it! What the hell's he doing?

In the end, Mazeloff thought with some irony, Gardner hadn't even needed to reach for the sheet of yellow paper. The President had known what was written on it in his own large handwritten letters, and he had repeated the words by memory.

Gardner had written the words several weeks earlier, and he'd shown them to Mazeloff even before the results of the New Hampshire primary had helped him to reach his final decision to say them to the nation.

Mazeloff curled his own body up into a ball as he listened. It was as if he wanted to become invisible. He watched in despair as Gardner leaned forward, his hands folded tensely on the desk in front of him, his eyes lowered from the teleprompter. He looked into the camera and finally honestly connected with the American people as he spoke his concluding words to them, "and therefore, I will not seek and would not accept the nomination of the Democratic Party for another term as President of the United States."

"You've won, Jack," O'Connor said.

They were in a hotel room in Indianapolis. Suzanne was with them and the television screen at the front of the room showed a round table of stunned news analysts at a studio in Washington beginning to discuss Gardner's announcement and what it would mean to the presidential politics of 1968, but Cassidy was barely listening.

" 'I will not seek and would not accept the nomination of the Democratic Party for another term as President of the United States.' " O'Connor repeated Gardner's words slowly, analyzing them like a high-paid corporate lawyer would analyze the words in a contract, looking for even the slightest flaw, but there wasn't any to find. It was done, just like that, and Gardner was out of the race. "My God, he has less guts than I thought he did," O'Connor said, his voice incredulous.

Suzanne leaned over to where her husband was sitting on the couch next to her and kissed him lightly on the cheek. "Congratulations."

Jack smiled at her briefly and then turned away, saying nothing.

"What are you thinking?" O'Connor asked, feeling slightly puzzled. After all, wasn't this what they'd all been working so hard to achieve? Here it was, and Jack's reaction to the news was only stunned silence. Something was going on that he wasn't being told about, O'Connor thought. Secret meetings, falsified stories to the press about Jack's travel plans, private telephone calls to Rozier. Only yesterday Jack had disappeared for almost an entire day. Something important was going on that he wasn't being let in on.

Finally, Cassidy turned his head back to his wife, his eyes taking a long moment to focus on her as if he'd been somewhere far away. "I was just thinking about something funny," he said, a strange expression taking over his features as he spoke.

"In the war . . ." Cassidy continued, his voice low and reluctant, as if he knew that a moment like this deserved a better reaction from him, but he couldn't seem to resist saying what was really on his mind now, anyway. "In the Solomons," he continued, "our squadron was part of an attack force that was ordered to take one of the key islands in the chain. We were told to anticipate a major battle when we reached the final Japanese stronghold at the far side of the island, but it took us weeks of hard fighting just to cross the island, before we could even reach the enemy's final position. Weeks of tough, hard fighting, every day, every hour really, but the entire time we kept thinking out the final battle that we'd been told to expect, knowing how difficult and important it would be for us," Cassidy said. "But when we finally did manage to make our way through to the other side of the island, there was no great battle at all—there was nothing. The Japanese just surrendered. They laid down their arms and gave up. It was over before we even had time to realize what had happened." He paused then for a moment, remembering, before he finally added, "It turned out that the entire campaign had been decided by all the seemingly insignificant moments of battle that we'd been engaged in as we worked our way across the island, all the daily skirmishes with the enemy, all the small decisions and little moments of courage that we had thought at the time were of very little importance. But in the end they had made the real difference—and not the great, ultimately illusory battle that had supposedly lain ahead of us."

"Like Gardner," O'Connor said.

"Yes, I guess so," the younger man said, nodding at the telephone on the end table next to him. "What's the protocol here? Do I call him? Or does he call me?" he said, snapping himself back to the present.

"Maybe neither one," O'Connor said, looking at the silent phone. "I guess now Putnam will be in it by Oregon," Cassidy said.

O'Connor smiled. "I'll bet he wasn't told in advance either. I'd like to see the Vice President's face right about now."

"It probably looks something like mine does," Jack said, returning O'Connor's smile, but then Cassidy's attention seemed to be somewhere else again.

"Putnam will give you a fight, but it won't matter in the end. You'll win it now," O'Connor said.

Jack turned his attention back to his friend. "Perhaps, but don't underestimate the Vice President," Cassidy said. "Putnam's a powerful campaigner—and there's Gardner. He'll do what he can to beat us and that'll be one hell of a lot. Don't forget, he's still the President. It's going to be a fight, Frank."

"A fight you'll win, thank God. There's not a nickel's worth of difference between Gardner's policies and Putnam's. You'll beat him, Jack, you have to," O'Connor said, but, even as he spoke, something began nagging at him again. Jack was keeping something from him; he could feel it, something important. "What is it, Jack?"

"Nothing," Cassidy said. "There's just so much that can happen between now and Chicago, that's all. So much we can't control."

It wasn't like Jack, O'Connor thought, as he glanced at Suzanne. She could sense it, too, he thought, as their eyes met for a brief moment.

"California's the key, now," Jack said.

"You're right," O'Connor said, nodding his head in agreement. "A final confrontation with Putnam for the nomination. You'll probably face him in Oregon before that, maybe even in Nebraska, but if he's going to stop you before the convention now, it has to be in a big state—and there's nowhere else for him to do that. It will come down to California, now. Winner take all."

The telephone rang before Cassidy could answer him and Jack looked over at O'Connor, gesturing for him to take the call.

O'Connor stood, and with a formal dignity he walked slowly to the telephone. He answered it on the third ring. "Senator Cassidy's office. O'Connor."

A moment later, he turned to Jack. "It's the President," he said. Jack took a deep breath before he reached out for the receiver.

Winner take all, O'Connor thought as he handed Jack the phone. And that will be Jack, as it always is, but what was it that he wasn't being told? O'Connor could feel himself slowly growing afraid now, afraid that something important was being kept from him, important enough, perhaps, to change everything.

CHAPTER
43

When the door to the nursery opened, Jack could hear the sounds of the party going on in the front of the house, but then the door closed and it was quiet again in the room at the rear of his Georgetown home. Jack could hear only his wife's footsteps approaching behind him now in the peaceful nursery.

"He's a good sleeper, isn't he?" Suzanne said very quietly, looking down to where her husband, dressed in formal clothes, was kneeling above the brass-barred antique crib that held their newborn son.

"He's a good everything," Jack said after a few seconds of just watching his son's sleeping face. Then Jack turned to his wife and waited, while she knelt on the floor of the nursery next to him.

"You did beautifully," he said.

"Didn't I, though?" She laughed at her own words and at the great joy that she felt inside herself that she could no longer contain. She was dressed all in white for the early spring christening party, but the way that she was kneeling on the floor was wrinkling her long formal gown. She didn't seem to notice it though as she moved forward on one knee to see inside the crib more clearly. "Maybe it was all those plane rides that I didn't take during the last four years," she said. "All those political speeches that I didn't hear."

"Whatever it was . . ." Jack turned back to his child then and let his sleeping presence complete his thought for him.

"The doctors said that from the first moment he was born, his eyes were wide open, his arms grasping for life," Suzanne said.

She and Jack were quiet then, both content to just be there with their baby and to say nothing.

"I was in here asking him for some advice and counsel," Jack said finally.

"And what did he say to you?"

"He reminded me of why I was born, I guess," he said after a few seconds, and Suzanne nodded her understanding.

"When I'm with him . . ." Jack shook his head as he tried to find the words. "He's so damn happy to just be alive it makes me forget all the mistakes, all the . . ." He shrugged his shoulders then, as he realized the inadequacy of his words. "He just makes me want to be alive, too," he said, and then he slowly stood up.

"He's a good counselor," Suzanne said, as her husband reached down and helped her back to her feet next to him.

They were both quiet for a long moment then, and Suzanne could see the tension returning to her husband's face and eyes. "Jack, what is it? I know something's been bothering you."

Jack thought then of the document that he and Rozier had worked on most of the week. It was a press release, scheduled to be given to the press the day after the Indiana primary. Jack reviewed its contents again in his mind for what seemed like the hundredth time in the last forty-eight hours. All it needs is that one final sentence, he thought. The one that goes: "And therefore, I will not seek and would not accept the nomination of my Party as President of the United States." He could just copy Gardner's wording; that would make two candidates down in less than a month and leave the field wide open to Putnam. Summers would just smile and rake in his chips then. The Director would have won another in his long line of poker games with men who would be President. Cassidy thought of the typed copy of the statement lying at that very moment locked in the desk drawer of his den. He was half tempted to walk in there right now and do it. The statement setting out his authorization of Crossbow had taken nearly a week to draft properly, but it would only take a moment to scratch in the concluding sentence at the bottom of the page. Either that or walk in there right now and destroy the document once and for all, he thought, and let at least this one mistake of his first term remain his own personal secret. One or the other, but Jack wasn't sure which yet, or maybe he would just stick to his original course and make the disclosure public and then let the voters decide the final outcome. Three possible choices—quit the race, continue to hide the truth, or disclosure—Jack was far from sure yet which he would ultimately choose.

"Are you going to tell me about it?" Suzanne said, her voice breaking into Jack's thoughts.

"What?" he said absently, and then he turned away from her, back toward the second-floor windows of their Georgetown home. He could almost see the White House from here, he thought as he looked down at the lights of the capital spread out below him—almost, but not quite.

Suzanne smiled at her husband's evasive answer. "About whatever it is that you and Allen have been up to for the last week," she said. "I know that the two of you have been working on something important, while I've been busy having my baby and cleverly distracting the press from your secret plans, whatever they are."

"Oh, nothing," Jack said, trying to make his tone sound offhand and nonchalant. Then, turning to Suzanne and seeing her looking directly at him, he suddenly changed his mind. "I made some mistakes. I'm deciding now what to do about them. That's all. Nothing new for a politician."

Suzanne nodded, waiting for Jack to continue.

"It's serious though," he added. "It might even cost us the election before it's all over. If it does, I'm very sorry."

"Sorry for what?"

"For all the work, everything you've done. It could be for nothing now."

"I have enough," Suzanne said simply, her gaze moving from her husband to her child and then toward the door where a few feet away her family and friends were at that very moment celebrating the birth of her new son.

"This one's going to be rough though," Jack said, moving back to stand in front of her. "Believe me. It's Summers again, but this time, only one of us can win."

"You didn't tell me what he said," Suzanne gestured back toward the brass crib that held their child. "When you asked him what to do about it, what was his advice?"

"Not to be afraid," Jack said without any hesitation. "To do the right thing now and to not worry about the consequences, the same thing that young people always say."

"And was he right?"

"Probably."

"But it's difficult, isn't it? Risking everything that you've worked for now, just when you're so close."

"Yes, it's very difficult," he continued. "In fact, I may not have the courage to do it this time, but I'm lucky to have such good counselors. Whatever I decide."

Jack knelt back down by his son's crib. "I read somewhere this morning," he said, a small teasing smile beginning to appear on his face as he spoke, "that we only had a baby to help my chances for the presidency." His smile widened.

"And they called Tim ruthless," Suzanne said, and she looked closely at her husband's face. She was testing him, and Jack knew it. The wound that he'd suffered with the loss of his brother had to heal, and they both knew that dealing openly with his memory was part of the process.

"You miss him now, don't you?" Suzanne said. "This decision, whatever it is, you need to talk to him about it."

"Yes," Jack answered in a low whisper and then dropped his gaze to look again at his child. "Sometimes though, I almost think that part of Tim could be . . ." But instead of finishing with words, Jack moved his hand down and lightly touched the side of his son's head. "Do you know what I mean?"

"I know. Me too," Suzanne said, joining her husband. "Me too." She reached out and took her husband's hand and held it tight. "I think we'd better keep that our secret though, don't you?" she said, and her husband nodded his head that he agreed. "Whatever happens now, we can't let people think that we're starting to imagine things."

There was a knock on the door and Jack turned to it. "Yes," Jack said, and O'Connor came into the room. The flower in the lapel of his dinner jacket was a bright springtime pink.

"I'm sorry to interrupt," he said.

"The godfather has special rights," Suzanne said.

"We're about to drink a toast downstairs to your new son," O'Connor said. "We thought you might like to join us."

"Of course," Suzanne said, bending back over the crib to kiss her child's forehead one last time before she and her husband went downstairs to join the others. "A toast to Timothy Benjamin Cassidy."

Lopata looked down into a sinkful of greasy dishes. There were more stacks of filthy plates and silverware stacked all around him. The smell of the steam rising up from the sink made him gag and he turned his head away as he choked on the fumes. He felt dizzy and nauseated and weak and he needed desperately to go back to his room and rest, but there was something that he had to do first. Then he could leave New Orleans forever. So he stepped back to the sink and rested the palms of his hands against its stainless-steel base and waited for the weakness to pass.

The dysentery had returned with a new and terrible power. When he'd first arrived in New Orleans, the symptoms that had followed him from Muiriel had slowed for a few weeks, but the night after DeSavio's life had ended outside the French Quarter restaurant, Lopata had awakened with a sharply powerful pain in his intestines and the diarrhea and fever hadn't lessened since then. The only cure, he had decided, was not to eat, and the wrist that he locked against the base of the sink now was so thin that it appeared to be only dark skin pulled over a slender piece of narrow bone. The mere thought of food sickened him, and the job that he'd taken as a busboy and dishwasher at a French Quarter lunch counter, so that he would have enough money to live, had become a daily torture. The need for help, maybe a doctor, flashed through his mind, but he rejected it almost as quickly as it came to him. There was no one who could really help him now, he thought, and he had passionately hated doctors all of his life. They were only for the rich and for the weak, and he was neither.

He hadn't eaten anything in almost a week though, except for an occasional candy bar or a soft drink. And when he'd finally tried that afternoon to eat some real food, his body had rebelled, convulsing into a new round of dysentery. But he couldn't go back to his room and rest, not yet. There was still something that he must do that night, and he forced himself to continue washing the tall stacks of greasy dishes.

When he finished, his shift was almost over. It was nearly eleven and there would be a night man to take his place any minute now. Lopata removed the wet, filthy apron and carried it to the hamper by the back door and dropped it in with all the others.

Through the open door he could see several people seated at the tables on the patio of the bar next door, but his eyes sought the one table in the outdoor café that truly interested him that night. Three old colored men sat together drinking beer and talking, and occasionally loud laughter would spill from their table. Lopata smiled at the outbursts of laughter. Perfect, he thought, they were even drunker that night than they usually were. He checked his watch. The three old colored men came every Tuesday night to the bar next to the lunch counter where Lopata worked, and they sat every time at the same table and drank and told stories, and every Tuesday night, the tall, light-skinned colored man who sat at the end of the table got up at a few minutes to eleven and paid for his drinks and then walked the few French Quarter blocks to the place where he worked. He was a piano player in a strip joint on the Rue Bonaparte. Lopata knew that, because he had followed him out of the bar and down Bourbon Street the last two Tuesday nights.

Lopata returned to the kitchen and put his windbreaker on and zipped it up to his neck. Then he turned the collar up, covering the sides of his face.

When he returned to the screen door, the old piano player had already left the table. Lopata hurried out onto the street. Bourbon was crowded on another Mardi Gras night, the street filled with noisy, brightly dressed people, but Lopata could see the back of the colored man's white shirt weaving along the uneven cobblestone street only a few yards ahead of him.

Lopata put his hands down deep into the pockets of his khaki pants and followed after the colored man. The old man was drunk and he moved sloppily through the festive crowd, weaving from one part of the sidewalk to another, and Lopata had to stop several times and peer into the windows of the bars and shops that lined Bourbon Street or he would have caught up with the skinny, drunken old man too soon.

Finally, the colored man turned down the Rue Bonaparte toward the Rue Cardinal. For the next fifty yards there were no stores or bars and usually very few people. It was particularly quiet now and Lopata quickened his pace, timing it perfectly, so that he arrived next to the colored man at precisely the point that the street opened into a short dead-end alley.

Lopata removed a long-bladed jackknife from the pocket of his khaki pants as he came alongside the colored man. And the blade opened easily just as he'd practiced it. The knife went to the old man's throat, its silver blade illuminated in one of the gas lanterns of the Quarter, and the old colored man's eyes opened wide with terror. Lopata forced the man into the alley. Garbage cans blocked their way and the man's skinny body staggered into them, falling down and spilling them over. The old colored man lay in a pile of refuse, his eyes open wide and white with fear. Lopata reached for the pocket where he knew that the man carried his thickly folded wad of bills.

The colored man was whispering a prayer and Lopata wanted to kill him for it, but instead he simply took his soft neck in one hand and rammed the colored man's head against the alley's brick wall. Blood exploded out of the back of the old man's skull and Lopata wondered if he had killed him after all, but there wasn't time to think about it long. He reached into the man's pants pocket one last time to make certain that it was empty now and then he stood and reentered the Rue Bonaparte.

Within seconds, he had rejoined the thick Mardi Gras traffic on Bourbon Street. He walked along losing himself deep in the carnival crowd. He could feel the thick wad of cash in his pocket, but he didn't dare look at it until he was alone in his room. He threw himself on the bed then and began to count the money. There was blood on his hands and the blood began to stain the bills. So he stopped and walked into his dirty little bathroom and washed the blood away as best he could in the rust-stained sink.

Then he walked back out into his bedroom and finished counting the money. There was over three hundred dollars. With the few dollars he had managed to save from his job, it was more than enough, he thought happily.

He removed his flight bag from beneath his bed then and began packing his things. The rifle had been dismantled and its pieces scattered into the harbor, and without it, all of his possessions fit easily into the single bag. And when he'd finished with it, he carried it out to the street. There was a taxi stand less than a block away and he walked directly to it and climbed into the back of a waiting cab.

Lopata felt a stab of fear as the cabdriver turned to him. It was the same man! But then the old colored cabdriver smiled lazily, showing a double row of badly rotted teeth. No, Lopata thought, just another old nigger. New Orleans was full of them.

"Bus station," Lopata said and settled back into the rear seat of the taxi.

"Yes, suh," the old colored driver answered lazily and then pulled his taxi slowly away from the curb.

The taxi driver reached out and turned on the cab's radio then. There was a news report on Cassidy's victory in the Indiana primary and Lopata listened to it, smiling to himself at the small coincidence. The television, the newspapers, the radio, that was all they talked about anymore. Cassidy, Cassidy, Cassidy, the hope of all the nigger cabdrivers and all the rest of the poor deceived bastards in this whole fucking country, Lopata thought angrily. Cassidy was probably even the hope of that nigger that was lying now bleeding in an alley off the Rue Bonaparte. Well, I wonder what Cassidy can do for dying niggers. Lopata laughed to himself.

He could see the lights of the bus station coming up in the distance now. Shit, will I be happy to leave this fucking, dirty, ugly city, he thought. His business here was finished, but his final goal still lay ahead of him, he thought, his final triumph.

"Experts say that Cassidy's win in the Democratic Primary in Indiana tonight will have very little political impact in the upcoming and potentially more important primaries in Oregon and California," the voice on the radio reported, as the car slowed in front of the bus station. "President Gardner's announcement that he would not seek the Democratic nomination for a second term has removed much of the political significance of Cassidy's victory and made tonight's results in Indiana practically meaningless," the radio analyst continued.

Lopata removed a clean, bloodless bill from his pocket and handed it to the driver. As he did, he smiled to himself at the radio commentator's words. They don't know just how meaningless Cassidy's victory that night really was, Lopata thought as he stepped from the cab and then started into the brightly lit bus terminal—how absolutely and totally meaningless whatever Cassidy does now, will become very soon, he thought.

Denise was afraid to answer the phone. She watched it ring—eight rings, ten, twelve, more. She was terrified of who it might be on the other end of the line.

Finally it stopped, but the silence was even worse, ominous, hushed. She could feel her own pulse pounding in her wrist.

She ran to the door, looking back at the darkness of her apartment before she opened the front door. Jimi Hendrix's eyes stared down at her from the psychedelic orange-and-black poster mounted above her couch. She looked at it in fear. Out of concern for their safety, she let her kids stay at her sister's apartment most nights now and she was all alone. The ringing started again and the first sudden vibrating sound cut through her like a jolt of electricity. She turned away from her darkened living room and its insistently ringing phone then and ran. She knew that it had to be Grissum, or maybe Yancey, someone from the Bureau, someone who wanted to know what she knew—first Kit, then Jim, next her. She wanted to scream. The last few weeks had been the worst of her entire life.

She pushed the elevator button, but she couldn't wait for it to arrive. She frantically began punching the call button over and over. Finally, she ran to the door that led to the service stairs. She couldn't hear her ringing phone any longer, but the stairwell was dark and badly lit and the sound of every step that she took on the metal stairs echoed and reechoed in the narrow chamber as she descended to the subterranean garage. The garage was empty of people, just rows of silent parked cars. So many hiding places in the shadowy spaces of the garage, Denise thought in fear, as she ran from the safety of the elevator toward her own car. She bent down and searched the back seat of her dark green Mustang before she unlocked its driver's-side door. She glanced behind her again as she started the car's engine, and she turned her head and looked behind her one last time as she backed the Mustang out of its parking space.

It was dark on the street outside Denise's apartment and she drove erratically, watching the traffic behind her in her rearview mirror almost as much as she watched the road in front of her on the short trip to the downtown restaurant. As far as she could tell no one was following her, but in the darkness it was difficult to be certain. These people were experts in following people, she told herself. What chance did she have against them? They could be anywhere in the tangle of headlights on the crowded Dallas streets behind her.

There was a parking attendant in a bright red vest standing in front of Eddie's, and she breathed a grateful sigh of relief when she saw him. He spared her from the terror of parking on a dark side street and then walking all alone to the building's front door.

The restaurant was crowded and noisy, and Denise felt better as soon as she walked inside and felt the warmth of the room and the press of bodies moving around her. It was the kind of a place with far more men than women and Denise could see the male heads turning toward her as she entered the room. The appreciation made her feel even better and she began to relax a little more then. Maybe it would be okay now, she thought. Coming here had been a good idea.

She asked the hostess for Mr. Wellington's table and she was led promptly to a black leather booth in a private corner of the room.

Denise was surprised at just how much Wellington looked like the caricature that topped his column in the Dallas morning paper. A shock of unruly, sandy brown hair dominated his appearance just as it did in the familiar drawing. His relaxed smile was the same, too, and the jaunty way that he held his cigarette and let smoke curl up and frame his face. Denise paused by his table, but he made no attempt to stand, so Denise moved the chair that blocked her way and slid into the booth across from him.

"Would you like a drink?" he asked.

"Bourbon," she said, as she glanced around the room again. "Thank you for meeting me," Denise said, her eyes still nervously checking each of the nearby tables.

"I do most of my business here," the slightly built man said and then smiled reassuringly, but Denise's eyes were looking behind her at the door to the restaurant now.

"What are you afraid of?" Wellington asked, the smile fading, and Denise turned back to see a pair of shrewd reporter's eyes looking directly across the table at her.

Her drink came while Denise was still studying the reporter's face, trying to decide if she could trust him. She grasped the tall drink firmly and took a swallow of the harsh, smoky liquid. Her eyes watered as she set it back down onto the table.

Wellington smiled at her. It was apparent that she was not a woman accustomed to drinking straight bourbon. "I'm sorry about what happened to your friend, Agent Sullivan," the reporter said. Wellington had run a short piece on Sullivan in his Sunday column a few weeks earlier—young man dies in line of duty, that kind of thing. The column had contrasted Sullivan's actions to those of so many other young people who spent their energy protesting the war and experimenting with drugs. It had been a good piece. Wellington hadn't expected to do a follow-up on it though, but then Denise had called him. Maybe there was another story. Maybe not. He would see. Wellington inspected the girl from a reporter's point of view. Attractive; well-dressed; a soft, honest face; pretty, light-blue eyes; but nothing special —just another girl. You see them by the thousands in the big cities now, secretaries, clerks, vaguely ambitious, but with no special education or talent. In another year she'll be a good suburban wife for somebody. The faintly hippie clothes will be a little more matronly, the ambitious dreams and the vague thoughts of making some kind of a difference in the great-big, tough world will be forgotten. Wellington had her sized up and pegged within only a few seconds of meeting her. He was good at it, he told himself. He had to be. It was part of his job.

Denise reached for the whiskey again as Wellington scrutinized her, but then she thought better of it and set the glass back down on the table. "Mr. Wellington, I think the FBI may be trying to murder me." She blurted the words out suddenly and as soon as she did, she wished that she hadn't. She hadn't realized how foolish they would sound out loud, like that, without any preliminaries. Wellington refused to give away his feelings, but Denise knew that he wasn't impressed. She could hardly blame him, she thought. Here in this crowded, warm, safe bar surrounded by all these people, it sounded crazy to her, too. She'd thought of little else since the funeral, but she hadn't said anything to anyone and she realized now why she had chosen not to speak to anyone about it. No one would believe her.

"The FBI?" Wellington said, making sure that he had it straight.

"Please," Denise said, feeling a sudden panic flooding over her. "Jim was working on the Cassidy shooting. He knew more about the case than anybody," she said quickly.

But Wellington's slightly irritated voice cut her off. "Miss Richards," he said, with mock respect, "the Cassidy assassination thing is closed."

"Please," Denise said, lifting her hand up toward the reporter to ask for his silence. "Jim knew things." Denise searched her mind now for anything that might help her convince him. It had taken her weeks to even get her nerve up to call Wellington. After him, she had nowhere else to go. "Right after it happened, Jim took a copy of a file. Stole it really, right out of FBI headquarters here in Dallas. He gave that file to me for safekeeping."

"What file?"

"Strode's, I think," Denise said. "I'm not really sure. It was in a locked bag and Jim told me not to look at it and I didn't, but it was important. I know that much. So important that the FBI sent someone for it. My apartment was broken into and my roommate was killed." Denise was talking so fast now that she barely paused to take a breath between thoughts. "And the file was stolen."

"What did the police say?"

"There were other things missing and they just called it a burglary," Denise admitted. "But we didn't tell them about the file."

"Why not?"

"After their final report on the assassination was released, the Bureau tried to stop Jim from investigating the case. They put enormous pressure on him, but he wouldn't. He wouldn't stop. He thought that it was important to find out the truth. You see, Jim knew that there was another gunman in Dealey Plaza that day. He saw him. Jim didn't tell me everything, but I know that much. Jim saw him that day, and that man is still alive!"

Wellington paused for a moment now, not certain how to handle the woman sitting across from him. He lit a fresh cigarette and let smoke trail up and cover his face again. She probably isn't crazy, the reporter decided, just pretty badly shaken up. The man that she'd been in love with had just been killed. He was an FBI agent and he had worked in a mysterious and difficult world that she couldn't possibly be expected to understand. Whatever he'd said to her about his job had probably frightened and confused her and then, when he'd been killed, it was natural for her to be excited and probably more than a little panicked.

"Miss Richards, do you know how many people come to us with stories about the Cassidy shooting? It's down to about ten a month now. Down." He repeated the word for emphasis. "And it's not just us. Every paper in this city, every radio and TV station. We're flooded with stuff about it. Tips, photographs, theories, people who knew people who . . ." Wellington gave up in midsentence to show how hopeless it all was. "My editor's got a standing rule, Miss Richards. No more Cassidy stuff. All over, all gone, finished." Wellington spread his hands out in front of him to help him make his point.

Denise tried to say something then, but the reporter moved his hand out toward her to silence her. "An iron-clad rule, Miss Richards. We don't do assassination stuff anymore." He was lying, but it was the best way that he could think of to get rid of her. And anyway, it was close enough to the truth. It would take a hell of an angle to get his editor to do another Cassidy conspiracy thing right then.

Denise looked down at the tablecloth. She felt powerless. "There are other papers," Wellington said. "There's the police too," he added, with very little conviction in his voice.

Denise stayed quiet. She wanted to cry, but she began shaking her head back and forth, using the movement to hold her tears inside herself. She was damned if she was going to cry here, not in a public restaurant, not in front of this man. Alone in her car, she'd cry, she decided, but not now.

Wellington looked across the table at her. She seemed nice enough and he wanted to help her if he could, but he couldn't run off on every wild story that the people of Dallas threw at him.

"What is it you're saying? That the FBI wants this file back that you say Agent Sullivan took? So, the Bureau's going to try to kill you to get it?"

"No, I told you the file is gone. I don't have it any longer. When my apartment was broken into they took it," Denise said. "I'm not too clear on all of it, but just before he died, Jim told me that this second gunman was still alive and maybe still a threat to Senator Cassidy."

"And if he is?" Wellington said. "Why wouldn't the FBI want to know that?"

"I don't know," Denise said.

"And why would they want to kill one of their own agents?"

"To keep him from finding out any more about it, I guess," Denise said, but her voice was growing weak and uncertain. She was a damn fool to have come here at all.

"And why would the FBI want to kill you?"

"I don't know. Maybe to keep me from talking to someone like you, or going to the Cassidy family, or something, I guess. The Bureau can't be sure just what Jim told me or what proof he might have given me."

"What proof did he give you, Miss Richards?" Wellington said. He always thought that he would have made a good lawyer, and as he asked his ultimate question he used his lawyer's voice to make his final point with the young girl.

Denise paused for several seconds before she tried to answer Wellington's question. In the silence, she thought back over the entire period of time that she had known Jim before she realized that she had no real proof at all. "Nothing," she said finally.

"So, you really don't have anything tangible then," Wellington said quietly.

"No, I guess not," Denise admitted, and then she looked back down at her drink. "It's just that . . ." She tried to start over, but it was hopeless. She stood suddenly and reached down for her purse. "Thank you for your time, Mr. Wellington," she said and then turned away from him and started to thread her way back through the crowded restaurant toward the door.

Wellington raised his hand as if to stop her, but then, thinking better of it, he let her go. Poor kid, the reporter thought. It was probably a lot for a little girl like that to take. I hope her friends can help her sort it all out though. She could probably make a good wife for some nice suburban bastard some day.

CHAPTER
44

Less than twenty-four hours after the results in Indiana, the campaign was already beginning to take on the look of victory. O'Connor knew the signs. He'd seen it in the presidential campaign eight years earlier. You could see it first in the faces of the staff. Then in the way the crowds greeted you. They were bigger and more excited. The women wanted to get close to the candidate, touch him, while the men's faces grew more respectful. Even the reporters began treating the candidate with a little more dignity when they smelled a winner. The phones start ringing, then the telegrams, followed by the letters and the checks. There was a buoyancy, a kind of joy in the work. Even on a crowded campaign plane between Indianapolis and Portland, politics begins to be fun, a great challenge, a high and noble art. After the win in Indiana, O'Connor could smell it in the air and it energized him. The columnists could write all they wanted to about how meaningless the victory had been without Gardner in the race, but O'Connor knew the truth. There was no such thing as a meaningless victory in politics. Victories were victories.

He barely even noticed when the candidate excused himself once the plane was safely in the air to make another call to Rozier in Washington. As soon as the seat-belt sign blinked off, O'Connor sprang to his feet and walked up and down the narrow aisle of the plane, clasping and unclasping his hands behind him. New ideas were rushing at him. How to handle the war issue with the Veterans of Foreign Wars group in Salem. How to break the expected deadlock in the Mississippi delegation at the nominating convention in Chicago three months down the road. The wisdom of perhaps selecting Putnam as Jack's running mate when the time came. And California, always California, the key to it all, he thought, and it was only six short weeks away. Every time a new idea occurred to him, he would glance around the plane, looking for the candidate, but he couldn't find him, and O'Connor would have to return to his seat or hurriedly write down his thoughts on a scrap of notepaper. Then he would begin pacing the aisle again. And why all these secret phone calls to Rozier?

Finally O'Connor wandered back to the rear of the plane. He knocked once on the bulkhead that separated the candidate's private office from the rest of the airplane's interior.

"Yes," Cassidy said.

The candidate was alone, his suit coat off, the telephone that he'd used to call Rozier lying in its cradle next to him.

"Frank, good," Jack said, returning his gaze to the front of the private airplane cabin that served as his office. "I was going to talk to you in a few minutes, anyway," Cassidy said, and then he glanced at his watch. "Now will do just as well," he added with a small weary sigh.

There was only a single piece of paper on the desktop in front of Cassidy. With slow, reluctant hands the candidate reached down and slid it across toward O'Connor. "You should read this," Cassidy said and then waited as his aide removed the sheet of paper from the desk and stood reading it for several long seconds.

"You can't be serious about this," O'Connor said finally. Jack looked directly up at the old Irish politician's unhappy face then. "Sit down, Frank," the candidate said, motioning toward the small seat that was wedged into the narrow space between the desk and the airplane's metal bulkhead, but O'Connor preferred to remain standing. He just stood holding the single sheet of paper tightly in both hands out in front of him, refusing to look down at it again.

"Allen's scheduled to release that," Cassidy said, motioning at the paper in O'Connor's hands and then glancing briefly at his own watch, "in about seven minutes from now."

O'Connor could hear the sadness and reluctance in the candidate's voice. Maybe there was still time to stop him, he thought hopefully. "Why, Jack? Why in God's name?" O'Connor raised the press release into the air and shook it above his head.

"It was inevitable. It would have come out one way or the other and I wanted it behind me as soon as possible."

Jack's a very good liar, O'Connor thought, as he looked at his face, but damn it, he's not that good. There was something he wasn't being told. "You authorized a plan called Crossbow that was designed to recruit and train American agents for the purpose of assassinating political leaders of other countries," O'Connor summarized the opening paragraph of the press release, his voice incredulous. "Why don't you just go on television and tell everybody that you were just kidding about wanting to become President again and that

Vice President Putnam, no I'm wrong, that Bill Longwood is your first choice. It would be better than this." O'Connor dropped the press release on the empty airplane seat next to Cassidy then.

Jack tried to smile, but he couldn't. O'Connor was right. He could very well be committing political suicide, and he was in no position to tell O'Connor or anyone else why—but it had to be done, and in another five minutes it would be done. He could see O'Connor eying the phone on his desk—the phone that could still link him to Rozier and stop the release of the information, but instead of reaching for it, Cassidy picked up the press release from the airplane seat and looked over at his aide's face again. "Frank, please," he said, "sit down."

O'Connor sank down into the seat across from him. "Jack," O'Connor said plaintively. "I know there's a lot I don't know about and that's fine, my job is politics, not government. But damn it all, that's what this is, straight and simple: politics—bad politics. It could . . ." O'Connor stopped in midsentence and then tried it a different way. "I mean, we've got a little momentum behind us now. New Hampshire, Indiana, the polls look good in Oregon," he said, pointing out the window in the direction that they were traveling now. "But believe me, we're going to need everything possible going for us to beat Putnam in California, and if we do, it's over. You'll have the nomination then, but now this." O'Connor returned his eyes sadly to the press release lying on the desktop. "Call Allen, stop this thing, at least until after California."

Cassidy could feel himself beginning to waver. Everything that O'Connor was saying was true, but he would stick by it, whatever the consequences. "I've done the only thing I could do," Jack said, looking again at his watch. It was one minute before ten o'clock in Washington and Rozier would be on his way into the Senate press room. It was probably too late to stop it now, even if he wanted to.

"It could cost you everything we've worked for," O'Connor said.

"I know that, Frank," the candidate said.

"And you're not going to tell me why, are you?" O'Connor added, forcing an ironic smile onto his face, but then he nodded his head in acceptance and understanding. "And if I pushed, you'd probably say that I would just have to trust you," O'Connor said, looking across the desk at his friend. Cassidy started to say something in return, but O'Connor held up his hand to silence him. "You don't have to say it, Jack. I do," he said. "It just means that we'll all have to work a little harder now, I guess," he added a little sadly, as he started for the door and the main aisle of the campaign plane.

"And we'll have to start with our own people," Cassidy said, gesturing out toward the cabin full of staff workers. "I'll want to talk to them in a few minutes," he added and O'Connor nodded and then returned down the aisle of the campaign plane.

Cassidy watched him go. After a few seconds, he glanced back down at his watch. Rozier was probably almost finished reading the statement by now, he thought. Well, he'd had the courage to call Summers's bluff after all. Now, the next move was up to the Director—to Summers and to the voters of Oregon and California. In the next few weeks, both his own and Summers's public careers could be over, Cassidy thought, as his eyes drifted back out the airplane window toward the clouds that surrounded the campaign plane that was flying him west toward Oregon.

Rozier set the terms of his final meeting with Estanza. He told the Cuban diplomat the time and the place and even the purpose of the meeting. Jack's decision to release the information about his role in Crossbow may cost him the presidency, Rozier thought as he waited for Estanza to arrive, but it had at least personally freed him from having to meet with the Cuban diplomat in any more dark secret places.

Rozier looked out at the view of New York harbor spread out below the window of the restaurant at the top of the World Trade Center. It was bright midday in Manhattan and the sunlight sparkled off the distant waters of the Atlantic below the restaurant's tall floor-to-ceiling picture windows. Just then, he saw Estanza approaching his table from across the room. The diplomat looked older in the full light of day, his clothes a little less immaculate, the expression on his once supremely confident face a little less poised. But maybe that was just how he viewed him now, Rozier thought as he stood up to shake the older man's hand—now that the Cuban no longer held all the power in their negotiations. Estanza was far too experienced and skilled a diplomat to tip his own loss of bargaining power in advance, wasn't he? But the Cuban's handshake was decidedly weaker and he looked away from Rozier's steady gaze a second earlier than he had on their previous meetings. No, it wasn't just his own mood. Estanza knew that his government had lost much of the gamble that they had attempted. By revealing the truth about his own involvement in Crossbow, Jack had removed the negotiating edge from Castro's position. There were still some secrets left in the Cuban's possession, particularly the documents that contained allegations identifying the true conspirators behind the assassination attempt on Jack's life, but there was probably very little remaining that the Cubans could really prove and even less that would have any major impact on Jack politically. In fact, it was very possible now that any attempt by Castro to use what he had in his possession could create a backlash and stir sympathy and support for Jack. The Cuban knew only too well that the power between them had shifted. It was Rozier who was in command of the relationship now.

"Senator Cassidy's decision was unfortunate," Estanza said, as the two men settled down into their seats, but the diplomat's words were perfunctory, emotionless, and it was clear that he was only doing his duty, going through the motions as he'd been instructed by his superiors.

Rozier brought the waiter to the table then and ordered for Estanza, remembering the dry vermouth that the diplomat had requested at their first meeting.

"Yes," Estanza said, returning his gaze to Rozier's face. "And now, my government is forced to do what it believes that it must do as well," the diplomat said, but still his voice lacked any real conviction.

"Which is to release the materials that you have in your possession to the press," Rozier said.

"Of course," the diplomat answered. "We have no other choice."

"Or very little to gain either," Rozier said crisply.

Again, Estanza seemed almost to nod his head in acknowledgment of the truth of what Rozier had said, but then he remained silent.

"Senator Cassidy has instructed me to tell you on his behalf that he will not under any circumstances negotiate with the Cuban government concerning the materials now in its possession. But since these matters concern United States internal affairs, the Senator would consider it a gesture of extreme good faith, on your government's part, if the documents were delivered into his possession as soon as possible."

Estanza waited for Rozier to finish.

"Senator Cassidy does believe, however, that a new relationship needs to be established by the United States with the Cuban people and with its leaders. There are a number of areas, some contained in your earlier communication to him, that he believes should be reconsidered by our government. To that end, Senator Cassidy has prepared a list of items that could serve as an agenda for discussions between himself and Premier Castro. In the event that Senator Cassidy is elected President, he has authorized me to assure you that he would enter into immediate discussions with your government that should lead to a formal agreement between our two countries on the matters contained in that agenda." Rozier reached into his coat pocket and removed an envelope, placing it on the table. As the diplomat reached for it, Rozier was struck by the irony of the full shift in positions from the first meeting between himself and the Cuban diplomat that the envelope symbolized. At their first meeting, it had been Rozier who had done all the listening and Estanza who had supplied him with a mysterious envelope containing among other things the demands of the Cuban government. But now, four months later, he was the one handing Estanza a similar envelope containing an agenda for discussions between their two countries; this time, though, the terms of their two governments' future relationship had been prepared not by Castro, but by Jack and his advisers.

"I will transmit Senator Cassidy's message to my superiors," Estanza said, placing the envelope into a slim, white leather attaché case. Then he looked up at Rozier and smiled. "For, you see, I am only a middleman in affairs of this magnitude."

"I understand," Rozier said, returning the smile. As he spoke, Rozier's eyes again caught the outline of the New York harbor behind Estanza, and for a brief moment Rozier watched the passage of the ships moving across it.

"But may I tell Senator Cassidy that for now there will be no disclosures to the press of any information within your government's possession, at least not until we have heard Premier Castro's answer to the Senator's proposal?"

"Certainly," Estanza said. "For now," he added pointedly.

Estanza remained quiet as the waiter returned with his drink. The diplomat lifted the glass and raised it in a toast and perhaps in a hint of a salute, Rozier thought as he watched him—a salute to Cassidy's courage and to what the elderly diplomat knew would, if all went as Jack had planned it, be Castro's probable acceptance of the terms he proposed.

"I am very impressed with the way in which Senator Cassidy has acted in this matter," Estanza said. "But I hope that he hasn't forgotten one final but absolutely essential requirement for his plan's ultimate success."

"Yes," Rozier said, pausing to hear what that final piece of the puzzle could be.

"Senator Cassidy must win," Estanza said. "Everything that he has done, his entire strategy in dealing with my government, is dependent on it now. If he loses in his bid for the presidency, what you have proposed to us today is meaningless. I'm certain Senator Cassidy understands that and he must know, as well, if he fails to win back the presidency, my government will be obligated to make other arrangements with the information at its disposal than those we have spoken of this afternoon. And given the reaction in this country to the disclosures the Senator has just made, that may now be very difficult for him to accomplish. I hope he hasn't forgotten that."

"I'm certain that he hasn't." Estanza was right, Rozier thought, as his eyes locked with the elderly gray-haired diplomat's. Jack's plan to deal with the Cubans was courageous and bold, but it would all become meaningless without victory.

"Well, how does it feel to lose your first election?" The reporter's voice rose above the clamor of the other reporters in the crowded press room.

As he tried to answer the question, Jack hoped that how he really felt didn't show. "Adlai Stevenson said it best: 'It hurts too much to laugh, but I'm too old to cry,' " he said, his smile covering his true feelings.

"Part of the Cassidy legend has always been that you're invincible. Now Vice President Putnam has shown the country that you're not. How do you think that will affect your ability to win the nomination?" Before he answered the reporter's questions, Jack looked out at the crowded hotel conference room temporarily set up for the press on the top floor of the Benson Hotel in Portland.

Jack focused on his last questioner's eager face, and as the candidate thought through his answer, he marveled at the inexhaustible ability that the press had to ask the same question in seemingly endless ways. "I don't feel any more or any less invincible than I did yesterday or the day before," he said. "But I do believe that I will be nominated in Chicago," he added. Even in defeat, it was apparent that he enjoyed matching wits and trading comments with a roomful of reporters.

"The polls showed that the disclosures that you made concerning Operation Crossbow hurt you dramatically. Do you now regret releasing that information at the time you did?"

Cassidy was thoughtful, pausing for a moment to consider his answer. "No, no, I don't," he said. "I believe that in the last analysis the people of this country will understand, not that my first administration was without mistakes, but that in the future we will be dedicated to learning from any errors in judgment that we may have made. I believe that Crossbow was such a mistake on my part, and errors of that kind will not be repeated in my second administration. That should be the end of it."

"Do you think Vice President Putnam was too rough on you over the issue of Crossbow?"

"Vice President Putnam and I differ on many vital issues," Cassidy said, refusing to take the bait. "Events that occurred over six years ago concerning an operation that I mistakenly authorized when I first came into office and subsequently canceled are not as important as the vital issues of peace and war that separate us now."

"Did you enjoy your trip to Oregon?"

"I enjoyed my time in Oregon enormously," Cassidy said. "And I'm looking forward to returning here in the fall, with better results." Cassidy smiled.

"And California?"

"I've never lost an election in California, and that's one Cassidy tradition we expect to keep very much alive over the next few weeks," Jack said, dropping his hand casually into his coat pocket and then pointing with his extended finger at the next questioner.

"Why will California be any different from Oregon?"

"California will be different," Cassidy said, and, as he finished his answer, he could see Rozier pushing toward him through the crowd of reporters at the edge of the podium. "There's a call I think you should take," Rozier whispered as he moved up close to the candidate. Jack turned his gaze from the roomful of reporters then and looked directly at Rozier. From his friend's expression, Jack could guess that this was the call that he had been waiting impatiently to receive since his arrival in Oregon three weeks earlier, and that he had asked Allen to interrupt him for, whatever he was doing.

Cassidy turned back to the crowd. "Thank you," the candidate said, waving at the reporters as he stepped back from the microphone. The call was from Summers, Jack thought, as an anxious feeling began spreading through him. What did the Director have to say? Had the public disclosure of Crossbow forced Summers to show his hand? Or did the Director have some new trick up his sleeve? He would find out now, Jack realized suddenly, whether the gamble that had cost him at the least a primary and perhaps even the presidency had paid off or not.

* * *

Summers had never telephoned him in victory—but in defeat the Director was the first to call, Jack thought with some amusement, as he picked up the phone in the back bedroom of his Portland hotel suite. It was probably only in such a moment that Summers could make the kind of a call that he was making now, Jack added to himself then.

"Senator." The Director's voice was even more coldly formal than it normally was.

"Yes," Cassidy said and then waited. Since Summers had placed the call, it would have been inappropriate to do anything but listen to what he had to say, Jack decided, but the silence on the long-distance phone line quickly became long and very uncomfortable.

"This afternoon I met with the President," Summers said finally. "At that time I presented to him my resignation." Jack could sense Summers's deep regret underneath the formality.

"The country owes you a great deal, Mr. Director," Cassidy said.

"Thank you," Summers answered, but the words were hollow.

There was another silence between the two men then, and it was Summers who broke it again. "The resignation won't become effective until the end of next month, and I would like to delay a public announcement of it as long as possible. As you know, there are matters within the Bureau that need to be cleared up first. I believe that they can be accomplished best if no one knows of my decision until that time. I think you can appreciate that."

"Of course," Cassidy said. By the end of next month, Jack thought, we could both be out of a job anyway. The end of June was over three weeks after the California primary. If the Democrats of California reacted to the disclosures about Crossbow as the Oregon voters had, it would be Putnam or perhaps Longwood appointing Summers's successor.

"There will be other resignations among my immediate staff," Summers continued. "There will also be a complete investigation of the matter we discussed earlier concerning the Bureau's Dallas office. There may be additional resignations as a result of that investigation," Summers said. Then he paused and added, "I assume that you still consider resignations of personnel directly responsible sufficient? I believe we agreed that was the only way to keep the matter confidential. I told the President that I thought, in fairness, that both you and Vice President Putnam should be informed of my decision, but that no one on either of your staffs should be told yet. He's speaking with the Vice President now."

"Thank you for informing me of your decision, Mr. Director."

"Yes," Summers answered uncertainly. "Yes, of course." And then the line went silent, the call ended. Jack set the receiver down softly in its cradle, and only then did Jack let his own body begin to relax. Well, it's over, he thought. There had been years of valuable service before the excesses of the last decade, and the Bureau that Summers had fathered and nurtured and given its direction was an important and necessary part of the country now.

It had been imperative not to destroy either it or the man in the process of giving it a new start, but that had meant that there would be no blood revenge for Agent Sullivan's death. The punishment of those responsible for his murder would be only a loss of power, not prison or death, but at least the young man's life had not been lost in vain.

CHAPTER
45

Denise ate another dinner alone. She sat by the coffee shop's plate-glass window where she could see her parked car and the street that ran in front of the restaurant. There was a car stopped in the shadows at the side of the road about half a block away from where she sat, and Denise could see a man seated silently in the car's front seat, watching her, the same man that had been following her for almost a week now. She threw her fork down, letting it clatter against the side of the restaurant plate. This was ridiculous! There was no man out there watching her. No one was following her. It was just nerves and it was getting completely out of control. They had begun to notice it at work, too. Denise glanced across the expressway to the cluster of high-rise office buildings behind the shopping center where she worked. She had to get a hold on herself or the next thing she knew, she'd be out of a job.

Come on, kid, stop feeling sorry for yourself. Jim wouldn't want you to start going to pieces. You've come so damn far in the last few years. There's no turning back now. She stood up and reached down for the check. Come so far, she laughed at herself. What? Because she made a little more money? Dressed a little fancier? Had a better apartment? She paid the check and walked outside to her car. But it was good, what she'd done with her life, she thought then. It was damn good. And there was a future to it, a hope that it might get even better. She was not going to let it all go to hell now. Sweet God, that car back there pulled away from the curb just a few seconds after I did, she realized suddenly, and she watched the dark car moving slowly a half block behind her. Jim, tell me what to do, she thought then. She'd

586

begun asking Sullivan for advice and help lately. Sometimes there would be nothing in return, but sometimes . . . Sometimes she'd swear she could almost hear his voice directing her. Like now, pull over into the right lane and slow down, the voice seemed to say, and she did as she was told. Okay, so I'm nuts, she said to herself as she checked for the other car's lights in her rearview mirror.

She pulled her car back out into traffic and drove slowly down the Dallas streets, taking turns aimlessly, looking at some of the new construction that seemed to be springing up everywhere around the city lately. She had nowhere to go, really. It was early. Her kids were staying overnight with her sister again. They practically lived over there now, and her own apartment was empty, but she couldn't face it, not yet. She kept driving around aimlessly on the Dallas streets, taking a random right turn and then a left, letting the traffic and the streets guide her. She looked up nervously into her rearview mirror every few seconds. Sometimes she thought that she saw the car from the restaurant, the one she'd seen following her for the last week or so, but she couldn't be sure and she didn't want to believe it.

She turned on the radio, trying to relax. The music seemed very far away and she couldn't focus on it, but when she switched to the news it was even worse. It was all bad, more deaths in Vietnam, more protests and street violence in her own country. One violent incident in particular had threatened the life of Vice President Putnam as he campaigned in California on the final weekend before that state's Democratic primary. It was like the whole world was going crazy and beginning to pull apart. What had happened to that world she'd been raised in? It seemed to her as if the sane, normal, happy world that she had been brought up to live in had all ended on November 22, 1963. She looked up to see that she was driving through Dealey Plaza, headed for the overpass near the very spot where Cassidy had been shot. No wonder her thoughts had drifted back to that day. She looked over at the Book Depository Building and her eyes focused on its front steps, and then across the plaza to the grassy knoll where Jim had seen that second man that day long ago. Then she moved her eyes back to the road. There were street signs coming up in front of her now. East? West? She should just pick one, that voice inside her head that she wanted to be Jim, said to her. Just pick one and drive forever on it, drive to the Pacific or to the Atlantic. It would be all right. Was that someone behind her? A headlight flashed into view and just as quickly it was gone. Drive on, the voice said. It'll be okay, I'll be with you.

She glanced in her rearview mirror. It was dark again. She took a turnoff that would lead back to her apartment. There was nowhere else to go, she decided, and soon the tall, twin black-glass apartment towers loomed above her. She looked up at her unit, fourth floor, three sets of windows over from the southwest corner of the building. Her apartment was dark.

Hadn't she left a light on? She always left a light on when she went out. Was there someone up there? What the hell was waiting for her up there in the darkness? She couldn't do it. She couldn't go up. She moved her car past the entrance to the underground parking lot and continued on down the street.

Silently, a car pulled out from the shadows of the road behind her. Its headlights flashed on and flooded the interior of her car with a blinding, bright yellow light. Denise let out a small, short scream at the intrusion and she could feel the panic surging inside her.

She pushed on the gas pedal of her car and the little Mustang leaped forward. Without looking back, she raced her car up onto the expressway that crossed in front of her apartment complex. There were other cars driving alongside hers in the floodlights of the elevated concrete highway and their presence began to calm her. She tried to quiet herself down as she pushed her little car forward into traffic. It was real though, wasn't it? It wasn't only her fears. There had been someone back there following her. She was being watched. She was certain of that now.

The signs for the shopping center where she worked were beginning to appear in front of her. She glanced at the clock on her dashboard. It was almost nine. The stores would be closed, but she could go up to her office. She could lock the door and be alone and have some time by herself to think. She moved her car to the far right lane and took the familiar exit that led to the shopping center. She pulled into the deserted employees' lot and ran to the elevator that took her up to the administrative offices that overlooked the large indoor mall. She paused for a moment in the darkened reception area and looked out of the floor-to-ceiling plate-glass windows at the darkened shops on the floors below. She breathed in deeply, regaining some of her composure. Then she turned and used her key to let herself into the long dark hallway that led to her private office.

She reached up and turned on the hall light. It all seemed so familiar, so safe—the plants, the pictures, the burnt-orange color of the carpet. She walked to her office and used her key again to go inside. Feeling a little foolish, she locked the door behind her. She went to her desk and turned on only the small desk lamp. She leaned back deep into her soft imitation leather chair and caught her breath. She hadn't realized until that moment how really terrified she'd been. This had to stop, she told herself. I have to do something. I can't live like this.

Denise looked at the telephone in front of her. There was one thing that she could do. She could call Senator Cassidy.

Jim had given all of his files and information to the Vice President just before his death. Maybe his brother could use his power to find out what had happened to them. Maybe they hadn't been destroyed in Vietnam, as Jim had feared. Maybe they were still in Washington somewhere. Maybe if she talked to Cassidy, told him . . . Wait a minute, who was she kidding? She looked down at the top of her desk. There was a little pad of paper directly in front of her. On top of the pad the words FROM THE DESK OF DENISE RICHARDS were printed and below that there was a small cartoon daisy. Denise had to laugh. What was she going to do? Just write a note to Cassidy on her daisy pad and send it to him care of the United States Senate? If the Dallas papers are getting six tips a day or whatever it was Wellington said, how many must Cassidy himself be getting? My chances of even getting through to him are zero. She threw the little memo pad with the cartoon daisies on its pages onto a corner of her desk, but even as she did, her other hand moved defiantly across her desktop and picked up the phone. Why the hell not? All they can do is laugh at me, and if I don't do anything I've got no chance at all. I might as well give it a try. She sighed as she waited for the operator to come on the line. Operator, give me Senator Cassidy, she fantasized saying, but when a voice finally did answer she simply asked for the information operator in San Francisco. She'd heard on the news that Senator Cassidy was in San Francisco, speaking at a rally in Union Square. So far, so good. The San Francisco operator had a listing for a Cassidy campaign headquarters on Market Street. Denise reached for her daisy scratch pad and jotted the number down.

Then, without hesitating, Denise dialed that California number. It would be a little after midnight in California, but if she was lucky, she still might catch someone, she thought. As she waited, she realized that she had no idea in the world what she was going to say.

"Cassidy for President!" a voice announced confidently.

"Yes, I'm calling from Dallas, Texas," Denise said. "Is there someone there in charge of security?"

There was a long pause on the other end of the line. There was a click and then the young woman's voice was replaced by an older, more serious male one. "Yes, who's calling, please?"

"My name is Denise Richards. I'm calling from Dallas, Texas, and I'd like to speak to the person in charge of security arrangements for Senator Cassidy." Denise listened to the fear in her own voice.

"The man in charge of security for the Senator is in our Los Angeles office right now. Maybe I can help you, I'm . . ."

Denise cut him off in midsentence. "May I have his name and phone number?"

There was a second long pause. Finally, the voice on the other end of the line seemed to decide that a name and a phone number couldn't do any harm and Denise jotted down the Los Angeles phone number for the Cassidy head-quarters and then she hung up the phone.

She sat for a moment looking at the phone number on her scratch pad and recharging her courage to make the call, when she heard a noise. There was someone moving in the corridor outside her office. The knob of her office door moved against the lock. Oh, God, what do I do now? Someone was trying to break into her office.

The air felt cool on Jack's face. He could see the brightly colored red-and-gold lights of San Francisco's Chinatown ahead of him. California was going to be all right, he thought, as he sat back and let himself enjoy the night.

He reached down and squeezed Suzanne's hand. She was waving at the people clustered at the side of the road, but she turned when she felt Jack's hand touching hers. "I love San Francisco," she said.

There were fireworks now, twirling brightly in the air above the buildings. The fireworks flashed and exploded and showered the night sky with brief beauty and Jack waved at the crowd that lined the side of the road. California was a special place for him, he thought, as he smiled at the face of a little Chinese girl who was sitting on her father's shoulders at the edge of the road. It's going to be all right. The latest California polls showed Putnam still ahead, but the gap was closing rapidly. Was there enough time to catch him? Probably, but it would be close. The polls were already almost a week old, and it was Jack's sense of the campaign that he had at least moved even with Putnam during the last few days. But it was impossible to know for certain until the election itself, which was only hours away now. He turned toward the other side of the open car and waved. They were in the heart of Chinatown now, and brightly colored neon lights glowed out from the fronts of the shops and restaurants on both sides of the road. Jack could smell the Oriental foods cooking nearby mixed with the slight salt smell blowing in from San Francisco Bay. He loved this town, just as Suzanne did, a little like Boston in its . . . There were a series of quick explosions then, like rapid gunfire. Jack raised his hand instinctively to cover his face and ward off the bullets. He looked to his left; fear flooded Suzanne's face and she began clutching at him frantically. Her hand reached his suit coat and pulled it toward her. In the next instant, security men flanked the sides of the limousine. But the moment had passed; the sound they'd heard had only been a string of fireworks placed in the path of Jack's car. Suzanne slowly began relaxing her grip on the front of his coat. She'd been deceiving him, Jack thought, deceiving herself, too. In that moment the real deep fear that she truly felt, that they both felt, had come to the surface. The limousine was speeding up now. The crowd was parting to let them through, the carnival atmosphere over, but a final shower of fireworks illuminated the sky above them, falling in slow motion like big, brightly colored drops of rain. The limousine pulled away down the darkened city street. "I'm sorry," Suzanne said as she turned back to him.

Jack took her in his arms as the open car accelerated up a side street and away from the happy crowd. Ahead of them Jack could hear the anxious whining sound of the police sirens. "I'll be more careful," Jack said. The security people had told him not to ride in an open car, not after Dallas, not with the angry mood erupting in so many of the streets of America now. But he'd decided that it was important to do it, to show the voters of California that he wasn't afraid of them, and he'd ignored the security people's warnings. Maybe he'd been wrong.

Denise looked up at the knob of her office door. It twisted once, hard against the lock, and then stopped. There was someone out there. She kept looking at the door, but there was only stillness. She flung out her hand to turn off her desk lamp, and then she sat in the darkness alone, frightened, trying to decide what to do next. There was an angry scratching at the lock. She started to call out, but the words froze in her throat. She moved through the darkness and stood next to the door, her ear pressed against it. She could sense someone on the other side of it, someone within only a few inches of her.

The scratching at the lock continued. Thinking fast, she walked back to her desk and fumbled in its drawers for her office phone book. Finally, she found it and threw it open to the page headed "Emergencies." She dialed the number for building security. The sound at the door stopped. She looked across the room, expecting the door to open at any moment. In the silence of the empty office building, she could hear movement down the hall in the reception area. Then her phone went dead. Someone had cut the line! She dropped the dead phone down onto her desk and ran to the door. Outside she could hear the hall door that led from the reception area open and then slam closed. In a flash, she unlocked her office door and moved silently into the darkened hallway. She glanced only briefly toward the reception area before making a dash for the exit door at the far opposite end of the long dark hall. She had seen something moving in the darkness. There had been a figure in the shadows near the door to reception and it had started toward her. She threw the hall door open and moved through it to the service stairs. Then she ran down the stairs to the floor below faster than she had ever run before. She could hear someone following behind her. She threw open the door to the mall. Rows of dimly lit shops stretched out in front of her. She ran past unlit storefront windows filled with the ominous figures of mannequins. The sounds of her running footsteps echoed and reechoed in the enclosed space and she could hear the other set of running footsteps behind her. She was afraid to look back and see how close it was, but she guessed that the figure was within only a few yards of her now. She ran blindly then, turning right and left down the familiar rows of shops, their windows becoming a blur of reflected glass on either side of her. She ducked into a storefront and caught her breath. She could hear nothing now in the darkened shopping center. She tried to remember where the other set of stairs was that led down to the parking garage. And as the memory slowly came back to her, she mapped her escape route in her mind. She tried to step back out onto the mall sidewalk, but a man's body blocked her way. His big hands gripped her shoulder. Looking down she could see an enormous pistol protruding from a black leather holster that he wore at his waist. Denise screamed in fear.

Slowly the man's uniform came into focus. It was a security guard. Denise blurted out her story as she fumbled in her purse for her I.D. card.

When she found it, the guard compared its photograph with her face. Denise could imagine how she looked to him at that moment, but the young man only nodded his head and handed the card back to her.

"Do you think you could take me down to my car?" Denise asked, some of her composure beginning to return to her as she caught her breath.

There was a noise then on the floor of shops directly above them.

"You wait here!" the guard ordered, withdrawing his gun from its holster as he ran toward the sound.

Denise was alone again. She could see the open door to the back staircase that led down to the garage. She ran to the staircase door and within seconds she was in the darkened employees' garage. Her car was parked right by the bottom of the stairs in the big empty parking lot. She unlocked it quickly and jumped inside. The engine started easily and she stepped down hard on the gas pedal as she moved the car into reverse. The Mustang's tires screeched on the slick cement surface, the noise shrieking off the walls of the enclosed space and back to her. The Mustang shot up the exit ramp and onto the street that ran in front of the mall. The street was empty. She headed for the expressway, and once she was safely up on the high cement overpass that led back to downtown Dallas, she merged into the fast lane and checked her rearview mirror for signs of someone following her, but there was nothing. She breathed out deeply several times then and, glancing up at the rearview mirror again, she caught a glimpse of her own eyes. She tilted the mirror down so that she could see herself more clearly. Her face was surprisingly composed, her eyes clear and steady. She wasn't completely without resources, she told herself then, as she thought about how quickly she'd moved down the sidewalks of the mall. She hadn't run like that since she was a girl. But what do I do next? Her answer came in the form of a crossroads, marked by a large expressway sign mounted above the highway less than a mile ahead of her. She remembered from earlier in the evening that soon the highway would branch right to the east and left to the west. Without thinking, she stayed in the far left lane and accelerated into the western turnoff. She glanced back at the clock on her dashboard. It was late, but she knew that if she drove back to her apartment now she would never get to sleep, her mind was racing too fast. Her kids were safe with her sister, and she could call from somewhere on the road and let everybody know that she was okay, that she had just needed to get off by herself. She glanced down at her purse. She had a gas credit card, a bank charge card, and a little cash. She could get by for a while. She hadn't taken any time off work after Jim died and everyone had said that she should.

She looked over at the mileage sign at the side of the road: AMARILLO— 325, SANTA FE—575.

As she drove through the night west across Texas, and finally, a few hours before dawn into New Mexico, her thoughts of Jim kept her company.

The crazy things you think of at night, Denise thought, as she slowly began waking up. Of course, this one was even a little crazier than normal for her, she decided as she began to focus on the strange adobe ceiling and remembered that she was three hundred miles away from her home, sleeping in a motel room somewhere in northeast New Mexico.

No luggage, no change of clothes, not even a toothbrush, she thought, as she walked slowly into the bathroom. The bathroom floor was adobe too, smooth rounded stones that felt cool under her feet as she sat on the motel toilet. In that moment, she felt like a child, sitting, going to the bathroom in a strange place, a long way from home, a little helpless, but mostly just confused by the big world that she didn't quite feel like she was really a part of yet. Wild thoughts started coming back to her then, wild, unfounded fears that had driven her from her home and then thoughts of Jim being somewhere that he could still touch her life. God, it had been a crazy night. She reached for the unbroken roll of motel toilet paper and sliced its paper seal with her long fingernail.

There was a coffee maker, plastic cups, little packets of coffee and cream and sugar. She made herself a hot cup of instant coffee and drank it as she lay back down on the motel-room bed with the pillows propped up behind her back. Time to get sensible, she told herself. Last night was last night—and it's easy to get scared and confused at night, particularly after everything that had been happening to her, but it really wasn't that kind of a world where people actually did the kinds of things she had imagined the night before. She was a twenty-eight-year-old woman, with two kids, a good job, a steady, reliable person, maybe even a little dull sometimes, she thought, as the bad but strong instant coffee began to cut through her morning drowsiness and help her make some sense out of the world again. She was definitely not the kind of woman who ran off to California in the middle of the night without even packing a damn suitcase. She glanced at her watch, lying on its side on the bedstand next to her. It was late enough to call her office and start settling this whole thing down.

She picked up the bedside phone and placed the call to Dallas. The office receptionist answered the phone. "Administration," she said in her comfortable Texas voice, and just hearing it made Denise begin to feel a little better.

"Midge, it's Denise."

"Oh, God, kid, where are you? Everybody's looking for you."

"I'm okay," Denise said, feeling embarrassed. God, she had probably made a lot of useless trouble for everybody.

"Is Mr. Collins mad?"

"Mad? No, he's worried as hell, though."

"What, ah . . ." Denise stopped and collected her thoughts. "Did the security people find anything?"

"Well, we were robbed, honey," Midge said. "Although, God knows what they took."

"What do you mean?" Denise said, trying to fight the panic.

"Somebody broke into your office, all right. They found . . ."

"Midge," Denise interrupted her sharply. "What are you saying? There really was somebody?"

"That's what the police think. Scary, isn't it?"

Denise didn't answer this time.

"Hon, it's okay, nothing was missing or anything, just some creep. God knows what they thought they could find in here, anyway. I mean, I keep all my really big diamonds and things at home, don't you?" Midge said, and then she laughed.

But Denise stayed silent, her mind whirling, trying to make some kind of sense out of it. Finally she spoke, and when she did her voice was urgent. "Midge," she said, "do me a favor—switch this call to my phone and then go into my office and pick up on it."

"Huh?"

"Please. I left something in there last night and I have to know if it's still there."

"Oh, okay."

Denise waited in her little adobe-style motel room, over three hundred miles away from her home. As she did, she felt compelled to move the curtain next to her aside and look out the window at the asphalt parking lot just outside her room. Looking for what? There was nothing out there but parking lot and miles of desert. The phone clicked loudly in her ear, startling her.

"Okay, kid, I'm sitting at your desk. Everything looks like normal, a lot of unfinished work and a few . . ."

"Midge," Denise interrupted her friend again. "On my desk there should be a scratch pad with my name on it and a sort of a flower design."

"Got it, right by the phone."

"Good, perfect. Uh, on the top sheet there are two phone numbers and an address on Wilshire Boulevard in Los Angeles. Could you give those to me?"

"No," Midge said decisively, and Denise's fears leaped back at her with almost the full power of the night before. "There's no number or anything," Midge said. "Everything's blank."

"You've got the pad on the top of my desk?"

"Yes, but no numbers."

"Look around, maybe the sheet came loose or something."

"I'm looking. I'm looking," Midge said.

"Maybe in one of the drawers, or it could have fallen on the floor."

"Hon, I'm looking in the trash can now, nothing but a candy-bar wrapper. Are you eating those things again?"

"Midge, this is important, please."

"I can tell it's important, but it's not here. The cleaning people could have . . ."

"No, no," Denise said sadly, giving up now herself. "It was after the cleaning people were in there. Whoever it was that broke in last night took it."

"Took your phone numbers?" Midge's voice was skeptical, but full of concern. "Honey, listen, I don't think that any self-respecting burglar is really going to break all the way in here and then just steal some numbers off your pad." Midge made her voice as light as she could, hoping to help Denise see how silly she was sounding, but after she'd finished there was only silence on the other end of the line. "Denise? Are you all right, kid?"

"Yes, yes, I'm fine," Denise said, composing herself, but her mind was still busy trying to figure out what to do next. Finally she reached her decision. "Look, Midge, I'm going to go ahead and take the rest of the week," she said. "I was thinking about trying to come in tomorrow, but I don't think so now."

"That's a good decision, hon," Midge said softly. "You deserve it. I'll let Mr. Collins know."

"Yes, good, thank you," Denise said, her mind still off somewhere working through her alternatives.

"Hon, the police want to talk to you on the burglary thing. What should I tell them?"

"The police?" Denise hesitated. "I don't know."

"Look, I'll tell them you'll be back to work on Monday," Midge said helpfully. "I mean, it's not like this guy really stole anything. You get some rest and we'll see you next Monday, okay, kid?"

"Yeah, okay, Monday," Denise said, still shaken, and she hung up the phone. She turned back to the window and moved the curtain aside. What was it that bothered her so much? She looked out at the nearly empty parking lot and the seemingly endless stretch of desert sand that lay beyond it. Then it came to her. Whoever it was that had broken into her office could easily guess her destination now. They could even be waiting for her in Los Angeles.

CHAPTER
46

I t was smoggy in L.A., and Jack smiled at some of the grumbling comments that he could hear coming from his staff people, as the flight from San Francisco began to descend into Los Angeles International. The comments were good-natured though. There was very little that could really discourage a group of campaign workers when they smelled the possibility of victory, even in the smoggy air of Southern California.

Jack looked down at the houses below the airplane. They were voting down there already, he thought, and the trends that would carry either Putnam or himself to victory had probably already been set. If he could only see through the rooftops of the schoolhouses and fire stations and suburban homes that were serving that day as election headquarters and read the first early morning ballots he would know what the final outcome would be. He would be spared the suspense of what would probably become before it was over a long, tense day and night, as the election results slowly came in and were counted. The last polls were showing him dead even with Putnam and the smart money was betting that the winner in California would be the winner in Chicago at the convention, and in all likelihood would be sitting in the White House in January of 1969. If the experts were right, we'll know before the day is over the direction that the country is going to take for the next decade at least, maybe longer, Jack thought. And then he wondered: if he could, would he want to know the future? Would he really want the power to see through those rooftops and read those ballots or would he rather live it out and let it all unfold in front of him moment by unexpected moment? It would all be over too soon anyway, he decided finally. "They're returning you as First Lady down there," he said. And then he added, smiling over at her, "At least I think they are."

Suzanne looked down at the City of Angels spread out beneath her below the clouds. Her dark eyes were flashing with excitement, not just with the excitement of politics or power, but with the knowledge that her children were waiting for them in Los Angeles. She hadn't seen them in over a week, but Brian had flown them in from Washington and that was enough reason all by itself to feel the way she did, she thought, but she knew there was something more. "I've never wanted to win any election more than I want to win this one," she said.

They were both silent then for a few seconds, just feeling the powerful plane beneath them as it sharpened its descent into LAX.

"Are you all right after last night?" Jack said, bringing his wife's thoughts back to the sudden fear that she'd felt the night before in San Francisco's Chinatown.

"Yes," Suzanne said. "It frightened me, but it served a purpose, too." She paused then and tried to put her feelings into words that her husband could understand. "It reminded me of what the stakes are." She could feel her husband bending close to her and then his kiss on her cheek.

"I love you," he said. "Whatever happens next, I'm glad we made it this far together."

"So am I," she said softly and then, feeling a thin layer of tears beginning to cover her eyes, she returned her gaze to the city rushing up below the plane. "I wish it weren't so smoggy," she said, looking down at the brown air and trying to distract her husband's attention from her own emotions.

"It will be better at the beach," Jack said, understanding his wife's need for privacy at that moment and withdrawing his hand from hers and looking away.

"Uh-uh," Suzanne said, without much conviction. "Are we really going to see you today?" she asked then.

"I promise," Jack said. "There's nothing scheduled until the hotel. So, I don't have a thing to do all day, until we walk into that ballroom tonight and graciously accept victory."

"Not until Frank comes running in and tells you that Tulare County is looking soft or something and then you disappear into the telephones for six hours," Suzanne said smiling.

"Tulare County won't go soft," Jack said, returning the smile.

"Well, how about Mono County then?"

"Mono County is on its own today, too," Jack said. "The candidate is going to swim in the Pacific Ocean, play with his children . . ."

"And spend some time with his wife," Suzanne said, finishing her husband's sentence for him. "The hell with Mono County, right?"

"Right, the hell with Mono County," Jack agreed. And then he waited a beat before adding in a teasing voice, "Unless, of course, Frank thinks that we really need it."

Suzanne shook her head in mock despair then and watched as the plane passed over the San Diego Freeway and touched down on the long cement runway.

WELCOME TO LOS ANGELES, PRESIDENT CASSIDY! announced a big red-white-and-blue banner hanging from the side of one of the passenger terminals. When Jack saw it and the cheering crowd that waited to greet him, he looked over at Suzanne. "President Cassidy," he said. "Do you think those people know something we don't?"

But Suzanne was too busy to answer. She'd found the faces of her children. They were standing at the edge of the runway with Brian and she was waving and smiling happily at them. "Look, there they are," Suzanne said, and she could feel Jack moving forward next to her and joining her in waving out the window at their family. "All day?" she asked again, but not taking her eyes off her children.

"All day. I promise."

God, it was hot. Denise rolled her window down and stuck her arm out the side of the car and let warm air billow up the sleeve of her blouse. It helped a little. She brought her arm back inside the car and rolled the window back up and let the Mustang's ineffective little air conditioner continue its losing battle with the overpowering desert heat.

Directly in front of her now, she could see a dark speck growing taller and wider at an alarming rate as it came closer to her, faster and faster now. There was no way that she could avoid it. She reached up with both hands then and grabbed her frail plastic steering wheel and braced for the impact. The big truck roared by missing her by only inches, leaving the highway behind it flooded with rushing air. The little car shimmied back and forth in the aftershock as Denise fought to keep it on the road. When the truck had passed and she was back in control of the Mustang again, she took a deep breath and glanced down at her odometer. Two hundred more miles of this, she thought wearily. Jim Sullivan, wherever you are, you're to blame. This is all your doing and nobody else's. Then she shook her head in utter amazement at herself and glanced up at her rearview mirror, not to see the big truck departing down the long highway back toward New Mexico, but to look at her own face. She had to see if it looked as crazy as she was beginning to feel. Is this the way people start going off the deep end? But the reflection of her eyes in the mirror looked normal enough, the soft, blue shade blurred with a light film of tears from the hours of driving in the hot glare of the Arizona desert. They didn't look like the eyes of a crazy woman, but here she was on a lonely desert road, smack in the middle of the working week, headed for California of all places. And to do what? To tell Senator Cassidy's head of security that there was somebody on the loose who had already tried to assassinate Cassidy once, and might try again, and that the FBI had killed Jim, and was now trying to stop her from warning Cassidy? Kill her? It was all too preposterous. She might just as well turn around and go back now or just check herself into the first rest home that she could find, because if she didn't do it, the authorities in Los Angeles would certainly do it for her, but even as she thought about what a fool she was being, she kept her foot steady on the accelerator and kept pushing the car down the road that led to Los Angeles.

But the questions still nagged at her. What the hell was she going to do when she got to L.A.? Who would she try to see? She checked the clock on her dashboard and then the speedometer and did the calculations for the tenth time that projected her time of arrival in the city. It would be early evening by the time she got there, another hour to find the address that she had for the Cassidy headquarters on Wilshire Boulevard. But then what? Whoever it was that had broken into her office the night before knew her destination. They could be waiting for her. Maybe she should go directly to the police. No, that was useless. There was only one person who might listen seriously to the incredible story that she had to tell, and that was Senator Cassidy, himself. Oh, the hell with it, she decided. One step at a time; first I've got to get to L.A. Then I'll decide what to do next. Maybe Jim will come back and whisper in my ear, like he did the night before. Oh, God, I really am going off the deep end, she thought then, but she only stepped harder on the gas, and the Mustang shot ahead toward California.

"Senator, please don't go past that point out there." The Secret Service man in dark glasses and a gray business suit looked painfully out of place on the beautiful stretch of Southern California beach. In the distance, Jack could see several other Secret Service agents scattered around the perimeter of the small bay that held Jeffries's Santa Monica home.

"We've had a couple of crazy reports. You know, California?" The security man smiled at the candidate and pointed out to a small spit of sand that separated the stretch of sand in front of Jeffries's beach house from a narrow inlet of water that stretched back from the ocean in a long broad channel almost to the Pacific Coast Highway. The security people were using the inlet as a dividing point and no one was being permitted past it, either coming in or going out. On the other end of the small bay was a high formation of rocks, and more security officers crouched there, while out to sea directly in front of the U-shaped private beach several government patrol boats cruised slowly back and forth across the opening to the bay.

"Thank you, Dan." Cassidy nodded at the Secret Service agent. "You and your men might feel more comfortable in shirtsleeves today," Cassidy said, gesturing out at the agents dressed in their suit coats and ties. It was still morning and the air was cool with a slight layer of fog, but the hot California sun was promising to burn through the overcast soon.

"Yes, sir," the Secret Service man said.

Jack was in khakis and a light sweatshirt, and his two oldest children were dressed in their bathing suits. The small party was walking slowly down the beach near the tideline.

As he walked, Cassidy glanced out to sea. Jack's host was coming out of the surf. Jeffries's mammoth body was covered with gray hair, dripping sea water. Jack thought that he looked at that moment like some ancient sea creature arriving on land for the first time in centuries. There was a towel lying on the sand and Jack tossed it at the movie director. Jeffries caught it in one big hand and began drying himself vigorously.

"It looks beautiful out there," Jack said, his eyes moving back out to the vast expanse of sunlit blue ocean water.

"It is," Jeffries answered in his gravelly, self-assured, Irish voice. "But I'll bet you prefer your Atlantic, don't you? Your father always thought that it had more character."

Jack agreed with a smile and a nod of his head. "They're both beautiful, though."

"Well, I prefer the Irish Sea," Jeffries grumbled. "Makes your Atlantic Ocean look like a tepid little bathtub."

Cassidy mimicked the Irish brogue of his grandfathers, "And you swim in the Irish Sea in the first week of June, do you?"

"I do," Jeffries said. He wrapped the towel around his shoulders and the two men walked down the tideline, following behind the running figures of Jack's children.

"I haven't seen them in a week and look at them," Jack said, pointing at Erin and John Jr., who were busy now only with each other, playing with the sand and the lapping ocean surf.

"The ungratefulness of children," Jeffries said.

"Speaking of children, how are yours?" Jack asked.

"Diane's fine," Jeffries answered without hesitation. He had six children by three different wives, but he knew what Jack meant. "She sends you her best," Jeffries added. "She's in town and I think she wanted to come today, but . . ." Jeffries shrugged his big towel-draped shoulders then, letting the broad movement complete his thought for him.

"Thank her for me, would you please?" Cassidy said.

"Thank her?" Jeffries said. "For what? No girl of mine would have the bad manners to interrupt a man on his one day of rest, in how long? A month is it?"

"Well, as I remember, I had the bad manners to interrupt her vacation once," Jack said quietly.

"Yes, you did, but that was different. Wherever you stop, you make a little bit of history, not like the rest of us mere mortals. And young girls, even smart ones like Diane, all want to touch a bit of history in their lives."

"The rules are the same for Presidents," Cassidy said decisively. "That's one of the things that I've learned since I've seen you last. So, thank her for me, would you please?"

"Of course," Jeffries said and then paused. "A great deal has happened to you since you stayed with us in Connemara, hasn't it, Jack?" he added as the two men continued to walk slowly down the beach. "Both your brother and your father: that's quite a lot for anyone to lose in such a short period of time," Jeffries said, his voice rich with sympathy for his godson.

A breeze came in off the ocean, kicking up a light stirring of sand off the surface of the beach and blowing it against the two men. "Life's not the same," Jack said thoughtfully.

"No, I'm certain that it's not. It never is after you lose people that you love," Jeffries said, turning his body against the suddenness of the wind. The flying pieces of sharp sand died back down then and the two men resumed their walk, a lighter breeze barely stirring the sand at their feet as they moved slowly along the shoreline.

"I am stronger in some ways, though," Cassidy continued. "More certain of what I want and why I want it. For one thing, I need my family even more now than I did before," he added, looking up the beach at where his children had stopped for a moment to play in the low, slowly rolling ocean surf. Cassidy paused for a long time, weighing whether he should say the rest of what he wanted to say. "I know a little better what it is that I have to give," Jack said. "And this may sound too easy, but I want not only to move ahead now and do the right thing, but also to correct a little of what I did wrong before, even if that doesn't always mean making the smart choice, the politically wise choice, anyway."

"Like your release of the information about Crossbow?" Jeffries said.

"Yes," Jack admitted.

"Sounds like a very dangerous desire for a politician to have."

"It is," Cassidy said simply.

"Your father might not have understood," Jeffries said.

And then Jack realized why he had chosen to talk to the older man about it. He had needed somehow to know what his father would have thought about what he'd done, but hearing Jeffries say it out loud, it didn't seem to really matter anymore. His own feelings were more important now. "No, I suppose not," Jack said. "Tim would have, though."

Jeffries nodded his agreement. "Yes, I think he would have." The older man paused before adding, "Jack, do you really think that you can end the war?"

"Yes," Jack said. "But not without a price. That's the other thing I've learned over the last few years. There is a price to be paid. That's one way I think that both Gardner and I went wrong before," Jack said. "War is brutally expensive, and neither of us ever leveled with the American people about what it would cost to fight this one."

"Blood and treasure," Jeffries said, and Cassidy nodded his head in agreement as Jeffries continued. "Not fighting can be expensive, too, sometimes. My generation almost learned that lesson the hard way."

"Yes, I know," Cassidy said. "But it's a leader's duty to let the country know what the price is for the choices that it faces, so that the people can decide realistically for themselves whether they want to pay that price or not," Cassidy said. "That's why I'm looking forward to campaigning in the fall against Bill Longwood. We'll both tell the country what the price is for the policies we propose. Gardner didn't do that four years ago. I don't think he was just wrong about the war. I think he was dishonest with the country about it as well. He tried to let the people think that they could have it for nothing. He forgot to tell them about the blood-and-treasure part of it. I think that's part of the reason why he failed. Maybe why I did, too, to some extent. But I propose to end the war now, and I'll be as honest as I can about what that will cost to American prestige and our security. Longwood proposes to truly fight the war, and he's the kind of man who will be honest about what that will mean to us in both money and in lives. And in the end, the people will choose peace. This isn't the right war, if there ever is a right one, and they'll see that," Cassidy said.

"I do know this: If there is anyone left in this country who can really end this war now, it's you, Jack. There certainly is no one else," Jeffries said. "But even for you, it's going to be a hell of a struggle."

"You're an Irish pessimist," Cassidy said, smiling.

"And you?" the older man asked.

"Me?" Cassidy said, looking down the sand to where his children were playing against the backdrop of Secret Service agents with handheld radios and holstered weapons. "God, I don't know why, John, but I think I'm beginning to become just a little bit of an Irish optimist in my old age."

Lopata had waited in a Las Vegas hotel room until it was time. He was ready now. There was only one final piece of business to attend to before he moved on. He took a taxi to the bus station and began walking back from the station toward the city's downtown. He wasn't certain of his exact destination, but he was confident that he would find what he was looking for no matter which street he picked, and within less than a block from the bus station he found it.

The glass windows in front of the first pawn shop that he passed displayed only watches, musical instruments, and a few radios, but Lopata knew that he would find what he was looking for inside.

He carried his blue vinyl flight bag with him to the counter at the rear of the store. The glass case was locked, but Lopata could see several dozen handguns laid out on the shelf below the glass. He selected a small, black .22 caliber pistol and paid for it with some of the bloodstained money that he'd carried with him from New Orleans. The pistol had a much shorter barrel than the weapon that he'd carried with him since Dallas, and, unlike the long-barreled .38 caliber, the new weapon would fit easily under his clothes, hidden from sight. He bought a packet of shells too, and there were forms to be filled out, but the entire transaction took less than a half hour. When he returned to the street, in addition to his long-barreled .38, his small vinyl flight bag held now a loaded twenty-two caliber revolver and a cardboard package containing eighteen additional cartridges.

CHAPTER

47

Grissum's plane got him into Los Angeles in the late afternoon. Unless she'd driven all night, he reasoned, he should have arrived ahead of his subject.

At the airport the FBI agent rented a car using false identity papers containing the same name that he had used to book the plane flight from Dallas. His trip to Los Angeles had to be absolutely untraceable.

He drove northeast from the airport, using familiar freeways. Grissum had visited Los Angeles many times before and he knew the streets of the big, complicated city well.

At 5150 West Wilshire Boulevard he pulled over to the curb and stopped. In front of him was a glass storefront plastered with red-white-and-blue posters. Jack Cassidy's handsome face and signs saying CASSIDY FOR PRESIDENT appeared everywhere around the outside of the office building's glass front.

Grissum reached inside his coat pocket and removed a small slip of folded paper. He opened it and read the handwriting on its wrinkled surface. The address "5150 West Wilshire" and two telephone numbers were written below a small drawing of a flower and the printed heading, FROM THE DESK OF DENISE RICHARDS. Then he removed a cigarette lighter from his coat pocket and held the paper over its flame. As it burned, he opened his car door and dropped the sheet of flaming notepaper into the gutter. There could be nothing to tie him to Los Angeles now, Grissum thought, as he watched the last of the paper disappear into the flame.

He got out of the rented car and crossed Wilshire. He stood for a moment in front of the campaign headquarters. He smoked a cigarette and kept his hat pulled down low over his eyes as he stood on the street corner, but despite his nonchalant appearance he carefully studied each person that he passed. Several young women went by and Grissum inspected them closely, but none had the strawberry-blond hair of the woman he had come to Los Angeles to find.

The FBI agent waited for another few minutes and then he walked inside the glass-fronted building. It was noisy and crowded and seemed surprisingly disorganized. Telephones rang unanswered while volunteers sat at temporary tables distributing literature from big cardboard boxes piled haphazardly on the floor. There were a few semiprivate offices at the rear of the big open room, but the whole operation lacked order and supervision and had the look and feel of a gypsy camp. Could they really hope to elect a President this way? he wondered. But there was plenty of energy and noise and movement, and he took it all in with one swing of his practiced eye. There were at least a dozen young women in the room who were approximately the age of the one that he was looking for, but none of them was Denise Richards.

A young volunteer sat a few feet away behind a makeshift reception desk. "Can I help you?"

"Posters," Grissum said quickly, covering the side of his face with his hand as he spoke. There wasn't much chance anyone would remember him from just a brief conversation, but Grissum was determined to be very certain on this trip. "I'd like about . . ." He didn't have to finish the lie. The volunteer's phone rang and, as he answered it, he pointed to a table stacked high with campaign supplies in the far back corner of the room.

Grissum moved slowly toward the long table then, and nothing in the room missed his attention. A short line was waiting in front of the table and Grissum took his place in it. There were several volunteers nearby unloading posters from cardboard boxes and stacking them on the table next to other smaller boxes full of metal campaign buttons, and pamphlets, and bumper stickers.

One of the girls stacking materials onto the table called out to him as he approached her, "Take what you want."

"Thanks," Grissum said, and he reached for a single metal lapel button. It was a smaller version of the red-white-and-blue posters that were plastered everywhere around the room, except instead of CASSIDY FOR PRESIDENT, Grissum's button said CASSIDY IN '68. The FBI agent pinned it prominently onto the front of his suit coat and then gathered a short stack of posters in his arms and walked slowly with them back through the crowded headquarters to the front door. No Denise Richards, Grissum decided as he walked outside.

There was a coffee shop across the street from the campaign headquarters and Grissum crossed to it and walked to the lounge area at the rear of the restaurant. A short row of pay phones ran along one wall. All three phone booths were empty. Grissum entered the booth closest to the rear wall of the restaurant and closed the glass door in back of him. Then he called Dallas.

The CASSIDY FOR PRESIDENT posters had gone into the first trash container that he'd passed on Wilshire, but as he waited for his call to connect, Grissum's fingers reached up and nervously fingered the Cassidy campaign button on his lapel. It was the first time that he'd ever worn anything like that, and he started to remove it, but Yancey came on the line before he could.

"Are you somewhere we can talk safely?" Yancey said. Grissum had never heard his boss's voice sound the way it did now. It was heavy with fear, and Grissum knew that something important had happened.

In the late afternoon Jack and Suzanne made love. Afterward they slept together in the guest room of the beach house, the windows open, the fresh ocean breeze blowing the curtains inward and the sounds of the surf rolling in on the Pacific beach filling the room with its gentle rhythm.

Suzanne woke up first from her light nap and she lay with her head resting against a pillow that was raised just high enough for her to watch the ocean breeze stir the curtains of the small, cool, darkened room that she shared with her husband.

She knew without looking when Jack was awake. She reached over then and placed a hand on his shoulder, and the simple touch seemed to join them as intimately as the act of love had a few moments earlier.

"How are you feeling?"

"I never realize how much I need a rest until I finally stop and take one," Jack admitted quietly.

Suzanne looked over at her husband. Her eyes showed the concern that she felt about the toll that the campaign was taking on him. The press always reported how dynamic he was, seeming to draw endless energy from some secret source. Suzanne knew, though, that he was only human. But she could tell from the relaxed way his face looked, with his eyes still gently closed, that he was better now, stronger after almost a full day of rest.

"What are you thinking about?" Suzanne asked, bending down closer to the peaceful, handsome face of her husband.

But Jack only smiled. "Unh-unh," he managed. "I have my thoughts."

Suzanne removed her hand from his shoulder then, smiling to herself now at her husband's stubborn need for privacy, even from her.

"Well, I'll tell you what I'm thinking then," Suzanne said. "I'm thinking how happy I am that I married you, that I'm here in this bed with you, that you're the father of my children."

Jack opened his eyes. He wanted to see his wife in that moment. Although he never doubted her love, Suzanne rarely spoke of it, and he wanted to remember how she looked now.

"I thought you said that I'm just an overly ambitious Irish politician," Jack said, smiling up at his wife's darkly beautiful face.

"You're that, too," Suzanne said. "And you drag me and my children from one end of the country to the other every four years and make me do things that I'd never do if I weren't married to you."

"That's probably why you love me so much," Jack said, and he raised himself up on his elbows. "It's good for you to do those things."

Suzanne thought about what he'd said for a moment and then smiled at him. "You're probably right. It probably is one of the reasons that I love you so much, that and because you make such wonderful children," Suzanne said.

Jack bent forward and kissed his wife lightly on the lips before he stood and removed his bathrobe from the chair next to the bed and put it on over his naked back and shoulders. For a brief moment, Suzanne could see the scars where the bullets had torn through his back in Dallas five years before. How vulnerable he really is, she thought, as she watched him walk slowly to the window and draw the curtains aside.

"What do you see?"

"Oh, just one of those terrible places that I drag you and your children to every four years," Jack said.

Suzanne stood and put on a robe, covering her own body, and then she walked to the window to stand by her husband.

The sun was low in the west, the air gentling and cooling, the California seabirds just beginning to appear against the orange-and-red sky. In the distance, Brian and some of the others were playing a slow, lazy game of touch football. Behind them, Jack and Suzanne's older children were busy digging in the sand near the tide line.

"We do have great kids, don't we?" Jack said with pride, as he watched them for a moment through the open window.

"Yes," Suzanne said simply.

"Whatever else they write about us, they'll have to give us credit for that, won't they?" Jack said. "We loved our children and we did our best for them."

It was the kind of a thing Jack never said and Suzanne could sense his rare mood, and so, rather than say anything in return, she stayed quiet, and instead of words, she reached up and touched his back and softly stroked it, moving close but not quite touching the deeply scarred place where the bullet had passed a few years before. Someone who's been through all that he has, she thought, deserves his moments of doubt, or melancholy, or whatever it was that was passing through her husband's mind at that moment, as he looked out at his children playing at sunset on a beautiful Pacific beach, while he waited to learn his own political fate.

Lopata sat alone in the rear of the noon bus that ran between Las Vegas and Los Angeles. He didn't read or even look out the window at the desert landscape as it passed by. He just sat and thought about what he must do when he reached Los Angeles.

It was nearly five in the afternoon when the bus from Las Vegas finally pulled down into the darkness of the underground terminal built in the heart of the big Southern California city.

Lopata waited for all of the other passengers to leave before he walked down the uneven middle aisle, using one hand to balance himself against the seat backs, while the other grasped the little vinyl flight bag tightly to the side of his body. He was wearing a dark blue T-shirt and faded khaki pants and he passed quietly into the crowded, commuter-hour terminal lobby practically unnoticed. Lopata felt comfortable in the cool underground darkness and he lingered in the lower terminal building long after the other passengers had left. Then he walked up the cement ramp and through the main passenger lounge and outside. It was still light and he could see the big orange ball of the late afternoon sun through an opening between the tall buildings that surrounded the downtown bus terminal.

Lopata had never seen Los Angeles before, but he wasn't curious about the big western city that surrounded him now. He was interested only in the drama being played out inside his own head—the scene repeating itself over and over again, as it had now for months, until to him, the fantasy had almost become a reality.

He walked back inside the terminal. He bought a local newspaper and read its headlines. As he walked to the men's room, he hurriedly scanned the paper's front pages for anything that might change his timetable. There was a photograph of Cassidy on the front page. The candidate had arrived in the city that morning, the news story reported, and the picture showed him kneeling on the airport runway to hold his two oldest children in his arms while his wife stood above him smiling down at her family. Lopata smiled and refolded the newspaper, placing it under his arm.

In the men's room, Lopata used a coin to unlock one of the private toilets. He opened his flight bag and removed the twenty-two caliber pistol he had bought that morning in Las Vegas. He checked to be sure that the revolver was loaded with shells and put an additional six cartridges into the pocket of his khaki pants. He tossed the little cardboard box containing the remainder of the shells into the flight bag.

He inspected the pistol carefully to be certain that its safety lock was securely in place before he tucked its barrel into the waistband of his pants. He put his jacket on then and let it drop down loosely over his shoulders and hips, covering the pistol. Once he was satisfied that the weapon was thoroughly hidden from view, he bent down and checked to make certain that Strode's diary and his long-barreled thirty-eight caliber pistol were both still in place at the bottom of his bag. Then he hurriedly removed the few items of clothing that he would need that night and stuffed them into a brown paper sack. Only then did he return to the terminal's passenger lounge. There were lockers running along the cement wall outside the men's bathroom and Lopata used the last of his change to unlock one. He put the flight bag into the locker and put the key into his pants pocket. Lopata memorized the spot, so that he could return there easily, if he was given the chance. But he knew how unlikely it was that he would ever really return.

There was a line of taxis outside the terminal's exit doors. Lopata crossed the sidewalk and opened the rear door of the first taxi. He gave the driver the name of his destination and then settled into the vehicle's rear seat.

When Lopata saw the sign for the hotel, he told the driver to stop and let him out about a block away from its front entrance.

Lopata walked down Wilshire until he came to the entrance of the Garland, a small hotel located directly across the street from his final destination. The lobby of the Garland smelled like stale cigars and cleaning fluid. He asked for a room facing the street and then followed the bellman to the old hotel's single elevator.

The elevator creaked its way slowly to the hotel's third floor.

Carrying the crumpled brown paper sack as his only luggage, Lopata followed the bellman down a dark hall to his room. When the uniformed attendant unlocked the door, Lopata quickly handed him a wad of crumpled bills. It was the last of his money from New Orleans, but Lopata didn't care. Soon he would have no need of money at all. He tossed the paper bag onto the single narrow bed and opened the curtains of his room. He could see across the lanes of traffic on Wilshire Boulevard, and on the other side of the boulevard, across the long expanse of green lawn and half shrouded in palm trees, was the building that he had chosen for his final act—The Ambassador Hotel.

What was it? What could have frightened Yancey enough to make him sound like that? Grissum gripped the pay-phone receiver tightly in his hand.

"You haven't . . ." Yancey paused uncertainly. "You haven't done anything yet, have you?"

"No, sir, I just arrived."

"Things are changing fast here," Yancey said, selecting his words with enormous precision. He must be worried about a wiretap, Grissum decided. "The Director has ordered a full investigation into Agent Sullivan's death," Yancey continued. "There are two investigators from Washington here right now," he went on. "I met with them this afternoon. They made it very clear to me that Summers is serious about finding out what happened. Very serious," Yancey said again. Grissum knew what Yancey meant. There would be no cover-up on Sullivan. Yancey had miscalculated. Summers had decided that they had gone too far. Either Yancey had misread the signals coming out of Washington, or something had changed, and they were being left to take the heat for what had happened to Sullivan. But whatever the reason, the result would be the same, Grissum realized suddenly. The Director had decided that he and Yancey were expendable, and he was going to cut them loose. There had been no direct order from Washington to kill Sullivan. Grissum was almost certain of that much. Yancey had acted on his own, thinking that Sullivan's death was what Washington had wanted. That was the way the Bureau often worked. If something particularly ugly had to be done, something with more than the normal amount of risk attached to it, rarely would there be a direct order to do it, only signals. And Grissum could easily imagine the kind of signals that Yancey had been getting from the higher-ups in Washington like Hollis and maybe even Summers himself about Sullivan. That's the way that careers could be made, on the ability to read between the lines and take action when Washington wanted something done but had to be able to deny ever having directly ordered it. The Bureau called it "initiative," and Yancey had always had plenty of it and Grissum had simply obeyed Yancey's orders as he had many times before. He had known the risks when he had decided to go ahead though. They both had. And, Jesus, now they were caught in the middle of some high-stakes political power game that he and Yancey had no way of ever being able to fully understand.

"Washington is suggesting that if appropriate resignations are received before they get too far into their investigation, there's a chance that the investigation might be called off entirely," Yancey continued.

"I see," Grissum said, trying not to let his emotions show. Twenty-seven years in the Bureau, and it was ending like this.

"That will be a very difficult decision for those involved," Grissum added slowly, trying to give himself time to think. As far as he knew, Summers had never left anyone in the Bureau unprotected before. That was what Grissum had always counted on, and that was why he'd been willing to take whatever risks were required to do what he thought the Bureau wanted done. What had happened to change things? Why was the Director giving them away now?

"I want you to be very careful in completing your assignment," Yancey said. He was being told to continue, Grissum realized then. Despite everything, Yancey still wanted him to finish what he'd been sent to Los Angeles to accomplish.

"I think the subject is going to try to reach Cassidy, probably tonight," Grissum said, and, as soon as he did, he wished that he hadn't used Cassidy's name, but it was too late now. He was rattled, twenty-seven years and now the Bureau was turning on him.

"I don't think that's in our best interests," Yancey said. He was being less cautious now, too. "I think that we should continue with the plans precisely as we discussed them last night," Yancey added.

"Yes, sir," Grissum said. Maybe there was a chance they could get out of this after all, he thought. That's what Yancey was trying to tell him now. That was why the investigation would be called off, if they resigned. The Bureau knew that they probably wouldn't find enough proof to even file charges against them, much less get a conviction. How could they? No one could know for certain what they'd done. On the surface it was just an accident. No jury could convict an FBI agent for that. It was his and Yancey's secret. Only the girl could possibly know anything really damaging, something Sullivan had told her before he'd died, but once she was taken care of—there would be nothing.

"Stop her," Yancey said. "But be very careful," he added. "If she makes any kind of contact with Cassidy or his people, I want you to back off. Don't take even the slightest risk. If you can't do it right, don't do it at all. We've got enough to worry about as it is. With these investigators here, we just can't take any more chances."

"Yes, sir," Grissum said, and then he hung up the phone. What little margin for error he'd had was gone. He had to stop her, but he couldn't leave any tracks that pointed back to him or to the Bureau when he did it. Everything that he'd worked for all his life depended on it.

Jack wore only a light sport shirt and slacks down to dinner. A buffet had been laid out on serving tables around the pool at the rear of the Jeffries home, and Jack paused at the open sliding glass door to the patio for a moment before he walked outside and joined the others. Suzanne was still upstairs dressing, but their children were already busy attacking the plates of food on the long serving tables.

The ocean's evening breeze had removed most of the day's heat, and, as he stood in the doorway and surveyed the scene in front of him, Jack felt the air move his silk shirt against his lightly sunburned body. In the distance the sun was setting into the Pacific and the sky was lit up bright pink and red and gold in a final burst of color. The seabirds were still drifting over the horizon and Jack stood for a moment and watched their easy flight across the brightly colored sky. The Jeffries estate was separated from the last hundred yards of beach by a short white picket fence and, after a few moments of watching the flight of the seabirds, Jack's gaze moved out past the low fence to the shoreline, where the waves were lapping up and forming a gentle, white, soupy-colored foam against the shiny wet surface of the sand.

Out of the corner of his eye, Jack could see Secret Service agents scattered along the perimeter of the property. He knew that there were more agents in two armed ships that cruised just offshore and even more stationed in the upstairs windows of the homes that adjoined the Jeffries estate. It seemed like a lot of trouble for just one man.

The patio of the Jeffries home was full of his family and friends and Jack enjoyed watching them from a distance, unnoticed for the moment. There were Kay and her children and Brian and his family. It was beginning to look like 1960 all over again, Jack thought. Except, of course, for one very big difference; there was no Tim. But he didn't want to dwell on that. They had to go forward, and for now he wanted only to enjoy the breeze and the feel of the light sport clothes against his skin and the picture of the sea at sunset, framing the way that his family and friends were gathered together at that moment. Then he heard the rustle of Suzanne's summer dress and he knew that she was standing behind him. And in the next moment he could feel her long delicate fingers touching his shoulder, and, as he turned to her, he could see her face and smell the familiar scent of her perfume clinging to her long dark hair and he leaned forward to kiss her on the cheek.

"Is that the way you and Tim looked forty years ago?" Suzanne said, motioning out to where John Jr. and Tim's oldest son, Rory, were busy at the buffet table.

"Something like that," Jack said, looking back out at the patio and the two young boys. He stepped outside and crossed to his children. He bent down by his son, who held a very full plate of food.

John Jr. had the plate balanced with both hands, but it was swaying precariously back and forth. It began to slip from his grasp, but his father seemed to arrive from nowhere just at that moment and pick the plate out of midair, saving the moment, and John Jr. looked up at his father's handsome face in awe. "Do you think you have enough food on here for now?" Jack said, looking down at the impressive engineering feat that his son had performed with bits and pieces of food piled high on top of the plate.

"Uh-uh," John Jr. said happily.

Jack carried the plate to the children's table and set it down at the place next to Tim's oldest son. Rory was only two years older than John Jr. "Take care of each other," Jack said, looking first at Rory and then at his own son. Jack bent down and kissed the top of John Jr.'s head, but it went practically unnoticed. Jack turned back to Suzanne and smiled. Then together, hand in hand, they strolled out onto the patio and into the cool California night to be with the others.

Jack succeeded in fighting off O'Connor and his other staff people throughout dinner, but as the late Southern California sun finally set and numbers were beginning to trickle out of the television set in the Jeffrieses' living room, the candidate gave in to O'Connor's demands.

"The polls are going to close in another hour," O'Connor said apologetically to Suzanne as her husband stood and looked back across the patio toward the interior of the Jeffries home. "The networks are talking about being able to declare a winner by as early as nine o'clock. That means we have to be at the hotel, just in case."

"It looks like our day of rest is over," Jack said.

"Thank you for it," Suzanne said quietly. "It was all lovely." She glanced out at the darkening line of ocean in the distance.

"I should go upstairs and change into something a little more presidential," Jack said.

Suzanne was still seated by the long pool under the shade of a big beach umbrella, but the umbrella had been cocked back at a low angle so that she could see the dark blue sky and the first sprinkling of stars appearing over the Pacific.

"It's been a beautiful day," Jack said, looking out not at the night sky, but at his wife's face. She turned back to him then and smiled. "Yes, it has," she said.

"And it will be a grand night as well," O'Connor said. This was the part that he'd been looking forward to—the press interviews in the smoke-filled upstairs hotel suite, the trip down to the crowded hotel ballroom to thank the troops, the telephone calls to supporters in California and all over the country, as the campaign geared up for its next test in New York State and then the final delegate count in Chicago. It was all O'Connor could do to contain his excitement. "Well, should we be going?" he said, clapping his hands together. "We've got a ballroom full of people at the hotel," he continued. "They've been promised a peek at their candidate in the suntanned flesh—win, lose, or draw—and on top of that I've got a list of people as long as my arm, who've been promised a call from you tonight."

"You don't have to go," Jack said, in a low whisper that only his wife could hear. "We'll think of something," he added. Jack knew that of all the political rituals, the one that Suzanne liked the least was the few minutes spent on election night in a crowded hotel ballroom. Something about the chaotic time had always frightened her.

"No, I should be with you," she said. "Anyway," she corrected herself, "I want to be."

Jack reached over and squeezed his wife's hand. Then he turned and followed O'Connor through the patio to Jeffries's private study, where the telephone and a change of clothes waited for him.

"Next stop, the Ambassador," O'Connor said, and Jack nodded his head in agreement. "The Ambassador," he said, smiling back at his friend.

Lopata sat at the window of his room and watched the elaborate security precautions being taken at the big resort hotel across the street, but he knew that none of what was being done would really matter in the end. The wooden barricades, the police cars, the complicated lighting system, and the intricate police crowd-control measures would all be useless in the final moment, because all of the precautions that were being taken to protect Cassidy were based on one assumption, and that assumption was very wrong. That was why in the end he would succeed and they would fail, he thought. The security people could only protect Cassidy from someone who wanted to preserve his own life. There was no adequate protection against an assassin who had no regard for his own survival. In a week or a month he would be dead, anyway, Lopata thought, feeling the bone through the thin fevered flesh of his arm, as he continued watching the police and Secret Service personnel scurry around futilely less than a hundred yards from his window. He would be dead, not just because of the sickness that was draining the life out of him day by day now, but because he had stopped caring about being alive. Nothing, no force on earth, can keep you from death after that's happened—and that, he realized now, was exactly what had happened to him while he was at Muriel. He had decided sometime during those years at the Cuban prison camp that, after he had completed his destiny, he no longer wanted to go on with his own life—and that was what made him powerful now, more than powerful; it made him invincible in accomplishing his final act, he told himself. He believed that he knew the secret now—the secret that he had sought since he was a child. There was only one power, the power of death, and he held it absolutely. He held it and controlled it, and it was his. He laughed at the mass of security people milling around the hotel's front entrance, making the last of their arrangements. All of it, he thought, all the people, all of their expensive equipment and complicated plans—it all would be useless against a dead man.

CHAPTER

48

Grissum sat in his car across the street from the Cassidy campaign headquarters throughout the late afternoon and into the early evening. He sat slouched down in the car's passenger seat with his hat tipped low over his eyes and watched the activity that surrounded the front of the building.

He was parked at a metered space and his only movement for almost four hours was to get slowly out of his passenger door and press coins into the metal slots of the parking meter and then return to his post and continue to watch the converted storefront across the street.

As he waited, he would occasionally reach down and flick on his car radio and listen to a few minutes of news. A heavy turnout in the hotly contested California primary. Another Marine headquarters had been bombed on the outskirts of Saigon. They were still counting the bodies. Heavy fighting along something called the Mekong Delta in Vietnam. There was an antiwar riot in Boston. Stores and buildings were being burned and hundreds of people injured. President Gardner had returned to Washington and was preparing an address to the nation. The expectations were that he was going to call for more American troops to be sent to Vietnam, maybe even the long-awaited call-up of the half million American reserve forces to active-duty status. Fuck it, Grissum thought, and he turned the radio off. The news was the same as it had been for months. It wasn't going to change. It was a hard, shitty world and the only defense against it was to take care of yourself somehow and stay safely out of all the shit as best you could.

A woman walked out of Cassidy headquarters, an attractive young blonde

614

dressed in jeans and a bright yellow sweater. Grissum sat forward in his seat and moved the brim of his hat back from his eyes so that he could see the woman more clearly. No, not right. The hair was too blond and without the reddish tinge to it of the subject's, and this girl was too skinny. Okay, Grissum thought and glanced down at his watch, he'd give it another half hour. Then he'd drive down the boulevard to the hotel where Cassidy was going to speak that night. Already the crowd at the campaign headquarters was starting to thin out as the staff workers and hangers-on began moving down the street to the Ambassador. Maybe the girl would show up there. She certainly had enough time to be in town somewhere by now, unless she'd given it up and returned to Dallas. Grissum settled back down into place and let his thoughts wander to the hotel ballroom a few miles away and to just how he should handle the problem of looking for her in the crowd that he knew would be in attendance that night. If she was even there, it was ten to one she wouldn't have the nerve to approach anyone. That's all he had to be sure of, he decided; he just had to be certain that she hadn't contacted anyone before he got to her, because if she had, then it would be too late and he'd have to get the hell out of there as fast as he could. Just save his own ass then. The thing to do was to go there right now and make sure that if she did show up that she didn't talk to anyone, he decided. And then when the time was right—he would know what to do to shut her up permanently. It came under the category of "taking care of yourself," he thought again, as he slid over into the driver's seat of the rented car and started for the hotel.

Denise had seriously miscalculated. The outskirts of Los Angeles were a tangle of interconnecting freeways, and she found herself swept in a constant series of confusing circles by their traffic. She had been very tired when she got to the Los Angeles County line and she'd foolishly let herself relax, thinking that she'd reached her goal. But soon she found herself lost in the strange maze of freeways and unfamiliar city streets, still miles from her destination. The rush-hour traffic surrounded her and she moved very slowly toward the city's Civic Center. It was after dark before she found a service station and got directions to the address on Wilshire.

She got out of the car then and tested her aching legs. She was exhausted and she couldn't remember when she'd eaten last. Well, maybe she'd lose a pound or two, every little bit helped. She cleaned herself up in the ladies' room as best she could, using the small blurred mirror over the sink. When she was done she looked at herself closely in its reflection. Are you kidding? she thought. She looked like a wreck. Who the hell was going to take her seriously when she looked like this? The little gold peace-symbol earrings caught her eye. I look like a damn hippie, she thought, and she started to reach up to remove them, but the voice inside her head stopped her. Hell, no. You don't have to be a hippie to be against the war, or somebody in a fresh shirt and a neatly pressed suit to have something worthwhile to say. They're just going to have to take me as I am today, she decided. She returned to her car then. It was full of gas and its windshield was cleaned of bugs and desert dirt and she felt better than she had in hours. She pulled the Mustang out of the station and followed the directions that she'd been given toward Wilshire Boulevard. Soon she was headed west on Wilshire, glancing at the numbers on the street signs. She looked up at the clock mounted on the dashboard of her car. It was almost nine. Cassidy headquarters didn't make any sense this time of night. It would probably be closed, anyway. She was thinking better, she realized then, her thoughts no longer full of panic, as they had been during that seemingly endless nightmare drive across the desert. Maybe she should just get a room and try to see someone at Cassidy campaign headquarters tomorrow. No, that wouldn't work. Today was the election, and tomorrow the campaign people would probably be moving on and heading back east for the final round of primaries. She'd come this far; she'd see it through. She switched on her radio and spun the dial until she found some local news. The polls had just closed, the radio announcer said, as Denise continued down Wilshire Boulevard. Senator Putnam was expected to make an appearance at a downtown hotel later in the night after the results of the primary were in, the news report continued, and Denise reached forward to turn up the volume. And Senator Cassidy would be . . . My God, Denise thought, as she looked ahead of her on Wilshire. The lights of the Ambassador Hotel glowed out from its setting on the south side of the boulevard, only a few yards in front of her, the hotel where the Cassidy victory party was being held at that very moment. Either she was very lucky, she thought, as she pulled into the left-hand turn lane, or she was a damn fool. And only the next few hours would tell her which.

Lopata returned to the bed of his hotel room. The dark black .22 caliber pistol lying on top of it stood out dramatically against the dull beige color of its tattered cotton bedspread. Lopata picked the small handgun up off the bed and drew it up close to him. He would have to get very close to use a small pistol like this one, he thought as he checked and rechecked its firing mechanism several times. But that was precisely why he'd chosen it. He would have to get close enough when he fired it to look directly into the man's eyes. The closeness would make the moment personal, almost intimate, and that's the way such a moment should be, he'd decided months before.

He stood and began to dress. He stripped down to his shorts and then he opened the brown paper bag that he'd carried with him from the bus station. Inside it was a simple, white cotton busboy's uniform. He looked at it and smiled. When his boss in New Orleans had made him pay for it out of his first paycheck, he'd been enraged. He had even considered killing the fat old man and stealing the money that he knew was kept in his desk in the back of the restaurant, but now Lopata was glad that he owned the ugly pair of white cotton pants and the cheap white coat that was several sizes too big for him. It was perfect. What was one more spic busboy at a fancy hotel like the one that Cassidy had chosen for his final party?

He leaned down and looked out the window one last time, his eyes surveying the big hotel across the street, making certain that he understood the layout of its buildings and grounds. After a few minutes he turned back to the room and removed the brown paper bag from the bed and stuffed his khaki pants and windbreaker into it. Then he crushed the package into a ball and tucked it under his arm. He tossed the room key on the unused bed and left the door unlocked.

He took the stairs to the ground floor. The night clerk barely looked up from his newspaper as Lopata passed by his desk in the lobby.

It was a warm summer night outside. Lopata threw the crumpled-up paper bag with the last of his clothes inside it into a trash can. He still had his wallet containing his identity papers and the key that opened the bus station locker. He considered dropping both of them into the trash can, too. If he did, the authorities would probably never discover his true identity, and when he died later that night he might then become known throughout history as a mystery man with no name. The idea appealed to him, but if he did survive the next few hours, the diary and his identity papers might be useful to him. And so he decided to keep them, and he left the key and the wallet in his pocket. But in all likelihood he would never live to use either of them again. One way or another he would probably die that night, he thought, as he waited for the light to change so that he could cross Wilshire to the hotel. And then his hand brushed the hard metal outline of the pistol that was tucked into the waistband of his pants. The weapon was all that he really had left in the world that mattered, but it was all he would need. If he failed, he might even use the revolver on himself. He didn't want to die in some prison or at the hands of the state. Death was power, and he would use that power tonight, he told himself. He would use all of it.

"It's going to be a cliff-hanger, Jack," Brian said, as he came into the study where his brother was dressing. O'Connor was holding the phone up to the candidate's ear as Jack slipped into the coat of a dark blue pin-striped suit and somehow managed to continue carrying on a phone conversation at the same time. O'Connor pulled the phone away from Jack and finished the call.

"CBS is saying it's going to go right down to the wire. They've got the Field Poll and they're solid," Brian said then. "NBC is just reporting numbers so far, no analysis. So is ABC. The raw totals have you ahead by about five percent, but we expected that. It's all coming from Northern California. It looks like we're not going to really know anything important until the Southern California counties begin reporting and they're saying that might not be for a while yet."

"Well," Jack said, "get ready for a long night." Cassidy turned to his aide and said, "What's your feeling, Frank?"

"There'll be some shaky moments, Jack, particularly when San Diego and

Orange counties report, but L.A. County'll bring you through it," O'Connor said.

Cassidy nodded at his friend, acknowledging the older man's assessment. Jack's respect for O'Connor's judgment in all political matters was very high, but he still felt a nagging doubt. "I hope you're right, Frank. We're both a long way from home out here."

"You're still worried about the impact of Crossbow, aren't you?" O'Connor said, a touch of his resentment at the decision still apparent in his voice.

"Shouldn't I be?"

"Yes," O'Connor said without hesitating. "You're damn right you should be. It could turn all our expectations upside down."

"Well, we'll just have to wait and see, won't we?" Cassidy started for the door, putting the finishing touches on his coat and tie as he entered the Jeffries's living room.

His daughter was the first to greet him. "Dad, I want to go with you to the hotel," she said. "I want to be with you when you make your speech, like we did in Indiana. So does John."

"And I bet Timmy does, too," Jack said, laughing and kneeling down by his little girl so that he could look into her bright blue eyes. The face of the little ten-year-old girl looked very sleepy up close. "But we're all getting on an airplane at dawn tomorrow morning and going to New York, remember? So, you need your sleep tonight, love," he said.

"Can I watch on TV, then?" His children had exactly the opposite feeling about hotel victory parties as Suzanne did, Jack thought, and he began to feel himself giving in to Erin. He glanced up quickly at the ring of people standing near him, looking for his wife. When he found Suzanne's face, though, she shook her head decisively, and Jack returned his gaze to his daughter. "No, sweetie, you get some sleep. I love you," he said and kissed her cheek quickly before she could say anything more and he might find himself giving in to her power over him. "Where's John?" he said and stood up.

Suzanne pointed to a room off the hall where a television was playing loudly and a group of people were gathered around the set watching the election returns. Jack's oldest son was sitting in one of the big leather armchairs that circled the television, but he had long since stopped watching the parade of numbers and election analysis pouring out from the big TV screen. He was asleep, his mouth open, his head falling forward onto his chest, his legs curled up under him in the massive leather armchair. Jack smiled and crossed the room and knelt down by his sleeping son.

"Don't wake him," he could hear Suzanne saying from the living room. "He's exhausted."

Jack leaned forward and kissed his son lightly on the top of the head. On the television screen in front of the room a political analyst was declaring that the sleeping boy's father had the fate of his entire political career hanging in the balance that night and that he and the nation would probably know the answer within just a few short hours. Jack laughed softly. "Pretty dramatic stuff for a seven-year-old. No wonder he's asleep."

Jack kissed his sleeping son on the cheek then, half hoping it would wake him and that they could talk briefly, but his son barely stirred. He knew that his other son was in one of the upstairs bedrooms, and as he returned to the living room, he glanced up the stairs toward the room where his youngest son was sleeping. Whenever we're together I kiss him good-night, Jack thought sadly.

"Jack," O'Connor said, as if he could read his friend's mind. "We should go. We're already behind schedule."

Cassidy nodded. O'Connor was right. There would be time later. After the hotel he would return and give each of his children a final good-night kiss before he and Suzanne went to bed. Now wasn't the time. There were too many people waiting for his every move. Jack stepped into the hall and moved quickly outside to the waiting limousine.

A few minutes later the limousine was speeding down the Pacific Coast Highway. Ahead of him, Jack could see the red lights of the motorcycle escort and he could hear the wail of their sirens clearing the traffic from his path. Soon the limousine turned off the highway and began its way east on Wilshire toward the hotel. In its back seat Jack was silent, still thinking of his son sleeping in the upstairs bedroom at the Jeffries home in Santa Monica, wishing that he'd gone upstairs and kissed him good-night one last time before he had left for the Ambassador.

Lopata crossed Wilshire and began a slow walk around the outside of the long city block that held the big resort hotel that was his final destination.

The crowd in front of the hotel was larger than it had been earlier in the evening and the police were having even more difficulty controlling the traffic. But it was much darker at the back of the hotel; only an occasional police car passed on the residential streets that adjoined the rear of the building. Lopata walked around the perimeter of the hotel, noting each of its secondary entrances. A delivery truck drove up and he watched out of the corner of his eye as it pulled next to the loading dock that led into the hotel's kitchen. If there were security personnel watching the rear of the building, they paid no attention to the truck. That would be the best way, he decided, directly into the kitchen through its back door. Lopata took one quick look around him and started across the hotel's dark side lawn. He moved slowly at first through the thick foliage that separated the sidewalk from the rear of the hotel, but then he began springing from one hiding place to the next, his months of training on St. Christopher's Island years before returning to him now when he needed them. If he failed that night, he would probably never have another chance, he told himself, and the thought made him strong and careful, and he was in the middle of the dense garden area that separated the public sidewalk from the back entrance to the hotel within a few short seconds. It was surprisingly easy. And then, staying in the shadows and moving from one clump of palm trees to another, he was soon within sight of the loading dock itself, and he could see the door to the hotel's kitchen. There seemed to be no one guarding it. Was that possible? Or was it just a trap? Was there a Secret Service man or police officer hidden somewhere nearby? Lopata looked down the long row of flowering shrubs and tall fringed palm trees. There was no turning back now. He turned toward the hotel and made the last few running steps to the edge of the high concrete platform, and then, with a final burst of energy, he leaped forward and pulled himself up onto it. He crept toward the collection of metal trash cans that stood lined up against the back wall of the hotel.

Now he would simply fade into the background. He would become just another white-jacketed spic busboy. Lopata picked up a trash can, carrying it with the slow burdened gait of a tired pack animal toward the rear door of the hotel. Even if there was no one else watching the precision of the way that he acted out the role of a bored and tired kitchen worker, he was enjoying his own performance, he thought, as he passed unnoticed into the enormous kitchen at the very back of the hotel.

In front of him were the familiar stainless-steel sinks with thick black rubber spray hoses mounted above them. Rows of floor-to-ceiling storage closets obscured the view of the main floor area, where dozens of kitchen workers in starched white linen uniforms moved around long stainless-steel tables that held trays of food in various stages of preparation. It was a busy, crowded kitchen, almost precisely as Lopata had imagined it would be. He looked at the uniforms of the men working near him. Many of them had the hotel's name embroidered on their chest pockets, but many did not. There would be extra help mingling with the kitchen's normal staff on a night like this, Lopata guessed, and his own uniform blended in easily with the others.

The hotel parking lot was full and Denise had to park her car on a side street. She locked the Mustang and looked back through the curtain of trees that surrounded the hotel. It was dark and she was alone. She could hear footsteps near her, and the ominous sound frightened her. Was someone following her? She began running, across the street toward the hotel and then down the sidewalk to a narrow dirt path that led through the hotel grounds toward the front of the building. She ran below palm trees and between low, carefully trimmed hedges. She was afraid to look behind her. All that she could hear now were the sounds that her own body and clothing made as she ran along in the dark night. Soon she could see the lights at the front of the hotel and then the path began to intersect with other pathways leading from the hotel's bungalows and pool area. There was more light now and she could see other people walking nearby. So she began to slow her movements and then finally she dared to glance behind her. There was nothing, only darkness and the shadowy forms of palm branches arching over the path that she had just traveled. She looked up at the windows on the upper floors of the hotel. It is very strange to be really here, she thought. Cassidy was probably already up there, close enough for her to see him if he came to the window of his room. It all felt so unreal. She'd never really thought of Cassidy as an actual person before, she realized as her eyes scanned the upper floors of the hotel, searching for a glimpse of the man. He had always seemed like one of those larger-than-life figures who lived in a completely different world from hers. His was a shadow world of television and newspapers; like a movie star, he was some kind of an image that she could watch from a distance, but not actually a real man, who she could see, and who could see her, and whose life she might actually intersect with and maybe even influence. She laughed at herself then, at her own momentary feelings of self-importance. She was not the kind of a person who ever made a difference, she reminded herself then. People like her just lived and did their best and then, like Jim, they simply died unnoticed—unmourned by anyone but their families and friends. Snap out of it, she told herself sharply then. Snap out of it and move your feet—you haven't come a thousand miles to stand here and look up at the side of a building. But what had she come for? she thought then. And, embarrassed at her own uncertainty and confusion, she began a slow, timid walk toward the front of the hotel.

There were other people near her now. She looked at some of the other faces being drawn to the hotel's main entrance that night by the magnet of Cassidy's presence. A young, long-haired man moved past her. He wore a large metal button with STOP THE WAR—SAVE THE WORLD written on it. Denise laughed softly to herself. Well, at least she wasn't the only one here tonight with delusions of grandeur, she thought. And then she melted into the large crowd that was moving with her toward the main ballroom of the hotel.

They led the candidate in a side door when he arrived, avoiding the crowded hotel lobby. Secret Service personnel had the back elevator waiting for him, and the trip to the suite of rooms that was to serve as the Cassidy campaign's command post for the remainder of the evening was smooth and uneventful. The back bedroom of the suite had been cleared for the candidate, but even that room soon filled with aides and well-wishers and Cassidy retreated to the small balcony that overlooked the darkened rear grounds of the hotel.

As Cassidy stepped outside into the warm night air, he signaled for Allen Rozier to follow him. The two men moved out and sat at an outdoor table and chairs with the sliding glass door to the hotel suite closed behind them. Jack had brought a notebook and pencil with him and he began scratching more notes for the short speech he would give that night in the hotel's ballroom.

"Who have I forgotten?" Cassidy said, turning the notebook over to Rozier for his press secretary's inspection. Rozier took a ballpoint pen out of his pocket and added the names of a few more important California supporters at the bottom of the list.

The night air was hot and Jack could feel himself beginning to sweat under his wool suit coat. So he stood and removed his jacket and placed it over the back of his chair, and then he turned and walked to the metal railing that ran around the outer rim of the balcony. Below him, in the dense foliage of the hotel grounds, he could see shadows moving between the overhanging tree branches. Secret Service men, Cassidy guessed, and then his eyes were attracted to the quiet side streets that ran along the back and sides of the hotel. They were dark and empty, except for an occasional car. Jack enjoyed looking down at the quiet night and the little peaceful residential neighborhood, particularly after the crowded chaos of his hotel suite. There were times, he thought, when he longed to live in a neighborhood like the one that he saw below him now, in a simple apartment with just his family and a few close friends for companions and without the glare and attention of being a public figure. But tonight he was enjoying being precisely who he was— Senator John Trewlaney Cassidy, one of the leading candidates for the most powerful job on earth, the presidency of the United States of America. But had he learned how to use that power correctly? Maybe it was the power itself that was wrong, he thought then. Could anyone ever really be expected to use it wisely? Perhaps no one should have that much power and perhaps those who sought it were horribly flawed, and if they weren't when they began, perhaps having the power soon made them that way. Wasn't leaving the power to others even more dangerous though? If it was available to you, didn't you have to seek it and attempt to use it for those ends that you believed in? And if you didn't, hadn't you somehow failed yourself? But what of the consequences of the decisions that he had often been forced to make? The decisions with no clear answers? The suppression of truth to serve what he'd viewed as a greater good. The loss of innocent lives as a result of his decisions to protect what he'd believed to be other vital interests and values? How could any of it ever really be justified?

"What do you think, Allen? Do you think that only those people who have no real ambition for power are truly worthy of being given any?" he asked out loud finally.

"No," Rozier answered without hesitation. "No, I don't believe that."

"Good," Cassidy said then, answering his own question and honestly facing his own nature at that moment. "Because I'm afraid, if that's true, it would leave me out," he said. "I very much want the power of the presidency. I want to use it. I think that I can accomplish more with it than anyone else can right now," he said then. And as for the rest of it, the other unanswered questions of power and corruption, he thought then, perhaps that's what the next few years were intended to teach him.

"Easy does it," he said, turning toward his friend and seeing Rozier bending back over the growing list of names on the long pad of yellow paper. "I only want to be up there for a few minutes. I've got a plane to catch in the morning, and we all can use a little sleep."

"It's a big state," Rozier said, jotting another name down at the bottom of the page. "What else are you going to say?" Rozier asked.

"It depends on whether I win or not."

"You'll win."

Jack acknowledged his aide's confidence with a nod of his head.

Cassidy walked slowly back to his chair then and sat down. "You know, something very interesting happened to me up in San Francisco," he said after a few moments of silence had gone by between the two old friends. "I wanted to talk to you about it then, but there wasn't time. I received a letter from a professor at Berkeley, a historian. And I met with him briefly. I wish that I'd had more time though. I think what he's working on is fascinating. He's writing a book about what might have happened if that bullet in Dallas had been just a little more accurate than it was. His book speculates about what the world might look like now, if I really had died on that day in 1963," Jack said, and then he stopped to think about it for a few moments himself. "Interesting idea, isn't it? I hadn't thought much about it until I talked to him, but I wonder now what it would be like. I wonder if the world would be any better off than it is?" Jack went on, still smiling. He shrugged his shoulders then at the impossibility of answering the question with any real certainty. "Anyway, I told him that I'd like to help him with it, after the election was over. His theory is that our commitment to the war would have been far greater. And I think he's right about that. Instead of two hundred thousand troops, he thinks that Gardner could have committed half a million or maybe even more American soldiers in Southeast Asia by now, and instead of ten thousand American dead, maybe as many as fifty or sixty thousand could have died before it was all over. I don't know about that, but he believes that just my political presence during the last four years has slowed the pace of the war and kept it from becoming what it might have been without me and, if I can win back the presidency now, that I can save the country from an even greater tragedy. I hope at least that part's true."

"It is," Rozier said simply.

"You know, in Dallas," Cassidy continued, "I think now what kept me alive was knowing that I hadn't really accomplished what I'd set out to do yet, that I still had promises to keep. I can even remember that phrase coming into my mind that day as I lay there on the operating table—promises to keep. I'd forgotten all about that until . . ." But then Cassidy didn't finish his thought. He didn't have to. It was Agent Sullivan's death in Dallas that had reminded Cassidy of that other day five years before, and both men knew that without any further words needing to pass between them. And so Jack paused and just let himself remember back to that hospital room where he had come so close to death. "I remember lying there," he said softly after a few seconds, "and somehow I could see it all going on around me, all the activity, all the people, the doctors, the Secret Service people, but I felt so peaceful, so calm. It would have been so easy then to have just let my-self . . ." But again Cassidy didn't finish. Instead, he stood and walked to the edge of the small balcony and stood looking down again at the grounds that surrounded the hotel. "It was just like I was balanced somewhere," he added after a few seconds. "Maybe between this world and the next—and that phrase came to me, 'And I have promises to keep,' and then it became all that I could think about. I believe that in some strange way it may have helped save my life." Cassidy paused then, before slowly turning back to Rozier. "I wasn't certain then what those promises were," he said. And then, softly laughing at himself, he added, "I guess that I'm still not completely certain, but I'm getting closer to understanding. I think now that those promises that I had left to keep weren't to my country, or to my family, or even to God, but they were to myself somehow. Promises I'd made to myself somewhere, sometime."

"And now you're being given a second chance to keep them," Rozier said.

"A rare gift," Cassidy answered. "One that I can't waste," he said. And in the silence between the two men, the sounds of the hot Los Angeles summer night could be heard—crickets in a faraway garden, the sound of an ambulance siren moving away in the distance.

"But the only trouble with surviving, Allen, is that you have to face the consequences of what you've done," Jack said. "And that's been difficult for me to do the last few years, but I think that I've learned from it. It's changed my values, made me less concerned with just winning and losing and more concerned with something else." Jack wanted to go on then, to try to explain what he meant, but seeing the worried look on his friend's face, he added quickly instead, "Don't worry, Allen. I have no intention of losing this election. It's just that you can't go through what I have and not want to find some meaning in it. For better or worse, I can't simply be the kind of a President that I was five years ago, or the kind of a man either. It's impossible, and I'm not even interested in trying to be." Jack started to say something more then, but before he could, he saw O'Connor signaling him through the sliding glass door that led back into the hotel suite. Something had happened. Maybe the election had broken one way or the other, Cassidy thought, as he watched O'Connor's animated movements—and it was probably time now to walk downstairs to the hotel's main ballroom and accept victory or to acknowledge defeat. Jack looked out again at the tops of the palm trees at the rear of the hotel and breathed in deeply on the warm night air, showing O'Connor that he wasn't quite ready yet to learn the news.

Jack could hear Rozier standing in anticipation behind him. This stage of their life was over now, Jack thought, and within a few moments they would be entering another.

"We've come a long way together, haven't we, Allen?" Jack said.

"A hell of a long way."

"Do you remember when we first met?" Cassidy asked, turning back to his friend.

"Yes, sir," Rozier answered. "You interviewed me for a job as your press secretary when you were still in the Senate."

Cassidy nodded his head. "Do you remember what we talked about that morning?"

Rozier stopped for a moment then and let his memories return to that snowy winter morning in January of 1958. "We talked about serving our country," Rozier said simply, remembering the discussion as clearly now as if it had happened that very day.

"Yes, service," Cassidy said thoughtfully. "Not winning elections, or politics, or power, but service." He paused. "Whatever happens tonight and for the next four years, whenever you think I need it, you remind me of that, will you?"

Rozier nodded his understanding, saying nothing.

Jack looked back to where O'Connor stood waiting with his news. "Let's go see what our fate is," he said to Rozier then, as he stepped past his friend and back into the crowded hotel suite.

Lopata placed the two metal garbage cans down with some others that stood near the long row of stainless-steel sinks, and then he began moving in the slow, burdened way that he had adopted to cover his real purpose, as he walked around the edge of the kitchen to the double doors that led to the hotel ballroom. A security guard stood just outside the kitchen door, but he hardly turned his head as the small dark-haired man moved past him.

There was a line of people standing in front of a low table that had been set up as a temporary bar, and Lopata moved toward it. As he walked, he looked around the room. There were only three ways to enter it, he decided. They could bring Cassidy in through the big main doors at the very back of the ballroom and then lead him through the middle of the crowd directly to the podium and stage at the front of the room. But it was very unlikely that his security people would permit that.

Lopata crouched down below the table that was serving as a temporary bar and began emptying the waste baskets at the bartender's feet, pouring the contents of the trash cans into one large plastic container until it was full with plastic drinking cups and melting ice and crumpled party napkins. He set the empty trash cans back in place and carried the single container across the front of the room to where another temporary bar had been set up. From there, Lopata could see the second route into the ballroom. The stairs on the right side of the stage led directly to a side door. Lopata knelt down and filled a second plastic trash container. Then he carried the two loaded trash cans across the front of the room toward the kitchen, but as he passed the side door, he turned his head so that he could see the small lobby just beyond it. There had to be an elevator out there too, Lopata thought. And if there was, that's the way they'd bring Cassidy in, through that side door and then up onto the stage.

Another uniformed busboy pushed out of the doors to the kitchen then and Lopata stepped aside and quickly turned his head away, and the busboy passed without noticing him. But after the speech would they bring Cassidy out through the same door? That was the crucial question, and Lopata thought it through carefully, using every bit of information and strategy that he'd ever learned. He couldn't afford to be wrong now. He would never be this close to Cassidy again. He was convinced of that, and so he had to be right this time or his dreams would die forever. It was unlikely that they would use the same side door to take Cassidy out that they had used to bring him into the room. Good security procedure, Lopata had been taught, would require that the subject exit by a different route from the one that he'd used to enter a room. The theory was that changing routes would ensure that anyone wanting to harm him would be kept off guard and wouldn't be able to predict his movements. That left only two alternatives: back through the ballroom, or out by way of the kitchen to a service elevator. Lopata looked out at the ballroom, overflowing with people. They would never risk taking him through all those people. But with Cassidy, you never knew for sure. The man believed that he was immortal, but so had his brother; the memory made Lopata smile. He cocked his head back and scanned the perimeter of the crowded ballroom. It was filled with Secret Service people, men in dark suits standing alone in key places around the room, watching the crowd. They were pretty obvious, but there were probably others, less conspicuous, mingling with the people, talking or pretending to be drinking. Lopata looked at the faces near him. It could be any one of them.

Lopata passed back into the kitchen. There was a door at the rear of the kitchen's working area, and it led to a service elevator. The odds were good, Lopata decided, that Cassidy's security people would lead him out this way. They could bring a limousine up to the back of the hotel and Cassidy could exit through the door next to the service elevator, or they could use the elevator to take him upstairs to his suite. This was it then, he thought. If they brought him through the kitchen and out this way, as they almost certainly would, he would be waiting for him.

Lopata walked back through the kitchen. In front of him, a twin row of stainless-steel freezers formed a short dark corridor that led from the doors to the ballroom back toward the exit to the service elevator. This is the way he'll come, Lopata thought, looking at the line of freezers. At the end of the row was a small dead space, just big enough for a man to crouch in, hidden from view. Lopata walked over to the opening. He set down the trash cans he had been carrying and wiped his hands across the front of his clean uniform. He was startled when he saw a bright red stain appear on his chest. He looked down at his hands, and he could see that they were bright red from something in the garbage. He would step close, he thought, as he looked at his own hands and at the blood-red color smeared on them. He would step close as if he meant to shake his hand, just as he had acted out the moment a thousand times in his sleep and in his waking dreams. Their eyes would meet then, as they had that day on the New York street. And he would be able to see recognition in Cassidy's face, because surely Cassidy, too, had dreamed of this moment, surely he, too, knew the final scene of the drama that they were playing out together now. And he would wait for that final flash of recognition, Lopata told himself then, before he would act, but in the instant he saw it, that would be his signal and he would fire. There would be others with Cassidy, trying to shield him, but it wouldn't matter, they would find each other. And when the moment came he wouldn't repeat the stupidity of Dallas, he would fire at the man's chest this time, as he had been taught. The chest was a broader target, but one just as certain to kill as a bullet to the head. He would fire twice at the heart and lungs of the man and only then, if he had a chance, would he fire at the head and break that pretty lying face apart forever. But he knew that the third shot didn't really matter. He never saw himself completing it in his dreams.

Lopata walked to the small hiding place that he'd selected behind the row of tall stainless-steel freezers, the scene that he had rehearsed thousands of times continuing to flash through his head again and again, as he moved the final few steps across the deserted rear of the kitchen. He looked around one last time before he slid down into his hiding place. There was no one watching him and he felt safe. He touched the cheap .22 caliber pistol that was tucked into the waistband of his uniform. He didn't need to remove it and check it again. He was certain that it would work properly when the time came. He was happy now that it was only a cheap, poorly made handgun and not a shiny, expensive, finely-engineered, rich man's weapon of some kind. It was the weapon of a simple man, a forgotten man—an invisible man, Lopata thought—but at the right moment, used in the right way, it would become the most powerful weapon in the world.

CHAPTER
49

Grissum decided not to use his FBI credentials at the door; the chance that he might be recognized was too great. Instead, he waited in line, just like any other guest, but with one exception, he carried with him an FBI "safe weapon" under his jacket, an untraceable Colt revolver with a full clip of bullets seated into its firing mechanism.

He watched while Secret Service agents selected a few of the guests in line to be searched for weapons, but after a few minutes he understood the procedure. He waited until the two agents were busy searching one of the other guests and then slipped by into the crowded ballroom, the Colt revolver still safely hidden under his jacket.

He waited for almost an hour then, but Grissum spotted her as soon as she entered the ballroom. He'd positioned himself just off to one side of the room, where he could watch both the main entrance at the rear of the room and the smaller side entrance next to the stage. He was still nursing his first drink and watching both entrances when Denise finally appeared. There was no mistaking her when she came in the door. She was dressed in a pink sweater and blue jeans, and she was clutching a shoulder bag that dropped down off a long metal strap at her side. She looked frightened, her eyes moving anxiously around the room, but most important of all, Grissum thought, she was alone. Did that mean that she hadn't contacted any of the Cassidy people yet?

A speaker on the stage at the front of the ballroom was trying to restrain the crowd. "The Senator will be right down. Please be patient," he said, but the people in the room were barely listening to him. They moved around restlessly, pushing closer and closer to the stage in expectation of the candidate's arrival, and Grissum watched as Denise was swept along by the press of bodies that surrounded her.

There was a sudden stirring in the crowd. It was the most intense among the people at the side door of the overflowing ballroom. Cassidy was coming. There was a violent bumping in the crowd and Denise's body was swung around. Grissum caught a clear view of her face. It was white and tense. Grissum laughed silently at her. She wasn't much of an adversary was she, he thought. His bet was that she hadn't even gotten up the nerve to try to approach the Cassidy security people yet, but he knew that he was going to have to be certain about that part of it before he acted. He remembered Yancey's words of warning. He had to be absolutely safe—no risks, not with the Bureau turning against them. The stakes were too high. He would just have to reach her and find out, he decided, as he started into the crowd after her.

Denise pushed her way into the crowd, and she could feel herself being jostled and moved along by the people around her as they continued to push up close to the stage. She felt almost totally powerless, trapped in a sea of bodies. I should have said something to the people at the door when I came in, but I lost my nerve, it was that simple, she told herself, and now it was too late. She tried to look across the room then at the side door where the crowd was expecting the candidate to come from at any moment, but it was hopeless. She wasn't tall enough to see anything. She didn't know what she could possibly say to Cassidy, anyway, even if somehow she was able to get close enough to speak to him, she realized then, and she began to feel a horrible sense of failure. She'd come a thousand miles from her home for this. Jim, dear Jim, she thought then, and she could feel the love that she'd felt for him and still felt for him rising up inside her and giving her strength.

The crowd almost lifted her off her feet and she had to struggle to keep from falling. Cassidy must be about to come in, she thought. Then the loud chanting of the candidate's name began, and she could no longer even hear herself think. The inside of her head had become just a confused whirl of random thoughts and as she fought against the new rush of pressure from the restlessly surging crowd, she was forced to turn her head and shoulders back toward the rear of the ballroom. And then she saw him.

Oh, God! It was Grissum, and he was coming toward her. Did he know that she'd seen him? She turned and threw herself deeper into the jumble of tightly packed bodies that blocked her way. He was here to kill her, just as he'd killed Kit and just as he'd killed Jim. He must have a gun. In all this noise a gunshot would be almost impossible to hear, she thought, and she tried to claw her way through the crowd, determined to fight her way to the front of the room. "Cassadee! Cassadee! Cassadee!" the crowd was chanting over and over and the band was playing some old-fashioned political song so loudly that she could hear nothing else. It was a nightmare. She had become a wild animal, frantically tearing her way toward the stage at the front of the room. Finally she stopped and looked back over her shoulder. Grissum was still coming after her, moving slowly but efficiently through the crowd. He was only a few short steps behind her now. Another step and he might be able to reach out and grab her arm and pull her toward him. Who would stop an FBI agent? In terror, she plunged on again, but as she got closer to the stage the ring of packed bodies grew impossibly thick, and soon they pressed in on every side, hemming her in so tightly that she could no longer move at all. "Cassadee! Cassadee! Cassadee!" The loud chanting blocked out all other noise, all other thoughts. She looked back again and just then the lights for the television cameras flashed on, illuminating both the stage and the crowd at the front of the room in a cascade of bright white light. Behind her she saw Grissum's face lit up by the stark camera lights. He was almost close enough to touch her.

Denise turned her head away from Grissum. She could feel herself beginning to panic and she had to force herself to look ahead toward the side door of the ballroom, where the television lights were pointed. Denise tried to struggle toward the side door then, but her way was hopelessly blocked. She could see Secret Service agents beginning to move across the stage in front of her and start down the steps at the far side of the room. Other Secret Service agents positioned themselves only a few feet away, sealing off the doors that led out of the ballroom. That was it. Get to the security people, Denise thought, and she began to move back against the flow of the crowd toward the far side of the room where the Secret Service agents stood by the doors that led to the hotel kitchen.

Jack held Suzanne's hand as they moved toward the door to the ballroom, but a crowd of supporters pressed in on him almost as soon as he stepped off the elevator and reluctantly she had to let go of his grasp. The security people had brought them down a back elevator that led across a small lobby to the ballroom's side door, but there was a large crowd waiting for the candidate even at this secondary entrance to the room. Suzanne followed a few steps behind him. She saw Allen Rozier standing at the far side of the room and she glanced over and shared a smile with him, knowing that he would understand the strange mixture of joy and loss she was feeling at that moment.

A security man bumped up close to Suzanne and helped her toward the door that led into the ballroom. The security man had a radio receiver pushed tightly up against the side of his face and he was taking orders from some unseen central security official on the other end of the line. "After your husband finishes speaking, we're going to take him out the other way," he whispered into Suzanne's ear, as they finally managed to push their way through the side door and into the ballroom itself. The people inside the main room could see the candidate now, and they began cheering wildly. The band was playing "Happy Days Are Here Again," and Suzanne could barely hear the security man, so he repeated the instructions for her. "Through the kitchen," the security man shouted to be heard over the noise, and then he pointed with the hand that held his radio receiver across the front of the stage to where two other agents were moving into place. "There's a service elevator on the other side, at the rear of the kitchen area," the agent added, as the crowd at the door began to separate him from the candidate's wife. "Let your husband know," he called out to her and then watched her face closely for a reply, as the crowd continued moving them apart.

"I understand," Suzanne called back to him and then she followed her husband toward the steps that led to the stage. Jack was waiting for her, his hand outstretched, and she reached for it and let him pull her up the stairs toward him. "I'm supposed to tell you that the plan is for us to go out that way," Suzanne whispered into Jack's ear, and then she raised her hand and pointed toward the doors below the stairs at the other end of the stage. "Through the kitchen," she added, smiling as she caught her husband's glance. Jack smiled back at her. "It took the Secret Service to get you back into the kitchen again," he said, but only loudly enough for his wife to hear, and then he smiled at her even more broadly.

"Don't get your hopes up. We'll just be passing through," she said, but then she couldn't be certain that he'd heard, because as she spoke, the television lights flashed on and illuminated the stage near where they were standing and the crowd exploded in a new burst of excitement. "Cassadee! Cassadee!" they began chanting. And then, smiling at the crowd, Suzanne followed her husband across to the podium set up at the center of the stage. The people in the room only stopped chanting after Jack stepped to the podium's microphone and held up his hand. Then, as the noise slowly began to subside, Jack leaned forward playfully and spoke into the microphone. "They just told me that we've won this primary!" he said, and the crowd exploded into a loud roar of approval as Suzanne reached out and took her husband's hand and they both smiled out at the crowded ballroom full of happy cheering people.

Denise continued working her way toward the security agents stationed near the doors to the hotel kitchen, but soon she thought that she could see Grissum behind her, closing on her rapidly again.

At the front of the room, Cassidy gracefully raised his hand for silence, but the crowd refused to quiet, chanting, "Cassadee! Cassadee!" over and over. Finally the chant grew gentler until slowly it began to quiet against the candidate's repeated waves for silence. Finally, the room grew still and the candidate began to speak, thanking the people for their support and then accepting victory. And as the crowd began directing its attention to the words of the man standing on the stage in front of it, Denise looked back over her shoulder. She searched the crowd frantically for Grissum, but she couldn't see him now. She swung her head around wildly, looking at every nearby face, her mind racing.

Grissum could be anywhere, she thought in horror. In front of her? Still behind her somewhere? She edged her way toward the security people at the far side of the room. She was halfway to her goal, she thought, as she looked across the room. Out of the corner of her eye she could see Cassidy introducing the other people standing on the podium with him. First, he introduced his wife and then his sister-in-law and then, one by one, working from a long sheet of yellow paper he began introducing the other key political supporters who stood behind him on the stage. He was reaching the end of his list now, as Denise continued fighting her way toward the far side of the room, moving her head frantically from side to side as she pushed her way through the crowd, desperately looking for any sign of Grissum. Her head swirled with questions. What would she do when she finally reached the security people? Where was Grissum? She felt her nerve begin to falter again. She was only a few yards from the Secret Service men now, but she had nothing to say to them. She'd been a fool, she thought, and she turned her attention back to the podium for a moment and tried to bring her emotions back under control.

Cassidy finished introducing the final person on the stage with him. He placed a folded sheet of legal-size paper casually into his coat pocket then and looked back up at the crowd, preparing to say a last few words. Denise couldn't focus on what he was saying at first, but then the people around her were laughing and Cassidy's face looked relaxed, smiling as if he enjoyed the laughter. Denise began to feel herself relax then, too. She had been wrong, she decided. She hadn't needed to come here at all. It had all been a bad dream. But suddenly she felt a hand grip her wrist and her body went weak with fear. She was paralyzed. It felt like a ring of steel was cutting right through her flesh into the very bone of her arm. She wanted to cry from the pain and fear, but instead she turned to see Grissum standing with her. His grip tightened and brought her closer to him. She was within inches of his face, now, and she could even smell the powerful scent of stale cigarettes and dead alcohol. She wanted to scream, but she couldn't. She could only stand frozen in place looking with horrible numbing fear into his face. Behind her she could hear Cassidy speaking, and then another gentle ripple of laughter spreading through the crowd. Grissum's coat was open slightly and Denise saw the black metal butt of a revolver protruding from a small shoulder holster, just the kind of holster that Jim had worn. "You killed Jim," she said, her voice trembling with emotion. She looked only at Grissum's dead eyes as she spoke.

"I talked to the Secret Service people," Grissum said, gesturing with his head at the agents standing only a few yards away. "I told them you were upset and a little confused. I told them that I would make sure you got back to Dallas safely."

Grissum was a good liar and his face and voice were filled with conviction. "Let's go outside and talk," he said, motioning toward the rear of the ballroom. Denise wavered. Maybe that was best. Maybe she was confused. Maybe she should just . . . No. Sensing her uncertainty, she could feel Grissum's grip loosen for a moment and, with a fury of new strength, Denise jerked her arm away from him. She turned and dove into the crowd again, fighting to reach the steps at the far side of the stage. Get to Cassidy, she thought. Cassidy was her only hope now, but she could hear Grissum moving after her less than a step away.

Cassidy was finishing his talk and, as she fought her way through the crowd, Denise turned her head toward the candidate. He was smiling as he stepped back from the podium. Should she call out to him? The noise in the room was deafening again. He would never hear her.

Cassidy took another step back away from the podium and raised his hand to wave at the crowd. Denise's heart fell. Had she guessed wrong? Was he going to leave by the side entrance, the same way that he'd entered? If he did, she was lost. The side door to the ballroom was impossibly far away from her now. She would never be able to reach it in time.

Cassidy was waving and smiling at the people near him, while the band began playing the music from *Camelot*. The room was a frenzy of wildly cheering people, and then the familiar chanting began again. Cassidy seemed to waver for a second before he left the podium, as if he were trying to remember his instructions, but then he took a step toward the stairs from the stage that led down to the kitchen. Denise's heart leaped with excitement, Cassidy was coming right toward her!

Denise pushed through the last of the crowd, her way barred only by two final security men. Behind her she could feel Grissum's hand clutching for her shoulder.

Cassidy crossed the stage and started down the stairs toward the doors to the kitchen. The security men in front of her were clearing Cassidy's way, moving the people around her back onto the floor of the ballroom, and Denise had to fight to hold her ground as the security man closest to her reached out to urge her back. She could feel Grissum's hand on her shoulder again, but with a tremendous effort she managed to wrench herself free. Just as she did the crowd surged forward, pushing her past the final security man. Now she was the only person standing between Cassidy and the exit doors that led to the hotel kitchen. She looked up into the candidate's face.

"Easy, miss," one of the security officers behind her said, and then she felt him take her arm and try to move her back into the crowd, but she refused to budge. "We're trying to bring the Senator through here," the Secret Service man said, hoping to avoid a confrontation.

Denise could hear the people near her buzzing. What was this woman doing? Who was she? Was she crazy? Dangerous? She looked up the stairs in front of her now. Cassidy was just starting down them toward her. He was smiling, relaxed and happy, but his expression showed his confusion at seeing her barring his way from the stage. Denise was close enough to him that she could see, too, the slender figure of his wife a few steps behind him.

Cassidy froze in midstride, and for a moment his eyes locked with hers. She was terrified. Here she was, face to face with one of the most powerful men in the world. Now that she had come this far, what could she possibly say that would make any sense at all to such a man?

She could feel the hands of the security people on her, trying to move her out of Cassidy's path. They were right, she thought, she should just move aside, this is insanity, but she could hear Jim's voice then and for a brief second he and what he would have wanted her to do now were all that mattered to her. Sometimes a person's life can come down to a single moment, she thought, and this was hers! She could feel the security man's grip tighten on her arm. She would have to act now or she would lose the moment forever.

"You're in danger!" she shouted at Cassidy, and she could see his expression move from relaxed good humor to concern. Denise felt herself being moved aside by the Secret Service agents, and the movement broke her gaze with Cassidy's. "I need to talk to someone in security," she shouted.

"All right," the agent said, stepping between her and the candidate and then moving her back away from the stairs, clearing the way to the kitchen for Cassidy to exit from the ballroom. "You can talk to security, but just let us get through here right now."

Denise looked around at the people near her, afraid that Grissum would reach out and grab her at any moment. He must be inches from her, she thought, and then she saw him. He was backing away, trying to disappear into the crowd. She realized the truth then. He'd lied to her. He hadn't talked to the Secret Service people at all. He was afraid of them. He was afraid that if he spoke to them the truth of what he'd done to Jim would come out. "It's him!" she pointed at Grissum and felt a thrill of exhilaration rush through her. She could hear screams and confusion erupting in the crowd around her, but she didn't care. Grissum was turning and trying to run back through the crowd, but one of the security people rushed to the FBI agent's side and stopped him, spinning him around toward her. She could see his face now. It had an expression of fear and defeat on it. She'd beaten the bastard!

Suzanne hadn't been watching as her husband descended the stairs from the ballroom stage. Her eyes had been on the crowd, but suddenly she heard the sounds of shouting and confusion at the bottom of the steps somewhere near Jack. She looked down at her husband's figure with fear. What was it?

The Secret Service agent behind her pressed his walkie-talkie close to his mouth and shouted urgently into the mouthpiece. "This is Larson!" the agent said. "We're having a problem here at Exit Two. We do not have enough personnel to exit the subject safely through Exit Two at this time. Please advise. Over."

Suzanne could see the exit clearing, and Jack was making his way uncertainly from the bottom of the stairs the few short feet to the doors to the kitchen. She started for him, but then she could feel a hand on her arm. She turned back to the agent standing behind her. His hand slid down and held her wrist while he stood frozen in place with the radio receiver pressed to his ear awaiting his instructions. What should she do? Jack was almost to the kitchen now. Should she follow? God, she didn't want to be separated from him, not tonight. She turned back to the Secret Service agent. He was getting something from Central Command now, but Suzanne could tell from his face that he was having difficulty making out his orders. The agent had to press the radio even closer to his ear to hear the crackling instructions over all the noise. But then he jerked his head up, looking for the candidate.

"Senator!" he called out. "There's been a change in plans." He tried to be heard over the noise of the crowd, but it was impossible. Cassidy was too far away. He could never reach him in time.

The security agent clicked his radio back on to tell Command that it was too late, but then he saw Suzanne take several quick steps and reach out for her husband. She'd heard!

Jack turned and faced the steps that led back to the ballroom. He held out his hand for his wife's and she took it. "Change of plans," she said simply and pulled him gently toward her.

"Is this your doing?" he said, smiling up at her and motioning back toward the kitchen door behind him.

"You're not going to get me into the kitchen after all," Suzanne said as Jack passed by her and returned to the stage.

The crowd roared as he reappeared before them. Smiling, the candidate and his wife walked back across the front of the stage. Whatever the problem had been at the exit that led to the kitchen, it seemed under control now. The woman who had blocked the candidate's way was talking with the security people as she was being led away toward the back of the room. And the man in the dark gray suit that she'd pointed at was being taken off by security officers, too, but he seemed calm and under control. Everything was returning to normal.

Jack stepped back to the podium. He looked out at the joyous crowd for a long moment before he said anything. Then he leaned over to the microphone and spoke to them again. "I'm not that easy to get rid of, am I?" he said, and then he laughed and the people in the crowd laughed with him. The television lights were still on, and Jack's face, as he slowly raised his eyes to the cameras mounted above him, showed that he knew he was speaking not just to the people in the room, but to the entire country.

"We'll need your help in New York," he said, and then spontaneously he shouted to the crowd. "And then it's on to Chicago. And let's win there." As he spoke, he raised his hand in the air, forming his fingers into a brief victory sign, and the crowd exploded in approval. Then he and Suzanne continued on across the stage to the ballroom's side door and into the safety of the small lobby beyond.

EPILOGUE

.

Allen Rozier sat in his office in the West Wing of the White House. In front of him was a metal box about the size of an Army foot locker. The box was open and Rozier could see the materials inside it. They were mostly neatly stacked files and papers. He returned his gaze to a small red imitation-leather diary lying on his desktop. Rozier picked up the diary and looked at it briefly. For a moment he considered opening it, but he didn't. He knew some of what was written inside it and he could guess part of the rest, but whatever else the diary contained were things that Jack didn't want him to know about—and it was probably best left that way, he thought, as he managed to curb his natural reporter's curiosity and place the diary unopened neatly on the very top of the stack of other documents inside the metal box.

There was a final set of papers on Rozier's desk. The first was a Los Angeles County death certificate for a man named Antonio Lopata. The fingerprints on the death certificate matched those of the man with many names that the Cuban authorities had reported killed in the hills above Havana almost a year before the date on the certificate from the coroner's office. Rozier placed the certificate into the metal box. Next, Rozier picked up a Justice Department fingerprint report. It verified that the man who had died in Los Angeles last August and the ex-Cuban prisoner named Lopata were truly the same man. Rozier set the report down in the metal box on top of the death certificate. He took a deep breath then. He could feel the curiosity still churning inside him.

He knew or could guess most of what had happened, but there were still

637

a few crucial pieces of the puzzle that remained a mystery to him. It had been true. This man with many names that the Cubans had been holding at Muiriel Prison had been the second gunman in Dallas that day in 1963. Somehow though, he had managed to escape from Cuba in late 1967 and deceive everyone into thinking that he was dead, but why California? What had brought a man like that over three thousand miles across the United States to Los Angeles? Was he simply trying to hide himself away? Start a new life? Or was it something else? Maybe something to do with Jack's presence in that state early last summer?

One last document still lay on Rozier's desk. It was a receipt, and he reviewed its listed items one final time. Before signing it, he checked off the last two numbered items at the very bottom of the neatly prepared inventory: Death Certificate, Antonio Lopata, August 10, 1968; Justice Department Fingerprint Report, February 2, 1969. He wrote the date at the bottom of the page next to the signature—February 5, 1969.

Before closing the lid of the heavy metal box, Rozier scanned the list of documents that he was sealing away one last time. Even though he knew that he shouldn't, he was looking for any last clues to the questions that still troubled him. In addition to the original, the box held each of the copies of Strode's diary that the Cubans had delivered to Jack only the week before, and resting below the copies of Strode's diary was the statement Lopata had given to the Cuban officials when he had been captured in late 1964 and imprisoned at Muiriel, but none of these documents had anything to do with California. And neither did any of the other items contained inside the metal box. California just didn't connect to any part of the story, at least nothing that he knew about, Rozier thought then, still puzzled. There was a girl, whose statement he had helped take late on the night of the California primary; the girl, who had been Agent Sullivan's girlfriend, and also the statement of the FBI agent that the Secret Service had taken into custody that night. Those were the only two pieces of the story even remotely connected to Los Angeles, as far as he could tell, but the woman's statement had dealt mostly with the FBI cover-up and Agent Grissum's part in it. It had very little to do with the "second gunman" and certainly nothing at all to do with what this man Lopata might have been doing in California during the summer of 1968. Could Lopata have come to Los Angeles to finish what he'd begun in Dallas? The question haunted Rozier, as it had for some time now. Jack had been in California for almost a month in May and early June last year campaigning for the primary, Rozier thought then, plenty of time to try to assassinate him, if that had been what Lopata had wanted to do. But Jack had been in over forty other states last year and there was no proof that anything like that had been attempted in California or anywhere else for that matter. So, why was Lopata in Los Angeles at all? It was a question that didn't have an answer, or at least not one that he was ever likely to discover, he decided then. In the final analysis it probably didn't matter all that much, anyway. If Lopata had come to California to assassinate Jack he had failed, and whatever danger that he may have been to the Cassidy family had ended once and for all in the Los Angeles county medical facility early last August. Rozier was certain of that much at least. He'd seen the medical photos of the man's dead body and even visited the pauper's grave that the county had buried it in. He'd only been in Los Angeles for less than forty-eight hours, but it had been long enough to accomplish everything that Jack requested. He'd met first with the Los Angeles chief of police. The police chief was an old friend and political ally of the Cassidys and he had contacted Jack when the L.A. Police Department had come into possession of a diary—a diary that the police chief knew would be of great interest to the Cassidy family. And then there were the fingerprints on the death certificate that matched those that the Justice Department had for Antonio Lopata. No, Lopata was finally really dead all right, but damn it, Rozier thought, I really would like to know it all. I'd like to know for certain why he'd been in California and why he had died there. That's the problem with having a reporter's mind, he thought then. You're never satisfied.

Rozier placed the receipt on top of the materials in the metal box. Then he closed the heavy lid. There was a locking mechanism built into the front of the box and he hesitated only for a moment before clicking it into place. He was just going to have to be satisfied with what he knew, because this was the end of it. He reached out and touched the button on his phone and within seconds his secretary entered the room. Behind her were two uniformed Marine guards.

"I'm ready now," Rozier said. He stood aside and let the two young Marines lift the box from his desk and carry it toward the door.

Rozier followed them outside to the waiting limousine. As the guards loaded the box onto the rear seat of the big vehicle, another uniformed guard held its door open for Rozier to enter. And within moments the limousine moved out onto Pennsylvania Avenue and started across town.

It was snowing in Washington and Rozier watched the snow falling on the White House lawn as the limousine moved away from 1600 Pennsylvania Avenue. His mind drifted off over the last few months. They hadn't been perfect, he thought, but then, that didn't seem to be the kind of world that he had been delivered into. There had been accomplishments though. The Federal Bureau of Investigation had a new director and a new set of leaders at the top. Summers's resignation had caught the country by surprise, but the transition to new leadership had been accomplished smoothly. Rozier knew that the Director's resignation wasn't entirely voluntary, though, as Summers had told the press it was. Whatever had truly caused it was between Summers and Jack and that secret, too, was probably hidden away with all the others inside the metal box that rested on the car seat next to him now. Rozier reached over and touched the box lightly as he continued thinking through the events of the last few months. The two men in Dallas who had been connected to the shooting of Agent Sullivan had both resigned from the Bureau as well. Proving a case against either man would have been practically impossible under the circumstances, Rozier told himself, but their removal had been one of Summers's final acts. Rozier's guess now was that Jack had something to do with that result, too. Rozier would have preferred a stronger punishment for those connected to the FBI agent's death, but he knew that Jack had his reasons for accepting the lesser action. Absolute justice wasn't his goal anyway, Rozier decided finally. He was far too practical a man to expect that.

Rozier watched the leafless winter branches move by outside the window of the limousine. The two men who had actually fired at the President's motorcade that day were both finally dead, as were the people who had planned it. Sylvia Martine and Joseph DeSavio had both died the way they had lived—violently, probably at the hands of the very people they worked with in the underground of Cuban politics and New Orleans crime. Not perfect, but satisfactory, very satisfactory, Rozier decided again.

The formal discussion between the American and Cuban governments intended to renew normal relations between the two countries had already begun, and real progress could start coming from them soon. And although Jack had never spoken to him about it directly, Castro had apparently accepted, as the basis of the negotiations between their two countries, the terms contained in the agenda that Rozier himself had delivered to Estanza at their meeting in New York last spring. Rozier hadn't been present at the private meeting in Miami between Jack and the Cuban Premier in early January that had begun the talks between the two countries, but Rozier did know that it had been at that meeting that the Cubans had delivered to Jack the documents they'd had in their possession. And now those documents, along with the other important pieces of evidence related to the truth about Dallas, were safely locked in the metal box that shared the rear seat of the limousine with him.

There would be changes in Vietnam, too, within the next few weeks, Rozier thought then. Cuba and Vietnam—with a little luck, perhaps both trouble spots might soon begin cooling down.

The limousine slowed and Rozier looked out his window again. In front of him stood the tall marble staircase of the National Archives, its front steps lightly dusted with snow. Rozier waited for the limousine to come to a complete stop and then the two Marine guards, who had followed behind him in their own vehicle, appeared. As Rozier waited for them, he rested his hand on top of the cold metal box. He had carried out many assignments for the Cassidy family, he thought as he waited, but of all of them, this may very well be the one that he'd wind up remembering the most.

Rozier nodded at the guards and they opened the door. As Rozier lifted himself out of the back seat of the limousine, he could see the Director of the National Archives standing on the sidewalk. The elderly man was dressed in only a dark gray business suit against the cold snowy morning. Next to him were two of the Archive's security guards. Rozier pulled his own topcoat up around him against the cold and crossed the sidewalk to shake the older man's hand.

Rozier turned back and watched as the Marine guards removed the metal box from the back seat of the limousine, and then the small formal party started up the long front steps of the museum.

Inside the building they descended into a subterranean labyrinth of long silent corridors. Finally they arrived at a solid metal door that stood at the end of a dimly lit passageway. The Director of the Archives unlocked the door and opened it for the others to enter. At the far side of the room was a large metal wall safe.

The Director pointed at the open safe. The guards crossed the floor of the windowless room and hoisted their burden up onto the tip of the opening, and then they slid it deep into the yawning stainless-steel cavity. Rozier watched as the metal box slid up and disappeared inside the opening. The guards stepped away and Rozier moved past them to the open safe and examined its sides. They were several feet thick—stainless steel carved into a solid, underground concrete bunker built hundreds of feet beneath the streets of the capital. Rozier reached into his briefcase and removed a letter. It was addressed to the "Director of the National Archives, Washington, D.C."

The Director took the letter and opened it. The instructions it contained were brief, and Rozier knew them by heart. "By Order of the President of the United States, the item marked N.A. 7846327 is to be kept in the possession of the National Archives. It is to be seen by no one until the date indicated herein, and is upon said date to be delivered only into the possession of the then President of the United States." The executive order was signed and dated at the bottom of the page.

The Director read the letter carefully. Then he moved to the safe and compared the number on his instructions with the number on the metal plate that was attached to the side of the box. Satisfied, he closed the metal door and spun the heavy tumbler on its face, locking the thick underground safe under the protection of the United States government until the date indicated on the executive order—November 22, 2063.

AFTERMATH

Antonio Lopata—Died of heart failure and other complications arising from malnutrition and pneumonia in Los Angeles County Medical Facility, Los Angeles, California, August 10, 1968.

Deputy Police Chief Jacob W. Boyer—Died of shotgun wounds received in what police determined to be a hunting accident in Clear Lake, Texas, September 17, 1968.

Leo Green—Died of cancer, while serving his sentence in Dallas Federal Prison, November 19, 1968.

James O'Malley Sullivan Sr.—Died of a heart attack in his home in Philadelphia, Pennsylvania, January 23, 1970.

Randolph A. Yancey—Chief of security, the R-King Ranch, Austin, Texas.

Walter Edwards Grissum—Died from gunshot wounds determined by the Dallas County Coroner's office to be self-inflicted, March 13, 1969.

Ransom W. Gardner—Died of a heart attack at his ranch in Clovis County, Texas, April 30, 1970.

Diane Jeffries—Film actress, living in Bel-Air, California.

John Jeffries—Movie producer and director, living in the United States and Europe.

William Longwood—Reelected to the United States Senate from Arizona, November 1970.

Brian Cassidy—Reelected to the United States Senate from Massachusetts, November 1970.

Denise Richards—Businesswoman living in Dallas, Texas.

Allen Rozier—Presidential press secretary.

Suzanne Cassidy—First Lady of the United States.

John Trewlaney Cassidy—The thirty-fifth and the thirty-seventh President of the United States.

ABOUT THE AUTHOR

George Bernau was born in Minneapolis, Minnesota, on February 14, 1945. His family moved to Southern California in the mid-1950s. He was graduated from the University of Southern California in 1966. After active service in the United States Army, he worked for Universal Studios in Hollywood for several years developing marketing and advertising strategies for feature films and television programs.

Mr. Bernau left Universal and attended law school at the University of Southern California, graduating with honors in 1973. After law school he practiced law in San Diego with a major Southern California law firm and became a partner with that firm in 1979. He left his law practice a few years later to begin writing. Since that time he has worked on projects for 20th Century-Fox and several independent film companies.

Mr. Bernau lives with his wife, Laurie, and daughter, Erin, in Southern California.